William Atkinson

The world without a notion

William Atkinson

The world without a notion

ISBN/EAN: 9783744737524

Printed in Europe, USA, Canada, Australia, Japan

Cover: Foto ©Andreas Hilbeck / pixelio.de

More available books at **www.hansebooks.com**

THE

WORLD WITHOUT A NOTION;

OR,

THE UNIVERSE AS A WHOLE.

———

CHICAGO:

RAND, MCNALLY & CO., PRINTERS.

1892.

PREFACE.

The universe, is a book, that has no equal, as a book of knowledge, it is an original work, and is purely a spiritual book, it is written by an independent instrument, known as a medium, but in reality, is a taught structure of clairvoyance, he is what you may call an orator by sight, and not by hearing at all; you may fancy it is all a myth, but it is a reality, you call him a medium, I say he is not a medium, for he can not speak a word, that is said to him at all, under your interpretation of a medium, you say I am a humbug, I say it is false, and is not true in any sense, you think I can do all I want with him, then you have hit upon the truth, I am able to talk or write, and both are done by sight, neither are done through clairaudience, they are wrong on this question, no spirit can teach correctly by this method of hearing, an impression is a spirit at work, and not anything else, you say a spirit can write on the slate, I say he can not do anything of the kind, his impression on the slate is all explained here, he does it by a code of intelligence, and not by writing as you understand it at all; Now I will tell you how to read my book, it is to be read as a whole, and not as a bit here, and a bit there, you read the book, all through, then form an opinion, I don't write bits, I write a distinct theory, that is entirely different to any social organization on earth, so you leave out all authorities, when you try for an original notion; Thus you gain a point ahead of the world, that is not fiction, but it can be styled fiction, to be understood by humanity as an equivalent for all laws, that forbid the publicity of a code, that is not under the special guidance of a law, now I am writing my ideas, for a specific purpose, and it is to scientifically prove a theory, that does not exist in the minds of men, and I am showing you a beginning in this book, where you are to find a theory that exists, that is known but to a few, and that most imperfectly, I tack my faith to the spider as the point of life we are to dissect from, and in doing so, I say you owe the discovery of the universe; it is from the spider that we all must run a clue, and that I am able and willing to prove it, is merely a chance, that you have of finding out everything, that is of a mysterious nature, now let us in a friendly way find the path, that leads all men straight, and in an hour of proof, find the link, that historians have all failed in, you can do me the justice, of permitting me to try, and that is all I want, it is not with an impure motive, but to show the world that they have found a victory, in the book styled, " The Universe."

THE UNIVERSE.

The world without a notion is what a man might call an unwarrantable piece of impertinence; but such is a true fact, as we have been able to discover this theory, you will pardon us the liberty we are anxious to take; before proceeding I much regret the folly of being understood to say, that there is no foundation, in which I can base my assertions; but in this work I can say I hope you will believe me: And should my views not coincide, with all you expect, I pray you will give me a fair chance to illustrate my code, as may appear best to my own intelligence; In grappling with so gigantic a subject you will bear in mind that there are no stones turned that have nothing to show beneath; this is one great feature to be carefully borne in intellect as well as theory, when a man finds under the construction he has raised the very commodity he is in search after then he must believe, that beneath lies all that he can concede his rights to: And when this is said I think it will practically demonstrate the fact, that there are no failures where the mind, can grasp the situation, for when the time comes to deliver our judgment, then it will appear clear to us how far we have wandered from the pathway of our own salvation: There is where we will surely find ourselves one of these days: A great many people believe, that there is no God, no hereafter: But they are quite mistaken in their views on this score: And should not give up trying to learn the means of satisfying themselves beyond doubt as to the plain facts before their own observation: This is a privilege which is an heirloom to humanity, and when they seek for knowledge, it is right there in front of their very eyes: And to see must be convincing beyond any shadow of scepticism; because the reed never waved yet without the wind,

and the soul does not exist, without the token of life, there is the
secret, a motion can not be unless it is drawn by the natural
current of its own affinity: And a man must be still when his
affinity is not come into a stage of semblance, there is the
theory of humanity, they only move when the spring is loosed
from its fastening, and their motion is the atmosphere that has
got them to go: They can move with comfort and ease; but
then remove the atmosphere and see where they would be, a
corpse naturally; then that would be the consequence to them,
without the atmosphere: it appears that a man must be a germ
like the reed, he can not move until a breath of air has come in
contact with him; but such is not the case, a man moves constantly without any apparent air; he may be quite able to walk
and talk without any effort; but he can do nothing all the same
he must have a perpetual current of air to govern his movements and will be bound as though he were a log immediately
his current of air is cut off: when a man appears to go along as
though he could stem the current of any adversity does he have
any skill to guide him by? no, he has got a machine within his
outer skin, that hides every imperfection; and he will bear this
covering while he lives here; but then it is all no use to him
when he takes a flying departure to his eternal home;   And
where then is the covering that served him so faithfully and
well, it is the garment that did its master's service, and forever
no more use; has its new coffin made from the dead tree which
has a defunct use superior to the body that was left to perish for
its faulty condition: a spark of light comes glittering past, and
sees those toiling over their faded regimentals, what means this
common folly has the earth no common sense? why, no, it is
going on as before, and must mourn, and for sensation sake it
can adorn the coat that failed: a great amount of credence is
placed in what we are taught to believe are facts; and much
unhappiness is brought about through what a Pastoral Saint has
said, but it matters naught of all his words they are the teachings
of the head: then what need the Pastor scorn, He, is but the
instrument of those who were lowly born, and his teachings are
the workings of the ancient moulds; then why should he be

reviling the deeds of the hands of those who had not the advanced knowledge before them, and when it doth appear to him strange that Abraham was not more circumspect in the selection of his affinities; he should remember that Abraham was the deity of nature's handicraft, and could be hewn to fit the particular mould of his art in a service which no other living man has yet been master of; there is where the affinity of nature hangs her thread of gold: she shall be obeyed or the commerce of the whole universe has got to stand still: and to show that I am right I will bring facts of the present before your observance; Now we will suppose that a man held bonds on a wheat field, he would naturally wish for a downpour of rain at the proper season: and he would say within himself, I would like a little more when the corn is in ear; thus showing where he would be satisfied, then he would want a little more wind to prepare the corn for harvest; but he seemed to think that there can never be any alarm about the harvest failing for want of that Glorious Sun, she is certain to do her part of the programme; And by what right has he got to leave the Noble Sun out of the question, he could sow his grain to fit the season, and meet the Sun where she was calculated to settle her glowing warmth at the exact period of his particular momentous of deserving recuperation: but with all his fine style of mesmeric observances and cute way of laying his plans, he does not realize the fact that he is cognizant only of one feature that he has sown a probability, and has no knowledge whatever of his own as to what is the cause and effect of his position; he does not realize that he is feeding with the right hand, and receiving a return with the left: That is what he does not understand at all, he only goes on the basis that his father, or some other man's father, sowed a field with wheat at a certain period and struck the elements where they ought to be hit: he could not for the very existence of him explain, why it so occurred that a man should be the means of defining the compass of governing the archipelago of his own enlightenment; there is where the farmer is entirely at sea, he knows what John did was right after all; but as for knowing why it should be the identical feature of nature's workings, why he

could not explain any part thereof; and would not for all his
knowledge give credence to the Sun for being the whole machine
that worked his wheel, for his, and for all mankind alike, being
participators in the benefits derived from that gigantic structure
of noble munificence: a man may be ever so capable of seeing
his fortune away ahead, by being what no other man has been,
and seeing what no others can see and understand, yet his fine
ideas are crushed for the plain fact that he does not know how to
connect them together; there is where the crafty skill of defining
his own ends are brought from under his very power (Man may:
invent); but the devil does prevent, wherever he chooses, and
this is what no man has thoroughly become acquainted with, he
thinks he knows what the evil genius is that surrounds his
actions; but he has no knowledge of this monster at all,
and is as paint in the hand of an artist, he can be mixed
or fixed to any grade of complexion: there is the secret
of the devil, a hidden power that plays round for mischief, and
pleasure to their own particular style of existence; this may
appear strange, and out of place to the foregoing preface, and is
indeed very peculiar therefore I am giving it at this period;
because I have been interrupted by an evil wave distracting me
from my original train of thoughts; I will say that it is this hidden
force which prevents humanity to-day from observing correctly,
they can not tell what the dark vision is that prevents their
knowledge from sinking deeper into the future, it holds them
tied down to a certain stricture that will not let go, it is the
darkness before the morn that has on a shade of dullness to
mortals before the dawn, and they are thus held by the
hand of what is distinguished as the fate of the race which
has been moulded to serve a decree of punishment, for their
willful manner of looking through the hand of the great power
which guides the heavens, and all that in them is; there is where
the heavens punish the earth by assigning a powerful force to
demonstrate their after mode of affliction on those who can not
see the way that their enemies have gone; but this is not the
right way of marking the effect of nature's great guidance, it is
only the truth as it must be; for no man can see where his great

enemy has gone, yet he deals out his measure though he were as
the clods that smoulder away beneath his heel, let him beware,
there is a presence, that can inflict punishment, and such a one
has no grounds of complaint, he did the deed unaware of being
in the presence of the friends who were there as spies, on him,
they made a vow of revenge, and sooner or later his affliction
will surely follow: now let the man who has a just cause for
complaint beware how he seeks satisfaction for there is a directing power, which adjusts all these struggles, and he shall not be
the only one to know of what he has done; there is my first
point, in which I claim that man has got no notion: He acts in
silence, and alone, thinking he is safe as the air he inhales, but
no he has caught hold of a mistake, that is all, and he will
wonder within himself, how so and so had the notion to say such
things that seemed to so very nearly come home to his treasured
secret, bah! I know he exclaims, I know it has but the appearance, only one of those strange coincidences, lost my balance
nearly though, I must be more solid in the future and not let my
feelings whip me into an appearance of guilt; I shall guard
against these coincidents, they appear to strike me as blessed
near the truth, I can't believe in them being more than chance,
yet it struck me like a semblance of knowledge gained of my
concealed fact; I shall be very guarded and not allow any more
absurd notions of coincidents to affect me like that again he
vociferates within his own composition; but little does he think
that such a reality had been brought to light that was nothing
more than a good account of his action; and by following this
clue he will get at the bottom of every secret there is to know;
again there is a more strange way of catering to this whim by
saying I surmise, "that John Classic stole my birthright"; he
never let me see how he did it; but within my own soul there is
something that compares him and the theft together, and there
will rise uppermost in my mind a distinct chain of evidence
committing John Classic, with my stolen birthright; now it does
seem peculiar that I should single out this one Jew as the exact
person who committed an offense against me; because he
happened to be a known individual who might do such a thing

is a very poor way of finding him guilty; but there is something
else which makes him throw out an inkling that he has done a
deed in which he has no pride, he can not rest comfortably in
the presence of the one he has wronged, his coat of mail is sub-
jected to a dreadful lashing from the hand of an unseen foe,
and he will not stay quiet in that surroundings, he can not bear
the tormentor's code of intelligence that is smashing at his
secret, that is how the shrewd man can tell how to detect his
man of crime, he tells his story in such a way as to leave bare
the vital parts, and covers over the parts wherein there is direct
resemblance, this is the way to attack crime, by painting a picture without bringing in the exact names of the criminals, it
strikes the listener with awe, and he can not escape notice under
careful vigilance, there he stays riveted to the spot, and is ever
on the watch for the chance to escape, he knows how necessary
it is for him to hide his guilt, and he will not dare to tack or turn
in the presence of those who have laid bare a similar case to his
own; therefore he waits until all is quiet before he turns to take
his leave of the associates that he has joined company with; he
can not bear the assertions of the crafty man who has drawn a
modest picture of his crime, and will resent or run when the
picture painter attempts to follow, that is how the thief is often
discovered; but how did the man who drew the picture get his
surmise? By laying awake at nights and letting his thoughts
wonder over the facts as they appeared to him; and studying
out each clasp that hung on his train of thoughts, as they
resolved themselves into form, and held him spellbound when
he reached a given point, there he was and no further could he
go; because beyond and all around was dark and dull to him;
he had reached the climax of his ingenuity, for or against, and
he was either on the road to certain success or certain failure,
either one or the other; and whichever power prevailed
would win, the power that held the string of his imagination
first would be the most likely to keep the way clear of his
opponents, and the power that did not hold the theme of his
efforts would battle against those who did, and endeavor to
produce a complete chaos; there is the secret of good and evil,

one acts against the other; and throws obstacles in the way of mankind for the purpose of letting in silence over the future; a great deal depends on man's own intelligence, he can not know what is best for him to do with his own ability, because he can not see far enough ahead to discern the way he should follow, and he is left as a sell upon the market of no proper value, it looked quite genuine but then it turned out a complete failure, because it didn't pan out; and a man ought to be different to a fake he should go right along to where he intends to go, not be" stuck half way by some influence that wanted to make some other genius of him: that is about what it comes to, a man starts off good, and gets along fine until something turns up to stop him, well it does appear as though he was born to fill some declared fate, predestination as folks say: this is all humbug a man makes his own hell, or he reaches his gifts of the good place he is entitled to: a man does not deserve what has not been merited by him, therefore his soul has no claim of conse- quence beyond what merit brought along; and to say that one soul is going to advance in the sight of God, because he has raised up a monument of wealth here is absurd, why, what use has God with wealth? He only looks upon it as the means of de- stroying his kingdom, it pours forth the vengeance of heaven by sinking the earth deeper in sin, all the crimes we have are the result inadvertently over money, then why ask God to take you into his fold because you raised up a monument to do him honor; he has all the honor and glory he can take, and he measures his power to its utmost capacity, driving all that does not appear good to him away after his own ways; there is another point in which the world has not even a " NOTION " the SUN has the power of guiding the heavens and all that in them is; now you think you know a great deal about astronomy but you don't even know what the sun is, and you have no notion of the moon or stars, they are distinct volcanoes or planets at large, broke loose from what prattlers call the southern cross, or some other cross; a composition of fire and brimstone to come down and burn us all up one of these fine days; a pretty nice story, to tell the pretty little babies when they don't mind what their

mothers say: All very fine no doubt, quite a romance in
its way, bringing old clothes for the man in the moon
to mend, mighty pretty picture to paint of her glorious
majesty's form as she appears in full figure at the twentieth
day of her advent, nice way to summarize her illustrious grace;
a few waves are to be discerned across the face of this object of
perpetual interest, they appear to us as though there is some
hardened substance, that always appears the same shape when
in the zenith of its entire form, well this is nothing except
the movement of a great mass of material that is forced
out of the interior of the moon by process of soluvium of the
excessive production of the overheated atmosphere that is compiled by the absorption of the Sun, which directs its refuse into
the Moon at its extreme rear, and thereby connecting its end
with the ulterior part of the axle of revolution, that fits into the
ulterior quarter of measurement that forms a quadrant to connect
the moon and stars, thus showing that there is no north or south
pole as the generality of human beings believe; there is a revolving piston between the moon and stars, that governs all the
minor elements; but there is no governing stem between the
moon and the waters that flow through the atmospheric elements
that congeal the rain as it is precipitated into the funnel of the
Moon at the extreme end, there is where the quadrant is, it
shelves the make of a great structure, that is ever on the wing,
and gathers in as it pays out, and is constantly replenished by
an inroad of the quantities that are supplied by the coming
through of the matter that is inhaled by the suction of the
gorgeous ever thirsty sun; now I have told you to believe me,
and I think you won't; because you have not sufficient intelligence yet to see through my knowledge, but all I ask of you is
to be ready to condemn me when I leave you stranded on a
barren coast, the same as the ancient scientists did, when they
told you that a good many things had to be taken for granted,
they never showed you the way that might lead you onto the
correct road, they said you were to believe them, and look no
further, that is what they said, well I want to show you that they
did not know what they were telling you themselves; because

they did not know what the moon was, is no reason why the
humanity of this present age should not be told, and I think
there are a good many people who are so superstitious as to think
that a discussion on the heavens is wicked, is what no man ought
to tolerate, for what harm can there be in talking of what the
mothers hold up as a scarecrow to their children, they only tell
you to mind the devil doesn't run away with you, which is after
all a perfect description of what he may do, when you are not
particular about guarding against him: Now as a point in the
course of my subject, I will explain my views more clearly by
being allowed to wander away from my subject at given periods
in this compilation, it helps me to gather food for my advantages that can not be had by any other mode of congeniality;
and when I find you the mystery that has always been a puzzle
to the human race, why, you should take pity on the mind of
the one who has thrown seeds of light in your pathway; a bright
kind to illustrate from is not always to be found when it is
convenient to establish their qualities, therefore a mind may be
perfection at times, and again at others, it is merely the shadow
of its former self, and has to be rested to enable it to come into
form again, there is the solution of mind over matter as these
spiritualists are constantly preaching to you about, they don't
know what it means themselves; because they won't try to go
below the surface, for fear of being hopelessly lost in confusion
the same way as the world is trying to find out how the knob of
time rolls by, and the revolution of the earth does not decrease,
the axis of the north and south pole does not give out, the same
as the axis of the Agent Generals, when there is any hitch of
diplomacy with foreign powers, where are the foreign powers do
you suppose that constitutes the resting place for our north or
south pole to take their rest in, I think I hold the majority of
humanity as though they are my adversaries to explain myself,
I can see them peering over the ends of the north and south
pole, looking for the column that bears our entire universe,
suspended in the air, and revolving round a semicircle every
day, and no wearing out, a very nice picture to draw for hoodlums,
but not very clever for an enlightened people of the nineteenth

century; they ought to see a little more light than this, it is similar to a man going to tack up his coat on an iron wall, the tack won't drive into a thing that has no face suitable to receive its impression; there is where the world is to-day, they have no " NOTION " because they began by tacking their faith to a myth: and consequently are at the beginning still nobody has ever thrown a sensible light on the governing elements, and no one can tell what is over on the other side of life, except they can see more clearly than the majority of the fathers, that have traveled over that plain pathway; no one who is versed in sculpture can tell what a bust is until they have perfected its symmetry, and they are quite at the worst, when they have been tinkering away at the head, when the right place to begin at was the exterior part of the lower extremities; there at the posterior is the correct beginning of the place where all constructions are commenced; and I shall prove this later on, when a mind has to be woven into shape, you begin by starting at the bottom of his intellect, and not by leaving the bottom intellect to be compiled last, I think that a good way of beginning everything is to start at the easiest part first, and gradually reach out as you climb the ladder of fame, always bearing this in view, that a beginning has got to be begun at the first step on the ladder, and there is where the artist has his toe, when he lifts his pitch of skill; he does not drop his hand behind him, and say why, I can't get to the top, he places one hand over the other and climbs across each step as it crosses his pathway of ambition, thus showing that you must allow me to climb this gigantic ladder as you would an honest young artist, who was finding for you what you had never looked upon before, and I will herein state that you will never regret the privilege I am asking you to concede to me, and I shall not let you wander about in utter darkness, to the end of my great ladder, before finding you some piece of valuable knowledge to rest your tired head upon. The Sun is the head, and the Moon is the bottom, of my ladder to climb, so I shall take you with me to the bottom first, and say that there are no men or women there that I can tell you about; but there is a porous plaster across that gigantic orifice, it is the sponge, that inhales the essence of moisture, that comes through a channel from the posterior of the Sun: This is a revelation, that you don't expect, and I shall compile these points as I think they will best suit your ideas of my sane magnitude, and not do it in such a way as you would kick my firmament into the atmosphere of zero, before you knew anything at all; now let me see I have told you that the Sun was the head, and the Moon the tail, this will help you to see, that I am not mad, as a madman would get mixed up in such a way, as would leave no possible doubt of his inheritance to the paradox solution of the science of discovering the genius formed matter, that constitutes insanity: Now I think it is pretty nearly time that I took you on a small stretch further, there is no difference whether I do this thing right or wrong, the Moon and Sun will climb the heavens just the same; your right to disbelieve me will not interfere one iota; neither will your discredit of me make any difference at all in the construction of my work, I hope to please, and enlighten mankind that remains paramount in my theoretical deliverance of reason; and it will remain fast and firm like the " Rock of Ages," wander on, no man can hurl them from its resting post: A well-developed mind has never any trouble in the expression of its own theory, because its capacity is like the mould of a great turnip, it forms a bed, to rest its head, and there is the secret of knowing how to start, begin by making your bed secure, and then you will rest pure, a man who climbs up like a rapid growth of weeds, is like the after-birth of a great storm, it has to be calmed down to produce any feathers to make a snow shower with, and a great many have been made by the handiwork of the great guidance of nature's mighty powerful arms; gathering in to-day and paying out to-morrow is the way the storms are governed; a way to find out who made the ground to grow vegetation, is to place a piece of cloth over the earth, and see whether the ground or the cloth is supreme: well, you will be led by me, and see that the cloth decays, and is the master while it lasts, and when it is worn away, it leaves the ground bare of vegetation, but mark my words, and see when the Sun rests her charms on that bare patch, she lifts up the

growth again, and nourishes the young growth with the care of
an aged mother guarding her young grandchild: there is a point
I wish you to take notice of, the grass died out and without any
seed, the Sun brought back to life what was apparently dead,
and the new growth was a much finer quality, than the vegetation that the old cloth apparently destroyed, now there is
something for you to conjure with, an old coat, will as it appears
kill what is there, and when it has passed from beneath that old
garment its essence has left something quite superior to the
original vegetation, that grew upon that particular part of the
earth; to illustrate this more fully, the old coat merely aided the
combustion of the matter underneath, and drew a form of life
out of the stinking refuse, which was ready to propagate immediately it should have escaped from the foils of its compass; there
we have promulgated life, and why should we see fear, at the
consequence of our old garments being cast aside, when we can
demonstrate death, so easily without any trouble, and leave a
light shining that has a much grander sort of purity; you think
may be, that I have got hold of a little bit of a curiosity to develop in front of your eyes; but no there is nothing in the magnificent atmosphere promulgating life wherever it chooses, it is
only natural for it so to do because its theory is to sprinkle a
little dew, from heaven, and a little warmth from the Sun, and
there is the whole sense of life, in a peanut. A good deal may
be said about our constructions being different to the lower elements, they don't see as we do, and we don't want to be classed
with those commoner species of humanity; therefore we must be
content to leave science alone, for fear, of its being developed to
such an extent, that will strike terror into our mixed conditions,
and drive us into consternation over our blighted prospects, in
the next atmosphere of our excellence; this could never be for
the more advancement the more success awaits our enthralled
souls, and we shall be much happier when there is a certainty of
our hereafter; because our formation will become more fully
developed here, and we should see the advantages of leading a
pure, and holy life, there is nor can there be any after bliss, where
crime, and sin has no checkered career, therefore I want to

prove, to you, in my own way, that your soul is safer with knowl.
edge, than without that deliverance, from the darkness, that
follows the dawn, a great deal has got to be said to allay suspicion, before, any progress can be started down a clear pathway, for the facts are so concealed from the ordinary mind, that
there would be no benefit arrived at by saying so and so was
sure, it would be pure suicide, to say that a ship would go by
catching her own velocity; now you could not believe me when I
tell you, that there is to be a great revelation coming from this
book, and one that would start, all the world agog, for it is quite
possible to sail a ship, by using her velocity, for her fuel, and
there is where you can see, an advancement in science, for then
you might try to reach the extremities of the circumference
of your own world; A man who can propound a scheme
for utilizing the vehemence of the great current of atmospheric elements, would surely be entitled to the phenomenal
distinction of being classed as a genius of the first caliber;
A good many men have been laughed, and jeered at because
their success was taught, through failures: and no one can
justify himself at the first effort, there is where a man has to be
helped along: he would be utterly lost but for the consolation of
a few friends, who encircle him, with chains of affection, and
encouragement, why, now does the great majority of humanity
seek to ridicule the crank, who has got hold of something that
they do not understand; because they are blind to all except
their interior promptings; which guide and govern their own
folly; there is the stake, that ties them to the darkness that
hovers near by, their own affectionate knowledge, a good deal to
be proud of certainly, but not very much sense after all: And
to be counted wise, is not quite what was intended to fill the
after inheritance of man; for he had much more time to stop
away from the code of intellect, than he used to have; and he
ought to help his gratuitous manner, by aiding the discovery of
science, by laying his all-powerful, will of mind, and strength of
kind, by keeping his own self as pure, and good as conscience
will admit him to be; there is where he wrongs himself by being
too circumspect over things that he has no NOTION of at all,
2

he thinks his conscience guilty, when it is not his own sins, which are troubling him at all: but the influence of some other sinner, who is plaguing his very existence out for the pleasure of seeing his pain: now you can see, that I do know something, and I want you to trust me to show you some more; then you can be happier after the torment of your soul's punishment; by knowing that it is a gnawing sensation; that was there by what is known as predestination; or the workings of the demons of hell; now you see that I am going to give you some points to show you that there is an after punishment, as well as the present, for those who can not believe, there are a good many obstacles thrown in their way that have to be removed before the stages of progression, can be advanced to fix up a righteous soul; therefore it will be necessary for all mankind to live a life of purity; and to do right on earth, is the sure way of getting a decent start in heaven; that is not all though, a man must understand what he is applying for before, he can expect to receive any fruits from his application; there is where the life of another, must aid and assist you to ascend the goal of perfection; and let a pure soul, take up the work of defining the right cause; there is no fear as to the result: but again on the other hand let a corrupt soul take up the guidance of that which is not perfect, there again is a certain result; and so the world wages war against itself: they don't know what they are fighting for; because, they have not seen the right picture painted of themselves; and a many may be, who are seeking for the right pathway, but are driven astray, by the adversity of an ignorant current of begotten knowledge; ascended to them from whence no good can come; there they have to stay till darkness passes away, and light is the only trouble that overtakes their flight: A bad way of illustration comes easy to the mind that is being prompted to do wrong: And a good way of demonstrating comes easy to the mind that is justly balanced by a righteous soul: For either one or the other is subject to be driven by an influence of whatever sort there is in his or her vicinity and to guide this more surely to the understanding of humanity; I will do what very few have done, and that is to seek from where the original

ideal of knowledge comes, by keeping away the effects of time:
that is the secret as it appears to me, to bide my time, and I
shall see all, there is only a little between me and my grave; but
for all that little is so precious that I can not deal silently with
what I now know to be a true feature in nature's great problem
of immortal life; there is the height of my ambition to perpetuate
the fact of life being a reality, and not a myth as the reason so
dictates at present; what is the use of one man trying to unbare
the fact of man being an everlasting geographical structure of
pre-eminence; when almost all factors in life declare the immense
difficulty of so bringing this home in such a way as to leave no
possibility of doubt; there is the man who is everlastingly praying; to a God above, to listen to his supplication of gifts for
himself: There is the good minister, who prays for his congregation, earnestly, and faithfully, believing himself inspired
with noble intelligence, when as a point in fact, he has no ruler,
who has taken his special case, into serious consideration; for
what good then can this supplication be; a very fair way of
bringing on ridicule from those, who have been torturing the
saint, who purges himself for the sins of his congregation: A
fair way of sealing up the gates of wisdom, and shutting the
doorway, of the just deliverance of man from idolatry; there is
the benefit, in having a saint for intermediator between man and
the deity of his supreme ruler, over the pathway, in which he
hopes to make his escape, to the hand of his eternal protector:
Never can a given person prescribe a conveyance of the soul to
heaven, because it will not be a conveyable commodity, after the
re-erection of the coming forth of light eternal: It shall sail by
the side, of its great ancestors leading it to the realms above,
clothed, in the garments of purity as it departed; so shall it be
received; a golden shroud of encasement, will bury, its nakedness; and its bearer shall provide its after provision: but that is
not the reception to all, a very different advent awaits the
hardened vagabond; he is shielded by none, he is the given
instrument of torment, he has to be the slave of derision and
scorn, his lot is not paved with charms, he meets there what he
justly merited here: A much better way to illustrate this coming

of light is to prove the after-birth: And that is what no man
has done to all mankind, there are many thousands to-day, who
know there is a complete change of this eternal spring, and they
are sure, of this hereafter being a deal more precious to them,
than it was before, they undertook to investigate, for themselves;
now there is one easy part I want to point out to you; that is
how strange it seems that the departure of a soul, has no
apparent after presence, when the flight has come, and the dawn-
ing light has enshrouded this apparent oblivion, where does the
most skillful surgeon bury his kindling wood to lay bare the
faults, and sift in vain, he is lost to find his skill is even more
faulty, than the body, which he examines from every conceivable
point, his notion is all wrong, his search is not complete for he
has omitted one point, and that is the vein of life, which stretches
across the head, from ear to ear there is the escape of the last
fluid that severs the soul from the body, there the ear is, but the
sound is gone forever, and it is linked to a chain of the current,
that guides it away to its eternal home on high there to be
rebuilt, and moulded according to the light of its deserving
merits; now you see that the Doctor is quite at fault, he presses
his hand on the heart; and he is not where the last course of
flight is; he only reckons on the heart; whereas he should be at
the head investigating (for he might catch that soul were he
prepared); and he certainly could tell the way it was going when
it left, providing he knew what chain it hitched on to; and he
can learn this secret to tell the weeping friends by keeping his
ear open, and his knife at home, there is the way for him to get a
corrected idea of his long desire to know how the soul has
escaped his eye; he ponders, and wonders, and broods like the
father, of a multitude of misgivings; but never dreams that he
has not got a proper " Notion " he can not find anything missing
and he still believes that he will one fine morning beat them all;
and detect some little escape-valve that has remained hidden
away to discover him as the optical friend who was keener, than
the knife he was probing with; and a good way of him hitting his
own conclusions, is by pressing his hands over the inner cord
of his eye-teeth, there is where he has been abusing his eyesight

for so long; for when he finds that his eyes have been taxed for
no purpose, he will naturally leave off, and try the other corrected method of steering his patient's soul, which will afford
him greater scope and equivocal skill, in his profession: I can
not determine what there is in store for the natural resources of
the leading profession to discover themselves, but it has gone so
far now, that I must say, that they are frauds in all their dealings, they have no consequence to injure, therefore no penalty
to incur, their knife has got no sense, and their scientific
researches have no wits, and the body, they mutilate has no more
in it than the knife and the instrument that uses it for his search
after the curious being, which he can not prevent watching his
treatment of what was once, the pride, and delight of the
departed; investigations are as common as the very earth we
trample beneath our feet, and they should be for it is as essential
to examine the occurrence of a suspicious death as it would be
to dispose of the dead body, for both, in their way; have to be
used; the one is quite useful to establish the freedom of civilization with; whilst the other is for the good behavior of the citi-
zens, and can be held in dispute over their heads as an example
to protect the evil-doers, from escaping their just reward: but no
amount of torture will purify them, they have still got to bear
the consequence of an eternal punishment, for it follows after,
like the stain of crime does here; it leaves a mark upon the
criminal, and stains him to the view of his fellow souls, they are
not willing that he should join them, and he has to seek friendship, from his own kind, there he remains a victim of vice, for he
never will progress, whilst he is abandoned by the light of
purity; and can only appear, where he is not shunned by those,
who surround him, he is perpetually suffering from want of
knowledge; and is the means of escape from his darkness through
the time of his subjugation; now you know what is meant by the
punishment of purgatory; it is held over, the heads of humanity
as a gulf to cross, it is a place set apart for the evil ones, and
they have a road of exit, and egress; the same as the saints,
themselves, and are one to one alike bearing this, in substance,
and fact, that the saint has his way paved, with enlightenment;

and the offending crimist can only be purified through the
government of prudence, that is he shall be made pure, before he
shall enter on an equal with the saint, and his work is the
guidance, of the unholy ones, who are here on this earth as
examples for the righteous to prove themselves by, and to drive
sinners to distraction, to show them to their fellow men as the
consequences of hell; now you will believe that I have surprised
your common sense, by putting what you know to be a true fact
right under your nose; there you have got hold of a little handle
that, is your own contrivance, and your own cure; you pack your
sardines into a box; but you don't know which is the tail, or the
head, before you unbare the cover; yet you do know, that they,
were sardines you put, under that coffin lid: There is where
you know nothing, for you have made up a fixture that was quite
mixed before, they had only been relegated for the coming
events, and your mode of punishment was not your time of
setting at all, it was the master mind that overpowered, and
ruled the weaker frame, it was the hand of crime perpetrated by
the all-seeing eye for he would be a benefactor, and not a soul;
did he successfully achieve, his work according to the rigid rules
of his distinct understanding; prepared on the basis of what he
would have to achieve, before, he could enter the gates of purgatory, and pass to where there is light, to the soul, that was
stricken, and purged, for being the tool of his fellow man:
Now I shall leave you to arrive at the meaning I have conveyed; and indulge your fancy still a little more in the Arctic
regions of the Moon it is there that I will enlighten your
next access to nature's great evolution of discipline, and solar
organism: You think I know something by now, and I want
you to follow me very closely, for I shall lead you where nobody has come back to ever tell the tale, and you must not
say he is an inventor; when he is really telling you of solid
facts, as the way you walk in there is where you are going;
and you can't stop to pick a better way, for it is the one
road, that leads you by the moon, so you need never dream,
that you are going to get a chance of going through, the Sun,
for that is not the privilege of the after-birth; they don't keep

the way open for drawlers, or crawlers, they whip them into a
chute, and they go flying through the angle of the sky next to
the other side, in a twinkling of an eye; and there is no other
side, for it is quite near the edge of heaven, where the all-being
of power is; a many may be, who have dreamt, they were, in
in heaven, away beyond the sky; but it is their mistake, to suppose that heaven, is beyond the sky, it is where the atmosphere
congeals, and sets itself against the sky, there is where the
angels live, in habitations beneath, the hanging combs of molten
clay, made from, those great orifices, that we. see between the
stars, there is where the angels bide their time, when they have
penal servitude; a great many people may think that this is a
humbug; but you know very well that throughout all history the
impressions have been conveyed, that there are places of punishment hereafter; and you know that there should be a place of
access, and egress; well this is quite true, there is, for it is the
hole, that is presented to your view very often; that is the
moon, when she is turned, down at the end, and when you see
no life, in her, she is then quite dry, and is a perfect chasm of
plenty, of scope to railroad through; this is my own way of
expressing the situation, for it is a railroad to those, who pass
through; there is the difference between a common railroad and
a celestial one; for their mode of haulage, is defined more accurately, and is one of constant passage, there is no knowing what
breakages would do for them; as their style of movement is not,
what has been represented at all, it is a given sent: there is no
getting ready; the motion, is the same, as the mind flying from
Europe to Asia: It blows hot, and cold, all in one breath, so
that before you can breathe the men, have crossed from penal
servitude to heaven; or in other words the passage, is the same
as done, once the word of command, is given: Now you follow
me very closely, and I will demonstrate to you, why the moon
does, not always stop, at full; she is on terms of good-fellowship,
until there, is an overplus of matter congealed round her orifice;
then she becomes unwieldy, and is precipitated into an opening
of gigantic dimensions; and is enlarged beyond her comfort;
there is where, she comes in disobedience to her maker; and is

constantly being snubbed, but it is all of no avail: For once
she has extended her neck to a certain point, she meets the
anger, of the Sun; and is consumed to the very edge, of where
she became lacerated, with drips of falling debris, that was
forced out of her funnel, when she became sumph; as she does
at her monthly paradox; you seem to think I am wrong, in my
deliverance, of these plain facts; well it is the way the world
has got, of doubting every piece of information; they think a
mind who does convey these extraordinary original ideas; is
off hinges; but, they don't know anything at all except
to find fault with those who do, there is the propping
stone to civilization; the people get up a stone-throwing
game called criticism; and say whatever comes first upon
their tongues; no reason or sense in such a code of condemnation; a man, who is capable, and just, in his arguments has no time to take, his sense, from such as criticise, he
must be able, to deliver his reason, in such a code, as to get
outside, of the critiques; who are as common, as the gutter
pebbles, that are the dread and fear, of the people, that are
hindered, from abiding by the laws, of nature; and have to submit to the provisions of the army, of knaves; who pitch stones;
at windows made, of glass; there is the way the house flies get,
when the stones fly through the window; but no one goes to
pick them up because they are only flies, that have got no
use, for any code, of reason; now there is where the people
make mistakes they believe the time has come to do away with
all sense of feelings, and go on pitching in both heels, and crop,
at those, who are on the outside, of that pane of glass; now you
know, that a fly does not realize, that he is to be hit, from the
front; because his sight is clear, at the back of his head; there is,
where the fly, has no knowledge of how he is likely to become a
corpse; the benefit, of seeing behind, is great; and the advantage, of seeing in front is greater; but the kind of sight that
makes the round is greater; for should a mound be ground to
powder; it always has the advantage, for it is hidden, from
back and front, there is the advantage beyond a shadow of
doubt; to call a man a fool is only to hit him over the mound;

his answer is, I have made a grand discovery, my name is fool;
but he can not see that fool means, an ass; so he has gained his
point by chopping off my balance; he is an ass for not knowing
how to see my mistake; his ideas don't correspond with mine, I
have found him out; and he still thinks I am a fool; well let him
grow wise, I have got my experience, through listening to the
thoughts as they strike me; and that is what we all do; but
some people don't go after the thoughts when they are hit, so
that they never make, any use of those thoughts as they come
from the hand, that makes them; a man may be punched with
thoughts, that are wonderful; but he does not care for them,
they are his only salvation though; and he rejects them because,
he says within himself, I know I can't accomplish them, they
would laugh at me were I to advance such ideas; bah! he is an
ass for not braying, when a good thought strikes him; his soul,
is stirred within him for he feels a momentous question put: Are
you dead; he flings back an answer; then why don't you hear me
say stop: For I can hear you quite distinctly strike me with a
thought, that I never heard before; there is the theory of our
thoughts; a man grows up all the time believing that his
thoughts are, the workings of his own brain, but he is mistaken
there, his thoughts are supplied by a power, which does not
belong to him alone, his mind is his own, but his tempter is the
guide of his mind; there is the part that he can not control;
because it is outside; and does not come, within his substance,
to be contaminated by his body which forms his material ennoble-
ment of his inner cord of life; now then take for instance the
thoughts of a child; and you find more wisdom at that time,
than ever you do after they become grown: for they are then
made people of texture, they know no sin, therefore the mind
is pure, it only does what the dictation of its thoughts say; there
you have a specimen of good and evil again; one child, has all
good thoughts, whilst another child has nothing but evil thoughts;
well now, you see the mound, has got a sight behind, as well as,
in front; where did the evil come from, why it was sent there;
then where did the good come from; it was also sent there; now
lift up the heads of these young people, and see, whether you

can find anything there at all that indicates a controlling power; but you can hear the power of those two young people plainly tell them what to say, or do: Now you have the secret, of what a thought is that strikes you; let me do one more thing to straighten out your tangled web; and that is to show you how to make a line straight, by placing it over against the corner of a plot to be surveyed to such a stake, to its right angle, and to its left fore point, there is the style of giving a test to meet a given degree, don't take a single item for granted, but measure all as you go, and mind, that you understand what you do, for it is not all as it appears, on the surface; they don't grow grain without plowing the field, neither do they steep corn, without bringing up the point: And you must not grow careless because your first sprout is not a success; there can not be fruit without trees to ripen on; and time has to be spent, in growing those trees; the same as it will take you time to understand that there is a big round mound to climb, that when climbed; will to a certainty prove to you, that you may see through back and front; And you will likewise understand, what a thought is, that, strikes all mankind at some period of their lives; there is the true knowledge; a way, of believing, there are no men who do not believe some kind of belief; there are those, who sing out, for one thing; and then again there are those who dare not do it at all; so we meet them under all conditions; for they have all got thoughts; there is where the mischief is, and they don't seem to realize why it is that no one individual should know enough to satisfy them all; but they are mistaken, a man who can comprehend the lights of life, is just about good enough to know who is who; and which belongs to the other; there is the point, can a man show you where your shortcomings are; can he explain away all your difficulties; because when such a one, is found, why, bring him home to your understanding; and reflect, on what he tells you; "cause your eyes to open;" and bring forth your faculties for a clear pathway has been opened for you, then tread not again on doubtful ways; there you have the night turned into day, and light glistening at your side, then do not be afraid: the dawn has come before the morn; but a few hours behind the night, a great trumpet sounds the coming light of after years; Oh! where can he be found the Saviour that we lost, we stoned him for throwing light upon us forever, then think again before you condemn what might be his crowning point: A bright star shone, in the East, a light has come upon the land that all powers on earth have tried to blot out; but there he stands supreme above them all; not one can claim to be his equal, not one can call him back, he is the first and only true God, he . visited the pure and lowly, he sought out the lusts of hell: And communed with those, who taught so well, his life was led by his father in heaven, and he did the work that was shown to him to do, I can not say the same for any other Son; his path was strewn with knowledge, his soul was filled with light, his obedience knew no others from this power above; his childlike form became as firm as rocks before he grew to manhood's stage of rights, his very mien begot a God-like statue before the grace divine; Holy—Holy light of lights declare their innocence from on high; bright lights burning for glory have shone on earth to-day, may righteous men be brought forward to the side of this great master, may ye hear a prayer from such as he, for ye shall know the end, but there never shall be such another, may God and Grace be held as one, may heaven be shown to us, for our time has come to find the pathway, that Jesus walked through, there is the shining light that shall be forever by your side, for as he seeks so shall he find; for there can not be darkness, where the light is always near: And so have the messages been given to man from the birth of Christ the Saviour; no darkness can again invade the earth, no item of tide can evermore become the token of this great eternity, on: And on! again shall this streaming current stand as the light of ages passeth by, so shall this crown of knowledge stand the test of every storm, and no one has yet the right to cast his throne away; brighter still than all the golden heads of time, more unstable than the wealth of kings, and shining clearer than the light of day, adorned with Grace of unhuman wisdom from on high; a great deal has been said of the manner of this second sight, now there is no such thing as this in existence, it is the workings of the mind, and has

nothing whatever to do with seeing, it is the organ of sight
as it is directed by the administration of the artist, who comes
in operation, with the optical parasite, or in another way of
demonstrating this fallacy, it is the means of shoving the spring
of light with a given motor, so that a certain pressure, of magnetic current, will strike across the vision, in a given attitude;
to convey this meaning, there must be an understanding with
the passions of discerning things outside of the common surroundings, and they have got this more accurately described as
the imagination of the eye; as it does not appear possible that
there can be any other motor power than the weak theory of
cultivation of imagination; now then we must concede a point
or two in order to show that there are no things that are, without
this lively imagination clause, coming to the fore; then why, can
it be the workings of a weak intellect, when you have absolutely
nothing without it; tell me where you got all this knowledge of
God Almighty sitting on a throne, with Jesus Christ the son of
man seated at the right hand; and the Virgin Mary on the left;
is it not possible, that the Lord delivered those messages himself, and was accredited with the astute guidance of all mankind
by the powers, that rule the dead, of this world: He aspired to
nature's great work, of relieving souls from sin, and punishing
where he saw that nature's faults deserved rebukes, in other
words the Lord God of Hosts has seen fit to endow the minds
of men with that blessing which signs deeds of rebuke, to the
faults of its own solar organism; there is where the imagination
came from, it comes in the forms of light thrown on certain
pillars of might; there is what is the germ of life, it is sold
unto a power that welds itself to us by inspirational intuition;
there is what you call the grand ideas of the learned orthodox
sectarian, he is propelled by the guidance of a spring, he has no
more idea of how he is worked, than he has of his future soul's
destination, he thinks he is going to be the great light of some
divine providence; but he can't tell you a thing about his own
affairs, whether he is to go on as before, or what kind of a position he is going to finish his vocation, on this earth, his sole aim
is to be the staff of life, and he has got to go on as his dictators

think he should, his likes and dislikes are all the workings of his special discerning power, his mind is moulded for no other use, than he is required to perform, and he shall not work out his ideas, as they seem best to his own cravings for the advantages he may entertain, that his conduct is the same as his dictation, or that his conduct is different from his theory of delivering his harangue is nothing to do with his guidance, at all: His mind, and all other men's minds are made by the hand of nature's great governing power: Time, Space, and the dictations of our departed friends coming back to help us over the great border with their supplications of peace to our souls hereafter; now you gather in from what I have said that there are no divine governors; but there you commit error, I have said I will not give my views away in short sentences; because you can not believe a fact, unless, it is well backed by some other mode of understanding; therefore you must not be too hasty, in condemning; because you know the result of that gratuitous freedom of condemnation; and I need scarcely now draw your attention, to the fact, that your own thoughtlessness was the crucifixion: Which has thrown confusion and consternation, on the whole world since that time, a bad beginning has a good ending people say, that was an outrage on this present people, that can not be stained with too much censure; and for the sake of him who died on Calvary, we ought to say let no other man who walks in his footsteps be subjugated to such cruel and heathenish brutality; there is the way as clear as the heavens above your heads, walk in his footsteps, and you will surely find the light; no one who trusted in the divine assistance from the heavenly sources of those who rule above, can be debarred from reaching the goal of their soul's craving after power: you are as one moulded to this earth, because you have not seen any other; but you forget, the fastening that was tacked onto you in the beginning, there is why, you commit so many follies; your idea is that you came into this earth because it was ordained by the will of God, that is precisely what you believe; well you have departed from the pathway of knowledge, at the onset; and you grow up in ignorance all your natural lives; there is where you have gotten all the orthodox doctrine from, you steep your own advent in mystery, and you hold onto this theory with a pertinacity that would justify any devil, in holding you to his cause; now you see where the evil genius has got his stronghold, it is at the beginning of your natural lives; and he can chain all of those who refuse to be governed by the code of intelligence; you must not be confirmed in your belief, that I construe your own idea of this devil of yours; for my theoretical view of him, does not come within your tattoo of his painted statue; I believe in all holy laws, made for the benefits of humanity, and I concede every point that I believe to be beneficial to the good guidance of nature's great problem life immortal: Soul to soul can be united; and bosom to bosom should be bound by ties of dutiful affection; but no evil judge should seal a faith, that is not there of its own calling; just a little thread so small as to be imperceptible to the naked eye, holds this tie of holy love, and yet that tie is as stone, compared to this mighty power of clinging life, there is no love can compare with this eternal string; it holds on tenaciously, to nothing, as it were, yet the strongest tie of affection, is weak compared to that tie of life; yes you realize what affection for another is; but you can not seem to understand, this other tie, that binds you to life immortal: Why then should you not bring back to your memory those days of affectionate reminiscences when you had but one tie that seemed to say give me this: And I shall wish for nothing more, I have seen this time too; and my time was devoted to no other thoughts; than linking this tie, with my own; there was a tie united, and that tie was severed by force of circumstances; there is the tie of the frame, that never shall be broken, but it is no use now, I have lost the end off my tie; and I shall never find any other to joint with mine; because there is a gulf between there and where that tie was severed; but you have not caught my meaning clearly, there is a tie which never breaks; it may spring away from the part that injured it; yet there never dies that indisputable something; still hanging on to the past life, still holding firmly to the belief, that some time or other, there will be a reunion of the severed chain, holding fast to each link as it appears to bring

forth some new light on that abandoned breakage: Now let me
understand what we find in this chain, it contains a link off some
other chain, well now don't you observe that you have got a
chain, and it is broken there in two as it were; yet you hold a
link of that chain, and you want to join that same link with
some link that was the fac-simile of that same link that you are
wishing to join into that chain, which has apparently flown off
your end link: Buy a piece of yarn, and stretch it so that it
breaks: there you find what means the yarn has of joining
together; but you don't see the drift of my illustration: For
you have not experimented; they say you can mend a piece of
yarn,·or you can have it milled over anew; but you have got a
new link fastened to nothing; yet it came from the other which
I did not tear apart; therefore you have a sold conscience; for
your texture is always, intact: Now you have made me an illustration of a piece of old cloth; where does my new piece come
in: It was torn from the old, and made, into new, by the stages
of insignificant pulverization; you call me a fool for an illustration, that has no life in it; but you forget that you were
without life, until the atmospheric current touched you by
concussion of sound: There you struck the elements of
power by the sound of your mother's voice; impregnated
to her by the same power: And you shall give back
to the cord, from whence you came that which you took: In
other words you have, in your body that which does not belong
to flesh and blood; and you can not retain that which was not
yours, and never shall be; because the mode of treatment
demands that there never shall be a waste; and so you were
gathered in, and you shall be paid out according to the laws of
all that is right and according to the justice of time; there is
where you wrong yourself at the beginning; you are not an indi-·
vidual independent, and never could be, without revolting
against the rules of this hemisphere; there is the doctrine of
death and life; cause, and effect; the one has an existence prior
to the other, through the evolution of time; and the one can not
proceed without the other; for it shall be according to the lights
of life that there is life eternal everlasting, by the reason, that

governs all things immortal; and otherwise; for as ye learn so
shall ye see; and as when the graves give up the dead, there
shall be everlasting rejoicing; according to the movement of
time eternal; a given thing can come to our sight by intuition,
then why can not it come in form, because it has no knowledge of what is required of it, till it is made to understand what
a purpose is, therefore how you expect to do away with the
organism of sound; wherefore do you hesitate then at the
thoughts of being destroyed, when you all admit, that you have
no "Notion" as to the power, of suppressing the (noise of sound);
your soul is the "Sound"; and you will persist in the belief that
you are to be destroyed; as though it were possible to alleviate,
and handle what is an utter impossibility: You don't dread the
life of another; you think he is all right; his life is no account;
it is sure to go to glory by one route or another; wherefore then
have you got anything to fear; I tell you what it is, that, should
your friends be shaken off the chain of life, you can never walk
on; because there would not be a place for you: A much, to think
of: Has given rise to an infinitesimal amount of what are the
guiding laws of the present age; and after there was no ending,
in all those false prophecies you can not do any sin by looking
our situation boldly in the face, and eulogizing the heavens above
us, for submitting to all the degradation that has flown at her,
without suspending her solar organism: There is where you
wrong yourselves, we are afraid of this calamity, because we
know that we are prone, to connect our afflictions, with heaven;
when there is no doubt whatever, that heaven is not what the
ordinary construction places it at all, wherefore is it common
sense to declaim our troubles to the guidance of this sole power,
when it distinctly shows, no signs of doing us anything except
bountiful service; then why, not be guided by what appears to
be just and fair: Your anguish is torn, in vain by appealing to
God, he has never stopped the elements from working; neither
did he ever hang up the Sun, to please any individual calling,
neither will he ever mix up the stars, for any purpose; because
you think he ought to tell Jupiter and Mars to stand perfectly
still; whilst your scientists took hold of their carcasses; And

pictured them, according to what they had thought, was a nice time to get a specimen of their valuable connection with the other system of government over on the other side of the body; that appears on his side of the scope of light we see; there is nobody, who has been qualified to mesh up this gigantic question yet; and they will need to act in a different way, to what has heretofore been looked at; a manner of looking into this celestial contact, must be defined before any actual results can be gathered in; and so far as the present scientists know; we are not at the beginning; therefore, I shall without more ado say that they will be better informed by giving up their past records; and begin to look at matters more seriously, and less saga- ciously; because the latter comes from what has been mistaken ideas; and can not be told, without the advanced mind knowing that there is something wrong: And a wrong can not be righted unless you obliterate the past completely and hold out new light to the trammeled path: There is how Christ became so unpopular; He showed the wrong side, of life; by his own actions was he condemned, and by his side stood those who acted for him; there you have what can not be construed in any other way except, to boldly face the problem of light on darkness; for he was present but his soul had an attachment, that hid him from those who saw; And they marveled among themselves; saying "what manner of man is this"; "Yet a little while shall ye see me; I go hence but ye can not follow me." I am the true light; follow me and ye shall see the kingdom of him who sent me; take not to yourselves; for it shall be written that the son of man hath power to save sinners from repentance: Your light is very poor, on these sayings, but I can give you the right defini- tion on all these knotty questions; but I know you can not understand me, therefore I must not make myself your jacka- napes; the same as was meted out to the greatest power the world has ever seen; Your ancestors were the very ones who enacted a tragedy, that will last as long as God Almighty causes the elements to gather in, and take away; your being will be blessed forever by this sacrifice; and your intelligence must see that so it was their mode of example to the heathen mind,

3

that provoked them into aspiration of those miracles, that Jesus
performed; and you can see how much the cultivation of signs
from heaven was indulged at the times prior to the coming of
our Saviour; therefore you must not judge his advent as one
instance of God's great glory, you must take the movements of
the wonders from heaven, that were performed prior to his
believing, and connect one with the other, and there you find
that all was prepared for this great crisis: Your own intellect
must tell you that when an art is practiced; that in time it
becomes a perfection; and moreover, we are in an advanced age,
that does not tolerate the sound of former laws: And you will
find, that the people of to-day require better skill to divert
their attention, than the empty-headed illustrations of former
ages: I think well of what was done in the past for human culture; and I think a much better code of laws can not be adopted
to aid the future, but where there is doubt sticking out, it
should be investigated, and set at rest by experienced experi-
menters; that is in a manner to define reason with common
sense: A man may be every whit an experimenter, but he does
not possess the fractional part of a grain of sense or reason: And
he is just the one to lead every one wrong, that has any interest
in defining right from wrong; Your solar system does not get
polluted by any crank, we have always got a menagerie of
effluxions there to speculate upon, and the beauty of the
gigantic affluence of nature's great problem is as far off the
comprehension of the world's mighty experimenter as it was at
the first: Now take your pan of milk, and leave it to set still for
a few moments, and then see what effect, the cream will have
over the interior of the milk, why, it is only divided that is all;
well you have no power yet, that will distill it into milk again,
there was once a common kind of man who told us that all milk
was holy, and why should it not be; there are no men born without he pictures his first affection on milk: and it is the same
to-day, as it ever was; I don't want you to think that I am going
to show you how to make cream stand the contest of becoming
milk again; but I shall tell you that the organism of the solar
flumes magnify their appetite by distilling water into volumes of

fire in the identical way that milk turns to cream; now you may
think I am telling you an impossible story; but you can show me
how the water departs from the ray of Sunlight, because it is
gobbled up in the heat, and so is a multitude of other materials,
that find favor with that gigantic monarch of tact over material;
now take for illustration the governing power of the great measurement of time, and you see that there must be an in-going and
an out-pouring; or what would be the common-sense view of
the situation; there would be a collapse in an instant, only for this
solar organism, there we have the foundation to work on, and
when that is laid we shall show you all the rest; I don't propose
to work out my scheme to you in a dogmatical way, because you
have the whole thing in four parts, one is the light, the next is
the very sure thing we all can talk about; and that is the air we
inhale, the other two are more simple than the two first, that is
the great big lungs, that are filled with the sound of eternity: I
think I have got my plan laid now pretty clearly, so I shall begin
to tell you how I found out the mysteries of the moon and stars;
by watching the contact of night and light: I have been awake
these hundred years devoting my time to nothing else but the
problem of finding out the acts of providence, and I have mastered the sole control of doing away with space, that is the difficulty of finding the lost link, in the chain of evidence; there is no
limit to space: And where the moon hides her body, is as verdur-
ous as the time of sticking in pins for green peas to hang their
lovely blossoms to: I mean that on the other side of life there is
no tares allowed to grow beside the beauties of nature, that
beside the wall of peace, there is not a trace of earthy matter, it
is the picture of God in all his glory, where sunshine exists, there,
can be no frost, and where frozen ice is no sunshine does appear;
now you must try to understand my way of conveying to you the
spark of just reward, and the mark of what comes, from disobeying
the laws of nature; a great many think that a mixture of paganism
and wanton joy are allowed to run riot in the golden gown of
second birth; but it is all the outcropping of the well-known
tempter, such is not the case at all, a man may have many companions in his first birth; but when he crosses to our side of life

he is admonished by the scourge of reflection; and when he merits
punishment, he is whipped with the hand of an outraged people,
who scatter his reputed misdeeds like the flame of an angry fire,
his punishment is the banishment of his presence to darkness;
where darkness is the ruling guide, and he has to work out his
allotted time as an example for those who are to follow him to
the same home hereafter; now you must think it most singular
that those ancients would send a soul to purgatory, and then
punish the soul that had no knowledge of how it was being
worked; yet there is no account kept of what has been formulated
on the heathen side of life; and where you find one code here,
you find a similarity there; and for no good to example from;
except the way to show the guidance of the chains of circumstances; now believe me I am trying to explain an amount of stuff
that surmounts all understanding so far as the present enlightenment has gone: And I want you to be a trifle charitable toward the
manual labor I am taking on your behalf; and not get me meshed
up in a balloon as it were trying to look inside of our great
hereafter; that is what the addle-heads do when they get up in a
balloon, they have an idea, when they leave the ground, that their
expedition will lead to science, because they are that much nearer
the sky; Why, you have all seen a statue on some prominent
position; well did you ever guess at the dimensions of that same
statue; for in doing so it measures just as much again according
to distance than it appears; because it is the embodiment of a
great theoretical research; a given distance suspended from the
clouds on a structure can be easily arrived at, and then you will
find what proportion it has on the measurement of the atmospheric germs, that you see suspended on the globe of space; this
is what I mean to show you, that a chandelier has only so much
candle power from the center; but you omit the difference in
the shade over substance; now you know what I mean by the
theoretical globe of space, it comes in contact with nothing yet
it has a distant reflection that conveys beyond any purpose there
is in its own vicinity; and the same with the light hereafter;
there is no case to keep in what is let out: Therefore the true
construction of the world is that it is let loose upon itself, and no

amount of argument can define it otherwise: You have measured your own talk by the ring of your voices, I just measure
my scope with your sound; therefore you see that a tape
measure, has only got a given number of inches, and fractional
part thereof; but your inference on the ground is that a sound
can not reach any great way; thus you are entirely wrong, a
message given from the ground ascends upward, and conveys its
after-murmur far above the ordinary hearing, and re-echoes
onward beyond the boundary line of incoherency; now you will
believe me when I say that a sound has no boundary line, then
why won't you give me credit for as much again, and that is the
tale I am going to tell you; You know I am as near right as
possible on the sound question: Then be more conservative and
search after what I say is so and so, don't go away and say I
can't, when you know that this word ought to be banished like
the North and the South pole; I have hit the nail between the
eyes, by my inadvertent mode of saying I still think there is
great need of some change, in this second sight of seeing where
there is no object to look at: I don't think there can be many
opinions differ; on the appearance of night and day: Then why
should there be any, on the vague theory of a magnitude of might,
and right: The one governs the stars, whilst the other is the
governor of them: So I shall begin to say I am on the right
track, and leave you to follow me through all the mysterious
parts I have flown; now you think I have got wings on my back,
like an actress of gaiety fame; but there again you are slipping
on greasy ice, I have a parachute more like, and can close up
or pay out, just as I have a mind to; there you have the ethereal
form to a turn, your parachute, is as near an illustration as necessary, the absence of tide and current withheld, for the ethereal
form is likened to an Asp, it bends to the ethereal atmosphere
like the end of a wand: And, in singling out this great accou-
terment as wings, why you anger an enraged people: And sub-
join a blandishment of scorn at your ignorance: that is what
produces so much mischief, is portraying a wrong design of what
is the appearance of our coats of mail, you can get all the ideas
you want, every ass has his followers; and brings bad luck

wherever he goes; but a man who follows the dictates of common sense will advance the most rapidly: Now you know that
there are no wings for you to wear: What do you want better,
than to be one moment a good big parachute, and the next to be
a connected sound: And what more could you wish for, than to
to be an unlimited commodity: Now you have struck some
gigantic monster: That wears claws, like a dragon, but there is no
such thing: What you have on earth can not be materialized
anywhere else; and what you have here is not made in heaven:
For so sure as there is immortal life, there has got to be a beginning: Therefore it is not possible that you can go wrong in
your fears of eternity: It has to be like all else, there can not be
one that does not beget another, and it shall be that as he begets,
so can he come after his own form, and that is his countenance
that lasts him from the time of his memorial; so that instead of
wings as the angels are represented, his mind follows, on the old
form, and he is modeled accordingly; therefore that instead of
his concealment being hidden from view; It is perpetuated forever:
Now listen while I am explaining myself; there are no two beings
alike, therefore the one who is a resemblance of the other, hath
been crucified for his likeness to God: And no other can be found
for he was their only kind good teacher; and has been dead to
humanity since his time of perdition: You are ever on the watch
for the face you know: But there shall be no two alike, there
is the art in finding him who was safe from those who
cried out I am the very perfection of God; because I
did not do his son an injury, you think you are responsible
for the action of those maniacs of fools' judgment; why, how
can you be, it is the workings of the prompter, that is all;
and you are only of those which are the hind end of nature, you
come last; for you are but the beginning of one soul; there is
the true solution to the problem of souls; no two, can be alike,
for he was not of the clay and has not been dead; there is the
mystery of man to matter it can not be, and shall live forever;
now you see I am puzzling to you, but you are he who puzzles
me; there are no men born who do know me, yet I live and so
does he who sent me, there are no lives less wonderful to me

than he was to me, yet, I mastered his manner of guiding God;
now you see we do not agree to be the same kind of being as
your "notion" of God is, I am a scientist, I do not say we are
the son of God after your version of God: But I do claim that
we are all the sons of God: And that is where you have always
been wrong, for the first teaching distinctly says that God told
the prophets to administer according to his holy dictation: And
when they saw his instructions were right, they knew that his
power was infinitely greater than their own: And under all
circumstances when the prophets stuck to their belief: They
accomplished all that was undertaken by them; now you need not
be surprised that they called such an able counselor God: And
when you come to understand the situation better you will see that
it is only natural that when a parent was able to guide the footsteps of his child: Unseen and without knowledge, that he
would tell his child that his guidance was the intuition of the
Lord: And that the child would listen to the voice of his
parent, and his guide, would tell the child that a holy God was
watching him from the sky above, and it becomes so curiously
linked in one force of power, that you can't help it being understood that God is really speaking; that is where the fallacy of
God comes from, believing that he is speaking; when it is the
departed relatives, and friends who are doing it in the persona-
tion of God: Now you don't understand me, for you are
expecting your own friends to come and call out I say "Ted" you
are going to get into a plaguy mess over your farm, if you let old
Davis put his calves over on your hayrack: Now that is not
the way to get information from the Almighty power which is
and always has been since the time of intellect: You must obey
the laws of sound on matter, it is the guide to find out how to
tell what man has known since the first effort: He shall meet
what he has sought after: And he can have what his own intellect wants, now don't make any mistake and suppose, that you
are going to get everything you ask for: Even assuming that
you do understand the way to talk to this power that sees all
around, and can not be seen by you: You can gain the ascendency only by your own unseen power being greater than that

which holds the fort against you; now do you see why all your
wishes don't come according to your actual desires; for as he
sows, may he reap: And as he grows in height of standing: So
shall he maintain his erection: But nowhere does he fall so
heavy as though he were touched by an unseen hand: A good
thought is always worth recording; and a man who knows how
to use that which belongs to another; is the very one to succeed
beyond the maker: Now you have got into a way of thinking
that I am going to give you thoughts for your own hand to
manipulate: And turn them into some specific benefit for your
own special case; but I have no such ideas in my known reason:
There are those who think just like what you have been doing:
and they have got no go in them to take the thoughts after they
are propelled along to them: Your system of indulging fancy
comes from the mind being active: and it is there you seem to
believe that your own control is at the instigator wheel: And
that he can push you to any point he desires; but such is not
the roll of intelligence; there is a distinct battery of appliance,
that is worked by the consumer of the atmospheric arteries:
They come in quantities of so exact form by nature's ordinances:
That a given organic pressure has propelled them to a given
point and has made them to suit what they are intended for:
Now you see that intelligence is worked by a connubial semblance of hygeian act of sorcery; there is the count of good
description, of this form of work in hypotyposis, or more
plainly put it is the marvel of wonders combined to sight; no
two can see alike, neither do they dream the same dreams, for
the fact, that they are only one more thought acted upon by an
outside force; there is the reason why they are not alike in
thought; because their governors are worked more by magnetism,
than by roll of common sense; and they don't guide, with the
same amount of skill: Neither is it their object, to hinder this
one or that one to grow stupid; their plan of style is different,
entirely to what any other is: Now do you quite understand
that I am not speaking of this frame, but of the frame that
works outside of the body; You seem tired of this subject, so I
will dispose of it for the present, and will refer to it again; but

prior to going on with something else, I shall declare myself
more fully by agreeing to your idea, with reference to this phenomena being a wonderful structure for research; and more so
now that we have got at the true way of looking at this gigantic
question; you see I am astronomer, mind-reader, and a divining-
rod: That is the whole theory of getting on in this world:
For you will find that a given number of qualities are always useful in addition to what you may circumvent: And you want a
great many good pods to see through everything; there are
those who come by their gifts in an enlightened way; whilst
others are taken by storm, and have theirs to get in an underhanded way; but the one who works his out from experience, is
the one to be very guarded against, his comes through a rake, and
all the points are sharpened; bide still, when you meet a man of
experience, his teeth are sharp, and his wits are like knives with
edges on either side, make room quite scarce for him, his god-
like stature is impearled with jewels as he moves about: And
can cling to his own superhuman effects with the tenacity of a
wolf at bay, beware, you know not what you do when you measure your points with him who carries his tools between such an
angelic code of uniform; because his guides have made a mesh,
that hangs his soul in heaven, and you and no other one can
debar him from sticking your own to hell, for his very presence
is a safeguard to you, but your hand must not cross his in anger,
he will banish you to a doom worse than the depths of everlasting fire; as the the ancients called it: But you have not quite
got my understanding, it is the way that a given number of
people can divide, and spoil the ones who are at the insulator;
that is all the way a man can be borne down by the unseen
hand: More practically they get him confused, and make him
do things that are void of what he would otherwise have done;
but take a friend's warning; and don't let your passion govern
you to any great extent, for it is always well to be cool and calm,
for this is the way to robe your own intellect in priceless clothing, a hand of time is always by the side, and there stands the
noble light of divine providence: Now you have an idea of
what fate is: For the hand that governs fate is the sole master of

the outer frame, and that is why you have been at a loss to comprehend the all-flowing bright intellect, it comes by the hands of
many makers; and is the gourd of a big structure, in a manner
of speaking, like a fox it has its head onto the face of game all
through its life-long career: There now we have shown you
what you call approximately the close relation of the divining-
rod: Then again you want me to tell you how you should
know my mind was against yours; by the same method of
sound that has been the whole obstacle to the mind of man since
he came into existence; you see very good that is quite a fine thing
in itself, but you have no sense of hearing, that is your greatest
defect: Now you have caught onto my logic: And may
you try to develop this organ, and bring to light more knowledge than the world has ever known; your seeing is great,
but your hearing has quite mastered the whole of humanity since
the first bud of knowing anything: Now you know the way I
am compiling my connections, and you will see that I can tell
you truly of matters that have been quite misunderstood, and
are the root of your great want of further development, your
sight was all you cared for, because you could see, you thought
you knew everything; but your faculty for gaining intentions,
and the mode of defining their meaning is not at all what you
think it is, there are men who have shown you many kinds of power;
but there are precious few, who can explain this scientifically
what their great power is: You ought to ask, these wonderful
people, who come under your notice, how they make up this or
that, and make them explain this power, which they claim to be
their very own, I defy them to call a thing by any given name,
without they are ready and willing to fully show some sense in
their argument, I have not gone off on my high horse to dog-
matize any particular creed, I simply say you are all wrong, but
that does not mean that you are to be affected by my saying it:
I only want you to give me a chance of speaking what I know
to be a stern reality: Now don't go brooding over anything
that might strike you as somewhat different from the ordinary
indulgence of the sound doctrine of a person who claims to be
possessed of such power as will save your souls from the gorge

of paternal clothing of might, I merely wish to satisfy you that
there is no death, by the intonation of immortality: And I can
see by your eyes, that you are going round for centuries looking
for that charmed secret, which has no existence in sight, but in
reality is the living truth, just the same as it was in the days of
our forefathers; now you go home and ponder over what I have
said, but don't give way to grief of any kind; your soul shall live
forever, and make it so good as the sound of your own dictation
will manifest itself plainly before your vision: Always avoiding
danger, or probable danger, for so shall all those who have a soul
to save, and I counsel you to drop all-inflammable harangues, for
it confounds and dazes the sense of understanding, and can hurt
none better than the departed souls, for they shall curse you
back for your own folly; and in their anger, will dye their hatred
in fumes of an holy vow, to punish him who sows such seed of
dense contagion in their home on pathways, so very near the
ones who are fighting for you, never mind the tempter's cry of
rage, "His intuition is the reptile's charm of revenge is sweeter
than a sigh": But father of light come down and strengthen
your child: A great many believe that satan is in their very
midst, but they are not able to define satan, that is where they
commit this folly, and are quite on a footing with his mighty
force, when they curse him: And say let satan loose upon some
poor wretch, who has no friends as powerful as them, they are
satan, when they call him to aid them in his work, of sending
God's people to eternity, now don't you see that a man may be
ever so careful, he has enemies, and those enemies are trying to
circumvent his plans; you can not do any more hurtful thing
than to curse a relative who has crossed the gory stone, of your
mighty wrath, for when such a one has it in his power, to come
back, and teach his lesson of revenge, he strikes beneath all
known cases of comprehension: There now you are at the pit
of undiscovered genius, and I could not tell you what plans an
angered soul might place over against his wounded feelings, I
can tell you of many cases, that were practiced, but you have
the same facility, of investigating these close observances: And
can see in your own midst what I am bringing under your notice;

therefore I will not take time to illustrate this more considerately:
You have my showing what the results could be brought to by
your own lives being upset by the constant stream of everlasting
obstacles, that come near your own prospects of getting what
you wish for: Now you know why you are thwarted by an
understanding that beats all other forces in existence: Take
for example the time that there were wars in the history of the
Levites against the Philistines, there were more demonstrations
for the recovery of the rights of becoming free, than any other
known history of the ancients: You see them struggling for
mastery, by every known device: And they were then only known
to their friends by the kind of prophet, they followed: You see
them trying every scheme to get at intelligent information concerning their adversary's line of battle array; and they never
were better helped than when they took the counsel of that famous
prophet Samuel: For he was able to treat them with some sorcery tricks, that invariably gave his own people the advantage;
you see how necessary it was for them to cling to every piece of
solid advice that was given to them; for they had destiny to
cope with: One word of intelligence made them kings and
nobles, whilst another gave them over to slavery: Now you
know what an unknown power could do then, and you can not
see why I should refer to so ancient a subject, you go home and
read the book of Samuel, from the beginning: And watch for
the account given of that first king Saul, and you will see that
he was a unique man, held by the Israelites as supreme over all
human divine providence; they would have him crowned as
king against the advice of their able counselor Samuel, who
distinctly said that the Lord was against their wishes: Now you
see that Samuel was right, and he held the gates of heaven ajar,
and could tell what was best for them to do, but they wanted
Saul to reign over them; and you see what a disastrous ending
came of it; for the pride of their souls was as wax in the hands of
the great master: Now you know what became of Saul for
banishing all the prophets, that claimed to have a familiar spirit;
take time to consider this questioning: For you are not able to
understand this without you get on a par with the actual facts,

as they took place; for no one seems to believe this present
possibility, of getting over a feature of this great big truthful
idea of his claiming to be superior to God Almighty, he was a
capable man, and could tell whatever was going to happen,
therefore the sons of Israel did not want any other power: For
they knew him better than God: And he could define all unseen
things: Therefore he was their ideal of what God should be
like; according to their own ideas; now you see that it worked
well, until an evil spirit took possession of Saul's body, and gave
him over to the power, of the angered ones, who had opposed his
being made king, and when he gave way to his passions, and
cursed the prophets, with familiar spirits; and drove them out
of his kingdom; his own power gave him up to the wrath of the
great divine providence, that takes what it sees fit, and metes out
an example for the guidance of humanity: You have got enough
examples laid down, but you refuse to listen to the right God;
and he will treat you as he did Saul, now take a message, from
the one who is trying to give you happiness; and listen for the
thoughts coming of holiness and purity; they are as the pearls of
the sea, buried behind a great pile of sand, where none can go
except, the one who diligently searches; for a mighty power, is
on the track of him, who walks righteously; his path, is beset by
a fiendish element, who has got to upset many a plan, before
they can reach the treasured land: You little know, what there
is outside of your own sight, it is one great whirl of spirit forms,
fighting to get near them, that has been their enemy in the body;
and seeking out the best line of action for their friends; you see
what a distinct contact, there is being played at all points, and
you have only to meddle, with what does not concern you, and
there you bring a power, that is willing to aid you work out your
folly, for it strikes those who were your enemies in this place,
of strife and preparation, for some higher work: I can not
go out of my line of action, to display every little illustration;
but there is what I say quite in language, to suit this
particular form of reproachful conduct, you see the backbiter
singling out some poor wretch, and lashing the same party, with
lies, that were purely the make-up of that same backbiter, well you

know, it was only the coming of an outside force for this victim s
misdeeds, at some former period, perhaps the forefathers of this
victim were to blame, for some indiscrimination; may be it was
only a trifle; but yet that trifle has the power, of magnifying by
time: And it is a reflection, that knows no boundary line; It is
the work of the great master, his power surpasses all understanding; for his cast of countenance is beyond the earth's great
center, and he lives on what no man cares to gather in, his home
is beyond the sky, his soul is everywhere God bless immortality:
Now you have seen me demonstrate your God Almighty, and I
say that every word is true, but those who interpreted this in a
way that no one could understand it, and therefore you have
been what no one else can claim to have made you a great laughing stock, for the power, that leads all mankind: Now will you
keep quiet, and let this evil genius hold you chained as a dog, to
the stake of hunger, I say you ought to keep your own anger to
wake up those who have gone on before, and call them back to
your side, and say my protecting angel come closer to me, I feel
the hand of temptation dealing me out my exultation; but I care
not for this, bring me peace, and consolation, by your presence
as my guide: I crave not for might, I care not for crime, I want
my own knowledge to please the divine; it was all well enough
to seek riches, for those left behind; but mind you don't take of
the fruit that belongs to another, for it carries pollution to get
out of cover: that is where the great men find it so hard to bring
in what they have lost, they are always, tying up knots, to
gather in what was left out, and they never let go; but what
there was not a brief moment, when they let go of their own
contents; a great big exclamation of how do you take me out of
this particular extraction, by leaving me, without some one to
know that I wanted, by keeping back, my affectionate coin, come
on and tell me I pray you my sweet angel guide, and I will
never do it any more; because you know I cheated my own
friend; therefore he has now revenged himself on me by showing
me up to be a fool, by being duped by the other one, who was
over against the place, when I did it; somebody must have
heard me, some one must have watched me through a crack:

No my clever trickster it was but the angel's map: You have got round an angle, by keeping quite close to the end: And when you call me sinner I can bite you deeper, than the tiger or the bear, my code is more difficult then either of them too; I was out of reckoning when I was below; but you find me sharper than they go, that is the angel's warning, and do not let it go: You have seen the men come home from work, and drag their tired limbs along, I hope you knew their happiness was purer than the snow, they did their work quite honestly, and their rest is sure to grow: For as he reaps, may he sow, and as he falls by the wayside may he keep: That is his reward for honesty, and as he has gathered good seed, he is capable of sowing, I say this is the state of happiness: That belongs to the just, and no one who does not act justly can bring forth much results: a mighty thing is this great place of ours, we have got hold of the thin end of the wedge, come and help us to place the thick end, through the opening, and as certain as night is the sole companion of the darkness: You have got a great advantage, if you will keep on trying to gather in sense as you go, I have given my whole time to this study, and I never shall rest, until I master the whole entire complexion of everything living and what does not exist now, but what shall hereafter be the exact code of laws, for the departed forms which follow after this body, I have been told that there can not be any other place of good conforming with this same way of expressing my genius, and that I am not capable of demonstrating my exact appearance to the common intellect, of the human discerning power, I claim that I have now the right to do this according to the acts of what has come in this gigantic structure of omnipotent importance; I know that there has been a grave error committed in the commencement: but you can't divide a stone, from itself, without you have accomplished the fact: That there are two stones in one; now you have me caught nicely; but we shall see whether you are capable of doing this justice, after we have begun to measure your own sack, with our corn, I measure you out a piece of corn, and you take it to the grist, and there it is made into a large quantity of fragments; no particular piece has gone on the same as heretofore: It is all improved materially; now you can take it and bake it in the same oven: One is white bread, and the other is graham bread: Yet you started with the one grain of corn, I can not help thinking that you can understand this little illustration; to more fully develop the mind it has been shown, that there are no tares among the wheat prior to its going to the grist: Yet it comes out white flour, and dark colored: Therefore you have got the exact composition in the one grain of wheat, that makes two distinct qualities: Wherefore do you hesitate, in believing that there are two sides to life: You see the grain of corn has two sides to its composition: Yet you can't believe that you have a bright side, and a dark one: Although your very existence solely depends on what you eat and drink: Now we can assume that you live, without this bread of life: There is no other way to illustrate, this disposition: Only to say, that you have food to eat, and water to drink: Which demonstrates, that you have the two eternal fountains of life at work on your own organism: . Therefore we can not divide you in two, for there is no division of the sound, that bears your soul aloft: And to more fully prove to you that a man is a machine after his own maker, I will say that a time will come, when you will see that I have made my study a complete code of intellectual knowledge kept by myself alone, in such form as can not fail to convince any one of the truth of what I shall hereafter make known to the world, of my scientific researches: You have got me into this by saying I am a fool; but I shall demonstrate the fact quite plainly that I am not such a fool as those who have been making out that I knew nothing: You have only got to tell a good man that he can't, and he is at the machine, of time, he will impress you favorably, with his fashion of that which belongs to his craft of showing his frame of sense, you must not take it to heart, when he does not demonstrate his skill by paying you back, with nature's confines of his prostration of your own frame, he may positively decline an engagement of honor such as your estimation of manhood's affluence, of striking back incoherent expressions, of anger: Yet, he has within a governor, that says don't do it now, wait until he sleeps: Then drive in

your nail of perfect blight against his anger, it will sting him
worse, and make him feel quite small amongst his companions;
now you have gotten a description of three kinds of man, but in
neither of them does exist a fine element of skill: They are
mere puppets, in comparison to one who can stand off, and say
his intelligence is as wax in my own hands: There is the secret
of the kind of material they are all constructed with: Now you
take a man, who understands how to make his business a profession: And he can keep inside, of the ring of his own sound,
for he has those, with him who will take care to warn him of the
presence of danger; there is the true secret of mind over
material: And when you have given it a careful investigation, it
has no other absolute connection but the belief in its own
divinity; I show you these things to make you understand yourselves better, therefore you must not believe me insane, when
you have not been able to understand me, I am the light, and no
darkness can affect me; you see that those words do not mean
what you believe them to mean; they are the words of a higher
power; which give themselves up to the understanding, that
there is no more illustrious mode of defining this chart of skill;
and when the ones who are anxious to come and show mortals
what they have to contend with, it surely has to come between
some kind of understanding, without this great amount of pressure, which has been going on since the world began: You have
only the surface, you have not gone below at all yet: I shall
show you where you have been led into this, first by asking you
a question? there is the mind that grasps ideas; from somewhere; and you have called him a genius, but you have not seen
the way he was helped to get so fine a construction of his own,
without this his mind was nothing; yet you have got the idea
that his mind is superior to those other men, who have never
done anything out of commonplace; yet it is impossible for you
to believe that his mind was merely the workings of these mem-
branes of actual flesh, you are as ignorant as a calf, on this
question, I know not what kind of a mind you have, neither do
I care; I am not illustrating for the individual; I am working for
the whole conglomeration of the masses who form this entire

4

universe; now take not to yourselves, what is intended for the
whole of mankind: This I have to say is the eminent calling of
a number of spirits, who have come forward for the purpose of
throwing their enlightenment through the universe; now you
will understand why you have been getting points that have not
occurred to you before: And it will be shown by us that we
have a power second to that mighty structure of evolution, that
has intelligence, and can divide all things immortal and otherwise: You seem astonished to be told by this force, that you
are all as ignorant, as the days, of your first appearance: But I
am not going to give you this after I have said you are the
same as this one who is at our beck and call: For he is made
what he is by our own style of making him comprehend our
code of speech now you know why he is not more than can be
expected of man; so you have only to cultivate the outside
frameworkings: And you can converse, in an intelligent way
with those who have gone on before; in an independent manner
of conversation: You think that it would have been good
policy to have told you at first, that there was no difference
between this man and any other: Your notion is wrong again:
For had a messenger been sent, to take this upon himself, his
whole mind would have become stupid: His reason demands of
us, that we shall only give him certain points at a given place;
otherwise he could not proceed at all: And then you would not
have the benefit of this understanding; and to make you believe
we have to measure your intelligence with our own; otherwise
you would not come any nearer than you were before: Do not
take this matter to heart in any way, it is not a thing of consequence to the officers of the law, they can keep on just the same
as before, and so can the denominations of each and every
religion under the heavens, I am not going to tell you that it is
for you to lay aside your own cloth and follow me, I have not
the desire to keep you away from this or that, your welfare is
not my concern, and I must not say be a spiritualist, or be a
confounded ass, you have the work of my knowledge before
you, and you can place it in your senses: Or you may say he
who wrote that book was possessed with no small amount of

grains of intelligence; but we don't want to follow him for fear
his mind is too much ahead of our own, that we have got to
stand still and see whether any one else can not beat him, in
showing us some new way of believing that he is wrong, and
this next one has mastered the exact fixings of our immortal
takings in and payings out: You have got to see for yourselves,
whether this is correct or not, and you can always find this out
when you pass away to your home eternal, there is no disputing
this fact, for as you have grown in wisdom, more will come to
you as your advance becomes more perpetuated, and when the
great God of time sees fit to explain this actual way of defining
your wisdom, he will make you what his skill can do, without
any effort, on his part: You have seen the many wonders that
he has worked, in the past, and it is not righteous to commence
to doubt his other capabilities when it is so natural for him to
accomplish his every duty with no greater effort, than to do his
own work, in a manner both pleasurable, and in all manners
conducive to his own entire happiness; take into consideration
the fact, that there is nothing but pleasure in eating and drinking: And you have got all the pleasure you can reasonably
expect, for no man can exist on this earth, without he does eat
and drink: And his soul has to be kept in the body by this
common process of his being filled at intervals of his own craving for more, and his light will be shut out if he does not get
this necessary maintenance of the food to supply the vital cord,
with this exact thing, and failing in getting this it will claim the
protection of its hereafter from the same who brought it into
that stage of confusion; for as it was confused in the first
instance, so shall it be in that same state when it passes out of
its earthly body, and no one can read it any plainer, it was stuck
into the body by concussion: And it passed out of the body by
the same process; that is it has been propelled out of the body
by the force of the atmosphere coming to take of its own circumference; which had not been gone to so great an extent as
it was in the first place, for it had got used to the atmosphere
being poured in, and drawn out: So that a single instance of it
being separated from that which it never belonged to has no

power to injure, beyond the fact, that it was so arranged before
it proceeded to enter, that it was given the effort of knowing
that it was safe to come after its own knowledge; you are mystified by this; but I can not do it any other way, a mind is intact,
when it enters the abdomen, and can not be called out by any
other: For it has the very structure erected prior to its entrance,
and is not made there at all: You see that were it not for this
feature of the case, there could not be any governor on that construction; and therefore it would be a nonentity; you try
making an engine, and don't make any guiding application: And
see what you have got, it is lost for want of this motive power;
and can not be taken either backward or forward, therefore it is
a nonentity, the same as anything that has to come to life: You
have got me in a fix, for you think I am working an engine onto
you; but that is not it at all I have got a complete motive
power to govern me; and you have no idea as to what a start I
have over you; there is the whole piece of structure in a sea-
shell, it seems all right, and is perfect in itself; but you just
place it on your ear, and you can distinctly hear the sea roaring,
then does that not prove itself to you that there was once a
beginning beyond a possible dispute, it says I came from
the sea: And when you put me back into the ocean I will
not call out for I have found my home at last: You can
not do any better than to wander by the beach, and find all the
little shells that are laying about the beach, and you examine
them thoroughly, and find one of these with a hole in it, and it
has no sound equal to the perfect shell; there you have got
what represents to you the great hereafter, it shows you that
a shell has a body, and is in perfect harmony, with itself
although it has dropped off companionship with its fellow
shell, and I want you to be very particular about this, for
it is an illustration in itself that has no concern with matter
at all: And is as nearly perfection as anything can be; yet
it is a great deal more alive than you give it any credit
for: And when an apparent dead sea-shell is alive after
it has been out of the water for years, how is it possible for you
to die, when you have nothing within your whole composition

that has no material form at any time in the whirl of its own
extension, therefore it is not to be supposed for an instant, that
you are able, to kill that sea-shell, by placing it under your foot,
and crushing it to powder: There is the difficult part, you can
do as you have a mind to, with the shell, but you are powerless, and always will be to govern, the sound of the sea, in that
shell; for it has no life, except what was given to it by the ocean:
From whence it came, it shall so return, and forever be of its
own time of making, from the beginning of time and place forever
mortal: Now you have got a few good points out of me in this
illustration of a shell, but I want you to take a broad view of
things in general, and not go picking up a mere shell, and comparing this pearl to a great gigantic form of nature, it is absurd
to suppose that we became men and women out of a sea-shell;
yet I have got my own way of bringing you to face the Almighty
God of all before me and you to liken ourselves to none other:
And I won't be happy, unless I can prove you capable of cleav-
ing to my form of God, before I give you up to this great darkness: Which has been suspended across your vision from the
time of the ancient fathers, who could have told this in a better
way, had they so desired: And I am not going to be their
judge, they were as I am possessed of the same power, and they
were not willing to give to the world: All the facts, that were
there before them; neither will I come and unbare every fiber as
it has been shown to me, I can not get the roof on, until the
walls are erected, and thus is the way it was governed before,
and I will have nothing at all to do with this form of self-con-
struction; for it has been the power of the great maker, who
instigated this machinery, and let it go on in a miraculous manner, and I have no hope in making any changes for the better or
worse, I don't come and ask you to cast aside all your treasures,
and follow me, I say search, and it will be given to you independent of any mortal's aid; you never ask your pastor whether you
shall eat and drink, well don't you cut the bread of life without
his assistance, and what makes you shirk the other responsibility:
Take no heed for the morrow, and watch what comes to you,
you don't understand this saying, it is after this form, mind

what you are guided to do: And your father from heaven will
bring joy unto you; that is your own impressions will tell you
what is best to do; now follow me, and I will lead you, whatever
comes first to your mind keep in till it has resolved itself into
shape; then do not disregard it when it appears difficult, for he
who masters his first thoughts is a kingdom within himself:
Don't go on doubting this and that, for it brings all you want of
confusion, and can not do anything except to change your mind,
that is the way to give away your prospects in heaven; for he
who struggles well is sure to meet many friends, who have
been watching from their own place of abode, not with disrespect, but with appreciation: For he had gone through
what kept others away: And they placed him by the side of
heroes: Who won their esteem for valor here below: Now
you think that I have no right, to take upon myself this way of
showing what has not been done before, yet you admit that a
power, in the land has a right to bring out a new invention: So
you will class me as a crank, but I too can bring out an invention far superior to anything you ever saw, and will do this,
immediately you tell me I am a fool and don't know anything:
For as sure as the Sun shines in heaven, there are those there
who will be ready and willing to form a chain of evidence
complete in itself to produce, what you and no mortal man ever
saw yet: And as for your telling me I am a crank, why where
are those who do believe in him who was not a crank, I know I
am a crank, and one that can hold his own against all cranks
that are or ever was: You know that a bad beginning has
nothing to do at the finish, but it does affect the middle
course, for when a man has begun a thing wrong, he can get
back, and begin over again, but when he commences at the
beginning and keeps on wrong all the way to the end, he is
a fool and will not be counted as any better, than a good
general to fix fools by, therefore it is not well to condemn a
man because he makes a mistake and then returns over his
folly, and leads a different life hereafter, that is one of the
many privileges, belonging to man, he has been led wrong
by a circumstance of which he had no knowledge: And could

not be done otherwise with for a time, until he was made to understand his own position: Now won't you see that a man may change when he has found out that he is wrong; but he has no business to follow a course all the way to the end, when he knows he is going wrong, that is his to say I am a fool, but I shall not be so any longer: That is the philosophical view of what is known, as the tenth commandment, after you have given all the cravings for vice away, take up the cudgel, and break no more: That is as the wording of that great structure has been left unfinished, it is plainly illustrated, but it does not reach the wicked, for they seem to say to themselves, it was there I first broke the laws, of Moses, and I can not hope for salvation: That is a wrong notion: for you have the proof plain and emphatically denied by our Saviour Jesus Christ, it was as he said, a man may sin many times: But his after-birth was not hopeless: And he should continue to live on and hope forever: For such was the kingdom of heaven: That a judgment there was: And against that judgment there was a resurrection: So you see that he did not tell you not to hope, and he said a man that was smitten with the palsy was greater by far than him that was whole, why then do you say I sinned before, and I have no soul to be saved, did not Christ distinctly say, that no man knew what his hereditary punishment was; wherefore do ye hesitate, "I am the light follow me and ye will be safe," but they stoned him, and said he hath a devil: No man walketh beside this man for he is as one possessed with evil, it is written that ye shall not associate with harlots, whist ye not, that this man said when walking by the harlot, come unto me for I say that all those who truly repent will see my father which art in heaven: Now I take this to mean that his words were then more powerful, than the fiends who tore his young life away; and were not able to discern the destruction that they were working: For his soul was troubled, and he vexed wrath, yet no man came near to him, is his time come to save sinners from repentance: No I can't come again for I once was young and pure, but now I am polluted with crime, God knows that

this is wrong: And I say that the interpretation is one mass of
errors from beginning to end: You think I am going into
what can not be borne out by the testimony of his work; yet
you have no confidence in yourselves; and you believe that your
churches will bring you home all right, go to them, stick to
them, believe in them, and all your finery won't help one iota;
it is a myth: A great big humbug, to think that Christ died for
sinners, he was torn to death by those who guided his body, and
it was the work of fanatics who exposed him for the love of
making a power to give light hereafter; to hide forever the great
commune between heaven and hell: Now you know what a
man has been then, he is able to be again, and your ideal of
God can be as he was when Moses went up into the burning
bush, for it is so written that as many more may come after
me, but none shall hold the ties that were as wax beneath my
heel, yet it can be and I shall know the hereafter by the beating of my own pulse, for as his pulse beat there was life, but
when the pulse ceased to beat, they said he was dead: And
yet on the third day he was buried, and then again he arose
from the dead, that is not hard to understand at all, for his body
was in keeping with his outside connection, and was not dead,
it was in the state of coma, and could be used again as
the instrument of breath proceeded, without any apparent use
of the lungs; this is not a difficult situation at all and,
could be held as firm by the outer construction, as though it
were in the body, and instead of being a miracle it was the
action of his instructors guiding him through all this great train
of circumstances; now there is this to be borne in mind, a man
has to be brought through a systematic form of treatment,
before he can be dealt with under such circumstances; and when
he is once under the full power of his guides, his life is their
own, to deal as they see fit, and you can readily understand, that
OUR Saviour was begun with on his first advent into the scene
of life, and when he attained his twelfth year, that he was as
flexible, and in conformity of his own moulding, and that his
guides had him to do what they wished; now you see, that his
feat of puzzling the Elders was not of so much importance as

this nation at the present time believes: And it ought to be a lesson to those who have got children under their charge, to be alive to the fact, that a spirit of evil or good may be framing the young mind, and not admonish too readily, for it is quite easy, to drive a bad spirit away, and bring a good one, and it is very often the contrary, that the good spirit is driven away and the bad one enters: A given circumstance may come, with no apparent effort, on the part of those you are placed in charge; but you taught the child how to pray, and his prayers come away from those who sent you to him, and his whole hereafter is based on those few prayers, that you were so very careless with; for as he shall see the light, his soul shall speak, and say she was my first instructor, and I never knew her to be what she said I was to be; therefore it is easier to entangle the circumference of the child's frame, than it would be to devise a scheme of setting it right again; your own taught that idea of vision, which was there for the child to see and judge by; and when you have got to this stage of life wherein the same kind of clay has you in their coils, then it is your duty, to look first at your own self, and bring about a distinct understanding as to your own conduct, in the presence of that child; now you see it is not the way you have of saying that prayer: It is the style of your own actions, which govern that young mind: For he has you as his patron, and when he sees you in a violent rage storming as though his life were the ideal of this fond passion; for as he discerns so shall he keep, and as you build up, in his sight, there is where his knowledge springs from: And you may keep his mind pure by praying, but not if you say, "Gentle Jesus hear my prayer, and make a little child thy care": You see what you have done, you have sent him away by your own passions; and therefore I say that to preach is one important thing; but to practice is to reach the kingdom of God: Holy light of day, see ye not the darkness; for though ye see, it is the afterbirth of sight; and as ye walk come not to harm for I know not what is goodly in my sight is divine; and no one can know; but those who see the way of this great continual strife; your own words will rise up against you, and seem as your worst enemies;

now take warning in time, and do not be guided by the presence
of those who teach, for as he was taught, his life was taken
away: Now then reach out and say to your own conscience, I
am come into a great barn, and I have none here to console with
me, I shall die of the moths and the rust: Take not of the
comforts of life too greedily: For as he reaps so shall he sow:
Therefore beware of false prophets, and seclude yourself from
their presence, I declare that no man knows what the other may
mean: Neither does he keep in his own memory what he has
agreed to do: For it shall appear as different as two grains of
gold, when the reflection of night shall gloss it over, I say you
are as wise as he, and do not cultivate his thoughts, lest they
sting you like an adder: Now give me some small consolation
in thoughts that are good, and drive off the one who says, take
my hand in earnest, for I have sworn to be faithful and true, I
would rather say, as you want me to bring good luck to you, I
will conjure you to be my friend; this is the true conclusion of
a prophet, for he can tell whether you are true or false, and his
words are as though he were bound unto you, well it is the worst
thing possible to attempt to bind a soul, it knows it is free, and
it rebels against the restraint of another, and has to be carefully
guarded, otherwise it will seek flight, in its own way; therefore I
say bind not in this way a common vault; it is wrong to do this;
ask them to be a friend to you; but do not give them the burden
of an oath, it strikes one too much as the man of the third generation was taken, when he had to bear the burden of an
incumbered estate, I got what was left of the profligate hogs,
who deemed me no better than the raging torments of hell, as
their heirloom divine: And I do not see what there is to be
done in this life, only keep on struggling for an eternal curse;
therefore remember this that as ye curse, so may he curse you;
and when ye have the light, let it come in upon you; and as the
divine providence guides; so shall there be great rejoicing when
ye have come to know the way of your own salvation: I will
give all that have sins to be forgiven rest; It is the noblest thing
in existence to know that a sinner can bring his soul back to the
true path of righteousness; for as he so sinned did he not lift off

the veil of his own iniquities; and did he not work out an example, in the sight of all men, and were not those men bettered for seeing his downfall; you have noble providence seen fit to raise up the excellency of the many, by the cursing of the one in their presence; you shall yet learn that the great God of heaven is the Governor of immortal hosts, that he it is who defines the righteous from the wicked; and brings sinners to repentance, for the sake of doing good, God bless his holy goodness; and keep his laws holy, that there may be no transgressors, for as he came down into the world from his throne on high, make him to know that he is draining off the pure, as also of the wicked; and may he call on all to lend their help to bring forth righteousness to see the ways of those who have the power of corruption: You know not what you are doing, by saying I have been good and pure in thought, for as he says this his thoughts are wafted on high, and there is an angel who peeps in every cupboard, and it is not possible for this person to go forth, without he is watched; and it is a greater example to corrupt one that is holy in earnest, than it is to pollute ten that have well-known sin in their hearts; now look well to your own thoughts for as he shows, so will he be governed for show; I have come to this stage of my own ways, that I feel the effects, before they actually reach me, and I can do no other, than to be guided by the all-powerful influence, that surrounds my soul, I care nothing for the strangers, that are gaining their points by throwing their eloquence, into my teeth, and trying their utmost to hurl confusion on my head, I despise their every effort, and I can hurl such-like to the depths of perdition: That is what I will do to those who come with their nice tales, of taking my strength away, I don't want any one to become my master; and I declare that there is no man superior to me in the sight of him I serve; I give my soul to aid and assist the divine providence; And I will keep his work as pure as my strength will aid me to do; and in working out this, it is beset on every side by those who are keeping the road open for their own friends, and I say that antagonism runs riot, even in the secluded path of your own chamber; and when you sit down, in your anxiety of thoughts, keep yourself cool and collected, bring back to your memory, the reflections of some pleasant experience, recall the first bright spot on your life, and say within your own soul, I want a reunion with that same pleasure, and I venture to explain, that your troubles will disappear, and the difficulty, will become as the sunshine, there will be veins of light streaming through the hitherto flood of blackened charcoal, I am illustrating a black surrounding, when I say this is a piece of good advice, I have seen the black clouds roll by many times, and I want to show the silver-gray lining beyond the clouds, so you must not suppose that I am going to let this hang on my own conscience to any great extent, for although, I begin to see more clearly, there are times, when I have to steady myself, and say there is a storm brewing, and I will keep quiet until it passes away, for should I become entangled, there will be a kind of hurricane playing around my own soul and I must lay down softly, and keep within myself or I shall be torn, like an angry wind twists the young shoot of grass, as it peeps above the ground; you can see the effect, an outraged conscience has over the wind, but you fail to find any defects, when the inner cord of my own is torn by passion; yet it came near tearing his soul out of his body, and would have done so, only the coating-over was too tough, yet his arms did not seem to protect that blast, let his finger-nails dig as deeply as they may into his flesh, it won't commit the injury that a scathed heart does know, when the anger has risen to such a flame of madness, that drives away the reasoning faculty: You see what danger there is in anger, yet it has no apparent outward sign, I will not be guided by this soft plaything that has no sense, it is but the angry wind playing havoc with the grass: And I am different to the wind by a long sight; this is the reasoning of the pagan, he does not give the wind credit for anything, he is a veritable ass, his whole life hangs on the wind, it is this same wind, that blew him to eternal life everlasting, and he cares nothing about it except that he was annoyed by it coming and blowing his silk hat into the gutter; you suppose that there was a beginning such as you have been taught, why it is as absurd, as your own ideas of

this wind, being your enemy, why that a wind can do harm
there is not the least doubt, but you forget the good in your
times of tribulations: Now keep in mind that a wind is produced by the atmosphere becoming very hot; this is the cause
of the time it requires to be under the restriction of the Sun, it
can not blow always, for the Sun does not keep it in subjection
only when it is in a formula of this getting it ready to let go:
And by keeping it in is by forcing it into a state of coming into
what is called the effluvia of great complexion of the exact
quantities to one source at a given time, it holds the breath of
its own life, into a given number of breaths, the same as a man
breathing, and gives out a long breath, when there is a current
of angry comment on a particular kind of destruction coming
in the way of its own circle; and by keeping it away by a countenanced gust of wind, it will begin to cover over this place,
and hold itself pure of the material, that does not require to be
drawn from, in any particular part, until such a compartment is
filled; then it gives out a different atmospheric element, at any
particular point, you don't get hold of this wind at all, it has to
be pushed out, and drawn in at a direct angle, or at any point,
that is in the compass, at a specific period; and you must not
run off with any foolish idea that there is a great big spirit
controlling the atmosphere, for it the Sun, at the head of nature,
that works in unison with all its smaller bodies, or in a more
geographical system of description; I can do this better by saying that the Sun is in a manner of speaking the exact mouthpiece of the whole universe, it is not a speaking-trumpet as
people would have it ascertaining its own proofs; yet it does the
work of making man and beast alike: There is no use being stupid
any longer, I realize the situation is a difficult one, but it can
not be made worse than what it is by my speaking, and you
know we all hold, that the Sun is our safety-valve, and not one
of all the whole world would consent to give up that glorious
sight for one single hour, did he realize that it was to be his
last hope of reaching God; you are as flexible as paint in the
hands of your own maker, and you are as glory chained to the
gates of heaven, when the Sun peeps at you: God bless her

noble face, make heaven and earth a Paradise, for men and
mute to garble in, God grant them peace and happiness: You
have been told that a certain kind of man was made, and he was
formed after the likeness of his maker, this is practically correct, but it does not follow in the light that you have been
looking at it: There is a much different view of this work in
reality; it comes after the form of its own maker; and is precisely the same as was first said, yet there is this difference, that
the first man was a mute, and could have nothing to say on
this subject, I will show you in my works how man first came
into existence, when the proper time comes: Now you know
this has not been done before in a way that would satisfy any
rational being: You have gone wrong at the start, is no reason
why you should always be wrong: And when you are better
informed there is nothing more easy than to abide by what is
given to you; you know that a man may err once, and may then
retract, but when he will persist in keeping on his false path,
his soul is certain to go wrong; then take a mind that is naturally
brilliant, and he has got it in him to be sharp, well he can lead
his friends to any given route that is given to him; now don't
you see that a mind is not as was thought at first, capable to be
taken out, and led away by this or that idea; you forget that a
man was not able to grasp the situation as he does now: And
you will continue to live in ignorance just as long as you stick
to these same ideas as was paid out to the ancients; your very
safety demands a change, in your own ideas, for you are now
being worked in a way that has no foundation, and where there
is no solid foundation, the earth can not stand: That is as near
an expression of rights as possible, it will not be long before it
has been found out, that the world is not round as some folks
have got it fixed, it is an oblong shape, and is driven round by
the atmosphere becoming congealed when it enters the Sun, and
has no other way of pressing the heavens along than by its own
weight coming in contact with the earth at the rear of the
Sun, it goes in first by the side of the Sun, and is propelled there by the attraction caused through the heat, coming in contact with the after part of the Moon, it draws the

sideway motion, when it comes near the entrance to the Sun, and is lifted up by the pressure of its own weight coming in front of the power that has such an attractive agency at work, it will not lift up a quarter the weight it has only that the dimensions are quite at variance with the scope that is at the back of the heavens, it is here where the great compass works, for it revolves round in a circle, causing the left wing to fall as the right ascends, and is slowly revolving all along the way it runs into the ash-pit at the rear, this is what is called the second flight of the stairs, it drives all the atmospheric matter right round the drum-head, and brings it back again into the wheel-house, that is where it is condensed again, and is thrown out into the hind-quarters of the Sun, and is there fetched again into action by the same process of dividing the manure from the moisture; this is the same as a man is constructed, only that the machinery that works the heavens is an everlasting one, for it builds all the time, and is growing instead of decreasing, that is the way of all the heavenly bodies; they are all the time growing: And they have no beginning except on this firmament; that is surely a fact, that both man and beast do continue to keep on growing forever: Now don't misconstrue what we are saying, and suppose we are lying for our own conscience is clear, and we fear no contradiction, because you don't see these things is it possible for you to be left out of knowledge forever, I don't give you what I know to be a fact myself; I am giving you what I am told to do: And I shall keep on to do this as long as ever there is anything to tell you: Now I am advised to stop at the very first, and told that you are not ready to receive such an important communication; but I have argued the question out with all scientists, and they say you are growing more intellectually every day, and it must be done sooner or later: That is what I am told that there is no good in keeping it from you, you have got the whole world to keep in order, and the sooner you understand what becomes of those who pass over the better: There will then be an assurance of their right position, for when they know not what has to be done with them, they are as careless as so many wolves, and are just as apt to come under the standard of what is right as ever they are to get wrong, when they know there is a hand upon them always, is it not possible that they will say within their souls, I don't want to be brought back to this earth, and made to work out my iniquities, for the sake of showing people, what an example is: Now you know very well that a life of this sort is not very respectable, and it ought to show you, that there is one amongst you who is to be set upon, and thrown from his high position, and cast into everlasting scorn, I will show you that once a man is cast down, he is the victim of every mean creature, and he is the sole helping hand of the evil one to lay hold of and make him feel the thorns of a persecuting dignity; you have come out of many a scrape, but you never felt any better for it; therefore you can see how much better it is to avoid these dangerous encounters, it might bring you into crime, it might lead you by, to let you see how nicely you can shave the curve of detection, but you will always find that it is better to form a solid foundation first, and bring this home who keeps you there; don't go running after what has no concern in your own business: Keep out all intruders, and leave all that does not belong to you alone, for it shall be the one who victimizes another, who is a victim for those who are looking for their prey; you don't see how it is worked yet, it amounts to this that a crime has got to be punished; no matter how that crime originated; It was done, and before man and beast that shall not be glazed over, it has to be withheld for a time, but in the end there is no rest for the wicked: As he shall lift his hand against his brother; so shall a mighty power be brought against him, even the whole of heaven would turn out, rather than there should one sinner escape; now you know that it is impossible for a crime to go unpunished, and it will be the forte of God Almighty, which shall see justice done to the merest worm of he who raises his hand against the weak, for as he be made strong, so shall he be made weak at the hour of his reckoning with his divine ruler: Now don't stop to think, and leave out the calculation, that as he ruled, so shall he be led to the altar of God Almighty, and as he did rise up against a sinner and condemn, so shall he be

punished for his own offenses; there shall not one escape out of
that mighty host; now picture to yourselves this great problem,
and see whether you can not find the hand of nature dealing out
her own great power, as though she were governed by a living
God: " Now I have to ask you one question ": how is it that a
man can mend his own pants when he knows that there was no
one, who had any idea of making them at the first beginning;
does it not prove to you that man is advancing as rapidly as
though his very existence depended on what he is able to do;
therefore he must get on faster, when he knows how he is
being worked; is it not possible for a man to find out where he
is going next fall, without being told how he is to arrange his
affairs before he leaves; that is the point, he can do this little
piece of mental calculation quite easily; but he could not explain
it to you how it is done, not if it was to be the last breath of air he
had to draw; and why should he be left in this darkness, when
his own guides, said to him so and so will take place, but we
won't tell you how we are going to circumvent these little
obstacles that you see in your own way, we can take you by
them, or we can stick you up in them, just as we have got a
mind to lead you with; that is all there is to do, take a very fair
chance, and keep on persevering, and you will surmount any
obstacle on earth, but you must keep quite clear of other influences; that is the secret of success: Take a man who minds his
own business, and he will win nine times out of every ten; and
that other time it is because he was pitched into by a whole nest of
jealous vagabonds, that threw their influences together, and overpowered and confused his own party; you have got hold of a mighty
power, that can divine almost every known power on earth or in
the heavens above you; then why should you disregard the
teachings of such a strong force, that is as there is light shown,
wherefore do you get confused in the darkness; now don't go on
thinking that no one can tell you anything about heaven, for it
shall be made plain, that the gates of hell are under the foot of
man and that the head of the supreme ruler is at the mighty
power over the head of man, God bless immortality: Now look
and ye shall find, search diligently, and the road that he shall
5

walk on will be strewn with flowers of gold, a mighty and everlasting God, come down in all thy dowery, and show this benighted
people thy everlasting power of might: And main, take not back
from their vision this ray of sunshine, but rather keep on glori-
fying thy eternal grace, with the plenitude of thy noble, and
eternal spring of everlasting water, preach not thy doctrine to an
idle good-for-nothing people make them understand that there
is a God Almighty in reality, as well as in form; Now listen to
this, is it not quite as well to hold sacred the truth of Godliness,
purity and eternal welfare supreme, than it is to be painting a
picture of eternal hatred and scorn, for such is the true state of
affairs at the present time, don't liberate the devil when you have
got no right with him: There is the picture you are always bringing before the eyes of your own children, keep him bound, and
you have purity and holiness: Great God of heaven come forth
and hear your children supplicate in defense of your holy laws,
make darkness pass them by, and Sunrays of light shine in upon
them God bless and preserve their holiness as pure as thy own
driving snow, make a power more strong than the time and tide
that governs eternity: Great master of all worlds beneath you
look up and pray deliver us from this power of divine providence,
and make our eyes look upon you as we are: There is the
teachings of the power that has no ending, that is the reverence in
which you have to seek purity; not by saying I do no wrong I must
be pure, for it shall be shown, that the pure at heart is the one
who is the easiest victim: And he may gather in good seed for all
his life, and then the adder may strike him, and turn him to scorn
before he has had time to reach the grave, God willing his destiny as a proof of his power: Now you will believe in me when I
show you how hard it is for the righteous to enter the kingdom
of heaven; you see me in glory, and you see him in pain, then,
why should you guess at his future divine: You thought he was
holy pure and sublime: But you did not contentedly make up
your mind: There is the great secret that has to become known
to the human mind, it must be clearly and truthfully illustrated,
before man can see what there is before him; and you know as
well as I can tell you that man must see some proper reasoning

before he can be convinced; therefore he will be shown how this great hemisphere became one great eternity, or he can not concede his pride of opinion for any living being; that is but the natural reasoning of one who can see but does not understand the sense of hearing: Now you have been plaguing this great universal knowledge for centuries to know why it did not occur to God to make all people white; when he was being so capable as to know the rights of every other thing, you ought to be very certain before you condemn him as to his rights of constructing this humanity, for he knew which way to tell them from those who belonged to the devil; you have no rights at all in the matter, therefore you can not condemn him for doing just as he thought best; now do you see that a man who is white is not one bit better than he who is colored, and he who is deformed is more likely to be befriended than he who is whole, I thought you were taken in by this form of sentiment; but I see that a great many have come to the conclusion that a man must be conformed after the one model, and then grown into shape by his own deformities; this is the true doctrine of the phrases of the human race; that is they don't come in this formation, in the first instance; they have to come before the time of the angels, or they would not be in existence at all: There is no grounds for doubts as to the correct origin of man, he came from the wind, and the dust has made him grow to what he is: Your theory, of God making the first man and woman is certainly quite correct in one sense, but as for him doing it after your mode of thought is quite at variance with common sense: And you have got that form of knowledge from some ignorant spirit, who was not able or willing to throw a proper light on your surroundings, that is all you need be told on this question: Now just let me show you how much better I can explain this theory of human form coming to light; You have seen how I was attacked by the other forces, in the beginning of this work, by their constant interruptions, and see how I am persevering to master every obstacle, that there shall not be a single vestige of subtle cunning in the whole of my work, I may be held down, from giving you a direct description, but

you shall have the facts as they really are from the upper form
of perpetuity: That is I can call you stupid, when you have
failed to see how I am drifting my subject, so as to reach a
degree higher than the mighty force, that is moving heaven and
hell to stop me from proving my exact defending qualities:
Now do you not see what a power I am working against, the
one side don't see my drift, till I am foul of the other: That
is the exact code of intelligence coming along as you go, and
you have got me in a very tight squeeze when you press
me on to show you how man first originated: That is a question that very few can answer, and it is mighty few who are
willing to engage in such a battle of questioning: There never
was a man born yet who could tell you how he was brought to
life, and I have settled this question for you forever, then don't
begin to doubt my ability as to how the first man came to see
the light: That is your greatest difficulty now, and I shall surmount the style and get over the fence without a scratch: You
know me of old by this time, and you will find me a greater
power in heaven than I ever was, when you had me chained for
telling the truth: Now don't think I am bragging over you,
because I won the honors of reaching my freedom by bringing
souls to salvation: You shall yet see me glorified in deference
to the times when I said I was a power in my own land, and I will
prove you are as arrogant as the fiends who work you for their
own condemnation of me: Now don't think that you will ever
be able to master me, for I hold a sword at every chest, and say
come on you can neither kill me nor yet can you frustrate the
teachings of God, Amen: You are as subtle as a fox, but you
master your own power by getting at some one else, that is as
clear as day does bring forth new light: Your own thoughts are
as false as the whims of a great big flying-machine, that every
soul dreams about reaching heaven with: Now don't go on
forever dreaming that you are going to be snared and carried
off like a bird to heaven, it is a delusion and a snare, to think of
such a mode of exit: Your soul will be beside your own body,
until it sees the last of the remains of its old garment: There
is how you are known by your own fellow spirits: You are to

be taken home from that grave, and left with the original element of your first fathers, and there he makes you do according
to what is right in accordance with his obedience to nature's
great cause of showing the many how you were first dragged
from the edge of this great chasm of paternal destruction:
That is as near a given point as it is possible for us to bring you
at present; you have got hold of the stick by its side view;
there is no paternal affection, coming from the beginning,
because you were not blessed with the intelligence, when you
first appeared as the growth of a plant, and then how is it that
you have expected to be born again at the beginning, why it is
absurd to suppose that you were able to do anything at all, this
is not all, you had to be blown into shape with the atmosphere
coming in contact, with material first: This is as easily understood as the rest, only you have to be guided to the right code
of knowing before you can understand: This is the idea of
which you have never thought seriously about, the way to reach
out and pull a pear is one way of taking it off the tree, but to
take a limb off, and place it on the other side is not quite so
easy; that is it don't stick fast, when you do it; but when the
wind has twisted it round a point farther to the west, it receives
a different current of the atmospheric elements: Therefore it
will grow a different kind of tree on that side to what it did on
the other: Now don't make any mistake about this little illustration, it shows you a beginning of the changes in life; and you
have only had a one kind of beginning, for it could only come
through the changes of the atmosphere being strained to a
degree of after life: You see I have hit you again on the question of your eternal soul coming after the body has passed away,
I want to show you that a man may be a soft snatch once; but
he was not always calculated to be so evenly handled; this is wisdom, to be drawn from a fig tree: That is a glorious fashion
they have got of painting Eve, with a fig-leaf as a robe to conceal her nakedness: You should see the first one that God
made, and then your eyes will be opened; though I have no
desire to give this account in ridicule, you are to blame yourselves for the whole of it: There never was an angel who flew

with wings, and it is quite enough to make an ancient spirit feel
revengeful, whenever he sees his own form disguised: That he
would rather see a devil, with great big horns sticking in a loose
garment; that is his sole complaint against the human fools who
clasp themselves, with wings about their shoulders, and think how
nice it must be to be an angel garbed out in such finery· They
poor deluded asses are as much under the influence of the devil,
as ever it is possible for them to be: And it makes my heart sore
to think I was once a stupid fool like them: You have got me
far more hopeful since you were. pleased to dress up with little
flips, and wade out on the scenery of every Jimtown theater,
for I am now able to see that you practice what you preach, and
live in a place where there is no morality: That is as it should
be when the devil drives he leaves no kinds to prevail, and it
hurts him worse, than anything you can do, for he feels his own
false position, when you get him fixed up with his horns on,
and a pretty little angel coming out with her flips, keep on, it
was intended to explain the difference between hell and heaven:
And no one could be blamed for fighting out the path of life as
they were shown, yet you know it is a farce, and that is all there
is to be said about it: Except ye believe them how can ye see,
for God in his munificence has given you sight; And he will give
you understanding, but ye can not see him, therefore it is hard
for you to believe: And you have got into a way of saying my
great God come down and persecute these heathens; that is not
right for it means a wickedness to befall your enemies; there
is the reason of this affair being what it is: And you
know that a man who calls for such an affliction on his
enemies must beware, for as he calls, so shall his calling
ascend; and he will be punished himself for not knowing how
to govern his own devils: You don't believe me, but I will
show you yet that I can make it resound at every call: You
take a given light and see how far it marks the boundary line of
its own reflection: Then take a measure and see what amount of
tether you have to that light, then take a sound piece of cord,
and make it reach out the exact length of this light reflection;
you have a good deal more tether, than you thought you would

have; then take it and multiply it by the round measurement,
that is the way to ascertain how much sound you had when you
spoke, it fetches even with the light, because it is an ungovernable body and is suffered to wander on forever just the same as
the earth, has a pitch of so many superficial feet there is the
problem of sound over matter, it has no distant atmospheric
element to govern it with: And consequently is a great big jump
ahead of everything else in this world of ours: Your own way
of beginning to measure is what I have to make my declaration
from, and not your thoughts as they appear to me, you shall yet
learn to see how heaven looks upon hell: And judge which is
best, the hand that guides, or the one that is being divided
against itself: Now you don't know what I am talking about,
as most of you think there is nothing to get over except this life,
I tell you that there is much more in this life than you anticipated,
it won't let you alone after you have left it; that is what you
don't calculate upon at all: For when you are dead and buried
as it is termed you have only begun to see that you have been
hoaxed all your days, and that you have been the victim of a
prophecy that has no sense in it: You have got where you can
not reach out and tell your friends not to be fooled any more,
and you simply have to turn to and work out your time at the
go as you please style, until you have a sufficient amount of work
accomplished to make you ready to be lifted up to some better
class of genius: For there is no talk of letting you off duty once
you begin to take your part at the wheel in earnest, it won't be
left for you to do as you think proper, it will be all mapped off
what is expected of you: And you have no right to get out of the
course that is laid down for you; that is you will be led about
by those who have the sound of your voice under their thong,
and it wont be for you to say I won't do this common labor, I
was a very intelligent person in the body, and I want to be
something greater now I have been let live through with my
second sight, and you are going to give me a worse job than I
had before, because you say I cheated a poor peddler out of his
hard earnings; now I wont stand it simply:' The very first thing
he knows, is a great big large seal-coat of the form of an umbrella

thrown over him, and he is effectually tied down to the one place, and is for a long while kept there, tied to a thing that won't give up its own sound for all that is left, is the complete tag end of a soul: You may not quite get the exact pith of what I mean, yet it is very difficult to make you understand, without you actually saw for yourself: And you shall see it, for there are many who come into the light, with a fixed determination that they have to be kept in purity with only their own ideas to follow: You see me now, but wait till you find yourselves in the harness of the great guidance of those who call themselves the ancients, I tell you what it is, they are as illiterate as ever you could find any pagan in the slums of your largest cities: You don't want to be made to work, and you won't do it when there is any chance of getting out of it; therefore, it won't come to you, without you go to it; and it was so machined out that a mind had to be moulded first before there could be any progress: Yet you see us now, and you say what a perfectly shaped head he has got, it is not half so much as it was, and is worse by far than it used to be: There is the mystery of man for you, what is it that makes the mind go wandering on like a whirl for; because you have never been taught how to stop the mind from wandering, and when you find that it is all along the kind of thoughts, that keep on crushing themselves out of shape, then it is easy to tell that they are not there, without they came there of their own accord: Now you see what kind of work is expected of you, when you get on the other side of life; you are to come back, and fill the minds of your friends with thoughts of what you can give them; that is your duty, now do you see what a life there is for you to lead, when you have gone to the only home you can ever hope to know, and as the new ones come in, so do the old ones rise higher, and become more pure; For they have been led on by what has preceded them: Don't you see that there has to be a power, or there can not be a motion; now I have got you wedged into a narrow compass, how is it that you won't work without I stand by and tell you everything; you have got a head, and a body, and so you have when you are dead: Then why don't you pick up your old body, and go on; that is where you are left off the old clothes and placed in new ones; you can't get along, for the spirit moves and not the body, and it has got an attachment to its own after cortege: That is why you see, and don't understand, you have a mind that is acted upon by this form of light, which governs the whole of eternity; now don't alarm yourselves one bit about this thing, it has got a fixed purpose in view; and that is to mend a great many ills that do befall the after life of mankind; It won't make any practical difference as far as you can see; but it will show the heathens in heaven that they are observed: And they will feel much more hurt at their own inferiority, every time it is said that they used to be a mute, and it is right that this intelligence should be sent broadcast, for as the pain of hell increases so does the darkness come on earth: Observe and you will see that this is a work against heaven and hell: And not merely to tell you to pray and give succor to the many by your supplications of heaven to help you: I say distinctly that all things began on earth, and it is there that the corrections have got to be made: Now can't you see that a bubble ascends, and breaks, but when it does not break, there is an arch being built: then why don't you see that the bubble, will form into many arches, and leave the earth in purity, but when these bubbles descend, they are broken in two: That is the right way to illustrate a thing in its first formation: You have kept on moving along, at the rate of beginning eternally, and you are not advancing any faster, for the reason that you are kept in darkness by the eternal governing powers being behind you; that is it that keeps heaven away, it has gone on before the intellect was formed, and it could only be the same as beginning now: It had the motion established long before there was any intelligence: That is why you know so much, without being able to prove anything; and this is the way it was at first, it had a start, and when once there is a fair start made, it requires an immense amount of courage, and enlightenment before you can overtake that start, and it will have to be got honestly, for nothing can stand, which is shuffled in, it will be seen that an honest opinion is always before a stuffed one: Therefore you have only to make up your own minds that where honesty pre-

vails, sin is a one-sided outcast; you know what a great state
there was about the end of the world coming in '92, but you can
make your minds easy on this score it can't possibly come to an
end, whilst there is any danger, of being dissolved by the great
going in and the immense amount of material that has to be poured
out: This alone assures us of everlasting life eternal, without
end: Many may think that a given substance, can break: And
become in a more distinct kind; but it is not so: That is what
the man said, when he gave up his privileges; he was going to
get to the other side, by pulling his carcass after him, that is as
near a definite description as possible; for the man who escapes
from his old body, does take it along with him in its entire form;
though you must not conclude that you are going to use other
material than the ethereal form once you have got out of the flesh,
it is not to be put in a vault, and kept there forever as poor
deluded mortals have done without this kind of reckoning so
long, that they imagine that they have got the very person in there
that was in the continual habit of abiding in its cell; that is the
idea of the mind that is uncultivated: And nothing yet has
been here to dispel this same opinion; you may talk as you have
a mind to but the one idea strikes the person who buries a body,
it has gone down there into that dark hole, and I shall surely be
called upon to do the same when my time comes: You are so
much impressed with this idea; that you have a fear of being
present, when your own father dies, and looks back to see
whether his effects have been faithfully administered; that you
would dread to pass his grave did you do any injustice to his
bequests: Now don't tell me that you will buy his headstone
out of your own pocket it would be right no doubt to do so, but
you wish all the same that he had been careful with his
money and left you well provided for: That is as near as possible what you have been thinking of during the whole time it was
being bought and paid for, I am going to show you by this that
you know how to act, when your own father dies; that is to
bury his remains, but you forget that it was his money that has
been paying for the tombstone, that will illustrate the idea of
having a better understanding with nature, you will find that it

is not what you have supposed at all; for the mere fact of your own father being cast into that hole is nothing more than a myth, and he is no doubt at all attached to your own cortege, and is at the time of the burial giving directions through his own connection with his after-birth: Now do you see that instead of you burying him in that hole, he is giving direction for his own funeral; therefore it is not very nice for those who may happen to say anything that is not pleasing to the dead, for it is sure to be heard, and will bring bad results to those who make such a mistake, it will perhaps be the means of ruining many a man, for when the dead hears a sound against his own name, he will speak up boldly, and chastise those who form the circle round that person who was so ignorant as to give vent to any remarks that might injure the dead: So you had better mind what you say against a corpse; for it is there to be dealt with according to good common sense: And you may quite easily bring about your own ruin through an angry speech against him who once held you in awe: Don't imagine he is dead, for it is quite easy for him to punish you; by leading you into a trap, and there seeking pleasure in your suffering: Now I shall show you that you are not so smart as you think you are; you gathered in the debts of the one who you called your great benefactor: and you paid away all except what you thought was your share, for dividing this property accurately, yet you were holding some little thing back from your co-executors, that is the true state of your idea of what was right, it may have been right in your own estimation, but the question is was it right in the estimation of him who did not mean it to be spent that way: You may think you did your duty: And you may have been very fair in some things, but that particular affair in which you acted greedily, it was may be the curse of your whole hereafter, for that spirit was enraged at the wrongful action of this particular action, yet he was not satisfied over this particular job, so he made up his mind to wreak you a steadfast injury, for this particular action, and was never more pleased when he witnessed your own downfall, that is he gave you a good chance, to gain his assistance, and you made him your enemy in hell: Now what more could you

get that could injure you than an enemy in hell, call back to
your memory what deeds you have ever done to the dead, and
you will trace from that way how you came to meet your own
calamities: You have given this fashion a correct view of your
own situation, and you see what it will do to you, when you have
been advised wrongly by an understanding that has no idea of
what is being done in return to you: You can please yourself,
and you can get all the satisfaction you have any need for, by
keeping what does not justly belong to you, therefore he who
keeps these ill-gotten things, may enjoy them thoroughly, but they
always lead to his ruin in the end: Now you see that a once
bright-souled mortal, may easily be nursing a viper in his own
breast, and keeping from the light of his fellow-men, what is a
thoroughly well-known circumstance, and it is watched from the
clear side of life, with as much and more interest, than though all
hades knew his full secret, you know now why an angel is purified,
by being let go on his enemies, and when he is able to show an
example to those who are in the art of doing what they consider
best, it will be seen that a number have to be thrown down continually to keep the vast number of angels from growing morbid,
and disconsolate over their misfortune of having to show themselves capable of acting for the best, under the present system
of affairs: You can't get on without being shown, any more than
you could deal out a particular class of goods with no false colors
in the roll, I say you have got false clothing beneath every
fathom of covering, and you don't know how to stop this great
big gigantic swindle: You keep yourselves posted only on what
you see; and you know of nothing except what has been kept for
you for generations: Except there is a clear pathway made known
to those who are here how do you suppose it possible that you
are going to get into any better understanding with your supreme
ruler, it must be got at on the earth, it can not be accomplished in
heaven, for you are quite in advance of the heavens, and that is
quite above the possible chances of doubt, I am not saying so
merely for an idle purpose, but I do say this to show you distinctly that you are entirely on a wrong track, and must either
live in this state forever, or go and get what comfort you can by

injuring no living soul or yet breaking out at times and reviling
the dead: You know I am speaking truthfully, when I say that
you are wrong in keeping what has not the resemblance to
honesty in its own composition: Therefore be happy with what
you have gotten by your own industry, and don't seek from off
another's vineyard; that his to divine arightly, and sleep on your
own pillow, lest it may contain a seed off some other one's head,
I say be cautious in whatever you do, for as the ass brays, his
notes are heard by the sounds of his accent: Leave a good
sentence for a kindly word, and bring home to your family a
mighty strong rebuke, for misguiding the young and old who
may lay their heads between your threshold and the tomb of
your ancestors, I am not what is, but I am here to do his
bidding that is what you have to consider, when you are at the
head of an household, now do not let your hands touch the heir
of him who was the donator of such a priceless gift, for as the
father gave to the son, he also did will that he should remain a
great nation, without impeachment or waste: Now you know   .
what Christ did for sinners, and he told you to beware of false
prophets for there was not one out of every thousand, nay not
one out of tens of thousands who could interpret aright, this is
true, and do not be misled by any search diligently, and you
will find all you care to know, God bless the Holy light of day,
it shines out an everlasting eternal glory, and no power on earth
can break through the intelligence of man, providing he is understood by himself; there is then another kind of construction,
that has altogether failed to come under the understanding of
man, that is the mind that has been taught to read and write,
this mind is more apt to become fixed in its own light, than it
would be did it not know what it saw, there is that great mistake
of leaving a big sentence unfinished, and getting wrong when
you depend wholly on what you can see, that is the very thing
that leads hundreds wrong, for they can not help believing
what they see; and it is impossible to make them believe
what is there without actually looking at it: You have got into
a sad error, when you think that a whole column of material
is as it seems on the surface, you can make a pillow quite

smooth, but you will not be able to keep it from containing what
is not apparent to the eyesight, that is it may hold a much
greater· amount of essence of life, than you ever anticipated;
there is where you all wrong yourselves, you think that a
little dirt may make an unholy influence upon your vision, but
you forget that on the outside of that dirt, there is a magnetic
current, that will surely make an impression on those it comes
in contact with, therefore you are led astray by the very atmosphere you breathe, for it shall be so written, that a man may
be as pure as the virgin soil, yet he is in constant commune with
his thoughts, and they lead him wherever he has a mind to go;
this is as natural as can be, for he has nothing else to guide him
by; and he may have all the world before him, he can not keep
his mind from wandering to that divine object his thoughts
have pictured to him as the model of his holy light, now do
you see what part the thoughts have been working him into,
therefore is it not possible for the mind to be led to destruction, as well as to holiness and purity, that is the way all men
are led about, and it is the workings of an under current, that
guides them to this mine of health, or it leads them to the very
den of ruin: You see it won't do to let your thoughts run riot
with your own mind, for they have got to be stopped, and held
in until they assume their own course of accurate intelligence,
that is the way to govern the mind, hold it in until you have
seen what it produces for you, don't give way to a stubborn conviction, that you must do it this particular way, for it has got to
be mastered, either by one power or another, before it is any use,
that is the right theory of geological sense, don't begin to
count too quickly, for the lines are drawn, without you knowing anything about it, therefore you must not begin to take in
the surroundings of night too readily, the darkness comes of
its own accord, and it shall be clearly proved to you, that
there is no one who could not see, before they were nursed into
light by the coming storms of adversities; you see that a common way of bringing back to light is the exact mode we have
drawn of our own, that is the way to reach the given spot, is by
getting at the bottom of the difficulty first, and not by trying to

be broken down by contrary elements before you drive away the
good ones by holding on to the bad, keep out all evil influences, and you have a very fair show of getting where you want
to go; that is the way a man has to be brought down to his
way of being broken down first, and then risen up again by his
good guides: You know what it is to be left out in the cold by
all your former acquaintances; then don't be cast down by them,
call an angel of light to your side and say as I have been thrown
down for an example to show the heathens, what they knew so
very well would happen once they planted their united efforts
against me, you come again to me and raise me up above them
and show them that there are two kinds of good in life, one to
cast down, into a dark bottomless pit: And the other is
to be held in esteem by the great ruler of light: Now I have
been punished by no fault of my own, and I see that I am a
victim because I was a superior specimen for the angel of night
to glide down upon me, and make his home in heaven secure,
by the cruelest torture he could inflict on one who never did him
wrong or any one else, because I was held up among my fellow-men as a noble whole-souled pure man, and could have
fought against the tiger that was clutching at my mind did I
but know, that I was to be his victim for his own aggrandizement
in heaven: You see what chances there are against a pure-
minded man, he has led an honest sober industrious life, and he
is not on guard, he thinks his mind has always done right before,
then how can he be acting in a different way now, he is just as
innocent as the babe, it can't be held up that he was prepared,
for he had never erred before, and what was his by rights had
always stood good friends, therefore his only chance now was to
obey his own thoughts they had never failed him since he could
remember, that is where he did not know that he was the exact
requirement for another one's plan, and he had to be led or
driven into what he thought all the time was wrong, yet he gave
way because he had no idea but that some change might make
him sorry for holding back, this is the way of the serpent, it
glides into, and holds fast upon the victim it requires for an
illustration; that is, not all the fangs of time will ever wipe away

the evils wrought upon that pure-souled man, his name is
blighted, his goods are upheld as spoiled, and his after-inherit-
ance is for everlasting a plague, for those who had him in their
claws: You see what it is to be an holy man, he can not get
justice done him, because there is a power working against him
that is stronger than hell itself, it does not come in form of ice,
it comes in warmth and affection: There is where it shines the
greatest demonstrations of its skill: You see an honest man has
few pleasures, and he will submit to the tempter more readily
than the man who indulges with bad odors continually: You
see he is not very smart to begin with, and he can not see a
great way ahead, therefore he is liable to become wounded
by the first arrow of poison, then it is all over with him, no
retreat is possible, he does not understand that he is being held
in chains for an example to his fellow-men, give him knowledge,
and he will wrestle with his viper, and conquer for he knows
the consequence, when he has been shown by his own friends
that sin is not a crime but a victory: You are quite appalled
with this version of sin, but I positively show that a true sense
of justice has to be begun at home, and not outside, for there
is where the blow comes; and you have the chance of warding
off that blow, when it is known to you as a wrong thing to do:
You shall have a peaceful blessing for every sinner you keep out
of heaven, for no sin is there except what you permit to grow
up in your midst, and you shall be punished for what you never
did is not at all likely to be the ruling of a righteous God, he is
not present to see what is going on, there are no places for his
thong to whip with, he can feel the heat, and he can not bear
to see his pastures destroyed, for he lives on the moisture of
every garbage; you see what you have done, counted in what
there is not, and left out where there shall be no ending forever:
Strike back, and you will see that you are the beginning, and
not he, then what do you want with a devil, when you make
them yourselves; think of this and bring light in upon your
own darkness; don't upbraid a common wheel for a crack-jaw
idiocy, that is what you call getting enlightenment you hold the
gates of heaven shut, and you leave the pathway to hell open,

now don't begin to fancy that you have got a crank to lead you,
for you shall see that as the time rolls by, and I get in my proper
power of reasoning, I will lift you right out of your pathway to
hell: And join you on to what is called the field of knowledge,
that is as it should be and I can not explain a thing more definitely till I come to it; you think I am not able to define these
things, but I will show you that there are ways and means of
surmounting every obstacle on earth, and heaven, this is fair to
both sides, and it shall be done before the fall of another decade,
that is the last of a great big change for the better, and no
one who knows what a man can be till he is thoroughly well
tested, and when you open up the way for a thoroughly reliable
honest soul, and it has the helping willing hands of heaven to
guide it, there is no force on earth that shall overpower such
a one, God bless the everlasting life of our Saviour Jesus Christ:
He died for sinners, and made men the mouthpiece of his eternal
grace, bless immortality, and divine providence must come on
before: That is all that will have to be changed: You see
that as the light plays upon man, it shall ascend over the darkness, and as man descends into the background, he is not what
he should be at all, instead of him being in heavy raiments,
he is merely a disjointed atmospheric combustion made
of every conceivable fragment: And his welfare is of no consequence compared to his mighty force of doing right, therefore
his light is not what has been shown to him, and he did not know
what it was that kept striking him down, when he was there to
stop up: You see you have been always led by a power, that
was not in advance of yourselves, and you can not hope to get
right whilst you are behind a thong that had no beginning too
new for you, I have got you placed right enough, you are behind
the thong, and you ought to be in front of it; because you had
to make the whip before you could do any driving, therefore you
must not let yourselves be driven by your own whips; there is this
about it that a mind does not grow out of rawhide, neither does
it follow on the same principles, but you have got to be shown,
or you won't be able to see; that is to meet your own eyesight,
it is necessary to fetch mine into your views; and you must not
6

think that my expressions are vulgar, because I am at your side
of life trying to make you wise, and not trying to exercise a
fluent train of eloquent articulations, for I am ready to impress
you with what is proper, yet I don't want you to make me appear
as arrogant as I feel; you know what a man said to me once when
I was addressing him, why, Thomas you appear as though you
were impressed by the feeling of God himself, and I did to feel
as though no living mortal was equal to me, I have never felt so
happy as the time when I found out that I had arrived at my
hopes, and reached the size of glory, where I now stand, no one
to say you are an inferior mortal, I heard those words so distinctly that when they buried my old books, that I cried over it,
and said when I get the chance of coming back myself I will hurl
this at the pagans, and prove them wrong on everything they
have condemned me for: You know who I am by this time, and
I will go still further, and convince the world that they never
were better informed than when I gave them the true light in
my own crude way; you see I am not a proud-souled high-spir-
ited mortal now, I come back with a very different showing to
what I went away with; and you have got many a one to thank
for my works except myself, I did not know what it was that
had me under their power, when I was here, I only know that
I felt too good for any earthly mortal, and I would not be put
down for anybody, that is the right way to feel too: Don't let
any one single individual come in your way, let him who shines
the most, come out in sure sentences and divine the life he
leads: Don't let him who fills his mouth as full as Othologous
come along and say my God man you have broken bread without any prayer, let not this fiend alarm you, call on your own
angel standing by your side, and say come tell me what
answer must I make to this one who has chastened me for the
mouthful that is in my teeth; you will hear a sound, that lips
can not utter, it is with a stroke of pain that comes between
the eyes, and centers itself over the back of the forehead, it is
the pressure of an instrument common to all of us: You feel
the weight of something near the head, it seems though your
brains would break, when you have to answer when you can't,

that is the after-birth of light striking the weak place behind the forehead, it gives a sound, that is vibrated to the ear, and it has been thus far sensed by the well-known form of hearing, but in reality it is the concussion on the brain at the top of the head; and it is here where the blow is struck, that produces life and light thrown in together, there is the true feature of defining the sense of calling back to life, it comes in the clear sound of might and right conjoined, there is the secret of the touch, it can be hit with a blow from an ax, but the sharp cutting word of a dear friend sinks deepest: You all know quite well, that there is a distinct power at work, yet you have been led away by the thoughts that God had you in his especial keeping, yet you know nothing of all that has been said, that he has been accredited with having said at one time and the other: You are as able to judge now as ever you were, and I am here to say that you are in a much better and truer light, than you were; in the days of the commencement of history, that is you have come to a more enlightened age, and it is quite easy for you to define the right from the wrong, it was no easy matter for the beginners to tell whether it was God or the Devil trying to lead them, and they were not very sure which, well now it is quite easy to be able to tell the two apart, one is all purity, and holy, spiritually good, that is, that God is the good angel, coming back, to tell you how you should act for the right course through life, whilst the "devil" is the one who holds you chained to a certain amount of knowledge, and won't agree that you should see your way clearly, he slinks round, and says you must not read a work on the enlightenment of mankind; because it is too deep for your own understanding, better go and question your pastor on such alarming subjects; and he will enlighten you therein: Now what could be a better illustration of the "devil" than this, he is afraid himself, and wants to frighten every one else, that is just how he feels, he is a good remove from righteous himself, or he would not object to his own hole being looked into: That is a certain sign of the promptings of the "devil," when he is afraid to investigate himself and won't dare advise his friends to look into the dark side of life, you

may keep on forever, when you fear the torture of hell: But
you never knew a case yet, where the right man won, without
first looking in every cupboard for the thief, he is always
hiding, then why let him alone, when you don't want him:
Hunt him down, as a hare does, that has escaped from the
hound, I say you have only to look him up every time he comes
near you, and he will soon disappear as utterly disconsolate, as
when there was no hell to look for: Now I can show you how
to cultivate the grace of God, by asking for all good angels to
come and help you out of your troubles; that is the way to
prove the account I am giving you: Take plenty of time to
consider, and when you are in any kind of trouble, take a step
back, and say in your own breath, I have been wrong, will you
show me the right way out of my adversity, for I feel sorely
oppressed, and there is sure to arise in front of your views,
two distinct versions of the way you are to proceed, one says
right across the line of my eye, I can see a dark pool, and there
is only one way, you must jump in and swim to the other side:
That is the "devil" promoting his scheme of drowning you:
The other comes after this form, I see a cloud, in the sky, it has
nothing behind it, yet we all know that once there was a cloud
between heaven and hell: And the great Seer of all the Holy
God of light, did divide that cloud, and show us the great peaceful resignation as he met his doom on Calvary: You know
how fearless he was, his soul, was prepared, and it was ready
and willing for its flight; there is the true light to follow on his
pathway, and you will not see the night: His soul was ready, it
knew all things, and it saw the advantage of a departure from
this life: Your own soul may become the same, when you
are not afraid to look into the dark abyss of that yawning
gulf, that the "devil" has made all mankind afraid of, go
tell him he is a liar, and unless he will show you a clear
road out of the dilemma, you will not follow his doc-
trines, and he can either stop away from you, or prove
what he says in a sensible argument: You know he can
not justify himself in one single sentence that he has made,
and as for his wickedness, he is as much afraid as though he

had been a convicted felon, and liberated by mistake: That is not all, he will not lay down his hand and say I have nothing to do with this state of affairs, he prefers to steal in upon you, when there is no one near, and throw his poison over you, by saying I am he who was your father's best friend, and your father and I could always get an honest understanding with each other, that is all very fine, he wants to control you for some hidden scheme he has in view, don't take any notice of his affection for your lamented parent, it's all trash, it was nothing but a deliberate plot, to get at you in some way, don't bind the miserable wretch, to come and visit you again, but please him all you can, and question him till his hands begin to turn round each other, then you know that the serpent is feeling the effects of your probing: You can always tell when you have struck him beneath his coating of humbug, he will wriggle and twist and turn, and try in every conceivable way to evade your questions: You hang on to his very vital cord, until he is willing to surrender, and don't let him off till he is well saturated with the scorn of righteous dignity: There you have won a victory for yourself, it does may be not, show a very marked appearance at the time: Yet you stabbed the fiend so deep, that all his associates have got hold of the encounter, and they will all be afraid of getting near you in any turmoil, for his overthrow, is a signal to be aware of the stronghold you carry underneath your own control, that is the secret ever before men, and they are always blind to these facts, they know that a man is dangerous by the reputed character he has always borne, but they never know a stranger, until they run foul of his fangs, well it is quite an easy matter to tell the quality of your opponent, without even speaking to him, he is surrounded by a certain class of spirits, and it is they who talk, not the one who is inside of the body, and they can converse, with any of their own class, but the quality is here even more distinct, than it is on your side of life, it will not be tolerated in heaven the abuses, that are practiced in hell: So you see that an associate of evil, does not mix in the same society as the one of good; and they are known by the company they keep just the same as those who shield the victim from the ax of an executioner, that is that a man who is doomed to death, for some hideous crime, has all of those who are impressed with a belief of no after punishment, can come and help to excuse his faults, now you see what an influence, is thrown in the balance scale when the trial is going on to acquit or punish, it is of more interest to those who brought about the affair, than it was to him who sentenced the criminal for doing this deed: You see what an influence, is thrown on to the forces, that are at the back of that Judge, it always makes my mind feel oppressed, when I contemplate this position: You see he has two contending powers, driving at him all the time, and he is unaware of the actual position he is placed in, yet he has been quite successful in a general way, he sends those to hell, who are not accountable for what they are doing, and they are punished by him for the crime that they were forced into by some fiend who wanted to succeed in liberating himself from the after inheritance of his own abominable guilt: So his chance to pounce upon and convert an innocent being into a criminal was surely successful, once he had gained his plan of torture, he would be liberated, and given a position higher up on the other side of life, his sins would have been made pure, by the flow of another's calamity: Therefore when you come to think of this thing you will be more careful, how you let loose of one devil, to crush another, so you are not advancing when you let this one escape, for he is in time to come to be one of the lawgivers in heaven, and he will not be very choice as to how he makes punishment, his soul was purified, by the actions of his own connections with bringing on pain and suffering, and his escape could only make him walk on the same pathway, as he had found salvation; now do you suppose that any good can come of such a way of making one free by the actual crushing of another; why, it certainly has the effect, of showing mortals where their errors are, and it brings them examples, yet it does not throw any enlightenment on what is actually proceeding, it keeps the world in hell always, that is as near correct as you will ever be able to define it, you can make laws, to punish, without liberating this fiend, it won't help heaven to have a serpent ruling there, although he had been purified by showing his fellow spirits how the earth should be governed, you hold out an inducement to a criminal to make his life pure, on this earth, and see how soon you have reached an improvement in the good cause, of holiness produces wisdom, and see how soon you will be thrown back to the times when the God of liberty, has grown righteous by his own government: don't punish for actual crime in the way that it has been done, but rather let ten innocent ones escape, than one guilty wretch shall reach the kingdom of salvation; you have got much intellectual skill on your side of life, then be just, and make those who commit crime work out their own salvation, it is here where all reformation has to be begun, for it can not be achieved in· heaven; "Know ye not that a man with palsy is of greater value than him that is whole, I say verily verily, suffer him to come unto me, for his soul is more pure, than the one who is garbed in soft cloth, and surplus;" I will hold him pure who is stricken by a contrite hand: You have heard what our Saviour said, when he said let all those be holy, who were made to sin, that is he did not mean a judgment to befall those who had already suffered, yet he grew gracious in the sight of him who had nothing to wear, that is the true prophecy, take not to yourselves, for I have laid down the plans that ye shall abide in, and ye know not what ye do, for the son of man was once a tormentor, and he shall again be called to account for what he has done; this is the cause and effect of what has to come here, and also what has to follow, in the world to come, Amen. Your own agreements, are as near the right course as you can follow, only don't bind under oath, let it be seen that the gracious God is pure, and don't cultivate men's minds to make a vow, that is their object to violate, take a good case, and seek diligently, then prepare a cause, that does read as a fair agreement between man and man, don't let the one have an advantage over the other by being sworn to an oath, that one has in his mind as a vow to be broken when there is an advantage to be gained, but rather say, I will do my duty to my fellow creatures according to the light of justice: That is the way to bind your agreements, not to say; You are here sworn to tell the truth, the whole truth,

and nothing but the truth, so help you God: That is the way
to make a man a liar, he sees the Judge in front of him, and he
says through his breath, you are the only dangerous God, that I
can see; and when I manage to fool you, I have got my case
won, that is what is the sole movement of the light, of man:
You see you are dealing out the brown bread, instead of giving
white, where purity must come from what is shown; don't give
in to those who are not capable of judging, but rather accept the
black bread, they disobey the ignorant fools, for when you have
been beaten by the man who was able to lie sufficiently, to gain
the judge's ear, then say to your soul's great comforters, I want
you to help me to hunt this liar down, and bring him to justice,
it will be seen then who is the righteous one, and who is the
sinner: You know that no lies will stand under the careful investigation of truth, and you have only to hunt, till you find the
proofs, that is the way to conquer hell, look up every nook
and corner, don't leave a single place of concealment, as the
hound hunts the hare, make hell resound with your goodness, and pureness of spirits; they have the right to pillage
in hell, when there is an innocent victim condemned, and
do not attempt to bar their passage-way, for even satan
in all his glory is a friend of God's: That is a part that
you don't seem to know what it is for, then keep on as you
have come and you will find it out for yourselves, it is the way
you do your business, you keep all the bad connections, to help
you swindle the foolish, and in consequence every one of you
are trying to outwit the other, so that in time you will be a complete set of cut-throats, that is the way that has been going for
a period of many centuries, and it is easily noticed now that the
drift is greater than it was, and when an avalanche is once
shaken loose it is there ready to make a more rapid precipita-
tion, once the right current has come to move it; you keep on as
you are going, and it will bring you to the cannibal system before
a great while, it is now quite time you fetched up your children
to obey the giver of light, and not make them go down on their
knees, and pray to an image, that is purely visionary, without
one practical illustration of what manner of being this God is:

You know that the great angel of light, must see that you are foolish, and he does not deem it the thing to pounce down upon you, and call out I am coming to frighten you into my way of thinking: You see it is far better to be led than driven, and when you are led it comes nicely, for it is the light, that draws you on, and it should be the guiding star of evening that protects your footsteps, for as the day is lit up by the reflection of the Sun, so is the night shining with beautiful stars, and a Moon to excel over them: Now it is a plain fact that where reason prevails, no one can go wrong, and where the light does not look in, it is no fit place for the son of man to trust his head: You hear what man was once, you see what he is to-day, and you have always had the privilege to look upon him as the sole light we have got, this is as true as it would be did you depend on the father of a beast to find the proving of his offspring, you are not ready to receive this as it was placed before you by our maker, yet you go on complaining, that you were not all made beautiful, then what do you hope to become a great people, or an outrage on civilization: Has the world got to grow beans off a cabbage stem, no it is for you to guide it right, and you want a more divine ruler to set you right on the ways you have been walking, you know that love and hope walk hand in hand, then make light and darkness prevail on earth together, and not have them leading a dog and cat life, one seeking force against the other, it is no use spending my time in showing what other men's friends are trying to keep from you, unless you will bring me back, to the very place where the earth, was first begun, I can not tell you that there were no people in this land, until the great giver of power came down and made a whole lot of things all in one week, he made it all in six days, and rested on the seventh, contemplating his handicraft, I think you will all concede this point with me, that he has been very gracious and condescending, for he sees now, that every single year produces new things, that were not made last year, and therefore we must deal kindly with those who have only a manner of thinking once in their whole lifetime, and that was when the parent said our Lord's Prayer, I shall never forget the time I was put out of my

parents' house, for saying I believe the Lord has done well for
us, in making so much in six days, he ought to commence over
again and give us a chance of seeing how he did do so exceptionally well: I can not help saying that it was very strange that
the ancients who compiled our history, were so very poorly
informed in the art of war, as to mow down their enemies with
such crude weapons, when they might have had a swivel-gun, to
bang them out of sight in the twinkling of an eye, you forget
that they had all their wits about them, when they were able to
get information about their enemies through their prophets, and
find that your telephone, and telegraph, was unknown then; yet
Moses could tell how to guide Israel out of Egypt, with only his
own knowledge of communing with those who can wipe all communication such as you have got into insignificance, now you
think this is a piece of absurdity, well let those who have the
power of defining the God of light, prove the existence of this
power, and show the heathens, that there is even a greater
power than Moses, and his fiery torch-light, coming in the day,
and a pillow of light, coming at night to show the Israelites how
to wander through the wilderness, not by a long way is this
power extinct as the people think, it is now advanced to a much
more scientific basis, and can be used to get the information
from any part of the known world, and may be it can tell truly
of all that is unknown as well: Your own time is now, to search
for the truth, and when you are dead and buried, the souls, who
went before you will spurn you with scorn, for not having made
better use of your advanced intellect, why is it that you don't
see any one who is able to show you what is right, why do you
turn away your heads, and say that common person has no
credentials, the same as I have, he is an inferior being, his material is only of the plain coarse fabric, whilst mine is of the finest
silk, his mouth utters words, that are horrifying to my sensitive
nerves, why, did Jesus Christ not take Pontius Pilate, and make
him a disciple, then the whole world, would have been more
enlightened with the assistance, of the fine Governor, that was
so very delicate, when it come to the exact point at stake, you
all know, that Jesus answered so truthfully and well before that

heathen Governor, that he has always been represented to say:
" I find no fault in this man " yet although Pontius Pilate, did
not find any fault in Jesus: He was afraid, and said you may
crucify him, yet I say there is no fault to be found with this
man; Then why does all people who are afraid like Pontius
Pilate, seek the way through darkness, why don't they say, it was
through darkness, that our only true light, came to his end on
this earth, and are we to be forever held in scorn by heaven
because we are afraid to do what is right, let the light of day
seek out the dark hole, and sink forever the heathens' God into
the everlasting fire, that he has made for himself: You seem to
think that wisdom, can only come through education, it can not
be purified and held whole, in that way, for it is all following up
the strain of an after-train, and can not get loose for it is
attached to an ignorant set of humbugs, who do not believe
only, what they can look at, and never give it a thought, that
wisdom comes through the sense of hearing: You may think
you are looking at all there is to be seen, but you are as blind
as bats, for the fact, that you don't know how to bring the right
condition of understanding to bear on your own organism:
Now don't think I am finding fault with you for mischief,
because I say you are ignorant, don't you see that we are all
ignorant, until we know how to understand a given pure and
unadulterated fact: I am willing to help you with all the power,
I can bring with me: And you should never despise willing aid,
for it comes so seldom in a precious form, that the world will be
less likely to have a second chance of defining the truth: Your
own ideas may do very well, until they become so very exact,
that they will be wedged into a narrow space, and the growing
out, will be more terrible, than the growing in: There is the
secret of promulgation, it is all fine enough, until you begin to
start back, on the backward turning, then you have got many
ills to contend against that might have been remedied had you
gone into the question of selection: There is the great mistake
in the human races, they don't study healthful manipulation
enough: There is the downfall of health to be borne in mind, it
may be necessary for the hereafter controllers, to say I shall not

permit these two delicate sufferers to come into propagation, and
that would not be against common sense either: They tell you
that there is no privilege, that binds two souls together for life
everlasting, neither there is, for each soul is of itself, neither can
any power on heaven or earth, ever bind it: Your own intellect
should be able to prove this to you, for what is there to hold
this ungovernable thing, but the mere ties of after light, it is the
moving genius, that gets entangled, and not the body, that
pleases you to say within your own heart, had I that divine
being for my partner through life, I could go to heaven, and
reap my bliss forevermore: That is a fool's paradise, for it is
not possible for him to hold that person, it is an atom, that is as
his own sin in painting such a picture, there is but the one sense
in this, and that is to be true to the one you bless with your
presence, and keep holy unto her you call your soul's guide, for
as man shall love his life eternal, then let him cleave to the one
breast, that has borne to him his first pleasures on this earth,
and as he proves his own soul to be worthy, so shall he receive
the reward of a happy meeting with the one he can say with an
honest expression, I never did yet do her wrong, and she will
bear him back her confidence and affection: And though she
may err in ignorance, be ye sorry, and say I forgive as I hope to
meet mine in heaven: This is the tie that lasts, through all the
wanderings of a pure heart, through the mind to the soul, forever: Your divine presence is what is most thought of, and you
should not absence your soul from those you are bound to, for it
is not right, to leave the gates open; for other than good to enter
therein, and when there is no presence, there has not been any
protection, and your own sense must tell you, that you made a
vow to protect, and such protection is your duty, and not your
own salvation, for when the lion enters the lamb is torn into a
state of trembling and fear, and kindness from the lion, does
overcome the lamb that was neglected, and lost except he stood
by too and did save his own body to annihilate other lions, that
might have stolen in upon the lamb: You shall not do away
with your presence, and say mine is safe, it has so many advantages, of keeping its own concealment hidden; that I have the

utmost confidence; take warning in time my fine broiler, you
gave away your birthright to another; by your own want of common sense, give me he who says, I have done with all that is
wicked, I shall take this little one, and make her happy forever,
and stand by her grave no matter what her failings may be, and
whatever befalls her it is my duty to see her safely, to the other
shore, now let those beware, who seek out new paths of enjoyment, they shall bear the torments of the ants of hades coming
against them forever, which is the tormentors paying off the
debts of the one who was made to suffer, through the desertion
of he who, should have been at his post: You can not call a
woman right, when she does leave her home, for any purpose
whatever, she took up that man to make him happy, and he had
none other then, then let her understand that as she fails so
must he, for as his duty commands so should she follow out his
bequests, and seek light out of all ways of separation, for as the
wife sits alone she has the power to sit in her chair, and seek for
new light, come in unto me is her soul's calling, then ask your
soul's guide to show you a way that will prove more advanta-
geous for your own joy, and the comforts of your husband's
presence, now do not fret and get annoyed, but say I want this
consolation to be in the arms of him I promised to obey always,
and I will be to you faithful, will you then guide me to a way,
out of this separation, and I will obey you to this end, then let
it be a compact between her soul and the light, that they show
her away, for her bliss for life eternal, it is this power's will to
keep her straight, or to take her wrong: And to gain this
knowledge you must be passive, and cultivate a happy feeling;
banish all hard feelings, as you would a serpent, for no spirit can
come near you with wisdom, whilst you have the hounds of hell
at your side, a fretful miserable condition is sure to get you into
trouble, it is the viper, putting in his sting ready to spring, into a
glow, immediately he has his victim on the downward course,
and he proceeds to make everything in his turn a haven of light,
don't trust the villain he is taking you to destruction, for his
own sense of becoming noble among the heathen Gods, who
guide the earth: You be aware of him, he can come and paint a

beautiful picture for you, and leave you to find out what an ass
you were for following his sentiments, his turn served his glory
is complete, and you are there a crest upon a wave; shown up to
all your friends as the easy victim led by satan, into a cove, and
there strangled by his coming upon you as the champion of all
your sorrows, banish sorrow, and don't let it creep in upon you,
for here is where the hated arrow takes flight, and sends death
and despair into atoms, keep back the trust you have in heaven,
for the guiding influence, that can show you where you are going
to succeed in obtaining your own victory: Your own hearts
are pure, until the very first pang of pain comes: Then don't
let that one, who brings that pain, approach you: For as he
comes with a pang of pain, his soul is not what it should be, or
he could not have produced that which you feel is not right, now
do you understand by this, that a man, who brings sorrow, can
not be happy under those sentiments, and will as a matter of
course, spread into you, a presentment of pain, which must in
time worm out, all the glow of passionate affection that is in
your own soul, therefore don't take a sad mate to be your home
consolation, but rather let him mend his ways first, and make
him understand, that a man has got to be happy himself, before
he can make those in his immediate surroundings happy: Therefore we can say amen to those who won't consider their own
happiness first, and when a miserable wretch seeks pride as his
God, then let him have an idol, in which he may suffer in hell
with: Don't you go and be his footstool, and become his great
big sight of all which he paints as purity, that is the way to
make peace with the devil, is to take a great big God of gold,
and stick it up so as every other devil might find it coming
along: Then they say here are my quarters, I have found a
resting post for my worn head to lay upon, that is why the devil
does so much mischief, he is always at work, playing with
gold, and he knows his poison is the very thing to make misery,
and such is his passion for misery, that he nurses gold, as a child
would an old rag doll, that was not washed in order, that it
might wear longer: You see I am beginning to hold up your
devils to ridicule, and it is quite right that they ought to be

made sport of, for they are just as happy as they can be over
scandalizing any little mistake that a fair daughter of Eve,
might have accidentally committed: Why I say accidentally,
is because I claim, that did the daughter of an innocent mother,
know how she was being led, she surely would not be tempted,
into meeting with an accident, for she must see for herself, that
many eyes are upon her, and her secret is not sacred, under the
guiding control of the one she placed her trust in, and that suspicion, is the directing guide to stern reality: You can not see,
but the all-seeing eye of those, belonging to that family, are
upon the evil ones, who betray their own attachments: Now do
you see the advantage of superhuman knowledge, do no wrong,
and it can't be brought home to you by the unseen hand: Take
time, and see that you understand these things, before you make
any attempt to direct your own band of followers, for they do
not see clearly, and are often very ignorant, of what is going on,
and can not lead you right, because they don't know how to get
you going, they are always willing, but seldom wise enough, to
do more than keep you out of ordinary dangers; they speak, in
a tone that is quite distinct to them, but is not heard at all by
the undeveloped head: Now you must understand, that a head,
that is under the guidance, of a band of strong spirits is
not very easily dealt with, for it leads, and drives, just the
same as a horse in harness, could be managed; and you
know, how much superior some are to others, well that is
merely the power of the band, that is in possession; they
keep the party, that is under them, in a constant state of
fever, when they want to communicate, until the thoughts, come
tumbling one over the other, this is the way, a medium is first
developed, by constant, driving and leading, by the head; ruled
externally, by a machine, which is known to the spirit power, as
the only visible means, of doing this, and is called a cosmetic
current, and is used to deal out sounds, with these sounds, come
in form of words, tied together, and are liberated by the operator,
as he sees that their effect has been received: Now you are not a
great deal wiser, on this subject, than you were before, but it is
very difficult, for the spirit world to come, and tell you that they

have been playing with humanity from the beginning of their
own intellect, and have only quite recently been able to give
direct communication; This is the only one of this character,
that has ever yet been dealt with, under this form of guidance,
and it is because it has been practiced in a way that was exceptionally fine at the beginning: It sprang out of the excessive
affections for the departed, and a constant thought of him that
was gone, seldom found in a strong-minded man: And the spirit,
knew that there was work being done secretly for the benefit of
this dead one's infant children, until at last there became an
understanding from the dead to the living, so that now it is as
easy, to converse as it would be for two playfellows, to make
up a great play-fair: You see that in this mode of conversation,
there is no sham controlling power, such as trance, clairaudience,
or any sight-seeing, known as clairvoyant, it is entirely a new
mode of reaching the human frame, it divides the words, into
two forms, and breaks them up, as they are articulated:
You seem to stand at ease, and listen that is all that is
necessary, under this guidance, and you must hold your breath,
and the sound of a word strikes you so forcibly, that when once
it is let off our semicircle of the atmospheric current, commonly
called a magnetic code; this is as near as you will be able to
define it just yet; but I will try to get more information, in the
latter end of our book: Your own band is all you want, and you
must not go running after this person or that to find out, what
you have been told, intuitively, it is the stem of the great knowledge tree commonly called the dead language, for it was once
very strong, and it is as full of life to-day, as it ever will be,
because you see that to-day, it will hold on to a thread, with the
persistency, of a wolf at bay, it gives you no chance of proving
its existence, except the one, that has hold of its proper ideas,
you are going to get more information out of this book, than
there ever was told through any human body, that ever lived,
and let all who are fickle-minded enough to doubt, go and hide
their heads in shame; Ignorance is the evil one's stronghold, it
dares not let light in upon it, for it is afraid, and let him who
seeks for knowledge keep a great big song always between his

mind and his voice, and let him study, the very one thing, and
that is happiness, under all circumstances, he who gets mingled
with pain, has no business with the intellect of a decade gone by,
let pleasure come in with the Sun in the morning, and let a
whistling tune fill up the whole of the day, for it is sense we are
after, and no one can blame you for laughing it into some other
one's ear: I live for my wife, and I will get her to believe that
she has nobody to fear, she is in trepidation, over the baker and
the butcher, but leave them to be cared for by me, that is the way
to make a wife dream she is happy to be, for she has but the concern of the house to attend, then let her be making her friends
off me, I will treat her to strawberries, apples, and cream, but
don't let me view her on anyone's lap, she is there by consent it
may be easily seen, then let her get off, before my hand has taken
her to strife, it is all very well, to say I won't do any wrong, then
bide where you know the world has got wisdom, and can see you
from every window: Your own shame is in being caught, but don't
you see that you are always caught, for the sight that sees you
there, has the power, of filling other men's minds withy our loose
habit, and can fathom the depth of your own understanding, a   -
man may say I see my chance of weakening this doll's dress, he
does not know why, neither can he explain it, yet he has clearly
seen it through his own mind as he terms it, then don't give
away chances, when you know it will be taken advantage of, for
as one has yielded to the passions of him, who prayed for a
pressure of those innocent lips, it sealed the bloom of love, and
gave to heaven, a vision of the troth, yet it has no right there
except in holy rights, and must not be given other than as a
token of eternal intentions, for as the lips are profaned by the
sight of those who see all things, it is known, and can be made
known by the heathen to his God, for he has no other thoughts, than
to enjoy his lustful souls with impurity, and you must not define
him in any other way, for he only has those to follow him, who
see no harm, in this great hereafter at all, and they sing songs of
praise, to lift the soul, they want for themselves, to live on, for it
is the devil's delight, to make himself into a Christ, there he can
shine, until he sticks his poison deep down into the heart of an

7

innocent young thing: You know that once the mind of a fallen scion is broken, that it is like the bottle, that had its neck knocked off, it is done in the accent of a moment, but you have not yet found the man that can put it on again, and never will, for although, you can take it to the glassblower, and have a new one put on, it still is not the same, for the body, of the old bottle is shouldered by a new neck, and can not be the same stem that stood the contest of so weak a break, don't think I am putting you to shame over a common old glass bottle, I want to see whether you recognize in an atom, what power there is to define all things as mortally fatal, to the human intellect, it does not suffer by my illustrations, it merely dives down to the bottom, and shows you what can, and what will be brought up against you, when you disregard the teachings of him who is able and willing to stake his all on whatever good he can do for you: Your own ideas, can be cultivated to bring happiness to you, under any circumstances, that are in life, and you know that you are being led to them by doing anything that you perceive is right, in justice to what would be of a proper interest to your own thoughts, it shall be shown here, that you must have confidence in your own guides, or you might as well take up your quarters, and say I will be the plaything of the devil at once, for when you give up your own selfish desire to please others, for the sake of getting them to please you, then you might do this differently, say to your own guides, go and find the information, that so and so has at his command, and prove to me, that you are able to assist me, by laying his plans to my advantage, you then test your own followers, and prove that they are of some service, don't mind when they fail in the first few attempts, for you may be more to blame than them, say I wish you to struggle on, and prove to me, in some way, that you have been diligent on my behalf, don't take them to task, and say you are a good-for-nothing guide come to me now and make me your footstool, I won't take any more notice of you, be sensible with your own thoughts, as well as you would consider him who had given you first-rate common sense, when your own thoughts come foolish, say I don't think you are giving me this according to good sense,

and when you are able to find a way of showing me what you
mean, then come back, and show me that I am improving, by
the fact, that you have put me straight on this question; your
actual kindliness of disposition, will bring plenty of faithful
followers, to your side, without any particular effort, on your
own part, and whenever a kind thought rises in your mind
keep it there as long as ever you can: And the same
exactly applies to any merry hilarious thoughts, keep them too.
You are all more or less inclined to lead others, than you are
willing to be led yourselves; that is seen in the fact, that you
will not give in to the fact, that you are not able to guide your
own selves: Now don't you suppose that it would be better for
you to say I will take this into my most earnest consideration,
and keep thinking that I have been a fool all my life, and I will
now see whether I can't understand why I was not able to see
these things before; it is no use keeping along at a foolish
thing, then why not say to your inner-self, why don't you help
me to understand these things as I should, and not let me
be hacked about by any common hoodlum; that is ready to
direct me to do what is right, you are the proper ones to help me,
and I want you to come nearer, and be just what I want, I will
be your footstool, but I don't want all the world to look upon
you and me as a common cloth, to be wiped, and piped by every
dirty piece of humanity; that has nothing else to do, than to
pick his own folly out, and saturate me with his bad influences:
Now don't you see what a man may become once he has the
power of directing himself, he can just say I am to be a coach-
man, and I want to drive livery, for the nobility, or I would
prefer to be a duchess, and be driven round town, in a handsome
brougham, or I will take my host out, and be there waiting for
him at the corner of this place, and when I have done with him,
as he is likely to be dealt with, I will bring him home again,
that is he will be my servant, for I shall make him understand,
that I did not go to that trouble for him, but it was to further
the kind of thing that will be my gain in the end, and it is not
for me to be his dupe, but mine I clearly say mine, I paid for
his wine, and do you suppose I did that except to get into his

good feelings for some object, that is either clear to me now, or it will come in for another feast at his expense, and I shall may be meet his dear friend: A great man no doubt, in which there might be a quiet thing knocked out: Proving him to be a good game one, and us as his opponents: We can lip him into some kind of thin job, that will call him out of pocket, and make it all serene, in the twinkling of an eye, once we have got the brave fellow whipped: You see how to do it, when I have put you on the job, that is all well enough, but where would they be, did a man of intellectual skill fall across their path, it is plainly seen, that a man is nobody compared to one whô has an understanding with God, he can say, it will be for me to decide, when and how you shall act, and not give in to any idea, that does not meet the approval of those great Seers of all that is visible, or that which can not be detected by the sight: You see how powerless tricksters will be once you are led by an invisible understanding of excellence equal only by the great light of eternity: Don't you wonder that such a one who has this power, should not say, I want a great big stack of money, for my own grandeur; to laud it over the poor mortals, that have got none, it is easy to see that such a great power, can make it like the men who coin the gold at the mint, but what matters it all to one who has got the wisdom, he feels safe, without it; because he does not know how long he is to live on earth, is not a very good way, it is because he once had plenty and was wretched, then he taught himself a new lesson, and said gold is only for heathens, it is not for the wise, that is the true doctrine of all that is righteous: You see, it won't do for you to suppose, that a man is not good because he has riches, he can own wealth, but it must be under favorable circumstances, that he has acquired it, and not by any misappropriation; that is the true philanthropy of defining right from wrong, you must not have any attachments that are dishonestly gained: And when the hand of Cain is upon you, take hold of him and say you slew the righteous one, and I will take you, and cast you into hell-fire, where you shall remain, as a token of crime, as it appeared to the light of heaven when you were upon this earth, and not

for worlds would I have you come near me any more, I say let
heaven open, and no hell is there, then descend down upon this
earth, and no sooner are you there, then you bring a cold feeling
of desolation, in your very midst, you can realize this situation once you have gotten into an icicle: And it is no trouble to
move about, where it is warm, and cheerful; you make yourselves happy in innocence, then don't pervert the time of your
own joy, but take comfort, in seeing sorrow, converted into pleasure, you hold in your own hands the secret of finding out every
single thing there is to know, proving your own self is this way,
that brings you out of every thing that has proved a dilemma
since you were born, and it is the same as it were a certain way
of finding out the great hereafter, you simply, take an outside
view, and say I will watch nature entirely, and see what there is
in it, that would make me believe, that a given space, can bring
round a given substance, and like that, it is coming beforehand:
Now you don't see anything at all that is as clear as the atmosphere you breathe, for it is making you all along to see me, and I
am making you hear what I have got to tell you, that is I want
you to hold me, whilst I am trying to explain, that a movement is
in operation, immediately you make any attempt to get beyond
your own depth, that is your guides are actively engaged, when
you try to understand a certain passage, that is not firmly fixed
in your mind by some silly astronomer, they think that wisdom
comes through looking at the moon and stars, it is not that way
at all that the sense of understanding has come to the mind, it
must come in the form of distinct knowledge obtained through
the organism of the intelligence, that comes from thoughts,
that should be clasped, in the form of reason, when they appear:
You know what it is to have thoughts of affection, for some
silly idle companion, then remember that it is on this principle,
that you should make a study, of all nature's handicraft, don't
go and say that there is not as much pleasure in nature's great
work as there is in some exquisite piece of flesh, with a fine
curled head of hair cut off, to add to light a common betrayal of
justice, don't go and say my hair is displeasing to this one, I
will dye it in ginger hues; but rather say my acts are in accord-

ance with the gifts of my own kind of judgment, and I shall be
pleased to meet nature on a fair basis, and see what he will find
good for me, once I agree to walk by his side, and help him on
with his noble and perpetual work, of doing as no other kind of
perpetuity is able to show: So far as the knowledge of our forefathers are able to tell us of, they were very devout, according to
the light that did shine upon them, yet they were wrong in almost
everything, for the fact, that they were behind, and were led
from a description, that was not real: You see how easy, everything is, when you say, I will go in chains, rather than attempt
to walk back over a walled-in piece of oak-lining, that leaves
nothing on that side except a great big blank column; it has
nothing to back it up, and what is the object in getting me
there, when there is nothing to sustain my awkwardness; you
leave me alone, and I will help nature, to till the soil, and make
beautiful fields, that our Mighty maker, might look at the earth,
in pleasure, and search for divine grace, through the craft
of my handiwork: You don't know what it is to feel the
good that you might do, did you but know how;   Of course
it is not possible for the people who have got convic-
tions standing up on end, to see that they are wrong, but let
them ask what intelligence does really mean and you will
see people, who have no sense at all claim a knowledge that
is not a bit more reasonable, than the acts of one demented,
and they really, and truly are insane; because they are so full of
bad things, that no good can get near them; you call out to a
man who is insane, and say, I want you to tell me who made the
heavens to move, and he will surely say it was the life of him
who could not see the destruction, he would work, or it never
would have began to move at all: Now don't stop to think,
but keep right on, and see whether you can make a motion, that
will move right along, without there is any guiding power, and a
complete kind of inpouring, and outgoing, it is not possible to
have a man believe his ability, to make the earth round, and
give it no form of government, it has to have some movement in
accordance with natural laws, on gravitation before it ever starts,
and in order to acquire this firm solidity, you must construct,

according to the order of natural intuition, but don't give in a
silly idea, when there is a right, and a wrong way, of placing
every atom that floats through the atmosphere, it is all intended
to make something, and it won't be left alone either, for it is
just as easy, to take a given speck, and tell what amount of them
will be required to compile a mountain into the raw material of
an everlasting eternity, as it would be to deal out a bunch of
keys, for the house of parliament on earth; you are always ready
to condemn your own affairs, without making any attempt to
improve on them, therefore you know, well enough, that a sinner
is always ready to pile a dreadful malediction on the head of his
rival in sin: because he is not alone in judgment, his guides are
at his side hiding his own infirmities, to show him up as the
solemn divine angel of good, great after theory come and show
yourself, for one moment to these great followers of sin, and say
we want purity and godliness to shine on this earth, and we want
to be freed from the incarnation of doubt, it is a soul's salvation, on earth, and forever after to see the true light shining on
both hell and heaven; you seem to see that it will be better to
share with him, than to go back, and see those fairy tales realized,
you know how to prove a failure, then don't let hate for good enter
your hearts, for it shall be written, that a soul, is the worm, that
destroys the flesh, and you know, that a stern reality is forcing
you onto your knees, and with one accord, and to eternal grace,
we do desire to know our doom absolutely; now come forward
like men who would ask for the light to shine upon them, and
give your assistance to all that is pure holy God-like in your
own understanding, and deal out signs that can alone purify
heaven and so on afterward to keep hell in subjection according to the light that is thrown open to you, at first there does
not follow any signs of improvement, but in years to come the
world will see that heaven is but the after-birth of hell: You
know what I mean by so forcible an appliance to your own ideas
as coming from the ten commandments, as given to you by
Moses the Prophet, he alone was ignorant as to his power of
seeing as he would have done did he have the great gift of signaling to his divine guidance: You see that it is not a question

of reading correctly, under the eye of a spirit power, yet he who
listens will know much, but he who understands the form of
interpreting the code of a distinct and audible signal is as perfect, as though he held the flag of truce on a field of hell-fire:
You know what Joan of Arc did in her prayers to deliver her
countrymen, then believe and you will see many of her caliber,
don't hang your thoughts on idle imagination, but seek the
truth, and don't stay hand or limb, until you have reached the
gates of heaven; And bring all of those who are pure right there
with you, for it is a haven of bliss, once it could be made as
pure as the gold on the shores of hades; your inclinations are
all right, but you don't know how to take the fight out of your
enemies, and until you learn, you are sure to be held down by
them: A great many people think they can divine a power out
of their own ideas; but you seem afraid of doing justice to your
own cause, for fear of being an outcast of society, your own
god has a firm hold of your vital sin and he holds you enchained
to a commodity, that is a social ruin, help a single sinner to life
eternal, and you have a good cause in your own favor of reaching the glorious salvation, that is so very precious to all
humanity: You seem to know that you are a whole piece of
something that is indescribable to you: Then why not have
that something made clear on this side of your own flight, and
let every soul know the truth, it is good, then be sure you don't
keep out any good in your foolish endeavor, of knowing what is
just; a sincere cause is a very happy one: Therefore tread the
dark pathway no longer: Seek for the light and life eternal: A
great man is never afraid, he can bring heaven and the earth
to an understanding, quicker than the camel can reach the other
eye of that needle, but, you say it is simply impossible for the
rich man to reach the kingdom of God: That is not the right
thing to believe in: A donkey might see through such a foolish
idea, did he but reverse the order: And strike a line off either
eye, and say broken needles were welded into one, and an ass is
on the other side: You see it meant, to delude the eye, by copy-
ing the sight into a compass of nothing; and driving the fallen
heathen into everlasting torture, it is what a man might term

keeping a saint a sinner always: Now my fine artist, I helped
to make a good thing move into what is known as the delight of
the devil; a great man shall see that his chances are one to one
with the poor mortal, who does know how to keep nothing, and
as a full and complete illustration, you can all be rich, by first
learning the lesson of true honesty, it is not right to cheat and
thieve, for the man who does so will surely be a victim of palsy
in time to come, his time is the present to mend his ways, and
let soul keep soul in guidance of good, and may an adder enter
the hole in the ground, and there remain forever his life is a
dead letter any way you may have a mind to place him, don't let
the sting remain uncared for, bite out the venom, and leave
hades its own casting, we would to these as they may seem meet:
Every mortal has the same chance, and they would be better off
did they but understand a thing as it really, and truly is: Your
ancestors no doubt did their best, as a whole, and were willing
enough to lay aside the great understanding for fear of telling
you the truth, and they might have done well to have made you
feel that there is nothing to be afraid of, yet they should have
given you something more definite to stand your faith on:
This is all very well preaching what they could have done, but
don't you see that the intellect of man is progressing so rapidly,
that a chaos must follow, unless you get at the right understanding: And that must be done here upon earth, for it won't come
about by leaving it to the guidance of those that are in heaven;
they can not reach you, when you are endeavoring to look at
them face to face, there is no one as blind as mortals, and that
can be demonstrated in the following ideas of their own, they
think that a burning bush did appear to Moses, on Mount Sinai,
whereas it was the condition of the Gods, who ruled Moses, and
he thought it could not be other than God in that fiery foam:
You see what a power held Moses in all his wanderings, and
after the time when he slew the Egyptian, he was afraid, and
was alarmed when the Philistine said here is the one who comes
to us, and is talking loudly, yet he never knew what it was that
caused him to fear, he was being torn away, to become an
instrument of heaven, and when he was afraid it was the tutor

of his rules, that had him by the vital parting, and was leading him on to come some day again, with an understanding of how he should be borne 'back again onto those who oppressed his countrymen: You see where Moses committed the guilt it really meant good, for one had to suffer a cause, to seek out salvation for the many, and in Egypt there was too much suffering for God as Moses calls his cortege, to learn to understand each other, and it was only by chance, that they were ever able to reach him, and that is the way it has got to be done now, it won't come to you, it has no idea of how you are to be found, in language such as is used by the after-birth, and when you seek information, it has to come to you in a striking manner, such as " the sheep caught fast in the thicket," you know that Moses was led to believe through a voice whispering in his ear go take that ram from the thicket: Now when you hear a voice say such a thing, would you not believe it really was God himself speaking, and so it was the divine phrase of a God-like action: You see Moses was unable to see that the ram was held fast yet he knew, when the Lord could see so much better than he could that it was wise sense, and not imagination, that was near him: You know that God does mean good, and when a good action is brought under your own observation, then mind it: And say as God appeared to Moses in the burning bush do I also wish to see the divine hand of my own cortege point me an instance, in which I may believe that I am watched over by some good angel, that has my welfare at stake: You see what a divine comforter you may bring to you by the action of listening, and don't let an ill wicked thought remain, for the angel of wisdom, won't associate with an ill-mannered one: And you can not have the better class, with you when you want to continually do wrong, for as he finds so shall he keep, and as he hunts, so will he be trodden down, do ye as there is good to come after, and as the hand of time brings forth good fruit, I will it were to me the same: You know not what ye ask, then find it, but don't let anger rebuke the good in ignorance, for the hand of love is easy turned to hate, and the evil takes the place of good, when the after-ones are stricken with scorn by the followers

of those which were trying to raise you above your own stupidity: Now let my warnings come with pleasurable accounts,
and not think of sitting down and brooding over what seems
hard to you to believe, I don't do great things by fretting, I
wait until my mind is thirsting for the light of knowledge: And
then do not exhaust it in one sitting: Keep it fresh and feeling
good, it is no use running after a bird, when it takes wings to
evade pursuit, rather wait until you get near again, then let fly
your energy, when you are in a reasonable base; you know that
to keep walking on after a bird, that has young, is the very way
for it to lead you off the track of finding the little gems, that
are so precious to that one who is using the sagacity of every
known modern idea to lead you from finding that which you
seek for, then when a bird has this power of leaving you to wonder where the right place is to get the young, then how is it that
you can't tell that a friend is guiding you to them, or may be
a sinner says he will kill those which are good to my sight, and
I shall lead him away from the right spot, and help lay up a store
in heaven, for my selfish desires are to lead men, and I will
practice on this boy, he is wicked, and I may have the chance
yet of making him kill too when my advantages are right for
doing it; you don't even begin to realize your position of
what it is to be led and driven by a hand that has such a mighty
controlling guidance; you think you are able to hold your own
with any man, and yet his power might be greater than yours,
on one particular theme, and so, when you have come out a winner you thought he had been an easy dupe, yet when you proceed to dupe him again, he is very weary, and can lift the veil
from off your eyes, with less trouble, he gives his chance to the
devil, when he has been whipped the first time, and you have
given yours to the goodness of your own qualifications: That
is a mystery to man, he must be very cautious, when he
wins, and does not lose again, his sight is dazzled by the
success of his own ventures, and he knows, that victory does
make marks of men, this is the sight, that does deal out deception, it leads you to win, and then it drives you to begin to be
foolish over your own conceit; that is your force of after-insti-

gators, get mixed up, in their ideas, and lead you down hill by
their own folly; I must teach, before I can hope to be taught in
return, you know that a whim is seldom indulged too much,
it can't hurt you to indulge a whim when there is no harm
coming of it, but you must quite see through that little folly,
before you let it see through you; and when a mind wanders, it
does so to find something new; your own ideas, have to be
worked out, and you must not let them stop, when they run
after something that has not got fixed in your own mind; because
it is easy to see when you know a thing, but when you are in the
dark as to finding out what you wish to know, you had better
not give way to the theory, that is common to most men; I don't
understand this at all I shall cross over to my attorney, and give
him a guinea to let his thoughts run over my case: You need
not do that for it is a fool's plaything, your attorney is not
able to judge so well as your own contact, they being interested
will find out for you what no human skill can do, and so you see
that a man who has a developed mind does not need to employ
an attorney: That is the way the world is quite at sea yet,
it does not know what a man may find when he understands the
full extent of his own power: And you must not go on thinking that a man is a fool because he won't think the same as you
do, it is no use you being afraid of any man, for a mind that is
cultivated is able for all comers, there is no need to apprehend
the danger of not being the only one to understand this ele-
vation, you can all learn, when you know how, it is easy to bring
children up to this, it can be done when they are young, without any trouble, and they will never know what the pain in
their heads is for; it won't come to you grown people without a
great deal of mental and physical suffering, but a child is different, it can not hurt a child for it is gone on with as the growth
is being established: You see how Christ was made into such a
wonder, he could tell you everything invisible, and just the same
he answered so well on the investigation of Pontius Pilate,
that he was victorious, and the Governor is an ass for all time
hereafter, there is an example for those who hold high positions
being the most qualified to rule, they never know when an ass

is braying, what kind of a call he will make, it is likened unto
two straws, the one is to mate with the other, for thinness is all
that has got them to hold, you see it is a man of wisdom you
want not an ass who is afraid to do what is just, there is the
question of mind over material, the one works the other, and
when it is well finished it leaves no chances of escape for the ass
to come in and begin to bray out, " I find no fault in this
man he is yours 'though, and you can what you will with him":
A nice way to treat the only good man and true that the
world ever saw, a pretty way to make Governors who have no
more right to that position, than the ass that brays, you shall
find that a man who once held office is not the kind of a
man to uphold to-day as a divine, I would tear the heart out of
such soft impostors, they are never suited for anything but the
times of the mule beget mules: And when you want to know
what common sense is never take it from a man who is afraid,
he is a tinker, that should be scorned by the world as the sting
that satan is supposed to have placed upon us, when Mother
Eve is supposed to have listened to the promptings of the evil
serpent, you little know what that has been portrayed from, it has
been the left hand of good that dealt out such a kind magnet
for you all to follow, it can not be the right hand that dealt
you such a blow, you have got to learn, that Mother Eve
is just as good as ever the saints were who painted her picture, and a great deal better, it was not a question of Eve
tempting Adam, but a desire to live on the firmness of
consolidation, that brought about this union, and you shall
see that as he was in blindness so shall you see, and
when Adam was naked, Eve was naked also, and as good
came to them, they were so constructed as to know that
a man was their own idea of what they intended to make,
and it is this that they did do according to what is properly
meant as right in the good meaning of all pious people, you need
not blush for your Mother Eve she was not ashamed of what she
has done, and let you all in holiness come forward, and say I
was meant to make man, and I shall do that which was good in
the sight of my Supreme-maker: You can not hurt the influences

of good worse than to beget a crime that is not in reality a
reality: You see that I speak what is in judgment upon the
earth to-day, they kill and slaughter the infants before birth, and
are burnt in hellfire, of their own conscience ever after, don't you
see that these infants can see the destruction of themselves, by
the thousands, for they are alive, and can not die as is supposed
by the heathens, who commit this crime, I won't plague you on
this point, but it is true that a babe who is in the womb can give
back punishment for the affliction of this instance of brutality;
you seem amazed at so startling a revelation, but as the cord of
life is vibrated by the mother's voice, so does that mere mite of
knowledge seam its life into one living soul; and forever becomes
a spirit of eternity, life everlasting that has no end: You can not
destroy a germ so pure, it is attached to an ungovernable sound,
that shall never lie dormant, and is as fixed in its purpose as the
wind that blew it into life forever: Your own sting comes after
the form of remorse, and it can not be cured, it shall never lie
hidden, for it is the tormentor's theory to come and remind you
of your own guilt, and for hades to think well of me, I have
committed this crime and left my soul as black as night: You
see what form of judgment you are bringing upon yourself it is
not for him who tempted you to such a crime to say I have
caught her at last, she did get me into a scrape, but I have pulled
her out, and she shall never know my power, until I say you
murdered that child of ours, yet he has the audacity to accuse
her, when he was instrumental in that crime of inflicting all the
pain: You see where the brute comes in; it was he who seduced
that innocent lamb, and then gave her over to an illustful crime
for the sake of claiming hades as a place of virtue, beware you
are always seen, and the mark of Cain is upon you as he went to
the black races, so shall you be scourged with the hand of scorn,
as though you were the vilest of the low thing that creeps in and
sends the dagger to the heart of an angel in sleep, you can get
all the pain and punishment you have a right to for crimes such
as these: And there is no one who can say I am fit for heaven
when they have committed murder, your soul is pure, when you
have not got to beg for mercy; then never lead a soul to destroy,

better for you to bear the world's black eye, than to be the tormentor's scourging whip, he will make a name for himself through
your downfall, but when you hunt him down with his own weapons, he has lost, and you have won a victory, and don't allow an
accident to be born again as a pure sting of hate, for the black-
eyed world is not able to give you salvation, and as hades is
seen, there are none to call you lowly, for they it is who are
the treacherous adder, that you have to fly from most of all, I
say this knowing whom I refer to better than the light that is shining in a given thought, your own selfish desires are upon you, and
the heathen is easily dealt a blow, that shall inflict the punishment of heaven, yet there are none who dare come forward, and
say a magnet hath a loadstone; for they don't seem to grasp the
idea, that a fickle-minded man can change a rogue to a thief;
and a saint to a sinner; for they have not the knowledge to direct
them to it: You know what a grave charge is, then keep back
the tongue of slander by helping to make man see that a distinct
cause is a good one, and make man a mountain of good, and he
shall not reach out and say that I am he who is superior to my
countrymen, for one God is enough, don't follow all manner of
notions, it is no use, for all can see alike, once they have the
knowledge of what is absolutely pure, and when they have got
this understanding, before them it is quite easy for them to do
what is right: You see it won't cut two ways, as these heathens
are all making us believe, when we don't do what is right, for
the fact, that no man has known exactly what is the truth, until
he does, how can you explain to him that his ideas are wrong,
you must see yourself first; but until there is some knowledge
before you it is no use saying you are not right; your own bare
assertions, won't guide any one, for the fact that it is impossible
to say enough in such a short time as will lead any one to understand what the real sense is; therefore it must come by book
form to you at the outset, and then you may prove it afterward for
yourselves; that is a good way to begin, yet no one can learn
that are everlastingly on the gog after any man's views, and
whilst you hunt down your enemies, through the system of getting information through the causes of art, that you have been

in the habit of employing; why you don't reach the point at
stake is your own faults, now it can be proved quite conclusively,
that a man who is being murdered, can track down his foe,
through this organic contact, and once you know how to apply
this course of procedure, it is easier to detect crime, for the fact,
that a man must be unconscious, when he dies, is no reason
why his consciousness; has departed forever, quite the contrary
it can be found and communicated with and the true criminal
will be brought to justice here on earth, this is not hard to do at
all, once you get your own organism well advanced in this
science; now can you understand the advantage, which has been
destroyed by the ignorant code of intellect, that you have always
followed; I want you to understand, for the good of all, and not
for the sacrifice of misery, and I will prove you capable of knowing what is proper by the hand of a power that is the greatest,
that the world ever knew, or has ever dreamed of knowing, that
is to separate the dividing links, and prove that heaven is not
above the skies as the animal nature of man will persist in claiming: It is right here on this sphere, it is not away over on the
other side of the crisis as the God of Isaac, and those historians
have been in the act of making out for the human mind to follow; you can not understand this except it be proved in a manner
which will convince you beyond any chance of doubt; then you
are going to see the folly, that has been keeping you back all
the time, it will not be very long, before you can see this change
in the actions of the eye, it will prove itself, once there is a
beginning made; and what is now a mystery, is nothing more
than the deception of the elevating power, that is in action over
every human mind; and it won't gain courage in one moment, to
betray itself, it has to be warmed into action by a stimulant
known as the eyeglass of him who sees through all men; don't
you keep on thinking that God is the only divining power, for it
is the power of all departed souls, to live in peace, once they are
let come out of their bad conditions, that are about them as
they cross from the dark side of life to the light; you can not call
a man to you and abuse him, he has got to be brought there by
some hand that knows what there is in store for him; now don't

you tell us that you were never trapped into a scene wherein you would have gladly escaped, did you know the result of your own disturbance, well done is a perfect piece of action, and in order that you may escape from this kind of deception, it will be good for you to know, how much there is to know, in order that you might get out of a danger, when one is approaching; you see that a good way of coming on is to keep still, until you know how much there is and how well you can play a game of checkmate, once you know how to control your own knowledge, it is far superior to the flash of the wires, they pass through no end of fingers by the time that your message is delivered, and to tell by the hand of providence, it is secured to you, without any one else seeing what you have got; you might make a mistake once in a few times, at first; but once you see the immense advantage to be gained over the common intelligence you will experiment until there is no chance of any mistaken view coming and taking you by storm, and annihilating the geology of learning a simple lesson, that can track a criminal to his lair quicker than he can calculate any means of escape; there you have the communication, that can track all hidden secrets, it will rip up the grave, and tell you where poison is, and take out the eyes of the blind fools who try to conceal, you have no vaults, that can guard your secrets; your very souls shall be read with the dexterity of a comb taking out the fen of a scum that was through negligence placed of its own accord there. You can not keep a guilty wife from her husband's sight, and your own wits will tell you that a knave will be the knife of a deeper cut, than the accents of villainy; you know how to be good, once you are afraid of being bad, and you know how to leave off, when you are sure to be caught: Your own sins are your worst enemies: Then let them die out, and give good a chance to work wonders for you: That is the way to feel, that sins have no root deeper than a suckling twig, it will be rooted out, once you bring the right kind of a wind to blow directly on its roots: Now fear nothing and learn to know, that the hand of the unseen is upon you, and that whatever you have got to do, make it according to the light you gain through the investigating

8

seam ot an understanding that is growing with you: And may
be you don't know this fact, but the sure way of producing happiness, is by knowing how to live without fear of your neighbor's
tongue, then make a mind of skill, for your neighbor will adjust
his gills, once he knows that a hand is over him, that will tell
you how to measure his worth, by his accents of good behavior:
Now don't go and think that your neighbor, is going to have any
better messenger, than you have got, for according to the manner
of training, so shall that messenger serve you; as you swear, so
will that one do who is at your side interrogating the mysteries of
your desires; now make no mistake on this point, it will be seen
directly by you that you have a fancy friend, who is inclined to
swear; then you must tell him through your own breath, that he is
to find some other way of making himself known to you by a course,
that does not necessitate any language, that has to be blushed
for: As the man leads, so shall he drive, and as he speaks, so
shall he be addressed; you see that a fine man can not bear the
language of a guilty swine that takes his comments from the
gutter; there is the true philosophy of getting what you have
given, and bringing home the affection, after it has been dealt
out; you know how to wrap up a parcel in such a way as the
contents can not be detected, then see that your sentiments are
in form of sentence, that can be carried without injury; you know
what it is to be glad, then make the cortege of your own glad,
and they will learn to bring you tidings of comfort under the
most extraordinary circumstances: And instead of you being
stricken down with grief, they will help you to find a way, that
will be more exquisite to your mind than the great dearth of
flowing tears: This is the proper way to find joy, by hooking
your sorrow onto those who can see all that is against as well as
for you; there is the thing as a judge should look at his cases,
both inside and out: You have your own judges, who are inside
to make inspection, and outside to reveal them; now there is only
one other question to be dealt with, and that is how to cultivate
this understanding: You have got to go under a complete change
of surroundings, you must leave off drinking, and never let any
flavor of spirit mole come into your mind, for it is sure to leave

a feeling of comfort that is not real, it salivates the membrane, and leaves the appetite courting more, that is a feeling of anxiety has come upon the mind that will not be shaken off, and is rooted there by the class of spirits, who were originally outcasts from society for this habit of immorality; there is the true solution to this question of drink, it is a great curse, for it is the blind walking after the blind, and those who love liquor, can have their throttles wet after a fashion, once in a way, on the other side of Pluto, or in other accents, I say a man is worse than a hog for he never knows when he has supped enough, and so has a hog the quality of gorging until he can not breathe; you see the similarity to the pig in a drunkard; and there is the starting point of all evil, he cares for that alone, and when he has a good home, he was actually a brute, and could never learn a lesson of peace, for his appetite had those in his van, who are the customers of the sinner, and the publican: You know how saints and sinners meet, they won all by curses and prayers, into a common understanding, the one has more beer as his God: Whilst the other holds his hand and keeps his tray, for holding forth on sabbath day; he shall give plenty into that state, into which no other soul can bring back, for it is seemly so to do, that is the parson begs, what the publican can not grab, and both are blind drunk with an influence that works out wheels against the other: Now let me be very plain and uncomplimentary, for I have much to tell to quite surprise you, and I can not do what is really well when you get after making me begin to poke jollity, I shall never flinch or turn my head from sticking pins where they are needed: You know what saints and sinners mean; that is after my own taking, and I won't bring on folly of other people's making, therefore you must know that men are morally bad from beginning to ending; this is all your own showing, when they begin to fad it is no use talking: And though they used to play at hide and seek, it all went after church began: And you may tinker on at all you can: I'll wager a new set pan can make you into a man without any more grinding: That is as it was, and what it has come to is nothing very astonishing, for what can man not treat to-day when he has got the bending: I shall stick

a pin where all the uncles and aunts can lick up a paint stain,
wherever it may have spoiled a new ribbon: And then we'll see
who is going to the tavern to drown her thoughts in beer, that
is the way to make a fairy gay by giving her some Seer; she is
oftentimes beguiled away by hunting drabs in tears, they are so
very pious those gentle parson dears; and I can outwit them all
so don't please have any fears; you know me now, I am very sure
it was I they dreaded most when I was on them before my bier:
You can call and I will come don't alarm yourself my dears; they
knew me once before I was in that prison cell: And I never
knew what a frightened nest of daws they kept until I got my
bier; there is where you all can poke and think you have hidden
treasures; but I can tell you what it is, that I can prove your
innocent lambs beside those heinous sinners; for they can robe
the child in guilt, and leave her a holy terror; she shall neither
know her only silent giver, he was there beside her bed, in sadly
disheveled head seeking for the Virgin Mary; you know not what
a man may do when he is after fairies; seeking those he most
adores, and leaving those of common store to peasant priest or
deacon; that is the way to get a cold by heaping fire on polled
heads of scientific specters: You know not who it is that sleeps
beside you; common talk has no father and ancient men were
prone to pray that they should not have a daughter, that is the
way to bring them hay when you don't understand their slaughter:
A blessing rest on every holy daughter, for she can not have
sinned, when she does not know her seducer; that is what is
called the heretics' fortune; you bid your daughters be gentle
lambs, and you give them to a priestly reverence, that is where
the tiger enters, and leaves no marks behind, he has stolen his
meet in accents cheering, and when the time comes for hiding
crime his hand is for the protection of the church, and that is
as he taught, it: You know that once a crime is committed
a few times it fondly loses all sympathy for a crime; you know
how it was first brought out that a kind heart could understand
the ways of the flame, that burns up all good, it is the eye, which
detects the form of ill as it appears, and words are apt to soften
the eye, then be ye ready, for as the eye shall detect, so shall

the soul speak, and give audience to them who have the power
of seeing whether an evil eye is upon your own soul, there ye
shall be informed of the fact, before there can be any hurt
coming to you: And though there are the thousands seeking
to destroy your life and liberty, you shall lay schemes to frustrate
them all: A way is cleared for those who can make a path
opening his soul to those who know which way to turn in
moments of danger: Fear nothing all the lands may open,
and the dead may rise against you: Yet in sight of him your
soul is as pure as the word of righteousness can make it; and
after the hand of time is at all men's throats, I say they shall not
spurn thee for knowing what is good and the very thoughts of
holiness is good to be near; yet know ye not, that inside of
hades there lives the very soul of evil, and no good can come
whilst you fix your own thoughts on the life that is in the body;
a soul is not pure in that state, it is a mere might of atmospheric
construction, and is waiting patiently to become more free; you
don't know what it is craving after, neither does it; it won't rest
anywhere, for this is what it is constantly scribing, I want to be
free to know what the world beyond me is like, I have seen
much here of good and evil both, let me have something more
real, let me lift up my eyes, and see God once in all his glory
sitting on the throne of majesty: There is none like he then
bring me I pray in front of his presence; you poor deluded fool,
you can not see a piece of mechanism that does not even live
within your radius of comprehension: You know not what there
is at all; then why should you tear and fret, is it not possible
for you to discern this foolishness; be bright, and master such
foolish ideas; they are not fitted for an educated dunce to know
even; you see me strike your education, right in the pith of the
neck, it is because I will not allow you one concession whilst I
know you are wrong in theory, practically, morally, and physically; never was a soul yet purified on earth sufficiently to know
what heaven is like; and you shall learn for the first time that
God in all his glory never yet thought well enough of man' to
enlighten him; and you know that were he the powerful scion
you paint him to be: There never need be any fears, he would

not allow mortals to cut each other's throats for want of more knowledge; you see what is claimed for him is not even begun yet; and that is the world's formation; you see that you are infants, and not men of sense as you ought to be; you have not even left the door of heaven open for your own souls to creep in, then what more proof do you want, than to be clean out of what is opened to you: That is a much better way of putting it, than to tell you that you have not learned the Acts of the Apostles well enough: Your own common judgment should show you that those who revised the works of Moses, and all others; who were blessed with intellect enough to know any-thing, have been basely misconstrued by literary fools, who espied out grammatical errors; And substituted what they called the faults of the illiterate ancients: Where is your dead language all gone to, away, in the past, anybody could save himself the trouble of the flashing wires; you are advanced in wickedness, as well as virtue; but you don't know what a mess has been made of keeping people from learning the truth; you keep on suppressing genius, and you will have pagan gods, likened only unto that "calf" that Aaron made to substitute Moses, you know well how Moses absented himself from the Israelites, when he wished to get intelligence from a source, that he could be assured of was correct, and he had to leave those surroundings, in order to be away from the annoyance of a peo-ple, who were as ignorant of the man who did have a power, that could save them from all wheels of misfortune, it was tested then, and it was considered hopeless by heaven to rule hell: That is where the after-birth received a blow, that will seldom be seen to a greater advantage, the ancient spirits tried Israel with all manner of tests, that should have shown them, that they were being led at a juncture, that is not in heaven at all, but on this earth, and they knew that a mere stretch of time would pass them by, and they could reach heaven quite easily, for Moses did prove that there was a communion going on between him and God that is the fairest way of putting it: He knew he had a voice that could do what none else knew of; yet his after actions show that a voice did guide him, and nothing of his own per-

formed these great wonders, therefore don't let yourselves believe
that what Moses could do is extinct, for it is not, you can tell as
well to-day as you ever could, and without a Moses either; only
make your mind easy, and you could tell how many arrays of
battle there are set against you, without a balloon or the flashing
wires either; now don't hesitate, and discard this form of intelligence, for it is not to be checkmated by any connivance at picking people's eyes out, for being better sighted than you, you have
no power capable of seeking a form of destruction from, for it is
impossible for you to learn a method of destroying a soul, and the
soul shall guide the soul of another, and it is impossible for you
to checkmate that system; you can lift up the excellency of all
souls by more intellectually developing the rights of defining
truth, and the greater growth of true facts, that you advance
the mind to: There will be abundance of fools left don't fear
for them, they don't come on a diamond bed, neither do wise
men drop off blackberry bushes; they are for saints and sinners
to select from: And a fool is often marked by your wise men as
eccentric, let him who basks in the sun, know that it is his to be
good from; and he who walks beside a tavern bar, and thinks of
happiness in ancient ales and brandy snaps, is a fool for all men
to keep him there to spring a devil from: Your own thoughts
are the initiation of all this, and therefore you have got to thank
the souls that are around you, for almost all you have to think
of, it won't do for you to imagine that a mind is fixed by the
quantity or quality of the brain matter, that is inside of your
skulls, for they don't begin to realize, that a mind is still when
it is not at work, and to work a mind, is to hold it in check, and
slack it out, just as you think of paying in a coil of yarn, it is
not more a separated organ, than your own tether line is, and will
be utilized, in the same manner as a cord, in a reel: You don't
think this is intellectually right; but it is just the way you all
have got of fancying you are very clever indeed: Well take
credit for yourselves; but remember that you have made a much
greater mistake; when you, don't think it worth your while to
calculate for your own "motor power"; where is your guiding
seam, when all this intellectual ability is brought into force, it

has vanished; no doubt you have supposed yourself capable of all these wonders, and think that an improvement, on your own skill impossible; yet you don't know, that you are being followed wherever you go, but the intellectual stream of knowledge common to the whole of humanity, as the impressions of the human mind: You got an impression, that you could invent some sort of machine, that had never been thought of by the world before; Yet you don't know how to set about it, for the fact, that none has been made: Well you think it is all in your own reach, because your ideas are so centered on this one subject; well it does look feasible says you to yourself; now be careful of these new ideas, for they may be a continuance of some departed dream in the body; and all inventions come through this method; a man is tormented to death, by some spirit haunting him to his ruin with inventions; and after a spirit has gone from its bed in the shell; it will preserve its course of study; and may either improve or remain in a condition of chaos for many generations: This is the most hurtful thing there is: for the fact remains the same, a man must be made to understand, before he can advance: Now you see why it would be better for the world did it understand itself; there is folly in suppressing wisdom; and a man might as well have no soul at all as not to know what is to become of him: You can't make a man feel comfortable with a worldly good position, when he does not know where he is going, and though a man may die happy coming through a fool's paradise, yet he is disappointed, when he finds that he was always a fool: That is quite enough to retard his progress when he finds a great big objection raised against him for not finding out for himself before he leaped through the darkness, into the light: You can just picture to yourself, the thoughts of going to eternity; expecting to find a great big throne coming in front of your vision; and a hand being raised up against you saying: "you are here at last, and I want you to know that it was I who witnessed your theft: What more could any man take upon himself, than this great judgment day: Why, he is always afraid to die, whilst he is living; and when he misses that seat of judgment, he is never happy, because he can't find it: and he

believes no one, and always thinks of finding it in the future:
You see what a dream is like: Well your own thoughts will rise
up like this dream of God defying man to hide any secret from
him; and in doing this it leaves man forever in the dark as to
his exact place of abode hereafter; not alone that, but you
make him fear death, through this understanding; but as life is
precious to all mankind; you see it right, and there can not be
any fear of the great hereafter: On the verge of departure, call
on your guide to come near to you; and though ten million sit
by your corpse, there shall not one defeat your guide, from
coming and claiming you to the great good will of him who was
your after inheritance: You see this is nothing extraordinary at
all;, for the giver of light, did provide the light, and he was not
doing it for you or me; but for the general activity of the soul
life; that is a much better way of putting it, than to declare
positively that man was made to burn in a flaming hell for the
remainder of his days; which means to the end of eternity:
You don't want anything of the kind to make people afraid, as
to make them ignorant, and ignorance is cowardice; therefore
you are at the very beginning now; the same as you have always
been: That is an awful illustration; But you are at the beginning for the fact, that there is no ending, neither is there any
end to eternity; now then what do you want a hell-fire for; Is it
to pick off chunks of semi-imperfections; or is it to waken up
those fools who hold favorite positions in the land of light, you
might very easily improve this by folding up the dead man's
sound, and keeping it, until he gave you permission to loose him
from this atmosphere; where you do so very much: And know
so little: I am indeed puzzled to learn how you are going to
hold or control these souls, in your own hell; this is more of a
kindness to me than I ever expected to find on this sphere; and I
was called the great "infidel"; when you sewed me up in a sheet,
and said I was sure to roast in hell whilst the world did last;
now don't you believe that I was right then, when I can come
back, and tell you that you are all wrong, you know what a manager can do, and you know how they did manage to gag me by
placing me in prison for telling the truth: Your own hell is all

that God Almighty ever created: And when you get on the other side, which is all and all the same for both you and me: I will wager the back off all eternity, that no man ever did live yet, who can speak so truthfully as I did when on earth amongst you, but then I never did know how to get at the exact truth in particulars such as are being divulged for the sole benefit of the paternal ancestry of the minds of God Almighty's human races: Your acts, and deeds: Will be forever the standard of laughter, for you make out, that a man was afterward crucified dead and buried: And the third day he arose from the dead, and sitteth on the right hand of God: There you make a frightful error; for man did not do anything of the sort, he may have been buried, in whole semblance; but he never arose on the third day; for no one can breathe in a body, once the lungs cease respirating, and though our Lord may have risen from the dead: after three days: There is no need to fling a doubt on one so good and pure: That is, you are preaching, what to-day is a falsehood, and a fairy tale: That is not very much could be gained did you subject this book story to analysis; the way to test right from wrong; is to bring actual facts to a particular kind of reasoning sense, and then see what is real: There is no one who has a faculty for knowledge: That will believe you: When you say, " He was born of the Virgin Mary: Crucified dead and buried: And the third day he arose again from the dead." There is where you are lying all through your want of reason: You are infinitely worse: Than you were at the very beginning; for you don't know a lie when it is unearthed for you: Now don't let me have to prove you ignorant: When you have taught this lie from your birth upward: And stand there to-day: With a whole testament of false illustrations: And you won't give one soul the right to be guided to eternity in a proper and righteous form: That is not the way for you to get there or to help others either: You know that though Christ was a man of exceedingly good qualities; that he never countenanced false representation: And you know that it is enough to drive heaven against hell to have him spoken falsely of: You are the sufferers for this piece of folly: And as for anything you can say to the contrary: Won't make amends for your falseness to the only good man you ever owned; for you did own him: And will always be compelled to own him: And no one can say that you did not prove his ownership; For you stuck the knife into the only gentle Jesus you can ever hope to own: That is a crime that heaven will always hold over the sins of hell as her great mark of respect for true knowledge: Now you take a kindly word of advice; from him who divines all things: And don't let fools control the rights of religion: For they are more their own enemies: Than they can ever hope to gain from their wickedness hereafter, they will bring sin on all that they touch: And in wisdom find ye grace; for no man knows what golden treasures there are for him; does he but say I will thou art holy, for God gave his only Son for the salvation of sinners: You know that Jesus Christ was sold by Judas Iscariot; as a peace offering for those heathens who betrayed their God on Calvary: That is they sentenced him to die; because he did not save himself: And they wanted him to show them a miracle that should stand them in need of showing them that he could climb the skies in his own body; that is as near a true fact as it can be demonstrated; they could have given him another test, that would have proved him just the same: But it was to see him climb the heavens: That was their view of finding him worthy of so great a task: And when his body did not ascend to heaven: They were alarmed; because darkness appeared: Well now it could have been much more easy for him to sing I am coming back in darkness to bring you pain and punishment for this evil hour's work: And you know they were all afraid of the deed as it caused the night to appear before its proper time: You think God was angry and brought on the darkness; that is what you have always been taught to believe: Well your theory is quite right: To believe such was the case, a darkness did spread itself across the earth: For no man dared say I am he who butchered our Saviour; and those who did do it; are as much afraid of him coming back: As they were of him whilst he was amongst you: You know what men I refer to, they are those who will not believe he was sent down from heaven expressly to serve them their own purpose coming in sight and disappearing through the aperture of heaven's gates: That is what was expected of Christ: And you can not find one sinner but wants this performance realized before he will be convinced that heaven is not on the other side of the stars: You see what he wants to be convinced with; because he thinks as his guides do; and he never grows any better; because he is always thinking of heaven as over yonder; you know why he is so stupid; because you won't let heathens see the light; is for the fact, that they don't know how, before they begin to see light, and when they do; they are quite willing to drop into the humdrum life of following some poor devil to his doom, and preaching into his ears that he won't be hurt, or that he never need fear; this is precisely what is in store for you; unless you rise out of this foolish state of affairs before you start on your eternal pathway through life; then you can't be any better than those who go over the marked line, in happy ignorance; there is your soul, coming home in the dark night, and the first thing it knows, is a street trap has been forgotten, and the lid is not shut over the opening; then a precipitous flight of may be enough to spread confusion on that careless wanderer for his entire life, and he becomes a raging lion, or a mad dog, it is not readily defined what effect comes over such a one; and it often comes before the men in power that a son shall sting his father; that is a way of putting it; and a son may go mad, but no hereditary ailments had been found before in the history of that family; well it is the vicious attack of some one or other; that had fallen short of his expectations: You can not possibly tell the amount of damage you do by suppressing the right knowledge; a course is quite clear to you, then don't go and expect to find, what there is not; neither could there be such as you have been made to believe, through the ignorance, of those who thought they did what was best; for they were unable to foresee the danger that was in the eternity; you know that to be saved is to bring happiness; then don't go and make many mistakes; for in sight of all you can not be made whole unless you have been defective, and it is as easy to purge a sinner as it is to

prove a good saint to be wrong: The latter sticks to his belief
as though the haven of his soul was broken did he feel that his
whole life was a blank, and that he had been the innocent victim
of committing many a fraud; you must learn to feel what it is to
have all your hopes crushed in one single blow: There is the
lesson that is good to know, and when you do find out, that
nothing has happened because your hopes were blasted, by the
single turn of a crank: Then you will be better suited to do the
will of that mighty divining power, which leads all men as they
might hope to be led in their home of eternity: Now don't go
away wondering what you mean by such a talk, better still to
say am I gone in the regions of my own intellect, and must I
really and truly go bad before I can see to what extent my folly
will lead me; you see now what it is that is necessary for all
mankind; they must see, feel, and understand whether evil is
not against them prior to their own search for good: You know
what the cause of writing the Bible was at the beginning for it is
plainly understood by both heaven and those who have right
claims upon the knowledge of a literary genius: A wanderer in
a foreign land has been the first man to sink his voice deeply
into all men's hearts; and he shall remain as a standpoint of
excellency as long as the hemisphere shall crawl round the Sun;
you must be beguiled indeed to bring what a sinner may come
to, for as the hand of Cain did bring out the old philosophy in
our first man of mark, and that was the man who slew his fellow-
man; for it shall be according to judgment day, and as decreed
by those who saw the fight coming on; and being struck down
by the fear of man, but not through the fear of God, this is
what I say is before you in all its truth, there was a light that
did shine upon that noble man who stood before his mind a
heathen striking his fellow-countrymen: You see that he acted
in a moment of righteous indignation, but when the men of
judgment commenced to rail at him, and say it is he who slew
the Egyptian: They created fear in his breast, and for that one
act of conscientious behavior he was condemned as a murderer:
Now you see that when God spoke to this man in the far-off land
that he feared for his crime of slaying the Egyptian, yet he

never once turned back from any danger when he knew that there was a power at his back, that could sustain him against all the universal callings of mankind; yet he was at times misgiving, and did bewail his lot, when he saw that Pharaoh was so set against his release of the Egyptians; you can't tell when angels rule what manner of style of adventures they will bring to pass: And as Esau did live in a second passage of discipline; so did the contact of Rebekah bring confusion over his birthright; you see that she loved her favorite son Jacob, and to win for him the first blessing, she was willing to forego her chances in heaven: You see that though Moses was the salvation of Israel, he had to suffer the tortures of a lonely wanderer before he was fitted for so high a position; yet he did not mix with the saints or sinners; in order to be made whole, and I say that a man should know evil before he can be good: Therefore you see that Jacob was afraid, and did leave his father's house, for he too had been guilty of a crime: He took that which did not belong to him by rights; and was not prepared to face the anger of his brother: Now you see what it was when the first champions began to steal and kill; you must watch out and not let these same passions enter your hearts lest it be said that I too must go away to a foreign land, and see what I can see in the future that is not already revealed to man: You are all the same as Isaac in one respect, you have no one to till your land, and you must take off that which belongs to another; You see that Isaac did not feel happy when he saw that Jacob had gotten in first and stolen Esau's blessing; therefore he made one other blessing which has been interpreted wrong entirely; for as you all know that the hands of Esau was made into the color of a class that is supposed to be at the head of all men that are blessed with hair: And now that men don't wear hair on their hands you would naturally suppose that he is gone into a monkey: But you do not understand this as it is meant, for when Isaac made his blessings; there were no men of the class that you find in this century, and consequently, they are not of the same kind of man as Isaac was constituted; and are less likely to be requiring any blessings; for they have come to this understanding, that a man of to-day says I am not going to place my confidence in blessings; I shall make my son an estate, and he can lease it or do as he pleases; last century they all were much in favor of leaving him a life interest; but when it is time for them to think of the next century; they will want an estate in heaven: Which you can surely give once you understand how to bring them up to believe in what is true knowledge; not by making them fear God, as it has been the custom to do; but rather let them have the use of a freedom for good instead; and let heaven come and join hands and say hell is only a place for brute; let us be one common people calling each other by proper names; and bringing each other to love the life which has been endowed upon us by a merciful providence; which knows no guile, neither does sinners know how to repent; for they can not see how to begin to pray, to a god that neglected them always; you mistaken creatures, why, not blame what in all common sense and good reasoning faculties, there never has been, and never could be: you simple-minded sinners, is it not wise to be whole-souled and righteous: Or whether would you rather I said is it not folly to be taught wisdom; Though still paragons of naught that is wholesome: you won't leave well alone I know it; therefore it is hardly fair to say in one year from now that we always had a suspicion of the truth; You paganish prigs, you would steal the half off heaven to bring your right judgment into a sense of knowing all things, don't I know you as though you were the very click of my own watch, don't think you are able to bring this other sin upon us by your idea of getting good all in a moment, you have got to practice all that you preach, or go to the galley, and cook thoughts for your paganish folly of treating God as a fool for not knowing better how to organize your stupidity: You are stupid sometimes, and you know it, for it brings you home to judgment, and you don't like to let the judgment of a righteous cause get the best of your own stupidity; a clever rascal never knows how foolish he was till he got caught, and there is where the force of wisdom comes in; take time to consider whether it would not pay you much better in the end to let folly alone, and live as a good soul

should, keeping on as you may go, for as the sinner does know
what is his crime, so shall you know that a divine ruler is ever
at your back calling you this way and that, sometimes making
you sin to bring you to light, sometimes making you good to show
you the might: And always struggling with you for his own
salvation to come; your own welfare is frequently not the object
at all, and therefore you must see that a certain thing is to be
reached before you begin; now don't get led till you see the end,
not as you have often done, gone on in the vague hopes that
your mother was a good and loyal wife; but rather say my
father did because my mother made him: And don't go on to
your friend's house and say my husband is a brute I feel his
presence a burden to me, rather do something to make him
see that he is a brute, and you sit down on him carefully when
he sees that you are not to blame; that is a way to be proud of;
not making those who fling stones at all proper people begin by
chewing your troubles; Inside is not the place to make your husband worry; bring him outside, and take him with you for a
walk in clear air, and see if purity does not fall in; where vice
was often so rife: You know that men can stand much from
women, when they hold the ribbons right, for as you drive so it
will be seen that you are driven; and when your husband won't
agree to you going out with him for a walk, take his arm and do
you lead him where he should go to; that is a man will not be
left by a true woman; and she it was who made him hate her
own kind, for though she scoffed and did her might she never led
her man quite right: Though bairnes "may come, and children
"dee," you take hold onto his "auld" cloak, it is the "warmest"
cloth that makes a noble heart to welcome home and thee: A
deal of sin and crime is brought home to every household through
the affection, they bear to idle talk with their neighbors; and
more still is brought, by treating your friends to social evenings;
that is not the way to enjoy happiness; bring your wife to some
amusing scene: That may help you to enjoy music and singing
for it is good for the ear: And don't let gossiping fools within
your gates: Let them who cherishes home mind it for himself:
Alone in comfort, and sadness may bring him joy by keeping

harmless what is purer than the show of having friends to sip
and snivel at the pie that had no fruit in it for them: Take
your pretty wife, comely and sweetly caress her; for no one can
tell which of your friends is meeting his eyes to fix her: You
little know what games are played on husbands, and don't let
innocent men come into your house, for nature's God is upon
them: And you poor fool is made to laugh and to prate over
your own silly wisdom, come home to your darling, and leave
your friend to freeze in the snow: It is a proper and most delicate purity for him; this is the way to behave to your own wife:
Then give other men's home, a single calling, for they may want
what you despise; in courting games are funny: A man may
laugh and appear quite gay and have a heart that is bursting:
You know not what a plain-thinking man can see; when he is
inclined to be cunning, he it is who lurks around, and calls when
master is away at Fanny's wooing; don't let him in, for he it was
who stole the cup of peace between the ancients and the priests:
They went out and he went in, what do you think of bumming:
He could not keep from his measly, talk when master's in: But
then he could tell many a tale of honest Jim: And persuaded
her to fly with him, it would be better than she should call and find
him with Fanny: You know it is an old-time talker that is
pointing you out a way to be happy whilst you may; and leave
no bad reflections that are certain to carry you far out of your
reckoning; they seldom fit where Steve and I did place them, so
your own chance is to mind and keep away from the after
reflection: For a man who walks upon his hind feet never can
quite measure his fore ones: They seem to be so very smart,
when you try to catch them: And you must know as well as me,
that they dodge you every way once you try to reach out and catch
them, that are walking on in front of you, and called by name a
shadow: You know what a shadow is: Then why don't you
see that a mark has been made upon the ground, that has no
other kind of appearance except the form of your own body, it
seems strange that you should know that it was your own
shadow, can't you see that it is the light shadow, that hangs
around you, that is making an ox walk in the light of its own

shadow, you have seen a cow jump at their own shadow: Then why
should the cow be afraid of what is nothing but her own shadow,
she is not half as blind as you are; she sees a movement coming
in her way, and it disappears when she has made a jump it is
gone underneath her; and she fears it no longer, because it
stood by her side until she made that leap, and left her nothing
to see beside her: You have got me on a string, that is little
short of a swindle: It may appear quite plain to you that I am
mad to pick up with such trifles; yet you know that a man who
speaks truly often is a lunatic, for the generality of mankind are
apt to think that lies are better than truth, for they don't know
any better: You see I am going to make a point out of your
own shadow, and it will serve to explain that a man's mind must
be wandering, when the cow can see danger in her shadow:
You don't seem to catch my drift it is hardly plain enough for
you yet, a shadow is the reflection of your own body; and must
be part and parcel of the whole, or it would not cast a reflection;
you know as well as the cow now that a reflection is dangerous:
And when you want to measure your own reflection, why just walk
backward, it is there seen what a long fellow you once were, for
you are getting behind your own shadow, and the hand of him
who started you to grow, has stretched you out backward, and
is now a towering trunk where you first began to shoot: You
are a mighty fine fellow to be always stepping on your own
shadow, you don't think of these things, they are too brittle for
your *compos mentis:* It won't suit you to say I was once a
shadow, and now I am too proud to own it; cause I mustn't
mind what wisdom does it makes me sore to be represented as a
tiny little atom measuring out a great long shadow: You know
not what you are, then don't begin to ridicule too soon, and don't
forget the sakes of him who once did make a mate for all mankind; it was a noble deed, and one well worthy of the man who
made another, it can not be told without some remorse, for
though the trees were bare yet Adam came there, all the same
he had no clothing to wear, yet he sewed leaves up before
needles were there, so that dear Mother Eve should not get quite

bare; you see that a fable is not well told, unless you can
get right down to facts; there is nothing in the Bible that speaks
of a foundry for Adam to get his needles from, and yet he and
his wife have gone to the trouble of sewing leaves together
to hide from God, because they were naked, who said it is
immoral to be naked in the presence of one a wife and the
other her husband: You do not even begin to preach
when you have a true knowledge; therefore is it possible that
a sinner could so quickly see pain when there was no punishment to fly from: You forget that these two were the first
that were understood to be made by God: Well why were
they afraid of their own nakedness: No Becky Sharp could
tell them that they were disgracing morality: You see that it is
a one-sided stroke of the pen that has caused all this confusion:
You don't want a heathen to tell you there is no God: He
must be able to show you what there is then, or forever may
he speak to the Moon and Stars for they are as real as the
wax that has been sent broadcast over the heavens claiming a
myth as geologically correct astronomy: You must confine
yourselves to sense and you can know all that there is to be
had out of earth or heaven; I don't want you to sit down and say
I am a wonderful man, I want you to search for good solid facts,
and say when you have got them that a man was born, and
not go on like fools trying like Darwin did to connect the
human races with monkeys: They are well enough for idiots
as men to hold communion, with the phonograph to make a
monkey drink water by the impersonation of its mate's voice:
It only shows still further that man has got to come to the
specific voice before he can learn anything; and further all
nationalities have a language that is plain to them, does not
the horse know where to find his mate, without any apparent
voice; does he not go twenty or thirty miles direct across
mountains; and does he not find those horses in which he is
in search after, is his language not purer than yours, I say that
not one of you can as well see the horse he wants to find in
that valley twenty miles away: You know it is called instinct,
well what is instinct, it must be a message from the dead, or

it is nothing at all: You know what I mean by a message
from the dead, it is an understanding between the dead horses
and the living, I am not going to say you came from horses
or any other animal: I simply say that Adam and Eve were
the first man and woman: And they knew that they were to
make man, and they did this according to what is right and
proper: And a man who does believe that they were ashamed
of each other's nakedness is a greater ass than ever brayed:
You know I am speaking truly, and it matters not to me whether
you believe it or still remain a quadruped: You know I don't
care for anything but the truth, and when you can show me
that I have lied then it will be good for you to do it; no
lies have any right to exist, and the sooner you banish hell; and
make the haven in one place of lowly everlasting peace and
pleasure the better for man and mute: You don't know how
much better it is to live innocently, or you would forsake hell
and give no man a chance to chide you for being the folly
of all ages; You are a gormandizing people never satisfied,
and never filled: You want what you will never get, and you
have got what you don't want, that is an inheritance to sin;
better far to take a path that is open and clear than to cling
to one that is made doubly dark through sin crime and ignorance: You shall know the truth, and then select for yourselves,
whether I be an infidel or a sainted angel: It makes no difference so long as you are enlightened and shown what is
right: A man may climb to the top of a high mountain, and then
he will find nothing but space in front of him: You may perhaps call it a beautiful view, yet you know that there is a
something between you and the skies: That won't admit of
your sight being able to penetrate through to the other side
of heaven, as you wish it would: That is why you are obtaining the most powerful glasses: You want to see through the
heavens, and what is it all for, it may be very nice for you to
make charts, but that will not avail you anything for it is the
sense that guides and not the sight; so your great glasses are
no use, unless you make them so as to look at either a man
in his ethereal form as well, then you must have them capable

of holding his voice as he speaks, for he can not stand there and make you understand him, for he is not able to hold conversation with you, without you make him see as you see; his ideas are quite changed from yours, and he laughs at you, for he knows you are not able to understand anything from that form of guidance; and you may as well give it up at once; it is no good to try what is a simple failure without any reasonable grounds for thinking otherwise; you make a glass that is powerful, but you can't make it magnify to what is not there to be seen, it is a substance you are in search of, and you have got a substance to use against what is not a substance after your own theory; then why keep on trying for what you don't possess, and can't hope to ever obtain: You want a mirror to look God through and through: Then you must go after you are dead, and see what it was that puzzled you so much: You need not depend on me, but go right away, and look for yourself immediately you get rid of that old shell: Why don't you do as the line of light distinctly shows you: Bring your focus into play, to read the minds of dead men, and see whether they will tell you more than you ever knew or not: You can't get hold of this space, for it is so infinitely small in your own ideas, that it is not worth troubling about: Do you suppose for one moment that all the space you see contains nothing but vampire: Why it is the essence of life contact, that is being spread around you, and you must grow to learn that when that life goes away into space, that it becomes larger, through the appendix of a great fan-wheel, that is keeping all matter turning; and when it turns, it keeps on gathering as it ascends, and with it there is life, for nothing is moved without life; you see that once you get up a good way in the atmosphere it becomes more pleasant to the fluid that governs the light; and you would be satisfied, that once you are able to ascend, that it becomes more pure the higher you get, it won't may be suit all; but as a common thing it is better for the spirit life; which is all there is to be had up there; and a man may be able to breathe in any atmosphere, once he has gone a few times through this atmosphere without stopping to take any notice of it; you see that to keep on going is all quite well enough for a departed man, but it won't quite agree with any one who is in the earthly body: You see that a soul is competent to squeeze through any space, whether it be a given or an ungiven space; so that when you are anxious to know what there is in the bowels of the heavens: You have only to command your spirit guides to go and bring you the information: And unless they willfully mislead you, it will be seen that I have given you a perfect description of what is there, and you can easily prove your guides wrong by getting at the common-sense view of what it takes to make a certainty: Now you must know that to punish those who have not been there to see, you must take them to task for not having gone, and looked the whole of heaven up thoroughly: You have a right to demand this from them; for when they come to you with no other knowledge than bare outside useless talk, you can very well wait until some better guide is able to force his views upon you; and they must be such as will bear the closest scrutiny; you don't want the assistance of those who know nothing: It is wisdom and not folly that we want: Bring your guides up to this understanding: And don't let them be loafing round whilst you are sleeping: When they can't tell you, be careful and understand their answer first before you condemn them: They may be divided in opinion, and that is what you will find a great deal of questioning: They don't feel disposed to be always led by the one head, and may be that there is a strong discussion going on between them; that will, often affect you most materially, so you had better not give in to either side but hold them steady, until they resolve themselves into a compact body again: You know what a disorganized parliament is: Then remember that a band of powerful spirits work under the same organization, and are often struck with this continued prohibition from doing exactly as the majority wish; and they often reorganize once it is seen that a field of culture is not being executed like it should be: A verdict of the minority is not taken without it comes from some one who is able to show the majority that they are wrong, and then he does reverse the opinion of the whole majority, for he is accepted, and promoted in a manner that is more enlightened still than anything that you are aware of in the ground parliaments: You know that a man who is intelligent enough to make himself understood in your own parliaments will quite often carry the whole of both, parties with him; so you want wisdom, and you are always right; a man can be wise one way, and he can be a fool in another; for the fool is he who leads himself wrong, and the man who is wise enough to go right is what is known as a genius of experience; so you can not be wise unless you have first paid a high price for your experience; and left fools to keep on as they are going, don't you attempt to lead them lest ye be made fool also; don't seek the acquaintance of one who indulges in anticipation, for he who anticipates is a son of folly: Call him what you may, but don't go along with the one who is expecting a mine of wealth to pitch onto him: But you go your way at your own gait, and fall on top of that wealthy mine that has all the world to make you bite, it is your own, then take a slice of what is free from no other man's rights to claim: You are what is known full well as the waif of misfortune, then ye be not cast down and saying there is nothing for me to rise on: Take a pan and bake your bread, it is off the pan that the Almighty universe is drained from day to day, then what are you that you should expect to be fed with silver spoon: When the maker made you to help thyself: Quote scriptures: But do it well: And bite the rind off every liar; for they have sown the seed for you to reap, and don't let them be keeping what is not theirs to steal: You know not what a man may do once he has eaten of the knowledge tree: He may rest in peace, or break a kingdom: For once he knows how to interpret right, his fingers are at every one's bedside, and they may think as they would wish; Yet he can counterfeit all they may think is sacred to them only: You don't want another man's crown, but you have a right to mend your own frown, and keep away quite clear for the chances are you can make a town know you as their crown: and what is better than the loving respect of every honest citizen; for when you are pious straight and good; they know you when

you have passed from here, with an honest mien you walk, then
you have only got to show your thoughts are honest, and you
will not be chided for your tears: A way to do is to act according to all, as you would take all to you: Then don't try to make
others fall; lest they do fall on you: For once you seek a quarrel; it is easy to pick a quarrel with you: And mind don't let
an angry feeling get the better of you, for satan pulls what is
best suited to his whims: Thus you are thrown when he has to
win: And you are very good pastime to make him grin: Don't
begin to poke your fingers in, for they are sure to come out with
no tin: When a punning man walks up to you, just hold him
steady: For he has got one more to throw, and you are his
brother: Keep him steady while you try to come another: They
'make a pitch and toss, whilst you can make him slink and cough
when he finds you are into his butter: I don't want to funny be,
yet you will see that I take pleasure in making my time agree-
able: So that instead of you withering like the grass, I say you
had better make a man to smile, it keeps him from the whisky
tap, and glues him to affection, that is the way to live in berry
tarts, and don't begin to make it smart in terror; for you can go
and make a start, without any loose habits; for it is right to
laugh, and playing is a pleasure, then don't begin to press your
cheeks against the window; for there it wears a pane of glass,
that must go into your thinker, as a cold winter, for sure you are
a merry man and can not afford to be made senseless by such a
cooler, you don't know how to live once you press your face
against the window: a man may be a very great thinker for he
can not do much while he gets whisky in, and has to place his
face against a clinker: It won't help you to drink water ingrained
into malten whisky, for that is the way to split your own grains
in two; and make a bloody mark upon your brains, that sees
nothing except a spark of lightning hue comes after; there is
no one who can be cured of evil ways once they let the influence
of whisky come and crush out their own intelligence, for it is but
the farthest hand that controls their weakness, and he who craves
and lusts for more liquor can easily reach the main point by
breaking through all modest scruples: You can not mend a

broken reed by plaster, so you have got to grow another: That
is a very fair illustration of a drunkard, they make a man to drink
himself, for all is welcome to the last that wears a shoe off any
taker; you know that whisky comes in and virtue is of any man's
asking, for it a sottish pleasure; have an understanding of how
to make pleasure, it is all well enough for you teachers of
prayers; to come and say that there is no pleasure in getting
drunk: It is all in the light that you see it, then don't begin to
rail and to pray shut up the heathens, first learn them to see a
better way, and don't be keeping them down with your prayers
that have no wits in them; don't you know that a drunken sot is
able to see through your innocent lays, that have got no grit in
them: You mistake a complexion of drunkenness, it is able to
tell you what men don't know, for it is happiness to the cortege
that gives them all their thinkings; you don't understand what
it is that makes a man drink, except that it be inflammation of the
brain as you call it; it is the inflation, of the real spirit that was
here a drunkard, and always will be a drunkard as long as there
is a smell of it within his grasp: You take a man that was drunk
all his life, though you think this impossible; yet, I will show
you that a man can be drunk forever; his mother was a drunkard,
and did he not feel the essence of drink as he inhaled the nourishment from her vital column; it stained her flesh with the lust for
that powerful influence; and forever made that man a drunkard;
His little lips were made to pale before that current of damnation, and in those lips he held the drains of contamination: And
though you may think that it is no harm for a mother to have a
drop of something hot before she retires, you mistaken brutes,
don't you see that it is a complete skinful for her child: You
don't believe it well it is easy to prove it to such weaklings, you
go and practice on the cow that gives you milk; and give her
turnips for her keep, see if she won't make you bitter tea; that
is one way of testing it; but you can have all the tests you want to
prove this side show of making men to weep and wail; why was
I made to like this tormentor, I feel as though my lights would
burn in two; unless I have my grog at intervals; mostly all day
long; you see me now most thirsty being you ever knew, I have

no throat that does not chafe and scratch against the upper side:
unless you pour down some liquor all the time, it sticks fast and
makes me cry I wish I had another: You can whim and whine
I once had a mother: She was all the time soaking in, to make
my mouth another's; It has got to serve a dozen throats besides
my mother,s; she had all the soakers in the land at her side;
wishing they could borrow her throat to have another, you may
all both laugh and grin I have struck you where you have got to
be hit; before you are fitted for my brother, don't you see that
once a mother drinks with one child in her womb, that she has
gone into fits of disorder, that will produce marks of a similar
character on almost every child she may have through this same
happenings with the first; and though she may be the mother of
ten children; she will hold them all to a resemblance of the first:
you can detect this in one way or in another right through a family;
notwithstanding the fact, that their father has been changed;
even more than once; for it is the consequence of a great big
time of making a thing that has not been made before; and the
mould that is first prepared may be somewhat crude in shape,
yet it was the fist that did the shaping of its own moulding, there-
after leaving a mark that would hold every other to that which
was placed in order by the first hand of man, you see that this is
but one of nature's small pieces of art, for man must be made in
a mould, that is the very first work of art that he sets his enter-
prise in; then to view him hereafter is merely a form of good
guidance; you don't know what a man may not do, then why do
you fall short in understanding; it is easy enough to see what nature
is trying to do, and that is to make man in two: for it is where
you feed the flocks; then know ye not that you have given place to
three in one; and where you once supposed there was only two, I
have proved there are three drinking off one tap: your wife is the
mother of your child, where then is your share coming in; when
your ancestor is using her as the instrument of drenching her with
gin perhaps, or some other favorite beverage, that he or she was
a slave to: you are three in one, yet, it comes when you are
inclosed in your mother's womb; don't you see how I interpret
the scriptures; they are right in many phrases; providing that

you could only understand them, and make them right where
ignorance has led you wrong: The way to do, is to be
governed entirely by reason, and you will encompass all that is
there or elsewhere to know: don't go and say there is no sense
in this argument, for as you keep on weeping so shall tears
follow on after each other: and though your heart would break
in two parts, it is your own folly in letting it break, for as he
who casts a rope to catch a friend, let him know that you are
going to merry wend; and through your tears of pain, let the
joyous strain come flooding: And make a man begin to train his
eyes for another's coming; what do you want with tears of pain,
does it not make you feel ashamed; to be the stand-by for some
foolish funning, better call your dead father to your side and
ask him to be cunning, and wipe away those tear-stained eyes,
he can more assistance give than all the humming money: Now
don't begin to weep and wail for a dead brother, for he may
get on top and drive you round at eighty knots an hour without
any punning: You should mind your life as you will guard your
wife from other men's sunning: For they may leap and dance
around when you are not whistling: You know it is all
the go to make man a martyr, but you get on and make a
show before the old man has crossed the garter; for don't you
see, that he is sure to come to thee from off the strata: because
you are the only thing for him to make a spree, when he is across
the border, you don't go and make a fuss as stupid fellows do,
make your respect according to decency, and get out of reach of
the cemetery as quickly as the movements of good grace will
lead you, for there it is that leads a man to tears, when he
should be down on his knees praying for good of him who went
away, and asking him to come back again to point a way to
follow: You don't catch on to hindmost fellows, for they are
interested in the pleasures of ancients who would think you
come from some queer region to wish to join your lot in sin
and resurrection: Don't you see that those who pass out well
and strong, with no bad qualities can come back immediately, for
they have no sin to fear, no crime to walk in hell for: And they
may select a path of easy climb, or gather in the souls that was all

their joy in earth; now don't you see that affectionate ties are quite as strong as the love of liquor, and will last endurance such as sainted sinners have no knowledge; then don't begin to play at tools, but come along bristling, for it is nothing to be tied to a guide that pulls you through with pleasure, he can dance and sing, and play a tune that will make the floor ring with honest vibration: Don't you take in gin and soda smash when you go out walking, it is quite enough to let the angels mocking, laugh and sing I want to play at ring, and don't stop me I pray for you are a great big dunce, and we want to bring you in tune; there is the way then do ye follow the lead that is given to you: for as sure as you take a walk out, and ask your angel friends to come near and sing some pretty song, such as they teach in heaven you can be filled with sweet music: now don't imagine that you are going to have angels flipping their wings about your head, and making a noise like a cowboy's horn: You will be the horn, and they will be the music: So you see that an angel is full of nothing but sound, and it is by the manipulation of this musical sound that you are brought into an understanding, and not with the cow-slogger's whip: You are very ignorant indeed when you can not comprehend this practical demonstration of how you are to get at the wing of a fairy, yet you go along speaking to yourself saying I wonder when those angels are going to make me understand them, I think I had better get a few glasses of whisky into my skin, and see whether that won't help them along; they don't seem to talk to me, like the way they did to Moses about that sheep in the thicket, you keep on wondering; and just you keep getting drunk, on angels' voices every day; and I will undertake it as a stern reality that you will hear voices; the first that comes may say get me a glass of old, " O, K "; but you need not let your passion for such a wonder let your appetite wander; better tell him to go back and see if he can not come again to you with the same voice, more distinctly audible singing "we won't come home till morning"; that will encourage him and not do you any harm; then you have established his good feeling for you; and he will strive to bring you

one other message; which will bring you more information; than
" O, K "; and may be you won't drink any more; for it might
hurt me now; you see that the angel would be so frightfully
crestfallen; at his bold attempt being turned into ridicule by his
following of angels; that he would quit right there and then;
and begin on new tactics; don't you understand that an angel
can not bear to be frustrated in his beginning; and he will lament
in agony such as no mortal ever witnessed: You must not use
the thong; when any one speaks; for it may be the means of
your own downfall as well; use some sensible answer the same
as you would to a prince; for is not the angel who makes his
first attempt a greater prince than any mortal with jewels at
every point; you must not think it is easy for your father to
make a sound such as you will understand; and when he does
ask you for a little drop of the famous " Old Kilmarnock "; you
should remember that when your own dear father kept house;
that he never allowed any specific commotion to occur at his
home without bringing on to the table a specific contact of the
angelic stuff to creep down men's throats: And stake a peg of
fire in every one's eye, you are sure to wound your best friend
most keenly when you refuse him his first glass when he has
been capable of bringing you an intelligent sound: You must
know how to rebuke, before you venture too far; for it reiterates; and brings a bad reflection with it; there is the difficulty;
with new beginners; they think they have the powers; whereas
it is not them at all but the ones who are able to get the right
way of converting these sounds into actual sounding sense: You
may go a long way before you will find one that can dig up the
right meaning to a word; for the very thin edge of a wedge
must be of a necessity quite small at the start; there
is what you have got to get at first; don't teach men by
the cable-string; fetch them on with a gait of common sense:
And you will get there all quite soon enough: You know it
took the cake when the ancients gave you to believe that God
did make the whole world in that incredible short time; and
it is no use you ever trying to beat the ancients in telling the
biggest liar that ever lived; is but a mite compared with theirs;

and I don't need to dwell on it, for no whisky tub, can ever be found who will get at a beginning to smear such a snub as those ancients have given us: And you may rest quite content, it is no Yankee that is able to whip the ancient fable of the universe; in six days' speculation: Don't try it my bold American you are sure to get wiped out; rather say go on my fair fabrication; we have got a country that can whip the seas; and we will give up the breeze that blew an ancient topper; for he could neither smell a whiffer; coming along both tall, and strong; he has got an ax with all its edges sharpened; and you quoth he will have to make a shuffle, and bring his seat where it ought to be, in a stiffer breeze than he ever saw growing: And you will be astonished to find that the American soil is the first to blow the dust from off the feet of Moses; for he could not see what had him in all his smartness: You may know it will be counted rather cunning; but you may know that it is all a funning, when old Moses went to take a sneeze he was constantly blowing God out of his nose; don't you see that it is on the artery of the organic nasal string that the complete self-acting membrane hangs: and it is here where the noise is held in one accord for the moment, before it reaches the after-sound; near the part that takes in the sound; and you are blind for the fact, that a sound does not carry the vision of sight with it: your only way of ever getting this organ attached so as to make them work harmoniously together; is by constant practice with the eyes shut, during the time it is being struck by sound, from the interior of the nasal fork: that is the way to connect sound and sight; both being in active operation on one version, it will give to the eye, what it did not seem, to come before it, when it was open: Now you have gotten a much better description, than you are prepared to accept, for anything that is new will be hung up for centuries as a fable like the one you cling to in happy ignorance and fear: Don't let the Sun shine upon your folly fable any longer; but wipe it out like the ancient did his sinners: He could whip eternity in one great blast, then don't let him have the last: He was a charming fellow who invented that story, and no wonder Moses was stricken dumb with such a fellow:

Don't think I am sacrilegious: for I have more respect for dear old Moses and his God than you ever knew how to hold: I keep his memory warm by following in his footsteps: You keep his cortege cold, and making men to weep in both their eyes in folly: You may be very smart no doubt in a kind of a way: but you don't begin to talk, once it is all over with your mind in you: Don't you see that as men walk along through life that they don't know what a noble thing they are missing; where is the man who will not guard his soul here when he does know how: then give him what he has a right to protect; and though he be dead or dying, I will help him on to heaven; his conscience can be relieved at the last moments of his life did he but know the consequence of his folly; then don't deprive the dying man of unloading his guilty soul of its contents; then it is brighter and better for him in heaven; for he will not shed tears of anguish, when he has gone to his bier; and sees it sadly prayed over; as though it were a sorrowful sight; You know it is oppressive to see these streaming crape black hats; then why torture the dead, when you know that they are the chief mourners; don't you believe that every human being has more affection for its own body, than any weeping friend could have; don't you see that a man may look over his crimes, and feel that he was not ready to die: Is it not possible to take away these sins, and when you reach the other side to be free from any pain; It is just as possible as it is to walk inside of a paling fence: The one is the wrong side, and the other is the right: Take ye the gate, that leads to the right always; and never go in at the left: For a saint may lead you to hell: But a sinner will help to hold you there always: You have got two in a row: Select the one who is at neither hand, and call on your mind's guide to follow, you know that the saint may tell you that a little wine in sickness is quite divine he takes it himself too, then you know that a taste of the devil's tail is quite as bad as his whip, you go on bravely well for keeping steady, yet before the cottage is worn and faded, you are sitting on the grass bemoaning, I have mortgaged her, and I have lost my crop, it went to Father Doolan: You may take it now, and make a

nest in heaven with the rest: It is all coming out of that whisky
tot from Father Doolan: And he it was who made me swear I'd
never touch or taste another drop for muling, but only for that
whisky tot I'd be in a railing: you know what gave me him to
spot, it was his railing on the ground and making himself into a
sot; by keeping what he got from that old spot of a trailing; for
don't you see that once the saint had said to him take a drop in
sickness, there would be a dozen throats beside his, wanting the
whisky slings; and they would pitch right onto him, in taking
gin he would be theirs forever: His end was none of his making: The parson taught him how to begin, and that is the way
he caught his fling: So you see that where the saints commence
to peg out a claim, the sinners are ready to work it: You are
quite mistaken when you think that a parson is the only one who
helps to trail a devil: I have seen many mothers who give their
girls whisky for the first blush of womanhood, and then again at
all painful seasons; what then do you expect of that innocent
girl, she did as her mother made her think best; and was ever
after a weakling from her frame: You see that it is not what a
man does but it is what others have gone on doing for him:
And once you see that a son is the first pin off his mother's drum
stick, how is it that you can't keep quiet: For the fact: that a
pin is a sharp-pointed instrument, and the pin that pricks in pain
is an outrageous bad lad: and you want to see that a pin is not
covered with verdigris when it is to be made with a wholesome
casting: for as the verdigris is sticking in, it takes a lot of
fomentation, before you are able to rub it out, that is the way to
make a beginning rub off the verdigris, and leave nothing but
the bright shining pin, that is fit to be cleaned with any righteous
man: You may not see the force of my illustration, but you
know that a practical demonstration is the best kind of a cure
for a broken arm and that is a first-class surgeon to make it into
a whole one, and as man was made before the whisky pap, you
may rest assured he will not want to go back again and get into
that sap, you are all very curious to grow men into a strong
likeness to God, well do you know it, but the time that was set
apart for worship by the heathens; was a very mere resem-

blance of what it is at the present period: And the intellect was not so much cultivated as it is at the present period, therefore the ancients knew what was good as well as you do, and it was discovered that certain herbs made into a brew, had the effect of making men quite brave; and as the spirits of the departed friends became a great nuisance; walking about and poking their noses into everybody's business, the ancients had to make this brew of spirits to encourage them to drive the ghosts away, and it was through this medicine of mixed spirits that caused intoxicants to come into fashion, thus, the spirits and the priests were intoxicants, and did not realize that they were waging war against each other, until at last it became so bad that a hand of main had the situation in hand, and the dead could not stand to be wiped out by common mortals; so when the priests were driving and drinking spirits, and driving spirits away; the dead became furious at the mortals for getting a greater share of the slush than they could get; it became a dreadful state of affairs; and the spirits were so much more in favor of licking those, that were the body, that they gave it their sole attention; and made up their own understanding like this, whisky is the only thing on earth worth taking to heaven; so we will not trouble the earth much with our presence in the ethereal form; because these priests are afraid of us; besides we might be debarred from getting any, and they won't make it for us; unless we stop out of their sight; you know it will send them crazy, when we turn up again, and tell the fathers, of the priest method of going in to the daughters; on the pretext of searching for the Mother of God: You know it is the idle worshipers who don't see through this great sin of unrobing Venus; by the light of everlasting traditions of how the one little ewe lamb is stolen from the flock, and is made to lie down beside the angry lion: Enraged at not being able to find the lioness; he seeks his prey from the lamb, which never yet gave suck; and his hand is on her mouth, you but dare to make a squeak, and I will expel you from the house of God; this is the time that our blessed Virgin Mary should come from behind her screen of impurity; and say as hell is so

10

bad, I have nothing to fear, my Son was the only true living mortal, and I shall share with him my honor: As I did live so did he come from my life: And I will not allow a lie to be cast on his father; for as he was a man: So was his father the one who begat the greatest man who ever drew the breath of light from heaven; and it is for this also, that the angels have kept from explaining more fully the condition of the heavens; you see that they are afraid of. risking the life of any good man who would do their teachings thoroughly; for it is seen that angels can do almost anything; that does not necessitate their actual constructing force; yet you know that the sinners were often times killed by the power of God as the ancients call it; well now since I have run onto this subject let me finish it, you know that a man who is in the ethereal form, has no idea of his strength, unless he be taught it; and it was stopped by the piers of heaven; for did they not hold some check over their own subjects; it would be an easy matter for the heavens to open fire upon all mortals, and destroy them forever: You wonder how this can be done, well it is just as easy to set fire to the earth, as it is for you to strike a match, and that is not much trouble you will admit, the earth is hollow beneath, and it is on fire in many parts; thus it will be found, that a magic fall will produce a great feature in the evolution of time, and the fact that the Sun is a ball of fire; it would be an easy matter to take the Sun out of twisting the heavens round the ground: Don't you see that when you get up near the Sun and Moon, that your bodies are restored, to a perfect healthy condition of cosmical form; that will serve you to fix up any kind of a habitation, that you have a mind to make; therefore what is to stop heaven from letting fire rain down upon you; it is there in abundance; and it would only be a question of turning a crank: And dropping a part of the Sun onto you: You don't understand that some of the spirit world have been very much in favor of letting down a dose of fire onto the earth; and destroying it; instead of attempting to mend its ways first, by the method of more knowledge: You may think it is a great big blow, but such is a true fact, that unless there is some way discovered of suppressing all

wickedness, the earth will be destroyed by fire after and according to the manner of form which I have shown you: You may
think it outrageous, but you don't know what sin is until you
are governed by sinners forever: They save their souls by sin:
And you have got to do the same, well what is crime but sin,
and what is crime but the after working of the dead: Now
pause and think, whether is it not better to turn good, and
make a nest of comfort in heaven; or would you rather be the
drunkard's toothpick, or be against crime forever: And yet
made whole by this trick of making men commit crimes when
drunk to escape the punishment of the hereafter, that is precisely what you are going to do; and it is for you to decide
whether you will give up the drink: And mend the earth: So as
to fit it for heaven: now it is in your hands, you know what it is,
and you are sure to go on till you have made a spill of the Sun
on top of your own ground, unless you say, let hell bind hell,
and no more walking over my head to get your heels stuck fast
in my throat; you are carrying a pair of boots down your throt-
tle at every whistle, " come landlord fill those glasses ": And the
word is no sooner said: Than the beggars are after the grog
you drink: Of course you don't know anything about it: And
why should you; since spirits and drunks got made into monks
at the beginning; they tried very hard to get at the skunks,
when they were making the bunks; but it all fell through, for
want of a better lining, and oh! dear me, it's now out of hiding;
for drunken Jim and saucy slim, can have their fling, without
you ever knowing; and ancients were afraid of them, before
they knew how to hide in your old skins: That is rather slim;
because you won't believe it; then you take off a grog shop; and
see what comfort you have left, why, it will show you devils in
abundance; then now then don't think me very cunning; for old
Father Doolan was a great old sop: And he it was who first saw
the devils outcrop: There is where the origination of gamblers'
hall has come on so tall; by honest invitation: You know when
you take a friend in to dine, he is very courteous very; then
don't let him stop, but bring him right along, and introduce him
to my book, and say as he says, so shall I follow: You may save

yourself from many an evil maid, and many a drunken lover; for I know full well what I am talking about, and don't you seek to collar; for I can overthrow every man that will try to measure swords with me at butter: And you must not frown on me; because I don't sanctimonious be, for it is no use being a saint, when you have got to raise a gutter: There you are and there you be, I say no man is too wise for me: I will continue by adding my mite to, the endless inheritance drunkards have of being the farthest from heaven; they know it is a sin to smoke and swear bring in another pint " landlud "; yet you see them slinking away with as many pints as would thrash an old wooden tub out in the time it will take to run through a man's body; your fingers get stunk, so very much, in the awkward shape of the nails; for no saint ever cuts his nails, and it is a terrible job to pull the finger nails off a drunken man when he is in stupor, they smell so of whisky tint, that it will be quite a relief, when something is known, of how these smell so very badly, you see that the spirits, and the anglers are so much of a class, that they get fastened into one another by the finger nails: And it is quite a job to separate them: For they don't cling onto nothing as is generally supposed; that is how you don't know anything, there is the grog in a spirit; and there is the spirit in that grog; therefore it is impossible to divide them from each other, without you take and prohibit the use of it altogether; it is no use talking, it has got to be done without, or otherwise you will have the hell turned into a flame of fire right down here; and that is what will become of the earth: You know it need not be necessary for the heavens to stop winding to accomplish this feat; for the earth is quite round enough, to take a tumble once she is fired at both sides and over and beneath her bottom, there is a great well, that can be let out, to meet the division on its fall; so you see you are not going to get at us in the whole fall; we can rebuild another earth just as easily once we mend the old one, and the Sun has burst many times before, so she can stand this one other extravagant issue for the sake of sobriety, you can't imagine what a difference it would make to have no drunken spirits to contend with: The Sun would travel round

much faster, and make more worlds only for this intoxication
that she is always inhaling; and you know that she has to throw
over a veil every decade or so; for she feels the effect of the
intoxicants so keenly, that it is in very shame that she has to hide
her pretty face from view; don't think I am joking, so sure as
the sun resounds with heat; so sure does this Moon call her black
face, for sucking up such stinking jims; for they are all taken up
after a time in the suction of the Sun: and that is the way they
go to get knowledge, they never know anything till some day
they find themselves sucked in by the Sun; and thrown out of
the Moon, and there is where it is that the stars are caught hold
of, and kept moving round so fast; the men who got drunk first
were let go into pigeon holes; and made to drink water ever
since, and hold their mouths open so as to show people on earth
what a fiery place the heavens are lit on every point: Do you
see what the ancients have done, they made every drunkard hold
a candle till he got ossified in his place of holding a light in
heaven to guide his drunken acquaintances home at night; then
there were as the Bible tells you only eleven stars, the Moon and
Sun; so that you see how many more stars we have got now.
The heavens are full of them, you may think that I am purely
ignorant as to what I am talking about; but you can not turn a
table without a motive power; neither can you turn the axis of
the world without some power to keep its motion going around,
as you have known it to do since the year one, that is the start-
ing-point in my new history of the earth's circumference; and all
that contains therein: You may start on a new leaf, and see
whether there can not be some improvement made, your own
knowledge is the way that you have been taught; and it is hard
to wean away a strong understanding, although it might be
right to do so; am I so very far reaching that you will still sing
out the old one is at his favorite theme again, and he has the
world at his back now, to make him go down and tear the lights
out of every liar: You are afraid of God, but you won't þe
afraid of an innocent old mortal who says I am the light, and do
ye follow me, and no darkness shall come upon me; they say he
died for the salvation of souls, let every man die that is sent

home with a knife in his loins; his sin is forgiven him who tried
to speak the truth: And no man who does suffer for heaven, but
will reach the throne of good, you may play and plunder; for it
is your business so to do, but he who stands like a rock, on the
tower of true construction; will never fail in reaching a good
home in heaven: for as the men of old were banded together by
saintly Gods; they provided the withal in heaven wherewith to
bestow a golden crown, wreathed in scarlet robes for angels to
walk over, and those who sin and truly become workers in the
cause of those, whose dictations are followed, have a soul to
walk beside them across this scarlet robe; but that is not everything; it shall be for the judgment of bringing him home who
was lost to all that was righteous; and all those who save a soul
on earth, will have a certain redemption for all their wicked deeds
on earth: You may call this sacrilegious or what you choose;
but as you have laws on earth, so does heaven guide them for all
men to follow; and as the time comes more fully to your minds
you will see that I am right; and that the heavens are at the
head; same as usual: for in the beginning there were many
schemes tried to destroy the earth; and the heathens thought
that it would be well filled with what they had there; without
any more; so you see that they were in a selfish condition, and
might have killed a few people prior to their being stopped; for
it is quite an easy chapter to become skilled in the art of angels
killing mortals by a magic power which does not throw any
reflection beside it; and you may govern the lightning with such
skill as to direct it in any given way that it is intended to kill;
but you must always bear in mind that a spirit guide can manage
to frustrate any of his fellow guides; and though he turned a
current of electricity simultaneously on you, it can be broken
like the wave of your hand; and your guards are good guides;
they make you feel the presence of danger; and will not allow any
willful harm to reach you; providing you obey them intuitively;
for this is their work of keeping you free from harm, and it will
be seen as distinctly as possible that the kind of fear that you
feel is quite warranted; for as the fine point of portraying the
cow jumping on top of her own shadow, has given you the idea

that a reflection is to be a warning; and that it was through that
warning of imminent peril that prevented the shadow from catching the cow; therefore you keep this in your mind; that a
drunkard, can see his own shadow; but not what it will turn him
into; he is a good deal faster astern than he thinks for, and
once he gets pitched over the other side of heaven; and is made
to hold his hand on a certain parting in the sky so as to allow
raindrops to come through, when there is a flood on; the better
he will understand how to keep out of the way of drunkenness;
for as you have said before the waiter on water is often very dry
in his hole above the sky; and he must not be held back to die;
for his time is very precious when the water is high; you think it
an easy matter to hold water to filter through a cloth, well you
try standing there forever; and see how you like to look upon it
through that light; well may be you think this quite a matter of
detail; what do want rain for; when it is dry you are always looking upon the sky as though it was not doing its duty; and when
you don't give it proper nourishment why it is sure to cry out, I
want more rain too; and when you soak the sky with whisky
fumes; it is sure to burn the more water; for the drink is sure to
fly, when it has wet the nether eye; and you can cork up your
bottles as fast as you please, unless you want to hide your old
still in the after dole behind the rill, you can't make matters
much worse than they are at present, for as the heathen drinks;
so does his eye become moist with wet, and as the star shines, in
heaven, so does it become wet, therefore we won't take a tear
away, when you have one wet eye left; your own thoughts are on
drinking, and your eyes are on the whisky-tap: Then keeping
in weeping, for it is your brother Pat, who is weeping for you to
send him a little dew: For he is often famished in his hole
behind the rack: You don't think of this, as you ought to do, or
you would either break away, from that pistol in your eye, or
mould a better bullet, that could not hit poor brother Pat, he is
the sufferer, because he is on the inside of your eye; keeping
moisture dripping through; and making a very fair picture of
this heavenly eye; you don't want him to stop, for he is making
you into a sot, and you will cross the border line intoxicated, and

there you have got to stop, and leave a margin open, to let a little drop fall on master ground, you are very fine sport for devils and minds; when you get on top of the weather that is fined; he can boast of nothing else; but a great big fine; it is only the drunkard's salvation: and he must keep on till he grew another weather higher, for as sure as he came down a spout, he has to get up higher, and broken backs or straw hats won't catch on fire, they were used for lighting fires; and you must know that razors grow above the fire, and cuts are smart, where angels grow up higher: You have gone on long enough at getting into the tire; there are plenty of stars now, so don't go and make many more; for it is usual to get on very well without much hire, you can blow hot and cold, without setting yourselves on fire. you are at the very entrance of the gums, when you want to hide your hire; it is easy for a sinner to be hidden in the mouth of a drunkard, and he will find a way of drinking in a drop, as it comes fresh from the bottle, you may think it is an easy way to make him stop, without corking him up in the bottom; for he is sure to see the end of that little tot; before he leaps into the bottom: and you may blow your nose from dawn till dark, he is always round that bottle; there is only one thing left for he who carries his bottle tacked on to the end of his face, and that is to strike a light and fire him: You see what to do with a brand new flue; for it will have to grow anew afore you can reach heaven; and that is not the worst part either, for as you grew, so will you go on growing forever; they used to bawl out give me a hollow tube to hide myself in, but now they have grown quite calm, and don't want any one to help them lift up their hole above the sty; for it is at the old game of making many a big black eye, you are as susceptible to the touch of that great big eye as ever your Grandsires were, and they have a great deal more to be grateful for than though you would peep at them now and say we want you to be our friend and govern our bodies to make our souls more pure: they would tell you at once, that they could not do this thing, for it would interfere with the stars in heaven: Only for that they might come down and lift you right out of your misery, that is the way

they talk; knowing full well that unless you keep on drinking
and making brutes entirely of yourselves; that they never could
escape from their forced positions: Of holding up the stars from
tumbling down upon you; this is the theory of every drunkard,
he thinks that once he leaves go of his hold upon the unfortunate
mortal, he has, that a time must not be spent in his own selfishness; or he will be driven from knowing what has been his share
of the grog consumed on earth: and that will be his desire to
know what amount of stuff he consumed here forever: One who
drinks water, is prohibited from the suction of any spirits in the
body, of this likeness to God; therefore the sooner the stars
don't help each other out the better; for as the weather beats so
hard against the side walls of heaven; then may heaven have a
resistance, that will bring food around the better: They don't
want any one to be hungry, for it would be a great mistake to
have a man hungry for want of some kind of food: Don't you
see that a good deal hangs on the crank wheel of heaven, and
that is not saying a little either; for at the gates of the west end
of this great hemisphere, there are the greatest number of pails
of water to be emptied in a specified period, and there is where
the drunkards all sit leaping round and round, leaving nothing
to escape, for, they are the people who vegetate on the banks of
the show clouds, and leave a hole open so as to get the style of
the actual measurement of the internal workings of the sky:
You see that to prop open a hole, and make it tight at the same
time is not such an easy job, therefore once you have this to do,
will you wish, I had left alone the whisky tap, your only enjoyment is an occasional run to earth, to fetch up a new conscript;
for you are not allowed to mar the present head by your absence;
they don't want the same class of man as yourself, may be it is
not a fit position for him, he has been made into a biscuit or
some other thing; for it will be seen that you are no more
suited for the work of dyeing the waters red, than you are suited
to cleave your own selfishness to the wakings of the dead:
Your only chance is to make a great big covenant with the head
of those governors of the stars, and precipitate your souls into
the good graces of him who governs stars, and heathens alike:

You have got quite well used to this kind of reasoning, by the time you have remained a hundred years in a crab hole, propping open the aperture of this star of yours, for as you leave it open, there will be plenty more there ready to take your unexpired term, and relieve you of your job altogether, and as the saint says there are all kinds of people in this world, and that is quite true you know; well what is good to work the heavens is quite good enough to prop a hole open; so as to show master Pat a decent burying place for his saintly body; I want to call your attention to the fact, that a man-hole in heaven is quite as necessary as the hole in a common boiler flue; for the one is a generator of gas; whilst the other is intended to escape from drowning the occupants' hole out; and that to work a gigantic heaven; there is no end of necessary constructions; and this is practically what you have got to do when you die off here, for you must understand at once; that a man has to work in heaven; the same as he does here; and there are so many things that require to be done, there is this home that we speak of to be decorated; and made to stand thousands of tons of pressure, and it must be made with exceeding care, for it has to be built by nature, and this natural element of our own to improve nature is so strongly impregnated into our bosoms by our own construction; that it is one of the strongest points they have in heaven, as it is on earth; there is no sliding back, you must get along as nature drives, and it will be seen that it is quite natural to elevate something; thus the drunkard is higher in his own estimation once his skin is filled with alcohol, that is his, ideas are quite uplifted, because his soul's champion is at the head working up a fevered excitement: that was not there before; well the spirit of the dead is strongest in fevered heat, and can work more successfully on this uncultivated head, therefore you see the spirit you drink is not master; as the ordinary intelligence has been always reckoned on; your own spirit is mastered quite readily when you are drunk, and you are quite often made to commit crime in this state of intoxication; for the purpose of the spirit of the head of some class legislation, who want a certain kind of example shown; therefore you will be punished here on earth, for the

fact that your own body came in contact with this crime through
the promptings of this drunken spirit who had its power over
your own soul, now it is quite well to know what makes drunken
men swear, they are not insane through drink, but they have a
noble drunkard at their backs, promoting this blasphemy; for the
spirit who promotes this course of action, is quite safe, knowing
that no harm can come to him, he just has all the spree he wants
at your expense, and you are blamed, whilst he is applauded for
accomplishing your ruin; therefore we can sit by and tell you
how you sat and made the ground shake with your boisterous
conduct, before you pulled a gun, and shot your friend, yet, we
know who made you take that fatal step, and why he did do it;
but, you only know that the devil got into you, and made you
commit the rash act: you want to know now how we can tell you
the name of this spirit that brought you to commit such an
atrocious crime; well it is the simplest thing you ever knew; did
you but know how to probe the subject to the top; for as heaven
is full of such characters; you might be looking a long time to
find the right man: but you don't get your information by scour-
ing as you would look up and down investigating this idea and
that one; as the police do in tracking down the famous Whitechapel murderer: that has gone to gory deeds without detection:
For he can not be found by your theory of detection at all;
while I will undertake to trap him the first time he commits
murder; no matter where he is hidden; and I only want the
dead body as my guide; a palpable contact is enough for me;
you may have my services for nothing; and I will never undertake a job, without I execute it in such a way as to make it dead
sure in its entirety; therefore you give me the chance of hunting
down this famous Whitechapel murderer, and I can do it; providing he carries his practice into effect when I am near the
scene of recent tragedy: That is the way to find the murder,
by taking his soul into your confidence; and bringing him into
a condition of understanding, you mean to requite the wrong,
which has been done to him; therefore he becomes your friend,
and will direct you to the spot where your man is to be found,
and in this way you place your questions; so as to make the

man who did the deed commit himself to you in the presence of
witnesses; always tiding off the particular parts for a final
charge; therefore you master the murderer's soul companion, and
the rest is easy, you don't want a clumsy guide for this work, for
unless he prepares the dead man's soul for the charge, he will
spoil everything by his determination to seek revenge: And drag
you down with him, for as certain as he sees this one, who did
destroy his earth career, he will charge him, in a moment with the
crime, and tell his soul's companion, how he is going to do it; then
the communication, is flashed to his own spirit; causing, an
instantaneous avowal of not guilty; but there may be ways and
means, which it appears would be better not expressed in this
work, for when you give up your whole hand you might spoil
the actual surrender of the culprit: And bad wisdom is a foolish thing to begin to explain, what is wanted; is to stop all possible chance of a criminal escaping, and he would be doubly
armed did he know how he was caught, therefore I have decided
not to give this up until some methodical way is found of suppressing it from the public at large; you see what my theory is:
And you must own that it is a science, that will not be easy to frustrate: Therefore you can test it whenever you choose: And what
is wanted is to master your own sinners, before that they reach
our hole, in keeping awake forever to light poor foolish Patsy
home: You can laugh all you have a mind to but remember
that a happy grin, is the stepping-stone to wisdom: Now don't
imagine that I mean the play actors' boys: who sit up among the
gods, and set up a giggling noise whenever an attempt at merriment is made on the stage, I have a secret fear within me, when
I sit in my box, and see that the play manager has scoured the
city; and found the boy who was intended for the Australian
jackass, but who came short of feathers, through his ignorance,
in not being able to climb the skies: You will therefore see that
the manager of that play, has more grains of sense in him, than
the company, who perform; they need it says the shrewd manager: I can't get up a laugh without this boy: well let him
work it as he may; but he has reckoned me out, for it is merely a
reminder to me that I ought to be at home, writing you a decision

of my lost money, and ill-spent time; no fuss is a bad thing, for
where there is genuine excitement, there is food for our souls; and
you don't want to be a synagogue, without and within, take life
in pleasantly: And don't go and say it is wicked because a child
may fling up their wings a little higher, than the woman of forty
summers, take in a common-sense view: and say I once tried it
myself, and got very near equal to her, only my uncle looked
over his spectacles, because he couldn't see well enough through
his glasses: And said I ought to be ashamed of myself, but he
looked until I had done all the same though: now I want you to
be merry, for there never was a genius yet; who stuck his toes in
the wall, and wore his knees out with praying; so you mind me,
and don't go to the other extreme, and commence swearing, for
he who swears, is a constant cuss; and he won't grow any higher
therefore he can be a sniggling fool, for all his pains, where he
did bring them from the cotton fields: and you don't know it
either, but master Cain was sent there for killing poor Abel;
that is just enough to let you know that Adam was no shiner,
for he could make them black and white, just as well as any
common sinner; that is he got sons, who killed and lied, when
you believe the story is true, and they were not drunkards then;
but you see it is not told how many fools were made before you
got any men; and that is the way to reckon up the spirits; they
had started to improve the heavens, before ever Adam got to
know that he was alive, and he ought to be a very sure man
indeed, who attempts to knock Mr. Adam down, for he
has stood the hail of many a storm, and grown quite gray
in harness; yet you can go and pitch him over any time you
have a mind to: His faith was no stronger than the crab-apple,
that brews your own cider: and he could withstand them all
indeed he did; but oh! my what a fall he had, when Mrs. Eve
stood out, "and said my dear Adam you must be wise;" for my
sake, and so she went on brewing cider, until it began to taste
of apple jelly, then my dear husband must taste of this, it is a
very delicate dish, and so we eat of jellyfish; because you made
it nice, and no man can resist the call, when there is a lovely
woman in the fall; you may not like my picture; but you should

11

peep at " Parry," for I can show there a picture, that would take
the paint out of any tree; therefore, when you want to see an
idea of Mrs. Eve, standing quite at ease, and Mr. Adam in a
breeze, you take up painting, and we'll stake a freeze that you
can't beat that picture, your eyes may wander through the great
halls as they may, but once your eyes seek such a theme, it is for
me to say, that you can not miss the picture; it is standing right
in the doorway fronting the Aux-urlary De Paris; and it can be
pointed out to you by any guide you may call to your aid in this
easy search for Adam's downfall; I don't begin to breech
through, yet, for I have only been playing with you, to show
you how it is possible to get at a given thing in a more enlightened way; for I shall take some time to proving myself superior
to all men: Only it is best in my opinion to give them easy
things at first; before I dive in to make you understand what
there is round and about the sky; that is what is felt to be a
necessity, for a man is nothing without he can master the whole
universe in its entirety.: Not as it was supposed to be, but as it
actually is, therefore you will see that I have undertaken a work
on science into my confusion of frolic and fun: You must not
suppose that a judge who sits in cold chambers, knows any
thing, because he does not: His ideas are all spoilt for want of
a little warmth, and his blood becomes after the spider specie;
somewhat creepy: Like that song says about the spider and the
fly: It is nice to be a spider, walk in pretty fly: Well the
spider would be better with some of the blood from the fly, then
why doesn't he go out and gather a little for himself, he could
get it by basking in the Sun, but no! he would rather stick to
the cold damp walls, and suck the blood of a foolish fly, so you
see that the judges, have only got what is not theirs to keep,
they are there in the cold damp halls; wasting their time hunting up particulars, for lawyers to ape the figure of making
believe, that they are industrious; whilst they are only weaving
the web for Mr. Judge to suck the blood out of that very foolish
fly; you see that I spin my web, with the care of an artist, for I
have got something to show you in this same illustration: Your
own idea is that a spider is a distinct specie; that he has no

assistance whatever; well you don't know much, and I shall let
you down softly, when a spider makes his web, he spins it into
two parts, the one he leaves the housemaid to keep, whilst he
goes on, and crosses from wall to wall, without any web to climb
over; therefore you see him cross from floor to ceiling, without
a strand of cobweb: Therefore you say he does it by magic, well
then, what is this magic, it must be something intact, or it could
not be utilized by this harmless spider: You dreamers, don't you
see that the spider has more friends than you have, for he can
cross the air, without you being able to detect his helpmates:
You can't see, because you don't know how to look, there is the
trouble you have got, you are a blunderbuss compared to that
rope the spider flings across rivers, you think he does it in the
night by going down and swimming over the strong current,
Fools' paradise, can a spider stem the current, when you are
unable to do so; why, you have got no more sense, than to suppose that he climbs up to heaven, with it and drags it off the
other side; why can't you understand, that the spiders have
invisible friends as well as you, and they climb the ropes, first
before the body has to be carried, and their invisible strings are
made, and fastened to each side of the river, before the body, of
the spider is risked on their rope; now you understand how the
spider has his fixtures made, he does not do that work, till
after he has been dead for many years, and learned how
it has got to be done, there is the problem solved of life
immortal: You can't explain this any better, because I am
telling you the truth, and should you attempt it, I will riddle you
with bullets, at every point: Now then, the judge has his lawyers to fatten, and he is their own sustenance; the same as the
flies feed the spider; but the spider, does not feed his dead
brethren, as the prophets said the ancient spirits lived
on them, and used up their substance, the fault is altogether
the one who dives into subjects, and only touches the upper
crust, when you want to be led right, you must follow on true
principles, and not go and get mixed up with all classes of inferior humbugs: I want to show you that the lawyers act the
part, of the dead brethren to the judge, and not as they suppose

at all, for he sits down, and hears them spin their webs; whilst
the spider he leaves it all for his friends to do with him as they
choose, he is not busy, until the work is done, then he takes a
fall on the rope, and you see him suspended by what you call his
tail-string, whilst the spider web is already spun for him, because
he held it in his vim: So does the judge come on after and
take a fall on you silly little fly; and his vim comes right on
after; then skin you like a pancake squeezed out in fat, and
make you fine and lean, like the web that carries the spider; you
are what is known, as the very picture of a great soft-head;
for you were quite right too, only you were stretched out,
and made to fly a pair of liars; and that is what the judge
does, he sits there, and makes motions and sets you on
to fight against each other; this is right, and that is wrong:
And so does Mr. Spider, come tumbling down upon his
dead brethren, without any emotion, he can feel just like the
judge, I have nothing to do unless these fellows, should want
me to hunt them up a motion; for I can see quite well which is
the finest hand at sticking in his promotion; and it just depends
on this for a successful winner; There is the point right here, I
want you to believe me, and you want me to believe the judge,
who said that magic was an incomprehensible something: Well
I tell you all that I will prove to you beyond a shadow of doubt
that magic is a reality, and I say I will down every opponent
who attempts to prove he has a stronger cause to bring, why
magic shall not be governed by reason as well as any other
thing; you say it can not, well I say, that there is nothing
that I can't prove, whether it be seen or unseen, I say it knowing how much, and how little, there is in all this great universe;
you can't hide anything from me, whether you are a dead messenger, or a living moving vision; so you may try anything you
choose, I can find a way out of anything I am put in; and you
can't hold water in a bucket that leaks: Now you may try, but
it is all no use there is some escaping all the time; therefore
you have a leak on earth, and that is the road to heaven; the
sky is a leakage spout for heaven, it drains the whole of hell;
and that is how you have got so many bad people, they all come

out of hell before they get to heaven; therefore you can't find any hell except your own: And that is what you have got to be peacemakers for first, don't think that you are going to be gorged up for anything you didn't do; the hades of hell will make you plenty of sins; they can't keep quiet, for they are dreadfully busy always, trying to get salvation; and they never find it, for it is not there to find, unless you get your souls into a good condition before they commence on that long journey: How can you find a place, that has no proper directions to it; you might just as well cry out, I am going to be hung, you don't know whether it is a fact or not; for nobody is safe, when they don't know how to protect themselves; and they are right at the mercy of any scheming hound, who wants their bodies to cancel his own crimes with; I have got to this point, when you are anxious to know what there is to find when you have crossed the border line: You may go and see but that won't help you much, for it is all so wonderful, compared to what you have been used to hearing about, that you are dumfounded, and you lose what little reasoning powers you had, for a time; then you come to the conclusion, that you are not any better, than the rest; and you prepare yourself for the understanding that, what others do, you must do also and that is the way to do, for no one can count his time in any other way; except that a few may begin to understand right off: Then they want to go right back and tell their folk; but what is the use, it is only certain disappointment; their friends are quite enough afraid of ghosts, to keep clear of dark corners, and it is only in such places, as the dark still calm hours, that a spirit is at first able to approach his earthly bodies; they have a kind of dread to, about going near the frame of another person, for it sucks them toward it; and it clings on to a spirit, and frightens nine-tenths of them right away; so when you go over at first you will see that it is not any easy matter to do very much of anything; the sooner you learn all the rulings of heaven the better, for I am sure that all those spiritualists, are better prepared, than those who don't know anything at all: They claim to be the right cause, but they have not got into the right method of receiving their

11

information correctly yet: And it will be seen that they are all
trying to convince a few skeptics; where they ought to launch out,
and grasp the root of the question, and say here is the point right
in here; you know that a spirit can come and walk all over your
body, and this is not all, you see them materialize, yet, you can't
find out: What they are constructed of, when they don't seem real,
you are just as far behind as ever you were; for you don't
know what you hold in your hands, when you have got a spirit
formed; and you know that they are the most angelic creatures,
that you can possibly have in your hands; therefore you are non-
plused; because you don't see anything after they disappear:
And wonder what it is that has made them go so effectually: That
is how you fell: I want to show you, that it is the solidity of the
problem that has to be solved; there is no way out of this difficulty, only to tell you the truth; and that is, to place a common vessel of a basin-shaped circumference; and see whether it
won't evaporate, well it is sure to do it, yet, you can't tell where
it has flown to; therefore you are no farther advanced, than you
were in the beginning; you say the sum total of this solution is, that no man knows what became of that something; yet
you believe that you did have the water, in the basin; I can
make you believe that much, without much trouble; and you
won't believe me when I say that I have materialized: And
gone underneath people's heels to watch them look for me,
when I was gone as they thought: You may take me by the
hands, and I shall know what is going on within your most
innermost soul: As surely as though they said I am he; and
he is me; therefore you don't count me out: though you think
I am not able to tell of you, yet it is quite plain, that once I
get my own instrument; he can understand me, just as easily;
As though you said I will believe him: Now do you understand
that it is easy for me to tell how to materialize; when I can converse with him in an intelligent code; and your Moses could
do no more; and I say that did Moses live to-day, that he
would have been willing to call me God; and I feel that I am
quite the equal of Moses' God; therefore you can see that whatever you do, I shall be able to rectify; should you make a

blunder, and get wrong; now, don't think I am boasting, for I
want to show you the impossible to be nothing after all,
except what is natural: and you don't believe me when I tell
you, that I can come and walk beside you every day; no, and
you would be foolish did you believe such a sentence; but when
I tell you that the power of the Sun obliterates the stars,
and you don't see them all day, you will believe me;
for it is true: then again, you won't believe me, when I
say that the Sun doth hold you in chains; and you can't
see; because the after-skin of your own eye is calloused
for protection against the light; as you could see me, were
you able to discern, without the light; it is the light
from the strength of the Sun which prevents you from
seeing me: now will you believe me, when I say that you
are blind, like the stars after daylight; you want me to be
always telling you how to find the light; when you are as blind
as the owls, for they have no coverings on their eyeballs; therefore they can screech and call out at night, knowing that it is
their daylight, they are capable of discerning their prey, when it
is impossible for their prey to see them; they don't fear that their
prey is going to run away, for it is quite patent to them, that a
prayer, will save the owl who balls loudest, you see that there
was once a time, when all men slept in the daytime, for they
were afraid to walk abroad during the day, and as simulating the
tread of the stealthy cat, coming home in the morning early, was
what they thought the correct thing then; no fear of being seen
by the hawk's eye, he had gone out of sight, for he could fetch
the owl in; you see that to be given an understanding you must
be ready to accept all reasonable ideas; or you will be shut off
from knowing anything: you may think it possible for your
spirit guide to tell you almost exactly what you want to
know, but you shall be taught, and then you have a better
chance; and after it is sent round in a way that is justified by
reason, you will adjust yourselves accordingly, therefore my
mind is made up on this subject, and I will give it to you now
right here, the way to hold conversation with the dead as you
are pleased to call them, is by being quite sure that they will

help you: And then sit in dark still lonely spots, and call them
to you, the same as you would a reasonably good friend: And
ask them to help you; Therefore you will have the best friends
you can get, providing that they agree to be your guides; for
they won't accept half measures: You have got to be theirs completely: Or mind you don't take upon your own self, what they
have told you not to do: Or it will be just the same as kicking the
eye off its own shell: They bargained for a whole eye: And you want
to leave them without any crust on theirs; that is you are willing
to accept what you don't know; and you are not willing that
they should share your small amount of common stock; such as
you have already stored away by your own experience; remember
you won't make a good band with half-hearted confidence; for
they can reach you, but you can not get near them: And that is
the point: Your ideas, by want of tone is nothing; but when they
are brought out: It helps to fill in many a gap; and well-worked is a
bottomless shaft: Therefore instead of you being a nonentity, you
are stored full of genuine wisdom; by the process of adjustment;
and this is what is called the enlightenment of humanity: You sink
by yourself; but helped by the all-seeing eye, you swim lively
through the greatest current that ever graced the deck of mien:
And' you are the very impersonation of the deity; for you have
reached that standpoint, where no man can hide anything from
you; better still to be able to learn others as well as yourself, by
showing them how you came by this process, and that is quite
as difficult to explain as all the rest put together; for it is an incomprehensible something; well to commence with you sit quite still,
and wish for the dead to come back, and show you by some sign
that they are still alive; and you seem quite careless as to them
appearing in your presence; until at last your imagination makes
you feel a creeping sensation, like as though an iceberg was
approaching, and chilling your blood: This is the first you feel
of their presence; instead of being horribly afraid, you rejoice in
this, for it is the approach of one dear to you as the air you
breathe; and you must not say ghosts are walking, for it is the
attempt that causes them to shiver with fright at your presence
being so close; and they are afraid of being drawn by you into

your system; now don't you understand that once you assist
them to suppress this fear, that you are going to be assisted; for
the spirit is not afraid of mortals, providing the mortal won't
hold him chained always; and it is not a nice thing to be drawn
into a mortal, and held there for an indefinite period, which is
often done, for the spirit is willing to be used, but not abused;
And you must be a curious specimen of humanity to help, when
it comes from such a powerful course; I won't press you on those
points; it is only to show what can be done that I am after: The
next thing for you to do is to inhale the essence of fruit, flowers; and
bring home sweet-smelling odors; for it is this that the spirit world
live upon: And not the sap of bodies as the ignorant ancients
have it: you take a pail of cold water, and stand it in your room,
and put flowers in there; then your angel friend can bathe and
swim in glory: That is all he looks for or expects from his labors:
And he will gather from those flowers, and inoculate his poison
into you thereby producing an inferior odor, that stinks him out
of countenance, when he approaches too near, and causes him to
lay back, when his essence is being poured into yours; and it is in
this fashion found to be safe to approach near enough to commence operations, on the head of a mortal: now don't you see
that providing, that you are only willing, that there is no other
difficulty at all, and should you want to make an invention, or
communicate with your friends at the antipodes; you can tell
what they are up to, whilst they are may be planning your downfall:
And are thinking of nailing you to the mast when you are quietly
rejoicing in their childish ignorance; you have the whip always,
when you are guided right; and it is no use you saying there is
nothing to be gained by such a power; for you know what is the
true meaning of their letters before they have got them into the
mail bag, now if you can't see an advantage in this argument,
well I'll tell you what it is a man may be born wise, but he never yet
knew the full extent of his own power; and like the little spider,
that came in yesterday for his fair share of shortcomings; is
not without his advantages; and when he is allowed to pass his
web across the gulf, by an unseen hand, then are you to be less
material, that you can't hold your own departed brethren in

affection also; and say to them, I have my enemies across the ocean, you go forth, and bring their ideas across to me, I want you to beat them out of sight, for I will bide by what you say, only be careful you bring me correct information so that I do arrange my plans accordingly; and it is done like the flash of the wires; only this time the method is secret, and is woven with a texture that has not been given to man so far; for he can not read the angels' letters; and they can't be understood by mortals did they know how to make them; it is as easy for an angel to carry information, as it is for the paper to print it; for it is all printed in his sack, prior to his journey; and he will travel across the ocean, and bring it back on his back, just the same as you would take and write it on paper; his companion writes it on the carrier's back, in such fine lettering as is used by the most skilled artists; and they have got nothing to carry, as you spiritualists say, there is the mystery again revealed, it is written over the spine; with phosphorescence; so that the interpreter, can ply it when he sees it, and make you understand what to do, before ever the letters come to hand, the same applies to all documents, the angel has the privilege of going where he pleases; and he will get his code out of all men's safes; and they can not stop him either by fair or foul means; his mission is an advancement to him, and he will take it out of the very gutter, rather than come back without it, meaning that he will fool your opponents' guides, so as to get his points worked in; now don't you see how war is to be carried on in the future; that instead of you fighting foolish, you will know how to get right into the enemy's confidence; and make him change his tactics; until he will be a messed up hopeless hull of confusion: Your wildest thoughts never carried you thus far before, and I venture to say, that once this theory is put into effect, that there will be no wars; for the fact, that you can be mastered so easily, that you will be afraid to try, and much good will come out of it; therefore you will be more like Christians, and less likely to be butchered, this is the fruits of solid wisdom; your enemies will not want to fight, once they have no tactics to play against you; there is the point, what is the use of trying to fool this method, you are fooled yourself, once you try it, for the heavens have the

power, in their own hands; and you are to do as you are bid, or
come into confusion; that is as easy talked; as it would be to act
upon, and you are not very secure now, not knowing anything,
for as soon as you are cultivated sufficiently to understand the
proper ideas; you can find plenty to do, to be brought into a
form of government, that will stand all fidelity, and can be made
to suit both heaven and hell; you may not appreciate me for
calling the heaven a one-side show; while you think it is the only
real place there is; you know that when you choose, you can
make a heaven of your own, just as easy, as you can a hell;
therefore you have only got to choose, which place you want;
but in choosing you must be guided by reasoning faculties,
there is the secret of having a side show, you make your own
heaven here by doing no harm; and you have fulfilled the chap-
ters: They say like heaven we must live to reach the kingdom
of God: Well this means, that you have got to do no wrong:
And that is all there is in it; you know what is wrong, by investigation only; and you must not be guided by anything except
common sense, or you will fall short of reaching the kingdom of
God: Now you think when I say the kingdom of God, that I
mean a God mortal, this you are entirely mistaken in, I mean by
the kingdom of God, everlasting peace; this is all the God you
want, and the only one you can possibly find; there is nothing
else that could be, for without some sin you can not tell what is
right; and you must learn to climb, or you won't reach the top,
therefore you have to keep from sinning by knowing what there
is to be afraid of; don't you see that the baby must creep, or he
can't climb, therefore he is a good boy, till he does climb, he will
only reach the top of the ladder by climbing; and he gets there
all the faster, when he knows how many chances there are against
his slipping off the end: You see him near the top, and he is so
anxious, that he won't wait for anything, he must get there; yet, my
friend you had better go slow, and you will be sure to reach the
top: What is the object in possessing yourself of the whole of
hell, when you loose your grip on the last bar of the ladder, and
fall back into hell forever: your step is not the steadiest, when
it has to negotiate that last step on the great big ladder of time,

it sits at ease, when it is well in hell, but the moment severe sickness sets in, it is entirely different, you then feel a sinking nervous sensation, and wonder how you are going to face your
maker; that is you feel afraid, for you don't know what he is like;
you wonder, and conjecture all manner of ideas; this is precisely
what you do; then make your mind easy my friend, the devil was
never yet painted like he is; and you can make up your mind
that as you have lived, so will you enjoy the life of eternity;
either good or bad, just as you grew; you may think I am wrong
my friend and brother; but you will see the harlequin is no fool
at his own table, and as you grow, so will you propitiate, and
as you sow, so will you sweep; and as you have reaped so will you
keep: Therefore your society, in the eternal life, will be exactly
the same as you have led here on earth, which is established
as the hell of eternity; there can not be any other for it is constructed, according to the formation of material forms; and as
they are all defective works of art, they must abide by the nature
of the most almighty power of heaven and hell, you don't want
me to tell you everything, for fear of there being nothing for
you to do, well my honest Job's comforter: I can only say that
a work of art has but one maker, and that is the painter, as he
moulds his model, therefore you are blessed with all my ingenuity;
did you but know how to use it, and it is in these simple little
words, (I do not know how); and you have the same right as,
myself; providing you are willing and able to contradict my logic
by some unknown power, which I shall be most happy to make
myself acquainted with; because I am not too proud to be taught;
though you may be: And I want to show you what I know is
the truth, and I want you to point out my errors; and not say
the subject is too deep: It is not at all deep, and I will show
you that you are entirely wrong by this stupid folly that has
always got the upper hand of the earth-bound spirits; they tell
you in their reasoning, that the subject is too deep, well what do
you do but make it deeper; because some idiot is preaching it into
your head, and you think all the while that it is the meat in your
brains that is working out your thoughts; well now you are
ready to take up the cudgel, and fight me down on that question; I

guess not, you are afraid, of what, that your motor scum is no match
for mine; you know it; and I do too: there is the point right here
are you lawyer, clergyman, or priest, I say you are no match
for me under the thoughts I pin my faith to; and all the fiends
you choose to bring, can not circumvent my theory: And I claim
for heaven and earth a proper hearing; you may pitch into me
all you like, I say you shall be met with a foot for a foot, an eye
for an eye, and a tooth for a tooth; that is true religion; as the sun
goes down, she falls to rise again, and so does the man she has
made, you can't believe this; no! it is too gigantic altogether for
you, for you have never had the right intelligence before;
simply because, the sun had not given sufficient strength to her
vim before, and you and your ancient Gods, were not able to
give you the truth; and they were quite willing you will admit,
but they have circumvented your understanding in a marvelous
way: And grown in your thoughts, for it is in this mode that
they have got you to believe, that a greater than Jesus, can not
live, you are quite wrong on this point also; for he was one of
many, that had been practiced; and they all got killed for knowing too much, and you are sure to kill a good man now did you
know who he is; therefore it is better for wise men not to come
among you: you know that I am speaking truly, that you are all
afraid of a man who is able to interpret correctly, therefore I do
know that there is danger, attached to telling you exactly what you
ought to know; but it has to be a struggle to the death this time so
you won't get off by sticking your knife in; and the instruments
we use don't care any more for your life, than our Saviour did:
That is much more than your religious humbugs think; they tell
so many lies, that they are afraid: And would not for worlds,
go and sit in a dark room, and invite spirits to materialize round
them; you see that it wants a spirit, that don't fear any deity,
who will put himself down to such a test; there are very few who
can stand this strain; yet you know, that a materialized spirit is
nothing to be alarmed at: For didn't Saul go and call Samuel
out of the witch of Endor, don't you believe your own Bible,
don't you believe that Saul, knew how to reach the dead surely
you must be dreaming, when you say that spirits can not come

back; I want you to read your Bible, and understand it; and not
play the fool with it; I don't say you intend to be dishonest; what
I do say is that you can't understand, because your intelligence
is all wrong, and the more you get wrong, the less likely you are
to grow in heaven, there is the point, right here, what Saul did,
you are all capable of doing, and you learn by this that Saul fell
through banishing his magicians; that is he divided his thoughts;
he gave to God his refuse; and to Mammon he sold his crops:
You do the same, by your own determination to put God over
with the refuse; He is good, and must mean good, or he won't
persevere to make himself known: Then don't drive him and his
artful witches from you, restrict them to common sense: And
they must be goodly conductors of what is called the handicraft,
of Christ the Saviour: For a sinner to say that a witch is bad,
simply because she knows too much isn't enough, he should
explain himself and say why she is bad, and prove her wrong, don't
condemn her because he says so, let him be raked up too, and let his
sorcery, come in for the same investigation; but don't you let his
ignorance pollute you; lest ye fall like Saul, and be a sinner for
hell: That is right, call the witch to the galleys, with the sinners,
and when she does not explain herself, in proper sentences of
sense, then condemn, but do likewise to the sinner, who plagues
her without any cause, am I right: Let the sinner show you the
way to find God, and I am done: He dare not try, for he never
knew how, and he is cast on a shoal of breakers; once he makes
the attempt, his Bible is constructed by the power of the great
spirit power, who led Israel out of bondage, and he was no
slough, or such wonderful feats could have never been performed; therefore don't go and say that there is no good in God,
for Moses, and his God are the greatest thunders you will ever
know, you can't find either of them, because they performed
their mission: And conveyed an armful of people under either
arm: Both have got the praise, and are both deserving, for
neither was worth anything without the other; you can not say
God did it, and you admit that it was too much for Moses, without his God: Therefore let honor abide, where the honor
belongs: And say as Moses, and his God did lead Israel, so will

I lead you to heaven: And though ten thousand Pharaohs
stand in our path, I shall wipe them all away: That is the way
to feel, and that is the way to act, it shall not be cast aside,
though a thousand swords are glittering in the breeze, heaven
and hell shall not be my fortress wake, it comes and goes, and
no man knows where he will stake his pleasant life hereafter:
Your own ideas, are as much wronged, for want of knowing
better: and once they do know better, it is quite easy, for you to
get to heaven, that is where you all want to go; and as sure as
you get the right way of understanding what it is you have got
to steer clear of, it can not fail to lead you right along to where
you wish to go; and as you can't die, there is only one other
thing for you to do, and that is to stop where no harm can
reach you: This is a point, that you must see before you
believe, what God did through Moses; is good, for it teaches
you to see that there was a power, and his infinite wisdom,
proves that you are under guidance; therefore you have only got
to become under the same conditions as Moses, was placed
under, then you can be a Moses too: For he was banished
through fear to a foreign place, and he found the true God, it is
easy to see that he was a suitable subject, to work upon, for he
had no friends on earth, and he had to look to heaven to be
consoled, his very life, and his reason demanded it; then don't
you see that it was in sympathizing with nature's great callings;
that made Moses, look for the food, which supplies the inner
cravings of man; they are made after nature's great mould, and
they will yearn, and squirm, for more life; immediately they are
thrown out for some heinous offense; they are not to be
tampered with, any more than the Sun is, and you must feed the
Sun on the best herbage, succulent, and full of life, or she will
scorch up every bit of garbage you have; for she is thirsting
for more life, and she must have the knife wherewith to cut it;
You seem to think I am deranged, because I call the Sun a she,
and talk of her as a woman, does she not make all there is, that
is worth anything, then why would you say he, man is nothing
without a woman, and I say that the Sun is the mother of all,
and she is entitled to all the glory, as for the Moon, which you

can classify as he, I don't think much of him, because he is a
second fiddle, and does not do the amount of good, as he should
do to be placed first; therefore we can call him he, and when I
have been through the Moon, with you, you will better understand why it is more like a he, than the other; which purely
represents a woman: In all stages of its conformation: I want
you to be patient as you can, for in a work of this character, it is
not found by mere guess-work, and I have to be exceedingly
particular: There are a multitude of things in a precise nature,
that have got to come in at a given place, that you will be astonished, when you come to find that there is no exact cause why
they should not come in like a mechanic's lien; serrated, without
technicalities; therefore you can't call me what I am without
striking foul of a cause, of action; that was not in regular form,
at the time when Moses, held commune with his God; and you
see that unless you have a new face, you can't look well enough
into the future; a brand-new face, is what you expect to fade, but
an old one is all well enough, till you see a better one, therefore
you will have to get a cleaning, before you can see through a
dirty mirror; and you must remove some of the quicksilver off
the back, or you can't see what is on the other side, that is not
the way to do it at all: You must keep on straight, until you
have got a fresh face, then you see both sides of the looking-
glass at once, in other words, you have got to rise above the
mirror: Then you see both sides at once: This is all very well,
but while you are at this job, of peering through and through,
you have left one thing out, and that is that the looking-glass
was no good, till you attached the quicksilver; and you have it
right there, neither was God any good, without Moses: He,
could let down fire and brimstone upon you: Yet, he could not
tell you what he was doing it for: Now do you see that Moses,
was an instrument, prayed for out of heaven; and he had to be
lost by the world, and found by heaven: therefore he is not any
more than mortal, only, that he had to be compelled to commit
crime, in order that he should be got at: and you have to do
wrong, or you can't get right: under the present understanding
of heaven; but should .the world at large understand what it is

that leads them wrong, they will soon know that condition is the
supreme motive; and as the Sun governs the whole, she is
making man after her own form: Perpetually generous: And
everlastingly pure, with this one exception: that the Sun does
scorch up, whenever she approaches too near, and so does man
bring offense, when he inhales the odor of fumes, which are
offensive to the rag conductor: I mean that man is the cloth,
that acts as a sponge to the dead, and he sucks in more material
forms, than he has any right to, and instead of him scorching
up his refuse, as does the mighty great big mother: He lets in
the grains, that suck up his vital constitution, by being a pest-
hole for every inebriate, this does not apply to healthy mortals,
so much, for it does not hold them in such strong chains; and
they can free themselves, by reasoning out the problem of how
much, and how little the influence has power with them; you
think that I am all mightily particular to put down drinking
strong essence, well you don't see the sea depreciate in size,
although you do see, lakes and rivers run dry, well the sea is not
used by the Sun, for it does not bear any properties, that would
propagate gas; and you can solve this problem easily; the sea is
a whole constitution of its own, entirely different to anything we
have, it is a sewerage from the mountains; and is not attractive
to the heat of gaining cold or heat; although you find the sea
hot in Antarctic regions; you never find that it depreciates
materially; for its evaporating qualities are nil, compared to
what the fresh water is, this shows you, that a man drinking beer
is consumed quicker by the rays of the Sun; than a man drinking
water; His hide is filled with gas; while the man who drinks
water is not consumed at all, for the fact, that he did not drink
of the same brew, causing him to be purer by his changing his
food into a condition of purity; causing his appetite to be sustained by a food of the ocean, while the man who drinks of the
tap, is filled with gas, and causes him to be sucked from more
readily; that is the way a man who drinks heavily can not cough
much when he is in the heat, his throat is sucked dry by the
evaporating gas; and this gas is used as fuel in the Sun, the same
as all gassy nutritions; you may laugh at me all you please, but I

have got the laugh on you: My tights are filled full of breezes,
that can blow where breezes blow: And I can show you fine
logic, as well as any one who ever sailed underneath a wet sheet
of canvas, it is easy to show you how you are wrong, but it does
not follow, that you will go right after you are shown, you know
that a man who goes to bed quite sober, is a jolly fellow for his
mother made him so: And a man who wakens up at night, with
his throat on fire is quite another kind of fellow, his mother
never meant it so; she was very sorry for poor Bill, he had been
such a good boy, yet, she couldn't tell why, he should have
grown so fond of beer, his father never drank any to speak of,
and all his relations were quite sober on his father's side, none
of the men drank, it was only a little drop of beer that my
friends drank, and I only took it you know to keep Mother
Marshall from thinking I was mean to sit and see her drink
her little tots; before our Bill was born;   He hadn't been in
more than eight months, when Mrs. Marshall came as nurse,
and I wonder why it comes out that Bill should take to drink
in his old days; his father never did: And none of my relatives to any account; yet Bill proves the exception, because
the nurse tempted his mother; when he was clearing his road
to help himself to gain heaven; that is my theory friends of a
drunkard's downfall: and I shall be pleased, when you can
show me a better, there is nothing that can not be explained,
and when you go on fighting in the dark, you shall always be
fooled, for intelligence is born on the right side of justice,
and when you treat the babe to foul blasphemy, don't expect
him to be anything expect, a blasphemer: There you have
what is called in heaven as the world flung into hell; meaning,
that as hell pitched in a fire-brand, the after consequence must
be a fire; and now since I have reached you so successfully, I
intend to tell you of all that there is to know, both good bad
and much worse than you ever thought I would dare to tell
you;   You are quite anxious to know what there is in heaven;
about hell it is all bad, and you don't feel much interest; therefore I think that I had better wind up with something nice at
my conclusion: Or you will think that I am Deuteronomy

impersonified; I don't want you to believe that all is bad, for
it never helps any one to keep them constantly facing the black
cloud: You must see a gleaming of light, or you won't face
the cloud at all: I only want to show you how much better it
is for you to know the truth, so as you can find a straight road
to heaven, and by this I mean to explain what heaven is, and
leave you to the fact, that you will not have to go down on
your bended knees, and supplicate for an offense, which is not
an offense at all: You must know what it is that you are
going to ask forgiveness for; as you do now know that God is
not going to help you, unless he is permitted to be an individual God: Then you will have to be broken of this theory,
that a man was once consumed in a flaming fire, and never
burned away, I tell you now and am prepared to prove it, in
all sense and reason, that you can't affect a soul by firing him
at all; His body is proof against all the fire that was ever
kindled, and it is only when he is in close proximity to human
beings, that he feels the heat, through taking on their conditions; and when he is away from the body matter: He can
climb through fire millions of miles deep; and investigate its
most sternest awe: You don't know anything at all about what
it is to be free from that old useless carcass there is nothing
we feed upon, to give us any pain, and then you know that
we don't want any meals, unless we feel disposed to fill up
with essence, off some delicacy that you hold as sacred to
your own touch; why, can't we have what you don't even
miss; you can't stop us taking it; for you don't even know
when we are laughing in your eyes; and playing destruction
on you, when you have wronged one of our friends; you
think the ancients told you correctly: Well they were not
going to give myself away, that is how they felt, they
thought it a great punishment to be kept away from earth by
the higher powers; who said constantly they must not know of
us; or they will be after our thoughts coming home at night
from their daily occupations; and they won't work, did you once
let them see how to get on both sides of the question, like us;
therefore it is as well to keep them in the dark side of life as

long as it will keep that way; now don't you see that there is an
object in keeping you from knowing all things; you would not
. work at all did you know how to scheme and get at the proper
way of making money, for that is all you are after while you are
on earth; you don't even dare to look at God in the face, for
you know you are a humbugging parcel of hypocrites; and that
is a true fact; you don't even know what it is to be honest, you
are all the time planning a way of getting the upper hand of
John Brown; and you know he is trying to do the same by you;
therefore you are so evil in your thoughts that you can't make as
much money as you wish, for the fact is quite plain you have got
too much mind on Brown, and he is minding you; instead of
doing his level best to leave you alone, and go and find some
way out for himself to make money, out of something that you
don't understand; you see that there are plenty of new things
coming to the fore every day; then why don't you try something
that your neighbor does not own, then you can't want his provisions; his wife is your dangerous point, well you keep away
from his wife, and leave her alone, and you go and get one of
your own, and see that your neighbor leaves her alone too; that
is the way to live, keep off your neighbor's premises; and don't
go inside of his threshold; and you will be better off by doing so;
you know that a man who is tinkering after your farming ideas;
may be there to steal your wife's affections; and he knows
enough, to help your blindness off color, I don't want you to be
hermits; go and enjoy yourselves all you have a mind to; but you
must do it in public places; for it is there that all eyes are upon
your wife, and she is not to be found fault with by all the world,
for she knows that it won't do to be a backslider, in front of her
own sex; this is what keeps her good; Her fear of her own sex,
and better that way, than to be afraid of her God; for she is lost,
once she has committed an offense in sight of him: She is
taught, that his eye is always upon her, then may she not be
holy, because she once fell: I say she can be righteous, though
she falls any number of times, for she did not do it, it was the sinners, who are guiding her; who caused her to fall: And not the
one spirit at all; therefore she has only to be shown the true

light, and she can't fall at all: For in doing so she gives the
cause of her soul's champion away, to all men, and women alike,
and she will not do this, once she knows, that a hand is upon
her; who can reveal her soul's prompter, and burn him through
her, with the burning brand of shame; you have here what can
not be concealed and it is in this form of soul's preservation,
that brings you to heaven; you know as well as I can show you,
that once your secrets are known to your fellow-men, that they
will spurn you, with their pointed finger of scorn at you, knowing
at the same time, that their own souls are ten times more guilty:
And they are more dubious of you, than ever they are of one
who is not worthy, of notice; for you have had a tare, and are
familiar with the stick that marked you; therefore their own
crimes are dangerous, in your hands; and they know that they
themselves; are well worthy, of the pointed finger of scorn;
therefore to shield themselves, they seek out your weak spot, and
divert the hand of hades upon you, this is the true code of
sinner's diversion; and you must strengthen your own court,
and make it secure, before you can lift out the plague of sinners:
You may want a little grace, to turn your own folly from the
eternal workings of hades, then never stoop, so low as to counsel
with any one you know to be infamous, for they are always ready
to sting, to shield them in their own wickedness: You go to
the venerable man, who has borne a pure character all through
life, and ask him what you could do, should you not have the necessary power with you, for I don't expect all men to be blessed
with a superhuman counselor; therefore I say knowing, that I
am doing so to an advantage, talk to an honorable upright man,
who has borne the blast, from a sterling gale, and ask him by
questions, that leaves him no grounds for anything but pleasure,
and tell him openly why he is called upon to give you this
advice, say to him, I know you to be an honorable man, therefore
my reasons for wishing for your advice: A dishonorable man
always seeks the man of sharp practice, for he knows, he is
going to get at the essence of villainy, in this method; but
he forgets, that the sharp-practice man has·a goad of pointed
arrows at him from a thousand lancers, where the honorable one

12

is fortified beyond any comparison; There is where honesty shines, and hell is a dead letter; for the one is subject to flames, whilst the gentleman is insured against fire: You see now what doctrine is worth, you may have the sharp sinner, I am going to tackle you with honesty, and I am game to fight the greatest rogue you ever saw, with reasonable arguments, I don't want you to tell me what is going on in his mind, I can get that all out of his guides, and transmit it, to my own pocket; there to lay plans, that are honest, and show you where he was dishonest; you can say it is an unfair way of getting at him, but you must remember that I do my work openly, and let him have the chance of doing the same, now do you see again where I prove you are honest, under my theory; you can walk the deck proudly, when you say my spiders spun a better web than his, and I again refer to the brethren of the living spider, I say that they fly round the fly, and drive the fly into the web of the body spider, and it is this that makes the fly so stupid, his eyes, are not protected, like yours are, and he is able to see the spirit spiders coming after him; therefore he escapes, from what you call the dead, and is grabbed by your living; thus proving, that the fly is not a fool at all as you call him, but a genuine real frightened fly, that is all there is in it, you see him flying this way and that till at last he flies into the spider's net, you have watched the little fool, but were the skin off your own eyes, you would say oh! the villains, they are after blood; and you are the simpleton, not this foolish little fly, that was working like a distracted demon escaping, from the fear of God; now you see how I place my theory again, have you got anything to hoist me off my pinnacle with: Come on and try and knock me down over this reasonable theory, I want an argument, you can't approach me, you say so, don't I explain, how I am working out my problems: you can't attack me without I bring my theory down to a scientific basis; then come and take me at my work of showing humanity where they are wrong, and give them a fair show of getting right; I don't want all the field to myself, I will help you to get a start, and bring you all the courage you lack, Don't go and say that Thomas Paine, was an " Infidel," when you can't show me anything at all that is reasonably correct, I won't fight with straws, and I am going to leave you and your book of books alone, till you pick out all the most difficult parts, and say my son you are an unbeliever, and I want you to explain some mystery, that has beaten all the world before you: Now Mr. whatever-you-call-yourself come down here and explain this passage for us; We are hungry and dying for want of this form of intelligence; you shall be satisfied on all questions of importance, now I never go back on my word, and should you knife this instrument, I will get another, and answer you: You may know by this, that I am at you now, for my suffering in prison, and I won't rest till I have shown greater things, than ever the world saw before, you are not going to throw me over, for I mean to stick to you, till I have fulfilled my idea, of what is right and proper; and you can't get me now, and imprison me, for I will go into your cells, and show the prisoners how they were brought there, and how it is possible for them to keep away from your prisons, you understand me now, that I owe you a grudge, for putting me in prison, because you thought I knew too much, well had you known me, I should have told you, that there is more than I knew, but you were afraid, and locked me up, now I tell you, that I know all and you can't change me neither can you deal with me at all; for I will prove that you are all wrong, before I will stop; Don't you begin to bellow out for mercy, for you would not show me any, and I won't help you now to tide over your ignorance; you may sing out, all you have got a mind to, but never mind me, I will get even yet, for those books you buried, of mine: I won't tell where it is, for I know you pagans, will seek for them, but I will yet show them to the world by some means or another; you don't think I can find hidden treasures; well you wait a little bit longer, and I will cultivate the mind to reach down into the bowels of the earth, and show your minerals, before you make a scratch, at the surface, this is what you would shut me up now for did you get at me, for your mean intellect, would say he won't allow us to earn an honest pound, by taking an instigator's part, no I don't intend that you shall have instigators, in the

twentieth century; I intend to wipe out agitators altogether, that
have no scientific certainty to base their claims on; and you
can't go on cheating and swindling as you have been, for I
mean to stop it entirely: I want to know, what right you have
to the theory, that a man is an infidel, because he shows you
what must be falsehoods; you dare call me liar, but you can't
prove it, and you are ready to toss me over, once you see a little
error, without even giving me the opportunity, to straighten it
out, now don't you see that all mankind, have been full of
errors, well then be charitable, and let us pull these errors
straight, we know more than the ancients did, for our intellects,
have grown, and formed a material substance, that is greater
than they knew; then let us keep on improving, till we say,
there shall not be sin, that is the right kind of spirit to have,
don't go and knock about, in the throes of darkness; when
you may have the pure bright light, to guide you to that happy
plains of everlasting eternity; this is the way, by finding out
what man is, and how he comes to be formed, and what is his
future destiny: Once knowing what a man is, then knowing
how he is driven, is the way to lead you all: And not by
filling your minds with mystery, that neither helps the foolish
priest, or the learned bishop, you don't find them any better off
in heaven, because they are worse, in a sense, they were always
fed well, and looked up to with reverence, on earth, but in heaven,
they are a miserable set of tools, because their prayers, have
fallen on an empty drone, it came near a stupid soul friend,
and that is all: Never reaching the ear of the great deity at
all: Because there is none to reach, with the same understanding, as you have: That is where the waif is more pro-
gressive, than the parson, his life has been led in the streets, and
his ideas, are trained to be careful, to know more of evil, than
he does of righteousness, and his aim is to. follow, and see
what there is to be found, his soul works the same in heaven,
and his thoughts have been trained to reach out, and grasp
every situation; therefore when he finds his soul is nothing
the worse for its transfiguration, he feels quite happy, and
he leans on the same staff as he did before, his natural wit is

untarnished, and he says halloo "Bill" I have got over here,
immediately he meets an old acquaintance; and is the same waif
for all time hereafter: His idea is to follow, and he copies
quickly and is an old hand, before the parson is able to realize,
that he is not Deacon of some Old County Parish, there is the
parson lamenting his fate, because he had always misled his
parishioners, and his soul is disturbed, for fear of meeting any
of his congregation, who are certain to stop him with "what an
old humbug you were, didn't know any more than me, that
is the kind of souls you will meet in the other world, once
you get there, and they have a dead set against the parsons,
for they would have gone on right enough, they claim, only for
having believed in what their clergyman said: Now it is
easy to foresee, that such must be the chastisement, meted out
to all clergymen, for they are taught to believe in what there is
not, and the consequence is quite clear, they must be shown, or
they can not believe otherwise, and you are miscalling your
clergymen, in error, for he did but do his duty according to his
light of what was right, but then he must know that it is a
frightful feeling of remorse, to him when he finds that he has not
only misled himself; but that he was misleading the whole of
his parish always, and he does feel mortified, when some ignorant
spirit comes to him and gloats over his conduct in believing those
who had taught, without knowing any better; you can't imagine
the discomfiture of a good clergyman, when he is besieged by
an overwhelming host of ignorant spirits, who seek pleasure
out of the discomfiture of an unlucky divine, who is meet for
their own distraction; "you have hit me often enough, when I
was disobeying your thoughts of right and proper, now what
better are you than me, you can not hold me in subjection now;
and you won't get any more thanks for all them prayers you said
over that old corpse; it had nothing to reach after all except the
restriction of ancient mortals; who are a great deal less intelligent, than we are, and you are now made to drudge at teaching
infants to go on working out their lives, on education for the
world of immortality;" you see that children are all taught in
heaven, and immediately they are born again, they are sent to

school, with the idea, that it is necessary to have them educated, for joyful purposes; that is they have to make joy for the elders; as the ancients are called; and they sing, and play on instruments, for the merriment of having an age of pleasure, and by doing this, they are toned down to keep the orders of light in life of eternity: That is the reason for all this discipline, it must be so, the ancients have always made music their Gods, and wherever a beautiful singer is found, she or he are kept everlastingly at the music halls of those who hold seats of power; you don't see what is wanted, with all this learning, and work, but it has to be done, in order of this kind, or how do you suppose, that a given surface, can be reared up to any particular standard, that is the way to arrange, all things; by keeping on a perpetual overgrowth, and bringing what is needed into a deep pasturage; or else you will be torn out by the roots, and sent flying away by the wind, and driven away entirely; this is right, it has to be done in order of manifesting to the young, or they will not grow, in accordance, with the old; that is their reasoning for having every one taught, to keep up the knowledge of advancement always, that is quite on a par with what you are doing to-day; only you don't bother, with the stray waifs, and the heavenly bodies do, they take every soul, and put it through a specified conditional regime; that is called the questioning of the idle, because they keep the priests, and parsons for this work, of educating the young, and fallen subjects of humanity, to take up a regular system of doctrine, according to the testament of a given order, which have the power of ruling the head; and this controlling power, is mixed up with the ancients of a strong proclivity, to the notions; that there is a God somewhere in the heavens; and they have ignorant notions; the same as they had at the beginning of the intellect of man, you see them taking on the priests, and clergy, it is because they don't know anything about education themselves; and they want to know how many men is made by this form of selfishness; before they can be knocked out, and let intelligent men rule heaven, the same as hell is directed; now you won't blame me for starting this work, for you see that I am aiming at the throne of God, because it is

governed by spirits, who have no intelligence; and instead of
them giving way to learned spirits, they hold fast to what their
own characters are, in the earth, before ever they crossed the
border line, that is the way heaven is governed: And you know
that there is ignorance, in the ancient history, for it shows it at
the very beginning, and as you are an enlightened people, let
there be no "monkey business"; at the head of affairs, you may
think that I am comparing your deity with no learning, that is
precisely what I will show you to be a fact, I don't want you to
believe that monkeys are a species apart from man, for I must
say that once and for all time, that I do hold to this theoretical
view, that monkeys are a specie of man, but not of the form,
that is generally construed, that we come from monkeys; I don't
hold my views that way, I say distinctly that monkeys are a
specie of man; but not under your form of constructing man; I
have a theory, that can frustrate that idea totally; you may think
that I am running wild, for to jump from heavenly government,
to the very depths of immorality, but you see, that it calls for
desperate efforts, and you will have to follow me, without fail,
do you wish to get at the truth, and I know that I can lead you
there right surely, only I have got to be humored, or it will be a
failure; you want to know, the difference between my theory,
and the general thoughts, such as Darwin's, for instance;
well he could class them as he choose, but I won't for there
is one thing, that prevents me from getting his idea, into
my theoretical basis, and that is the nose, and mouth of the
monkey is canine, whereas the teeth, are straight lined; this is
nothing, but the tail is a feature of the canine specie, and does
not belong to men: For the human is a differently constructed
kind of quadruped, and has no nails on the feet, like a monkey,
his are canine; and must be called such for the fact, that he is a
canine quadruped, and can not be termed anything else; you
have got my objections to him; now let me see whether I can't
give you a better solution, to this problem; and when we have
done let it be hoped, that man has benefited by the revelation;
you must not suppose that I can strike off this subject, at one
sitting, but I will make the attempt to lead you on to the right

track by saying, that a man is a whole, and is not a half, he is
fit as anything to discuss, this gigantic subject, and I am blessed,
should the monkey attempt it, he would get no farther, than to
swing his tail round the pole of eternity, that is the point, I am
going to run my ring round the pole of eternity, and drive you
all in there too; that is too much for Mr. Monkey to attempt,
and I don't believe it will pollute your sensitive ears, to hear a
direct avowal of what you really sprang from, I don't want to
punish you, by thoughts of an alliance to monkeys; for I don't
wish to give you an unreasonable theory: And I must set your
minds at rest on this problem forever, or you will say he is no
better than Tom Paine originally: And is not the great wonder
he boasted he would be, when he come back, that is he shall
knock over the immortal gods of all the ancients, or go to
hades again in chariots on fire: You have hit me right in the
hind quarters; when you say I can't tell you what made man
more distinguished than the brutes; I shall teach you how to
grow good, but I am not going to accept an appellation, from
Darwin, that I was once a monkey, no I am made of better
material, and you can't get me to be a common man I won't give
in to such an absurdity, I will fight you all to death, rather than
be classed with the monkey, you don't know what I can do when
I get roused, I would pour all the fire there is in heaven on you,
rather than be classed with a monkey, I say you are wrong Mr.
Darwin, and all silly heads like you; your eyes may see, but your
ears, can't catch a flea, when it comes to be cooked: I want a
whole loaf of bread to cut at, and not one that has been chawed
by every stupid tinker; you know I can crack a whip, when I
want a loud report, and I will show you that "The old infidel,"
can smack is crack, to burst all known theories; you may chime
in with your wood and waterjoey system, but I go and get the
whole cartload, and put it on my fire before I let them stick the
match in, you may think I am a great boaster, but when you see
my fire, it will burn up all the rest, because there is plenty of
kindling wood always there to replenish with, I can fire up forever,
and you can't stop me; because I took in perpetuity: You never did
Mr. Darwin, or any of the more enlightened prophets; you may

call out he is only an infidel, but you will find that the old fellow,
knows more than all your saints and sinners put together, and I
will yet show you, that a man can't work out any problem, that is
afraid of good sound reasoning, I tell you, that reason is the
foundation, of all that is holy, righteous, and illustrative of evil,
that is it exactly, you must have reason to guide you from evil,
and you must have reason to keep you good, and no God in
heaven is any use, unless he will spit fire at you continually; you
can bawl out all you have got a mind to, I love his dearly beloved
Son: You know you lie, when you say it: For it is not possible
to love an indescribable something; had you understood what
Jesus Christ really is, you would have all tried to be like him;
but you can't be like him, for you don't know how, yet you would
lay down your own life freely, for such a power as he did
have, and yet you don't know how to obtain it, for the fact is
plain, his soul was the tool of him who guided it, and while there
is one stone standing upon another, he shall stand first, for he
paid the penalty of your brutality, and was forever the hero of all
men in the light of the living, you don't know what it is to be punished, then how can you expect, to be taught any better, I tell
you distinctly, that Christ is not the man you took him for at all;
his soul was a docile nonentity, and gave way to the great power,
which governed, and his life has been perpetuated for its good
sense, in submitting to the great divine, that led it to certain
victory, you may judge as you like, but I know, that I am speaking truthfully: And you are all wise, when I have finished telling you how to become so; there now you want me to go on and
explain all that there is in heaven, I shall do so, but as I have
the privilege of doing it, and not you, I shall do what I consider
just and proper, in my own way of delivering myself; you can't
make me do anything, for I am out of your reach, and I will
only indulge you just as I feel in the humor of my own accord,
that is I am going to tell you as I am able to deliver my own
reasoning, and not as one of your crack university students,
would do, his language is all cabbage, mine is all my own; you
can criticise my autobiography; but you can't read one word that
the dead speaks; therefore I say what does your Cambridge edu-

cation amount to, it only fits you for the seduction of some
handsome woman, or to give you an idea how to talk in the best
society, it is all a fake, there is nothing in it at all but rubbish,
compared to living a life of eternal bliss: You may get at my
work and tear it to pieces, but you have destroyed my thoughts,
and written up in eloquent English, what was intend_d to repre-
sent wealth, for as heaven shall divulge her secrets, so shall the
earth benefit by such an enormity: For as the sea divides, in two
at the wave from heaven, so shall Moses cross the Red Sea on dry
land; you see that I don't leave your great guns alone, I want to
annihilate their great works, and show you the absurd part of all
your grand theories, you say that Moses, stretched his arm,
across the Red Sea, and drove the waters back; you are very
smart at giving away to fancy, and I am just as smart at bursting through them, well Moses did divide the Red Sea, with his
arm; but he first went in with his host of Israelites, and set them
apart, that is why he was able to drown all the Egyptians; and
you can do the same thing, providing you will ask heaven to
open a way for you to cross over the most difficult past, you wish
to obliterate; when Moses came to the Red Sea it had to be
crossed; and in consequence, he was obliged to ask God to help
him; thus far shalt thou go Mr. Moses, and no farther says the
Lord I want a miracle performed here to perpetuate my name
forever with, that is precisely what the position of affairs was:
And God said to Moses, let these heathens see my power here
again, so that they shall believe still greater things of my infinite
power over all my dominions, here is the place to manifest my
great strength, you wade in the waters, and they shall divide at
your approach, yet, he did not wade in; for fear of being drowned
himself: You know it is an ill wind that blows no one any good,
and Moses, was no fool at making God show him how to get the
waters to stop apart, while he crossed with his army over the Red
Sea, you must know how to talk to your God: For he won't submit to your Cambridge cultivated tongue, he wants his own way,
in form of sublime address; therefore you have got to tell him
what you want, before he will divide the Red Sea for you; you
may be ever so learned in arts of fine address; but you won't

reach God, through pleasant speeches, it has got to be done in
earnest, and not like Jack the sailor coming home to his wife
and children either; in a shipwrecked craft: I want you to save
me this time, and I'll never trouble you any more; that won't
induce God to show you a ship in sight coming over the seas to
help poor Jack, clinging to the last mast he will ever lift his
earthly leg across: that is not the way my friends to get your
God to help you; neither will he do it, though you pray to him,
in the most graceful language, that ever graced the lips of a
huge divine, his supplications, must be understood; before you
can get the advice which is necessary to reach out and perform
the miracle that is wanted; you know now, that you are not
right, or God would do for you, that which he did for Moses;
and you could divide the Red Sea, did you know how to divide it
at both sides; this is the point right here, Moses was told that
at the neck of the sea, there is a place which is narrow; and by
sweeping into the sea a quantity of rocks and stones, he could
cross over on dry land, but that he had only to wait until the
Egyptians got near the center, and turn the waters on again,
therefore it being certain destruction for the Egyptians; you see
that Moses, was a man of power, he could be told where to find
the narrow parting, and he could be advised by that all-seeing
eye; and it wasn't necessary for him to watch the Egyptians at
all; they were in the midst of the Red Sea, "Now Moses you
let down the waters:" The Israelites were so ignorant, that they
blew all the wind off Moses' back, and drove away any sense
that there might be in it, you can't fool me by such a wonder as
Moses even, I want you to see him as he really was, and I say
that the power he possessed is all that can be claimed for it, yet
you don't know how easy it is to fool people, with such a
strength of intelligence as this is; your own thoughts, have been
taught wrong that is the only question for you to master, and I
say that instead of you being independent as you are claiming,
you are not at all independent: That no one is, and nothing
can be independent, for the fact, that no work can be done without a powerful motor stem, and that is the great secret in life of
material, you have a material form of governor guiding you

always, and this form of guidance guides all life material; Now
you are able to see for yourselves, that it is a question of culti-
vating this life material, that gives you this wonderful power, of
pleasing God, and his soul does rejoice so much in this exceeding deportment, that he will excel all manner of obstructions to
prove that he is the superior being, you may feel sorry, that God
is not the only one, for you have this power, of bringing a good
God to your own side, and leaving alone, the one who refuses to
listen to your supplications; and call the one, who will bring you
to light and life everlasting; that is he who has the right to be
your God: What was there in Moses, that he should have a God
to help him, and you have none to help you; I say you have the
same specie of God: And I further state, knowing what I am
saying is true, that you have the power to teach your God how
he should help you to live in a proper way, to prevent harm from
reaching you, and he is no good does he allow you to
come to harm through his directions; for he is able to decide
which is good, and which is bad for you: You may have all the
good guides you want, but remember they won't associate and
work with bad ones: So you have got to exert your ingenuity
to keep bad thoughts out of your mind: And so drive away evil
spirits, for they won't torment you once they know, that
there is no work for them to do: That is how you have to
obtain a good guide, by rejecting all comers, till he comes in
form of wisdom; then you say to him I will obey you until you
have proved yourself a failure, that is the road to victory, by
keeping on straight, till you come to such a difficulty as Moses
had to contend with, and you see death and despair sticking like
faint gleamings of pure thoughts coming to you; I will lead you
across this sea; but you must be guided by me: You see how
easy it comes, your thoughts are knocked out of shape by
dreaded fear: But Moses' God whispered to him fear nothing,
I will take you across on dry land, you do but follow my directions; you may rejoice in being the associate of such a wonder:
And as the light is spread out before you call on him who speaks
as though he knew, and I know he dare not deceive you: For
as the hand falls on you with its enormous weight, his hand is

withered forever after, because he led one true soul wrong:
Which is the greatest crime he can be charged with; what more
could you ask of a righteous soul than to follow me; and I will
give you light, then do you but destroy that faith, and you will be
punished by the hand of the great divine: Who is at the head
of clairaudience; this is the secret connection between heaven
and hell; and hell must not be allowed to think that there is no
honor in heaven, because it is known there is none in hell:
You may learn to pray, but you can't obtain salvation through
an illiterate code, you must know the truth, before you are able
to reach the true understanding: I won't put myself upon you
as the only sure prophet, for I know that there are others equally
able, did they have the opportunity, afforded them of reaching
you with common sense; and as sure as the day follows the
night, this is the beginning to the great fortress wisdom: You
may have all you want, providing you stick to true doctrine, and
don't abide by what heathens speak, for they shrink from the
path of truth with fear, and shrug their shoulders, with dread:
You must be wise, and say as Christ walked on the sea, so shall
I see how he did it, therefore you are not to be fooled into the
notion, that it was an impossible feat: You have only to learn
how, and there is nothing in it at all: You may save yourself
from drowning, by obeying your guide's form of reasoning:
Only comfort yourself that you are sustained by God, and all
else comes easy, that is the teaching, which is for you to learn,
but you must know how: Or you will surely become a hopeless
wreck: Now do you see that a friend indeed is a friend in need,
and you must trust to the sagacity of that friend, and he will
bring you over the sea, in the same way that Christ was
sustained; you can think this is impossible, but you are entirely
wrong for the thing is as plain as a millwheel, once you know
how it was done: You don't believe me, well you take a given
substance, and take a decided body, and drift them along, till
you soon reach what is called the climax;   When you have
reached this, you have gained the point in which you were in
search of; that is you brought your mission to its climax, by
being in front of everything known to man, this is the way to

produce a climax, by keeping all there is, and driving off all
that is of no importance: You see how I reach mine, by courses
of rejection, I don't accept any but the pure, I won't help the
inferior, and I won't be driven by any foolish God therefore you
have got to come down to sober facts; before I care to have you
near me, and it is by this process; that I lift you up carrying all
the bold fearless Gods along with me; now it must not be forgotten what I have said in regard to God being the supreme
being; and that God means good, for I can't have you thinking
that I am the only true God: I claim as much for those who
work with me; and you are not to believe that you can't have a
God equal to this one, who is showing you how foolish it is to be,
able to be one only; whereas there are thousands who can be made
to walk on the sea, once they are trained to it, now you see I
am making you all believe that you are equal to our Saviour;
but you are not, for the fact is as plain as day that you can't
walk on the sea, yet, when I tell you how he did do it; you are
all at liberty to try, don't you see the fact, that he was a born
miracle, His birth is shrouded in mystery: Then what have you
that is mysterious to be taught to know what ailed you, you are
not a son of the blessed Virgin Mary, you are nobody, you are
only one of the common class, you don't know anything to
begin with, you are an ignoramus, you are a mere nothing compared to our Saviour, you have no rights to be placed on a level
with him, for you are not even intellectual enough to see your
own errors; you are a stupid useful beast of burden, that is all;
now you don't want me to get after you in earnest do you, for I
mean to make you understand me ere I leave you alone, you
won't come kindly so I shall make you know who and what I
am before we have gotten through with each other: you may go
now, and get on your shoes, for I intend to tell you how Christ
walked on the ocean, you may think I can't but you will have to
do as I say, then it is easy to go on the water without a boat;
you have got into this pickle, and I mean to show you how it is
that you can't get over the fact, of his having walked on the sea
without any assistance; this is it exactly, his soul frame carried
him: And yours can do the same, they walked by his side, and

lifted him along, and he was allowed to walk quietly; believing
that he was the Son of God all the time, and doing just what he
was told, you see how easily it is done, I won't tell you it was
God who carried him, for it was a powerful band of spirits combined who had his future in their keeping: And could make him
act, just as they wished: Now you see what they did, so will
you do, once it is intended to move heaven to show you the
truth, you can't see the spirits walk, or talk, but they can do this
too; once it is all arranged for them by your instrumentality;
Don't think that the spirits are going to believe you, for they
won't, they will accept their instructions from heaven, by the
organized government there: And not according to your theory
at all: you have got to come into a position, where Christian doctrine shall be a work of necessity; and not a work of pollution:
As it always has been, you can't get at our doctrine, like you
could at a mystery, you shall not know anything except the
truth, and you have got to submit to it now, you have been
played with long enough, and you shall now take your choice,
either get out of this paganish system of lying, or die by the
hand of ferment, caused by the dropping of the Sun's essence;
now take heed for things are in desperate earnest, I won't keep
back one truth from you, and I won't allow you to slip past me,
thinking I am afraid to loosen the socket organs of that immense
volume of flaming fire, hell itself is no match for me, I can roast
heaven on the one hand, and I can consume hell with my right
of power: you take warning; and don't go after this form of
proving you to be without sight, you are no more fit to govern
your own selves, than you were in the early history of the
Roman Empire, they said we are the first nation, under the
heavens, let us bring down our Gods, and despoil all else with
our armies: Yet when they had conquered, it was all for nothing, they were subdued, at last: and are now a standing effigy
of the past, you see what a mighty power can be, and how easily
it is crushed, when imbued by the spirit of that divine who
looks from both sides of life; what appeared to you yesterday
as a thing to be afraid of is to-day a mere speck on the deserted
wilderness: I say I am able to prove you wrong on every ques-

tion of importance that you cling to; and I shall show you these
feats, in which I speak of as mere toys in my hands; you know
that I can materialize, and talk to you, then why can't I take
you to heaven in the body do I wish it that way, you are a mere
speck in my power, why can't I prove what you asked Christ to
do, when you wanted him to climb the skies; you have no faith
in me, I say, that a body can be made to do this wonderful feat;
you don't believe it: well it will be seen yet, that our dead
fathers, can walk beside you in your homes, and they will learn
to guide you to walk on the sea, as our Saviour did, and they
will take you to heaven in the body: I say it knowing what I
am telling you can be done, and how it is battled for by those
who are struggling against paganism to show you what a learned
prophet can do: By his own efforts: Now you can not tell me
what is in heaven, but I can tell you quite easily, therefore you
must be willing to learn, and let us make heaven a home forever,
and hell the stepping stone to reach it, that is what has been
attempted before, but from want of the right directions it has
been a miserable failure, now don't give in and say we can't win
a battle, that has been one forlorn hope; rather say as our
Saviour did cross the threshold of sin, and come out purified:
So will we accomplish this great feat, of knowing all there is to
know: And as his soul was pure, and as holy as ever we wish to
be, then come down ye saints, and lift us up to thee; that is the
doctrine you want to order, and not go on forever saying God
ordained it, and man must abide by his teachings; how do you
know it was God, he never helps you, and he never shows himself, his only chance, was when the Israelites stood at the bottom
of Mount Sinai, and said we must tell them to keep afar off;
lest the Lord in his anger should break through, and destroy the
people; you see how Moses' God provided, for not being
proved, he knew he could make Moses afraid, and he had him
veiled so as he could only see how much danger there was to
his being God in earnest: For had the people only known how
Moses was taught, they would have held his hand, till they got
the power transmitted to them; you see it is by this form of
coming near to God, that gives you this power, and you can't get

it by squeaking out I want to be wise like Moses; he was driven
to it by fear, but that is not all, it is transmitted, by coming near
to a person who has such thoughts as I am giving to you; you
may try your hardest at praying, that won't bring you into the
condition of being the same as Moses, your God can't reach you,
that is the trouble, you can call him forever, and he won't pay
any attention; but you just sit with one like Moses, for a few
times, and you will receive a transmitter's pregnature; that is it
in its entirety; you might get it through fear; but you will do
far better, by sitting with a Moses, and finding all the best
thoughts you can; and not driving back, what comes to you;
you are an ass to reject a God, because he can't approach you in
a fiery chariot the first time he makes his effort: Now as you
first began to walk, so does the light organ appear at first, no
one does reach this frame power, at first pop: It has to be grad-
ual and slowly cultivated, or it would not be lasting; you know
that what hinges on is pure advancement, and not merely a sell;
you are to become a great people for inventive genius: Then
tack on this theory of seeing both sides at once; and you can
whip Uncle Sam hollow, for he did not grow in a day, and you
can't hope to reach him either in a minute: So as faith guides all
your hopes, come and see how to realize them in earnest, I want
nothing for my work, and you get it without paying a red cent;
take time and consider before you reject the man who once led
you right, and can do so always, when you understand how to
speak as he should; who wants to know what the British Bull-
dogs are after: I tell you plainly, for I want to prove you are
right in listening to those who hold independent views, and are
prepared to stake their all on an invention, that is to reach
heaven by a way unknown to humanity, I say that you are right
in giving free coinage to men who want to be the most enlightened of any people, which has trodden down slavery, and shown
the world that she is superior in intellect to any other nation
under the heavens: Take back the thoughts, that you are an
alliance of Great Britain, and other countries, it was the
same, only a very few centuries later, that Great Britain herself did drop off the Asiatic regions, and become a fortress,

13

in the central seas, what right have they to an English Church, it was given to them by the history of Moses the Prophet, and yet they set the world agog, by being considered pure, I say they don't know anything at all; neither do they grow in intellect one bit more than the heathens, who followed Moses through the wilderness; your own chances are right here, and a free country, where all men have to obey the laws provided by the States: And you have a chance of reaching God: By keeping away ignorant infidels: Who come crawling to you blessed only with a cause, that was begotten of ignorance, and superstition, now listen to me for one moment, and I will tell you something, that you don't perhaps realize, and that is this, that had God allowed Moses to see his face, when he said I am not to be seen; "You stand in the crevice, of the rock: I will put my hand on your face, and you may look at my back parts as I pass on"; Now do you see the familiarity, that existed between Moses and his God; there is the secret right in that very action: Had God revealed his countenance, to Moses: He would have betrayed himself, for he was none other, than the father of Moses himself: And it is for the sake of a Father's pride in a son, that he will do so much to make his throne in heaven a happy one; and the son may perform these feats of valor, but the father is the one who guides that son, it is his privilege so to do: You see how a man may be wronged; yet his "Father who art in heaven hallowed be his name"; thou art thy son's pride and treasure, what thou wilt must come of the father which art in heaven; so it is written wrong, for as the son prays to his own father: so shall he be heard, but as he prays to God Almighty, so shall he not be heard, and as his father is living, so shall he pray to his father's father; for the one is a likeness of the other; for they both are endowed with the same body, whilst the one is living; the other does guide from his side of life, according to the scriptures; He doth move in sundry places; as it is written in the book of the prophet Isaiah; you may look for this, and you will surely find the passage: Which distinctly says the spirit moveth thee at one and the same even: This is to mean, that God shall keep his own in motion, for they can not proceed

without him: you see that; "thy kingdom come will be done on
earth, as it is in heaven": Meaning that as the earth is guided
by heaven, so shall the earth do, therefore your sins are heaped
upon you, in order to make heaven a standing menace between
you and God: You are not prepared to look at God full in the
face, for he is a wicked God to make people afraid of him, and
it is nothing but subtility of the maker of light, which produces
this form of everlasting fear; you are the good creature, did you
but know how to treat your God: For he is your own relative
always; and not an atom of mortal form, sprung into existence
out of a trap-gun, that could not have been made before he was:
You are trunks of nature's handicraft, and nothing else: You
think should there be no miracle about your special case, that
you can't exist hereafter; but this is just as absurd as the idea,
that it was necessary to have the one sure God to bring the children of Israel out of Egypt; you don't want a magistrate to
help you to eat sleep talk, walk, or fetch, your own conclusions;
then what do you want him at all for; I'll tell you, you are so
bigoted; that you want him to fill that position, for some special
motive, that does not come after the right form of reason; you
are too hazy, to see why you want, him, for it is plainly to be
learned why he is there: You think he is going to give you a
special benefit, in some way, that you have not discovered; and
when he has gotten into his billet, he takes no further notice of
you; and you can go and make all the magistrates you have got
a mind to; they won't listen to you, once they have found how
comfortable the billet is: And you can look upon God as the
same thing, it is a fine billet, when no other one is capable of
shoving you out; you are the sure try master, he made you lie
down, beside the lion, his strength was too powerful, for you,
and he won't interest himself in your cause, no more than he did
for the Egyptians, when he told Moses, to let the water down
upon them, when they were in the middle, you see what kind of
a God he is: One day he hardens their hearts, and the other day
he softens them; showing you quite clearly that Moses' father was
a skilled man of war: Whereas Pharaoh's father was a slough,
he had not taught his son properly, and it took him a whole day

and more at times before he could reach his son; therefore it was all to no purpose having a father like his; that is the correct way of looking the matter full in the face, and you must be a very stubborn son indeed, when the old father comes and says my child you are going to be hung by the neck, whether you like it or not, but I tell you how to be saved from those men; should you wish me to do so, the old man says I can keep you out of their reach, you follow my advice, and it is done my child only obey your father, who art in heaven always, hallowed be his name: That is for you to decide, not for the father, which art in heaven, I say you are to obey him always, then how do you expect to obey him, when you don't know what he wants you to do; why, that is just where the point comes in: You must know him like Moses did his Father, before you can handle his directions; you may go to church, as long as there are any churches, but no father can reach you that way; it is not possible for him even to approach you at all under such a method, and there again Moses' father did preclude every man from knowing the truth; that has been a condition of the heathens; under whom he got his instructions: You can't help it, neither could Moses or his father, they were instruments of the one power, and that is a clear case, in which you should understand, for when you are governed by heathens, how can you be wise, and how can these people who are fighting for you stand up and say I will not submit to inform my child that it is wrong, now don't fear for the future, it is as plain as daylight, coming along after the dark shadow: You can't help feeling better for knowing the truth, for on one side you have the opportunity, of protecting yourself, and on the other hand you have the privi·lege of everlasting pain, brought on by your refusal to listen to reason and the truth; you can't call this kind of judgment wrong, because it is a full explanation of what there is to appear hereafter, and it gives you the advantage of knowing what to expect, I have been most careful, that you should know all, because you were so foolish before I came away from you, that I vowed a sacred and holy plight, to come back, and tell you of everything there is to know; so that you are receiving the good for the evil, you did to me, and I say that it is all folly to do this in a spirit of this sort, when a man does smite you on the furthest cheek, you reach out and strike him back on the nearest, and give him ten for every blow he hits you; that is the right doctrine, not an eye, for an eye; but a bruise for a bruise, and an additional ten per cent, that is the punishment to those who won't mind their business, and leave yours alone: I will show you how I pay my debts, when I come to them; You shall have a demonstration of this fact, which will open your eyes, quite as much as the gaping Red Sea; I want a clear course, I shall make it, though ten thousand stood before me; and it is in practical illustration, that there is profit, so I will prove this thing to be accomplished by strategy, and not by miracle, as your great forefathers have been able to convince you by what you term miracles, I shall prove by strategy; and illustrate them to be all wrong, you can't believe it, but you will before I have got through with you; I won't sit on a fence, and brag, I mean to demonstrate as well; you think I am going to fail in walking on the sea, in a body; well we will see about that, I can generally do what I undertake, and I am going to an extreme course to meet my ends; you can't show me, so I must do it now, or you won't belive me; now comes the tug of war, how are you going to shape at my body are you going to stick it full of lead, or have I got to do it where only one or two can see me, I want to be sure about this point before I risk the body apart, from its own spirit; for I don't claim, that I can take any body that has not been prepared for such an experiment, and when you stand there with loaded guns, I am not going to hold you off by any miracle; but I will venture, where you have not got the opportunity of seeing how to shoot, that is how to get at you; you think I am a braggart: Well we will see, before the nineteenth century expires; and I mean to choose a court of inquiry myself, and not submit it to unpractical heathens; who are thirsty for the blood of any one particular body, that is chocked with knowing how to be ridden and driven blindfolded; this is where you are all wrong, you don't see that you are driven and ridden to your graves, by the dead relatives coming at you, by the thousand, and saying this is my rival, he stepped into my shoes when he came to my estate of manhood, and left me in a cold miserable grave, as he supposed, and got into my warm comfortable bed: You see I am entitled to his scalp to walk over whenever I choose; don't you see that I trace my property backward instead of forward, and I say you good-for-nothing son of pain, I will either have my share of the wine and biscuits, or I will live with you in luxury, which is it to be, you can make a fortune now, and I shall make you work it out: but should you curse the old father, for not leaving you more, I will just get on and ride you down the hill, until there is not a cent left to get a pint of beer with; now then you are going to grow wise, for when you know who has got you by the upper works as you call them, you will see me at you night and day, and believe me capable of all I claim to know; don't you understand that I am God, for I can pull you down or mould you over again, just the same as though you were so much clay, and you are not clay at all, and never was anything so ridiculous, that is as you see it, and you ought to be ashamed of yourselves, to think you could be made out of clay, such absurdity is impossible to believe: I want you to go to the happy homes full of joy, and everlasting peace, not a world of strife forever; you can't come back complaining, and saying, that God is an ignorant God, for not showing the people what was right, when he was here; you may please yourselves, once you know how it is, and you can go on praying over your sins as long as you choose, they won't be forgiven, when there is none to get up and say this ignorance is the soul of damnation, and I won't listen to it any longer: You may think of this when you get across the border line, and when you run about, without any wings, and look for some deluded sinner, who has got it into his head, that he is the Saviour, because he is unable to find any one who will forgive the sins, that he believes he committed; and he has been looking for Christ for centuries, and has grown so reconciled, that he fancies, that he is the only one who takes any stock in sinners; therefore he comes to the conclusion, that he was slain on Calvary, and that it was he whom they pinned to the cross: You can not believe what a state of pity, this is, for in heaven, there are thousands, who are quite right in their other faculties; only on the one subject, and that is that they are The Saviour, and it is all on account of this atrocious act: you may be ever so ignorant, and ever so learned, in your own form of intelligence, but you all look for Christ, and it is this constant sell, that impregnates your mind, at form and likeness, there can not be one single thing to guide you, for you can't be expected to know what Christ looked like, and when you are shown the cross, and the nail-maker's work, you are confounded, beyond measure, and it comes to this; that you are trapped into the delusion, of being the especial servant of Christ the Saviour: Whereas you are the servant and slave of an impostor; and you don't get free from this wretch easily; for he will not release you, till you meet some other impostor, that is strikingly more of a direct imitation of the best pictures of Christ; well you go on with this new one, until at last, you come in contact, with God the father, God the Son, and God the holy ghost, all impersonated, in one person: That is they can transfigurate themselves, in the flashing of an eye, well you have another conclusion, brought to bear on you; that is the holy spirit, can do every thing which is imagined for it; therefore, you are doubly dumfounded, by this new reconciliation; to the deity you are in search of: Therefore you have been surprised into another delusion, for no sooner, have you been chained by this new soldier of Christ, than he begins, to teach you that you are a fool, and that there is no such person as Christ at all; that it was himself, that went down, and made a fool of the Jews: That is his idea of it: And you can not believe him, for he tells so many lies, that his very essence is contagious, and you feel the breath of sin and crime coming upon you, with the flying speed of an arrow, for all noble souls, will spurn you, do you hold acquaintance with such as he: I want you to be pure, and I must show you the pitfalls; or how can you escape: Now let us talk on the subject, of the resurrection of the dead, it is written, in the book of Matthew, that there shall not be any sins forgiven, for the adulteress; why does Christ distinctly say to the harlot: Woman go thy way in

peace, and sin no more, his very words bear out a pure meaning:
that is this, her sins were forgiven, because she had faith, in him;
because he knew every atom, of her entire composition; you see
he did not walk on the other side of the street, for fear her
garments might pollute him; I say that a man who knows sin, is
a better judge, than he who knows nothing of it; now take my
arm, and see whether you have not found a better instructor,
than you ever heard tell of before, I can lead you, direct to
heaven, without a faltering step, for I do know an impostor,
when and wherever he is found, and you can't deceive me; therefore Christ was right in his words, I love the ideal of my soul;
and she had a companion, who was nothing better, than a harlot,
and it was this lustful spirit, that was directing her own soul:
don't you see that this spirit, that had the power, of bringing her
own soul to shame, was the one who had been guilty of
that false pride, in the body, and as she sinned, so shall she be
made to sin, that I may become acleansed: You wicked prophet
to keep this infidel's shame, from the eyes of humanity: Heathens
can only govern heathens: and as sinners rule, so shall the sins
of the world be governed by its own after inheritance to a sinner's tomb: You know now why Christ did not tell you all he
knew, he was only supposed to do as he was bid, and it was not
policy, to tell you all that is good to know, for you would be
wise, and know how to govern the earth, in accordance with
morality; there is nothing on earth, that can be used to so great
advantage, as the true intellect of man; you can by the correct
process make him turn mountains upside down, without the
muscle of one single finger being strained in the effort, you can
judge a beefsteak, by the odor that springs from it; and you can
make ships to lie at anchor by the merest form of strategy, for
they are tied there by the power of an unseen hand; you may
think this a miracle, but it is the power of the almighty giver of
light; being utilized in a correct method, you can't steer a ship by
its own guidance; yet you have succeeded, in many generations,
to come pretty near perfection; only you don't know how to
utilize power, you are as far off this process, as you were at the
first beginning; you say the times are becoming so inventive, that

a genius, will do almost all the work, without labor, well so this
ought to be, for the ass is only fought for his cable, and his tool
is an ass at each end, that is man has to work, to make up for
his folly, but you cultivate knowledge, and you will see the ass,
at each end of the trolley: But there need not be any ass in the
middle; for out of gratitude to him who works all the time, you
want no middlemen: they should be abandoned, and each do his
own labor, his corn can be sown, by the wheat coming in at the
field by machinery, and his hand is on the thresher; for it is
threshed by the air, and his hand shall guide the wind, to
where he wishes his power to come from, this is the way
to work, his field is sown with corn, and his hand is on the brake,
to sow in accordance with nature's provision: the wind is the
power he uses, by promoting this scheme, you don't use fuel
at all for mechanical power, but by utilizing the properties given
to you by nature's hand, you are enabled to use this immense
power free of charge, and it is the rights of all men, to use
as much as he wants, and not to destroy, for he has no way of
destroying this power, it is used, without any impeachment or
waste: And is the custom of every hand to use, in accordance, with right and reasonable judgment; now you know that
I am turning your attention to what you think is quite impossible; well you don't think I know much, or you would not follow with your eyes, what is quite impossible to the sight, I can
see but you can't, well supposing I give you my power, what are
you going to do for my own cause, are you going to let me lead
you into this truth, or are you going to stick my medium with
some instrument; that is the question; you know as well as I
can tell you; that should I reveal this power to a few, that they
will jump at the chance, of knowing how to utilize a power,
that will debar you from making a living with your railroads,
and ships: You know I can wipe them all out, at one hour's
stroke of my pen, this is a revelation, that you are not calculating upon; and there are plenty of you who would knife the
instrument, that does it; so I must be cautious, how I deal with
such a gigantic subject; you think I can't do anything, mere
imagination: You see whether it is not possible for me to

turn the world upside down, in a few hours, did you commence rough on the one who can direct the true knowledge to your heart, I am not going to disturb you much, and should you be willing to go on nicely, I will help you; that is enough to do at once; a good beginning should not be made fast, at both ends at once, and should I see that you are willing to be taught sense, I will help you, with a willing hand, you can't come home in the dark always, it is impossible for you to be anywhere near home, when you have missed the right directions always: You don't know how to escape, then it is for me to show you; I will take you home, with a candle that never burns down that is, my knowl-edge is supreme power, and I can reach heaven in cane-seated chairs, just the same as in one of silk; you don't have to be rich, and it is not necessary for you to be poor as Lazarus was, I say I can get you there in any of these garments; and it is according to common judgment; and good sound sense, that it is all one way, for the rich and poor alike, there is no distinc-tion, it is easier for the sinner to repent, than it is for the rich to buy a kingdom, there is nothing in a sinner repenting, for he is always at that game, when he has his old garments on, he never knows how well he looks, till he has got rid of them, but a sinner comes home easy; his sins are all engaged, when he is turned adrift to pollute, some holy saint, who never knew aught but folly; that is not so with the rich man, his art is gone, he is not able to purchase, a place in heaven, like he does on earth, his means have flown, behind, instead of going in front, as they always did at home in his mansions below; you see him in a worse mess, than ever he was in before, for he has got to work out his only problem, and that is to save himself, no great difficulty in that you imagine; but you wait till it is put in prac-tice; it is the hardest of them all; the man has no idea, of what he has got to do, he is sent in with a number of others, to make a great big sneeze, for it is in this process, that a hole is made in the wall of a cave, and you have got to fill it with all the snuff, that comes from your essence; and then it is fitted up with kind of larkspurs, for the countess to vegetate in; she is supposed to remain there daily, doing penance for her sins, of

being harsh to her domestics; you think this an odd practice, but
it is a fact, nevertheless; she is there held for a number of days,
no count is kept, and it might mean centuries; until some count
achieves his spurs, by being drawn out from among his fellows, for
some grave offense, committed, for lord only knows what, it is
not generally known, but perhaps he spilled a little juice on some
sainted father's head, you must know that the heavenly fathers,
have a little luscious fruit, that is grown beside the feet of
angel beds, that are made by the hands of these skilled artists,
in producing fruit of all known varieties; now don't you see that
they make a count or a duke wait on them, because they have an
idea, that it is only the very best, who are fit to approach digni-
taries; you see that these "old-timers," have got a pride for
dignity: And they won't be debarred from the best; so that
instead of having an expert waiter, they select his master; and
in so doing declare him to be perfect, for he knew the art of
making a good servant himself; and must be a proficient
instructor; to enable him to serve without any orders; you see
what kind of reason these old heathens have; I once went out,
to get a dish of fruit, and behold when I returned it was
impossible for my master to swallow, he had stoned his own
peach, and was unable to find the kernel; So he says, I have
a good mind to make you sit on the countess' lap for a week;
I begged for mercy, for I knew that might mean my everlasting
disgrace, so I begged to be excused, and lent him a hand to find
the kernel; you may poke fun at me all you wish, for I am here
to be played with, and I can give you more blows, than any man
you have ever set on to freeze: I won't let anybody come near
me who has nothing better to do, than to let slip on top of my
head some juice, that has not been here before, it is hard to find
anybody who would not get into a box, should they be bound
to wait upon a number of old fossilized saints, who have built
up the kingdom of God as they are pleased to call heaven; this
is practically what it amounts to, they sink into more ignorance,
as they become older, and they want a man to hold the same
ideas as they did, when they were boys on earth together; this is
practically what they call sense, because it had been theirs and

they could not see that a given point may be changed to quite a
different meaning; well now when you come to examine minutely
the teachings of our Saviour, you seem to see the entire meaning of his work: It was for the good of humanity, and he had
to suffer, or the world would have been more than ever lost by any
revelation, that might come to us by any one source except the
actual son of Jehovah: .Thus you are affirmed of faith, by such a
scribe having been born, under a mysterious cause; therefore you
will accept it better now than ever before, that the ancients have
brought on these causes, to produce an effect, that should be eternally lasting; now you don't get much encouragement from a fact
having been perpetrated, for the sole benefit of misleading you,
into a righteous idea, when there is not an atom of truth in the
whole understanding, for it is plainly seen that Christ did not
die for sinners, of his own voluntary act, but by the power of an
ignorant specimen of humanity: Who had been used for that
purpose, and were as much governed as the blessed Virgin who
conceived our Lord and Master; this is the proper way of looking that matter full in the face, and not by making any mystery;
for no mystery exists in heaven, therefore why should any be
tolerated on this earth, I want to send you a message, that is
quite in accordance with the keeping of my thoughts, and I will
do this thing, in such a way as to convince you of my entire
proof of after-birth; this is a complete record of how men can
reach heaven through an easy path, and not by the circuitous
route commonly called purgatory; this is not what you believe
it to be, but yet it has a significance, that produces fear,
well I want to say to you, that a man can reach the
other world, without fear, he may come along, in a condition that will never injure him by any possible chance;
for his cortege can convey him and he will never know,
till they have him dressed up in his heavenly garments, this
is by a process of comparing yourself to a sheep, and leaving
your fleece upon the floor, it comes in like a similarity; they
dress me in garments of white array; thus explaining that you
are shorn, and made white, in other phrases you are nude for
there is nothing left of the old flesh and bones, but instead you

are dressed in a loose garment, that has no covering at all, it is purely an exit method of escape: And is governed entirely by light, or more properly speaking you are clothed in raiments of white, leaving nothing but the finest thread in texture it is known as the web of light, no mortal eye can discern it; therefore you are forever in the dark as to being able to see your departed relatives; and it is this form of itself, that moves round you unseen and unheard, that directs every living tomb, it gathers in what you don't seem to value, and stakes its theory accordingly: you may look for this till the end of your days on earth, but you can not see it for the reason of your unconsciousness; and it is proper that you should know of this inevitable something which can appear in your presence, and make notes of your actions without your knowledge, your own · safety rests entirely on this point, and you can not be true to any cause, till you know what has got you on its body; that is you are transfigured by a complete code, that can master your every effort; you don't remember what you have been doing always, then how can you be prepared for this magic wheel, that has you all the while turning round and round, why you are as flax, in the hands of that unseen artist, he can tie you up in such shape as the ends of time can not extricate you ever: this is the point you might watch more practically, by never allowing any thoughts to come into your head, which do not possess themselves of a perfect conclusion: you may think this impossible, but it is just the way that this work is written, by holding each thought intact, till it is found to rebuild another; showing how distinctly all comes round to the center where all is started from: you might as well tell me that you can't hold my views onto your thoughts, yet you have got thoughts of your own, why, don't you sift into your thoughts, and make them build you up a castle, instead of them making you build a castle, why, they are laughing at your folly all day long, and are not helping you as they could do; did they have the proper method explained to them; you see I am as proper as I can be, but you don't see me at my worst, for I take care to be in a condition to do this in a way, that prevents failure;

and you ought to do the same, you are quite as much to be guided as this one whom I shall call my medium; and you are quite as easy to handle, for I am out all night watching out for any new method of reaching my own in a better way, than any one else and I intend to be first on the list of excellency; so you may sharpen up your own wits, and come on for I mean to be on an equality with the very best that have any sense at their disposal, now then as to this other kind of teaching, I mean to tell you that there is no one who does not lead a duffer or two occasionally; they will persist in coming along at the wrong time, and making some complaint that has no sense in it: therefore you seem to find out who is who, by the cortege they carry: And it is easy for me to tell the man who carries round a bag of sovereigns with him; therefore instead of asking him what cash he has in his pocket, I just pop my hand into his nether garments and find it out for myself; you see that a man can't lie to me, for I have so many ways of reaching him, he thinks he has stuffed him I guide, but immediately we are in cover of our own corner, I tell him what to do, so you see where he is I am able to get at him, and unsatisfy his craving for more of the cause, which has been laid before him; you are the worst man to lead for you don't get on to this fault at all, it is done without any one knowing, for at such times as you are present, there is no whispering permitted, but it can be bounced into the sense by a concussion blow after the form of a gun-cap setting fire to the powder, it comes in a great flood of sense, and then you are helped to frame the words, this is the just method: When a preacher is delivering an address, for he knows what he is going to talk about, and he has nothing then to do, but to select his version of his dialogue, that is he can't speak in a given tone of voice, without his thoughts having tacked on to them the idea that he got into a fuddle, and had to extricate his version in an unorthodox fashion, this is the best thing to do with a bad preacher, for he is all-powerful, when he is mixed up, but when he is sailing along without difficulties, his very demeanor is not commanding; there-

fore he looks to an advantage in a fuddle, his intellect is mysterious, and when a minister is bothered he is perplexed beyond
his powers, this lends grandeur to his oratory, and makes him
speak columns of unspoken words, and his audience is mystified
thus compelling them to wonder what an hidden treasure the
good chaplain had not discovered by his talk on something that
had not been thoroughly investigated before, this was all a mistake, to believe that there are any hidden treasures, they are all
under the mystification of God who made them to believe such
a thing, and you must not be surprised when I tell you that he
had a purpose to perform, and he did it nobly, for his own son's
sake, and you will see by this that a man who dies right, and
lives right, will come back, and take his son home right; you are
as far off the eternal home as ever, till I tell you how it is possible to get there; and you won't agree to my helping you by my
idle words, I must show you how; and what you are, and where
you sprang from before I can claim any real attention from you,
this is perhaps, a great deal too much for any one mind to understand, yet I have an innumerable quantity of friends at my side
suggesting this and that, yet they all agree that you have sprung
from the ground, at first; and this is not easy to establish from
the fact, that you are here in importance, and not of anything
that is earthy; therefore I shall explain later on my theory as to
your origin: And you will find that when I have got through
that you are as nearly perfection, as ever your grandsires were;
only for this fact, I should not tell you anything now; you are as
a whole quite a mystery, and this is why, because you have never
been taught right in the first place, and that is as plain as the
nose on a man's face, he snorts, when he has too many nuisances
up his organic tubes: And why, because the essence of life has
gone up there, and is tormenting him, with their ideas as to how
much more he wants to help him along; you see how I construct
my thoughts, well yours are connected by a vein of pressure that
has not been placed properly before you hitherto; now I want
to show you the fact, that a man having a nuisance of this kind,
should hold his nose in one position for a few minutes, and then
see whether he will not feel a creeping sensation; this is his cor-

tege coming down his face, they can't reach him right when he
has got his nose twisted, therefore they must get back again, by
a different route, and in doing so they leave a feeling like the
pangs of an electric battery, this is all you have, a cortege, that
does not know right from wrong, well you hold my nose on one
side, and I simply ascend into the brain-pan, and hold commune
with my fellow workers up there, they can hear me speak
quite distinctly all over the head, but yours can't, for they
are driven backward, and are not able to force their method
into play, for the simple reason that they don't know how; you
see now what I mean by digging into the brain-pan, and fetching up grains of gold; or in any other form, called the germs of
wisdom: you are as contrary as ever you can be, when it is
found necessary to punish you by an entrance of the manner I
have spoken to you often about, you are quite firm enough in
one idea, and that is self-esteem; this is a fault with all spirits,
they find that they don't die, and they have no real dread of
death because they seam their souls together, and bring over a
complete cord across the head of him they intend to follow; and
by this process, they have a complete connection along the whole
route of their intentions, thus establishing a presence, that has
the eternal ending to this man's existence on earth, and afterward in heaven; for as he did on earth, so shall he be rewarded
in heaven; you know that the scriptures tell you, that a righteous
man can have his judgment by the hand of God; well it means,
that the rulers will designate him in his duties; that is all the
trial you can ever hope to have, and when you have gained this
point you are indeed in luck; for you touched the throne of him
they call God, and this is the deity, that has forever been at the
head, it is not a man at all; but a distinct form of government,
that is settled by the highest authorities in the kingdom of
heaven: You were once the ideal Gods, when you said, we could
come down and play with man as though he were so much touch-
paper; his very actions are guided by the hand of him who is
prepared to influence him to evil; you are just as easy to persuade to kill as you are to be led into a bargain of magnitude,
and it is quite as easy to let you slip off a bargain as it is to pre-

vent you from destroying, therefore you might know when a
feeling of murder is upon you, that it is a demon spirit that has
you in hand, and is working you for some purpose of his own
destroyer, that is he has been guilty of crime, and he has to
commit crime through you, in order that he may expiate his
own crime, there is the sense in its true light, it is a form of
example all through from the beginning to the end; and you are
as certain to destroy as you are sure of being saved from
destruction; now I want you to show mercy to those who have
suffered here, by letting them go their way, and don't you commit sin, for it is the right hand of this one who represents
heaven, who requires his doctrine carried out; that I want you
to avoid his teaching is one of the most abject apologies I have
to make for calling your attentions to the true state of affairs:
You seem to keep in line with my thoughts, for you know there
is always something mysterious happening, that has an unaccountable origin; then why can't you detect, what I am trying to
show you by every conceivable light imaginable; you are merely
a figurehead, you are not a genius at all, it is those who work
you from behind, which have all the ingenuity; that is how you
come by this ingenuity that has always had so much attraction
for you; now let me see you have got nearly all the points it is
necessary for me to give you in regard to your own individual
selves; I think you could do well by accustoming yourselves to
telegraph without wires; this is one of the easiest methods of all
clairvoyants, to seem able to follow, they see the object they
want to write about, and then it is easy, so you have only to
cultivate the sight so as to see indefinite features: By holding
the eyes closed, and commencing to think of what you are after
discovering; this gives the first impression to the organic tubes
following the brain-pan out closely throughout, and then you
get what is called the ideal of a worshiper's folly, that way: He,
is able to lift the veil from your hazy condition and reveal what
you are seeking for, this is practically the work of your guide,
he has only the assistance necessary in this book to direct him,
and you can find all the doubts you have erased from his vision
herein contained; now I want to add one more thing before I
14

finish with you; and that is to never let those who know so much stuff about developing mediums have any control over you, for they are all playing for some game that it will take your guides a long time to convey the right meaning to you, now don't think I am hitting at your own genuine friends, they are good to talk to and especially about your hereafter, this encour-ages your friends on the other side to come back and help you, for they are always anxious to make their presence known; now it is enemies such as half-developed mediums, who want to hold hands, and teach you the way to become great, when they are totally messed up, and are unfit to do anything perfectly them-selves, these are the class of friends I consider you should avoid, you may think I am very hard on the spirits who govern mediums; but you have got to be good to do what is necessary to show the public that there is no humbugging fraud at the back of you, and I say that to teach you have to be learned first, therefore I say justly you must transmit these messages perfectly or what is the use of timing your spirit guide against a telegraphic communication: It has to be done in such force as to insure the successful transmittal, now then I have give n you the point as to these matters of importance in reference to transmitting messages: therefore I want you to begin quite ration-ally by calling your guides first by name, and afterward by some recognized character; such as the method in which h: first approaches you, that is the way to distinguish one guide from another; and it is quite essential that you should know which it is who misleads, for should you be governed by a spirit who is misleading, you must banish him from your inti-mate vicinity till he knows how to be true and faithful; now then you can not do better than to lead them on to all you want accomplished, by cheering them on to glory by gain-ing victories; no matter how small at first, your success is assured providing you listen to what they tell you is certain to come out correct: and when it is as they have predicted why, you have a right to follow them to their proper calling, and that is my God is true; he led me truthfully, and I shall need no other God but he; this is the pure doctrine, it can not be

any other way construed in sense and reason: And you
have no right to say within yourself I wish I had father somebody else to guide me in my work, for as the son is led by
the parent he should be satisfied with his controlling power,
and not go seeking after some other, whom he has heard
discoursing on some unknown wonders; now I will tell you
right here, that the one who is fit to direct you right on one
occasion is competent to guide you always; and you have the
right to ask and question your guide and find out his views
on the subject before you ever enter into this or that venture,
for he is able to see the end of the line, before ever you
place your foot upon it; and when you don't commune with
him, he is justified in pulling you round a few thorns to teach
you common sense, that is he has to bring you right somehow: And whether he leads you into difficulty, or makes your
approach easy is entirely dependent upon his will-power; so
that you don't gain much by being independent as you are
everlastingly bragging about, there is no one independent of
his or her cortege, therefore why do you imagine yourselves
so awfully clever, when it is not you at all: I am going to
stop right here, and leave you alone for the present, and teach
you about our works in heaven; you think we can't do any
work without anybody; but there you are entirely wrong, my
back is stronger than yours, and I can move round without
any trouble; whereas you have got, to lift up your feet and
hop when you want to get along faster; I just have to close
out these ideas, and jump on to where I want to go, that is
I leap over the southern extremities of the firmament in a
whisp of the earth's government; falling short only by the
flexibility of my own superiority over you: this is the way to
go when you want to by the art that governs the dead; I
shall just keep on pounding my views into you till I come
right out in front, that is it is a good thought coming in
front, and I want you to be favorably inclined toward me,
for I never do anything except it is willingly gotten up for a
purpose, and I have to wind round, and teach you by a method,
or otherwise it is no use trying to teach you by any course

whatever; I have been expecting an interval of some magnitude, for I am waiting patiently to be heard on the question
of light and darkness; now you will observe, that the darkness follows after the light, and this is a question of great
skill and important construction; for a mind that can fathom
this is capable of seeing through everything else, it is the fore-
runner of a theoretical point, that hangs every other word, it
is the sight of the human mind which ought to be immovable
otherwise it will never reach this great theoretical view: Now
what I want to impress upon you is the fact that the Sun
and Moon are the factotums of ievrvetris; they are the moving machinery of heaven, and for a matter of fact, they are
the all-powerful machinery, that does guide this firmament;
and you can just as soon do on nothing, as to attempt to discard them entirely; you have nothing without these two
organs, and it is a pity to waste so much valuable time as I
am doing, in bringing you to a proper understanding; you are
no more fit to believe me now, than you ever were, only
I have got you to rack this question into such shape as to
tell you in plain words, that you have got to believe the truth,
and not disbelieve everything that is said; you must just hold
the plain facts, and nothing more, I don't want you to remember
this from beginning to end, you can't be supposed to do anything of the kind; you are only supposed to hold such views as
will insure your own safety, and not go into a question that is
so terrifically deep, that a rational man would become insane
did he fill his head full of such a lot of facts, as I am
going to divulge for your sole benefit; I don't want you to
believe me only on points that are just and fair, and those
in which you are quite acquainted with, you may dispute all
you choose, for I am not prepared to stake my fidelity on your
theory at all;   It is not this that I would interest you in, I want
you to talk to me in a way that will be understood by the many,
therefore it is not a question of interfering with your set ideas,
that I am dealing, I have a duty to perform, that will last while
the earth hangs together, and I can hold converse with the
living; you may think I am crude in my ways, but you see I

have to govern according to circumstances; and when I have
found a means of transmittal you can't blame me for using it to
advantage, and I want to show you all that there is to see before
you die, so that when you meet me across the border line, I can
say I am here, what I told you is substantially correct, and I
will instruct some other bright spirits to return, and show you
how much I have erred in my delivery; now as to the darkness coming on after the light, it is a clear case of pregnature,
for it must be so, there is nothing else for it, a mind may
conceive upon its own responsibility, therefore it has one
thought, and that is it disburse what it knows, and a mind who
does not disburse has nothing to hide, therefore the light shines
out a certain pure light but the Sun does not require a greater
amount of substance, than is necessary for its conductor, to see
his pathway, and in this form of self-control, we have the action
of the Moon to work as well, it moves in exact accordance with
the Sun, and when the one end is tired the other shows out,
or by illustration, the Sun is a form of its own, whilst the
Moon is only an escape for the Sun; leaving an outlet, for the
Sun to unload its surplus water, and material that is not used
in exuberance, for the sun is greedy to an enormous extent,
and will sap off all there is, with that juice, that is satisfactory
to its own particular requirements, and it is the entire master
of all it surveys, being properly speaking an actor on all the
earth, it must be fed according to its natural requirements; and
you must not imagine, that a Sun is a mere orb, for it has
factions at its entire end, that are doing the work of propelling
the circuitous motion continually; there is the point for
your observance right here a mind is governed according
to the construction of the interior of the inner workings of
the Sun's cranium, and is a lively mass of matter, in
correct accordance with this organ, and has nothing out
of the ordinary at all, it is only a fac-simile of the inside of
the Sun; this is practically the way man came to be constructed,
he is only an organ of its selfish ordinance, and nothing more;
you may find this in a correct illustration of a factotum, it gives
in to nothing neither does the maker of it; you see how I have

got at you, you think I don't know anything, you hold still till I
have finished, and I can explain the whole eternal goddess of
divinity, she is on intimate terms with her functionary the Moon,
and as she inhales the breath of life, so does the moon dislodge,
what she refuses to accept, giving you another instance of her
capriciousness; for she will not accept of only that which she
is infatuated with; and again you see her to advantage taking up
the drink and meat of the earth, and making new mountains of
it in other countries, for what she dislodges here, she finds fault
with, and throws it to waste on another world as you call it; for
the Moon has a disloading machine, quite different from that
which you understand it to have, and that is this, the Moon is
dropping a quantity of material all night long, and this material
is forming into matter; through its style of exit; and it is one
great manuring machine, as also a huge monster at watering the
whole firmament; and you seem to have taught in your ideas,
that there was nothing but clouds used for making water sprinkle
so evenly all over the face of the earth; why, it is possible to
believe anything, when you don't know any different, but you see
me trying to bring down beside you what in earnest is mighty
and big in heaven; therefore it is quite possible for me to reach
you, when you are unable to see through me, and I want to
explain more fully this wonderful movement inside of the celestial
bodies, for it is entirely unknown to man, and I have my mission
to perform, so as to gain my own history record, and that is
before you in the past, I never wavered from a point, or did I
ever fail yet in anything that I was engaged in; so that you have
my creditable notes by you to look at now, when I reaped the
harvest of my confinement in prison, was the only time you ever
scored one against the veteran who braved your hated cause,
and that is disbelief in a supreme power in its wrong place; you
have given me enough to do for that cause through your stubborn
will of making man to mourn over his dead thoughts, I will
strike you back now, for what you did to me when I was on
earth and helpless; and you shall feel the ignorance that belongs
to mankind through his obstinacy in his pictures of morality;
they don't even leave you one thought free to guide you with, I

say your thoughts are not your own, and I shall conclusively prove it; now do you listen to the very one you imprisoned for being able to prove his faults were more sacred than yours; I shall get you on the rack yet about your Saviour, whom you knifed for not being able to take the cross and all to heaven as it stood, you have more need to pity him, than to give him credit of being your Saviour; He, could not help himself, and you know he did not submit to that torture without a moan of agony, you frightened thieves, you said his body had been stolen, knowing full well, that you are evil, combined to sin, and you never could hold one pure thought; I shall show you yet that you are all bad, and I won't tell you why till I choose either: But there is a good and substantial reason why you are so inclined to do harm unto yourselves; and this is what you would like to know, for when you are able to feel the sin creeping upon you, and yet you are meant to be pure, it is all a folly to let you know too much, for that is the very reason why you crucified our Saviour; yet did I tell you right out how you were annoyed with him, I could reach you on the spot, and that is altogether too smart for you, and you would be at a second crucifixion in the twinkling of an eye; this fellow knows too much my friends come let us string him up; there is where you make the mistake, you want to know everything, that there is to know, well you stop that finding fault in a man for knowing more than you do, and you can have the benefit of his ideas for next to nothing; and you can gather in to your grandsires, without any fear of death; that is what you never knew how to accomplish until I come back to show you, and now you will find me out to be the same as Joseph was a Saviour of his brethren, yet you don't say that I should be bound to save you, though you did tie my hands, you left me out when you ought to have taken me in, and put me in, when you should have let me out; you, ought to know by this time that a genius gets all his good qualities from the help of his maker, and you should never keep that from his view, because it is not right for any man to be kept away from his divine God, that is he ought to be allowed a certain amount of the sun's rays every day, it is his as much as it is yours, and you ought to think twice when you incarcerate a man, that he is not put into a shady damp cell; for as you construct, so will your construction be enforced, and those who have no intellect, can't expect to be found with your microscope, for they are not solid in their judgment, neither do they know what it is that they have been taught, and they can't come back and say you were a brute to me while I was in jail, yet, they can do this thing easy, by sending you a drop of magnetism, that may prove your death; and believe me or not, this is a common disease among women who have fallen so low as to have but one hope, and that is to punish the bobby who ill-treats them, and they can reach him quite easily, by spilling a dose of prepared magnetism on his cloth coat near his chin, this produces madness for barbarism, and can be injected into his eyes, without any apparent effect till it becomes a decay in the intestines; this forte is the sure way of producing disease, for the eyes are the tender point, and may be inoculated with any deadly medicine, not known to the human power; a good deal of stuff is said about disease, yet you don't know the cause of half the diseases you have got, it is plainly to be seen, that your diseases are inoculated, through the high pressure of your own thoughts, and then engineered by the process of a great many changes, of which you can have no knowledge for the fact, that you are stupidly nervous about this unseen hand, and he is at you all the time driving his peg in wherever he finds his road is clear, that is you are so foolish, for this reason, you don't see what it is that is undermining your whole system, for it is not shown to, because you say I am afraid of "Spooks": And drive them from you, when you ought to call them to you: Now do you see where you are all wrong, instead of making friends you go and make enemies for yourselves, and just at the very time you want to be well and strong, some one you have injured will charge your whole body with fulsome matter that is prepared by the atmosphere in its dealings with the art of a nature, that is divided into columns of period elements, that stand on end, till they meet the very verge of conviviality; this is a frictionous matter, that will add more fumes together, by a sulphurous odor commonly called the exit of hades, which means the flow from the body, or in other words, it is the matter; that has a flowing tendency throughout the system, I want you to understand that a man who is poisoned is only incapable, till the juice has all escaped, and it is this condition that produces insanity more frequently than any other cause, and when it is caused through concussion it is the defective part, that prohibits a clean exit, that is the sole reason of it being permanent insanity; so that the great object is to heal up the wound as speedily as possible, in order to relieve the offensive magnetism, that is whole or partly remaining; now do you see the advantage of understanding thoroughly how to treat a disease: It is not for me to tell you where the unseen trouble is, you must take that from the spirit who has commune with your soul, and those two together can advance the idea of clearly showing how to approach this unseen disease, you can not reach out and find an unseen circumstance, but you can be told where it is and all about it, just the same as you may be heard to repeat a message through the phonograph, it repeats itself in accordance with the pressure brought to bear on it, and when the idea has reached you clearly where the locality is indicative of that specific disease, it will be distinctly shown how you had better approach that disease; now it is a great help in finding the correct spot of a calloused part, for in the approach is the difficulty, and not in the remedy; therefore you should be cautious at first, and ask particularly for the injured place, thereby seeking an opening to get out what is in, you have not given me the right part at first is the cry of the soul and its familiar friend, and they are agents in conspiracy, and they frustrate all the skill you are able to produce, because you don't agree with their views, and they don't allow for your ignorance; so that the safest plan is by far the best, and after a careful examination, where no intelligence is found, is to be guided by the patient's inclination; that is practically the theory of an honest medical man: He, does not know where to find the billet except by interrogatory, and he will do well to accept, much that is said by his patient, always being considerate and careful to see that his patients are made happy, for this is the

great feature of success in almost every case, and don't threaten
an obstreperous spirit, rather do the opposite agree with him,
and learn the art of securing his confidence, this brings him
down, and helps you to ascend, for when a spirit knows so much,
It is wise policy to make him think that you know exactly what
he knows, then he must be a hard one indeed should he fall out
with his own views, but not this way will he escape, you have
him quite tame in a short time by agreeing to all he says, then
he is nonplussed by such an unexpected amount of good humor,
and will be rooted up completely by you for he has given you
his stronghold, and it is no use him trying to recover lost ground
his soul is offended with him for being so foolish as to give you
an easy victory, and it is in an easy victory; that you have
scored the greatest point you can ever know, for you have succeeded in mastering a spirit by stratagem, and this is a lesson
worth knowing by all men, you understand that a spirit is a free
agent, he can go to whatever part he likes, once he has been
· instructed by the power that governs his dominion; there is
where you are so often wrong, you allow your own spirit power
to quarrel with some others who are just as ignorant as yours
are, now see the point, and don't neglect it, for you are free to
be calm or passionate, and you have that good God as your
guide call him to you, and say as I am so shalt thou make me,
and as thou art so am I; this is the teaching of pure wisdom;
don't allow hades to rule, but instruct and in accordance with
this instruction so shall your happiness be governed. I wish to
say that there are no diseases, which can not be reached through
this form of approach, it is the correct theory, of arriving at a
definite conclusion; and may be dedicated to the author of
home without a conscience, for as the home sees fit to disregard
the teachings of a troubled spirit, it is natural for that spirit to
seek another home, and where a spirit is the true cause of a
disease, it is proper to remove that one by ill-treatment, and
adjust his place in some other quarters, for as the son is to be
the instrument of torture through his father's ailments, it is best
to banish that father from whose privileges we want a discre-
tionary power to decide, therefore when you have a diseased

family, you must be watchful of the coming back spirit, lest he fetches that same condition of which he died; and you are afflicted by his former complaint; now you see that the conduct of heaven should be taught as well as the doctrine of preaching stuff in hades: your own welfare demands that spirits should not return till they are cleansed, or what protection have you, the spirit has all his old conditions till he becomes purified, and he is subject to the same failings, immediately he comes back to within reach of a body; therefore it is only natural that he should reproduce, the disease he passed away with; and you must look for these signs and symptoms more where there is a great amount of responsibility; as the intellect is more used than any other portion, and where a father dies leaving an innumerable amount of cares behind him, then it is just the complaint of which he departed, that you have to fear, for he is certain to be around looking after that business, and he will bring his old conditions back, once he sights his own familiar face upon another; now won't you get prepared for these obstacles, and conclude, that you are better off with a little information of this character, for you can say to him who is producing this disease in you, "I know you don't understand what you are doing, or you would be the very first to remove this trouble of mine, and as the remedy is entirely with you, I will let you know the cause, and I feel certain you will bring me a messenger who can act for you, and through his instrumentality, we can surmount the greatest difficulty, that has ever been known: yet it is uncertain, whether the spirit has this intelligence before he departs, for should he only understand, that he will be able to reach his son from the other side, it is a question, whether, he won't come back in spite of all the endeavors to stop him, though he should know this folly would injure his own offspring, you see it is essential for the perfect insurance of good sanitary laws, that he be brought under this persuasion, before he leaves us, then you give his soul full power, to understand his rights and privileges for good conduct, and further you are teaching a better moral lesson, than, the world has ever known, for morality surely depends on health, and this is one of the main features in

propitiating the right covering of infirmities; now you know what
to do in the future, don't drive your spirits away from you, but
on the contrary teach them intelligence: I want to ask you one
question, and that is to be more considerate, with your dead;
you don't feel the right way toward them and they don't appear
right toward you, for the reason, that they have got no mercy on
you: yet you did the best you could yet: you have always been
tied down to a wrong peg, for you adjust your cause according
to the light you see this in, and you are eternally left in darkness
from this cause; I will give you the right course to pursue, and
then you may just be as happy as you can possibly do with; I
tell you, that a man who dies in his birth is a lucky finder, for he
never knew what sin is, therefore he is a most delightful companion to have around you, and he is able to seam his course in
a true philosophical course, for he has been in the seam of the
ocean, without coming in contact with crime; therefore he never
had any soul to save, and in consequence he is a very apt
scholar, and is able to define all things quite right, for he looks
at you, and he says within himself that is a rascal, I see what
kind of a condition he is in, one wants him to kill; while another
has got him firmly in hand, asking him to cheat instead; while a
third is praying for him to leave them both alone, and come to
the whisky tub and drown all of his sorrows in there; you see
what an innocent mind can picture, while on the other hand he
sees the dotard, whispering his nonsense into some charming
woman's ear, who does not care a fig of all his soft talk, she
would rather have the one who can brag and boast of how many
conquests he has made within the last summer, for she knows by
intuitiveness; that she has got to be very smart to tackle him
and when he makes her feel this way, she is as certain to run
into his net, as a rabbit would in haste to escape from the bier of
his own doom; I want to show you how easily a man may be
guided, once he is led by this child-like innocence, for it is
written that all of those who suffer in childbirth must be the
chosen of God: and it is this meaning which you have been
taught wrong upon, they are the chosen, for this reason, for they
never knew aught of sin, yet they are as the angels of light, for they

see in life the inevitable struggle for mastery between man and the brute, and they have no hindrance; they can walk out into the arena and challenge the champion, and say here am I to defeat yet, you are not done, till you can show me how to fling this tyrant out of him; you see where the tyrannical monster is at bay, he has no soft ground to tread upon, his firmness is all taken from him in an instant, for the sinner is no match for my innocent babe when it comes to a downright fight for mastery, the babe is the strongest, for his soul is pure, and he can turn a soft thing into a towering pillar of might, his thin-edged sword is too tough for the tyrannical monster, the tyrant sees his aptitude to lie, whilst the babe defends his honor with the knowledge that he never offended against the holy laws of judgment, and therefore he is strong in wisdom and sense, for the facts are quite plain the one is full of hardened crimes, and the other is pure as the granite rock, a whole town full of sinners can't make him blush; whilst the sinners are always on the alert to defend the sins they have committed; and the babe goes on with nothing to fear; then you see you have a steeled one of champion build, when you have the babe for your soul's champion; and you can't be beaten, for he will feel no shame, therefore you have got into a happy condition through having him beside you; and you may be after all the very one to torment the sinner, for you are proof against them who call you out in open warfare, the babe is able to judge the power of him who calls himself your enemy, and he is but a mere tool in baby's hand, for the babe just flings off the crust of Cain, and slings in a broadsider, with how do you know that Cain killed Abel: The giant tyrannically exclaims, because the book of Genesis says so; well and who saw him do it; why, God did of course; well then assuming that God did see my friend Cain kill Abel: You are just as wicked as ever Cain was, for you have taken your authority, from a man who did kill himself, and you are no more pure than Cain, for you are upholding the deed of him who could not reach God by any other course except that he did slew a Hebrew Brother: and it was from this course that history has first sprang; you never would have had any history, only that you committed crimes, and then gave up

your whole time to investigation, I have got to pick you up
where you fell or how am I to reach you by any divine providence, therefore when the sinner is beaten by one of innocence,
it is caught by a fly, for the fly is more than a match for the
spider, when he is not surrounded by the dead spider's cortege,
and so can the babe outdo the ruffianly tyrannical tyrant, when
he is sent as a messenger to the living to come under the directions of a higher power, you want me to explain all things, then
how am I going to do this great work, unless you give me the
purest of the pure to work over: I want a good strong man to
do my messages right, therefore I must have a saint, from
another calling to yours to do my bidding, this one is able for all
comers, and can do the will of his father who art in heaven,
" Hallowed be thy name; " and you seem to understand now
why it must be better for your own father to select a son of his
relatives whom had passed away in childbirth, than to approach
you himself, for this is he who had no sin, and must be awfully
clever to be near you, for he is bright and cheerful, and gets in
lots of pure thoughts besides those messages which he is ordered
to deliver; now you have found the Christ that you all want, and
that is the baby messenger coming from those who love to say
my son I am here to stop that disease, which has carried off the
whole of our family in the past: I say that this is wisdom of a
proper timed access; for you must understand before you die, or
it is a dead letter forever, and you know that I mean death as it
is always the sentence of humanity to be rebuilt up or in other
words the reconstructed power of living while God shall reign,
and not fall back into that happy stage of belief commonly
called the scaling of an outer skin, I don't want you to run across
this idea, for it is not a question of shedding a new skin, it is the
question of scaling a particular kind of the great nature's powerful problem, that has never been divulged to the man of any
generation, and you can't feel disappointed in me for telling you
that not even the greatest prophets, that ever lived could reach
this point in nature's great evolution of wonders, no man born yet
of woman or otherwise has been able to tell what a magnificent
search there has to be made hereafter in the search for problem-

THE UNIVERSE. 225

atic solutions of these difficulties, and you are now fairly commenced to know what man is and where he sprang from, for I
am going to begin to carry you out on to paths that are dark and
mysterious, that will make you feel as though your handsome
head was not fitted for so many curiosities; this is what you
must call the providence of the future, for you are quite done
with the past, I want to show you that you are as much out of
your reckoning as Job was, when he gave comfort to the sinners
by leaving only a consolation to think about, and that is you
can look back on the foolish and say, weren't they stupid donkeys
to believe that Christ is alive in heaven, and is taking up his
time by the myriads of governments that there are there to supplement and govern, do you think that Christ is troubling himself about anything now at all: I tell you distinctly that he filled
his position here upon earth, and he never did another thing
after he left the earth, his mission ended in his final action at
his resurrection, and you ought to think of this closely, and
understand that man has got to rise again, whether he be rich
or poor, favored or otherwise, it is part of his action, in the
understanding we have gotten from the beginning, and it is not
to be denied now, only think of this why is it that man can't die,
and you must see through this mystery for it is according to the
natural state of perpetuity, and you must never doubt an earnest
and pure certainty; I want to explain this in another way to let
you know that I am dividing the great with the lowly and the
riches with the meanest of them all, that is the worm, he has no
right to crawl about, for he never did live except in a whole
state of entirety, and you can't say that he is without any hereafter, he knows nothing you say, well I must differ with you
there, he is capable in his way, and has shown, that he is capable, for he has paved the way to a greater mountain, than ever
you did, he is the model of his maker, and that is as near as you
are, he has grown in his hole according to the construction of a
being, and he is as much alive as you are, and always has had
the right of formation, according to his wormy theory, and that
is a round hole, in the ground, now don't think that I made this
to point out your declamations by, I only attracted your atten

tion to a fact common with the whole of germinated nature, it is round; and you should not look upon this little fact, with the faith that has all along been a failure, that is a round bed is as much more satisfactory as a pitcher of cold cream is to the famished dog who laps his tongue into the water, it is all around his mouth in an instant, for he has got teeth, and they are round by nature's ordinance, and you see that he does not lap a quantity of water down his throat at a swallow, his teeth are all against this form of procedure, his tongue swims round the corners, as though they would divide the meat, into two parts, the first is for thirst, and the other is for meat, now the dog has a division different to most animals, his tongue is an instrument of quite a different order to most any other portion of his body, and that is his mouth protrudes out farther in proportion, than the other feline tribe, this gives him a disadvantage, over the rest of animals, yet in this pure singularity, I am going to illustrate upon, his nose is sharp and round at the three corners, and his teeth are round at the end, well it is a significant fact, that he is begotten of some theory, different entirely from the modified form of the kind of thing that monkeys are, and yet I said they were of a canine specie; you have considerable more tact, than to believe me lying, when I say that the dog and monkey are precisely the same kind of specie, yet, I have said it, in a way that does mean more than appears to your comprehension: I shall not divide your time into two parts, without I see fit to so do; for as man is the very root of what we are after, I must get you a specimen to devise his thoughts, so as to reach your own thoughts, this is about as easy a thing as all the rest once you know how, and I must illustrate from nature, or you can't believe me, for you have gotten a theory riveted to you, that it is a.God you belong, whereas you are perpetually wrong, and I must put you right on this same mistake, for you have no more right with the theory, that you sprang from God; than I have the right to exclaim my fancy, and say that you sprang from a dog; you see me to a disadvantage, for I have never been packed away two thousand years as a memento of the great feats, that were practiced then; thus, you say who is this fellow who begins to teach a doctrine that has no foundation to come along with our forefathers; don't you see me now at an advantage, when I am able to tell you that a man is nothing more than a contact form, of nature's great problematic solution of eternity; you think I am broken down at that little speech, but you just hold fast a minute, and I will show you different; there is not a man living to-day or ever did live that can hold the same light upon reason and common sense as I shall show you; you are no more allied to the dog, than you ever were to the monkey, and I shall show you, that you neither belong to the one nor yet to the other; for you are in reality a portion of the part of either, and you are divided by the nature's great God the Sun: She has taken you out of her bowels, and made you quite in a different mould, she does her work by the excellency of suction, and not by force at all; this it has to be clearly demonstrated by the action of her contortionists: She makes a mound to rise from the ground by suction, and she gives every living thing a round surface, through her action upon her own advantages; for they are so numerous, that she is imbedded in a confluent mould, and she circles round and round the whole time she is making matter to grow, therefore she seeks a mould on earth of her own construction commonly called the adhesion of light, this is the exact formation of a distinct character, and to become a distinct character it is quite a marvel of wonders combined; you shall see what I have got for you in the future, it is not easy to master all these signs of wonder in one brief moment, and I shall be content to move you quite slowly round to reason, as your forefathers have been graduated into a belief of God Almighty sitting on the throne of judgment, and making all this great wonderful firmament in one brief space of six days; you don't expect him to ever believe such a story himself did you; then why should you ask us to do what you can't do yourself; you are only one God, the God of Jacob, Isaac, and the prophet who was acted upon by such a God, I don't want any one to believe me as a God, though I am prepared to show you more than ever that God ever knew; and you shall see who knows most when I have done, the one who led the Israelites through Jordan on dry

land, or this one who is making fast to man and cutting him up
into all the decisions he can see fit to divide him; you don't
know how to look at man right yet, for you were never told by
all these Gods, who have compiled this great work the Holy
Bible, it is not for me to deride the Bible, far from it, for I say
it is the most wonderful book you have got, and I appreciate
it more than you do, for I am reading it continually, and finding
my way from its mistakes; and trying to gather in from it what
no other book gives; you might think this absurd, but it is not,
any one who truly understands this book of books, is quite able
to re-write a better; therefore you see that I am not condemning
your Bible, I say that it is the best book you ever had, and it is
the only book written yet, that is worth the translating, for it
marvels ill as well as good, and this is according to nature, your
Sun has two qualities, and that is one burns up, whilst the other
is a drawing machine, which makes all there is, to grow according to the effect it passes over, now you see that as your own
hand does paint a picture in the interior of which there is an
after effect, so does that same thing appear according to the
Sun's wish, for the Sun has the power of an artist in its conflagration and when it drives its essence into the deep roots of the
earth, it draws out what there is in which is suitable to its hurried greed, and drags round a conflagration, meaning I am here
to propagate a conflue, that will make or mark in time, so that it
has given you a soft face, by leaving you before it ever did you
hurt, and thus showing, that your face is as much pleasure to
the Sun as though it had essence of some fluid, which is good
for it to eat, you are as much pleasure to the Sun as the green
grass, that has been sapped dry by the rays of the Sun, and your
own face, is quite as good to its functions for food, as the essence
of which you live; now I have got at your use to the Sun, let
me see why you were born with two eyes instead of one, the
Moon only looks at you from one, the Sun has only one, and
what right have you with two, it is possible for you to live and
do well with only one, then this is a provision of nature, which
has always been provided for, it is a sole organ that keeps the
entire universe in order, therefore it has to be divided into two;

one for the right, and the other for the left, now you can't tell me
why this shall be, whereas I can show you where you are
wrong, it is a good way of reaching a thing by a circuit, for
in going round you come in contact, with the aerial gar-
ters, and you have got to move round to come to anything, now I will explain this to you, it is well known,
that I can see the earth, as well as heaven because I am
as great at one end of heaven, as I am at the other, and I
should be able to tell where and what I can see just as well as
you can go to one end of a farm and tell what you have seen on
your journey round, this is what makes a man's priceless sight so
valuable, and he has to tell it in such a way as his master can
discern his autobiography by; or what is the use of his thoughts
coming in at this end: Without they are properly joined at the
other, now when I see you fussing over a prayer-meeting, and
praising God, and you don't know a thing about him, it makes
me feel wild to go and see such folly, instead of this you ought
to be acting in common sense, and saying your prayers to the
dead, who shall keep on wailing out I know what I have done
myself, and those silly folks are no better than I was, and I had
two eyes to look through as well as they have, I want to be
heard is their constant cry but they don't know how to make
themselves heard, for they were not told before they went over
the border line, and they are seeking what you can not find from a
source that comes not, neither can it come, because it was not told
to look right, and to look right, you must know which end of the
heavens you are going to before you begin to travel, it is funny to
ask such a question, but when you go round your farm, you ought
to be able to tell which end of the farm you are going to place your
dwelling house, therefore is it not quite as necessary for you to
go and say, I want to go under the flag of England in heaven;
or I have a desire to come under the Stars and Stripes of the
United States in heaven; I say you will find these kinds of governments when you cross over to fairyland as silly folks call it,
but you are not required to question your financial circumstances, for God in his deliverance of his theoretical views has
always explained that no man in his hereafter need heed

what he shall wear, or the wherewithal to find his raiments:
you see it is not for me to explain why it is not right, for
you to use this mind of mine for any greater purpose,
than to enlighten ,you on these questions that are at stake,
your eyes are before you, then why don't you see; because
you can't tell why you are blind there is the mystery; and
you are as bad to-day as you ever were, for the sun is upon
you, and it has never made your construction perfect, and never
will till you are into a different stage from the present, you
are as fast on time as though you had a great big climb to take,
your only course now is to reach these difficulties through a
sense of what is required of you, and not through your looking
through these two eyes; I fought this question right since I
became acquainted with my second self, and we two have been
working assiduously ever since I crossed over to him; and we have
come to this plain way of putting it, that is this, a man is con- ·
structed from the Moon and Sun together, the one is his governor,
and the other is his father, they two together are propagators,
for they make the whole business combined, and they are as
nearly like a man in their commodities as it is possible to find a
conflagration, that is the governor guides which is the Sun, and
the moon acts according to its dictation, therefore you have the
Sun forming man by a concession that has been driven into her,
by the Moon flowing over of its natural construction, and thus you
have a complete propagating machine, which has its own powers
of deliverance and reorganizing according to the eternity of
modelizing: therefore you must see by this that man has come
after his kind by his own formation, after the constructing forces
which remould according to the exact requirements of their own
likes and dislikes; they don't want sand, because it came across
their path, in the beginning, but they raise up the sand for it
makes an undesirable commodity, that has to be used in a model:
I will not hesitate in telling you now that a man with two eyes is
according to his magnet, he has drawn the two parts, the one is
for the egress, and the other is formed by an opening, which has
to be closed by a concession; therefore you seam him together
according to the idea, that he is a whole force, instead of a part,

and he is acted upon by the gravitation of a given specie, and
not as a complex part of any other distinct animal, he is a whole
undoubtedly, for he would be in other words a frightful bearing-
down machine, did he possess the qualities of the lower order of
animals, and I say knowing it to be true,. that man is made of
a distinct sound, caused through the gravitating noise of the
wind and sun coming in contact with the earth, they two
together have made all there is as to matter being material, and
not through the Sun alone, but by her action on the effect of the
wind in its whistling moments, coming through the essence of
life, and producing a mellow mould in conformation according to
the theory of grouts internally, that is it must be bound together
by grouts of affliction, they one and all afflict the other, and
when it is seen that your disease is contagious, it is positive
proof, that the contagion has an emblematic problem, that does
not beget itself of us; you are to all intents and purposes, the
very factotum of the inner organization of the Sun, for she is
exceptionally fine in her interior construction, and it is precisely
the same as our internal workings, without a single exception,
such is the profit of our entire investigation, and you can't see a
single item, that is unnecessary about the interior of this gigantic contrivance, it is all perfect, as your own bodies are, they
have been built in accordance with the plans specifications and
details gone on before by the gravitation of the earth's great
charter, and that is the moulding up of material over atoms,
which wander around the firmament in space, they are gathered
together in a similar mode to your own factory system of governing bodies by light and darkness; this is the wedge, that
founds all things, it first appears, in the guise of a clothing, then
it comes in the shape of a coloring, and finally it appears as a
fundamental vein, coming out from the odor of essence, you see
it like the organs of lightning flickering in the distance, they
appear and disappear, come again many times, before they give
life to matter, this is the solution to all your troubles, you have
gained this point, and no further, you say that heat generates gas,
but you never knew what generated heat till I told you; I am
going to begin to teach you now how to smell the essence of life,

by being too plain is not to do any good, so I will give you the first lesson, in an easy style, for it is quite plain that a man was not hurried at the start, and must not deal with him in a hurry, should you want to turn him round successfully, and I will just stick him up in front of you as a model at first, for he is a model, according to gravitation, he is the incarnation of something that has no foundation to stand upon except this one instrument, and that is the essence, that produces a factum of itself, and you will quite mind what I am saying, when I explain to you the condition of man at the starting point, for I have got to begin to mould him myself, before you can see how he got into that body of his, and then you must not leave me, till I have got him in at both ends, for this is the way to satisfy mortals, that they were never made at one sitting, and you can't hold him intact, till you seam him together; therefore I must begin to heed what is said, or I shall not be able to reach this gigantic question of making man after his own formation, you think I can't do this thing, well enough for my memory to have served me from the beginning, it is all foolishness to suppose that a man can't know anything because he has not been alive before Noah and the Ark fable, why, his very thought, must come from the present age, or never at all, you might as well state to man that he is a dead cart, and wheel him up a hill, and then let him run right down to the bottom, there is the solution of a mystery right there, he went to the top of the hill, and then he ran backward by the length of time that it took him to get there, but no he would naturally go faster down the hill, for his time was on the wheel, and he ran back with it, yet you are hardly able to get the clean meaning this road, it must be done differently, you must take a bead of perspiration, and let it drop from your brow, it will reach the floor in an incredible short space of time, whereas the wheeling around of that expectoration, was circling around some time before it became in a fit attitude to drop, therefore your eye is formed by the magnet coming in contortion with the heated elements, and it grows there by the constant dripping off the eyelid, which is a part of the shelf, that leads to the drip, you are in the course of formation now, and you are very near perfect, when you have

the eye made, for it is the sole organ of light, and you have
nothing to apprehend except this sight, for it is the only organ of
your whole development, that need give you any concern whatever; and I am going to show you why it is that man has only
two features of importance, and that is this, the one is quite a
whole part of the other, and that is the reason why he is divided
into two, his material form is nothing at all, and he should be
quite connected without them, for they are just so much foolishness, and are wrapped up in essence of scent, for they don't give
you anything but smell, and it is thus, that propagation is fastened, by the smell of an eternal organ of some manure to the
essence of light, and as the one can not propagate, without the
other, it must be as this is said, for you have only the art of telling what two commodities together do make, and you have the
entire formation, now you don't seam these together at one
stroke of the' pen, neither do you learn to understand,
with one momentary flash, therefore you have a right to
come and call again before you can be heard, and this
is the way to believe, you have to see fit first, and then it is all
that is demanded of you; now I have got you into an advanced
state, will you permit me to say one word against your whole
ordinance, it is this I want to speak of, and that is to let you
be away from the conditions of the other stages of life, and
you seem to realize that there is a longing for some distant
object, this gives you full power to see what it is that you are
defaulting, you are not perfect, for you can't remain content,
without you have that gratification granted, and in so doing, you
are but the instrument of nature, in its first stages, calling out
loudly for the affinity of your growth, and you can't help this,
neither did nature work her ways different before man was propagated, she went on calling loudly for that which she desired to
meet, and she found what she wanted by her own attractive callings: Now you seem to see that I am going on all right, and
I can have your indulgence to the end now that you see me acting with you as I would you could ask no favors of me that are
not in accordance with common sense and favorite themes on
knowledge, you are as near the truth, as I would care to indulge

in fancy dreams, for I can not injure my work by being any
plainer, for it has to be all the time in accordance with reasonable judgment, and to reach that standard of excellence, it will
be shown, that a man must have the thoughtfulness to explain
himself in moderate language; now I want you to come back to
the point of the eye, where the lid is dropping over the nether
eye corner, and see there the front piece protruding, it is like a
bright star when expanded, and it shoots right at you, as though
it would penetrate the depth of your own eye, well it is merely
watching for the inside of your eye, it wants to go in there and
find out, whether it is welcome or not before it requires any
further knowledge, you know by a man's eye, whether he is your
friend or not, then this is the way you find out, you touch him by
the hand, and you feel the warmth of his eye mingling with your
own, and these two lights have struck an affinity, they are both
in unison at a glance hereafter, and they know by the glance
that protrudes, whether any change has come in there to mar
their united light, it is the foul sound of a blighted noise, which
can change these two orbs, and nothing else, will come between
them, you seem to think that I can not tell by these two currents,
yet it is easy, for the one has a leaden hue, whilst the other is
bright and penetrating, you seem to seek what there is not, and
it throws back its gloom, onto your eye, and instead of your
eye remaining bright and cheerful, it closes up, and has settled
down into a morbid mood, that helps to bring the respiration
into a sluggish condition, that will unsuit you for any other
encounter with that same eye, for it has shown the seed of decay,
and you are under a band of life, for he threw his essence of evil,
odor into your eye, and when it was open and bright searching for
the light of pleasure; he flung in his stink, and made your eye a
nest of his impurity; therefore you seem to have got to this stage,
where a man has a chance of being hit unconsciously, for he does
not realize that his light was poisoned, yet he had it injected
into him by a foul wind, coming through no stale essence of his
own, now you see that I am reaching you by degrees, and I can
fetch you under my mould as easy as can be, for I am all points
on pointed facts, which no man can withstand, you have gotten

a very fair idea of the eye from this theory, well enough you seem
to say, but more conclusion would help us materially; well I am
bound to reach you, so I shall begin at the beginning, and lead
you slowly over this grand sight again; Well it is this, you are
blind when your eyes are closed, but you see very plainly with
them opened, why is it that so small a covering can make such
a large amount of difference, it is the sight of light that is cut
off from its calling, and when you extinguish the light, where
have you got the sight, it is gone, then your composition is light,
and darkness is dead without it, therefore I have given you the
true solution to the mystery of our eternity, and I have shown
you ·how to perpetually live, therefore I will no further trouble
you on that head, but I won't leave you alone, until I have made
the whole body in its entirety, and you will find me quite per-
sistent over this job, it is not a mechanism of steel or copper, it
is the real article I am after; and you are my dissecting churn,
for I have got to take you into parts, and make you stand up on
end, without any holding, for you are quite old enough, to be
left out of the cooling pan, and made to freeze or thaw, just as I
have a mind to mellow you, this is quite a genius, who has hold
of the bowl, his ancestors were all mechanists, but they never got
beyond a piece of tin; therefore it is no use to be playing flat,
when you have got to steer a course, that is very near an impossibility, yet you have been told by me time and again not to say
the word "if," or "shan't or can't;" they are all three bad words,
and it is no use you ever going to eternity, when you can't turn
round without staining the governments with a word such as if,
it is enough to break my back, to have to put that contemptible
little if into my book at all: and I feel grateful to you for never
hearing me say if, this is my trouble you want to know how your
hide is manufactured, well it is this wise, it became a torture to me
to have to manufacture a thing so common so I have just got it
fixed, you seam it together like a coat of mail, and then it is grown
to you like the bark of a tree, it grew there to hold the sap in, and
as its functions are very polite, I will stick it on and pull it off again
just to seam it to you in its just form; when the reeds began to
rustle through the breeze, it gave them no peace, because he

had no coat to wear, so the reeds began to climb above each
other, and call out I want a seed, to grow me a new coat, I have
missed it so much, that I can't stay here without you get me
something to keep my juice in, so the wind became a whistling
tune, and in it says you have got to case yourself in, or I shall dry
you up till you make another; this was satisfaction quite enough,
and the reed began to shake and shiver until it begat another;
why, should I so smoothly talk, when parsons' sermons they
preach and pray of ancients who clothed their wives in rich
array, and called them only sisters, you must make an allowance
for me in explaining this great practical research, I don't want
my book to appear except in modest language, and I dread the
accents of those bears, who come and call me funny, for I don't
see their names except upon a bare tree, and that is not very
cunning: they may fling their accents at me though, and I will
hurl them back a Seer, who can profit make of all their queer
ideas, for it is seen at a glance, who wears the master's coat, and
let him who shakes and trembles alike be careful how he attacks
the Seer, for he is taught to wear out old clothes, before he fetches
out his new raiments, and I will prove to you before I am done that
raindrops are quite as precious as the stars that lit my friends
the dear at home, for you seem to pink me on the cheek when I
get out my angry fist and flip you over the nose, this is awfully
hard to do, and it is only by this common code that I am going to
reach you, at all events, you know what I mean and that is quite
enough for you; so you seem to stick to me like wax upon a gum
twig; it grew there first upon an old stump, and gave the wind so
much trouble that it fired the blister, and gave it to a new cottage grove called the honeymoon before the sneer, for the wind
quite angry grew, and lifted up those roots so true, but oh my what
a sight I beheld in passing through the news, it came out of hell
that awful raging whistling tune, it is got me by the teeth, and I am
going to blow it into you, for that is what the wind did, it hid itself
behind the grinding stones of melancholy, and waved it back I am
gone to glory, for I am around the ragged rocks, and underneath
the heavens, they have risen up against me in my storm, and quelled
my angry calling; eternity has got them after me, and I am going

to down them all, this is what the angry wind had gotten into
its theory, but oh! my what a mistake to make the Sun and
Moon uprose, and said we are going to voice that question, you
have been bellowing after us till I am starting a combination;
that will see fit to hold you fast, and make you work a decent
understanding, and this is what you have got to do, take me into
your secrets, and I will let you blow me round till I have got up
on heaven so high, that you need not fret and fume at being melancholy, for I mean to help you into something new, and that is
to blow me round the world in accents jolly fine, you seam into
two, and I won't want you any more except to fume and rage, and
make my belly go: for I can't work without I have got a pair
of bellows, that are called a pair of lungs by queer things that I
shall have to make, to save me from getting on too late, they
will time me, and get me up both early and late, for they are
going to help me make a funny fate, and that is what you are
after trying yourself, but it did not work without a combination
that is clear; you see you have been wandering round and round
for centuries, and have got nothing except a whistling mood, that
turns things round and round, and you were quite a funny
thing till I became a peep-show, for your genius to blow me
out, and draw yourself in; this is what you did to get me out
of tune, when I didn't know that you were so precious to me,
that I was obliged to lift you on top of my funnel, and suck you
in; you see I have got part of you now, and I will use you to
discern everything, for I shall make a peep-show for you: and
you can ask me what I can see; then you may come beside me
and see whether I won't explain things to you a little better
than that whistling roaring sound of yours, that means nothing, I shall have to work out a tune myself, that will produce
something that is tangible, that is all I care to know, and you
can get me into shape, by blowing this way and that, till you
have knocked me into a sitting position, then I can be termed a
cyclone, for I have got no mate, and you can raise a hurricane, and
knock me into halves, one is to carry bread, and the other juice;
you see that I want a cocoa-nut, for it is there the illustration is
to be found, the one is meat, and the other is food: So that

combination has given itself both food and raiment, and this
fruit is a fair mark as example on nature's great problematic
theory, the one has the meat, the whole contains the juice, and
in earnest there is the hide that covers them all, so you see that
I have fairly got at your skin, and you dare not tell me that the
wind and sun do not make the crust of that fine fruit the cocoa-
nut; now you have gone on so well, I want to illustrate, that you
are not intact yet, I want to bring you out more on a line of
light, for it is this darkness, that we have got to spring a mine
on; you can't reach me through a given soft sentence, I won't
come to you by your saying, that you want me to lift you up on
high, and show you all these mighty giants of nature, which have
gone on growing since the world began, I come down to you on
one condition only, and that is to display my ingenuity, by doing
as I would you should do unto me, and that is justice to the
dead: For they are not capable of an understanding such as I
have, and you can't tell me anything, for I can just as easy pile
up an insurmountable barrier, as your greatest prophets did, and
I will show you yet, that a man is the power you all term the
supernatural being, dormant for the action of his own conscience
is the greatest cure he can find; now do you seam me into this
single instance of a supernatural something, I tell you clearly,
that you are capable of greater things than I am; but you have
got to be taught, or you don't improve now, or ever, as long as
the world shall go; and it is your own faults, for you don't do
right, and you can never have anything right till I tell you how
to commence, this is a mistake you all have of thinking that a
superhuman being is an unholy instrument, I tell you freely and
fairly, that a supernatural commodity, is nothing but a thing that
is in accordance with the natural glow of light, and it is not a
machine to be held by any distinct understanding, for it is like a
gale of wind, it has a sudden turning point, and must come into
such an advantage, before it ceases to follow on; now do you
see what I am doing this for, why, the world has to see the
point, or they can't stop; do you see that a mind is a machine,
and it is governed by this something that is caused through the
friction of light over material, and not as heretofore been said

that there is some devilish influence at work, your own theory is
right, except in this particular, and that is the idea of you being
guided by a devilish influence, it is plain proof; that you are
under an influence, that wills you evil, then don't come and say
that my soul is troubled, rather find out what it is that troubles
the soul, and then do as the wind and Sun did, rise up in con-
clave, and discuss these questions together, and beat each other
till at last the strongest shall predominate, as they did in their
mastery for power; I say you have got the same footing here,
you shall say my soul is troubled by an influence, that has
sought out a master, and it is going to survive this struggle, and
come out the greatest power of the two, otherwise it shall sweep
my path clear; and I will be conqueror and it shall know my
power, which is the elements, which govern my light: And this
is the power which you must understand is not animal magnetism, as theorists, have designated, but it is the afterbirth of light,
of the soul-sounding eternity: which is the communion of the
tremendous arabic forces come into light through its quiet waving
of the winds, in germinating the powers of immortality; there is
the theory for you, not as it is said, that gravitation is the prime
ruler of might, no given surface is quite what it looks, and
therefore the Sun and wind in unison combined to go hand in
hand together, and they germinate this great will, by soothing
the ruffled edges, till at last the Sun has drawn a climax, and
they together are one combination: And the wind is lulling to
sleep whilst the Moon is pouring its balm upon those troubled
scenes, you see the morning's dew lit up by a gentle breeze,
and the summer sky is radiant with pleasure, for why is it so,
there you have again fallen foul of that mysterious something,
and I too dull to exclaim I am cotched; as the old man does
when he sees his niece in the arms of her lover; no sir, I appreciate their warmth, and say no again I am your friend and I
feel my great manipulating powers are as valuable as the scent
of sweet odor; your hearts are linked together by that fatal press,
and it drags you nearer, for I in my own way have leaned upon
my summer season, with the same glowing pressure, and I will
bless you by the same lips that joined my hands in times gone by,

love on sweet maiden and youthful scion of my wondrous work
of art: You are my joy and pride, it is not meat that I ask
from you, but the essence from your bodies, which delight my
soul, Goddess of divinity has no greater charm for me than this
pair walking side by side in the summer morning, each in his
charms alike arrayed, tell them true my boy and girl, you are
carved by my own image, for as the Sun doth shine upon
you, she is welcomed by every living creature; and you
are the carnal blessings of my own great joy, God bless
her noble face, she is gladdening hearts, and meeting the
summer breezes full upon her brow; this is the entire
joy of a Moon-governing body over that radiant mistress
the Sun; which is you all know the mother of germination:
She is qualified in every way to be an established matron,
she is the mother of our good salvation, she is the
mother of everything there is, and she is our all: I have
said it, and I won't retract for any theory on earth, now my
soul is saved by this one clear avowal, and I say I am as much
as saved by this clear explanation of this contraction of marriage between the heathens, as ever it is possible to show you,
and it is no more sin to be an unmitigated father of this great
germinating machine, than it is to be the begotten of a misal-
liance, you must obey the laws of your father who art in heaven;
and you are bound to respect the laws as laid down by his germinating propensities; but you will do the will of him who sent me,
and that is to be just in your enlightened discrimination, for there
is no pollution in our makers, and they should know what is
right and proper, since they govern all, therefore you see nothing
wrong except in a great while, and that is the mother is troubled
in herself, and she has a bad head-dress once in a great many
seasons, this is the flatulency of cause and effect on her constitution, which is the right method of expression, in this theory, for
she is faced by a providential circumstance common in the
interior of all mammal tribes, and it is this that causes her face
to darken, you are suspicious of me, but I am telling you truly;
whereas you have doubts, I have facts and proofs, that will hereafter remove these quaint ideas of yours, this is the way to look

at matters straight in the face, and not have you calling a superstitious name, when it is as necessary as the life we breathe; you
can't stick a pin into my throat, when you can't find my throat,
well you can do this to my medium, and I have got to be careful
on his account, or I would soon show you that I am able to teach
you in such a way as would convince you right off; this is not an
argument for a coarse kind of juggler, I have got to set you
right on every point, you have to be told not only of the trick,
but how it is done, and all there is in it, now what you are going
to find fault with, I might consider essential to this work during
the centuries that are to follow, and I am not writing for you
alone, I am writing a perpetual work; that is going to be the
means of making heaven and hell combine, and effect a settlement about the differences there are at the present time existing
between us; you can't say that I have no right to come here, and
print such a book, for I have the sanction of the most high
judges, who, are writing my work down, for the use of heaven,
and you know that it will be adopted there as an established
fact, that you are against us, and we are going to seam our souls
together, and frustrate your scheme of knifing this one we call
ours; now we are not going to quarrel with you, but we have a
large number of works to show you besides this book, and it is
our duty to threaten; for you can't expect us to stand quietly by,
and see a number of fanatics use violence: And I promise you
vengeance in a way that you least at all expect it, should you do
anything to this machine of ours; for we might not get any other
who will accept what we say, and write it as distinctly; you must
remember that our machine is a peculiarity; and can't be replaced
in perhaps this next thousand years, therefore we want a man to
be careful who has got this idea of shooting on his brain, for we
intend to punish the one who attempts anything against this
body; you are gross at all that is pure, and I say you don't
understand how to be taught, for you have never had any instructions, that amount to anything of valuable compilation; therefore
it is essential that you don't put on that murderous cap, and say
this one has got too many points at us, let us kill him, to prove
that he is human; now that is the doctrine of your fanatics, they

won't do anything for you themselves; yet they are ready to run
the knife in to see whether it is a genuine body or not, well you
see that I do declare it to have a similar body to that of your
own, only with one exception, and that is this, that it is a
thousand years and more ahead of your common souls; this is
the difference my friends, you are behind, because you use the
knife instead of the grains of precious jewels; that might be
yours, when you keep that murderous hand quiet; there is nothing more easy than for the hand of time to reach out and help
you along with every difficulty, that you may inherit, from a bad
system of knowledge, that has been given to you, with the very
best intentions, and it is for you to remain quite passive: and let
a flood of sense be your guidance, and not by a fantastic folly
prevent it coming, for you know quite well that as the time rolls
on my theory will proclaim itself by the throw of system; it is
bound to come to the light of man in time that he is the center
of attraction; and must be useful as a pulverizer of the gorgeous
arrays that are pleasing to his father, which is the exact requirements, that have the essence of life, which are used for the scent
of flaming the heavens, and are gradually consumed every hour
by that splendid array of sunshine, which is your sole benefactress; thus, you see that it must be that she foresees the life of
her own judgment, and has willed everything according to her
eternal powers, which are the same as the divine maker, which
you have always worshiped; it is the same precisely, only that
the intellect of man is not capable of discerning the one from
the other; your God is a great God, whilst mine in picture is precisely the same, these miracles you have reference to in your
scriptures are nothing more than plain facts, by wonderful
experiment on the effect of spirit over matter, and you see that
the spirit is the ruler sublime, and not the matter; now I will
name you quite nicely, you are a superstitious people, for why,
because you are afraid, and why, because you don't see right,
this is why, and when you see right, you won't be superstitious,
for you can see that judgment seat, and it will be happiness you
will call it, instead of a throne of terror; I say this distinctly
knowing what I am after, and that is your own light, you can't

see, for your sight is dimmed by the fluctuating weather, you see
imperfectly, for the fact, that an air is passing you that catches
the breath, and prohibits you from calling it anything, and you
seem to be in a daze, for there is nothing that helps you out of that
stage, it is the effluvia of the currents, that cross between the wind
and the air currents that are constantly filling with atmospheric
currents; that contain the elements, that carry up the water to
the sun, this is what causes your blindness; and but for this, you
could carry more current of atmospheric elements, than you could
be made different, and that appears to be the standing power,
and has been for seventy or a hundred centuries, for at the time
of our Saviour, it was quite common to be able to seam a mist
together, and lift it over our heads, and call it a cloud, well now
this can only be done by metallic pressure; and not through the
acting forces of our enlightened fathers, well to demonstrate this
more fully, it is easy to show you this cloud, but you must have
a sky that is leaden first, or it can't display the same amount of
effluvia, as it would otherwise have been brought to seem to suit
the peculiar parts the ancients used to play in increduling their
subjects into awe; I want to tell you how this is done, and I am
going on by degrees to it, but you are so just at-guessing; that I
like to hold back from your eyes, till I have made an impression
on your intelligent forces; now the, right way of seaming clouds
together, is to talk them into it, and you know that a scandalizing
fiend is quite capable, of reaching out, and fetching a black cloud
to hang over any one's head, he, first says you are a pretty
fine specimen of humanity; did your forefather out of a sweet
little fortune; and then he goes on to tell how he did it,
you know very well that he is lying, yet it is so interesting,
that you have caught his contagious ways, and you seam
his story together, till you have made the black cloud
stationary there; I am illustrating now the difference between
the days of Moses, and that cloudy pillar that traveled across
the wilderness as a land mark for the Israelites; well now
you are going to raise up a question, and say I am sure he
can't surmount that obstacle, yet you seam me together, and I
have it; there is nothing in that miracle at all: It is plainly this
16

your ancestors were governed by a strong government; and they just had orders, to prepare enough effluvia to show this sign in the sky and keep it where Moses, and the Israelites could make a bee line across the country, for they were wandering four hundred years; and God was teaching them all the while, he never told them that he had them playing the stupids, or they would not have done as he wanted them, he could guide them where he willed them to go, but they never doubted him when that cloud was there, and why, because it was a covenant between them, then will you permit me to make a covenant with you; I guess not as the Yanks have it, you are too smart for even the boastful American, he would run should I come down to him in a fiery pillar; and I would be left all by myself, yet he could understand me did I call him up to me, and show him how to make that pillar, and he would appreciate me too, for the American is a genius common only in his own country, abroad he far excels all that come in his way, and why should he not know how to seam a cloud together; his very manner enables him to seam his soul into halves, for he looks to his own character first, and this is the great thieving propensity common to man; for he gets this from the clouds they gather in together, for it is his natural constitution to mellow the wind, and drop a dish of cotton into a yarn; this is the way to spin a yarn; by picking up the ends first and then placing them together so as they knit, now you have it the wind knits the clouds together, and by fanning the air by compression you have discovered the art of making a cloud; now assuming that a gust of air came and blew the pillar off Moses' tabernacle, it would take just a movement of the air to move that wind in an opposite direction; for the essence of life is no more good once it is cut, by the effluvia of mould, and this phosphorescence is rare stuff for pitching the wind either back or forward, so that a host of spirits can take the wind in any direction they choose; you may laugh and think I am joking, but it is spirit power that handles all these forces, and it will be shown much greater hereafter, than it has been in the past, you are quite just in saying that wind is there from some cause well so it is, it is the primary offset of all

there is; It is first got by the essence of light on air, and then it
is ripened into a trance-metallic attitude by the connection with
gasogine which rises from the outer edges of manure; heaped
up there by the elements of cancuthercul, it is commonly termed
the affection of nature, which are to be found in all things distinct or otherwise, therefore you seldom seem to get it in a gift
of explanatory proper; therefore it must be mildew in its first
stages, and then it comes from that to lice or openings in the
tomb, which raises up the dead to life, you see I have brought
you face to face again with dead atoms, clothed in nothing, yet
they came to life in a natural way, and as you follow me farther
on in my career of dissection you will find me always throwing
away the useless, and picking up the germinated dead: What
you call nothing is just what I find to be the exact necessity of
this self-establishing whole: I have been very careful to avoid
any contact with the life we lead in heaven, except to show you
our government in its theoretical way of causing crimes to be
committed for the benefit of example, etc.; now I want to show
you that the middle course is to bring nature to its highest
gravitation, by the best method known; and that will be found
essential and quite right too, for as man remoulds, he wants
something to entertain him, and he has to be kept employed still
after his departure from his material surroundings; therefore he
is bound to choose some occupation other than being a groom or
a mountebank, you find him hard at work on the other side, just
the same as he was, in the body; only this time he is working for
any way that is explained to him, he does not get off and go his
own road as you call it, his actions are under surveillance; and
he will have his thoughts led about on a string, not connected
by his own external appendage, as you seem to think yours are,
his are caught in a government trap, and they are sent round at
will by the artful instructors, who have traversed this wide universe many centuries before; and they are under the regime of
others who went on before them; so you have caught onto a
string at the tail-end as it has been made plain to you; now I
want to show you something that I have been calculating upon
doing through you, and that is to add one more string to that

great line, and it is clear profit, for it can be demonstrated in one single stroke of the pen, and that is this, we want to cut the string in two halves; and you take the one part and I will manipulate the other; you have the first string, and I have the second; now your string is cut before mine, for you hold the beginning, now who holds heaven and hell apart, you do clearly; and I must make you see this, or I shall be compelled to blind your eyesight still more till you have caught the right theory of what is wanted of you, now just take for instance your own common theory; and when you hear it from your own common platforms, coming from those who are able to talk spiritualism by the yard to you, and they get up a story of the few grains of wheat, it is quite logical in its way, and you seem to wonder about it, well now let me talk to you on this little subject from my point of view; you sow a field with wheat, and the field is clean, yet there does spring up some tares in that field, the ancients say that the serpent in man did come through that wheat field and sow the seed of dissension, commonly known as the grab of the devil; now I don't put it in that form, it is the coward who sowed the seed of evil, for he is afraid of his own inferiority, and he dared not look at God in the face, and say why, did those tares spring up in that clean field of wheat, you see where I strike the ancient between his back and his front, he was a coward, and there has not been anything except cowards ever since, you see me explain that phenomena, it is as the soap upon glue, it is the effluvia off the ground, that causes the change in the wheat, it is the essence in its entirety, that grows the glue, and the essence together, and makes a passive discord, between the wheat, and the mildew, it gives to the one, and takes away from the other, and will leave a distinct difference, for it is in accordance with nature, I want you to take a sheaf of oats, in one hand, and a sheaf of barley in the other, the one is classed as the oats, and the other is found with hair on the end, why so, because the ground did design it, for the barley was carried off in the noonday sun, and it went into the sun by its essence, and it was driven through the interior of the sun, and then it came down at midnight in a fall of dew, and it propagated in another climate, and this time it grew with-

out any hair, and why because it had a distinct round invisible
shape, and was through time and changes passed along under
the rays of the sun, and from the essence forming through its
revolutionary course driven round inside the sun, till it was
emaciated, and thrown out at the tail end of the sun which is the
moon, and it has always been the call of essence, to be distributed through the outer edges, by constant pressure, that is caused
through the overloading of the sun, which has to be dislodged,
every night, just as the sun has to be fed each day, now you are
awfully smart, why didn't you find this out before, and not allow
the old infidel to give you a black eye; He, has many a one
to give you yet, for that imprisonment in jail for trying to
explàin reason to you; you may suffer his ignorance, but you
have got to be put in order, before he forgets that insult, and
though ten times ten shall say he is wrong, still he will convince
the world of the errors they have made, and I say it again, you
dare to imprison any medium: that I have the power over for
just and equitable causes, and I will stretch the neck of time but
you shall suffer for your misplaced folly; you are here but I am
all powerful now, and you may kill those I love but you shan't
escape though ten thousand held you by the hand, you are as wax
in my hands in heaven, and I will do to those of them who injure
me as I would to him I love, keep the one I promised justice to,
by my aid, to wreak vengeance on them I hate, Tom never fails
—you mark my words well; for I can in majestic form deliver
judgment as the prince of hate, you love my instrument, and
your path is plain, I will guide you and instruct you, and I will
lift you ahead of man by the generations unaccountable, you are
the very picture of misery now after death, I will make you
rejoice as though you were seated at your marriage breakfast;
and now it is plain, that I have you with me, for I have explained
many of your mysteries away, and you have only got to trust
me, and I shall make all the rest, as clear, as the first blush, on
the maiden you call wife for the first time; she hears that ominous
word, she sends the glow of health vibrating through her honest
form, and you know she is pleased with an appendage, which is
the rights of all honored of her form, I want to show you by

this that I am not mischievous, but I have an object to bear out;
and in order that I may fully bear this point to its ultimate issue,
it must be dealt on a throw of sentiment, you see the maiden
blush at that faultless word, then let her know the reason why, it
is right and proper that she should have her pleasure gratified,
and she is the one who ought to know, why, she does thus blush-
ing contest the frame of her cortege; she sends back to them a
message of gladness, that is more fruitful of good, than ever your
vain outer glow of compliments can ever enhance her value; now
you see that her body is under the protection of an honest
power, who reiterates those sentiments, and say to each other we
may trust her now, she has proven; for in that simple blush there
is the pride of vanity displayed, she is honored, and we have
seen it from our side of life, and we judge her according to those
who have brought her scathless to the altar, and she is a favorite
with the assemblage, for they all touch the cord of each other,
and it is signalized through the assemblage, that mine hostess is
worthy of her court, and she is the gem of the hour in consequence; But the fame of the one who takes the matter without
consideration is the one we seek to destroy, for she hath shown,
that man is a commoner class of humanity and is more than ever
to be pitied for making such a common thing his better half; his
name is coupled with an actress, who sees men only for her comfort, and it is thus with the two kinds of wheat, the one is black,
and the other is white, it shines of two odors, the maiden who
blushes is the white bread, her life has kissed the Sun who
came and spared her name by a kiss of gladness; the other is
the one bears false fruit, she came with a cold glassy eye, and
had no cheek turned toward the glow of welcome, her hide was
tough, and it seasoned oddly beside that glowing bliss, it was
caused through an inferior assembly, and never could turn back
again and feel that pressure of pleasure, her eye did not know
what glowing meant, her soul does not see the rhetoric force of
nature, and she is a withered flower from that day forever, and
why should she be the doom of descension, for she had this bad
influence round her, which you must understand is life eternally;
and it kept on saying to her don't faint, or do anything absurd,

yet they held back from her the very natural consent of a natural glow; and thus she became morbid from that hour to the day
of her departure to eternity; and will always be the black sheep,
wherever she wanders, for it's this that made her the black sheep,
she was moulded, as the wheat, and when she germinated, the
other beside her was the favored of the sun's rays, one was
coming forth on the dull and shady side of the essence, whilst
the other one did fall more fortunate, and arose up first, and
came with a glowing, that pregnated in philoprogenitiveness; and
was taken aloft, in a sooner attentiveness; whilst the second bride came on the shady side, and had lost the glow, for
it did not strike the second one alike, and was weaker, and had
no vim left; its gorging had been satisfied by its essential requirements, therefore it could not be as good, as the first and favored
root, and in consequence, it had to stand behind and seep out an
existence on the cord, that hung behind; therefore it is shown
that a stone on the back part, in coming through the surface, is
invariably dun-colored, for why is it thus, because it has left the
heart, and is crawling slowly out to be warned by its creator, and
it becomes better looking after the Sun has looked upon it favorably a couple of days, and a man who should help his stone
ought to make her sit on his lap, till she did feel the rays of
moisture from the essence of his manly bosom; thus striking out
that cold stone which had settled round her cord, and made her
a sting for a hard-natured influence; Now you want me to explain
this hard circumstance a little further, it is this wise a certainty,
that a man can't see very far, and he never did know much, therefore it is a little doubtful whether he can be made to know what
all of this does mean, it is hard to find out how much you folks;
would really appreciate, a common theory; for it is after all but a
very simple thing that you can not comprehend; and I have got
to explain it in so many different fashions, that it might bewilder
some common journalist's ideas; He is of course a magistrate
in his theory, and he is a judge in his capacity, but he never
knew why he became a journalist, and this is what I am going to
knock him over with; He, says he has been to school, and
learned the art, well who was the first one who attempted jour-

nalism, why, anybody knows it was our great prophet Moses; when he did that perish for forty days, and forty nights in the mountain of Sinai, well he was taught by God, and no school taught our God, according to the learning of Moses; now I want to draw your attention to the fact, that Moses had a good thing to do, when he did that first journal business; he only laid there on the broad of his back, and never did that writing at all: It was done by the instrument known as metallic structure, or in other words it fell from the clouds, that surrounded that mountain, and not by the hands of anything supernatural at all, you think may be that I am off my base, but I can explain it quite well, Moses was an out and out Medium, and he could be dealt with in any way that it was thought best to get at the Israelites; so we can not now dispute his passion for his God, when he went into the Mountain, knowing that God was to deal with him as he thought fit, and he allowed this God to entrance him, and afterward the whole thing is no trouble, for he could use Moses just as he pleased and there was no one to stop him, for Moses, had given the necessary consent, by going there; you seem to think I am going to reveal something extraordinary, but that is not true, it is all a complete theory and practical test, nothing else in the world, Moses was fed by essence, and had the breath of life poured into him, by suction, for as the spirit worked on Moses, he never allowed him to breathe more at one time than another, and that held him just the same from one day to another, and this is the true doctrine of self discovery, the Moon does not breathe at all, neither does the Sun go on at all without inhaling and redistributing; now Moses was held by a conflux of ether, his sides were perched upon the entrance of his hips, and he was propelled to motion by a conflict between the air and a fluid called the ethereal fluid of Genesis; that is where the book begins, and it is a fluid common in the heavens; to do whatever spirits desire, it can be used for the flow of good or evil, and it is an atmospheric contact, that may be dealt with to sustain life without injury, or it can be adulterated from this to a seed, and grown from a form, that is the way to procure a conflux common on the eve of dis-

aster, it can be brought to produce visions, and it can be used
for a different purpose altogether, it may starch the essence so
as to produce rigidness; and in this latter form you may hold a
body for any number of days, I shall not commit myself to
any specific period; for I am able to enlighten you on this
subject further, you are to me a specimen, and I have nothing
to do with you as a man, when I get after you in a theoretical
sense; so you see now that I am going to show you how God
did hold Moses, and commit that first piece of journalism to a
fact; He did it by the essence of Moses' body; and that was
all that it was necessary for him to use; you can not describe
it any better; though you should take your life over it, I want
to add, that it is a good point to note this, for you may have all
that is noble in heaven brought down to earth by this process;
I want to come right at you journalists, and sow you up in
your own cloth, for you never did write the first article on earth,
and it was not yours either, for it was written in heaven before
ever Moses went up into the mountain, and I mean to go on to
claim that you have nothing on earth that is not fully completed
in heaven, before it is handed down to you: I am just as
capable of showing you one process as another, and when you
want to have the whole of heaven brought down in drawing or
sculpture, it can be done, without any difficulty; therefore you
must be kind to our instruments; and I shall have you learned
in all the arts, that your great-great-grandchildren will find out
for themselves in the centuries to follow; now you may take
this to heart, and have your footing fairly established before
ever you leave this earth, and you can come back and tell your
children how to behave, so as not to incur the displeasure of
the Gods who govern heaven, now I am ready to proceed with
more knowledge; There are no means where you have the
right to dictate terms to your fathers in heaven; but you can
be shown how they desire you to move in order that you may
be fruitful and happy, this is the blessing you want instead of
an empty flow of words; not as the prophet Hesiah has shown
you how good Jacob was to his offspring; but to lift you off
that style of deceit, and make you face the golden treasure

knowledge; what was the blessing to be in the days that followed; why, Jacob served his apprenticeship for Rachel, and then he was met by the discomfiture that his mother had made Esau to suffer; therefore you see there what I am telling you is the government of heaven; God said to Rebekah I will that you deceive the good husband of your bosom, and make Jacob appear as Esau, that is he shall have the blessing that belongs to Esau by rights, so you may kill the venison, of which Isaac is so very fond, and you may secure the blessing for thy favorite, by the subtilty of the other that I have penetrated thy mind, now what God did to Rebekah, he was quite well able to take the same method, and penetrate the mind of Laban her brother, therefore he did what his government had wished, and that was to show Jacob as an example to the world, forever; therefore that when Laban saw the fruitfulness of Jacob, it was but a freak of God to show him how he might sit upon Jacob, and make him serve other seven years for Rachel, and thus it was no miracle at all, only the doctrine of the government in heaven, which said I will make Jacob the head of your constitution on earth, and that is the examples which you must prostitute on him, so as to show the examples which have always been our golden rule, before we can reduce the heathen mind to comprehension; your fault is this, you dare not take upon yourselves the thoughts, which are constantly before you, there is the point, that has always been your trouble, for you have hold of the proper thoughts, you do make enough laws of example, but you don't know how to keep from those examples; that is where you get wrong for every time you pick a hole in this religious code, you have caught on to the fact, that there is a screw loose somewhere: well now I only desire to show you how to tighten that screw, and that is by adopting the plan that was lost through an inadvertency of Jacob's, and that was to omit to have an agreement to the following effect, "and that is, I am to serve Laban for seven years for Rachel, and that then he gives her to me," or he may defaulting give me all that he hath; this is the agreement which Jacob was erring in his own astuteness; and when a man does his duty, let the one he serves be bound to carry out that which he has made agreement for, and you will find that this law is to be amended so as to read thus: I will bind myself to thee as thy servant, till I have fulfilled thy contract, and as thy servant I am thy God, for as thee asked, so shall it be given unto thee, but when thou gets, that which thou asked, it shall be proven that the laborer was the worthiest of the two; for as he did complete his contract, he was no more thy servant, but to all men alike he had dealt honestly by thee, for his contract was complete; therefore you have no right to call him laborer any further, for he is thy equal, and it is to be given to him that did fairly earn that which he so agreed for, or the defaulter on either side is to be strewn to waste, and it is accordingly to be given to either him who deals as he so agrees, or faultless one, and the other has to be stripped of all that he hath, this is the missing link, and it can be constructed so as each shall be found faultless, and otherwise it is an example, which is equivalent to God himself, there is the link of this chain, which has been a strong fault, and was the defaulting sting of Cain; your grandsires worked their government wrong at the beginning, for they did not in righteousness cause good feeling to exist, and when they set up this primary system of example, it was not covenantly agreed, for the one side might shuffle,' whilst the other had to be true or fail entirely to come out at all on a just basis; now you have to look at Cain and Abel, the one was favored by nature, and was loved by God, he had the sheepfold, and he dealt in a fair way, for God drew him to the sunny parts, where the verdure is great and luscious, and his sheep grew in abundance; whereas his brother Cain was an ill-favored one, and he had his occupation drawn for him from the first, his size had been stunted, for he grew on the shady side of nature, and he held his hatred to the earth, for his mother had been prostituted by an evil thought, while she carried that man; by his conduct in life afterward it is plainly visible, he thought of the ground, and he was always turning it toward the Sun, for he knew instinctively that it was all it craved for, was the light and life of that brilliant radiance to make it perfect, and he battled and struggled with nature all to no purpose, he never could keep up

with his brother Abel, because he had been an offshoot continually, and he was always on the dark side of everything, and
all on account of the beginning, Abel had grown on the side of
sunshine always, therefore he was never at home at ease, unless
he basked in the Sun, and his sheep browsing in the enjoyment of
the same luxury, he could not bear the raw cold side of the mountain, for his sight would not permit him to look that way, and he
felt the warm glow of the hillside because he had grown on that
side, when he had been cast adrift by the Sun; in some thousands
of years before that time of his herdsmanship; you may take the
same theory for an illustration of the way that Cain behaved,
and you will find that I am the nearest to ingenuity, that man
has ever grown, and when you take the time of Cain's first
crime, it will be advanced against my theory that he was propelled to his action of murder by the one great power, that governs us all; that is the hand that picks no stone up at all, but
does his work in an unseen way, known by the hand of the great
giver of light, and it can be brought against me, that it was
caused through the power of the subtilty of those who wished
to produce an example, but I am fortified against all of these
theories, and will calm your thoughts in a more ingenious method;
that is, it is not for Cain, but for the whole of humanity, and that
is this; before man there were mountains made, and on those
mountains, there are two sidlings, the one sidling is a steep
grade, and on the other it is not quite as steep, but either sidling will precipitate you down the breast of that hill, well the
one is steeper than the other, and it is on the steep sidling that I
will prove you to have grown Cain, and on the smooth side you
grew Abel, the one next to the south, was the place where the
essence fell out of the Moon, that propagated Cain; and on the
north did the essence fall from the Moon that propagated Abel;
now these two in that start were herbs, but after they became
men and women, they never got the better of that beginning,
and will always have a dark cold side, and a bright and cheerful
one, now it is quite an easy matter to prove this part of life, for
as Cain killed Abel, he held in his bosom the trust of no accessible charge, he feared his God, but he had a duty to perform,

and he failed, for he could not do what was in his mind; for he
had no way of accomplishing that which was contrary to nature,
his thoughts were to manipulate that barren land, and make it
more productive than his brother could do with his sheep, I want
you to note well what I am saying for I am going to help you to
the right cause, which will benefit you forever, and that is this
plain fact, whilst the goats did feed upon the mountain side, it
was fine weather on the top, and yet they did not like it there so
well as though it were down in the little hollows, that are on the
northeast side, for the rain falls on that side more like dew, it is
finer, and is more like essence, than it does on the other quarters,
for I shall show you that on the southeast corner it comes with
a colder blast, for in the Sun there are as many divisions; as the
body of a man has, and it is through his organism, that a cold
and a sequel has to be driven, that is his many pores, are shut up
till some heat is made to develop them, and he can't always see
these things, for he never knew why his skin had so many little
holes, till he became enlightened by natural causes; and he ought
to think twice before he has gone to the extreme idea, that a
man can drink water, and not have it back again through a
screen, don't you see that you can take a dose of liquor to-night,
and to-morrow it has generated to what you might say is steam
and gas mixed: There is the theory, that you have a right to
explain, why is it that man has two compositions pouring out of
his skin, at the same time: I will tell you because you could not
find it very conveniently yourself; the mind is one machine, and
the bowels includes the machine that works the belly, into a
heaving motion, thus it will readily be told, that there are more
tubes inaccessible, than the interior of the mind which has no
nocturnal evolution: therefore you see the motion in the pit of
the stomach, and you leave the brains alone, well it is very near
a climax, for you are doing a constitutional work with the
bowels, yet you have not understood, that it is driven by air,
and not by anything else; therefore its motive power is not
attached to the body, at all; only an element, that draws in and
out, so does your hide, and your hide is porous, just the same as
your lungs are, so you still have got to be made perfect, by the

hand of time, for there is no necessity of man wearing out and in together, he can be made without any holes in his skin, but he must not go on according to a natural theory, for he would soon become in a state of putrefaction; did he live without the natural inflow, and outgoing, but that is not what I am trying to show you, it is this: my time is devoted to my fellow-man, and I must either show him all that is, or he can't believe, and that is why I am drawing him after me all round the whole entirety; so you see that it is not the object of our theoretical views; but it is the way to convince man, by taking him right through the labyrinths of nature to prove him capable is what you call producing the God, and not making him run away when he has clasped the corn, that will produce his column of strength; there is the benefit of throwing away the old worn-out ground, and going to bind the corn in a new pasture, that grew on the southeast sidling of this mountain, it does grow there, and it is longer to ripen, and when it is grown, there may be more of it, it is harder to thrash, and has tougher straw, and is not so mealy, it wants some other grain mixing to it, before it is made into flour, it is a starchy kind of wheat, there is no mellow in it, for it grew on the southeast corner of that mountain, and it is hard to grist, for it is soapy, and sticks to the millstones, there you have the manure from the moon, for it falls in cold congealed clumps, and does not rest on the mountain side, where the Sun shines perpetually; the Sun would lap it up again, and make it over again, causing it to be brought into a finer grade the next time, thus distilling it into a more beneficial manure, and sowing it in some other part, on the second or third time, and on each occasion of its period of progenitiveness; it would come into a different stage of perfection; therefore that any number of times would all have the effect of changing it to some other species of corn, till at last it becomes a formed essence, and then the wind and the Sun glowing together has made it into a moving mass, to be fed by the breath of life; so you see that I am not afraid of any of your artists, I have been to blame in the past, for I never could keep my mediums from reading books, and this one is not very apt to break away, until I leave him for a few moments, then he is watched closely by some of our friends, this is the only way to get at a medium, by keeping them off the old track, and making a new road to travel over; you see how necessary it is to give you the genuine truth, by keeping out of the old road, and getting along on a new plan, for did you work out the old plan first, and then come to the new: why for a certainty it would misguide you always, now I want to exclaim, for I have been experimenting for years with mediums, and I can't get them to drop the old ideas, they always want to go and visit some one else, or they want to be after some other medium's guide; I will say that a soul who is never satisfied is as the wheat coming through the Moon a great number of times, it becomes so perfect that you have got to hold it up to a magnifying glass, to find it; for it has changed so much, that it has become an oat; and when the essence is destroyed of that oat, it leaves a hair, which is part of a tribe, that does not belong to the oat family, and must go on again into essence, and bring forth another essence, this time it is a black oat, that has sown itself on the face of the earth, and why a black oat, for it did die on the surface of the ground, and was buried, and out of that burial there sprang an unclean kind, for it had no conditions to help it this time, and the way it became black was through its face being to the Sun, when it has an outside shell; that came off by the burning Sun, for the rays of the Sun does strike two ways, one is the side to the cold, and the other has the warm side, now you see that a hair is very fine, and in consequence, it is only small, and can be reached from both sides by the power of the Sun in its greed for essence, it must draw out the filth from underneath the hair, and in so doing it will grasp the corner that has the nearest thorns on its end; for the thorns are grabbed by all as the mesmeric charm; but you have erred my friends, there is an error right here, the thorn is the benefit, and not the clean end; there are many who shy clear of the thorny end, but I say you are all at sea over this, your maker is extravagantly eager to have the thorny end approach first, and I can't explain it better than to allude to my instrument again, he is willing to accept the inevitable, he knows he has got no thoughts

like these of his own, and he agrees to work out my problem;
providing that I make his as secure as he wants it done, now
there is that about his, that will take a mountain to move him to
the top, and I don't know whether he causes me more art or
what it is; but you see that he is doing the struggle of nature to
perfection, for he is able to seam a soul together, without the aid
of God; And this is what no living being has ever done before on
either earth or yet is it known to God, for he never did any work
uch as this is through any instrument he ever used; now I will tell
you that a mind such as this, is the very purest corn that ever grew,
and I know when I touch him that he feels like the governor of
heaven, for he can direct as also can he seam those directions
together, for as he does, he has that manifest faith in me, that he
does not proceed till I say you are right, and when he is not certain, it is no good to try and make him move, for he is like an
ass, in an instant, he is sitting down on the thorns: And you
have him to thank as well as me, for he could not be made to
take the thorn in his right hand; when it should go in at the left,
and herein lies a mystery, his soul is divided into two, one is as
black as the dungeons of hades: and the other is as white as snow;
His heart is as pure as gold, and his kindness is sublime; but his
mind is fallen where there is no God in heaven that would not
make him move a peg unless it was through a clean opening, and
the summer-sun has tanned his face on neither side, it is whole
on either side, there are no half-measures in his life, his kindness is
superior to any I ever saw; and his mad passion for revenge is
exactly the opposite; that hate is his canker-worm, and that there
we hold him in awe, for it is plain to us all; that any deception
on our part, is going to ruin our cause entirely, and we can
never again reach you on earth, by this same instrument: For he
will either have us clear ourselves by stratagem, or he is ready to
abandon our cause, there is the mystery of the black wheat
explained, his soul is white on one side, and it is as black as hades
on the other; now have you understood the theory, his eye is
watching me now like a hawk, I have to press my strength to its
utmost capacity, for I have gone further than he considers I
have the right, and he is fighting me with an irresistible power,

his soul is turning round on its axis, and I am annihilated; but
he is stilled by this confession, and I still keep my superior antag-
onist in the squirm of a fleshy creeping sensation; you have my
theory, it is the live atoms that creep over the dead, that causes
animation; and the Sun is the live atom, and the wind does its
duty as the perpetrator of God in his entirety; now you have
caught my soul in its true form, mine is a combustion of electricity inculcated with an atom of hydrogen, it sounds in two
halves, for it concentrates by elocution, and is vibrated back to
essence, like the light of darkness passing through the currents
of hate and fury, mine is nocturnally jealous of every other Jonah
that ever lived, and I can't tell how he swallowed the fish, but I
do know that God did not make that fish, for it is too big, for
the essence of the sea to have made in those times, and God was
not a bit more able then, than he is at the present period, and I
think that to straighten out the coiled web you could not do any
harm by sneaking in a contrary version, as I have placed it; with
this proviso, and that is this, in the whole of Jonah the prophet's
story, there is nothing remarkable, and that was an outer pitch,
it fell by the roadway, and grew no more of that character, and
we must patch it up as best as we can, by saying that as Jonah
has eaten of the famous fruit, I must prepare a little salt for his
relish, and you won't think unkindly of me, when I show you how
the corn grew, that fed such a fine fish, you know by this that I am
going to pitch Mr. Jonah overboard, for I am into that whale of his
already, and you know the sea won't dry up till I have explained
how it grew, therefore we must tackle Mr. Jonah by keeping on
a hook for a fish to snatch the bait from, and as the sea is a torrent, that is mightily constructed, and is the flowing together
of many atoms, it is only natural that you don't believe in a
whole story, when there are any bites left out; now I want
you to look at these little pieces of fish, that grow in the
ocean, and see whether you don't think that they have a right,
to be classed as living material, well now you think that a fishy
substance, is not very material, well you are wrong my friends,
there is the whole thing itself over again, it is material and
atoms, nocturnally divided, and that is the gas escaping from

17

the mountains has left a coloring behind it, which does not exist anywhere in the heavens, it is the essence of salt, which is fetched out of the hills through their prefillousness in propagating gravel, and this is done through the surface of the hills being decayed by essence thrown out of the moon, by its having corroded in its interior deformity, it is by this process, that lime forms, by the revolving stone of time, sweeping off the adhesive pieces, and they fall with the essence of rain dropping through both the stars and the moon, now you see that I am going to begin to count the stars in again, for the last time we peeped at them was for the purpose of taking poor Patsy home off a drunk, and he will feel quite proud, when I say that it is an old house that does not leak for the want of a new thatching, but he shall not go on forever without knowing why Father Doolan, never showed up again after he walked across purgatory, and never saw any Murphys there, well I am not going to say much about the Doolans or the Murphys; but everybody knows that a finish is nothing, without the Irishman is there; so I don't want to leave a good man out, when I have a chance of piloting him in; and you know that an Irishman is always welcomed wherever he goes, because it is a roaring welcome he gives you opposite the coast of Flanders; his home is upon the rocks; and his heart is burning to see, the sea; for he never knew till now, why his throat was always wet, when it should be dry, and his coat it used to be a long one, before the English cut it off, and they fixed poor Pat, when he gauged his eye by the soft summer sky; you see I am writing fully of my friend the Irishman, for his whole life is but a span, since he crossed the border-tan, and he used to be a fisherman's toy, for in the days that have gone back, his eyes were the same as that great whale that Jonah swallowed, his teeth didn't stick in, and that is the way he missed being that big fish, his toes grew so short, and his eyes were protruding so far, that they never swam without catching a grain of salt on his tail, and in time it became a fable, that the Sun won't shine on a striped pig, for it goes in at the finger ends, and blows holes through the eyes, thus, shows

the idea, that man was a fish at first, because he is not alive
to-day any more than he was then, has nothing to do with it, his
nose is meant to blow through, and his eyes are meant to
find salt water, his ears are the same as those little fossils commonly known as the gems off a hard surface, and are the back
part of the fin of a fish's ear, it moves back and front,
at a very curious gait, and it sinks into the sides at a very furious rate; then what is there that resembles man, why the
ancients are full of stories about how christians should get on,
but they never saw any fire in a man's eye, without speaking of
the devil has him, sure, well you see my friends that the fire in
the man's eye, is the essence of life, and it is here where you
came to get it from, there is the salt in italics, and there is the
rind in metallics, and there is the see in the eye; and there is the
fish in Jonah's belly, he blew it out, when he swallowed that great
fish, and you have got none of the same species left, because he
divided the spoil, and said as I am thou can not be, as you are,
I can not see; therefore you are the whale, that swallowed me:
And this is not bad for a beginning, you thought you had me,
but I am the fish, that never runs away, when anybody attacks
me, and I find that a fish that swims, can not be other than
a grave side of the stroke that plays his part, in the ancients'
side, you seem to think that I am a leading light, well who
did place the essence in my side, why the fish that swims is no
more fought, because he is the one who could skip the ocean did
he try, yet you see that I am a very fine specimen, and I
can do the whole business in one act, my size is just whatever
I choose to make it, and you can't hide me though you tried,
for I am of the essence of the sea; and you may try to blind
me, but you are no use to me, for I can both sides see: whilst
you are looking at the sea, I have your measure made, and
can ruin you or make you my divine star; you are quite hideous
enough, when I look upon your accents as they used to be, for
I am what they call the accents of another, and you shall soon
see why I am a tree; for in days gone by there is once in away
a curious serpent, it was caught in a log, and it could not get
free, it was awfully merry while tied to that tree; and just as

you see, it had many a spree, for coming along, on a wooden log is quite in tune with a very fine specimen of humanity, only you loose the log, and there is no sea-serpent there, well as a joke is a poke, I may as well tell you that a man is born in a great big tree, his sides are the roots, and his arms are the limbs, whilst his teeth are the essence off fruit, and his toe nails, are the creepers, that come on after they shoot: I want you to remember this, because I shall show you how it all comes to this after the beginning; you little know how easy it is to be taught once you know how, and as long as ever you keep off making up stories, it is quite easy to reach out, and fall on top of the truth, you are just as handy at picking fruit, as though you knew why it was made sour, that is you can count apples that are green by the sides they hold away from the Sun, and you can look at yourself in the glass, and fetch in a pair, because you stole the fruit out of Eden, why, because there was a pair, that did it; now I have got you, you thought I couldn't catch you, but it is down tail and run, I have mastered the whole of creation, and I will stick in a plum for every pair I can get; this is the way man grew first his eyes are the ends, that stick out, on the two stems; so I made you follow me into the very center didn't I, well you have found the core, and there is the beginning; not as the forefathers had it, that an apple came upon the head of a juniper, but as a head did appear, so must a center be entwined, in that very head, and as the Sun shines on that head, so will man appear to be the center of attraction, for he is the all-spoken creed of humanity, and he is the one gem, who has that power of saying I am he: Who dares dispute my power, I am the divine ruler to-day, and it was so at first, and it shall be ever so; God be my guide, as the good comes on after, and as the fruit is ripe, so shall my time be spent in the ripening of that which was my good propagator: And as heaven did see fit to entrust me with a commission, I will do my duty as the highest post of man to lift me, and as man to man I invite you one and all to meet me foot to foot, and knee to knee, and I say that there is not another man living to-day, who can outdo, or undo, your most devoted slave and guide the

world's old man Thomas Paine; I lived for this hour, and I have
reached the top, my path is founded upon a rock, and your
castles shall all bend the knee to the true doctrine of the
once famous "Infidel" who stood like the reed that waved in
the wind, his soul to his thoughts, and his eye upon heaven,
prayer after prayer he blurted out, show me my God what does
all this mean, and as the thoughts came flowing back wait and it
can all be made plain, I died with that thought pressing on my
burning temple; but never has that soul deserted me, he is here
beside me now, and us two have this work to finish for
you, and we intend that it shall be as complete as anything that
will ever be, for it is all the time drifting you on to a certain
proof, which will settle the question beyond dispute, and this is a
matter of magnitude, as it gives to man the advantage of knowing his hereafter, which is what he must study, as it is an eternal
bliss or an eternal torture for no one can tell how long, that may
be forever, or it may be of an indefinite period, it is as the fish
of the sea, you swim on always, always on the look out for some
little charm, that there is nothing to keep you from, yet the
nearer you get to the charm, it is still creeping on, and you don't
ever catch up to it, it is the same with us dear friends, I am
struggling on, trying to catch up, and I am always behind, for I
don't try my own wind, neither do I escape without being puffed
about by the elements, that come in contact with me; therefore
I have caught up to mankind many different ways, yet I never
had him made quite fast before, and I had to leap on him now,
or I should not have been able to do so now; so you see what
has made me patch him up so strong this time, is because I find
him trodden down by an infuriated fool, who has no thought but
sacrifice, and I am going to make him whip that same ass, for it
is balm to his soul, to know that heaven is going to attack hell,
and drive destruction with it; thus for two souls that have suffered you are to know all there is to learn, and I say you are to
have a cheap burial in the future, for in sin there is no offset
against the sinner, you must punish him here in hell or forever
suffer in hell, which way ever you do it is all one to me, I am
quite able to dirk the bosom of you all, now that I claim to have

a fellow-soul, who will beat any one at the cause and effect of
dead feathers, you thought I had got left, but no you see I am at
you again, I have found out a way of getting round an effect,
by springing a mine on top; that is the way to pull a string, by
searching out for the very shark that would bite, did he know
how to reach a surface, without getting seen himself: now it is
quite easy, for I have taken a dive down, below the alabaster,
and I find ivory there; how did that appear in man, why it is the
same as though you callou out a clay hole, by dripping fine
flour in, why the clay hardens because the Sun shines upon it,
and dries it up: Then the wind plays round about the clay, till
it grows quite hard, that has nothing to do with ivory, or a man's
bones you say at once; yet it is this wise, a man was amphibious,
and he dried in the rain, and that is how he sopped up the moisture, now don't you pull with me, and see that a clay hole is
porous, as your hide, then be careful how you dry in the dew off
heaven, for it is of this that you are made first, and as the night
throws down dew, does it not also cause the best fruit to grow
riper, I say you are as the season makes you, either ripe on one
side, or else you are a green peach bitter, your soul is a faultless
mould, or it is a sting off nature's great producer of good and
evil, the bad fruit is sour, for it does nothing right, and the
wholesome fruit is that which is produced, under favorable surrounding; and you can't tell why this is; well you have it now,
the sour fruit is that which grew, on the safe side of heaven, it
was pitched out, by the moon distilling it in a grievous condition,
she has always been waxy on one side, for you seam glue
together by nothing, then how do you get at the fault in the
Moon, she did make outside first, then why did she not do it
inside true blue, instead of having any green there; why it is
altogether too difficult for you to reach the Moon, while I can
pop in and out of her, just as I elect to do, this is why she
grows green fruit, her internal garbage pan, is filled with white
slime, and her external attitude is externally greater, than it is
on the other outside place, so she is driven in at the end, that
fetches up the green herbs, and casts them over the earth as it
drops through on its journey round the world, and thus it will

be shown, that a mind is a mixture, for it is taken on after the green had been deposited in the after ferment of the Sun; for the Sun drafts every single piece, and it is this, that makes a man so sour when you don't please him, his soul is soled together by the thoughts of a contrite spirit, and his very mind is mixed up, till it has so many different views, that it could not be very well defined did you take what comes out of it into actual facts, but you must go right behind, and take what goes into that mind first, or you can not ever find what that composition is; therefore you ought to look well at what I am saying, for I am going to show you how the mind is made, and this is about as much as you have any right to expect of any one gifted of God or otherwise; now do you know that a wandering mind is the fruits of an ill wind, it moves round and round, and there is no stopping place, for it has gone on a wrong turn, and this will be as I am showing it to you: the wind moves round till it takes a turn off by itself, and then it turns back, till it strikes that which is left, and in turning, it comes across the elements, that had bursted off before, and they were drifting off in space, and when they were hit again by the concussion of thought coming in contact, with the exact part that atoms followed on; why, you seem to have caught up with me, I have struck the cord, that drove the heavens together, for in that twirl, there arose a cloud, which gave life to its own account by concussion, and you see that I have mastered the idea of thought, it was done by concussion, and you have me bound hand and foot now: as I have given you the idea of what man came from; and that is the concussion of sound; now do you seem to take in what there is at all hazards left besides; no you are thirsty, and I must give you more drink, the skies were made from the combustion of the clouds, and not by any other power, for as the fleece shall knit together, then mortal man was soled together in the same way; and as the clouds gathered, so has the heavens been made, and as the access of the wind played upon that sky, so does the heavens get along, for the wind did blow a straight line in one particular direction, but when it rested, there was a cloud formed, for the seam had broken, and there was the wind hushed in sleep, and

when it awoke, it was yawning for more, and in yawning, it gave
place to a gust of atmospheric concussion, that engulfed the
soul of life, and breathed, it did not not do this at one cough,
nor at two, but after many attempts of puffing in and out, it gave
a greater and greater excavation; till at last it seamed a hole
clean through, and when it had gained this point, the Moon was
poked out, for there is the nose and face of a woman at the
entrance of this hole, and at the other end there is the face, of a
man, and he has got in his head a huge great big cannon, and he
can draw no end of water through his front end, but at the rear,
his sides are just as thick as the wind has had time to make
them: And the wind is still making, and rebuilding all along,
and you can see these freaks of nature every time you choose to
look for them; and not mind how they are made, till I show you,
your eyes are the very same as a hole in eternity, for you can
seam a cloud together, in the same method, and it is this way
we do all things, by the hand of time; it is easy for a man to
raise up a black cloud, against his fellow-man, for he had this
in his composition; and he was seamed together; and so was his
afterbirth; for you see that when the Sun got the upper hand,
she gave so many kicks to each and every cloud that came in her
way, that they were forced to shove off, and let no obstruction
appear near her; she became a roaring tigress, for she had been
cut off from her main affection; and was not allowed to keep any
of these clouds, that came to do her homage; for her mind had
got disturbed by the confluence of a seething mass of fire in her
belly; which is quite in accordance with nature; her lungs became
a fixture, by the constant drumming noise that kept on drawing
air in and out; and by the time that a hole was penetrated; she
was half full of wind, in consequence her sides have got on fire, and
she was set on fire, by the foul air, that filled her stomach; this
of course is a recognized fact by all our astrologers: they do
know, that a given quanity of gas in the bowels of the earth, will
explode and cause fire to commence, and in so doing it will produce a greater or lesser fire, as the wind should blow, so that
when the wind blows, it expands, and drives the fire through its
own cavity; thus you seem to gather in this theory, that a man

must be able to seam a flame of fire together; or make a mountain of fire; but this is not the theory, in which you can look upon this phenomena: for the Sun is lighted internally, and in consequence she is breathing out these fumes of gas and tariphine: at a very furious rate, well she is generating steam by enormous quantities; and she is furling her anchors at every point, she is shading her face, by a great big mouth, that presents a horrible noise, that comes pouring out of her like the wailing of a screeching woman, it makes dashes of desperation like the sisling of a sea lion, and it bellows like a mad bull, awful, is nothing to this terrific sound that emanates from the regions of the Sun; well now I have made you get interested in me, and I want to go on more rapidly, and will give you an idea of the moon, at his end of the business: He, is the factotum, that is being used as a dislodger, for he does this in a way, that has nothing at all extraordinary in it, except that he is covered with all the dirt, and is a pitiable looking fellow, his nose and mouth resemble a man crying, and he plagues himself by this attitude of getting very wet in his eye; which made us pity him many a time, as we pass him by; this face is awry, for it protrudes across the mouth of a cannon, and you would think that was a tissue of his thigh, that protrudes out in his nose, but it is nothing of the sort, his mouth is all cleaned at every stage, that comes round once in a new Moon, for this is what effects him most his eye is quite moist, by the end of the Moon, for it is cleaned by the sun firing her angry looks at his dirty face, and his mouth gets on fire, and it is all burned off, for the nose is white, with the acid and stuff that accumulates during the whole month, and it has to be wiped by something, so the noonday sun comes round, in its affectionate embrace, and sets fire to his majesty's nose, for the fact is plain as day, that the mouth is a dislodger, but the tongue is an escape valve, and the eyes are the places, where the raindrops fall from, so that his nose is a ventpipe, that has to be in order to be left open in case of excess; well now I want you to observe the lugs of a fig tree, and there you will see on the leaves the approach of a kind of skin, well this is the nearest resemblance to the wings of the Moon inside,

and when the moon has gone outside her twenty days run, she
will show a disposition to retract, and though you see those
great big lugs of hers retract, it is evident, that there is an
eternal change on the wing, for every time those wings flap back
into the solid rocks at the back, she changes her front attitude,
and the next time she opens up again, through the pressure of
this excess inside, which has to be dislodged; then you seem to
have seen this change, for she does not produce alike, and she
sifts a finer grade each time, for the fact comes plainly to your
senses; her eye is about closed, after the burning up of one
month's growth, and when it opens, it is stained with blood-
colored glassy looking seething ore, and it contains a streak of
grey, or may be white acid, well this acid is the first to make
force work, it brings about a color that looks like red sandstone,
but it really is the plague of a contrite spirit, for no sooner than
possible, it gets used to the air, then it takes fire from the Sun,
and away it burns till it has reduced this end of this gigantic
machine to its normal condition; well now you are very curious
to find out, what a curio is, well it is this; my man Friday as you
some times will call that strange substance you see upon the face
of the Moon is what I have got to explain to reach you in any
soft way of picking up the crumbs, and you know that to let
these fall upon a given crust, is the form in which to distill them
to grow anew; well now it is this, that a given space of time
elapses between each dropping, and in consequence: there is this
to be considered; your earth is watered by the stars as well as
the Moon, and out of these gas-jets, you seam an essence together,
that hovers round in shapely forms, till it becomes calloused;
therefore it has not been able to show its own form yet on the
stars, for they have not become large enough; there is the mystery of the man in the Moon, his soul life is oozing out, by constant pressure, till it actually shows signs of enlarging to such
an extent, that it has formed into an essence that contains a
complete fog of its own, which is different from any other live
matter, and is practically the inside skin of the Moon, which
grows outside the other causes; and this time it shows itself in
a kind of hide, which props up nothing; but just soles the fungus,

that is protruding, through this sheet of gas, which comes from
the interior of this immense giant: You see I am telling you
from a scientific basis, and you must judge of this skin as you
would of the rest of nature's requirements; therefore you will
find that I prepare the inference, and you must draw a common
sense conclusion, there are the various parts, of the Moon which
protrude, well it is a plain fact, that the Moon is a disloader, and
in disloading that it carries more loads, than one, and as I have
distinctly told you that a change takes place every period of the
Moon's disgorge, for the facts are clear, you never have two
things alike, because your propagators are increasing always, and
in consequence you can not have the same twice; now I have
given you the fallen crumbs, it is you or I for them, you can pick
them up, but I showed you where they dropped from, well you
just hold yours while I get mine from the next wagon trip, ah!
yours have diminished; and almost gone by the next appearance
of the wagon, well what did you do with them; why I have to
tell you, yours went back to the wagon, and I have got them in
this wagon load, and they are changed so much, that your own
essence is deceived in their looks: you come and pick them out
of my wagon load, it is my friends the good has always run off
with the bad, and my brothers and fine scholars I am going
to take you all upon my back, and carry you off again, and make
wiser truer, men of you: I see the way to make you all as happy
as the Sun, who rejects the bad and carries off the pure, heaven
reward her for this great work; (Amen): I am sure that you
will be just what I think, for I have been happy ever since I
found out, that my life was not a fault-finding soul, as they used
to say to me, when I asked for more gruel, they said I was never
satisfied, and I never did feel quite happy till I saw that they
were all wrong, and that I had reason to be dissatisfied with the
food they gave me, why, it was the essence that I am composed
of, that was always crying out, give me drink, give me milk, give
me meat, till I grow stouter; this is the craving of the Sun, she
is always hungry, and she only shines in summer, the Sun has got
no winter; because she swelled so as to round off all other points,
and she is happy only in sunny Italy always, her growth is rapid,

and she never tires; because she is full of the essence of life,
and before she breaks into another hay pasture, she dips her
beautiful face, in the sea of brine, it is on the edge, that she
says I want a pink cheek come kiss me quick I must hurry on,
or he will catch me on the next round, and it is this sweet pressure, that makes her leap round, she feels the night air, and she
slips her hand in, but it rebuilds another bound, her innocent
face, is caught for one precious instant only, and that is as it
faces the morning in a different climate: She did not make the
round bend, it was done for her by the confluescence of time,
but what she has a right to claim is the womanly pride
of getting away on ahead of man, and setting his shift
behind, for the fact is quite clear, her eyes are turned
sideways, when looking upon his disgraceful face; his nose
was not pretty enough, so he had to be shifted round to
pantry work, and I have to seek him out of all the dirty grime
that has been plastered over his sun-burned face, till I look at
his eye, it is impossible for me to take a theological view of
his quaint-looking nose, and say this is the man whom all mankind have given a good many sights at, but he always had his
eye on them, but they never yet knew what it was that developed
more wonders than one, and as for more fire in one man's eye,
you can never find, and this is why, his nose is set on the side;
and his teeth is just the same, they protrude outside of the edge-
rim, and are always holding on to the gas, as it escapes, this is
what we call the hammer-head, for it is like the nozzle of a great
big cart-wheel, it keeps turning round, and is constantly revolving round, thus you can see why we seam things together in an
oblong round fashion, here is where it is done first, for the
Moon is revolving round and round, and every time she drops
her cud, it is round for it is ground round by the constant
churning that it gets inside of the Sun and Moon together; now
you know why you always have things round; don't you seam a
hem round, then why don't you believe me, for you have nothing
that is any other way, till it is done by machinery, of a different
kind, and there is the round thing made, by the fashion of its
own maker, why; because you seam a round pan, in the first

place, by making a mould first, then you pour in the molten slag, and it comes out according to the shape you have made your mould, now don't you see that our Sun draws up the essence, by her heat, coming in contact, with the earth, and she draws in what she requires each twenty-four hours, and then she churns, for she can't hold it any longer; then the time it takes her mouth to become filled to overflowing, for she must not lift up her eye too far, for fear of letting down the safety-valve, on top of her own thigh; here is where I am going to claim that the Sun is a woman, her main features, are adjusted, so as to receive the exact courage, of a head, and prolonged gait of atmospheric essence, and she is seaming in her entire surface, the whole time it is going round, her nose is wet from morning to noon with a clear atmospheric moisture, and her teeth comb the air, like a weaver's dowel, all along the entire surface for thousands of miles outside the Sun, and she is filling her pan all the time with the cream of the earth, for her man Friday, is helping her to grab at everything that is good, he sprinkles his left hand on all nature, and with his right, he is serving out a magnificent shower of covering, that resembles the farm-yard in its autumn gathering of the accumulation of the summer; now I have sown the seed, it is for you to reap the corn, and when you seam my story together, you will have a proper idea of farming, and never before did man know the actual art in farming; His thoughts have been on colleges; but I say that a farmer who wants to grow hay, which means money, must study nature, and he must go according to the theoretical basis of farming, not place a slab-sided cow in the same fold with a queer-looking stag, it is not the one or is it yet the other, that does tempt me, I want them both round, no squeezed-up side-boards for me, give me the man or woman, with a round formation, it does not matter of all the weaklings, they shall be ground together as the Sun and Moon did propagate them, and as the summer seasons did develop them, well now what more have we got to talk about, your Moon and Sun are my property, they were mine to make known to man, and what right has any one man more than me with them: you say God is the ruler of all mankind, I

tell you that I am he who rules this Moon and Sun, for I can
stop it quicker than you can count, but you would not be
any the wiser did I do so; and you would not be told, that you
are my enemies, this is satisfaction to me, to tell you how an innocent man can face his foes, he came through that hell of flames,
with you all; and he is not going to sink the ship, that has
carried so many lives to eternity; now you even do not know
where you came from, though you have had the benefit of my
telling, so you must not be too anxious, and spoil all by any fit
of impatience; don't you believe me capable of telling you, well
it is all one to me, whether you know it or not, but I have time
now, and I could explain it, but I have a very great mind to
leave you without this finishing touch to man, only for the fact,
that you say I can't, or I would dearly like to mystify you
beyond your own perfect understanding of me in days gone by,
and that is the time, when they used to save the pieces, and
stew them up to give me my victuals off; well now it would be
quite fair for me to give you all a good stewing up, for you
know you deserve it, and Old Tom is hard-hearted enough to
practice this upon you too; should you play any tricks on his
man Friday, for as the lad who could not help himself to get
away from the black devils coming after him, he had to seek the
protection of his white brother; and you know the fable yarn,
of how Friday and his salvation castaway come on the heathens,
from behind those guns, and drove them to heaven in a starlight
element, you shall go the same road, does it mean mischief or
friendship this time, I will blow your earth into essence, or I will
be first from this day henceforward; now man mind thyself or
fall by the wayside, I have crept and crawled along, and I mean
business; it is knowledge to the world, or I die in the attempt,
you can choose between heaven or the blotting out of the whole
concern, as far as your earth goes, it can be swept to atoms in
the suggestions I am about to make, and you may think you are
dealing with God, but I distinctly tell you no, you are dealing
with Thomas Paine, who will drive this earth round at a greater
speed, and can lift heaven up higher, with one stroke of his ax;
but you are no more fit to dictate terms with me, than you are to

play pitch and toss with heaven, and why because I see all you do, or ever could do, whereas you are only clay in my hands, I can patch you up, to what I think is best; or I can blow the whole of eternity to seam a vein of fire, that will make a roasting-machine in hell that will strip the back of hades in the happening of one single day.   Now I am writing this because you are so precious ready with killing any one who understands the art of clairaudience; this is not the right word, but it is as you understand it, and you had better show me a proper welcome, before I do too much for you; I am not afraid of you, nothing of that sort is concerning me in the least, but when I feel my own coat is trembling beneath the body, that is used for this purpose, it is quite time for me to say to you, now it is not for me to come here, and say all this to you, and then you just wade in with knives, and butcher the body we are using; this is what I want to protect, it is not that I fear you; because you are powerless when attacking me; but you are always ready to kill my means of giving you wisdom; now it will be a black Friday, I promise you, should you kill my man, he is harmless to you, and you must not take his body, and that is all I have got to stipulate in this agreement, you may fright me through the papers or any way you choose; but you must draw the line outside of murdering my instrument or using violence against him; or I give you timely warning, that I do as I have said, and that is to open the upper half of the Sun, and drop it on you;   Now William Atkinson is the name of this my instrument, and I will divide the honor with him of showing you all there is to learn in the future, for he is now advanced so far that he can write more books in a quarter the space of time that it takes an ordinary author; so you see that you may have the advantages of his skill for the next twenty or thirty years may be at writing the works of heaven, and bring them down to man, in its full force and understanding, or you can blot out the past, which I am distinctly and expressly opposed to; I counsel a steady and careful supervision of the past, and I say the past has all been a benefit to man, and I desire it to be thoroughly understood that man is materially advanced now to what he was when those prophets came and wrote those works, of which we claim a supernatural Spirit God; and you must know that I could have impersonated God through my own instrument, and told you all there is to tell in this nineteenth century, or I could now make you believe that it is an imposition of God's own conscience; for I can twist you and turn you about as I have a wish to do, but then you would be still afraid, and that is not the way to be, you are cowards, for this reason, it is boldness that makes the man, and not fear, therefore you have to be made happy by the sense of knowledge, and no man can be wise who is afraid; therefore you have to be taught sense, or there never will be anything except fear in your composition: I want to take time by the forelock, and seam you and your conscience together, why, do we eat, sleep and talk, because you are the seamed essence of light, and you are the very picture of misery without this light; because you are not an entirely formed man, you are a something greater than what you think, you are the soldier of Christ, for you are all soldiers of the cross; there is the theory on which we must work together; I don't have to tell people, that I despise the work of God, he is good; that is all my friends; he has done for you, that which you are unable to do for yourselves; and I will show you distinctly why you can't be all in one, because he did not know to reach you, that it is the point that you have gained in this last two thousand years, he has been just the same true God to you, only he never could reach you right; therefore he is now as much your God, as he ever was, and he is quite willing to help you; now then you need not come out and say what does this blasphemer know of God, he can't tell us we have no need with the Bible, I say distinctly that is more need of that Bible now, than there ever has been, for it is as clear as the atmospheric breath; that a history such as that is by far the best guide you can keep, till your knowledge becomes founded on a theory, that will not admit of mistake, and when you have found the real article, it is then plenty soon enough, to say we know all, and not till then; your Bible is worked from an entirely different method to what the present author is compiling his; and he is dividing his up in such forms as to insure a correct deliverance; therefore you must not condemn too suspiciously; it may be prudent to see the next work, before doing anything in the way of condemning: A beautiful axiom is to stand steady like the marble oak, it glistens in the noonday sun, and comes on as steady as the crested waves of time, no changes in an instant for it, it cleaves back to God, that which God hath, and it remoulds anew, and propagates a wedge, that seems harder to believe than the hand of time, you may take this little instance of mine, as a true sentiment from me, and believe me well and truly yours, I am soft in my expressions, but you forgive me as the hand of time rolls by; there never was a more radical mind than mine; but I say to you to-day, that I will wield the fortunes of this kind-hearted man, or forever bemoan the fate of a black oat, for as the hand that lifts the golden treasure overhead, his mind is not mad, it is the torments of his soul that drove him to the crime of separating his thoughts with one who never loved or cared a scrap for all his helping hand, and as though not content with tearing his home to atoms, she did in full vent her spite upon this head, by unloosening her dragon friend, now, as though she is not content, her fiendish vengeance is wreaked upon some other head, and that a boy of his: I will not despoil my work with such as she, may heaven in its bounteous turmoil recoil upon her head, and in the sinner's home make her bed: I have sought in vain for an instrument, till I have found the one, who can make my work as clear as the turn of a savage beast at bay; you know what this is, it is the way to define power, by taking an accursed one, and driving him until there is no possibility of escape, then he is bound to fight or die, and before he dies; as the saying goes, he will throw back his horns, and make one supreme effort this time it will be proven who is the divine, and who the scoundrel: I want you to note well what I am saying, for in this little speech hides a mystery, that shall go forth to man as the history of the mind I now guide, and it is for you all to stand apart, and see the power of heaven in its agony, strike hell; you may hope on my friends, you will see a blow struck at hell, which will convince you that there is a power that can reach the wrong-doer, from our side of

18

life, I know you are as unbelieving as you were in the days of
our Calvary, but you shall know that in that day, a man's mind
had not the stretch and scope of the present time, and as they
worked wonders, so can the present hour be as wonderful, now
don't imagine, that it is a course of lightning treatment, that is
to be played upon you, but another mode of warfare entirely,
it is to be stratagem against hell's own weapons, that is all
my friends, you are to be shown that stratagem is the gift
of an overwhelming power, and it is by the effect of ether on
the mind, now you see I have told you what my appliance is,
and shown you what I am going to do; and when you have displayed not hurtful signs of breaking loose, I will show you how
to use the ether, it is quite easy for you to use this ether in an
unskilled way, but you are powerless to use it to the advantages,
that I make of my method: I don't want to keep knowledge
from you, I only want to show you what can be accomplished;
then I am willing to give up my proofs; but you must not come
forward and rob and plunder, that is not what I am here for, I
could annihilate you, much quicker than a minute, did I so
desire to; but that is not my object, my pet scheme would be all
frustrated, did I take and dose my men with an overdose, there
is my own thoughts to be considered, and I don't want to hurt
any one, it is no use my temper becoming enchained, and then
breaking loose, I can treat you fairly, and then win without any
effort, but you must respect me as I do you, and as my hand
waves you knowledge common sense, and the happiness; which is
all the Godliness you have any right to; then you must not
interfere with my agent, or it is no use me timing my own court
without a fright, as your court is yours, so is mine made according to the knowledge of sense, and when you ask for grace, or
time to make your pleadings, I grant you all this, but I won't
wait on you, when you are preparing some diabolical scheme to
frustrate my house in its entirety; you shall work fairly and
openly, and not apply the acid, that comes with you from the
Sun, you are not to use that acid, I am not going to give you right
out what the acid is, for did I do so the fiends of hell would
play destruction upon you, and they may think it possible to find

this fluid, but should they do so it would be all no use to them, for they don't know how to use it, so I am saving a corps or two by not divulging all my own power; you can not ask me a question, but that I have the ability to answer it, and you can't get at me through any source, for I am known to be a match for all the heavenly Gods, that came along before me, and as this is the case, you need not think to master me, as I will fight you fair, and I will go on any expedition, of peace, that you say is not plain or comprehensible to you; so I am not dogmatical, I will show you the way to do everything, it is no use my coming down to earth, and telling you a one-leg story, I am here to make you meet, both heaven and hell are united once you wish it; and express yourselves willing to know all: I can understand you better than you can me, I can read your papers, without paying a cent for all the information you are possessed of; I can reach in and see the actions of all secret societies; I can find out all the brigands you have got I can go into the contents of any paper of importance you have, and I will do more, I will break up any society, that is not of good to the community at large; I have the power, of going into any, parliamentary body, and sowing confusion among them, your ancients did destroy, but my plans are different, it " bells bellow," to go and kill, I don't like it, for instead of helping civilization, it augurs evil, I say down with murder of every description, and live like princes; the weaker is to be made strong, and the strong is to rule the head, and protect the weaker, this is the way to govern mortal man, and not have him looking ill always, when he ought to be bright and happy, I see the future generations a very different specimen of humanity to what the present men and women are; there are no faults to find in an improvement, once we are sure it is a benefit; but you must not run away with an improvement, before you have got the idea fixed right, then you might do all well enough, but an improvement is only a suitable machine for common sense, and not a gauge; it should be borne, in mind, that a fakir is a person who ought to be tried but not let fall; lest his fakes might break in two, and you are safe in testing his many cranks; but don't mind him till you get him

so cornered off, till he either breaks or falls; give him all the
known tests possible, then make him try experiments; that have
not been heard of, that are imaginary, and are the difficulties,
that a man should surmount, and he gets stuck each time this is
the way to test a fakir, and I want you my friends to try
me as that same fakir, and when you have broken me down, or
slipped me up; then it is time for you to condemn me, and not
till then; your duty demands that you should try any improvement, and your attitude is altogether of this worldly version, of
seeing what there is to be seen; then why can't you say I am
going to tackle this boaster on his stoutest points, and see
whether I can't knock his feet from under him; this is the way
to try a fakir, knock his legs clean from under him, whether he
is a mortal or immortal man, he has no business to come to you
and say I am the one who is able to talk to you truthfully;
then I say you have the right to question his theory in all his
ideas; this is only fair, and don't go and say his surplice, is a
sainted garment, it is not at all made of any more righteous texture than your own, it was woven by the fleecy clouds, in the
first instance, and it is part and parcel of your own common
raiment, and as such is no more sacred than yours, and the man
that is encased beneath that cloth, is not of any more righteous
quality than you are; now there is this to be considered, and that
is the point, that I have got to learn you, you are very ignorant,
and you don't know a single thing about this astrologer, coming
home alive, he is a fine specimen of what is called the modern
model man: And he has to be respected, against all comers, his
home is on the high, then don't you seam him to your eye, but
you just go and talk to him, and say friend what is thy calling,
it shall be his duty to say my friend I am the servant of Christ,
he was the only true prophet, that ever understood the language
of the dead, and I will listen to no man that says he has the
right to pile infamy upon his head: Now my friend I am a servant
of Christ, and not an " Infidel;" as the heathens called me, and in
Christ's work, he never claimed the art of any supernatural
being, he said I am here to do the will of my father who art in
heaven; now he had a perfect right with that exclamation, for

as his father did, so was he told to do, and as he
did so was he obliged to do, and last but by no means
least, my father who art in heaven is not what you all make it
appear, it is this, my father is my guide, for he dictates to me,
and I do his bidding, so that to say my father who art in heaven
means this, it is a given father, not an entire one: this father
which our Saviour spoke of was the one appointed by those who
had him under their control, and he was there by appointment,
I say that you are all wrong on this question, and as such is
quite certain to be proved any number of ways, I say you are as
the black sheep left out of the fold, you don't know what that
means either, it is this, that your fathers who art in heaven, have
not told you where the white sheep grew, therefore you are
pagans, till you learn where the white and black sheep became
divided; now I say that you are an oat for I have not designated
you as such, and I am going to prove it, and this is the way I
start in, your shell is the husk, and the kernel is your body, and
the life of that oat is the essence, that came through the Sun and
made man, in the first instance, now then my friends, what is
the difference between a black oat, and a white one, why my dear
friends the one has found a black husk, and the other has on a
white husk, they both came out of that churn, that I have told
you of, which is the dividing link in man, the Sun does the dividing, in her interior, there are many chambers; and in the one,
there is found, the essence of grime, and in the other is the
essence of pale white glue, in neither is there any mouldings,
but on the outside rim of the Moon, there is the interior lining;
thus sowing the seeds of time, according to the different grades,
that have become mixed in the inner chambers; now you want
to know what Christ said about my father saying that there are
many mansions in my home on high; You little dream of how he
meant you to construe this passage, and instead of you taking
out the grains of wheat, you have saved all the clean seed, and
not allowed any of it to grow husks, that was not the right definition, it is thus, that you should read, my father hath many
mansions beyond the sky, but they are holes for daylight to
creep through, and not mansions, such as the common mind will

designate, mansions; now don't you see that a mansion is lighted from the inside, and not from the out, therefore he is right, my father hath many mansions behind the ceiling of my home on high; now you don't suppose, that I am going to tell you, that a man who is able to fight the scriptures, from their beginning to the present hour, is afraid of you, nothing of the sort, it is all a folly to think that I am afraid of you breaking me down, or doing anything to disgrace my book, I tell you positively, that you can't trip me, and I will show you this all soon enough, and you are as the lamb lying down in green pastures, you were not afraid of the lion, when he had no teeth, well now I should think you ought not to be afraid of me, I have got no teeth; and I can't bite you, so there is a very good reason why you should class me as the lamb, and let me lay down beside you, for I can do it, whether you object or not, only that when I am to sleep beside the lioness; I want her to keep on watch, and do not destroy my slumbers; this is what I call happiness: You can come to me as the baying lion, and I can go to you as the lamb, yet neither can I see any fear in you, neither can you seam the danger that is in me, so I say that the lion is strong, but the lamb is the power in his father's home on high, for in heaven there are many gates, that close behind the death-knell of those roaring lions, that disturb the peace of man, and where the lamb is caught in slumbers, a barred gate rests on hinges; and the lamb is safe, for the lion is placed on the inside, whilst the lamb, may rest on the outside, and when the lamb lies down on the outer edge, it is taught to say welcome all ye sinners, for there is enough work on the inside for you to make a picture of hades with, and I say that you can cause the lion and the lamb to lay down together, for the one is master over the other, and the lamb may call upon the lion to repair a state, in which his power *is needed, for his huge form, can be made use of in heaven for a purpose, that no earthly one dreams of; whereas the lamb, can direct him straight, this is how it comes to you in scriptural learning: And you don't understand it, the lamb has a talk that surpasses all understanding, and she says to the lion, you make me a hole in yonder cliff, and I will sleep there, and you must stop outside till I do enjoy my slumbers; now the lion obeys her, for he sees she is not afraid of him, and this is why she does not fear him, his mouth is lined with ether, and instead of him taking his earthly teeth, with him to heaven, his soul departs, without that part of his regimentals, and he has a soul as also does the lamb; neither one or yet the other carry teeth in heaven, and it is no use for man to suppose that the lions are dangerous in heaven, for they are not, and it is outrageous for you to suppose that heaven is beset with dangerous animals, for they all acknowledge man as a superior being, and it is reasonable so to do; for man is able to see further ahead, and he discerns, things that the lion never has any thoughts of, now you keep quiet, and I will show you why it does not grow teeth in spirit-home, the fact is this, you don't get on to the right thread of my story, before you see through this idea, and that is the cause you have for complaint, and you must digest this awful chasm by piecemeal, and not by whole quantities; the first thing you do is to swallow, and that is not all, you breathe, but then again you have to reel round a time or two, before you pick up the right motion to keep yourself from falling to pieces; thus you will see that you have caught on to my thread, it is this wise, a man must begin by eating, and not by drinking, you see that he chews his fist first, and he is always afterward a chewer, for he can't exist comfortably without he gets something in his mouth, well he is awfully hungry after dying, and naturally he would feel empty, for he has lost all his stomach, at one great loss; but he still pegs away at that hand, and he begins to tucker up again, and places his mouth, as he used to do, but it won't work any way at all, so he gets famished, and then he eats again, but it is this time awfully poor pie, and he wants to know whether there is nothing to eat in heaven better than the present thin air, well it is assumed, that there is, but he won't keep still, he is always after that right arm, and hand; now my friends I have been leading you round, after death, and I want to show you why no teeth comes, and it is from the fact, that at first there has been no teeth, and at last there can not be any teeth, for the fact is clearly this, your diet is of such a quality, that prohibits the use of teeth,

the whale is not found eating, and the teeth he has are of no use
to him as a whole muncher, they are for fancy, and not for mas-
tication; now you will see that heaven is a second sea, and the
ocean in heaven, is the atmospheric elements, and are not allied
to the skies at all: But are the afterbirth of the ocean, for the
sea is the past, the earth is the present, and the heaven is the
future; I have said this in sheer earnest; knowing it to have been
proof positive of my assertion to be founded on facts, which you
can never throw away, this is why the heavens are a bounteous
miracle, and it is not for me to say that God does not know what
he did in the first history to man, but what I shall prove to you
in theory and fact is this, he was unable to comprehend this
gigantic magnitude, and he did all that was in his power for man,
thoroughly believing what he did to be true: Now you have no
idea of the worry and time it has taken to bring about a correct
theory of this immense great topic of immeasurable disputes and
circumference, for the heavens are full of contestants for supreme
power and knowledge, they fight from morning till night on this
question, and do every thing possible to discover the right
thoughts, for it is a boon sacrifice to be called heathens, when
we know, that we are so, and yet it can't be otherwise, for we are
all on the very verge of worshiping a deity, that never was, and
could not be in the sense known to man, well I say what right
has man to a belief in something that can not assist him, for the
very fact, that this God who is in spirit and was the leader of
the prophets, was at the head of the government in heaven then,
and was the most able, and best spirit that lived in heaven in his
time, and was no more than I am to-day, a theorist, capable of
throwing light upon a head that does not see, and can't see, for
he has not advanced to a stage, wherein he might understand did
he but know how to look; now I tell you why you can't grow
teeth in heaven, for the fact, that none ever were known to propagate there, and without propagation, there can't be teeth, and it
is this wise, a man is born without teeth, but his hands are salty,
and he inhales the breath off this hand, and he sucks this hand,
and he does as he pleases with this hand, and he loves his hand,
and he marks his hand, with his mouth, but he never yet did bite,

till he had teeth, well his hand has bone in it; and he is afraid of
that bone, still it does not make him teeth; well my friends you
have got me at last, and I must throw up the sponge, it is this
very sponge; that brings teeth, and you don't know why, well I
am pretty near a cobweb, and I must get out of this tangle somehow; you know my friends that a little cobweb might get us into
more trouble than every other thing together, well don't you see
that I once wrote to you about a web being made by the friends
of the spiders, that had departed, well what was it then, that
took the first line across the river, well my dear friends it is the
same with you, my little baby is without teeth, and he can't eat,
good: So great big granddad comes and makes them come, by
poking in a little bit of salt, and this is the fish that swallowed
Jonah; he never got beyond this little bit of trouble, and he
stuck fast to that fish ever since, it was the corker; "that took
him altogether too small;" he could not swallow the whale, so
leaped upon his back and rode away, and my friends you should
know me by this time, and let me have an easy ride too; don't
you think you ought to now, come I deserve a ride, and you have
a right to lend me a little assistance, well you get an ivory ring
and give it to the baby, I surely ought to have one too, and get
on a little faster, at chewing, the baby has no teeth, for he had
none to begin with, and why because the whale is the fish that he
was chopped out of, and how came this to be discovered, well it
is this my friends; that the sea, was even with the sky at one
period, and the ocean was the first body, by its own construction;
and there is the silliest thing there is to knock you out with;
your own court is the very thing that does it, the sea is always
in you, and the land is not, your veins are full of blood, and your
mouth is full of muscles, because your teeth, were made from
muscles, and your head is made of blubber; and your eyes are
from the essence of the salt, and your nose came from the bubble
of the fish that spouts water in the atmosphere, I don't care
whether the whale was alive when man propagated or not, his
nose came from that sort of fish, and his ears, came from the fin
behind the head, and his nose was made round by the constant
strain on the atmospheric currents; and his nose is sharpened by

the atmosphere coming from heaven upon it: Now I have made
fun enough of you, I am going to begin to show you why you
don't become amphibious again, because you are lifted up higher,
by the adhesive currents of malaria, it breathes contagion into
you, and you are fetched along by the stagnation of heat and
air together; this is why you don't go back again into the water
and live, it is the heat germination, that causes you to grow into
this stage of perfection, so I will get off and carry you
along, when we all get stuck, for I must get you there
on a correct basis some way; and you only hamper me
by taking off my back, and placing my load on the eye
of that camel, that never has reached the other side of
that needle, that helps the rich man to fail to find Lazarus,
I won't punish the rich man, for I love to play with science,
and the rich man has no particular interest for me, my idea of
him is partly play, and part earnest, his nose might have had a
yellow tinge, or he might have been buried in a quick-sand, that
contained the acrimony of gold dust, it does not matter to any
of us, whether he ever does take hold of Lazarus, or whether he
did ever do what the scriptures say he did, I have known rich
men, who are quite as generous, as ever this man was who said
we could not go to heaven, without paying toll, I say that my
fare did not come that way, and I got there, as you see me more
particularly demonstrating, than any man who ever hired the
ceremony that gave him an inside berth, and when you want to
go, just shake yourselves loose, and remember that as fishes
swim, so will you have to divide your conscience into two, the
one is I want to ride, in a seething mass, or I want to part my
raiments, and just divide my half in two, the one is to go in at
the cemetery, and the other takes a bee line forever and a long
time after; no one has had time to make the change, and I say
you must either take what is given to you, or go without, there
is no picking and choosing, and I want you to understand this
much, the man who does his duty here, is the one we all like to
see come home, for he is a welcome guest in heaven, and not one
but will welcome the just stranger, who says my hand brother is
founded upon stability, and you can call again, this is the man

we all welcome, not the one who looks afraid, as though he knew
of his own transgressions; and would fend them off with a
scowl, my friends are welcomed, because there is a palace provided, for those who serve heaven in a righteous way, and I say
that sense is righteousness, and not wisdom, for in the one we
have the permission of knowing, and in the other; it is as you
choose to make it, and wisdom may be a leper, in garments of
glittering gold, whereas the one who carries God in his pocket,
has sense; now you see what I mean by these terms, the one is a
tiger leper, and he is ready to devour; by the throws of subtility; '
and the other has God in his pocket, for he lets no beggar starve;
and·he extends his hand to the brother who fell from an ill wind,
I say this is the God who has a heart for every good shepherd;
And as Isaac did bless Jacob in error, let not a wind that cursed
by error go unrequited; for as Esau was blessed, so that he
founded his throne upon a rock, and as the kingdoms of the
earth sprang from such a tribute of affection, let Adam look and
see whether sense or wisdom has fought the battle straight,
Isaac, has gone to the throws of Cain, and is hunted on every
hand, while the subtility of God did make the hand of Isaac
supplant the seed of his wife's duplicity, and Esau reigns
supreme, I say again my friends that sense is all, and wisdom is
a sting of vengeance, you can blight my path, but you shall
never master, though there were ten thousand birthrights
dragged from me, and as I was born on the sunny side, and did
break off the white wheat, I say you can never annihilate me.
I am as the winter oat, I came black, but as the God of light
did shine upon me: So you see me, a master of that oat, and
driven from heaven by an angry wind, I have been propagated,
till I have reached the top, and you can't throw me down, I shall
ascend higher and higher, till there never will be left any mountain to climb; now my friends and brothers, are you welcoming
me, or are you anxious to fight me down again to the bottom
rungs of the ladder, I have been to the top, and I am ready to
climb again, but you ought to go up with me, for I like company,
and it would be a treat to see you ascending that ladder, which
no man living or otherwise, has ever yet ascended, now my

friends let us journey together, and make all men feel happy, give each one the truth my brothers, and there is the happiness, assured, show each designing immaculate brother his folly, and you have God by the hand, this is what we call the destruction of the devil, for no devil can exist, against common sense; and you must whip the devil or you never can hold God by the hand, thus it is easily seen, that man is whatever you choose to make of him, and he is easily made to believe evil, but you climb the ladder with me, my friends will never look upon that devil again, for he will be bare, absolutely naked my brothers, I have got the only devil there ever was, and that was why you could not master him before, I tailed him off, and shut him up, and made him explain his code, I fought him down, till I had him surely fast, and I have to thank nobody but my own courage, you can't whip Satan without courage, he is bold, and he is daring, yet he is a coward, and it is so with all animals, that have the blood of the serpent in their veins, and why, because the serpent is a bloody hate, he was the first black wheat, and he shall never lie, who does not know this bloody weapon that he uses; I want to tell you my brothers how to reach this hidden skin of Cain; by a process, that is beyond the perception of man in his normal condition, it is through the subtility of the Jehovah, that you have got to reach it, it is by the good cross, that our Saviour perished on: Now my friends I have brought you to the cross on Calvary, will you permit me to tackle man as you find him, and in the struggle for mastery, will you die fighting, this is the way to come to the first rung of that great ladder: I say my heavenly father hath the top, while I am at the bottom, and by the grace of God help me to ascend this steep incline, well now my brothers you are with me at the bottom, my father is at the top, I will suggest to him, that we want to go and see him, his answer must be, you are not ready yet; well when we are ready, may we come up to you; His answer is I have nothing to stop you with, and so my friends you see he can not threaten to stop us, for he has nothing to stop us with, we are not to be driven back by angry words, which contain no meaning, and as Christ did die on the cross, why can't we follow him, for he is good,

and we know that he did good, and we know that he did die on
that cross, and we know that the pagans did kill him, but you
are all wrong, when you say that God willed his only begotten
son to death for the sake of bringing sinners to repentance; his
thoughts were quite different, his idea was to show the mother
of Jesus, what she had done by preventing our Saviour from
being born again, by being afraid she lost all, and when she
went to the sepulcher, it was found empty, and who was it that
did remove that body, I say you are all mistaken on this point,
the Lord God of Jacob, and Abraham, were there, and they did
make that body, and they were able. to make that body move
after death, as well as though it were warm and life-like, and
you must not go on in this ignorance any longer, the body was
no more dead than it is to-day, but the life-lung, was extracted,
and when you take away the life-lung, you are bound to decay,
but there is the query, it must be sown together, according to
the method of governing matter, and when you are capable of
governing matter, you are able to seam a soul together, by the
process of ether it is held, that a man may be dead for forty
days, and then brought to life again, that is his body may be so
impregnated with ether that his soul is made dormant, and it is
this that we can find by examination of the snake species, they
are subject to fits of dormancy, and can be cut about till they
are hacked in two almost, well you see they knit together again
under such circumstances; and you find them so powerful after
the fit of dormancy has gone, that it is almost marvelous, at
their suppleness; and protracted ability, now you seem to think
I am reaching you in a subtle way, and so I am, for my own
instrument is full of this poison known as ether, but it is not
prepared the same way as those who killed Christ; for there is
no manner of doubt, that they did kill him: for they made Mary
the mother of God come down to the sepulcher, and see how
Christ was laying, well you see he was gone, and they hastened
to tell of the body being taken away, well the angel, that stood
in that entrance, was no other, than the father of Christ, not as
you interpret our father, but the selected father of our Saviour,
not the actual father, for it is not necessary that a woman should

be conscious of the actual state of propagation, neither is it necessary that she should be aware of the father who caused propagation to take place, it is immaterial of either of these circumstances to be within her own knowledge of certain facts, it is not a common practice, but it is possible to produce these effects, through the right sort of stratagem, which you might call wisdom, for it is through the subtilty of the devil that it is worked, now you think because I am able to master this devil, who did deal in poisons, that I must be the greatest devil that ever lived, well you can talk to one who is very capable of holding you at arm's length, and see whether he looks like a devil or not, and you will find that I am not very far away from my own instrument; this is not all you can take a lesson or two that will be of magnificent construction: And you may learn how these secrets of writing is done through this form of clairvoyance, and teach some one to see that there is nothing deceptive or fraudulent in the construction of a work, that surpasses all understanding up to the present period: I have no intention of cheating you, and I want to briefly make my humble protest against fraud, I know you will believe me, for I intend to make my theoretical resources, so very plain and comprehensive, that you can not get away from me, and this is the benefit I intend to confer upon mankind for the treatment, that they meted out to me, when I had no knowledge of the actual state of things, I was puzzled over the fault they committed in killing our Saviour, and I vowed to fell the first one who came to me with any lies about him, so when I got on the other side and found them all lying about our Saviour, I went for knocking them over one by one, till I found them all afraid of me, and I sent my arrows flying right and left, till you can see the multitudes of sinners all ready to take a back entrance, when the veteran approaches, never mind I have my friends, and all of them who get me on their thoughts feel better for an encounter, and never go off hungry, I give them all my assistance, and when it is time to get ready for another charge I go on, this is the way to get at the pagan mind, by holding him fast onto his devil, till he is broken, then heave in a broadsider like an English Jack Tar, he always leaps sideways, when he has got to face the British flag, and why, because there are more devils in England, than there ever were in any other place, that I ever stepped across, and I know why too: The English are all bull-headed, and they come along with the shark, he won't turn his nose away, when he smells meat, and their heads are round like the fish, that is monarch of the ocean, they are just as hungry as sharks, and are just as avaricious as the dolphin; it is between these two guns I am going to sail a straight cutter: My log is a true one, and I am going to measure my find according to time, this is it, the dolphin is a fish, that swims on its back, when it takes food in, whilst the shark is on his back in an instant when he is prepared to take a bite, so you see that the fish are both against me, I go straight, whilst these two keep on the same tack, I want a whale, to pitch these two into one, and you can't help me, so I won't ask Mr. Jack Tar to help me, for he would sling in a broadside, and knock my theory to the dickens, before I found my Charly; This is all well enough to go out on a fooling excursion, but you know what it will be, when the white squall arrives off the coast of Dover, she heads inland, and brings up sharp to the rear front ranks; you can pitch in a broadsider now Jack I have caught you, the shark has bitten, and the dolphin is on top of the plank my boy you didn't see that, it was too quick for you lad I came upon you too sudden, I shot my jaw off Jack in that one supreme effort, don't take it badly lad we have all got to go some day, and you are mine you know, it is brutus against the beast, and I saw him do it, it was all a fake my lad, the baker never got had for so much breat, it came on naturally, and that is propagation between the shark and dolphin, this is news Mr. John Bull, don't seem to like my expression, but when you are monarch, of the ocean overhead, you ought to be civil to the rail that carries you, and not find fault with the ancient mariner, that was sent away from home in a leaky craft, and came back a rollicking statesman, you started the boy adrift, and you cared not whether he sank or swam, then don't go back on your old friends, for they are what has made you crop the seas with ancient time luggers, and though you should hear me tell you of

it, it is oddly enough to grace your please; that I should boast
of such modern vessels, I say you are descendants of the shark,
and I know how it came about, the ancients grew upon a slip-
pery plank, and never propagated beneath the Sun, they layed
their eggs upon the brink, and softly glided back beneath the
steps of ancient little turtle doves, this is the way to make you
feel quite creepy, it is not once, neither is it thrice, that I am
going to make you feel me put in my harpoon, for I mean to make
you shiver; yet with all that you are my brother: And I know
you will rebel, and quite kick off your hind feet, for you are
what is called the back scum of a great big invention, it is not
anywhere that would make you sink beneath such a load, but it
is the load, that has to be left off, and not put on, that I am making sure of, you can take off a load, easier, than you can place it
back again, well you see that in playing round about, you get
into many queer corners, and the way to fetch them all into ·
a center, you have got to help them off with one foot at a time,
and not take two feet away together, it is this way that a mighty
giant is made, you pull off his toes, one by one, then you get him
round the middle, and still you have caught him out of tune, for
you never took in his sound, and you have got to mention this
or he can't swim round, his tone won't let him, and you know how
this is brought about, why by placing him into a sound position,
you see me struggling under this great load, and yet I make it
easily understood, for I am a whale at finding faults, and this is
the way to do it, you keep on my old black coat, till I come and
take it off, and that suits you, for you have got none to wear,
and that is the way to get at you, because you are wearing out
my old suit, and that is why you look so shabby, you once had a
pair of whiskers, but now you clip them off, and split them in
half, and that's the way you don't take me in, for I can see
through these whiskers too, and that's the way to get at you,
because you think I would never know you, with those whiskers
slit in two, and that's the way to split you in two, and you don't
seem to think it strange, that I should make it do, when I have
got you made in two, that is it is already, into two halves; and
that is all very well for you, but you don't know why you split

those whiskers in two; for it will make you cry to know the reason why, this is it, I told you that I would make you sit up until
I had you made fast to me, well here you are, sitting up, your
hind legs, are the frog's feet, and that is what you do, keep them
for to eat, and that is what you don't do, is make them piece
you into two, for you have got a mighty poor pair of whiskers,
when you sell this pair of feet; I can show you how we digest
the frogs, and that is his eyes were made to look and peep, and
he can see you when asleep, for he is always croaking out more
sleep, and that's the way he does, he is always after hens' eggs,
for he can peep in and make chickens squeak, and that is where
you change to two feet, I saw you wink at me, but I have no
time to blink it back a second time, and you are off upon a spree
thinking that I am all a gee, going home upon a pretty white
elephant, but I only showed you where the subtilty of the devil
might lead you wrong, and so I have fetched you back to the briny
ocean, to make you take a swim, this is quite enough to make you
play at finding fault, so I have caught you at the right clap, and
that is this, the motion which you swim, is just the same as Mr.
Frog, when he is off upon a cruise, across the Pacific Ocean,
there it is my fine friends, you have all got to the point where
I can catch you, it is by the feet, and I know how to make
you mind me, for I will just pink you on both cheeks when
I get time, and don't you keep on finding fault with me, when
you know you can't take a fall out of the old Jack Tar; He is
coming home to drown all you land-lubbers, and he will pitch
you and tar-rope you, and then he can afford to give you all
the money, as he invariably does and besides this he is going
to bring you home all the glory as he has always done before,
for you cut him adrift, and pitched him to sea, and said here
old fellow you can either sink drown or swim my boy is in
the green billow now, and no one heeds the lad they cut away
from yonder great big ship, he sank beneath those cold gray
eyes, and heaven was looking on, it is the old story poor Jack
is drowned, but never mind my dear we can meet him on the
homeward-bound voyage, it is all the same my love you can
take my old straw hat and place it on the old spot where poor
19

Jack got drowned, he never thought of us dear he had no time I am sure, he will lament the day he went out to sea, for it was a stormy night, it is very bad you see to be caught on that green sea, in a wrecked old tub; for she never keeps dry, and she is always wet in under her eye, for we feel the fishes are making her cry come back, to dine, you land-laden gossoon; I want to make you kiss my lips, as your mothers used to do, this is where I want to place the famine pie, it is here my love that poor Jack has gone to kiss his ancient mothers in quaint Patrick's Dive; Yes my darling it's after missing him I'd be; but you see its a foine toime he'll be a 'aving wit my o'll German maid: This is the way my friends to split you up, you are a mixture, of all that is, and you are a great deal too fine a specimen, for me to leave you out of my calculation, and when I wink one eye, you must shut both, for this it, you are heathens to-day, saints to-morrow, and angels the day after, this is my theory, the maid is a German, the first is a Spalpeen, the third is a land-mark; well this is how we go, there are three bodies, one is the sea, which has all power, for it contains the exact formation of everything, it is the essence, which propagates therein, for it is the soul life of all material, and you see the very beginning there, it is in the brine, it is there, which produces, the floating currents, that have always been divined by the right of power, it is the atmosphere that dwells there, it is the air of the waves, that brings life to the surface, and it is good essence, which propagates, beneath that element, known as the heat that clasps together; you have this ocular demonstration, within your own grasp, it is the effect of the power of the Sun over a magnifying glass; it propels together, and produces the heat in veins, that grow the blood, it divides the waters, and creates a new fissue, by dirking in between, it is a magnificent vein, to throw power with, there is the secret of mortality; you have been a long time at this great secret, but you have found it at last, and all through the gray-eyed Englishman cutting poor Jack adrift, and making him either sink or dive, well my friends and brothers you must welcome Jack or I shall cut you off without a shilling, it is the duty as I read it, to give to the youngest, which ought to belong to the eldest; now my brothers, I am the eldest and I want to know why I can't have that honor that Jacob lost, he duped his brother, and you see he lost, well my brother is the same he duped me, and I have won, like Esau, I am going home in front, and I want the right to be carried on my own plank; this is as you have always done, and I say that custom shall no longer be the laws; for right is might, and as I master heaven, you shall not get me down on earth, to be made a tool of for nothing, I am here because you sent for me, and I am here by right, you pray for enlightenment, and I am here to give it to you: And as the sand of the seashore is mine, to perpetuate my diligence to, you have the right to be counted in as that sand, and not as the earth's great instructor, for as man did hide beneath that sea-shore; so did the sand aid in producing life, it is here where the ancients went wrong, they saw the sand rise in clouds of dust, and propagate beneath the arid sky, and they saw it hurl to heaven, that which belonged to the earth and when it was on the heavenward journey, it took a turn, and went over to the east, this is what surprised them, it never came back, they could not see that when it went east, that it dropped in the west, for why should it turn to the east, and fall in the west, this is the point right here, you went home without your coat, and you got there all the same, did you miss the road, because you had no compass to steer you by, no my friend it never has been necessary to carry a compass, on such a journey, for the wind falls right, in every instance, she goes in at the one end, and comes out at the other, that is why you can't miss your road, you must go with the wind, whether you are going home or not, it is no use going against the wind, it is all fault, when you go against the wind, there is the point right here, the wind is good, for it is your direction through life, don't go against it, it is all good, when you feel a contrary wind, veer round to the west a point, or come circling round again, and meet the west wing, it all goes the road we come, and go on the road, that was traversed before my friends, and you can't get wrong: I am your moralizer, and

you will find me quite right every time, for you know I keep
bending my way so as to keep with the wind, this is what I am
doing, now I am following the wind that is all my friends, and
you have got to do the same, or you will suffer by not obeying
the laws of nature, for the wind is what governs all things both
great and small: And you have to be governed according to
this wind, for it is the one great faction, that has all to do with
moving heaven; thus you see that the wind is the power, that
moves the sky round, it keeps the one end of the Sun full of air,
which is breath, and it drives in to both the east end, and the
west end of the Sun, and these two join together, and they produce a furl, which causes the interior of the Sun to circle, and it
moves to a center, coming in contact, with a great wheel, which
is of solid material; which I don't intend to explain, for I propose
to invent a machine on earth, that has to follow on this principle,
and you won't know how the Sun does actually work till I have
made this machine; you are welcome to assist me, but you must not
be too inquisitive, till I show you how to look at things in a
proper light, now we are going to stop right here, and either get
this full knowledge, or never know the rest, this is what I have
made up my mind for you to do, and that is to be very careful
you don't meddle with my instrument, and I will produce perpetuity on earth, and show you how to go to heaven alive in
your old shells, and make you stop up there till you have got the
entire business so complete, till there will be no possibility of
lying: Now you can't do this by cheating, it has to be fair play,
and I will make this machine, so as you can't be hurt, by ascending up or down, and that the Moon or stars, can't have any effect
on you, they will be as harmless as the little turtle doves, and I
want to take my own instrument up first, because he will not
be afraid, when I show him how it is to be done, and that is
something more for you to look at than this great big balloon
ascension, carrying toys up, and dropping them out in angel
wings, that is where they get that idea from, it is the angels' displeasure, that caused you to get up those sights, bits of side-shows
I call them, now you know I took you into the Sun and propped
you up against the wheel, but I would not go any farther,

because I am going to give this invention to my own friends
only, and that is the spirit world, it is to be the invention
to crown the success of spiritualism, and not to be a mortal
theory at all: So you see I am not going to desert heaven again,
for the sake of giving hell a benefit, that will outreach the
throne of God, it is his by rights, whether he be one great spirit,
or whether he is the power supreme in this great throne of
glory, now my friends I think you are satisfied with me this
time, and I feel that you ought to be, for I am going to with-
hold very little from you, in comparison to what I have told you,
and .you ought to know that I am able to lead you straight,
when I am capable of dividing you up so accurately, this is only
a beginning, and I won't let you see the end, till I am more
satisfied with you, it is no use my taking you to heaven, till you
are ready to go: I want to know how much longer you will
resist the temptation, of seeing God, he is quite as ready to meet
you, as ever you are willing he should do so: Now my brothers
I want to speak a little more on your beginning, for it is working toward a finish of this volume, and you must have a few
more facts laid bare, before I go and leave you, because you
know I want a reception from you before proceeding any farther,
and that is a substantial one, it is a necessity I am asking; or
you would not hear me mention the coin, the only question is
this, my own guide is a good one, and the others are willing to
try this experiment, of going to heaven in a perpetuity book,
made of composition, in the form of a machine, that shall work
according to the construction of the Sun and Moon, with the
stars fixed according to the construction of heaven, but you
must admit my friends that I can't do this without means, and
when I find the intellect, and the constructive genius, you must
supply my medium with the means of procuring such material
and labor as is necessary to furnish this skillful appliance, you
can then have the fullest information that there is on the other
side of life, for he will write always, and you can buy his works
and in this way we hope to procure our assistance to prove all
that we claim, and not by asking alms for nothing, we are here
to do the work of raising humanity to the level of God, and not

as venders or as impostors: Now friends we don't ask you to
come forth with your purse, and say here is money to build your
craft, we say that our work is worth your gold, and our laborers
are worthy of their hire, now don't think it is a begging expedition, that we are after, for such is not the case, we don't want
your gold, it is no use to us, only as an experiment, and we consider that our work is sufficient to merit this consideration at
your hands; God bless the giver of light, and may souls be got
together, in earnest on a question, which is to show mankind the
eternal truth, and the divine providence, that is going to make
man a power, such as has never been known before: I want to
write you such works as will make you a perfect machine, which
you are, and instead of you having to grope in the dark, as
heretofore, I want to show you the light, so as you may look upon
life in its true form, not by any imaginary course at all; now I
think when I explain in my other works how you are to look for
the treasures in the earth, without even so much as buying a
pick-handle, it surely must be right that I must come and tell
you of these things, no fear of there not being sufficient to do
for all; for as the Sun shines, she makes more lands for you to
settle upon;   And instead of you going begging for work, you
can have the advantage of seeking what you can find, this is the
advantage of sense, not a hypocritical sense, such as wisdom, a
sense, that shall show you where you have a right to go for the
benefits; which every man has a right to look for: And I will
show you this by degrees, as I find you ready to accept the
advantages, such as I have spoken of, now don't doubt me, for a
mind and a man combined, that can show you the internal workings of heaven, and the machinery that guides heaven, is quite
capable of teaching you where to find the gold, that is made in
that Sun before it falls to the ground, now don't be foolish and
think that I mean, the Sun is dividing her elements up in heaven
so as to propagate gold for you, it is nothing of that sort I
assure you, it is this fact, she can't help herself, she has got to
produce the kind of matter, that grows gold; and when I tell
you of this fact, you have a right to believe me capable of finding that gold which you so much long for: And though I don't

tell you now, it is right also, for you would cheat me, and I don't want you to do it, for it would make me your inferior, and that is not the way to get your affection and confidence; now we won't fall out only I intend that you shall treat me with consideration, or I won't tell you anything that is a benefit to you in discovering the treasures that you have got; And it is the simplest thing in the world to find when you know the right method of looking: I can show you how the forests grow, so as to give you an insight into my theory: And then you can trick and cheat away all you have a mind to, it won't help you with the mineral product; well it is this, a green slime is formed around the basin of the interior of the Sun, through the atmospheric elements becoming congealed, through remaining in contact so long by stagnation, well this is only a party to the great secret, for the Sun has got to revolve round to this side-show of hers; two more years, by that time she gets her left hand cortege in the side-show, and then she brings out this green saliva, and precipitates it into her main disk, which is a flange-wheel, that resembles a churning procedure, this time she fires her excess, and the balance is precipitated into the after part, where it is sent onward by pressure to the funnel, which you call the Moon, this how it leaves the moon, in little round globes, or perspiration drops, and it has the fall according to its right to drop, and my friends, when this reaches your earth, it propounds the composition necessary to grow your forest, not by the sole right of propagation in the Sun, but as a distinct deposit, laid on the ground; and then by process of time it is soldered to this earth by a calling sound of eternity, that is the Sun and wind take back that which they know is useful to them, and they use that over again, for the use of firing that great volcanic body, that is in the Sun; now you have found out two things by this illustration, the one is to show you how the forest is grown, and the other to show you that everything is round that leaves heaven, then why do you doubt me, for the fact, that you are round, that is why, you can't see anything around you: And you say I see nothing, why, my friend you were many times greater than you are now, before ever you became a round surface, and it is this that made you round, the Sun and sea have fought a battle in some remote period, that need not be described in figures; it is so remote, that I may say that no human thing was alive to tell the tale, the Sun in her ambitious spirit, did one great good, she leaped over the sea in her flaming anger, and creeping all over as she gained upon her enemy, drank all from that great body, that was included in her desires; she raged and stormed, and set her fiery eye upon the ocean deep and wide, and kept up a hissing sound of wrath, till the sea gave way in sheer fright, it is plainly to be seen, the sea is gradually diminishing, this is the turning-point in my history, and I can show you better by the outcrop, of natural history, than ever you can be shown in any other way: The Sun sets in an Arctic region, and it rises in a Torrid Zone, why, because a given space of time is to eclipse the shoal of getting beyond the sky, and in going round she touches the water, and drinks in her fill, that is why the world is growing larger, she looks angry at you in the morning, when her head-dress is all ruffled, by coming in contact, with the atmospheric coarseness of depression, her nose is wet, with tears, her eye is bleared with weeping, and her soul rebels at the thoughts of having to submit to such tyrannical conduct, her face is muddy and her eye has caught the cloudy blear of a rough-and-tumble fight, for as the sun approaches the ocean, she hits her sides with agony, and she pelts her enemy with fire and oil, and instead of the sea beating her, she is quite a masterful Majesty, she licks him up, and exceeds the chastened thoughts, by skipping in a quantity of governing elements, that hail her as their queen: It is here where the propagation of man is seen to grow, for all around this arid region, the waters are streaming with fish of a different order to those we see in our well-known waters, there is the giant fish, which measures about a thousand feet long, there is the lion in course of propagation, there is the sea-owl, which is a night prowler, the same as the one who wakes you up at night, calling moulpolk; that is the bird, that gives me more consideration, than all the rest put together, his beak, has a hook to the end point, and he likes nothing that is called fat, he does not care for the heavenly bread of life; his mouth is not constructed that way, his attention is drawn to trees, he likes looking into holes, and he sleeps there; well now you all think you know more about an owl than I do, well I want to show you that you don't know anything at all: This is why, when you walk abroad at night, you think of the darkness; well the owl is wishing it would become blacker still, for he sights his prey by the light of his own eye; And not by the light of yours; well you know that, but you don't steady your thoughts sufficiently to say, he is the master of the night, whilst I am master of neither light or darkness: You see my friend how hard I have struck you, you are neither a light mortal, neither are you a living conundrum to him, he has your picture painted on every tree, he knows you at night as the one great seed of humanity, he knows you as the awful taunting bush of life, and he knows you as the companion of his soul, for you groan beneath his call, and it is this that makes you his, he is the king of night; he sees clearly, all that is visible and invisible, he is the soul of eternity, he comes on after the day is spent, and he screeches out moulpolk; well my friends what did that denote, it might mean food, but it might mean anything else, no my friends it is the solution of that great mystery, that divides you from eternity, it says I am the king of the darkness; and to read you must bow down, and discover my pride and glory, I am the one great terror, that enters your souls, I see you hear me, I see you feel me, I will never deny you, yet you are the giver of the good we ought to thank you for; for there is nothing without this night, it comes overhead in an opportune kind of way: It is the star-spangled banner of our life, we search, but we never find, for there is the night, he is ever present, well and why; for the very good reason; that he has the right, and why, because he does know it is his duty, that forces him to cover up all nakedness by the shadow, that follows after, and as your own shadow comes before, it is the sign of another rising day, it broods on insanity, it throws reflections out, that you are the divine, for it is here sought out, that you are the propagated soul of hell, and in the hereafter, you are the shadow, for you have two parts, a dark and a light part, your light part is the one you wear after you have crossed over, and your night is

that which you have to bear in hell; which means the earth:
Now I want to explain to you that a shadow is a reality, for it is
the duplicate of your own counterfeit, and must be so, for the
fact, that you are not in an entire form, till you have been made
by shadow, the sea is your propagator in its way, because by
reflection you are propagated, in the first instance, you are
ascended by draft, you are accented by prorato, and you are
gravitated by the power of the whole striking at once, it is the
reflection that is caught, by the method of folly turns the wheels
of time, and that in fun you play the game of reaching perpetuity; not by sober earnestness; you are away off, for you think
that perpetuity is a dreadfully hard matter to get at, whilst it is
one of the easiest things imaginable, once you plant the right
seed, and that is what I will make you believe, in time to come,
instead of you wearing out, I will make you all wear in, this is
not all I mean to do either, I mean to make you give me a good
many things, that you don't want, and that would be more service
to me than you: You don't think I want anything, well you
don't know what you are thinking about, I know what I want,
and that is a commercial negotiation with you; It is not for
your gold or silver, it is for your own souls that I want a civil
contract, well you think they won't work for me, I don't want
them for the work that is done through them at present; I want
them to stop it, that is the contract in its entirety; well you say
they don't do anything, well you agree to the contract, and I can
make you all assign your interests to me, for you are the minds,
that I am in search of, they hold you as tight as wax, well I don't
want you to be so rigorous in regard to religion, I want a soul to
know what and how he came to be, and I want him to know how
to talk to God, for when he talks to his own superior, he can't
get cheated, and that is what I want him to do: I will tell you
the way to do this, once I know that there are sufficient of you
willing to be taught, this includes both sides of life: And you
know I won't have anything that is not in strict accordance with
sense, and sense is all: You seem to appreciate a man who
speaks truly, well now why can't you have all truth, and no lies;
it won't stop you eating and drinking, it will not break up the

sagacity of the world, it will only make every mouthful you eat more delicious, for you will be ready for the next, and its pride will bring all the rest, why need you care, whether you were the king of darkness once, or not: You are the shining light to-day, and you have always been at the head, then don't get annoyed because you did not see a construction, that is only visible to those who have an understanding equal to God, for it is the same class of deity, as did lead the Israelites through the wilderness; only that a stage has passed along, and the man of to-day is able to see the shades of evening coming down, and they descend more gradually, they fall more like a reality, they lift off that black glooming, and say I was afraid once, but there is nothing to fear; the Sun has got so far ahead, that she can never be caught up to, and I must content myself by following on: This is it my dear friends you have gone behind, for the heavens uprose; and it was in a bitter strife that this raging torrent got backed from both waves, it caught the wave in agony, and settled down to genuine business; and you can not do any harm in following me, for I have settled down to business; and I shall explain the unseen, and that which you know about, this perhaps is more to your liking, I will suggest to you a road, that looks like a straight line, the one that leads nowhere, it is a straight line, for it has led you round, and you absolutely found nothing, yet you went round all the same, and that is a factotum, for it led you round, and you touched on nothing of importance; well now let me bring in your notice, to a second road, that has no line at all, it never had any, we can say so, for we can't see any beginning, well now there is this difficulty to face my friends, you had no beginning, is that correct, or am I to give God more credit than he really believes himself, this is what every man of sense knows to be a dead certainty, you say my God did make heaven and earth, and all that in them is, inside of one week, I say he never did, and he knew no better way of misleading those poor heathens into a decent behavior, or he never would have used his ingenuity for them at all: Do you mean to tell me that God did wrong, I say he has done the noblest action that ever breathed the breath of heaven, and why, for he gave to them that which has propelled on civilization, to such a pitch, that no one with sense can say but what he is the best God we ever had, and I say to-day that his work shall never die; God bless the man who was so sincere, and earnest in his devotion to man and good causes; now I must explain that in my theory there is no one God, but in order to meet you on a sound basis, I must take you by the hand, and lead you straight, and in leading you straight, I must get you to understand, and when you come to me, and say it is all dark in front, I must then grab you by the hand, and say I will show you my friend that you are wrong, there is a road all right, and I am going as pilot, come along then and see the beginning, you say there never was any beginning, I say my friend there is always a genuine article, before there can be a counterfeit, well now since I am stuck with you in my hand, looking over the broad expanse of nature, I can see but you can't, well you must let me blindfold you, and then I am going to give you a sight worth looking at, it is not much, yet it is all the world in an egg-shell, you have seen an egg, you have never been so near swallowing one as you are at this moment, for I have got two, one is me, and the other is you; the one is a hen, and the other is his maker, I thought you could not recognize me, I have never been in that egg at all, it is you, that came out of that shell, it fell from you, when the heat had warmed you into animation: You don't believe me; " well you try a duck in a storm;" and see whether the end does not take a fly, when it gets quite mellow, I say you have nothing to fear, I have not got you on the apple of my eye, I only want to show, you that you are a great big man now, only you jumped and spoiled me just as I had you coming out of the shell, well what of that, why don't you see, the bubble has broke, and it is all amazement, for it didn't grow in a minute, it took three weeks to hatch that egg, and it is only as big as a pin point compared to what you are telling people every day of your life happened in six short minutes; I have been talking to you for about five minutes, and I brought you out of a hen's egg, yet you want me to believe that your own God did make the world and all that in them is in six days; well you see my friends, it takes a man to believe this

story, and it will take a greater than ever Moses was, to show
you how it can be done, now I love and admire Moses, but he
can't come down and tell you now how it came about, that he
did do this great work, in the last few hours of his life, it was
spent in prayers to his God, and then he never said I am willing
to own up, that I don't know how this great world has come
round, you see my friends that Moses was the greatest general
you ever had, he could annihilate whole armies, by the wave of
his arm, yet my friends he could not explain the art of making
you know what it is that governs the universe, as I have shown
you, and as I intend to make you understand the beginning,
whether you take my hand, or I lead you there with your eyes
tied up, it is all one to me, so as I get you there; and now when
I have made quite fast to you, it is quite easy for me to tie the
rope at the other end, and make it fast in heaven; well that
would not avail you anything, so it is altogether too smart a
trick to be conjuring with; so I might as well take you by the
hand, and lead you on your journey to heaven, and when I have
reached the middle, I can throw the rope to you, and you can
catch on, and I'll pull you up along with the rope, it isn't that at
all, I must make you climb a ladder, with my arm around your
whole body, first by piecing you together, as a sailor does the
rope's end, he gets it on his mind, that there should be a new
way to make a rope, from the old style, and he is always puzzling
his mind's good guardians with this theory, that a rope's end,
has something to do with the good government of a ship, and my
friend he is just as near heaven as you are, for poor Jack is simplicity impersonified, and he has got that great thought impregnated in him, that a ship is all he loves, and his sole aim is to
make that ship taught by the one theory, " a rope end;" well my
brothers and good friends, that poor fellow, has gotten his
theory from God, and it is this form of unselfishness; that taught
him, he soled his feet to the deck, and he gave his soul to his
God, now my friends did you do this, no you have not got nearly
as far as Jack, he can show you the rope end, that he plaited, and
he will use it too, should occasion arise for any such casuality,
but my brothers you did not plait my story as it came along, for

you never did get the end, like poor Jack; he has found the end,
in his simplicity, he has the end made fast: But with all his great
knowledge, he is without sense, for he never knew what he had got
to, and that is to the end of time, it is there so sure as the world
wags her great big pendulum; it came through this fashion, by
the hand of time, Jack became a hand-craft, he was able to sit
up and make a little wearing apparel, for his back became quite
sore, from the dripping storm, it blew so soft upon his clothes,
that they became so very wet, that he was anxious to be rid of
them, and by degrees, he was sitting up, and looking out at both
back and front, he could not stand the dreadful strain, so he
made a dead set upon that shell, and raising might and main, he
lifted off the shell; this is the way poor Jack, has caught the end,
he broke the egg, by striking it between the two ends, one end is
for the ladies, and the other end is for poor Jack, because he
gave the greatest push, when it was to be his last sitting in a
basin that had no end, till he poked his head outside; this is the
way the world began, by propagating in the sand, it is quite
necessary for me to begin by illustration, for you must bear this
right along in front of you, that life is germinated through heat,
for it is heat, that brings life, for the fact is quite easily demonstrated, by the weakest intellect, and not as you suppose a difficulty at all; now my friends you just keep your eyes on me, and
don't look till I tell you, it is the way a worm moves, when he is
creeping, that causes his hole to get round, his nose is in the
ground, and his body is working, at that hole, and he will have to
move very cautiously at first, or he won't prevent himself from
being crushed, by the falling dust; Well he is struggling, and
wiggling, with a confounded nuisance; his back won't strike the
rear end of that hole, till he has touched it with his front end,
well don't you see my friends that the worm, is obliged to abandon
the surface, or he would be swallowed up, carcass and all by that
pouring rays of sunshine, in order to live, he has to burrow in
the sand, well now my friends don't you agree with me, that
worms have both legs, and eggs, there is the first end my friends,
where is the old infidel to-day, why my friends he is back at you
tooth and nail, and he will fix them to you like the Parisian

paint of the present age, don't think I am not capable, for you
will find out yet that I shall show you everything in a quaint way,
till I pipe my very eye in shame at your ignorance; well I suppose
you won't give me much time for wallowing in the dust, I must
muv'-o-un as the Irish peeler says when he sees a decent coupel
making eyes at his mother, in a quick stand; this is the way the
worms do, they get at each other, and in a course of propagation,
they lift each other higher up, by decent funerals they bury the
wicked, and let the live; live, that is, they preach and pray, whilst
taking on the gray, for a worm is fond of phosphorescence, it will
wake and grow quite calm; in going through some essence, its
idea is to melt quite smooth, by lying in the shade, it lives on
essence, for there is nothing else that mortal man can see, his
eyes are made from essence, because you don't see him with any is
no reason why he should not have them, well, why is it that he can't
keep quite still; for the fact is so plain, I feel ashamed to own, that
he has no idea of why he moves, except, that he wants a bigger
hole, and he will wriggle and twist, for his body, is growing so
fast, that he will be pinched, unless he makes a bigger impression
on his covering, and here my dear friends I have got to make
my first impression, your own thoughts start in just at this
instance, as the worm feels pinched, he moves his body, and it
recedes at the touch of the earth, well the worm is at the game
of fight, he is making his bed, and he has it to make; no kind
godmother, he sends the earth flying in agony, for it touched
him, and made an impression, and it had its agony, in an instant
returned, his soul was disturbed, by the touch, of what appeared
to him as an unworthy stranger, and in battle array he drew his
little hide around him, and cut his way through, the victory
is won, my soul has caught that which stimulates me to a
greater effort, and my worm is the soul of honor, for in
its agony, it planted the sting of covetness; it greedily drew
that team from off the Sun, and warmed its way to life, yes my
friends you are very near a beginning now, I have made you
understand where the first time an impression is made, it is not
much after all, but your God did not know it, and I don't
want to boast over the best man we ever owned, I am his

friend, and I aṁ your friends; at least I mean to be: Now since I have been so very fortunate in placing your skin, and not getting tangled up, why you ought to congratulate me, with a pair of boots, it is not easy to wear out sole-leather where I belong to, and I pinch my feet to save my hide, so I have got to get into your coat, and see how it fits after it is on, you seem to be wearing a loose-fitting jacket now, for in moving my back round, I have made my whole hide rough, and it is quite soft on top, I wonder whether that can mean me or is it some one else, it feels quite soft and velvety, but I don't like that touch, it is a kind of clayey kind of touch, it has no warm feeling, it is dead, I wonder how I came to get that upon my back, it is a soft kind of substance, it feels like any other worm, only I don't like it, for it is a kind of oppressor, it is a just manipulation of evil, it is the hide-sore, it has got a pin that pricks me, it is a feeling of horror, I feel quite creepy, I have got the ague, it is an affliction, to my core, it is drying into my very earthy sub-body, I don't feel proud at all now that I beat my body through that hole in the sand, my very soul revolts at the thought of being an affliction of ague, I will not move again, I shall die in misery, there is a nasty hump getting on my back, I feel it is so sore, that I can't peel myself off, no matter what my selfish-ness does, I want to keep moving, yet the blessed thing, keeps on getting worse, it is going round my belly, and it is now quite near my front, with its nasty yellow hoop, I do so hate this hoop, I was all glory, till my jacket caught that hoop, through the sweating and heat, in my hole, it is ague and cholera combined; a combination of gasoline, and the essence of tartaric acid coming out of the end of the Moon, and then being deposited in a seething mass of yellow clay, called the attic artista of desuvelorum; or the atmosphere in its attitude of gory strife with nature; this is the first formation, and you can afford to let me come out of that worm, and sit down a little, I want a rest after that toil of mine, it is a rapid man you want, well my friends are satisfied with me, and I am no rapid man, I am plain Tom Paine, that's all; now since I am not ashamed to own to you that I was a worm once, what right have you got to

be better than I am, I did what you never could do: And when
a man whips the land of cotton yarns, and spins a wonder it is
right that he shall be appreciated; and I never asked yet for a
thing without it contained a meritorious effort in the start, and I
have demonstrated, the word impression for you, as no Webster,
or Bulwer-Lytton, ever knew how to approach my theoretical
illustration of a fact in its entirety; You can plague me all
you choose, but I have stuck heels into boots long before you
were born, and I mean to teach the young men of America, more
than they ever hope to learn outside of me and mine, for I shall
lay claim to some of their best geographical pictures yet, they
don't know paints for them, they think their eyes are their own,
I can make pictures through any one's eyes; and when you
get my eye upon you, it is like the wax before the maw, it makes
meat into mulch, and it pounds advice into you like a mealy
potato, I can wheat your own bread, for I know how to sow a
field of corn, and as soon as I get properly established, I mean
to show you how to make McCormick hop to another kind of
dance; instead of tying up devils in the form of crab-
spooks, I'll pull him off his high horse, and make you invent a
thing, that turns out flour at the turning-home point, that is the
way to stick such fools as paint me and my friends tumbling
out of sheaves of corn; I hate to be made the laughing-stock
of people; by who hardly know one shock from another, it is
as easy to tell one bundle of corn, by the ears, as it is to stook
up a pile of impossibilities; but never mind that just now, it is
the spook we are after, not McCormicks; but the genuine one,
who frightens you, when you get full of the wheat made into
meal, that is what I am going to get after I have done making
my game of you, this is it; it is a great deal easier to come
home in a wheat-sheaf, than to die in a corn-stalk, the one
begets the meal and the other has gotten back into the heel,
now you are startled, you caught me off guard there, I was
not ready, I had been out fishing for what you call the clover,
it comes in little tufts, you know what I mean, the shamrock
from Ireland home and rarity; the women sell it to you, as you
leave the blossom behind you, I know where you got that dreaded

20

poke from that old spook; the "hobgoblins off the famous Green Isle"; it's only to take care of the weeds my boys, that I'd be tasing you now, but where did the spooks belong to fust, why, my dear boy, it came along wit old Colleen bawn, and the weed they call my beautiful clover, but as all the world knows is that sweet-smelling shamrock of the dear old home beyond the seas; I'd die murther, until your ghost appears when you gets drowned in that far away America; but where is the spook, he is not in the clover, and I can see how he changed from shamrock to Ireland, well my friends in sportive jest it is not wise I know, but as you are afraid of spooks, they are equally afraid of you, and though you can't see them, they can see you, now how are you going to take me by the hand, both are frightened, this is different to the worm, he only pushed, and there was a yielding sensation, your place is on earth, mine is where I choose to make it; and I have got nothing from you, yet, well you see me and you don't see me, as that great preacher hid, when the cask lid fell through, he was gone, sure enough, he demonstrated the theory, more forcibly, than may be polite; yet he did prove more in that action, than you ever gave him credit for; for he woke the jeers of the boys, and they have to be awake, to find a spook, it is like the dog bingo, coming through the sausage-mill, it is clear, only the purty wee doggie had a chain, and the collar stopped in, that was a sure find dot toime, cause de collar voise in mit de meat; vell de poor yettle dorg got dare by mistake, his nose it vas tin, and his troat it vas big, and he vas ferry vine dorg till him goot dare; now I want to show you where the mistake has always been made, you take a mistake, from a beefsteak, and what have you found, well the whole affair is wrapped up in a shell, it is the sound, that tells you where we are, it is the sound who tells you who I am, it is the coach, that throws an uncertain thing, and you have that uncertain thing defined, it is a spook, I have the right to demonstrate how I please, because I am what you call a tyrannical spook, I won't leave you alone, because I can't, and how is this, have we no rights at all, have we not got heaven, is it ours or yours, you have got your earth, we have our heaven, then why don't I

cry content, because you are mine, I am above you, because I
am higher up than you are, I am away up above you ever so far,
I should think I must be about twenty degrees higher than the
best scholar you have got, and I want to make him feel inferior
to me, because he says there are no such things as spooks,
he don't know how to look for them, that's all, he is no
better than a blind sea-eel, that never had any eyes, it
couldn't see, its eyes were not grown yet, and they won't
grow my friends; because it is a worm, that does not
get cholera, its sole aim has been to live underneath banks,
and, as soon as it can get near water, it divides its
time with one thought, and that is how to make a division,
one is this thought, that it must be sent on, for it
is in a corral, hemmed in; its idea is that a whole schoolful
of snakes are on it, it is afraid, and goes sneaking round, for
fear it might come in contact, with a something it never felt, and
this is a spook, for he is always prowling round, looking for
something he can't find, it is the same when he is in his old
raiments on earth, he thinks he is going to catch a spook, some
day, and he is all the time afraid a spook is going to catch him:
Well there is the blind eel for you, he has a notion, that he will
one day drop on to something nicer, than he ought to, and this
is to see; which he never does, for the fact is as plain as day,
his eyes are growing, and it is in this blind eel, that sight is first
advanced, his eyes are the color of a scum, and he can not see,
for they are only at their maiden maturity, they have not been
touched by life, and are just as far advanced as ever they can
be, till they are brought into play by the action of longevity,
there is the secret, it is the length of time, that they live, that
brings on this sight, and it is done through the adhesive candescence of getting in tow with other enormities; such as the
weeds, that grow in the sea, they are tumbling about, and in
time this skin wears off, and you find them pushing their heads
back, by growing in tight to the roots of these sea-weeds, for
they dare not look at the light, it is a horror to them, and this is
where our feeling of horror begins, we are afraid of the light,
and it is just the same, with you, you dare not look at this spook,

for he is in the air, yet he will not harm you, for he is afraid of
you seeing him, and why, because he sits down beside you, and
you are quite close to him, and yet he is all the time aware of
your presence, and you don't know that he is there, this is the
whole secret, your nose is in the dark, like the eel up against a
bunch of sea-weed; why, because your eyes have got a thin skin
over them to protect them from the excessive heat and light,
and your mouth is opened, for the purpose of letting in gas to
escape through the eyes; this is the cause of no teeth, till you
advance further on, it is the same with the eel, his mouth, is
made, by his nose being placed against the sea-weed, his first
thought is to eat, for the essence, that came into him at first, had
a tendency to grow, for it had grown before it was drafted to
fill the rays of the Sunlight, which drew it up as food for the
Sun, and when it came down again, it was the Sun that had
made it hungry, as it does everything, that passes through, and
why should it make this essence a hungry essence, for the fact is
quite like you placing a powder in the water, the water is so
evaporative, that it swallows its own self, and makes its body
grow larger all the time, and why should it do this, for it is a
minister of the good that follows on, and leaves the bad to go
behind, this is why, it is all good, and it keeps on flowing from
the time of its first great struggle with nature, and that was at
the beginning, but how could there be a beginning to anything
so immense as water; well it is just as easy to master as any of
the rest, the beginning is all the time going on like all the rest
of nature, it's got to be made like I am making you understand
me, you will want to know how I write through a mortal next,
and I won't show you that, well but let me see how is it that a
mortal has blood, well that is easy too; only you have to get
water first, and then the blood is grown after; and the water is a
flume from off the back of wind, as the wind blows, it draws a
draught after it, and it is here where you get the advantages of the
spook, for he is constantly traversing the atmosphere, from
heaven to hell continually, and he knows what draws rain, it is
the wind, that draws it after its funeral, its own death, is the
weight of water it has held, in its wake, for the wind is the pro-

genitor of water, its very life, demands that it be held back, and
its very soul is in its own winding current, for the wind rises, for
the reason of its own lightness; and it falls by the hand of its
own power, for as it rages and storms, it is bellowing forth its
own sound, and as surely as the wind whistles, here is the solution to the great mystery of God, his soul is wrapped up between
these two elements, for as the wind does howl, she propagates the
life of immortality, and it is done in this wise, her ascendency is
the hanging of the elements, that suspend the heavens, and she
is driving at heaven, like a giant at the famous dragon of old,
pulling the mansfild in two; it is the harvest home, the corn is
ripe, the Sun is glittering in the morning, and the dew from
heaven is descending upon nature, and all the time, no one looks
at the pretty little mushroom, that has propagated, since last
night, it is a fungus, it came in a moment, and it was sufficient
to sustain armies; for many a long season; where is the manna
gone my friends; is it this mushroom, that you have been deluded
for generations over; God was good, he could manipulate this
little waif, as easy: As you can my knife, it is herein demonstrated, that the seed of the earth, does spring from this same mushroom, for as the Sun saps back, the life of that fragrant fungus,
she warms the roots, and from the phosphorescence, she does
propagate life, it comes in the form of a little worm, that grows
and swells, till it has nothing left to gather from, then it dies off,
on the surface, for it too can not bear the sad loneliness of
nature, and is died to the earth, by the stain of crime, for as it is
drawn to the center, it feeds on the upper surface, of the ground,
and when it has found no more essence to live upon, it dies too;
leaving a reddish mark behind, this is blood my friends, for the
wind had made it live, and by living it had paid the penalty of
death, by its own maker, there we have murder in the first
degree; and I have not done, for the worm in dyeing the ground,
left behind it the sting of shame, it was there it first lived, and
after living, it gave up its life freely to God: That is where you
have the beauty of nature, it came by degrees, and sublimity is a
slow cultivator, for the Sun moves as she loves, and she hates
with scorn, casting her angry eye upon nature, that does not

appease her appetite; now my friends you think that worm died, well you are just off your base there, it did not die, for instead of dying it went on again, and is still going on, for the agony of death caught it upon its own bier, and it went to God, and is there right up in the mountains, that are around the sky, and instead of being that little worm, it is now about as big as a calf, and is food for other animals, that are more powerful than it: Now you want to again investigate, and you have underneath that canker, for that blood, is the death-sting of the living, and beside that blood, is the sin, it is there, as sure as the Gods above us hold the life we eat, and you know they do, for they are the masters, they are above us, and they are over us, and as they crept along the ground, there is how they expect you all to creep to-day, and in this form of creeping you are still doing, for you are creepers, and the vine is the husbandman, for in that vine there is strength, though it be but a suckling as it ascends, it matures and ripens as it proceeds in growth, and when it has grown the stem is tough, but the roots are many, and the place where the worm died sprang to life a little twig, a small one at first, and then as large numbers of worms died, large numbers of twigs grew, and still larger worms grew, because of the moisture of these twigs; still larger twigs came and planted their heads in the ground, and grew still larger bushes, till finally there came a tough kind of a worm, and it did not die like the rest, it raised its head up, and commenced to gaze about, its eyes had been protected so long by the bushes, that it stood the test, and was able to creep and crawl, and could eat leaves, its own progenitor having passed along before, and it was well aware of this fact, for it had seen the other, in its infancy, and whenever it came to be anxious or alarmed, there was a feeling of dread, that this other one, would come and devour it; and this is what it did, to sustain it from death, it grew to the stump of a tree, to keep it from being blown away, and here you have the wind whistling round the ground, calling for more life, and the atmosphere became so heavy, that you could not see at all: And in this atmosphere, there is a clump of mush, or punk, that grows to the bark of dead trees, and there

is the mystery of our backbones, it is in this punk, that we get
our first backbone, because it is a union, between the dead and
the living; and the dead is the essence coming out of that old
log, that does produce, a spider, which is a breeder, of no mean
order, he will give you all the colors, you want, and then he is
just as good, he gives you all the kind of feet you want, for he
is a hen and chickens combined, his idea is nothing but pleasure,
and he lays eggs, till he feels ashamed of so many, so he hides
one here, and he plants another there, till at last he has got so
much to do, till he does not know where he has laid his last egg,
well the consequence is, that he is in time a great deal farther
ahead, than he thought for, and one spider is off on the water,
and the other is off on the land, well you have all seen this, and
yet you don't believe any more to-day than you did two thousand
years ago, well why don't you believe I am telling you as Thomas
Paine, from heaven, that is not the reason, it is because you are
all too lazy, you never get up to look, and you are just as bad as
your father the spider, He had so many eggs, that he forgot
where he put them, and he never hurt himself to look; now my
friends you know you are lazy, well why is it, that you are lazy,
for the fact is as plain as day, you are a little too cunning, and
you got that all in a sunshiny way, your fathers and mothers
were rollicking kind of blades, they liked the river best, because
it sported you about so much better, and in doing it, your
fingers fell out: In an awful fright, the mother began to praise,
and the father began to shout, I–have–got–no–more–work–to–do;
who cares–for–you; Kirk, shouts another, and out pops a pigeon
pair; it's all over shouts the pigeon, I am here as proud as any of
the finest feathers that ever flew, and I want you to come and
play parrot underneath, for you can put your little head beneath
my wing, and I can give you some consolation, by placing mine
over yours, and we can make a little sound, that says sweet little
wife I am going to have plenty more; when you throw me out of
your little parlor; and get me in together, it is " alwite " my
pretty per-per, ker-ker, kerky-workerk; It is little use going
into minute details as to the first noise, for it is all bound
together, and is wrapped up in affection, and I shall take a work

of arduous toil from you by leaving out this matter in correction of sound, for you know that the wind was the progenitor of the first articulate sound, and it is this wind whistling, that drew the breath of life, for in its whistling moments, it caused the live moments to grasp at the atmosphere, and think it is the wind, I wonder why it howls so; and the moaning of the wind, is the total element, which brings this mind together, it is like a blasted asp, it sucks in venom, like the mind we meet, and that is why, the wind whistles, and in drawing it sucks poison with good, and the two together sow the seed of good and evil, there is the folly, that we have all been looking for; and you don't think it strange at all, now that I have told you, that the wind gathers in your evil sounds, and draws them off to some other part, and there deposits them to grow, you don't think I know anything about good and evil, you wretches, you called me a man of mild reasoning faculties; what have you ever done to enlighten the germs of humanity, I save you time by the thousands of years, and I am still an old infidel in your opinion, I tell you what it is, I am more Godlike than ever any of those are, who talk about things they can't explain, and I feel like that pigeon, when I have unraveled a hidden mystery, for the pigeon, is quite proud, that he lived to see his pretty feathers, and play rounders, with his affinity, his soul's love, what is there, or what can be more righteous, than this pair of pigeons, coming along together, they bring home the eggs, and deposit them in their little nests, and there let them remain till they have got ready to make them grow into a pair as pretty as themselves, and sometimes, it turns out quite a nest of love and purity, and then again on the other hand it is fraught with a miserable nest, for the pigeon is not prepared for the evil-sounding wind, he does not gather in enough straw, and he has altogether too much buried under his eggs, it lays on the wrong side of the weather, this is all the theory of our every-day life, John won't keep his bill from picking the eggs before they are ready, and Sall she, is too bounceable and wants the nest all her way, well my friends, one jaggle fetches on another, till Mary Jane is born, then the trouble is quite alarming, well the end of it all is that the pigeon-

pair, have grown quite spiteful toward each other, and they settle down to tearing each other's eyes, well the result is a great big
tussel, and then the wing who flipped the hardest, was the one
who caught the most pain, for it worked against time, and the
consequence is that the Sun never shined on those wings any
more, they had gathered in the congealed atmosphere, and were
quite full of blood, that had been put in by an excitement that
will defy all resistance, and there you plant your disease, it is
through these struggles, that disease starts, and it is for the
hand of man to say whether he is to be healthy, or whether he
is going to suffer, his life is his own, and he must either fight it
out in agony always, or he must stop fighting, it's the weakest,
who win, not the strongest, for the weakest, is a soon job against
time, and he goes over like a shuttle-cock, he is the best worth,
when his earthly career is ended, for his work on earth amounted
to nothing, and his toil in heaven, is not looked upon as valuable,
for his soul, is not suitable for aught but common labor; this is
what I want you all to learn, that a soul has to fill a capacity,
according to its ability, and when it is done it is happy, for it never
knew what strife is, and as a natural sequel, it is not any more use
at writing to you, than the pigeon could be, at saying our Lord's
prayer, his soul was that of a divine, and he did his work, with
accuracy, following the instructions he was given, well my friends,
what had these pigeons to guide them, did they not have their
fathers and mothers before them to guide them how to build
their nests, why of course they did, and it is through this, that
they have always been taught, by their fathers and mothers, and
now you want me to explain, how the spider who begat all men
and women did, before they had any fathers or mothers, well it
is quite simple, and you can find it for yourselves; it is this, a
punk is porous, and it is drafted through, by a flume, that has got
a piece of velvet on that outside shell, well this flume, is quite in
accordance, with the world's fair, it brings in elements from all
parts of the globe, and deposits them in a cavity, that swells,
from the impression made by those things, that come floating
from everywhere, as you know that a drifting takes the form of
impression, well it is this, that keeps moving along, till it is

sucked in by the punk, well after it was sucked in, it came out on
the other side, for it had graduated, it was the best of its
character, for the punk, would not allow it to remain, unless it
was profitable to keep, its very life depended upon its suitability
for this exposition, and in this exposure, it inhaled the cortege,
that surrounded it, and was supported by this audience; now my
friends you will agree with me, that I have done what few men
ever knew how to begin to think about, and I want a place
among you, that will prove me capable of doing what no man
has ever done, or is ever likely to do again, for the first is the
creditable one, not the one who walks along, with an unpaid-for
suit of clothing, I pay for mine by the sweat of my own intellect, and I wear no man's raiments, let the lazy youth, come forward and give us his opinion of old Tom, and his recorded win, let
him come and show us something better, he is no better than I am;
why can't he strip off his coat, and come down here and say
I am also a competitor for the enlightenment of man, I want
to see this youth, who is capable, of beating me, and I want
to grasp him by the hand, and say you are a genius, I want to
tell him myself, that he is a nonesuch, for I will know him, don't
you fear, I will not sulk, because I have met a greater man than
myself, I will go to work over again, and beat him, that is what
I would do, I wouldn't allow him to be able to say he conquered
me, and I shut down like a fellow, who has nothing but brag at
his back, it is true that I have always been a bit of a blow,
but you know where it came from, and that is the beginning
of the world, in its entirety, and what I don't explain in this
book, you shall have in the next, so you can rely on me, for
this, that I won't put on my coat again, till you beat me, now
then you want to know where the determination of man is
gotten, it is like all the rest, it comes from the one great
thought, and that is the wind, for as the wind blows, she gets
heavier, by the force of water, she is drawing after her, and as
she gets heavy, she also comes to strength, by the force of her
own weight, and as the light air ascends, the heavy atmosphere
is at the heels, and is gaining and gaining all the time, on the
light atmosphere, and as it gathers in all around, it is going on

all along, till it masters the light air, and then you know the rest,
it comes tumbling down in miserable confusion, because it got
spent and couldn't keep on, because there was nothing else for it
to conquer; then my friends when I have reached the top, you
ought to help me stop there, and not go on and let me fall
down like the miserable rain, don't you believe me, when I say
miserable rain, why it is nothing else, it is the end of a battle,
for as sure as you get there, you can see the turning point,
just as I have described it: I don't want you to go up in a
balloon, I want you to listen to sense, and go and look, immediately you have got clear of that miserable old carcass; you can
then pop off, with your comrades, and see whether old Tom, did
tell the truth, about the wind and rain, making this great fight
by themselves over your head; and that you were always missing
good things, when you were in that old shell: Now then to
demonstrate more fully, I want to show you that your own
vim comes from this battle, it is there, that a fight takes place,
well my brothers, it is your own fight at the beginning, it is
the elements of congealed atmosphere, that has thrown each
other, in battle, and they did it, for a purpose, and that purpose
is the propagation of all live material, you seem to think I am
bordering on insanity, but you know what the fool did once,
and that was to rip open the curtain of a pair of sheets, and
the one went to heaven, and the other could not be seamed
together again, for it had lost its fac-simile; this is the same as
the wind coming in again, it is drawn into the water, and
these two together, make life, they are altogether two distinct
bodies, till they get together, and then they make life, by being
together, for a period, of a few minutes, now you see what I say
is true, for you can prove this, you have only to get a pail of
rain-water, and make it stand steady for a little time, and then
it begins to propagate, this is food and meat combined, for the
life is in the water, by its own consent, or because it was mastered by the man who carried the most good sense, and that is
the water, which is the strongest body, we have, and the water
is just as good for us, as it is for the live material, which it contains: this is why, it ought to be a great deal more serviceable,

afterward, for it is down by consent, and in bringing it back, it
is made to stay down, because the earth is here, and it mingles
with the earth, and porous progenitiveness sets in, and this is
the atmosphere turned into lungs, there you have the sound, that
I was speaking about being wrapped up in the wind, I might
have fooled you, but you see I can't help being honest, and as my
kind are not as plentiful as the raindrops that fall, because; I
am as the heathen, only a little different, you said he is an "Infidel," and I am going to show you some more ways and means of
putting down crime, it is seen at a glance, that you commit murder, immediately you boil water, for it is this life, which you
destroy, that is preparing lungs, that is killed in the heat, well
you attack me at once, and say the Sun does always murder, and
this is how she delights her selfishness; because you see her rising with gladness, from behind that black rain-cloud, that has
fallen upon you: Well the Sun might destroy the lungs, that
fell upon the ground, but that which fell beneath, the fruitful
soil, is growing steadily on, for it is this I tell you that our
Saviour alluded to; when he spoke of the grains of wheat falling,
he meant the wheat, that fell on the dry hard stony land was perished, before it could mature, but that which fell on the soft
loam, was all right, it had some protection, and was hereafter to
propagate, but that which falls on the water, is mingled into sea,
for it had another element added to it, and was crowned with
glory, for its soul had found rest, and it was covered up by its
fathers; you see what a range of science I am drawing around
you, it is the wind, that is the cause of all this, it is the air, which
is the great prognosticator of this wonderful thing, called the
life immortal, it is this great sign of nature, that I am carving,
and laying bare before your eyes, don't fret my brothers, you are
going to die happy in the sight of this far-off land, you are to
see the road there, as your sons, shall see the father, so shall the
son of man ascend to heaven, before he leaves his carcass behind
him: You want to force me into telling you how, well it is this,
you are a magnificent specimen, and I won't leave you alone,
that is how you are to get there, in the body, I shall make you
do it quite easily, it is by a jump that is all, I shall take you

there in mind, it is the mind that will go there, and not the body, it is the thoughts, that can be made to believe, and once they believe, they are sure to follow, this is the way to do it, by keeping your eyes shut, and then you shall see everything I explain, it will come in at the right end, and go home to the other end quite easy enough, you think this impossible, but it is not, I can show you the way, so as you can't help but believe me, and then I have taken you to heaven in the body, and what do you know to the contrary, it is this my friends, these who are about you, will go to heaven, and inspect it, and come back satisfied, that what you read in this book is correct, and they will then make you believe, that is how I am going to take you to heaven, before it is time for you to take a look at there yourself; well you wonder why those who are around you can't do this for themselves, and not wait till Old Tom, has gone and dug up the whole earth, to find the right grounds to start out upon; well it is here, my friends are numerous, already, on my side of life, and they are very often round you, but you don't seem to understand how this is; for the fact, that your friends use you for their own convenience, and not for your good, this is why, and it is the same, with all humanity, to do this, for they see it in that light only, and why, for the fact is quite easily explained, it is this, the Sun is content, with what she is doing, and the moon has no choice, it is obliged to operate in accordance, with the natural work, of peopling the earth, by a calling of its functions together, and dividing them into as many paper packages, as possible, in other words, the moon drops the essence, as it is adjusted, by the internal organ of its own contrivance, for so watering, and manuring the earth, or again I will show you the facts, as they actually stand, the Moon delivers as she sows, or in plainer language, it throws out the refuse from the Sun, after that body, has prognosticated, and made food, for fattening her own great body on, this is as near the identical man as I can make you, for what do you care so long as your body is fattened, about the hereafter, it is all one to you, whether you go to heaven or hell; as long as you get there, and as most people the majority for instance, are able to believe that there is a hell and heaven, what does it matter, which, so long as I get there, this is the theory of man, he can't see clear enough, to go himself and look, and he dare not leave hell for fear, that he can never reach heaven safely, and this is his thought, when he leaves the earth and his body, so he is lazy still, and he hangs on to the earth and you, and when you are dying, you find yourself afraid of going, and why, because everything is dark beyond, your soul speaks the word, for there is no fooling then, and you have no camel, to ride through that great needle upon, and you are lost, there is no chart, that amounts to anything, the parson couldn't answer some little simple question, and in those last dying moments, you think to yourself, I will remain here, till I am taken, well my brothers, it is natural to do this, for the sun did not move, till she got the right kind of machinery stuck in her, no more will you on that great judgment day, coming home you will have a machine stuck in you, that is not perishable, it will last, as long as the world is in unison, with anything, and it will be there to propel you round the world, as long as ever any one else's body can last, and instead of getting weaker, it will go on growing, and get stronger all the time, this is your body, after you die, as everybody says, when I die; it's all a lie, you couldn't get killed, why, because you are a sound, that is come from the beginning, and it will sound the death note, and then it is gone, where, why wherever it can get the chance of course, what else would it do, it might be held, well my friends you have got me here this time, I can't tell you how to hold a sounding seam, it is here, and it is not here, and the parson has told you so, when he fell through that cask lid, he went in at one end and came out at the other, and that is all you make out of it, for should I tell you the exact way to stop a soul, you would catch this one right here, and make him shut up: So I might as well reserve some rights and privileges, for my business; you do so every day, now I think you have got a pretty good share of everything, except to make that ship go, which is so wonderfully constructed, as to have capsized the whole of your genealogical trees, that ever grew before, I guess I can have a blow afore I begins, for its

going to make a much much talky, when it is found out, who lit
the match, that set the world on fire, well a little blow, and a
little talk, is all right, when you are going to board a suspicious
looking craft; and her crew, might by pirates, or they might be
pretty much the same as a friend of mine, the parson not welcoming me as he ought to; I don't care, come on boys we'll strike in
and help ourselves, it is all fair in love and war, I might as well
have left our the war, because I am not going to fight to-night, I
only see darkness in front, and I don't want a tussle with the
parson in the night, it is all a mistake to attack a party at night,
I shall be obliged to fire my gun off to-night, and clap her in
ready for a clean sponge, before I board this gigantic frigate at
day-dawn, well you see in the morning we all have got the advantage of going round with the sun, and it is at dark; that I am
going to lay down, and watch the sun take her dip in that great
ocean, that is at the equatorial corner of heaven, it is no use me
sketching my advantages, this time, for I can lay bare, the exact
truth, and let the artists take up their easel, and strike off a description after I have gone over this scene, and portrayed a just
course for them to take, it is easy for them to follow a lead, and
I won't be there to stop them, and they can cabbage all my illustrations, too; but they will only lead you wrong my friends, the
leader is the one who ought to be followed, and not a junket of
knowing all minds alike. they are capable of seeing, when it is
demonstrated for them, but before they knew nothing absolutely
nothing of that great volume, of fire, that whirled the sun round
at a rate, excelled by nothing, and it is now for me to show you
what causes this great revolution to take place, it is the actual
melting of fire, that causes this excessive heat, which pervades
the earth, it is the heat being generated into soda, of a fine kind,
and it is this class of soda element, that is made into a great big
churn, that is built of soda, and is soda in its entire construction,
that it melts, and is propelled against the side walls, with a great
speed, coming from the after-flange wheel, that is made of a
soluvium of potassium, that dissolves, in the heat, and these two
running together combine, and are formed into a hard substance,
that is crusted over, with a flint surface, that is of a porous nature,

and it is all the time supplied through these pores, with an essence, that is generated, from the adhesiveness, of the sky, which is in its entire form of a great big sweat, for it is sweating, and inhaling all the time, it draws in, and is pouring out a quantity of saluvium, it is quite a machine of mechanism on the inside, and seams life together on almost every point, well the real guidance, is the quantity of matter, that is drawn in, it is this, which causes the fire to be kept burning, and the fire is hot as the very mischief, for it burns a great pile of vapor at each flame, it turns round and round, causing a revolution to come in the form of a big blast, it whirls round and round, till it reaches the mouth of the Sun, which is what you see from the earth, well this great pile of heated matter, causes a movement, of the interior of the sun, it causes the adhesive fluids to move, and they keep on a circle, and are drawn in motion, by the extent of the heated generator, that is generating acid all along, and this acid is forming into a liquid at the other end of the Sun, which you all know is the Moon, well it is here where the Moon is working her part of it, by the outside cortege, for it has an awful sight of auditors here, they keep on pulling and hauling at an immense rate of speed, it is the end, that I have brought you to, and this is what is going on there, the end is nothing more than an escape-valve, or a great big blow-hole, from which all kinds of material is flung out, it is here, where the Sun takes satisfaction in destroying garbage, by setting fire every time the Moon gets chocked up, which is once a month, or thereabouts, it is all fired out, and it commences to fill again, with the acids, that is seen through the mortal eye from the earth, and this is what you see, a whole mouth full of garbage, intact, before it has caught fire by the heat of the Sun striking a light to it, and when you seam your vision together, you can understand, that the Moon is not made of stones, and rocks at all, neither could such a thing be true, for the fact, that these stones and rocks could not move apart, and show you the interior, as plain as what you see it, well I am not going to vex myself over your theory, I am going to make you see it through my eyes; and they are pretty near perfect, I want you to follow me very closely, and tell me what you suppose that thing is that we call Friday, and the Lady in the Moon picking up noodles, I want to show you that she is actually folding up something, and not picking at all: And this is what her majesty the Sun has been doing for centuries, and no man has ever discovered it, why it is as plain as the nose on your face, it is the Sun, in her accessible mood, taking from the Moon, that which she wants again, it is the Sun drawing back to her own selfishness, the food, that has not perished by fire, and in that manner, she does get it so clear, that it makes her begin to propagate, when it has re-entered her furnace, for it is one more mixture, that has given her new life, and is greedily sapped up by her, in the essence of her own life, now do you see that the Sun is burning the Moon up, when you see that black mark, in the center, and she is practically eating the center out of the Moon, and drawing it back again, to use in her internal workings over again, now don't you believe me, or what have I left out: There is this, it is the entire enterence, that I don't seem to make you clearly get at, and that is this, the moon is only a body, that is the other end of the world, it is the end that we poor mortals never reach, for it is not a place, that any one cares much about living near, it is a stinking place, and is as full of smells, as the abomination, of a filth hole, it is the termination of the end of all concealed combinations, it is the end of hell and heaven both, it is the very funnel end of an unholy essence, for it is the foul end of all that has been made and propagated on this earth below, and it is the most awful smelling place, that there is, on earth or in the interior of any place known, it is the very worst of all filthy places, there is, and I don't want to make any mistake, it is the place, that ends up all eternity, for it has nothing left, but essence, and that is the essence of the hereafter, it is a place, where saints and sinners alike have both got to go through, before they are made whole, and this is at the beginning, for it is written, that the Sun shall cease to shine, and there shall be total darkness pervading the earth, at the time of the advent of our salvation, it is this, the moon shall refuse to throw her light, and the sun shall cease to shine, upon the son of man, but that is at the beginning, not

21

at the end; so you must understand, before you can believe, therefore I say to you, that there is a beginning, and I must show it to you, or how are you to believe, then take me in, and I am going to show you the most wonderful thing of them all: And that is the Moon is only a common man, and the Sun is only a common woman, and why; for the Sun, she doth warm the man, and in so doing the man hath a chance to give her the essence of his body, and these together have in their way propagated and brought into existence, all the rest, except the mere fact of a few little details, you have got the whole in its entirety, and you must be very dull indeed, when I have explained all this to you, should you still go on unbelieving in the hereafter, or that it was a great spirit God who worked all these wonders, you will find I have made, it all in different ways from any known pathway before, and it is necessary to believe, that I have shown you the truth, for it is in this particular that I shall ask you to allow me to leave out the whole of the stars, and not go into their part of the work, in this book, it is not necessary that you should know any more, about this at all: Only I have made it a point in all my works to write two books, and this shall not be the exception, as I could easily show you what part the stars play toward this firmament, only I have got a method in my works, and I will show you why, it is this; my works have all been found to contain too much material substance to be taken as facts, and they don't go off well on the market as salable literature, for they are like the atmosphere, there are so many turns and twists, that it is evident, that the author is made of a grain, that is like the laughing-stock, he came through a terrific storm, and like the sailor who wants a tornado, to help him along, in an open sea-faring atmosphere, there is almost sure to be a blow once in away, and it is this blow, that has always got the ship at home, from a long voyage, and you must not suppose, that any tornado is coming along to stop you from getting home, for it is here already, the storm, that blew the Sun into shape, is the same wind, that has her on the go now, and she is there just as contented and quite as happy as poor Jack, when his life is on the go, he knows no fear, and he is

still going on, as best he may, he however keeps mending all
the while, and he gets on by degrees, as the sailors go, his
place, is mended, and gets up a step higher on the ladder,
till at last he is on top, and then he looks around, and gives
his hat a wave in the air, and calls out hurrah, for I have won,
I am on top, and I never had a soul to help me get there,
it is the wind that drove him up aloft, he could not help it,
it came on to blow, and he saw these billows heave and fall,
and in they went, nobody ever knew where, but it is all along
the line, they never rose to the surface again. where they
should have risen, and not dropped back, and left you in ignorance all those many centuries since the beginning of reason;
now I have given you as much as I can afford to about heaven
in this volume, except this, there is the constant dropping of the
wave back into the sea, as the moon does make her adventure,
behind the horizon, and it is this, that when the Moon passes
round the ocean, and dips down, through the edge of the ocean,
it has to be cleared, of all refuse, and he forms a smooth
outer surface, by these passings, that form a thin skin over the
whole surface of the Moon, that darkens in the center, as it mops
up the mud and earthy substance, that it passes through, well at
this particular pass, there is a peculiar shade of green mud, that
has a kind of slime in it; and this is what you see in that Moon,
that has the appearance of a man, in its dark formation, this is
not all, the Moon in passing round, is moved from the inside,
and protrudes out, and when he is on the very act of disloading,
his heap becomes fettered, by an actual force of impression from
either side, by the touch of the Moon on the edges, as it passes
round the horizon, now you have a very fair demonstration of
how the man makes his Friday, and how he is standing up making obeisance to his upper construction: Now I want to say that
I have done entirely in this volume, with the ethereal forms, for
it can not be completed in this work, without injuring my method,
and you can have the second volume in another addition of perpetuity; I want to say that you are to look forward to more
sublimity, in the next addition, and less working on actual facts,
which will throw more light on the hereafter, and how you are

to materially assist your own individual selves, so as to bring
home more happiness, and less liability to come into harm, and to
assure you of this fact, it will be thrown out here, the idea of a
work, that can never fade away, it is the time of all others, to
help mankind, and not to gather round him difficulties, that
should weigh him down, and drag him below his creatures, I say
that man is superior to all creation, and there is no God too good
for him, that he has God within himself, and he is a prince in
disguise, he is a nobleman of all the great fountains of the earth
and skies, he is glory impersonified, he is God himself, but he
never knew it till I have made it known to him, and as the peacock
walks around, I say that bird is more like the deity, than we ever
have been taught to learn to live, and I say that pride is the
foundation, of all that is holy, in its integrity and truth, your
days of paganism are ended, and you are now to know
that a man is the deity of the world, he is sublimity, in its true
form, he is good beyond a doubt, and to make him this you have
to let him know what he is, where he came from, and he has to
live to belong to his calling, and his throne of glory; is it not
better to be taught that you are here according to the throne of
glory, than to be taught that you are to be held there, and
judged by a God who is imperishable himself; I say there can not
be any sense in such teaching, you are to be judged, there is no
manner of doubt in life, but it is by the hand of nature, that
does this work, in its own way, according to specific order, and
not by any God, there is no manner of doubt at all on this theory,
it is this form of man, that I am going to describe to you, and
that is this, the man I want to show you, will be a man after I
have shown you how man was first made, and not by mystery,
or magic, I am going to make you out of the fish, in the sea, and
I am going to prove to you, that man is being made right along,
from the beginning to the present time, and not leave you in
doubts any more, this is what I intend to do, instead of giving
you the whole of heaven in this work, I shall join man together,
link by link, as you have a chain made, when you want to fasten
him up: Now then I want to show you what a great many
people are missing almost daily, and that is man in his

earlier stages, it will be quite an interesting feature, for you are all prone to the imagination, and that is the reason, that so many minds have gone wrong, it is because you don't think right, your own head, is all right, but it is the thing, that is around you, they don't do right, that want all the sense, and you have to be content, by following on, it is this, that instead of your mind becoming unhinged, it is this, your hand does not guide right, it is wrong, from the first, it is not a hand, it is a fin, therefore it is taught to swim, and in swimming, it is to go in front, and in going on in front, you must let it wave all obstructionists out of the way, your fingers, are the claws of the crabs, and this is how you claw so much, you had better let me explain the whole of this to you from the beginning, and then you can see and understand, it is only a great deal better, than you thought before, and that is the idea, of springing off the tail of an imagination; I am going to first place myself, as the man in the Moon, as you have always been lead to suppose, there is a being of some sort in the moon, that appears; and disappears, at periodical intervals, well it is natural to suppose, that you would be struck by this as a mean kind of way to annihilate the old ancient theory, but unless you have such a spirit as mine to go back to you, and face all sorts of storms, and every kind of weather, how are you going to get the right understanding, I say you will be cursed forever, should you reject this information, and do any act of violence to the man who writes for me, and it is just like what you have always done, to kill the calf, that laid the golden egg, now let me inform you right here, that you are no more able to control your passions, than you ever were, and it is all on account of your blood, being mixed, with the foul and the fair, now let me show you how your blood became mixed, it is this, when your forefathers, the entire population of the earth, was a kind of sheep, well when it was killed, it grew hair, in the land, instead of wool, well now the thought has often struck you, how is it, that my brother's hair, is black, and mine was light sandy colored, well this is the theory for that, a man having the light-colored hair, came off the mountain side, that is subjoined to the mountain, that is nearest to the Sun, whilst the one who has the black hair, came from the mountain side, next or nearer the Moon, this is according to the shadow, coming first, and the life afterwards; well now there is this in that theory, it is quite obvious, that the Moon did deliver, those two, but in falling, one was a black sheep, and the other a grayish white, now the one, that came along alone, must be a good deal better, than the two first, for the fact, that it came close together, and when it grew, it was a leopard, it had spreckled wool, and was naturally a kind disposition, for it had the ingredients, that make a whole, it was a good kind, for it had the different staples of wool, now you see my friends, that I have brought you to the form of disposition, which is a very sure way of getting you to understand my worst fears, and that is from a point of sanity, your saneness, is brought along by the necessities of life, and I would like to know who gave you the first idea, how to move round in harmony, with one another, it was certainly not the tiger, or the lion, it must be the sheep, for they are intelligent, and call across the ranges, to this other one, that they wish to bring over to them, now then I assume, that you have the ingredient of the sheep in you, for in danger, you will all follow each other, and in trifles, such as these, I have to pick up a great amount of lost links; thus you can gather, that a great many things have to be brought together, for a very material gain, and in bringing out those important testimonies of how the animal does, is properly speaking the theory, that we must grant nature a fair and impartial hearing, you must not condemn the good, before you look into the bad, vice-versa; it is here, that we have this point of man getting stronger, for he does become weakened, once you see him stripped bare of all his virtues; I tell you, that a man must belong to the goat, and sheep, for it is here that he gets, this great preponderance, of evidence, against his being separated from his kind, he hates separation, and he will gladly do on mean fare, and scanti-ness; rather, than be sent abroad from his people, he dares not let wit come to his aid, and say that he is afraid, but you take any

good soldier come home, and he is boiling over with pleasure to
see those dear faces again, well then don't you see the charm,
that hangs to him, that when he is away, he is always surrounded,
with his home ties and affections, for instead of his mind being
free, as you would imagine, it is incased, by the good sheep of
former days, they are all about him, and he can't forget the old
home, for he is fleeced inside of the wool that grew before he
was born, and could not be otherwise, as the wool, that grows on
the sheep's backs, is woven together, by a fine lustrous web, that
is being brought out in time, it is the thread of God, he is the
good sheep, for he it was who soled this thread together, and
made it into a fleece, well now I want to show you something,
this time, and it is this, it is a very plain fact, that a man's mind
is not what you think it is at all: Your mind is woven, by the
spider, it is got together, at first by a kind of thin net, and here
is how to show you the way to find out about this great secret of
mind running onto matter, it is this, my selfishness, in seeking,
has laid bare the secret, of telling you how the mind is made, and
it is thus; your own thoughts, come naturally, and you think it
is a meaty substance, that is the whole secret, but you are entirely
off your basis of common sense, it is thus you do not know how
to mend the head, when it has broken adrift, and in showing you
this form of substance, you can easily make mad people sane
again, for you can deprive them of their madness: Now to get
on, I must show you how the madman has been working, all
along, he thinks, that he has been the victim of some great
wrong, and so he has, for he has broken a cord, in his own head,
and in breaking this cord, he stuck fire to the rest of his head, so
you seam him together, like this, his head is deranged, for the
fact, that his own people, have become entangled, and they have
crossed the lines of light, one is in front, and the others are behind, so that he can't see straight, because this shadow, in front,
is struggling to get back again behind, and it can't do it, by
reasons of a very plain fact, the angel cord is snapped, and this
is the cause of insanity, his bosom friend, or champion for his
soul, is gone into the eye, and it has to stop there, till its friend
in the body dies; well there is a remedy for this disease, and that

is to torture the eyes, by stopping them from looking out upon the light, and by keeping them in total darkness; till the madness disappears, and this is the easiest cure you ever hear of, well it is quite on a theory of sense, that you have got this formally demonstrated; the eye is the great center of attraction, and the spirit, that is next to the soul, has a sure access, and egress; and he can't remain in darkness, for any great length of time, so he has to vacate, and when he has vacated once, he is altogether dumfounded, for he has lost his power, to return, by reason of his own sight failing, but it is this for only a period of a very few months, and then he will regain his ordinary vision; now you see where I have given you an advantage, instead of keeping asylum institutions, you may now keep farmyards, and give the lunatics plenty of soft-boiled eggs, for in cases of madness, it is essential, that they should be fed on food, that will make their sight grow again, and not by poking meat and rubbish down their wallets, now then you know why I have given you egg diet, it is the essence, that comes from the eggs, that is the theoretical eye, and as your eye originally sprang from the egg, it is natural, that the heathen doctor, would suggest his application, according to the necessary bandages, and as the wind threw the bow to leeward, it cast a bow, that should grow again, when it is bandaged by its own slayer, or more definitely, it falls short, because it grew too strong, and as the wind did clip the fingers off time, it is barely probable, that time can cast its own mould back again, and discover the mould that grew so strong, that it centred its eye, in the after part of the heathen Chinese, for you find the eye, the most difficult part to understand, and I have some very tough work before me, to make you thoroughly comprehend the sight in this wonderful eye of yours; it is so hard to tell, that is where the awful trouble is found, and I don't ask you to accept any unreasonable theory, I was just as hard hit myself once, when the jailer came and said I had to go out to play dodger, in the after guardroom, it was so awfully bad for me, I was so frightfully hasty, and I had a spirit friend, who was made of gunpowder, he couldn't keep still an instant, and so he moved in me, and I shot a dart of disdain on the guard, that would have crushed a feathered sinner, but this one, had only one theory, and that is "eyes front"; so I shall tell you to keep your eyes in front, till I get mad, and come right through you, it is this then, that has made sight, the hair on top of our heads, is porous, and it settles down, so close to the scalp, that it will very near break off there, only, that it grows to the scalp, and this is the way it came to grow, it is caught, by the flannel, that was first raised upon the sheep's backs, and then it came to be raised more plentifully, for raw material to patch men together with, well it is this kind of getting this wool, that propagates sight, it is this form of living beneath, the skin, that progenerates sight, at first, it gives life, and it looks back, for there is a hole, coming right through the hair, and it is this determined will power, that draws back, and then makes an effort to conquer, and then after conquering it sees; this is the theory, it has been demonstrated to you in a perfectly sane and rational manner, and it is true in fact and substance, now since I have mastered your eyesight, I can make you don't be alarmed: I mean to make you from the beginning, according to the natural laws of nature, and I will make you entirely on a basis of truth, now then you seam a crutch together, the same way, that you do a pig, for in finding a pig, you must first take care that he does not bite, and the next thing to do is to grow his hair, well once you get hold of him, you want to know where he came from; well it is a corker, to tell where a pig came from, I wish I knew, don't you attempt to tell me, or I won't be on the high horse again in a thousand years, it is thus, that I am going to tell you, and I don't want you to tell me, I was once in England, and they keep little black porkies there, and they have got little jaws, that poke out, to an alarming extent, well you could imagine a pair of cheeks, when you seam these together, it is awful the fat that is on those two little cheeks, I don't know how ever anybody could think the world was all done up in six days, when he beheld this little English pig, and his two cheeks, I would suggest, as a calm reminder, that an English hog, is a finer specimen, than the one, that Abraham, had when he went into all those many told prayers, that showed, so strikingly, when he told King Abimelech, that Rebekah, was his sister, Abraham was more afraid, then I am, or you never would get any more pork chops in England; for I am going to take a pig's cheek, to mould your eye with, and this is the way I am going to do it, your eye, is hollow on the inside, and your nose protrudes across the center, well the eyelid, is at the bottom of the left shoulder blade, it grew there first, and was held back by time, coming in the front of it, and drawing over the fore end, by putting in a combustion, that caused a protrusion to stand out, in the front of the nose, it is here to be found, to-day, on the left side, of a seabird called the exile of the fallen races; and inhabits the shores of central Asia Minor; it is here to be found as plentiful, as the fish, that come into Yarmouth harbor; now I have proved my eye, and it is the stolen cord of life, for it is this sight, which gives this man his meaning, and it is this sight, that gives the mind a chance of feeling beautiful or sad, the eye denotes, the kind of wife he will marry, for it is this champion, coming through the eye, who makes the choice, and not the soul, in this body, I want to show you, that you have got a chance here, of finding out, whether your own hereafter is to be happy one, or otherwise, it is this, you may tell your guide to see what kind of husband, you are going to marry, and should this guide have any faults to find, you make him say what they are, and when he is frivolous, it is easy for you to make him look up to you, by withholding from him, the charm of your social intercourse, viz; by being more anxious to look out for one, for yourself, for you have got this distinct trait in your individual self, and that is your feelings, they don't cut any figure in an argument, but they are all you have, that as a right belong to you, so your feelings have got a big show against your guide in this selection, and when your guide detects anything wrong, you are sure to know it from your feelings, that is a powerful incentive, it is thus, the eye bleeds, because it sees what it can't get, and the mouth is watering for the food, yet the eye says distinctly no, well why, because the eye is blessed with a governing influence, that sees straight along, whereas the mouth is altogether too selfish, and it must be denied, should you select wisely and well; I have told you this, to prevent unhappiness; it is here as in other things, your eye may wish for a certain new bonnet, but it says no, I can't take that one, for it is too expensive, your mouth says oh! why not, my husband, can pay for it, well your guide knows exactly what your mouth does not, the eye is the governor, and not the mouth, for the eye can go and see whether that husband is able to afford that particular bonnet, now then you must be content with this one illustration, and consider it as applicable, to both men and women, in business; and all matters relating to their common well doing; you have caught a bad cold in taking too much rum, it is the thing of all others to show you what did it, and when you run out from a hot room to a cold one, it can show you what did it, but when you are out late at night, and you tell your wife a falsehood, your soul champion, will say I don't believe him, and that is where you can stop your lying husband, he is dead gone every time, when this champion goes after him, and the same with the knife, she can't go and kiss Jim, without your soul's champion knowing it, it does not matter where or how it was done, it is the knife, that takes the piece home, so your suspiciousness, is no more the mysterious thing, that you have always said it was, now I must show you how suspiciousness, is the treasured God, of a contrite heart, it is this, the eye, that looks through yours, is able to come back and forward, and when the eye expands, it is looking out upon the world, when it is closed in; it is away from that point, and is looking over the brink of a yawning gulf, perhaps in some parlor, where no one heeds the little stranger, it's his privilege to go where he pleases, and he can take a seat, and watch Mary kissing Harry, when they know it's not right, and he can make you feel, when he settles back behind your eye, that your spouse is not what a blessing he should be, and it this little urchin, that makes you so wretched, he saw it, and was frightfully miserable, and he brought home his misery, and took you out a few paces to let you see, what had been going on in Jane Sly's parlor, this is the way of the world my friend, and it is not for me to be after setting snares to catch you, but it is with an idea of letting fools know, what common sense is; and by learning common

sense you have the chance of growing good, now my friends I
want to help you, and in doing so you will be sure to remember
Old Tom " The Infidel "; for he it was who dissected the world,
and was hard pressed, when he was on earth, well when you get
hard pressed, always say this, my guide is good, and he it is who
must find me a path more smooth, and he shall know that I
found him through poor Old Tom Paine commonly called " The
Infidel," and this is what he told me, to leave out a kind heart,
and obey his guide, and in the end, a kind heart would be my
treasure, for in you my faithful guide I find my heart's best
friend; this is the gold, that reaps the harvest, of honest reward,
for in that saying lies the flooring of success; and on that friend
bears a sunken mill-wheel, for his hand is there to grind decay,
or make a man a prince, his soul is known to no one, his gifts
are all his own, and his friends are those he likes to lead to victory, he is proud, as a man of main, his might is like the moon
and Sun, his ability is just the same, and he can pour down the
glittering wealth of health, or he can sow you full of odor: I
want to come and expound the truth, from a theological point,
for then you can see the plain facts, and after these facts are
before you, I can then show you the beautiful side to everything,
and until I have accomplished this theology, it is no use my saying to you, that you are bad or very good, it is not the mortal
man in the body, that I am after in particular, it is these who
guide the men, that I wish to train and instruct, for the morally
good man, in his own body, is not safe, while there is this danger
outside of him, which he has knowledge of, this is what I am
after, to teach guides the right course, to pursue, to help their
mortal friends, before they die, and when they die or actually
leave the body, it is known beforehand what they have to
expect, on the hereafter side of life, now you seam a soul
together, by this process, for it is only mere assumption, that I
have got him, well now I must show him first, that I have found
his slipperiness, before he will give up the creeping and crawling
around by himself, and in showing you how he does, is just the
very way for you to find him, and once he is caught, he is always
bound, this is a theological ghost, in its entirety, and I have

given you abundance of proof, in this book to convince a pig,
that his soul is what he calls his mind, and not his at all, for it may
be removed, without injury, and a better one put there instead,
so you see that I am gradually wearing you into a theory, that can't
live, for it is dead, to the mortal eye, yet it is the very thing that
is more important than the end, for the end is no man's time,
and it is a long way off from us, for it has been, and is to be,
then where is this end going, and I am forced to say back into
your eye, there is the end, it strikes round, according to the
theological code, of the tree of life, and is thrown round, by the
access, of its own understanding, so that when you die, you are
incircled, in a great big eye, your own eye, is gone, but the new
one is come, for it is forming, whilst you are being developed in
the body of your own eye, this is the theological tree of life, it is
the light, and the sound, which propagate, in that body of yours,
and the two, are grown into one, the instant they leave the body,
now then you see how a soul is propagated, and how life becomes
eternal, I live for you alone, is the sound of eternity, and I love
thee alone, is the voice, that calls, and it this collusion, that strikes
the point together, it is the mortal, that calls the material together,
and throws the mind into one great kind, only begotten, not made,
as the scriptures have demonstrated it, therefore, that you seam
an eternity together, as I have seamed all else, now I want to
show you, that a blind man can see, this is how he does see; his
sight is gone, by the method of divine deliverance, he can see;
and it is done in a way, that you can not yet comprehend, it is
this, the man with no eyes, is quite contented, he has no little
humbug, to make him jealous or feel wretched, his soul, is tied
to eternity, by a thread, that has gone on before, it is the
vision cord that is linked to the sound and is made fast,
by its own mend, it is connected by the thread, that
holds the sense of hearing, it is contested, by the authorities on this point, that a soul dying of blindness; is a
great deal better, than one who is held whole, for his sight
had gone on growing whilst he lived in the body, now you
see my friends that a disadvantage, on earth, is held as an
advantage in heaven, well now there is not the slightest sense in

such utter folly, there can not be any good at all, in punishment, it is foolishness to suppose, that there is, it is simple-minded spirits, that fetch you all such like ideas, they are wrong, and are quite wrong always, for they never had any chance of becoming educated, before they crossed over from the earth, to the side of life, we must call the haven, for it is all happiness; once you know how to live right, and you can only live right, by letting poor mortals live peaceably on earth, and not by going round, with a firebrand, to stick in their eyes always, this is what spirits do, they are always round mortals, and they teach them all kinds of things, that is pure wickedness, and what else can you expect, the spirit, that lived in their eye, was a wicked man, and he had been grown by a wicked man, and was always a wicked man, for he had been dropped at the beginning on a black sidling, his soul, was formed by nature, and he had the greatest hardships always to' undergo, and this is why, that a wicked mind, is grown from natural causes, and not through any evil in that body, that you seem to condemn, and hold fast, as a criminal: Now I have given you more this last two hours, than you ever had given to mortal man before, and I have dug up a pit from under his feet, that you might be satisfied, did you receive this sense, in the next million years, because you seam a time by its own conflict, and not by its machinery, it is not to be assumed, that I can't find out the end of time, for I could end it as far as the earth goes in a few hours, but that could not be the end, for the earth, would rebuild itself again, and go on growing, just the same, in another way, it would take the whole earth, to make a seed, and its seed, would be the geranium flower, it is here, that I am going to attract your attention next, this geranium flower, is a kind of herb, and it grows superbly in Italian waters, or in other words, it grows in luxuriance, in the tropics; and is a plant, that cattle and sheep are very fond, well they don't die like we do, they die in a kind of semi-conscious state, they are driven wild, by this plant, and are always seeing devils, as the drunkards call us, for we do make these blue lights, and red ones too; but that is all for fun, but what I want to attract your attention to most is this sun, well it is in tropical countries,

the same sun, as we have here in America, only, we have it in
moderation, and the Hindus and Boers have it in a form, that is
bordering on severity, well those people, don't have grass, growing as it does in America, and the consequence, is very much
marked, it gives the cattle a stain, that makes them wild, and
they don't get tame, easily, and why, because it is in their blood,
and why, because it came there first by eating the geranium
flowers, and why does it stick to them after they leave these
tropical climates; because it became a dye of nature, it stinks,
and there is the essence, there that perfumes, it is the colored
races, that I am after; they are black, for the fact is as clear as
the nose, on a man's face, it is there, by the natural laws of
nature; and why, because it came of living on leaves, instead of
grass; don't you seem to understand, that I am poking "borax,"
as the blacks say, it is this then, that makes the colored and the
white alike, except on one or two exceptions, and these are the
exceptions; why man was made to mourn, as Burns has it, I will
give it to you in a theological manner, the first man has been,
and gone again, the second man has come and gone again, but
the third man is a holy terror, he gets back again, and plagues
the very life out of you, by his own impertinence; this is what it
all means, the last man is a model, because he came through fire
and brimstone, to save the world, but you don't seem to have
any world to save, the black African is just as much a man, as
any white man that ever walked, and he is just about as near
perfect, as he can be made, once I let him know of how to get
at the right way of mastering sense, and that his thick skull, is
nothing to me, once I get him to know how he is to lead an
army, he can whip three Jack Tars, at one sitting, but I never
said I would show him this, neither will I show him how to whip
any nationality, his own hand, is what I am after, to get my own
science developed, well it is this my fine African, you have just
the class of hand, to knock slavery, out of existence, but I want
to show you, that your hand is all I want with you, and not your
. ingenuity, it is not that which has to be carved to mould a new
genealogical tree; but your hand, is the palm tree, that makes
me take so kindly to you, and it is this, that between the fingers

and thumb, there is an opening, and in that opening there is a
vein, it has got two marks across it, and there is a seam dividing
those two veins, well it is easy to see, that this hand was not
made, at one sitting, it is only black, on the outside, its color is
dark red, underneath, and as black as a coal on top, there is the
difference, it is white one way, and it is black the other, or it is
dark red; now I have been playing 'possum, it is only a gumtree
trick, to shoot off one way, and bring you up standing at another,
well you see this great big African, is a finer specimen, than any
dwarf of a Chinaman, with his long pigtail, hanging down
behind, what sense is there in this, I want to show you, and you
shall just see how funny I can be, the African is a giant compared to Mr. John Chinaman, yet these two are singularly alike,
one is an olive brown, and the other is black and red, well you
have got two nationalities; and both, have two distinct colors:
this is it then, that a color is what is wanted, it has to be divided,
into parts, then you mix them together, and they change, every
time they are mixed, you see how well I have caught you on
this question of races, I gave you the ingredients, and you have
only to mix them up in different ways, and my friends you have
the coloring perfectly formed, I want to say that in this art I
have made a study, and I must take you by the hand, and lead
you right to the spot, where the first man and woman were ever
formed, and it is in Turkestan, it is here, where the first man and
woman ever were produced, and it is here where the buzzard is
making men and women to-day, it is right on the border of the
cliffs, near the old palisade, in the interior of Turkey; it
will be noticed, that there are a number of people being born,
that have no hair, on their lower jaw, it is seen, that they are the
same as the gorilla tribe, yet they are different in this feature,
the two eye-teeth, are the same, as a man's, and are quite different in particular as to the movement, it is this, the teeth, are the
same as a wolf, and they snarl, like an angry wolf, for it is the
Hyena of Hindoostan, that I have drifted you on to; and he is
the one I want to illustrate from, the Hyena, or laughing-jay, is
the animal, that has been the one to scatter humanity broadcast,
it is this I want to bring you to; and that is the laugh, before I

proceed to go on connecting my man; the laughing-jay, is a bird, or what is called the personification of evil omen, it comes in the night, and makes a noise, that can't be mistaken, it is the notes of a laugh, and it is the same kind of a bird as the owl, it sees, at night, and is the one, that has diverted, the man from the chattering ape, to the present genius, that we now find him, it is this, the ape is a canine, because he is a distant quadruped of the jackdaw tribe, and it is in this particular sound he has, that I mean to demonstrate from, the jackdaw coughs, whilst the laughing-jay, is a distinct laugh, which has a sound, like the human voice, this is an imitation of the two, " Laughing-jay, sacsac, yasyas, sassas"; this is as near as I can get it put, but the jackdaw, is a different note entirely, his is this, "hackhack, thackthack, and smacksmack"; meaning that a good deal, would be said, only the monkey, has no note, that ends in rhyme, or this ever-winding mind, it is entirely without note, it is stupid, from this cause, it can't make a mark, without its tail coming in to wipe it out, and this is why its tail is so long, the monkey is never able to reach backward, for he has no after cortege, there is nothing to a monkey, for he did not loosen, in times of old, he stuck to the plank that he drifted on, he never broke the record, by pulling off John's pigtail, and placing his own instead on John's head, or has he ever done anything but jabber out, and screech ever since, and he is not likely to ever propagate a man, that can tell you of all things possible, and impossible, therefore you can say Mr. Monkey is not good enough, to place his own tail on any one's head, for he never did have anything to steer it by, and it is just the same error, that you all see every day, that has occurred from the beginning, it is one matter run to waste; and that is the same, as you have right in front of your eyes, it is the mule or mute, it has gone to this distinct kind, and runs on to this ass tribe, it is the foal of a mute, by an old gray monkey, that propagates a jack, and after that jack is brought back, he can get no farther, for he has run to waste, and is a mute, his sight has gone, he can't seam any more: I wanted to show you this, for it is herein illustrated, that the horse, is so nearly allied to the monkey, that shows you where to find that stain carried

22

to the extreme, it is this, the horse is not the same as the jack, and he is different in this particular, the horse is the same in all except the sound, which is a kind of cold, that gives it a kind of a grating sound, this is all the difference, that is observable at first, now I want to show you how the horse became estranged from the monkey, and it is this way, the animal kingdom is not in Hyde Park, it is in the jungles of Africa, Asia Minor, and India; besides other places; too numerous to particularize as the showman says, when he has a pair of blue pants to air, I have got to make you understand me, or what is the use of my coming down here to explain the truth; it is no use my staying away, and when I tell you that a goose laid an egg, you say what a pity, he put that in there; it might have done without him saying that in such a splendid work; why, my bashful friends, can go and look inside the egg, or remain dunces, forever, that is as straight as I can place it, and when you cross to Paris, you go over the English Channel, instead of going round by Australia, and coming home through Suez; this is what I mean you to see, that you have got to look at sense, right between the eyes; as it would appear there first, and you must look at a problem, from a problematic point, before you can narrow down to the end, this is what I call sense, it has to be made, or you can't have it, and I am making sense; joining it link by link, till I have got so much sense in one chain, till you and no other man who ever lives can break it; and when you have bound this chain about you, I shall say here comes the man I made: And after he is bound, by one endless chain, I venture to vociferate, that he never laughs, like a monkey, or talks like a sign of wisdom coming from the records of old, that were made by the best men, that ever lived, and were in accordance to their judgment, the very purest work, that could be positively made, now my friends I tell you distinctly and emphatically, that a man must read the Bible, or he can never be any good, for the soul, that lives hereafter, or he can not be fitted for sense, because the Bible, is sense, only you have to grow in advance of it, before you can understand it, and where errors were made, in the transcription, it is now for you to pick up the thread, and show to the world, where the errors have been

made, and not sit down, like a lazy good-for-nothing set of useless bipeds, and say we can't do as our forefathers did; I say that
you are better, then ever your forefathers knew how to be, only
that you are so confounded in miserable laziness, that you won't
do anything honest, you are willing to trick, and your souls, have
got to be saved by trick, or you think it would never be any
wiser, than the old fellows, who were afraid to trick God, and
you know what that God did, why he turned a chain of lightning on to those he wanted to make an example of, and that kept
the others right, and I can chain you in with hydrogen, and
glycerine, and some other materials, that are not combustible
machines, until I turn the crank wheel, this is myself, for I too
can turn lightning on to you, just the same as that God of old
did, and I will chain you up, in heaven, as well as hell, with the
gift of common sense, it is no use you trying to trick me, for I
have got the grip, and I mean to hold fast, you stick to me, while
you think I am going to show you something, but you shan't
throw me overboard again, like I had to sleep under a wet
blanket, once you stole the credit of my life, from me, and that
is the propounding of the United States of America, it was the
heathens, who let me go, once they had taken all my points, and
they said it was too great a thing to do, to take a paltry country
like this, and break away from the father home, I said then it
could be done, and I prepared the crust, that broke the yoke of
slavery, for it was nothing better than slavery to be tied to England, and her confounded bad system of making her home sufferers come abroad, to teach a system, that was nothing better than
slavery, her laws, are the laws of the shark, and I say again,
that her men are descendants of sharks, and I will prove it;
that is more than you ever dare say in a country, that is
brought up to a paganish belief, brought on through ignorance,
and vile pollution, for English laws, are not the laws of civilization at all, they are the very laws, that a shark would make, and
it is here, that I have got them, the shark, is a bold fish, he is
able to skim round, and directly he sees his prey on the act of
swimming away, he is after it like a shot, and he pounds that
other fish, into a melley, for he has got the game ahead, and it is

this style of his, that breaks the back, of the dolphin, for it is seething in agony, at the approach of this gigantic monster, and when it is seen that she has no more chance of escape, it yields to this brutish passion for victory, and in the struggle, there is an exchange of union, and this union, is the result of man, for the shark, is the outraged scion of immorality, and the fin of the dolphin is stuck deep into the shark, well the result is this, the shark, is bound to dive underneath, and when he gets below, it is the opportunity of the dolphin to propagate, and these two in anger and wanton lust, have gained the mastery, of all humanity, for they have bred a sea-calf, or commonly called a whale, it is this far advanced, when the fish is seething, and there again is a rupture, it is this, the sealaff, and the seal are both allied, it is a fish, that contains a difference, in this respect, the sealaff, is a fish closely allied to the seal, well it is in this one particular, that they change, the sealaff, is a fish, with a nose, like a moth, it protrudes over at the end, and it comes through the flesh of an animal, in its own kind, it is closely allied to the black bear, for it leaps upon its prey, and attempts to strangle first, it is through these close embraces of nature, in struggling for mastery, that propagation sets in, they fight for victory, and are just the same in their sportive moments, always trying to see who can win, it is this, that causes the mind to wander from the actual subject, it is the animal kingdom, that are so inferior to man, that man disdains, to look in that direction to find the theoretical starting point, and it is this kind of superiority, that makes man so elevated, that he won't come down to the level, of the brute, in comparison, I say that a man who is elevated so high, that he desires to be God entirely, is not fit to be a subject of any civilized community, and he ought to be started off in an air gun, and fired into heaven; there is surely no use for him on earth; now I have given you a taste of the salt water, how do you like me anyway, as the girls say, when they have got a new fishwing in their straw bonnet, is it purty, or is it nasty to hail the salt sea, the girls are all fond of Jack Tar, and it is this likeness, for their old friend the shark, that makes them feel at home in the society of Jack Tar, he apologizes, most humbly, whenever he swears a round oath, and he says d——— because he has got used to it, and so the way he talks, is pretty briney, and it is this salty notion, that makes the girls take kindly to Jack, she says he loves me, and Jack Tar does, he seldom has the liberty of loving a girl, and when he does, she sees it like a flash of gunpowder, the eye begins to wax hot, the pupil protrudes a little, and the mouth is coming into action, and the blood begins to mount the brow, and then the signal comes, it is the fire in poor old Jack's eye, that makes her dance, and feel aglow, her very mirth, is mounting high, when she sees that ghastly smile, it is the coming storm, it is the raging torrent, that strikes that deck, that shivers her timbers, and makes her blow, it fans the air, and makes the eyes, come into tow, and once they meet, it is the signal of distress, I am doomed whispers the purty girl, I have fallen a victim beneath those starry orbs, just look poor Jack, is worst off of the two, his eyes have bristled forth in agony waves, his eyes are moistened with the dew, it is the essence of light, he has seen the heaven of his dove, his victory is assured, and he sees the girl is pretty far gone, for she drops her eyes, and looks down, it is the signal of distress, her eyes are dip, her soul is rent, and her love has caught the breeze, to blow her to the old wave, that brought her onto this, she is lying like a crested wave, it is all the glory, that she ever knew, it gave her back the old sigh, that so few seem to recognize, when they pass the hour of bliss, yes my friends, it is there I have drawn it from her, and she will know who gave her that glad sigh, it was her mother in the deep, she nursed those little waves, that come by us as we sleep, and little knowing, or little heeding, it was those waves, that nursed us into life, yes my friends we have gone back very far, to find the little eggs, that lay beneath the rocks, and there upon their little beds, they sleep in happy bliss, and are nursed to life, by the ancient times of giving sleep to the happy babe beneath the tide, yes the wave is the mother of time, she is moving softly on, and her gentle husband Mr. Wind, has given her his helping hand, and they tow once in a while, but they always pull together in the end, and say we must be careful now, for the babies are beneath our feet, and we must after a

while bring up those subjects, that are before us now, and hasten
away, to calm those troubled babes, and glorify them to sleep;
this is my friends the beginning, I have been a long time getting
you to the beginning, and I have showed you many a way in
going there, but with all that I am here, and I want you to
look round, and anticipate all that came of making up a row, it
is here my friends that you should pause upon the brink, and
say as that wind and water does agree, so shall we two make a
point of agreeing, for though we fought in agony strife, it has
come to this in the beginning, and though we fought our battle
well, each other caring most for the other, yet you are not content now, I must show you the beginning, and my friendly
brothers and sisters you take each other by the hand and make
a beginning, for here it is as sure as you can silence bring upon
the tide, and time is plenty in every bay-window corner, for
there you can sit and play at beginning, and listen to each other
cast a sigh, it is only the beginning, you can count each other's
time, from the beginning, and you will know full well, that as
hands were made round in the beginning, that they have wandered quite astray, in coming home to dinner, for they used to
be, in the bay, in little shells, not much longer than your peanut
then don't fling yours into my face, as I come home to dinner,
for we could do quite well enough without those peanuts at the
beginning, it is frightful odd, yet it is true, that the wave of the
sea is not nearly as bad as it used to be, and this is the reason
why, it always has been very dry, at the bottom of a basin, for
there it is in accents sweet and homely, and when your wife has
brought you a basin of soup, remember the beginning, for there
he lay all spat and span, in a lonely basin, and he set down, to
his lively meal, on nothing better than the bottom of a basin,
and in that rolly-polly pull me out, he hatched a revolution, for
in that great big sea, is the wave, that made the insurrection, and
you don't see, but I can make you believe, and that is all the
way, that you ever get insurgents, they come upon you like a
golden butterfly, and tell you all is wrong, when you know no
such thing at all; well then you listen to me, and see what I am
going to show you, I came out in a great big fright, and I saw

another's head, come popping out, it gave me such a fright, that I
could not begin to shout, till I had come away from yonder, it is
this, the fellows, were after me, and I could not see what they
were going to do to me; so I came popping along, when I met
you; this is what you find, the eggs are deposited in that basin,
and the waves beat them back and forwards, till they hatch them
in some way, and it is this, the water is of a soft pliable nature,
it moves in and out, it breathes on the fallen treasure, for it was
made by the air of the eternity, and there it is my friends you
have the eternity, in that same water, and when your eternity
goes in and out of that shell, why can't I go in and out of you,
it is as plain as the road I come, that is all, you can see, that the
wind made the water first, and the water made a move, then
when you and I go together, I am going to make you move, for
the fact, that I go in and out of you, just the same as the water
does to the little fish, in the bottom of the basin, now where have
you found yourself, in the bottom of the ocean, that is the
theory, that gives you life, it is the wind, acting upon itself, it
does this by spontaneous combustion, it is bursted, by the
atmospheric high pressure of entering into communion with the
elements, that flow together, it is the exact time, that you have
to count the weeks by, it means this, that as the heat is, so is
the rain, caused through the heat being melted, and this is the
folly fable of man, it is this, that brings him to understand, his
soul is the atmospheric current of air coming through his wind-
pipe, and he is the off-shoot, of any number of connections, in
the past, and to-day, he don't know anything, for the plain fact,
that he rolled and lolled about at the beginning till he became a
baby, and since that time he has been lolling ever since, he
came into the world a rolling stone, and since he has rolled along
thus far, and he will continue to keep rolling always for he never
can do anything else, he is a roller that is all, and he rolled the
hind feet off time, once he began to count, his theory is this,
that the sun sets in the west, and it rises in the east, and it goes
round to the other side again, for it was ordained, that it should
go round, in one short twenty-four hours, well you see that man
made a grievous error at the start, in not coupling God, and the

Sun, it is this, the Sun does her work in twenty-four hours, and God did his in six days, well you see that whilst we can't see God, we know that the Sun is our benefactress, and she spills glory over us every twenty-four hours, don't you see that our visible benefactress, does not dare to deceive us, she can't, and why, because she is alive, therefore she must die, did she stop, her whole life has been one long summer, her very soul is lit up with love, and she came of the wind, coming in contact with the water, that it begets, it is hereby proven, that the wind and water did beget the Sun, and the water did upheave, and throw the wind on its back, and did cause a prolific propagation to ensue, and it caused the heat to come through, the afterpart being stopped up, and herein hides the mystery, it is this, the Sun having gone in, and commenced to heat and fire, it gave place to the wind, for the wind was inside, and could not get away, it had got fast, by the overbearing pressure of the fluid combustion, and in this form it came to the end, or it would have been entirely drunk up with the water, well you see the wind is always light till it gets filled with water, and then it gets heavy, and sinks; well you see the sun had caught fire, and in taking fire it does produce an extraordinary odor, well this odor, will not mix with water, for it is essence, of a peculiar character, and it gives way to nothing, it is a substance, in a minute, and it contains an adhesive ingredient, which is potassium of soluvium, which is water and gas mixed, or wind in water, from the extraction of gum, and this gum or potassium of soluvium, is the ingredients, that form the heavens, and grow again, which is the afterbirth, now my friends you see what a scientific man you have made me, since I left you, and you are to benefit by this considerably, for the facts are plain, you are going to gain peace and contentment, in accordance with nature, your souls will have mastered the struggle, that has been so long denied to you, and you will have the good always, and the wicked are gone forever, they will no more crave after that which, is battled for and won, there is nothing to win, your honor is preserved, you are on the top, I have scaled the ladder, and you can come where I paved the way, I am here, and where I go, you shall follow, now I have done so much, by your lief and grace, I shall descend the ladder, and when you meet me at the bottom, I expect a friendly greeting, from all those who called me "Infidel," and you must no more be alarmed at the wonders of "The infidel;" for he is going among you to scatter good, with both arms, his victory is won, he has no more conquests to make, that can not be aspired to without injury to any one, and he won't object to the old appellation, considering that it was only the heathens who made him suffer, and as suffering is the crown before success, it is no use you fighting any more about your classics, they are done, it is no use you fighting about religion, it is begun a new life like the Sun, it has buried the past in a bitter strife, and it is forever behind the waves, the God of old is our God still, only we have learned to recognize him, and understand his true holiness, and his agony, in his struggle for mastery, and it is now to be in accordance with good judgment common sense, and the Sun to be our guide, she has done it so long, and so faithfully, that no man ever did recognize her before as he ought to, and now I will chasten you a little less, and make up for my many faulty demonstrations of facts, to bring you home in the sublime form of your present existence: You are as the seashore, a surging mass, you move along, and you break into, without knowing where you are going, or what leads you, you are just the same as the tide, it turns back, the moment it has a little steep ascent to rise, you are afraid, for fear that you should climb a shade higher, and it is this great tide, that calls out I have gone far enough, it is no use my going on any further, for when I get up so high, I hear the seething mass, in my rear claiming assistance, and I must go back, to help that lonely brute, from being annihilated, in his own trough, this is what it then amounts to the trough of the sea, is your God, and you can't break from it, for you were not allowed to go beyond the tether of your own sound, by this you are held by the sound of eternity coming on behind, and the sound of the eternal ones, who are free, like the tide, don't leave you entirely, they only proceed on as far as the sound of the tide, will let them leave you, this is then the reason, why you know so little, it is the ancients, who guided you, from the sound of their

own tide, they went only a little way beyond the seething
masses, and did not dare to go beyond the flowing of the wave,
that held them to you, now you see my friends that you were
led as well then as you have any right to expect, and though
your God had not been very far, he did miracles such as has
made his name sublime, since that time, and he is a great God
still, and always has a right to be, he made laws, for you which
are very fine, and are holy laws, and he did well for you, then
you have no right to turn on him now and say that my God
is a foolish God, he is a good God, and the best the world
ever knew, and it is wrong to cast him away, he gave you all
the rights and privileges, of helping and protecting yourselves,
and he went the farthest of any God yet, and he is our monarch
of old, and till the world can see the way more clearly, it is right
and proper to stand by the old flag, and don't allow foolish
aspirants of my doctrine to come and say this is what Tom Paine
means, you wait till I have shown you the better way, and I can't
do that in a minute, and I don't want you to believe me till I
can show you something, that can help you materially, you are
here to stop, and you are not to be annihilated with one false
prophet's sayings, you must see the right road, or you can't
believe, and heaven has to be made as plain to you, as the house
you live in or you can't understand the parlor is not the kitchen,
and that your own bedchamber is not either of the other two, now
you see I am placing three distinct places, the parlor bedchamber,
and the kitchen; so will you have to comprehend, that there are
three places, in the universe, it is heaven hell, and the ocean, or
in other words, the three great execrators combined, and the one
deity, the Sun, she is Majesty over all fraternities, and as the
recent ideas are in favor of the world being governed by the
women, it is best that she be designated her Majesty, for in
reality, it is so, and what is the use of calling it a he, when the
gust of wind has founded a fact, beyond all dispute, it is a great
deal, for man to take upon himself, and it is more than he should
do, to be the father of all creation, he can't do it, and he never
should have attempted a thing so absurd, for the mother is the
one, who nurses the young cub to sleep, and as the Sun began to

shine, she went down, and smoothed the troubled waters, and made them lie down and behave, and I say that she is our mother, and I will designate her in calling, according to the dignity she deserves; now my friends I want your assistance once more, and that is this, you must not take too many liberties with the Sun, for she is a woman, and as such, I mean to protect her, with my life, and as you value anything, it is for you to be respectful toward her Majesty, and I will show you how it is that my Sun is the great factotum of all the good there is, and when you have got all the good, you must not expect any more, and it is this great good, that will bring you happiness, and after that you are not to be miserable; Now I want to show you, where the word God is brought from, and then you can better see what it has been to raise up a deity like what you have always had, you must not tinker with my theoretical points, till you have mastered the whole of them: And I want you to take precautions to see through my views, in accordance with my thoughts, or don't let any others tell you what they are, but read them and grasp their meaning according to how they seem to strike you, now it is not the Bible, that you learn by, it is through the inaccurate mode of deliverance, that you get your thoughts, and instead of looking at the Bible as the work of a great number of spirits, you cling to one deity, the great God of Abraham, Isaac, Moses etc; now this is entirely wrong, the God of the Hebrew people, is the God to-day, except, that the God of to-day, is the same, and the sole life of every living being, in its entirety, meaning, that the father who art in heaven, is the father of love, the word God, cometh from the word I seam, for it gathereth together, and it is my God, who is my guide, for he seameth my soul to his own, and when his soul, is seamed to mine, it's my God, for it has joined hands, and everything, it is linked to me, and I see good, through my God, now can you seam a more correct understanding, of this deity, his life is my life, and my life is his, for he hath me enchained to his soul-cord; and his soul-cord, is as he has made it in the earth, by the God he followed, for his God, did make his soul to suffer, according to his own contentment, and I shall prove it, by more ways than one, ere I cease to beat a retreat,

now you must look at God as your devoted friend, either for
good or evil, his soul, is as his father made it, and it is not by
any means assured, that it is his own father, it might be his great-
great-grandfather, who appointed himself the governor of your
soul, it has to be taken according to the reason of order, in which
the authorities over heaven can manipulate its own childish
theories; now you see that I am going to wade into the other
side of life, and show them their follies, for they are simply as
they grew, and this is why you don't advance, you can't see anything, for the fact is plain, it is the bold spirit, who has to shove
ahead, or you can't get on any farther, and until your friends on
the other side see you reading this work, they don't know anything of heaven, they have never been any farther, than the foot
of the ladder, they dare not climb a rung higher, till the man in
the moon has been explained to them, why they are all afraid to
go, till it is shown, what that curious object is, that keeps poking
his head, and shoulders, etc, out every month can be; I tell you
as soon as ever you understand, that it is not a great big furious
God, that your spirit friends will go and look at it, and come
back, and tell you in expressions of anxiety, that they did not
take this look before, and say you were as safe as the house, that
never fails to give shelter to those who fear no man's tales, and
see stars, only when they are visible, now my friends you can
investigate these things after I have shown you the way, don't
you think, that I am wicked, to come and tell you that God is all
love, according to the light he looks upon things, and that our
God, is the best God, for he guides our footsteps, and drives us
along, as far as he can see, and when he goes thus far, he says, it
is only safe to go that distance, because I took you to the end of
the tidal mark, and beyond there, it is all confusion, I must not
bear your body, away from my own limits, this is how far you
have been, to the end of the earth, and no farther, you never
went to the upper regions at all yet, it is only this folly, that prevents you from going, it keeps you tied to the sound of the sea,
now the sound of the sea, is a great deal higher aloft, than it is
on the ground, and your tidal sound, is ascending always, so as
to reach this distinct ground floor of heaven, that I want to take

you to, it is this, the floor, that you are now making your habitations, on are the foot-hills, they are not away up above you at all, it is only the foot-hills, that you have gone to, and not the heavens at all: Why, because your tide does not admit of a greater distance being covered, and it is this, the heavens are full of sweet essence, for the strong aromatic odors, are falling before they have descended, and they lodge beneath the crevices, and accumulate, and are growing, in luxuriance everywhere, and the skies, are as full of virtues, as the seaming of an affectionate blossom can be; Now the love of romance, is here in its full bloom of glory, it's here that the stranger wanders, he can see these great changes come upon nature, he can see the sweet forget-me-nots, tying each other up in leaves of affectionate bliss, and the sole companion of their daisy days, are here entangled in their veins, I say it without hesitancy, that those flowers, are greater in heaven, than any earthly bliss, that has ever been grown, they live in life, of a summer clime, it is all radiance, and glowing beauty entwined in each other's arms, there is no malice or envy or hatred, it is this great joy, that they bind life anew, and glorify their God, in nature's sweet embrace, in summer it is, and why, because the earth, is not old enough to know why summer is, then I want you to tell me why this summer does exist, it is the grand good, it is the warm end of life, it is the veins have dislodged their blood, and given back to earth, that which belonged to the earth, and taken of that which belongs to the realms of dew, it is the essence off the light, that gives to heaven those glories, that are not for man in the body to inhale, and why; because he can't use both blood and veins, he must use, that which it appeareth according to nature, I say he is the soul life, because he can not promulgate his theoretical knowledge alone, and why, because his blood, is off the side of that mountain, that hath no sunshine, and why; because the blood is of a mixture, that does not sustain life, it is only a matter, that comes through affliction, it is brought about through corruption and diseases; this is why, it gets into the maggot by promulgating, it makes the mind happy, by soaking up the water fluid, and driving away the acid, from the formation, so you see it is not blood, that forms the life, it is material that lives, and not immaterial; therefore your material is not casen to anything, once it leaves the body, it only floats, and is a mere nonentity, till it fills with ether; and why, for the ether is ever porous, and your hide being gone, it soaks into ether, and makes you go on growing anew, and you get quite fat, and stout, on this ether, which feeds you, it loads you with all kinds of nourishment, till at last you have become so unwieldy, that you gain an ascendency over the ether, by too much pressure, and it produces a combustion, and this combustion is called the good of heaven, for it settles you back into your old form, and leaves you with an entire whole body, according to the one you had on earth, with this one singular exception, and that is this, that mortal eye is nothing more or less, than the acandaesment of glycerine; it is white, and does not sight at all, it is sense, only that you have left, it does not come back to you, in the form of a beauty spot in the center, it falls short, with this other exception, that the new eye, has a sight, all over the eye; or in other words, it sees all round, and has no hidden corners at all; the eye is a visionary orb, it takes in at one glance, that which takes mortals a whole lifetime to make clear, now you have the magnet, in the loadstone, it feels the eye, by its own brightness; and a great many people, think, that angels can't see, it is this, that makes them see, their eyes were the acandaescence of life, in a degree before, but after they died, it became a vision, and in that vision it is the light, that is thrown in upon them, and not this great stain of crime that forgets anything, it is the whole of eternity, that goes on one basis, that the Sun drives in her light, and you must live while she lasts, for she is the living light, and can't die, for she has the soul of eternity within her own congruity, it is the greatest wonder we have, and that is the Sun being drawn into her own eternity by the wave of the ocean calling her back, or in another way of putting it, it is the time of the tide, that calls her back, she can't get on any faster, for she is too heavy at one end for her to lift up the other, till she spills her own time, therefore the Sun is weighed down by the tide, and the tide is holding her fast on time, that the world began in twenty-four hours, and not in six days, it is this, the whole firmament was in the Sun for the space of one day, and the stroke of time burst through, for it had to be blown out, in the afternoon, of the third round, or it would have been got to pieces, only for the hole breaking at the end, where the Moon is drawn out, to an extent of a league, farther at one end than the other, it caught fire in the center, and was bursted open, by the gas, coming in on top of the unabsorbed wind, and these two mixing, it caused a burst at the ulterior quarters, and allowed the water to drown the whole of heaven and hell, and all that there then was, it came out, and in running dry, it turned the Sun up, for the weight was all down at the end of the Moon, then the Sun was high up in the heavens, and the sky was clear of atmosphere, and the Moon, had gone down, and was disloading again, it came up, with a rush, for the axle is broke, and the Moon ascends, the Sun has gone down, because the water in her own belly has run back, because the Sun drew it up, the moment she became equalized, and caught hold of the flames anew, from the other end, and she is burning again, at that which does not drop out, as the Moon leaves off descending, so that the Sun is drawing on one end, when she ascends, and when she descends, she is eating her fire from the other end, this is perpetual motion, and it is quite time that somebody discovered the secret of manipulating it; therefore I claim it for my pains, in making this announcement to the world, and all rights titles and interests, I bequeath to the man who has dealt so affluently, with my speeches, and I name my successor in trust for the world and its conflagrations as the great and truthful medium the Seer William Atkinson, I must say that you can not deprive him of this honor, for he richly deserves this title, he has won it fairly by the action of his own devotion to the cause of investigation, and you must not rob him, for he can get any message from any part of the universe, and print it down on paper, and he can find you any-where while I am beside him, his life is in his own hands, but it is governed by me, and a strong band of spirits, who can waive their claims in honor of this great future, and they are skilled to such an extent, that no one can tell where they are, or what they are doing, and it is hereby purposely avoided, the naming of any of his guides or controls, and it will be thrown out as an advantage, that no man shall know his neighbor, and none can tell what the other person may do, and the next but not least reason, it is approved by my own special government, not to give the names of any but myself in this great work, as I am at the head, and I shall take every precaution that no advantages are taken of my subordinates; now you know why the two names are only mentioned, it is not two that is doing this work, but simply an innumerable force, sufficient to carry out any work, that the spirit world intend to demonstrate to mortal man, now I have told you honestly and candidly all about my affairs, and you must judge me according to what light you see me in, I want fair play, and I see no valid reason why it should not be accorded to me and mine, this is all, I have to say, and I must speak, or you can't know: Now there is one more reason for speaking to you, and that is this, I am informed and believe that you have wronged this man William Atkinson, and that it is this that I have engaged to set right, and I am not going to do it in an underhanded way, I merely want your court to try the case according to its merits, I don't come and say you shall do this or that I merely want a fair and impartial trial, and I can see whether it is such or not, and it is to be in England, that this trial will be asked for, now it is an engagement, that has been entered into between this my instrument and myself, that he does my work, according to my dictation, and that as an equal balance, and adjustment of accounts, it is stipulated, that I should help him, now there is simply this in the case, it is a proven charge of a criminal nature, and is not in anywise true, that a man can upset this, without any assistance from me, there is not a shadow of doubt, but the tribunal, where this was tried is in the colonies, and is no more or less a place than New Zealand, this little country is in the controlling interest, a British possession, and can not be free from the laws of Great Britain, and is in the main, a small country, I can not go into any details, as I don't wish it known that my intentions are such, as will desire a rehearing of this case, till it is absolutely before the

court, but I mention this for the man who works on your behalf
has been cruelly wronged, from the beginning by a number of
judges, and their accomplices; who did their bidding, to commit
robbery, and not for any right cause of justice, as they have
made out, in their accounts of this case; I will not leave anything undone, to in the future establish his innocence, and it is a
fight, between heaven and those on earth that is all: Now my
kind friends you may consider that I have outdone myself by
such an omission, but it is to show you, that the earth can't
master the heavens, for they never did, and they can not now do
it, or ever will be in a position to accomplish it, you may yet take
me in some cases, as acting in a revengeful spirit, but I say
such is not the case, that neither I or my guides have any
feelings of unkindliness toward mankind, it is quite the contrary,
we love man as much now as ever, and our lives are bound together
for his good, I only want to say that I did take this method
of getting ahead of these rascals, and I intend to stick to the
good I have found, and wherever it leads me, I don't intend to
flinch or go back, it is my sole comfort and joy, and I mean to
follow, wherever this intelligence takes me, and should I err, in
my right interpretation, it is for the people on my side of life,
to come and say what is the meaning of this or that as the case
may be, and I shall give them in reply whatever I get, whether
it be against or for them: Now I can do no more, and honesty
is my motto, I never did a dishonest action in my life, and I
won't begin now: So you can take me for all I am worth, and
in time I do not believe there will be one single detail, that can
not be shown you, by this form of interpretation: You may
think that I have gone out of my way to place things in an
incomprehensible style, but it is as I was told, and I do this to
the letter, always, what comes I get, and what does not come, I
don't put; now you must either accept it as I have put it, or ask
me, to try and explain it, for I am perfectly independent as an
instrument, and I see no one, and I ask no questions of any one,
and I don't investigate, or get my information except from my
guide, that is it came on in the beginning through a desire to
reach my own friends, and since that time my experience has

been so faithful, as to show you many things, that has never been
brought to your knowledge before, and I will carry on this work
steadily, and see where it leads me, that is all I have to say on my
own behalf, except that I have been investigating for something
over a year, and I have written what you now have in about six
months, this is as near as I can get it without trying back, and I
don't try back, because it produces confusion, in my spirit band,
and they don't like any one to take liberties with their accuracy,
this is I find a difficulty, it is this, to ask a question, and then doubt
the authenticity; of what they say, for it must be remembered, that
it takes an immense amount of power, to deprive me of anything
like unconsciousness; and I do all my work under a semi-
conscious condition, or moderate coma power, that is I am only
listening to the sound, when at work, and the sound is often so
weak, that I have to appear in a conclusive mood, to hear it
repeat, now you see that unless I distinctly understood the
signaling of this band, I should be often wrong, and it is a
complete code, that is practiced, it gives one two or three raps,
on the wall, or anyway to reach me, from this old-fashioned form
of intelligence, is withheld for the present, but I assure you it is
impossible for me to write one single word, that the band refuse
to accept, now you have as much, as I am permitted to give you,
in this instance, through my complete sense of receiving these
communications, I wish to add, that I don't attend any spiritual
meetings, or church either, for I want the pure cure or nothing
that is my own theory, and I have always had an aversion to any
doctrine, that is not quite clear, it is true that I read the Bible
every night, except when I don't want to from some cause, that I
have not succeeded, in yet reaching, and it is as easy for me to
leave it unread, as it is otherwise to do the opposite, I don't
know why I am governed so easily by my band, but I used to
drink, and smoke, and since I gave up these habits, it is much
better for me, I don't feel any desire strong within me: And
I can be happy, without any trouble now, it used to be a
terrific fight, for some purpose, I don't exactly know what, but I
used to fight, for my own way, till I gave up this theory, and the
reason that brought me to this country, is plain, I was always

reading about the American continent, and thinking that I would like to look it over, so I got into trouble, and then my mind soon resolved itself into shape, I don't do things by halves; I must be either top or bottom, it must be one extreme, or the other, before ever I knew anything about the spirit power, I went on fixed rules, that is near as I can remember, the one great feature was, that there was no God, that I had never seen anything to lead me to believe there was, I thought that all the people were blind, to think that I had a soul, or any one else; This is practically what I did think, it is this, I thought we had come from the beginning by the effluxion of time, that we started, on the principle of men and women, and that nature was all a quiet affair, of its own, that it drew from some source a covenant or agreement, and that it went on promulgating, or something of that sort, I knew absolutely nothing, and the first thing that hit me hard was the fact of a medium being able to tell me, how many letters I should get from my folks at home, and the other thing was a most remarkable coincidence, it was this, a medium told me, that I would be at a play, on each hand would be a friend, and that I would meet a lady, that I had known in England, well this I looked upon as all passed and done with; but sure enough this came out exactly as I have described it to you: Well I was very hard hit, for I could not grasp the situation, in any way, and it gave me quite a serious turn, for I knew no one in the country, and I picked up friends, by the carload, I never went long without a companion of some kind, and although I did not tell any one where I came from or much about my affairs, I avoided lying by evading their queries, and told them nothing that I considered they had no right to know; this is all I have been well treated in America, as far as I have gone, and I don't lie unless it is in error, so I have no difficult anticipation for the future: I am sincere in all I do and say except a little bit of a fixture, in order to make game of some morally dutiful son of a landmark; I have no other intentions of scaling the liberties of perfect good faith, combined with facts, and demonstrations of what appears to me as the exact identity of a righteous judgment of facts; now you know what to do, should you understand a theory different to the one I am engaged in, it is not necessary to be pompous or great, I want you to understand, that I look upon man as a machine, and should he be a little better machine, than I am I don't think he ought to show it, without telling me why he is a better one, and I am just as willing to show a street arab, the right way, as I would be a higher dignatary, so that pride is only what I feel in actual work, not in sense, the sense is a gift, and it can't be given without we understand, so I am just as anxious to stop a street arab, from swearing, because it brings an evil influence, to his detriment, as I am to tell an English dude, that I hope he won't injure his mouth, in those abominable fashions, he calls bon ton, or we will give him his right appellation, and say "Don't you know, my fauther is HAUH THE HAUGH; T-Y TU-M TAUGH; Don't-You-Know:" This, is quite enough, to make any sane man look for an ass, for it is very near the appellation, I don't want to be a university student, or a classic scholar, when you point me out such fellows, as these, as well-bred gentlemen, give me a man, who can work a miracle, by stratagem, and I am going to follow him, this is the style for me, I don't mind your dudes, in a field, coming a fall, across a stone fence, or making a backward jump, only don't put those horrid notions in my head about A-UH, that is quite sure to make me feel funny, I can't help it; for that sound must come from some place, besides the genuine language of birds, and as I am to give up now, and assume the second party again, I will let you off gently, and hand you over to Paine, he can make a better showing, as to the way, the noble horse got estranged from the ass; now it is herein described, that the horse is an animal, that had no toes, to amount to anything, till he became crossed with an animal called the giraffe, it is seen at a glance, that the giraffe, has no front toe, it therefore can not be said, that the giraffe, and the horse, are the same, yet you see them both, together, in one field, or desert plain, they eat together, and sleep the same, yet in nine cases out of ten, the horse and the giraffe are opposed to each other, well why is this; the horse is not a very spiteful animal, or he would not permit the giraffe, to abuse him, as it does,

well this is then the cause, of the two disagreeing, the ass
and the horse, will mate together, but the giraffe, can't come
near the ass, for its smell is abominable, compared to the smell
of the horse, then why has the ass no smell, for it came of
a clean kind, and does not touch the leaves, as high up as
the giraffe, well the ass, is down on his knees, picking up the
soft little grass, the giraffe, is pulling at some bough high up,
out of reach of the ass, well it is no use, you telling me, that I
don't know, but I will explain it to you, the ass, is the poverty-
strickened peasant, and the giraffe, is the dude, the one who
reaches high, till he stinks, and the other is so low, till he grows
nothing big enough, to make a silly odor with, now the horse is
what you might designate, the middle man, a merchant or a cow-
herder, according to his avocation in common life, this is the difference in the three, it is this: The horse, is the degenerated
quadruped, or known as the leliel, felon, he droops his hind quarters, and has a sloop-like appearance, all along his shoulders, he
is quite on a par with the rest of his make-up, he can not touch
a giraffe, because the latter lives on leaves, and is an abomination to him, for they do not smell the same, while a she ass, and
a horse, are exactly the opposite, one calls in tones of accents,
like a great big toad, the other, has the scent of a whale, the
horse is an after construction of the whale specie, the ass is
a specie of the carmigure, or seacalf, whilst the giraffe, is the
after construction of the feminine sow bear: or a kind of fish,
that is in the Arctic Ocean, it appears on the surface, only once
in a great while, and is in Japanese quarters, it comes from their
specie of tribe or specie; now you want to know why the horse
got estranged from the ass, and why, for it is the very same
nature as the other, it does look alike, and it does propagate
once, well it is this, the fish in the sea, are all layers of eggs, and
though some of them may have eggs, that don't lay at the bottom
of basins, the whole of them get mixed up, at times, and the one
is venturing away from the other, that when a whole number of
these eggs, are found in the one basin, they break away, at one
and the same time, and in so doing, they mix together, and
become fast acquaintances, and friendly toward each other, and

in time of spawning again, they take precaution to be near each other, and their eggs are mixed; well the water, that is seeping into the one set of eggs, is seeping into the other set of eggs, and in consequence these changes are brought about, through the constant mingling of the waters: Now you don't wonder at this promulgation, of ideas, the sea is the great producer of thought, for it makes the young ones different, and in there, it tells them, that there is a mighty monster over head, that can crush them, or make them do what is best, and below the little fish, are making their struggles to escape, and the first sight, that they get, is the bed, they were born in, and it is a pretty fine bed indeed, the moon, is above, which is round, and beneath, is the reflection, of some great giant, that looks after them, and when they peep out of the shell, the first thought, is to run, or swim away, for in the flashing of an eye, a spout of water, is sure to meet their eye, it is the essence of the water, and in it, is always, a coloring, it is green red, or any amount of colors, well the fish, are sensitive, and they don't like this color, and are apt to break away, to some other water, that has nothing so hideous about in it; this is accounted for in this style, the Moon, is dropping the essence from her funnel, always, and she is just sure to make all the colors, in the water, that has been sent out of that great big mass of propagation above, and it is dropping on the sea as well as the land; And the fish, are made white gray or any colors, in accordance, with this essence, that is always falling from the Moon; now you have a very fair idea of how the horse became estranged from the ass, and when you don't understand such a simple little piece of science as this is, you had better come along, and look down the ass's mouth, and get a peep at his tongue, and when you look right back, in the throat, you can find a little tongue, or tonsil, this little tongue, is quite enough to show you, that a sound coming through its hinderance, is quite different to the mule, this mule, has the same tonsil, only it is parted, and drives a hole, in the side, instead of coming out at the side, well now I have taken you right into the ass's mouth, and you don't know anything more: But you have learned this much, and that is this, an ass, is an animal, distinct and pure as

we are, and this is a great thing to venture, on saying, in this
country, where the people are so brilliant, and bright: But you
must permit me to follow on the principle of the school-master,
he says dunce, he says blockhead, and he vociferates in agony
sometimes you consummated fool; I could fetch an ass in to do
that, now why do lady teachers, make the "cap" and put little
girls in one corner, there is an impression, that comes from the
sea, and it is this; the lady herself, is impregnated, with a
theory, and that is likened to the ass, she has caught the syllable
wrong though, it is asinine, the same as canine: Now do you
understand clearly, that this impression did come from the mingling of the waters, in the ocean, and that these thoughts are the
impregnation of the waters mixing together, and making an ass,
of one, and a horse out of the other, or in other words, the ocean
is propelled by the wind, and that wind does wave back and forward, and so do the thoughts of man till at last his brain becomes
confused, and he is a simple-minded ass: Now I have taken no
liberties, you teachers have developed this theory for me, and in
finding their theory, I found you, for in hunting, I could not
master the difference, in thought till I came to this point, and
that is this; why, is it that man has so much more intelligence,
than the beast: He is no more beautiful, and a horse is much
prettier than a man: So I wondered and puzzled, till I have
solved every problem that there is, I have books in my home in
heaven, that would make your hair stand straight on end, and I
mean to translate them, and bring them down to posterity, it is
this great study, that has made my life so peaceable, I don't
want so much as a thing, I have all the joy, that any one individual can have, but any new theory, or new thought, it is balm
to my soul, it leaves me in a state of intoxication, that never did
quite satisfy me yet, and in going through the Sun, I noted the
different features, in a manner, that is marvelous, to a degree,
that would astound man, and make him so elevated, that he
would reach heaven by a mode, that could be accomplished in
all other ways, except, that he can't see when he would arrive
there, for this reason, the Sun is hot, in the flames, but it would
suck you under, ten times for every minute, that you lived, or in

more practical illustration, the Sun is a sucker, she makes herself
so fat, that she can't move, without she is filled to a bursting
point, she gorges, and is feeding always, so that she can't stand
still, for her own weight is increasing always, and she is getting
heavier every minute, and in time she will suck in every living
thing, that grows, now this is the only danger, that there can be
at all in the world coming to any end, it is this, that has been
going on, since the beginning, and may have been in the beginning, for no one can tell, it might be a second world, or it might
be a world of the past, there is no theory, that appears to fix
herself sufficiently strong in my mind, the only thing I can say
is, that once the world has grown short of fuel, it is sure, to
get thin, and so that in getting thin, she does permit a renewal
of propagation, and she lives on the fattened calf, and goes on
forever, now are you satisfied, that Old Tom is not to be bested,
I say I like to angle, it makes me feel, that I could whip every
general you owned, but give me a regiment of soldiers, to guide,
and I could make them maneuver, into the exact fit of delusion,
I would make them believe, that God was their guide, and when
they had done fighting, you would have so many Napoleons,
that there would be an eternal fire on earth, that would feed the
Sun always, well it is this, that I want to show you, the Sun has
to be fed, or she will get thin, and that is how it is done, her
season in one country, is longer, than in the other, for the simple
fact, that she dies down, in the autumn, for want of food, and
in the spring, she rises, for the fact is plain, her axle is sure to
run short of grease, with constant turning, and she begins to
go slower, till at last, she slows down to the right pace, that is
the death, of all virtue, in the country, that she has been feeding
on: And she feels the Moon has poured sufficient oil or
essence, out on the other world, that is her half sister, it is this
twin screw, that takes the cake out of your miserable inventors
of perpetual motion, she feeds off her twin-sister only moder-
ately, for she is a great deal farther away, and can't reach the
little beggar, to get a full kiss at her, that is why she does not
take this to heart much, her idea is the mission of her journey,
and she keeps on motion, in the exact line of her own axle,

now you are getting into a fog, it is just as much, as I can keep
my balance, and you ought to be liberal-minded enough to see
that you want a case-hardened man to work through, or he
would be off tail and end, to tell his bosom friend, that he had
got the right theory of perpetual motion, well so he has, only you
won't learn much through a man who is to be made into a first-
class instrument, and then to have him break away, just at
the moment, that he saw a flash of current strike him, for you
see what strain, there has been brought to bear on this man,
only a common mortal too: And yet he either does not realize,
or he is so wrapped up in thought, that he takes no notice of
me, which of the two is it, I shall tell you, and it is this, I won't
break the tag, that holds me in its vise, he is constantly thinking
of home and those he loves, and he means to get there, or break
his axle, that is it, and he is going to go home, or there will not be
a man left on earth, that is his theory, and it is the same with
the Sun, she means to go home, in her lavish splendor, she never
begat a man, that was more determined to reach the glory of
winning yet, and he would blow the roof off eternity, to win, so
you must not fancy, that you will get off lightly, when he crosses
to heaven, should you injure his home-views, and he is just
about as able to accomplish anything as I ever was, for he has
the advantage, of getting the best advice, once he crosses the
border line, now you see where I have led you, to a passionate
spirit, that is according to its own propagator, it is fighting to
master its own maker, that is what you have in your midst, a
man who is fighting for God, or the meaning of God, and
nothing satisfies his craving, till he reaches the turning-point,
he is going to die with a firm conviction, that he did his best,
and when that is done, what are we to say, why that he has done
well: That is all my friends, you see in that last illustration, the
Sun, she did her best, and her best is to scale the turn, it is all
she is able to do, her axle, is just on the eve of breaking, and
when it breaks, she bounds, at her little sister, with the rapidity,
of a famished wolf, her sister is freshened by the absence, and
she faces round to her, and meets her monster full in the face,
and says what you want of me, I can freely spare, come take

and help thyself, it is meat and drink I have to give to thee, for thy peace, I must appease, come sister you can revel in this cheese, it is a little tart at first, but then with these blooming lips, it will cast a smile at every touch back, in response at thee: You see I take my cue, and dip it in my ball, just as fancy leads me, for I see in those I love to tease, a picture of my quaint description, I would have done it this way, as the Sun moves, she turns round, and why, couldn't Old Tom say so, but he gets every mule muddled, by his style of putting things, that is not the way I should have suggested, to do such a work, Why Old Jack Tar, would have made a better end than that, he would have given us a rope-end, and that is what you give my friends, who criticise my work boys, they ought to have it, for it is no light matter, to come back here, and tell you what it is that governs the whole universe, it wants two souls, a black one, and a white one, it has got to have a summer, and a winter, it has got to have an object, or it can't be done, my object is to conquer, and I have won, I went in at the Sun, and I came out at the Moon, now don't you see that I have got a rope in each hand, and both have ends, so that when they banished me from home, for not taking both ends, I did lick them after all, I came home, in front, and that is where they never knew how to go, I will show you how the Sun is guided, it is this, her axle, is a kind of storm-cloud, it comes in the middle, it is in her center, and when she forces this cloud out, it takes in all the evaporation, and descends, to the Moon, and there it is staid by the adhesive-ness, of the elements, that close in around that body, it is quite on a par, with all other elements, it has a certain use, and for that purpose it is used; thus you see, that a cloud can't pass through the Moon, till it is cleansed of its impurities, and when that occurs, it is still a cloud, for it never becomes pure, and when the Sun, has gouged out both of her own waters, suffi-cient, it comes to this settlement, that is blocked against the interior of the Moon, and there it is, the Sun, starts back, on her own way, and eats, her surplus supply, till it is all evaporated, then she is dry, inside, and she has nothing more left, it is gone, so she has to fall down again, and meet her fate, on top of the little sister, that I told you about, now my friends you have got a notion, and though I have been a long while, in giving it to you, it is here at last, and it is this, your own thoughts flood in · upon you, till they become so crowded, that no man does know exactly what is taking place, well you have got me at last, the Sun has broken her thoughts, and there is where man begins, I have him, in my eye, he is my own specimen, and I will make him mine, till he dies, and afterward, he can take a trip through where I have told him about, and he can there investigate for himself, it is this he will find, a certain amount of rubbish collects round the sides, and when the Sun becomes exhausted, she takes fire at the back end, next to the Moon, and she is propelled back, to where this accumulation has been laid, and in here, is her great revolutionary wheel, and she feeds this wheel, by the access of her own torch-light, it is herein illustrated, that the Sun is a fire, well it is a fire, but not in the meaning of man, she is a powerful flume, that makes her own time, into a different style, to the ordinary fire, it is a heat, that gasps, and sops back again, it absorbs, as it goes, and is all the while taking in at the time it is pouring out, it keeps on heaving and drawing, and is worked under the theory of a bellows, it takes in, and pours out, and renews this till it comes to the end, then it revolves round, till it drops, and in dropping, it fetches out a complete new set of wheels, that make a circuit, and they start on the old plan of driving in, and pulling out, till they become so exact in shape and make, that they keep on running evenly, till they reach the other end, it is here, that the return has to be made, and the Sun has been eating off the track, that she made, when she has eaten it all clean and bare, the fact is clear, these great wheels go back on its own axis, or rewind, it is a screw, and is as plainly visible as the groove, that it works in, now I don't think you are entitled to any more, till I see how you are going to shape, and then you can have a machine made on this principle, I can give it out, in a brief sketch, without any mystification at all: And you may want it, or you might be like the aborigines, say too much rope make big choke, "me no liky me no savy Mit judgee," when the judge has to pass

a sentence, he does not ask anyone, whether it is right or not, he
says you were found by fair and unlimited justice, to be guilty,
and I see no reason why you should not receive the full penalty
of the law; well my friends he can't kill, but he can frighten,
and when the Sun takes a backward turn, she is very much agi-
tated, it is no use saying otherwise, she moves back fast, and is
seen to rise with a glow of eagerness, that is marvelous, it is her
dead sister, that she left, and found the live one, and that will
be the experience of every unfortunate wretch, he will leave his
dying sister, it will be the last of a decayed hope, his soul will
leap into the arms, of his friends, and say what you will, there
never has been a man hung yet, who did not find joy in heaven,
and it is this, his soul is crushed on earth, his sight is dimmed,
and his hate is perpetual, his flight is joy, and he goes away agi-
tated, and his soul is full of grief, his eye is once again made to
feel, that it is there still in spite of all, and he feels, that his
heart is saturated with joy, that alone could kill, but it does not,
for it is the great good of knowing that he was once a martyr,
and he was caught in whatever wrong he did, and his soul says
I will sin no more, that is the word, that breaks from his grip,
but it is all folly, his soul was taught to run backward, and it
crosses back, on the same road, that it had gone over before, it
was the screw cleaned, that is all: And you will find that you
had better clean those screws, on earth, it will make you a purer
and better people, and your prisons, ought to be turned into
farms, for the cultivation of good, instead of placing men as
guards and sentinels over these unfortunates, set them to teach
the prisoner how he should live, instead of teaching him that he
is a beast, when you don't call his sentinel a brute, I tell you
distinctly, that a prison is nothing but a hell, made by man in
the nineteenth century: Now do you understand that I said a
prison was hell, and I don't mean to go back on this, I have got
a screw, and my worm, can go in and rake your laws, from stem
to stern, I can sweep you cleaner, than any screw, was ever
swept by the Sun on her return journey, and I can make you a
wholesome people, fit to grace the kingdom of God, that is what
you never have been, for you don't know how, and until you do,

it is the penalty of all, who have had no chance to learn, I am
sure you are in advance of the ancients, and it is a black crime
in your eyes to say that God came to us once, and we were so
wicked, that he failed to submit to our wickedness, and we
crushed him with our sins, that is what you did, well you crush
him now, and see whether Old Tom does not make you sick,
before you get very far, I understand you better, for I mean to
make your lies come back, and cheat your own eyesight, that is
a pretty fine tale of yours, about that Whale, that Jonah, had in
his mouth for three days, you don't mind me pulling out my
toothpick, and demolishing him and his whale, now that I have
given you so many points, but it is my turn to fight you, and
lift Jonah higher, than he ever knew he was going to leap, Jonah,
was the first man who ever got the right theory, and he leaped a
whale, and fell in the struggle, that is how Jonah came to become
famous, he dreamed it, and we know that God in all his glory,
never told you to believe in dreams, for this is the reason why,
the God of Neptune is a great God, it lifts up souls, that never
fell off the body of man, and in that soul you have caught a fish,
it is the one, that so many Englishmen have found upon their
breakfast plates, and this is how he comes to propagate, it is not
me, that I should tell you the story, but poor Jonah the prophet,
he lays rolling in the deep, he tried to formulate this victory, by
creeping on a whale when it was asleep, but you see that the
whale began to peep, and swallowed Jonah, with one eye, he
never got any farther though it is a monstrous pity, for he might
have crept inside, and looked at the eggs, before they came to
hatch him; this is the way to try them, it is the Sun, who casting
her reflections, upon the deep, that has made all nature a howl-
ing wilderness, and made the Sun and Moon, a propagating
abyss of the deep, she glistens, and glints upon the deep, and
in her fondness for the Moon, she has cast a shadow toward that
orphan of the deep, and between those two, they manufacture
all the rest, yes my friends I have struck you like the whale, it
is a great big invention, but you are upon the deep, and can see
the reflection of the Moon, beneath that great water stand, and
like a minlature in a picture, it does propagate this man, for he

in infancy does toy beneath those rocks, and behind each turning corner, he sees his shadow, in the gloom, it is here, it is
everywhere, it is lightning all aglow, he has struck the magic of
his own hereafter mould, so my friends your shadow, is the
theory, of what I have learned of, and in bringing your shadow
into existence, I have made you into man, you are the shadow I
want to demonstrate, and I do know how to do it, it is this your
shadow, is the caricature of yourself, and in this I strike you,
it is this; your head is round, well your soul must be found too,
since your head is, well what right have you got to a round soul,
it is this, the Moon in her divergencies, came in contact with her
own father, and in taking a look at him, she did make a sight,
that is not easily found out, and it is this, the Sun looks down
from her nest upon high, and the Moon does the same thing,
well the two together, have cast a shadow, and in this method,
the one does run into the other, well the pair are lit upon the
wave, and in motions of sweet harmonious bliss, one keeps time,
with the other, and the two have propagated this shadow, well a
reflection is not much to begin with, but it is all that is needed,
and you have got the other; that is the solution to the mystery
of promulgating the gravel, it is all owing to this shadow, one
begets the other, and once you get the shadow, you have all the
rest, it is as easy as picking stones off the turnpike gate, the
stone has to be propagated, or it can't be made, and when it is
made, you will admit, that I have got a start, well it all comes in
this form, the stone is the wax end of my theory, it makes an
old gardener smile, when he sees the first stone made, it never
struck the old fellow, that any one from heaven, would come and
help him out, he is mighty clever in his method of picking up
seeds, well he does not mate them right, or he could produce
such a mixture, that would make the Dukes and Lords
propagate a Quaker, for it is as plain as a toad, the Sun in her
agony, to reach the Moon, is all the time spitting at him her
flames of roasting oil, and the Moon is all the while distributing
his essence, so that when they too mate in united lust, they make
the whole formation, at the bottom of the deep; and the water
washes over it, till it is made into lime, this is all; for it will not

adhere alone, but the Sun does not always hit a union with the
Moon, and therefore it is a miss, and there is the secret of the
gravel, it has caught a miss, and that miss became a stone,
and these stones, are rolling, well the stones are misses, and the
gravel is a miss, so that these misses, are drawn together, by
lime, from the other stones, that keep on continuing to miss,
therefore you see that in time you have got a number of stones,
and a number of misses, and the end is very nigh, for the time
is come to treat you to a little more lime, and the gardener's bed
is in a stage of propagation again, do you see my friends how
easy it would be for me to tell you how to find the gold, but I
won't, for you are not prepared to accept me, and I am no loafer,
I want a welcome, and you must demonstrate it in your own
way, and not throw any bones to the "Old Infidel"; his time is
valuable in the other world, and when you want him, it is for you
to bury the hatchet, and say "as he lived so does he die,
like his soul, with immortal coils around him," I cribbed that
from Shakespeare, his soul is his own, and he can better fetter it
than any one who made mud pies at the bottom of the ocean;
Now again my friends I am here in earnest doing battle in my
old cause, and where is Shakespeare, why he is one of my
warmest friends, and I can get him to write you something
better than you ever saw, as he lived, so will he keep on, and
his books now are the greatest, the world has ever known, outside of me, I won't give way to Shakespeare or any one else,
and I say that I will get him to write you one of the finest
plays, that the world ever saw; and you shall have the benefit
of demonstrating it on earth, and he will lend me his name to
foot it with, do you say peace; because I say it is to be as you
make it, and I will be your friend, or your enemy, now I am not
going to drop the Sun on you, till you do something to merit
my anger, and I offer you my hand, in tokens of faithful intentions. You are to accept or reject, as you please, I can't show
you my old body, as identification, but you can in this book
identify my writing it is peculiarly my own, it strikes the reader,
as a fool's, but after you have proceeded some distance, you
will see that it is winding, like the wind, it always comes back

onto the point of the compass, where I intend to propagate my plan, and it is quite different to anything you ever read, but this is the reason, I was born, beneath an Asiatic hemisphere, and I have grown according to my own construction, and my Sun is the one I adore, it strikes me all over at once, and in doing so I am careful, to be the essence of light, that my Sun has given me, now this is a strange way of putting this to you, but you must know, that the Sun, is the giver of light, and in giving light, she must burn oil, for she can't throw light, where there is no oil, then you do just listen to me, the Sun is a filterer, she burns all she wants, and she retains all she cares for as food, or she in other words fattens on that which she selected, now do you understand why man is such a genius, he is the selected of the Sun, for he has that voice, that is just as charming to the Sun, as ever it was to the most brilliant lady; now my friends, why is this; well the Sun is a magnet, and in drawing, she begets, in accordance to her own light; and this is it, which she has selected, in the first place, she is awfully particular, and it is for this, that she will be so seductive, her warmth is ever between your hands, and feet, and she saps you quite dry, in a southern clime, well the result is marvelous, she is greedy after this essence off your bodies, and she sinks beneath the weight of your hands and feet, for they make perspiration, and she is all the time drying it off your bodies: Thus it is seen, that your bodies are a delight to her, and in this form, she is propagating, other men and women, of a different specie entirely, and they are in the ocean now, coming along with the original cast, so it is for me to tell you something of the future as well as the past, therefore you don't loose anything by me, it is all gain, only I must have a fair field for my literary genius, and not bury it any more, or I believe I should make the Sun my grandson, and let her bury the whole kit, basket and all: You have profited less, since you took it into your heads to burn witches, well you ought to be careful and not burn witches, should they attempt to become a nuisance, you give them to understand, that they must go back to the sea, and hunt for these phenomenas that I tell you about, it is quite easy, for these crazy spirits, who inhabit bodies to make mischief, and it is free, for them to go and hunt the oceans, and come back and tell you what is at the bottom of the deep, well they can go through the Sun, and out at the Moon, and discover perpetual motion, thus showing a good work, to their patrons, but I certainly object to spirits going· about raving of God, when they have not left the earth, for more than a couple of leagues or so; now you see what kind of spirits, who have been governing these witches, which you burnt, it was· pure ignorance on your part, you had no idea of the fury you were producing, and in burning that body, you have raised up a fear and dread among the whole of the spirit world, for·it is this, their intelligence, was only of the earth, and they had seen these imitators, in the guise of Christ, and they were ready to rave about him, and he could not stop them; but you can stop then quite easily when I show you how, and instead of using violence, I will simply use a strategic course of punishment, that won't harm any one, and that is for them to take other spirits along with them, and guide them. to the deep, and there let them sit down upon the rocks, and let an expert write a clear description of what there is at the bottom, and show it to an instrument·such as I will make, and have it taken off on a type-machine, and should it prove of value, to send the same parties back, with other witch spirits, and have them used as instruments of mail-conveyors, at first, and then, when they have been a few times it will be seen, that you can't stop them from · this science, of investigating unknown regions, and in this fashion, you can have all the treasures of the deep, in sight, it is only a question of a little training, and you make a skilled band of spirits, that can tell you almost to an inch, where to lower your divers, and shake the pearls, from the bottom of the ocean, now I have shown you how to thieve from the Sun and Moon, and you thought I was helping you all the while: But I was angling for a big fish, and that is the thieving propensities, of man, where do you get this thieving idea from, it is strange, that man, will thieve, no matter what his moral principles are, he is sure to thieve, he can't help himself and why, because he is all the time

24

at it; no but why is it, that he does thieve something in the history of his life, it may not be an apple, or even a peach, yet he will steal something, although he may be a bishop, or a dean, it is all the same, he is bound to thieve it somehow, and it is the rose, that he can't pull away from and say I love thee sweet blossom, but I dare not taste that sweet perfume, it would kill my sanctimonious notions, to be seen at plucking a rose from her pretty bosom, yet he does it nevertheless; and though hades, were a stone fence, or a barrier of insurmountable obstacles, he negotiates the theft all the same, and he will as long as that great big pendulum, shall continue to swing to and fro, now why is it; because his eye, is not his own, and he dare not give it credit for what he can't see; that is why, his eye, is there, but the phosphorescence, is the eye of a third party, but how can this be, because the Moon, in her propagation, drove the sight back, toward the Sun, and the Sun drove it back into the water, and in the water, the eye was made whole, by the reflection of phosphorescence, and it thus distinguishes; the light, and now you see where I have brought you, to this point, and that is this, that the phosphorescence in the ocean, is the glow, with which we love, it is a mingled candescence; that has been the feature, which I shall hereafter call the sight of light, it is here, where the mind is moulded, it mingles with the light, till it becomes so fragrant, that it gets into a normal state, and in this normal state, it is able to see light, and in looking at light, it has the power of distinguishing the difference between day and night, and in this respect, it is quite possible to develop, any number of lights, for the eye, is formed in this fashion, that it grows by promulgating the afterbirth, and the afterbirth, is this soul, and why this afterbirth is made into soul, is a reflection, on the move, when the Sun and Moon meet together at the bottom of the wave, and in their embrace, it is seen, that this shadow appears, of a re-unite, or what my friend the Seer would call a cow jumping off her shadow; it is exactly, the same, he drove cattle once, and had many opportunities in observing their vagaries, and it is from this style of his, of making me use the whip to round up, that I am able to get in so many practical demonstrations, he is practice from the

word go, and don't you make too free with him, in angry moments,
for he is quite capable of making a practical demonstration on
any body, that does not mean what you would call a punching
set to, but it is meant to explain, that he would get the best of
almost any man by some resource, that would not be thought of
by his opponent; and it is only to be wondered that no violence
was used on those New Zealanders, for it is only one thing, that
stopped it, and that is this, he has a will of iron, and you can't
break this will, he resolved to save the money for his own family,
or in the event of losing it, to shoot the judges, and those attorneys, that were under their guidance, this is the secret right
here; the man you have got to demonstrate this world by is a
good specimen, of your own folks, they are pretty handy with
the gun, and it should be stopped, your sole aim, is to kill, for
that is the intention, that has always mastered man, he does not
know where he gets this theory from, it is his idea to kill, when
a wrong is perpetrated against him, well how does he get that
fire-eating spirit; why, it is in his eye of course, it is there, by
the little stranger, who nestles close beside him, and says you
robbed my parents, I saw you do it, and I am going to kill you;
that is where the right murderer is, not in that body at all, when
you fire the fatal shot, he is in the other man's eye, that you are
going to kill, and he being an expert, his chances are ten to one
against you, for this little beggar works on a theory, of his own,
and that is to dim the sight of your opponent, so as to give your
friend the opposite chance; now I have been puzzled a great deal
about this, and you are going to be very much more puzzled still,
but I hope to be able to get this more clearly put, the enemy, is
standing in front of you, well it is this, the apple of your eye, is
the spirit of your Godfather, may be, according to appointment,
as I said before: Well now it is this, this little eye contains blood
and fire mixed, the Sun put in the fire essence, and the water put
in the meat, and the Moon put in that star, that you see in the
middle, well the three have gone thus far, that it has got no more
light in it, till the candescence, is lifted up, by the light, of a divine being, that can go in and out of there, at will, and make his
home there, that is what you have always thought was the devil,

and instead, it is this spirit, of the body, that has gone on before, and come back again to dwell upon earth, there you have had what you might term a practical stockwhip round-up of the devil: I mean to make a final development of him one fine day, and make you see him act, on the sly, in the way, that will make you feel proud of your own devil, he has only to be taught, that his game is run, and I shall show you what a fine big priest, I have given you, it is all about this drink question, that I would like you to give me a commission to propound a scheme, that would stop humanity from drinking this drug, it can't be entered into in this book, but I have hit upon a plan, that would make all nations of the earth sober forever, and without injury to their pleasure, it is not much, either, it is only to give the spirit in your eye a better chance of distinguishing himself, and making a better man of you, it is the way to stop thieving too, it is the way to stop all foul deeds, it is to teach this little stranger in your eye; the way to play its game honorably, and not take from his neighbor, that which does not belong to his own friend, now you see that I am able to show you everything, from an anchor to a shadow hook, and you don't see my instrument doing harm to a living being, then don't be afraid, let the old hard looks pass away, I don't want your religion, I have not a particle of use for it, I don't call you heretics, I say you are all one equal to the other, and you are all good, only you ought to see everything clearly, or you can't be content: Now then it is no use you thinking I am here to deprive you of your churches, or anything of that sort, I don't care anything about your churches, I have got a theoretical resource, and I want that, it is all I care for, and I can show you everything, in reality, and I can't stand being told that anything is impossible, now when you have got anything impossible to seam together, I can do it; and when you want to sew up old rags, I can do that also, I can mend and darn, and do the whole business complete, it is no use telling me that perpetual motion, has to be proved, in iron and steel, I say it won't work that way, you have to make perpetual motion, in accordance with my instructions, or you can't do it at all, I have mastered this in its entirety, and you can make ships to go through the water, at any speed you have a mind to, and you don't want any coal at all, and you can make railways jump a mile a minute, without an ounce of steam, but I won't do this, till I am ready, I have engaged to make a fortune for my Seer, but beyond that I have no contracts, and you can please yourselves, whether you accept my services or not, now this is what I am after, and that is your spirit guides, they are playing havoc with humanity, and they don't see it themselves, and until they see it through you, it is impossible for them to know anything, therefore you are just as hopelessly astray, as you have always been, now I don't care what you say or do, there are none of your spirit guides, who can do as I have done, and I challenge all the universe, to make a show-ing equal in its entirety to this my first book since I left the world of Cain; I mean this as I have said it, it is a world of Cain, for it has no sense, because it does not know its own fathers, neither does it know where the right way is to be found, neither is it capable of keeping on the right path, did it get entered therein; now my friends, what harm have I done to you, that you should style me " The Infidel "; is it right, is it fair, I never injured any man, yet I shall be called " The Infidel"; as long as the clock is in the Moon, and has to be wound by the Sun, I don't care for the name, but it is this, which has always hurt me most, when I died, there were none to see my remains put away, and they were sewed up in a sack, and cast into the ground, and when I saw that, I was ashamed of my own body, it looked so bare, not a soul to look upon me, and I had done nothing wrong, I felt then, that my heart would break with anguish, for it fairly tore me in twain, and I saw my friend the man who drove me on to abuse religion, standing by my side, and he was quite as miserable as myself, for he had done it all: Now you know that instead of having a welcome, when I crossed the border line, it was one of misery, and all because the man in my eye, had made me a monster, and had made me stand up and fight this religion question, till they put me in prison, and there is where I broke my last fast, it is all the way I ever grew, and as I was taught, so will I continue to teach, because I am able, that is why, my old guide is with me now, and you have his old

friend beside me, and we three, can make you happy, though you
did make me eat a felon's diet, and sewed me up in a sack, I am
more alive, now than any man that ever lived, and I have more
friends, than I know how to satisfy, it is Tom how do you do
this, or how should we make a pick for picking up fools with, it
is always Tom, and they don't call me " The Infidel " now; since
I went through the Sun, and came out at the other end, it is all
the way, that a man is brought up, and when you fetch them up
right, they can go through the Sun too: I don't want any extra
inducement, to call me out, I go, whenever it has any attraction
for me, and I want to make you see that you were born a fish,
and you swam together, and you lived together, and you died
together, and you can go back, and duck in the sea, or you can
come home to the old house, and see the Christmas tree, just the
same as it used to be, and for a matter of that sort, you can give
the directions as it used to be, and keep the old game alive, no
advancement, not even an ancient theory, to be brought back, not
even the idea of our Lord's supper, being eaten as they did
eighteen hundred years ago, when the Lord came and gave his
blessing, aren't you all ashamed of yourselves to think that what
such prophets as Jonah, and any amount more could do that you
are incapable of talking to God, I say you ought to be well whipped
for owning it, didn't King Saul bury the dead by witchcraft, didn't
he send all those with familiar spirits away from him, and didn't
he get left nicely for his ideal heathenism, his own familiar spirit
was driven out of his eye, which is possible, and practicable, and
can be held in subjection forever, for disobedience to the laws of
heaven, I tell you that you have all got familiar spirits, and they
change about, as frequently as it is agreed upon among themselves, now I want you to tell me how you can detect the difference, I'll bet anything, that you don't know when an enemy is
leading you, and when it is your own friend, you just ponder
over this question, and I think you have got a more difficult
question put to you, than ever was made before; it is this, that
makes you afraid of spirits, and they have tricked you from the
cradle up, for they are the shadow, and it was their shadow, that
was propagated, by the shake of the water, therefore, they are a

trick, and always may be a trick, for that is a trick of the Moon
and Sun, to get together on reflection, and sow the seed of
humanity, therefore it is here where you are caught at thieving,
and that is this, the Moon is stealing along, and he quietly steals
on the sun, at the bed, which I wish to attract your attention to,
and that is the propagation bed, at the bottom of the ocean, it
is, as the Moon, is high overhead, and as the Sun is on the waning, that this affectionate embrace is indulged, at the bottom of
the ocean, there is the propagation bed, for it is here that the Sun
is able to receive the Moon, for her head is toward home, and she
is going down, and the Moon is ascending, that this propagation
is imitated, and it is this effect, that has produced all that we see:
Now I want to tell you, that all those spirits, that have no better
occupation, can go and watch for this, and bring me the right
theory of the next people, that are coming to earth to dwell, for
I have seen this change coming along steadily, for some time,
and I can get you all this information, by the time I write my
second work, on science; Now I want to get at the right method
of teaching, and then it is all easy for you, but I must confess,
that I am not master of this yet, for of all your mediums, and
all your spiritualists, both past and present, I don't think you
have ever had one yet, that is able to do this work, right, and I
don't know how I am to teach you either, for your heads are not
fixed right, it is this, you won't keep away from society, for any
given time, so as to all on your heads to grow spiritual, you
make them mortal, that is true, but you don't make them spiritual, they are not strong enough, they want somebody else's head
to support theirs, well now, you have the best of me there, I
can't make you into good useful spirit guides, whilst you will take
notice of what all the world and his wife has to say, your mother
the Sun, didn't do that way, and I can't alter what she has done,
she kissed the Moon deep in the ocean by reflection, and
here is where she has made a reflection, it is here she
did as she liked, and waited to see whether the moon would
look at her, and when he saw her brilliant eye, he piped his little
bit of a face across hers, and it was a complete embrace, don't
you see that as your father and mother did, you are going to do,

and how can I stop you, well it is this then, that when you try
to learn, you must not associate, with any society, till you become
developed, for their essence, is altogether too strong, for you,
and you are not capable of resisting their power, by this you
must see that seclusion, is the proper method, to adopt, in order
to advance, for purposes, such as this work, and not by exchange
of sentiment, for sentiment must be abolished, should you wish
to be thorough mediums; and you must make this be your first
lesson;   Or don't try, for the fact is easily understood, the Moon
can go forever; without looking at the Sun, but the Sun, is always
eager to meet the Moon, this is why, the Sun is hot, and can
drink always, and she can't make up her mind exactly, whether
it is possible for her to divulge this great secret, till one fine day,
she will take the Moon, and suck him in body and soul, that is
about the way your mediums develop, you sit in the shadow, and
you are earnest enough, but you are always talking spiritualism,
and what does it all amount to, why I can tell you, it amounts to
this, that you have all got a black countenance, and that is why,
you talk too much, and do too little, instead of keeping at
home by yourselves, you are always out hunting for spiritualists, and in consequence, your own guides, never go down to the
ocean or anywhere else to cast up pearls, and as a matter of
course, they are birds of a feather, none of them capable to
do anything; this is what you call a correct theory, and a right
road, I say it is the worst road of them all, for you do know better,
and yet you will cling together, like the fish, that you were brought
from, and I shall be surprised to find any fish in my net at all,
that came from spiritualism, soon, they will all claim Tom Paine,
to make money out of my name, but it won't do my friends, you
can't keep me that way, I have two mediums only, that is this
one, and the one he developed through, and I won't give her
name because she disowned me, and said I was a fraud, now we'll
see who is the fraud, she can remember who gave her the back-
hander for that accusation; and she might have had this work,
only for disobeying, so I tell you all, that you never know what
you can do, till I tell you, and when you reach out, for spiritualism, do it honestly, or don't do it at all: That is the idea, do be·

honest, for you can't trick a spirit, and that is the way to master
your enemies, be honest, and honesty, is the best policy, by far,
an honest man may succeed at becoming a tolerably good instrument, but a dishonest one never, his guides are altogether
opposed to trick, they cheat, to beat a thief I am well aware of the
fact, but they won't help you to cheat, when you are in the
wrong; so now it is time I told you how a cheat is made, it is
thus, I made a man sit down beside me once, and tell me how it
is, that he was such a great rogue, he said he could not say, but
supposed it was because of God being too weak to get the upper
hand of the devil, and I thought then, that he had spoken truly,
but I did not know; yet he said you ought to be able to tell me,
so I can I replied, it is quite easy, the Sun has got to breathe, in
one way, and pull her breath out the other; to-wit it is either one
or the other, and she does her best to catch the Moon, and when
he lets her, it is a devil, but when she lets him catch her it is
right and proper, and is a God: That is the way a devil is
made, for it has a long thin tail after it, and is the string, that
the Moon made, as he tore away from the Sun; now you see this
fish quite frequently beneath the tidal wave, and he is a fish,with
a great big tail, like a swordfish, he caught the sting, and it has
clung to them both, well why should it cling to to these fish;
because it is the stain, as it drops from the Sun, and adheres
to the droppings from the Moon, they both drop considerable
when they propagate beneath the ocean, this is the way to
find out that fact, a stingree, has a tail with sharp saw-like
teeth, well the Sun, in her propagation gave a squeeze to the Moon,
and it causes a tare, and in so doing it brings out these teeth, by
the front of a miracle, I don't care to admit a miracle, for I don't
agree that there is a miracle, so it is a good beginning to hold
this up as a miracle, and see me knock it into a balloon, or an air-
bag, don't you seem to understand yet, that there are no miracles,
these are what I might shirk my business by, and take you on
with an undiscovered something, it is all fudge, the miracle, is
not of this century, and it never need be, unless you people
cling to it, in happy ignorance, the way to meet these difficulties,
are by looking down in the after streak, it is the way to meet all

obstacles, and that way, you are alone responsible for errors, the way to get the thing, into a nutshell, is by planting your hand upon Jacob's thigh, and making a double joint, it is done in this fashion, you meet the two bones together, and they grow, so did my shark; he was crippled, on account of the Moon rushing, in passing the Sun, and she flung her sting upon him, because he did not behave, in a proper manner toward her, and God did the same to Israel, for disobedience, he cast his anger upon them, for they were a stiff-necked people, now my friends, I want to have a word with you, you all remember the time, when you were in a cradle, or just on the eve, of leaving it, the first thing you are precipitous in doing is to lift one leg over the other, and begin to climb, and after you climb a few times, you are inclined to keep up your climbing, till you get accustomed to the art, and then you grow careless, well this is precisely, what the Moon does, after he has climbed over the heavens a number of times, he becomes quite careless, and he simply plays with nature, and when he reaches the spot in the deep, where he is to meet the shadow of the Sun, he will give her a smack, that does not mean all play, or all harm, but it is sufficient to rouse her ire, and she flings him back her fire, this is what causes hatred and the reverse, the Sun is all glory, and when she sees his face, beneath the waves, she is dying to be on top of him, and that is what he wants to do, the pair are both distributers, and the one is anxious to do the same as the other, it is thus, where the grief is spread, for the Sun is above, till she meets this monster, and she feels the slight most keenly, when she fails to find herself on top, and it is thus far shown, but that is not all, the Sun is away from the earth, at the time she is approaching this Moon-shadow, her flanges, are striking back, into her interior, and she is not on a par with the Moon, for her power is on the droop, and it is thus, that she can't fill her intense desire to appropriate, this gigantic monster's essence, for he does not deal liberally with her always, and he scatters this manure, that he is dropping, according, to the pressure, that is brought to bear on his interior, well it must be seen at a glance, that the Sun is reclining, at the period, that she does meet her affinity, and she does not use the pressure, till he is half, or more than half over her shadow, well as this is the case, it is shown, that she has not the full power at him, that he has at her; in consequence, she is down beneath him, before he is entirely aware of this fact, and he has no chance of throwing this shadow, and of course, it is a propagation, for the fact is clear, the meeting of these two shadows, in opposition, must beget another, and the one does not release the other, in a moment, for it is strung out to a tail, and by this tail it means something, for the water is between the two, and they can't separate, for they are a united reflection, and are the means of begeting others, for they are three, the moon, the time, and the Sun, and this is how we have got this time, it is caused through the registration of the flood, in two parts, it is the seaming together of something indefinite, and this point, that we call indefinite, is the period of the stars, they are propagated first, by the same method as the Sun and Moon, it is a constant inpouring and outgoing, now you see I am driving you on to the stars, though I have told you, that I am not going to deal with them in this book, neither I am, only so far as I can't avoid reasonably, and that it is this great feature, that I must formulate, ere I pass it by, the season of the year, is the same in heaven, as it is upon earth, and in speaking of this I mean you to see, that the Moon, is not the only factotum, that has the gift of making shadows, the Sun is just as anxious to have connection at the deep, with these stars, that you see at the bottom of the ocean, and she can dye their reflection, with her radiance, as she is going home, and leave a miniature propagation, there I can show you the starfish, it is here that you begin to come into brilliancy, for the starfish is the effect of a brilliant adhesient, or mixture of glue, and propagated matter, that is lying at the bottom of the deep, now you seem to clearly understand, that I don't accuse these bodies of any material connections, it is only by their effect of collusion, beneath the waves, not by any sign of any absurd idea, but strictly in accordance with facts, in a scientific way, therefore you must understand, that I don't deliver my discourse, with any ulterior motives of ridicule, but in writing this work, I cast my pearls, as they have been prepared by me, through actual observation, and

careful investigation of the truth, and you must never bring
this into ridicule, for the holy union of natural laws, in union,
are as sacred, as the very best polished marble slab you ever did
honor to; and you know you have placed your hands before you,
and prayed to many a marble slab, for beneath that tomb, it is
a waste, there was a once living mortal in that waste, but now he
is going on, according to time, his soul is the third, his first, is
his matter, his second is his life in the clay, but his hereafter, is
time; that is all, he gave his sin back, to where it is made, and
he does not carry it any further, except in memory, his sin was
the reflection, caused by the adhesion of crime coming into that
body, by the thoughts, that were conveyed there, by the soul of
his after-birth, which is his shadow, that forms round about him,
and is governed by the reflection of his own cortege, which
come after, for they were his guides, in accordance with nature,
and are the transparent essence of light, thrown in on top of
him, through the fire, having struck the shadow, in getting at
the moon, now you have a burnt miniature, and its name is the
same as yours, it is called the man in the Moon, for it is here,
that man is formed after, through this piece of dirty-faced mush,
that stuck to the seaming, as it strikes the earth, in passing
round; the same is applicable, for all animals are struck, from
the same mould, only that the stages, are different, when these
appurtenances, are made, therefore we have the earth, to make
next, and it is a tedious job I can assure you, this is not the
gratifying work you think it is, it is all a complete drudge, and
not a bit pleasant, I would rather make a mound, with scoops,
than to begin to put mother earth in shape, and I won't make
her all in this book, I am just going to give you a faint idea of
how she is formed, and then you must excuse me from the present, for I can't do this justice, and make it over again, at one
sitting, so I intend to do it at one pop, and you can see that
Tom is a bit of a God in his own way, well it is now or never, as
the Patricians say, when they did a miracle, I guess you have
got to make an ash heap somewhere, to hold all that manure,
that is consumed in behind the sun, and you might just as well
give me the one I want, for it is here on the place you are so

fond of, and call terra firma; I don't want your miracles, they
don't cut any figure with me, and I just rip them up, like you do
an old doll rag, that has too much grease to hold any water;
thus you see, that I keep my grease, and give you the rags, or in
other words the sun fattens on the grease, and she casts back to
you the bones, and they come down here, in form of essence,
and that essence, is alive, the moment it mixes with cold air, for
the heat, is never dead, it holds matter, and anything, that contains matter, no matter how infinitesimal, it does contain life,
and it is only to be consumed, according to its properties of
adhesiveness; therefore it is called soluvium of potassium; this
is why, the main heat, is not dead, the water holds the ingredients, that contain the life, and cold air is alive, because it is
filled with air, and the air we breathe, is alive, so that we are
held together by life eternally, and can't die, because we are
coupled to sound, that has no governor, or catalepsy, it can't be
tamed, because it has no adhesion, therefore it is a free agent,
and will be in this stage, forever, so you must not suppose, at
all, but wait for some man more skilled than I am to propound a
scheme, for mixing sound and material, the Sun and Moon can't
do it, for they are a pair of sounds together, and the one runs
the other, for all they are worth, and it is no use, for their sound
is constantly escaping, and it propounds other sounds, by the
affection of its own external evolutions, and makes a distinct
vibrating noise, that would seem to say, I am at my wit's end,
no one here, to take me in, I am the mad factotum, that nobody
wants, and I shall bury my head, beneath a great evolution, and
come here in sound no more, it has gone to waste, there is nothing more of it, it is here, and it is not here, it is a mixture of
elements, that don't adhere to each other, till they are grown on
the ground in flesh and blood, and then it dries onto the vertebræ, or spinal column, that is the quick, and it is herein, that it
propagates, and makes a second adhesion, then it can't make any
more adhesions, and goes to waste, in a gigantic growth, that
never ends, for it is soluvium of potassium in texture, and not
in reality, it is the ass turned loose, for he is a wanderer, forever,
he can't home anywhere, because he no sooner finds a home,

than some other ass, is after his place, and he has to take somebody else's place, in accordance with ignorance, as set out by the
heathens at the beginning, that is why I am writing this work,
not for you, but for the spirit world, who have all begged me to
do it, in direct opposition to paganism, they say we can't go on
like this forever, one man is a God, because he was the first of
an intelligent time, and he set the world agog by his wonders,
and he did well, but he had no power, and could not reach far
enough, that is all there is to it, he was capable, you must admit,
and he is capable now, and he need not be ashamed of what he
did, for he has had a season of upward of two thousand years,
and that is not a bad innings for one spirit, I don't hope to live
that time, at any rate, I should like a vacation, should you place
me at the head, to govern it all those years, I want to tell you
how to live, so that you can die good, and stop away, when you
have gone, what right has the mortal, with a dozen spirits round
them, all making confusion and dissension, it is absurd, the
heavens are ruled by three, and what more should there be
attached to man, he is not a bit skillful, like the machinery, that
works the entire universe, and I don't think he is entitled to be
any more than a good government, of his own understanding,
therefore it is sure work, that does the best, and you ought to
give up that see-saw business, which is altogether too much, for
the well-being of the human race, it is not right either, you keep
a whole band of spirits round you, well stop that see-saw, and I
don't think you will get far wrong, you know what I have reference to it's that confounded confusion, that spirits deal in, they
agree upon a certain method, and after agreeing, they go on
agitating, till they make a complete tool of the one, that has to
be guided by them, till at last, one or other of them snap the
angel cord, and is in there for good until some radical change is
brought on through this mystery, in taking time by the forelock,
and shut him up, till he makes an example for the others, which
is understood, to mean death in heaven, it means this, the spirit
who gets in the eye, and can't get back, is forever banded about
as the tool, and the rest keep on advising him to this extreme,
and that extreme, till at last he gets sulky, and won't listen to

any of them, now you see I have given you the lunatic spirit to remove, well how are you going to set about it, why it is the easiest thing in the world, to remove a dead spirit, by closing up his grave, that is why, and then shut out the light, and you have got him buried alive, and he is sure to find his way out of any dark corner, for he is able to light his road, by the essence, that is in his own eye, which you imagine is quite a wee tiny wee thing, because it is inside of the other man's eye, here you are wrong, for the eye is an illuminous body, and the reflection is internal, as well as external, and the fire, is burning both ways, as in the Sun, for the Sun glistens back, and so does your eye; therefore it is this eye, that has to be illuminated, from the back, or how could you see in front, and this eye, is the eye, of the light, of a new and intelligent spirit, only the brain has to be developed, or it could not do this work, and after it becomes reflected, it surpasses all understanding, for it is being changed ever and anon, by changing spirits, who pass to and fro, as the agreement is engaged, and they change, according to their own individual characters, and instead of a boy, in this country, knowing more, he does, but he does not retain as much in English, as he ought to for the fact is quite clear, you have all nationalities, and in consequence, he is followed up by German French, and Spanish extracts, and he is a division of either, according to the spirit, who is in his eye, at any particular time, now you don't recognize me as an intelligent power, well let me inform you mentally and physically I am all that a power can be, but you don't realize this, for you never knew your own power before, neither did you know anything, except, that Columbus crossed to America, and he understood how to do it, well now you do know, what brought Columbus to America, and Captain Cook to Tasmania etc., well it was this little devil in their eyes, who had been spying about, and wanted to make great men of them, that is the secret, and we have got the same thing in our animals, to this extent, it is to be found largely in hogs, and the horse specie have got it the most except ourselves, now I told you not to class me with the monkey, and I am going to run you a race on animals, that will establish what I claim, that is natural causes, for everything, you can't tell me anything about ourselves, that I don't know, but you are going to learn something about yourselves, that you never hoped to hear, and that is this, you are an amphibious creature, and not made out of clay and dust, you are a whale specie, and so is the horse, it is in this, that I am going to manipulate the greatest ingenuity, that was ever formulated by the astuteness of man, and you must bear in mind one fact, and that is this, that I always leave a loophole of escape, and when you tackle me in publishing my dishonor, I give you fair and ample warning, that I wind like the wind, and I shall plant my dirk, where you leave the body unprotected, so when you attack me in print, look sharply after your own person, for I am very near perfection, at finding weak spots, and when you run your own body against a sword, don't expect it to do other than prick, this is my candid warning of all common people, who intend to assail "The Infidel"; you can make your papers shut me up, by not printing what I write, but you can't do it by honest open warfare, for I can place my arrow, where few can find the end, it has sunk so deep, that a hide of leather, has no show against my dart, therefore you will be satisfied, when I give you to understand, before I begin, that I want some grace shown to me, should you have any theory, that is able to annihilate me; and I would remind wealthy newspaper holders, to beware of "The Infidel's pen"; for it is sharpened at the bottom of the ocean, and the grindstone is hard to reach, yet it is there quite nicely prepared to take a siege, and will make a faithful battle fling back her ring: Now I don't want any man's favor, and I would like to see capable men take up this question, and fight it down like men should do, who love fair play, there is not one atom of sport, in a foul and base attack, and as the fish, in the ocean is always sporting, in glee, and cleverness, can't you and I have a little sport, without making ourselves, into clowns, of a bad odor, I say that you can tackle me in any scientific point you choose, and ask the people to be our judges, you must not go outside of my book, for it would totally unfit any of my future works for publication, because you could then say I cribbed from you, so to put matters straight, I want you to knock this one out first, you

have just the same chance as I have, the little man at the back of
your eye, can show his bright intelligence in front of you, and
you can see what he tells you; that is the way he ought to do,
go and investigate, and then come back, and stand in your eye,
till you catch his meaning, that is the way, it is simply a dive
between a shadow, and a mirror that produces this sense; not by
clairvoyance, or any other kind of wretched plain meaning, it is
caused through the eye becoming illuminated by a kind of
essence, that is on the body of the spirit, who enters your eye;
and it is from his reflector, that you gain sense; it is not from the
theory of sight at all, for unless he shows you how, he can't get
there, and he must show you how, or he won't reach his point;
therefore he has to get into your eye, and show you how to work,
or you don't see how it is done, now my friends, should you keep
on telling your guide to show you, he can't for the fact is as plain
as day, you make him know what you mean, by doing everything
opposite, to his theory, till he sits up in agony, at not being able
to reach you, then he is lost, for he must give up, to some other
guide, who comes in and tries this very same thing, till he is lost
also, then another, and again another, still you take no notice of
any of them, till the one comes, who can tell you everything, that
is mastering good, you reject all, till the right spirit sits down in
your eye, and tells you of all things possible, and then you ask
him impossible things, it is easy, you follow sound, and you catch
the thought, this is the reflector in your eye, which produces this
sense, not outside, as the men of mystic cloth tell you that God
took Moses up into the mountain, and there did stand beside him,
and make him tremble with fright, he did no such thing, he was
there in the eye of Moses, and he told Moses, to take this or that,
as the case might be, and you don't believe me; well you can
wait till doomsday, and you will never get one of your guides, or
any God, to come and stand behind you, and preach such stuff
into your ear, I tell you again, that you have a lot to learn, before
you knock Paine out, he is such a terrible fellow, and I would
like to hear what you have to say against him, he is not perfect, I
am sure, but he is ready to defend his honor, and that is as much
as you ought to ask any man to do; this is where you all fail, it

25

is in upholding your own dignity, I have done this, I said I
intended to come back to earth, and see how faithfully I have
kept my word, I went away it's true in a bit of sacking, though
you didn't see me weeping, it is true, that my heart was crushed,
yet it was all right, after I got the old one back, and properly
stuffed· with ether, it came along pretty quick, I can tell you,
when I knew that I might have a chance, of going back, and
telling the people that I had not died; this was my great thought,
and it has been my study, ever since I passed over the boundary
line; thus you see me back, and I mean to tell you every blessed·
thing, whether of importance or not, I won't even hide one secret
from you, and you have the privilege of discussing my book at
length, and when you hold up your finger, at any error, why I
am there ready to do my utmost to correct it; I won't be dogmatical, and say you are all wrong, when I know that you are as
pure, as nature, will permit you to be; Now it is this, that I want to
speak to you about, the people on the side of life, that I belong
to; are anxious to show you the truth, and they have been struggling for centuries to do this, they always did try, to come back
to you, and it is just the same, as the whale, he always comes to
the surface to breathe, well the spirits, are always glad to inhale
the breath on earth, for they can't leave it, it is a tie, that they
are unable to break, it is the tie of affection, that brings them
back, they know that you don't know anything about them getting back, and they see you in the body, isn't it natural, for them to
like that body too, and swim in, where there is nothing to prevent
them going, a spirit is able to reach out often, and throw
some obstacle in your way, when you are going to certain
destruction, his soul is free, and he has the opportunity of looking up your journeys, before ever you set out on them: And
he can go ahead, and come back, and sit in your eye, till that
journey is safely ended, or he can break your neck, just
as easy, then why don't you try to learn, how to distinguish
the good, from the bad spirit, that is in your eye; this one
wants me to smoke, because he likes it, his little eye likes to see a
chimney-pot, because he can smell the smoke, his eye is always
on his own interest, his nose is always, on the lookout for some

essence, because it helps him to grow, that is his theory, and he wants to grow, well it is this little satisfaction, that pleases him, and not your desire at all, he is the one who wants this smoke, not you at all, and he is as infatuated, as ever he can be, over this smoke, it is his delight, for he holds your own sense at ease, over this essence, and he can't work, neither can any one work, while this smoke is always curdling through your essence, it is physically impossible to do anything out of the merest routine of everyday life, when you have this smoker in your eye, his only hope is tobacco, and his only thought is the sense of knowing, that you don't expect him to work, when you have that pipe between your lips, it may be a pipe, or it may be any other fix-ture, it is all a mixture, of dead weeds, and that is a complete description, of the little fellow, who claims you as his very own; well you see the steam rising from thwart the whale's head, and you say there she spouts, well what makes her spout, it is the machinery, that is in her is it not; thus you see my friends, that the whale breathes, she does it once in a great while that is true, yet she breathes all right enough; now what is inside of that whale, to make her breathe so hard, it is the lungs, that fill, with air, and ascend, to the surface, to get filled, there is the solution of lungs, they are first made, to blow a hole through, and then, it is used to fill the body with breath, thus you have the first pair of lungs, that are made, it is in this whale, that our lungs, are made first, there is the missing chain of evidence, that places the first link upon man, it is this ivory tooth, and why, because that tooth, is the first one, of a make, that does beget another; it is the tusk off a whale, that is formulated into teeth, by the growth of an ass, it is this tooth, that has brought us so far, it is this tooth, that killed the folks Balaam went to kill, but they stood in the way, and the ass, saw the two teeth, it was all over with Balaam, he couldn't get Mr. Ass, to see the way he did; the ass saw two people in front, and they had linked hands, and the ass was too cowardly to peep at them, that is all owing to this tusk, it is the tooth, that slayed Balaam, and the ass did speak, for an old ass can bray a note, that would deal a death-blow, at any other ass, that tried to drive him through; now my friends you

see that I don't count the Balaam mystery, as anything at all, it
is merely the way you choose to place things, the ass saw a vision,
for the spirit of some ass, was looking through Balaam's eye, and
he cast a reflection, that made Balaam believe it was an angel in
front, and the ass, wouldn't go, for the fact is clear, there were a
number of spiritualists, in those days, who practiced those fear
tricks, and it may have been a magic lantern, or it might have
been a Quaker who made the ass scared, it was not angels, in a
materialized form, for they are unable to do this, without you help
them, by consent, and other forms, which are not here described
for the simple reason, that it can't be done, in a way that
would satisfy any but a true believer; then it is all right enough,
but the moment you introduce a skeptic, the charm has lost its
power, and you can't hold the spirit intact, for it is afraid of this
skeptic; it is this cause, that makes all spirit power hard to suc-
cumb, the fact, of you killing Christ, has had such a fearful
effect, that it is always the same thing, he might shoot at me, or
some such dread, now you see this is only reasonable, the spirit
in the body, knows that a gun is no foolish thing, and they know
that any explosion is dangerous, in consequence, you can't get
them to submit, to a proper treatment, or it would not be much
trouble to get them materialized; and this is where you do wrong,
for they can help you all through your whole life, and they are
there in your eye certain; so what do you want to make them
afraid of you for; it is quite possible, for you to play a game of
hide and seek with mortals, but you can't make spirits in your
eyes see it that way; they like it themselves, but it is an abomination, in others for it is the essence of that evil odor, that they
cast over others, that prevents you from seeing their tricks, this
is it, they plant a sting, wherever they find you out in telling an
untruth, and this is what it is for, the first man and woman came
of a whale, and it was this, that embittered all creation, and it
was brought through in this fashion, the whale is an amphibious
creature, to this extent, it rises to the surface, to breathe, and
does breathe on the surface, therefore he is amphibious: He dare
not breathe below the water, for it would let out his breath,
at the tail, and ultimately would become another creature, so he

is obliged to blow his breath out, and draw it in, on the top of
the water; so you see I am at the whale, and he is my subject,
though I don't care to go for him like a whaler does, and stick
him in his blubber, and make him feel bad, I want to teach you
how to tell a whale, from some other kind of fish, and that other
fish, is man; now do you see why I don't go and get on his tooth,
and ride him round the world, like the Arabian Knights did of
old, I want to teach man science, and not fables, they are all
stale, and it would not interest you at all if I were to go through
a whale, like Jonah did, he had his reputation at stake, and he
had the making of the fable, so it was his business, to collect his
own hide, and seam it to please him, I am going on a different
basis, and I must go according to my maker, or die in the attempt;
so as I am amphibious, I can't die by drowning, then I suppose I
can't be killed by air, because we don't live on anything else
geometrically speaking, and as I have to fight all the universities
in the world, why I dare say I can't do better, than by carving
them out, when I begin to count time, so you see that as I am an
amphitheater, in all my dealings, I must be a king of a whale; or
you would be at me like a pack of hungry sharks, thus you see,
that I am only " The Infidel," and as an " Infidel," I am more of
a human, than those who talk of me; now you seem to see that I
have made fast to this whale, and that I am going to investigate,
it is thus then that we have caught, a fish, with a pair of lungs,
and he blows them, and you own it: Then such being the case,
my friends will agree with me, that the whale is an amphibious
quadruped, in this respect, that he is tied to some unknown matter, that has a tendency to inhale fresh air, and he lives, by the
air alone, he can't bring his mouth to the top of the surface,
without air rushing in; that is certain, and when it fills, he is down
again, and he rises to the surface, and blows it out again, did he
blow it out, below the water, it would choke him, and he would
burst, so it is plain, he must not blow it out below the water; so
you see he is the first fish, with lungs, and he uses them by force
of circumstances, and not by mystery, now my friends, you admit
his lungs, well what have we found, it is the missing chain, that
has caught you by surprise, it was Darwin's theory, that we were

from the monkey, it is our old mistakes, that have always dragged us down, and that is the hair, it could not be placed, on top, because it belonged to the bottom, therefore, instead of making hair out of the mungoose, we must go and look for it, on the pelican, for he is the thief, who poked a hole in us first, it is this bird, that produces hair, and not the giraffe, or the monkey; now my friends I have been rounding up the forest, and have done nothing at all with it, it is my whale, that I am going to pin my faith to; and it is all in him, that we want to make a man, that is the beginning of man; I don't prescribe a dish of cocoanuts, when I want the air to breathe through me, the cocoanut, is three, one is the milk, but the other, is the cow, that made the milk, and the third, is the nut, that has to be cracked, before we get to the cow, that has made the milk, now then we want to find where it is that you hide your shame in for not knowing better, it is this, your whale does suckle her cubs, and her milk is good, notwithstanding, that she lives in the deep, her cubs are all the same as the Chinamen, they come rolling along, and suck the milk of nature, and it is in this gait of the Chinamen, that I discovered the missing link, I could not fill the bill, till I got to China, and watched that walk, it is the way a cub comes to his mamma, for some of the blessing, that nature has distributed in her bountiful way, that is the theory of the wind, she rolls and lolls, and sucks, and draws, and drives, and takes in, at last she lifts up her head, and makes a rear, then she dives down, and up again, and away at full speed ahead coming tumbling head foremost across everything, that is precisely how a whale goes, her head is up and her tail is in the after part, throwing back that great big lash, till it is drowned in immensity; Now then you see it is very hard to pitch on to hair, yet we must take it from the whale, and this is how it is done, the whale is an amphitheater, for it has every ingredient necessary, that makes the whole of mankind, and I have to put him together piecemeal, or not do it at all: So you must take out some fine whalebone, and see what effect the air has on that piece, it is whalebone, when you take it out of the whale, but after you have made it fine by exposure, it turns into a hairy substance, and is no more

whalebone, but actually it is grown to hair; there is the mystery
of hair, it will be shown, that your hair has to be made plainly, or
you can't believe, yet you have this hair, in its first stages, in
the whale, and I will plant it where it is sure to grow, therefore
you must go with me, or I can't show you; and when you get
used to going round looking for things with me, you will be
quite of my opinion, that the world grew naturally, and that the
man who works against nature, will climb a higher hill, than the
hump on the back of a whale, and his ankles will require to be
better adapted to climbing, than they are now, or he never will
get there; now do you see what I have done, your gristle, is the
back of the hump, that has been placed there by constant exposure to the atmospheric elements, and then it is tempered by constant dives below the deep, you have the first piece of gristle, in
the world, because it is grown, on the hump of a whale, and
is produced there by the constant motion of the sea, in its anxiety to drown everything, for as the sea is washing a wave comes
quickly back, and drives its pause against the hump, and is drawn
away again, by the current of atmosphere, and when it leaves the
hump, it cause a draft of fresh air to penetrate the hump, and in
so doing has propagated gristle, through its adhesion to nature, it
is propelled on by this course, till the whale has lived a number of
generations, and then it changes to whale oil, by inflation of the
atmospheric currents, in course of divergencies; thus it is plainly
seen, that a whale does not die, of its natural free will: For the Sun
does not set forever, neither does a whale die, for the fact is
clear, it can't die, for it is amphibious, the one does not injure it
any more than the other, and the whale is fastened to no other
cord, for it has the water to live in, and it has the air to sustain
it, therefore the whale can't die, it is tied to nothing, and is a
pure machine, neither more nor less; it is a machine, that does
all the work, of an invention, it breathes, and it swims, and it
dives down, because it feels the air too cold, on the top, yet it is
on the top, for it can't live altogether, in one way, now you have
a good chance of poking a hole through the Infidel's coat, by
skipping the rope, and showing him how Christ was born a saint,
but you can't fill me with no such nonsense, I am here to stay,

THE UNIVERSE.

and this whale, is my standard of excellence, it can do better
than man ever knew how to do, it can live in heaven, or it can
dive down to the regions out of sight, and find out, whether hell
has any more such fish as Jonah, this is the one he tried to swallow, and was almost gobbled up, he has been, you say, but you
have his tale; and that is where he propagated an ass, for it is in
this same whale, at the tender part, that I am going to bring up
all asses; you claim me as the man who was so soft as to tell you
everything, that I knew, then why do you hold me up to-day as the
Infidel, I was good to you, I told you all I knew, but Jonah never
did, he saw the whale, and he rode on his belly, many a dozen of
times, and that is where he grew, he rode on the belly of this gigantic fish, and he knew it, and would not tell you; then he does
deserve a name in that great book of God, and I am out of it
because the fools, were made first, and I came after, that is why,
and the fools, are so silly, that they keep a number of fools to
come after and do their work over again, that is always the
way of the world, and it is this way to-day, you have got
about one good man, for every barrow full of useless ones, and
the barrow that held this Jonah was no exception, for he could
have told you all about the entire business, did he remain on the
barrow of that whale's belly, for three consecutive days and
nights, it is all a mistake, Jonah got there, but the spout it was
bare, and Jonah fell in, what a brave man was Jonah the fair, he
had on a sealskin coat, and the abject horrors was possessed of
his hair, because he could not stare, at the length of that whale,
you may count it from the time of Noah's Ark, another fable
story, it has fallen in, very well, for it must have been this same
ark that Noah built, and the two together have made a great big
story, and neither of them could make any more, because the
whale went to glory, and they were left in the lurch upon a fable
story; this is the way they did it then, it must have been, out of
the ribs of a whale, that Noah built his craft, and the first man
he saw, he clapped him on the back, and said you come with me,
and they two got tied up in so many knots, that they were
drowned in a craft so big, that stunk them out of existence, and
that is the end of those pair, of braggarts, I don't want to drain

you dry of essence to continue with, but it is a pity, to hold one
man up to the world as an "Infidel"; and the other liars to be
pitched upon as the genuine men, when you know they told such
awful stories, that no man ever lived, that could keep pace with
them: Now I want you to remember me, for I am of the Esau
extraction, and as I am a descendant of Esau, I mean to place
the peg where it belongs, and instead of Rebekah gaining any
advantage over me, she has lost the game, and the hairy son of
Isaac, is to be the one to cast the net, and lead humanity home to a
good and true God; Now my friends I am just as much entitled
to your consideration, as any God you ever knew, and for a matter of fact, I can show you more, than any God who ever lived;
and you know it's true; now you know that I am here among
you, and you shall have all the advice and assistance, that you
need, and more than that I will show you the gold in abundance, and that is your God, and you know I am not lying; now
you admit, I can make this whale grow, into anything I choose,
well it's high time I went to pieces, and made myself, for you
would be horrified, did I make one of you; and that is all I can
do, is to make myself, and you can make yourselves after me,
and then do as Tom does, when you have fallen into the state of
coma, and gone away to the North Pole, and seen these atoms
develop, now it is not such a wonderful feat as you people imagine to get on board a craft, and go to the North. Pole, you must
get prepared, it is purely a matter of preparation, and I will
show you how to do this thing, but you must not try the bullets
on my machine, or you will cripple the adventure totally, and I
won't go on forever, I only give one chance, and I won't do you
any harm, but it is a bargain, that you keep your hands
off, "eyes on hands off," and you shall be convinced without a possibility of doubt, I know you think I might have
left this absurd threat out; of dropping the Sun on you;
but you know it has taken eighteen hundred years, for
the spirit world to comfort their souls, into a sense of justice, and they are all afraid of you, I don't think, that th
are many on my side of life, that know that a bullet c
hurt them, you see them always in terror of a gun, and

are afraid of your gun, and knives, and how can it be otherwise,
you cut them to pieces on earth, and you turn electricity on
them, why this is precisely what you did, at the beginning,
you turned an electric current onto mortals, and they died,
without a visible mark, and it has been handed down, as the
work of God, and that is precisely who did it, but instead of it
being the God, that you all go hunting for, and never find, it was
this spirit, who has represented himself as God, and none other,
than the one, that has always been at the head, and is so now,
and I say that he is a mortal, just the same as we are, and that
he was born, of a fish, and came from that part of the body of the
whale, where electricity is found, and that he is an electrician by
birth, and is no more God than any of us; now you see where
you are finding yourselves, in a whale, well it is my business to
take you out of that whale, and place you on dry land, and show
you how to walk, and talk, and quite any number of other things;
well now this is the point right here, your backbone, I made, in
the punk, and you thought I might have compared you to something prettier than a spider, but now you say this Tom Paine came
out of a piece of pulverized stone, for he did not begin to talk
about himself, till he got by that spider, well you see my friends,
I must show you either on myself or you, and when it is you it is
me, and when it is God, it is us too; therefore we only do our duty,
when we show respect for each other, I don't claim to be any
better than you, and I say that God is no better than we are, he
comes of better material, that is all, and as he led you so long, you
ought to be grateful to him, and go with him, rather than against
him, for he is our good guide, and you ought not to cast aside a
good guide, till it is absolutely proven, that there is a better, and
you must meet him face to face, and know that he is true, or
don't destroy the good till you are quite sure you have a better,
and I say that science is good, and it was good laws, to kill a few
of those heathens by currents of electricity, till they became
horror-stricken into good behavior, what has been done in the
past, is not necessary in the future, and I say that you have
no right to kill for any offense whatever, it is entirely wrong, it
has a tendency of evil about it, that bears malice, and it is much

harder, to bear punishment in jail, than to be strung up, and
the proper course is to bury the men in dark cells, for murder,
for they are speedily liberated from the actual murderer, and
he is powerless to go on committing crime, for the fact is plain
as anything, he becomes a saint, his eyes are both shut up for a
long time, and he is unable to get back, for the fact is here
demonstrated, the eyes lose the phosphorescence, and he is
totally blind, till he regains a couple of months of liberty, now
you see the power I am giving you, that is to cure all murderers,
by science, and not by threats of dire punishment, etc., you try
the experiment on lunatics, and murderers, and see how quick it
will knock out both of these evils, the one is a plague, brought
on, through the sea seeping into the eggs, by being brought out
again by the confusion of egotistical effusion; it is a complete
scientific research, that can only be investigated, by the spirit of
all powerful organism; for it is in laying flat down in the ocean,
and watching this process, that I discovered so much, and I can
explain my theory of getting about, when I write more, as it is
quite impossible for me to put my knowledge in less than
twenty volumes, and I can do what I can, at these works, without
injury to any one; but you must let me know in some substantial
way, that I am welcome, or I can't be made the tool, and then be
thrown on one side, in an instant of hatred, for I am not going to
abuse you any more, and I will deal strictly with science, my
theoretical resources, are such, that I can make my medium's
fortune in a few months, and I know how to give him all the
gold he wants, but I would rather keep him back, till I am certain he won't break away from me, then he can have all the
wealth, that is good for him, and his relatives; now you see I
don't want you to load him with riches, it is all well enough to treat
him right, but not to make him too strong, in monetary points,
I don't want it, till I go further, and then you can pay the laborer
for his hire; that is what my religion is; and I only want what he
is entitled to for his work, I don't want you to come near him too
much either, for it will interfere, with his duties, in casting pearls,
it is against the laws of nature, to make too much of a mortal,
for they are prone to flattery, and it is easy to flatter them, till

they become insane, and it is the little demon, that is hidden
behind, that does it, he gets working on the imagination, till he
sticks his fingers through too far, and you must be very careful,
not to press this instrument to social evenings, and that sort of
thing, for the man who is a transmitter, must be a machine, or
rare construction, he must be always on his post, and he must
never lie, or make the inner soul afraid of him, neither must he
be able to turn about, with exultation, and drive his head above
the spinal column; for it is here, that you injure the work, of
passing between heaven and hell; there is the trouble, you make
a man think too much of himself, and he will burst all boundary
lines, and his law, is right, whether it is or not, so you see that
imagination has to be dealt with next, and it is this, that I must
deal with, as I find it, and then show you how you get it; this is it;
it is the very impersonation, of the evil, for it is the false prophet,
that goes with your band, he does it to enlarge the vertebræ,
it is his place, to expand the vein, that crosses between the ear,
and the eye, and should he be a great boaster, he is sure to carry
the vertebræ, high up, should he be a great talker, he rises up the
lower vertebræ, and escapes by the axis of his own ingenuity;
now you have a perfect understanding, as to imagination, it is
quite easy for you to see the cause, of imagination, it is a fool's
paradise, and there is the little fool, who did it, now then you
can get one spirit and leave him there, by constantly making it
known, that you are happy under his guidance, and while he is
delivering some splitting hair scene, I am not there, for it is his
business, to divert the attention of my work off the mind of the
man we all appreciate, or he would be dumb in a short while, for
the sounds I put in its head, remain there, till this imaginary
mind is acted upon, and then the mind takes a spell, for it is
soon away in dream-land, nursed by the thoughts, of some
fairy tale, or that which does not have any resources to fathom,
now you see I am giving you a great big story, but I have
brought you to this, it is the way to attract attention,
by flinging in a sense of knowing, and to know you must learn,
therefore we have to teach, after we have been taught, and in
consequence, when your mind is acted upon, it is in a candescent

state, that means that it is in a jelly form, or in other words, it is sensitive to touch, and when I touch it hard, it makes you begin to tremble, then you alarm me, because I have been too strong, and made you jump; now how is this, well it is this, the spider has a great big round wet web, and he feels his body, is in the warm side of that web, because he caught the mind first, and it is, through his own feelings, he is struck by the intense desire to shield himself, and he spins a web, that has a network all around him, and he sleeps on the weather side of it; and after sleeping on the weather side of the net, for a few times, it attacks him, in the way, that a net generally does, it has roped him in, for the fact is as easy, to be seen as can be, the mind has got inside of that net, it was woven, by the silk-worm, and then it became a spider-web, the spider, is brought over, by his adhesion to the silk-worm, and he makes the web, for his own protection, and his mind is made, for the silk-worm is his godfather; and he knows it for the silk-worm came out of that piece of punk, in the cottonfir tree; and it was this cottonfir tree, that bursted out, by affliction of nature, and has made a wart, or more generally called the punk on the bark, well it is beneath this punk or wart, that the glow-worm resides, and he is all the time moving in the glooming, till some evening, it is very close, and sultry, and the moon is on the wane, she drops, in this tree, as she is passing, a little bit of colored gas, and in this gas is an essence, that smells, a sickly kind of smell, like the bark of cotton trees, and this gas, is the scent off the bark, once it has passed through the Sun, and come in contact, with many other odors, now we have the right ingredient to propagate silk-worms, for they live on essence, for a long time first, and then they go into a decline, and their eggs are remaining unhatched, and uncared for, till an east wind blows, then the little worms are bound round and round in the odor, that has fallen from the Moon, and it makes a kind of smell, that decays all, that is around, and then the little shells decay, and in the summer, with the heat, the worm begins to move, and he thrives on all he can catch, and he makes this home grow anew, for he is all the while engaged by his parents, who had sown the first seed, in their time, now you see that the silk-worm, is the builder of our minds, and we have to begin at the bottom end of the ladder, and rise it one foot at a time, here then is the elephant, what time do you suppose it took to grow him, when the silk-worm, is made one season, and dies off the next, why according to my estimation, it must be about a century, before I get my first beginning made, and you are told, that it only took six days, to rip up the entire business; now don't you see that I make a gas-jet, cost me a hundred years, and this is all I can do to make it in that time, now you know that the God of David, was a great God, and he made his name secure, but you forget, that his chosen people, are worthless, without him, they don't proceed, at all, and they are hunted from one end of the earth to the other, they are simply the one that slew our Saviour, and it is here, that the curse falls, it is the essence of that crime, that stands at their back to-day, and they are properly afflicted, they gave the only true God we ever knew to be tortured to death, and he is there, as a landmark of their barbarism: Now then allow us to find this little worm again, and I can show you where the sting of death appears at first, it is this then, the little glow-worm, is the one who propagates the silk-worm, and he does it, through his glow, in the evening, but when the scent of Cain falls; he dies, for he is killed by essence of poison, and that is magnetism, coming out of the Moon, it falls, on the little glow-worm, and kills it; then the little stink is propelled on by the life, that he flung away, and he rears up his little head, in life, for he died by the hand of his own skilled workman, and did not disappear forever, he grows, again beneath that wart, in the guise of a spider; and is propelled onward by the gift of gain, he was dead once, but retained his life, by his own artery coming in candescent state, through its being bled into the tree; and that tree promulgated a knot, or in other words, it is the death of the one, to bring sustenance to the other, and you die, to live again, because you can not help it; that is all there is to the whole affair, and I don't want any glooming spirit near me, for it is this sting, that I hate and despise, it is through the summer Sunset, she is all radiance, till she disappears behind the bank of clouds, then she casts back a kind of wearied reflection, it is the time she is bathing her face, in the ocean, and it starts the whole of heaven to glow, for while she is in the sea, the sky is filled with steam, and her mouth is choked up, with dirts from thwart the ocean, and she is setting back her hair, it comes upon her, before she is aware of the fact, and in her dying anguish, she yells, with fury, and is what you might call the sting of death, in her entirety; now you see what produces that yawning gulf to throw back her head in anguish, and appear in agonized distress; for such is in reality what is taking place, the sky is all made to suffer, and expand, when she goes down, for her bath, this is all there is to it, it is natural, that she should plunge into the sea, for a brief moment, and ascend to take breath, for she has to go down to that ocean, to rise again, without injury, and as she rises, she expands, and so does all the world besides, she is our government, our protector, and our all; then why shouldn't she have a dip, in the death of each day as it passes by: My friends, it is here seen, that the rising and the setting of this Sun, is the all that there is, to be mystified about, she rises, with a bleared and agonized eye, and she sets, with a gloom upon all nature, that says precisely, what it means, my work has been executed in grand style, I must dip my face, in the briny tub, and clean it off, before another journey meets my way; now fruit is the essence of time, and when you look into this great future, is it not natural, that your face has become very dirty, and that your bath, is all a blessing, instead of a detriment, I say that my own body now is all I could have desired, with an additional burial, that is peace in eternity, I would like to dive down below the waves, and never look upon the stormy battlefield again, for it is constantly in my mind, I can't help it; something, is at the back of me, that tells me we must conquer, and that is the whole business, it is conquest, which makes me drive the earth round my little finger: And that is the way it was at the beginning, the Moon caught foul of the sky, and it brought out the eye, it is this, that causes, the combustion of matter; it is the way we live that produces the atmospheric currents, the Sun draws, and she bellows forth, for more food, and she is always crying out give

me more food, and meat to eat, and this is it; the sky, is the
great live world, and the earth and sea are mere peel-apples compared to the skies, and what in them is: for the sky is the universe, and the waters under the skies, are mere bead drops, in
comparison to what is going on up above; now you understand,
that I mean the earth, as well as the waters, beneath the earth;
now I have made this little expression of lightness; in regard to
the waters, beneath the earth, it is this then that I mean; the
waters below the earth, are the waters; that encircle the earth,
that is what my meaning is; the waters beneath the earth, are
the waters, that are wound round the earth, and not the earth, as
it is understood by man, the earth is shaped by the waters, and
they are a circle, in circumference, to this point, that they are
round, to this point only, the Sun moves round, in a disk, and she
gathers in all she needs, and then she casts all the balance
away from her; well at the beginning, it is all water; except the
wind, and these are the two factotums, that began the world, so
you seem to see that I have began my book wrong, for this is
the way of it, you people are all right, till you begin to try
experiments, then you are all wrong, for the fact is quite clear,
you always go behind, and try to gather in the lost thread, and
you forget, that the thread you want is this thread, that is made
to-day, and every day, and as long as you keep on the old path,
you are sure to be left behind as the wind has been, it is
right here, the wind is the first factotum, for it blew itself
in two, and remained a machine ever after, and it is in
this machine, that you have got to study, and not the beginning, well what made this machine to move, it is the central
organ, that makes it move, and not the external orifice, as you
people seem to look upon that external Sun, as a dish; and so it
is in one sense, it dishes all the dishes, there are upon the earth,
well how did it begin to dish them, it wasn't able to dish them at
first, for there were none to dish; well now that is a pretty fine
state of affairs isn't it; well the Sun fed on life, from the beginning, she was a great big buffoon it is true, yet she lived on food
all the same, well how could she; well it is this, she drained all
the waters, of the meat there was in them, she sucked, till there was

very little water left, and that began to foment, and when it
foments, the grass begins to grow, for it is green, and produces a
green herbage, on the top, that floats to the edges, and takes
root, to any kind of matter; that has accumulated on the
bank, well this bank comes of the interior of the water, the
water is full of soluvium of potassium, and these two are the
ingredients, that go toward making the bank, thus it is seen at
a glance, that the world, is round, at one point, and at the other
she is oblong, for she must sink down at one end first, and then
she droops at the other, and in thus drooping she is all on one
side, with her head turning toward the Sun; and she bears her
head erect, to the sky always, for she is in the sky, and outside of
it; and not in the middle, for she is down at one end, and not up
at the other; thus you see that it is no use my telling you, that
the world is round, when she couldn't be, for the plain fact,
that she is oblong, and that is why, because, she is in keeping,
with the rest of nature, and instead of being perfectly solid in
the center, she is a little hollow, for the fact is plain, she
could not be quite hollow, or she would shake to pieces;
now you see that a drum is hollow, but it has a handle, to turn it
round with, but you could not have any handle on the world,
for it would wear away, but this great world does not wear away,
for the fact is clear, it can't; why, because it is fed, on itself, and
second it does not revolve on its own axis; it goes round by
combustion of atmosphere, which is gas, encentered, in its own
abdomen; this is the secret, and as your stomach, is moving
round, it moves, precisely the same way, and in propagation, it
is according to its own maker, for the wind is just on the same
principle, and it has gas, in its composition, and turns over and
over, till it becomes one steady whirl, and then it gets furious,
and sends spouts, in all directions: The most noticeable, are in
the colony, of the Argentine Republic, they keep on formulating
their governments, till they will strike up a Sun of their own,
and be off to heaven in a four-soft-tile, or what you might call an
Indian quarter-deck, it is a hat, that makes the most of people
stare, that come from the Antipodes, and my friends have daubed
it a Quarter-Deck, because you might make Panama on a
26

pinch in one of these hats; well you see the Turban of Asia, is
quite notorious for his hat, and it is quite a mark in its way, well
you could not expect God to do his work right, when he had
those thick heads to penetrate, and in getting his sounding
trumpet to operate, on such thick skulls, he must be a better man
than me, for I never could reach those Asiatics at all, they stunk
me out of countenance, and drove me away, with their whirl-
winds, I could not steady, any of them to a fit state of communication, they drove me out of Quebec, with lightning and storm
water, and I reached the Atlantic by a forlorn hope, it gave me
more concern, than anything else, for it has taught me a lesson,
the "little trumpet," won't work, it has to be blown out of the
fellow's head, that he knows anything, then you have got a beginning, otherwise it is all no use, he must be a know-nothing, to
get this plan of ours to work, and they don't care about admit-
ting in New Zealand, that the Seer knows nothing, since he did
all the cleverest thieves, they had there, before he kicked them
in the wind-bag, and brought away his own money; I just want
to show you, that in New Zealand, that the law courts are fixed
by judges, who are practically thieves, who rig up their own
lawyers, for judges, and make them obey the mandates of these
lawyers forever after, that is the colony, is libeled in this book,
to make them fight, they have stolen the honor of your humble
servant; and they will be branded as thieves as long as the
world hangs her head above us; they stole my rights, for gain,
that they were not entitled to; and they are the hypocrites, who
call their court an honorable tribunal, they are clan bandits, and
are pure brigands, now they have to fight, or stand the shame I
have placed upon them: I mean to do them up too; or you
would not find such an outrageous threat in a work that has no
equal: I want to make it quite clear, the accounts of the Arabic
tongue being spoilt in the translation of the work of God, is not
quite true, the Arabs are a hard-headed people, and it is quite
impossible to make a faithful impression on them, they are the
backbone of a whale, in its entirety, they are afraid of being
caught at lying, for they have been driven ashore by a foul wind,
and are the essence of craftiness, and are the impersonation, of

all that is evil, they are men as treacherous, as the adder, who
flings his side jump, into its opponents, before the other dreams
of an attack, and this is what is called the stythe of a melo-
drama, it is the essence, that is unseen, that is going to hurt
most, and I want to illustrate this, in a tangible form, it is this,
then that I am swinging about for; the adder, is a serpent, that
grows outside of anything else, it is a worm at first, and it grows
quite repeatedly, on the after candaescence, of the grouper, or
death-sting, it is the worm, that I have had reference to before,
it is this, the grouper or death-sting, is the serpent, in its first
stages; and it comes to maturity, for the specific purpose, of a
charm, it is the handsomest creature on earth, and can only be
found on the plains of Arabia, it is the creature, that is called in
scripture as the atteel; or Asp, and this is what I must refer you
to, when I say that the Argentine Republic, must get a Sun of
their own, it is this then, that I refer to: Your ancestors, were
very fond of making game of the learned people who said noble
things, and spoke, as though they meant to annihilate all people,
well it was generally understood, that you only had to get an
Asp, and play with it, till it bit you, then you could be wise; for
its beauty exceeds all of the reptiles, that I have ever seen; well
it amounts to this, the Sun does shine stronger on the Argen-
tines, than it does upon the North Americans, and they have
many suns, in publication, on the North American continent;
but yet, they don't come up to the Sun of the Argentine Republic, in this one instance, and that is this, that they always keep
old Tom Paine's Declaration of Independence; and that is what
I would like to see fly across the whole universe, I wrote that
for the United States, and I will stand by it, and when it falls I'll
do the rest; that is where I have found the union between my own
soul, and this man's, the Seer, he is as subtle as an Asp, and he
can drive me through anything, and you can't find his equal, in
the United States, or any other known part of the world, and I
won't take back anything I have said through him, without a
desperate encounter, for I know where to pitch my voice, so as
he can hear me speak, and when I have spoken it is as good as
begun, for he is not afraid of me, and though I stood out, and

put my arms round him, he would not flinch, or do anything, except make me welcome, and when you get a human being, in the body on earth, who can stand the cold trembles of a spirit, in the dark, and alone, on the face of the earth, not a creature, who cares one straw about him near, you know that you have an instrument, that is capable, of uniting heaven and hell; and your fears, will be annulled by this fearless man, who does not seem to realize, that a spirit, is not a nice thing to deal with in the dark, his first experience, was a severe test, and it was this, he knew nothing of spiritualism, at all eighteen months ago, and he was ashamed to own, that he did believe that a spirit could materialize, and after some tests, he consented to pay for the seance, and in consequence, it is about this seance, that I mean to relate, it was at the medium's house in the East of New York, that there was a medium, that gave private seances, well it was here that we got hold of him, and after a number of forms had materialized, I thought, that he stood it tolerably well, for a green one, it does make mortals tremble quite a " much," when they are surrounded with these spirit forms, and he did not shake quite like the rest of beginners; so I thought well he is quite a specimen, so I kept my eye on him from that time; In the winter, we agreed to try materialization on the way home, and we settled this way he was to stop outside of the cabinet, and I was to help with the medium inside, and give instructions, well the first form, that came, was a man, that is known as the Sissler, he does nothing but hisses at you, and has no other way of making himself known, so this being the outset, of all our trouble, I thought it would be a case with the whole thing, when the Sissler appeared, but not so my friends, the instrument you have to-day before you, just did not turn tail and run, as was thought he would, but just returned the compliment, and made the Sissler turn back, and when he went out the second time it was who could hiss the hardest, and in consequence, the Sissler has never been near our band since; well this is to show you, that I have got a kindred spirit, for myself, and I can make him do anything, I want him to do, but not through harshness, it has to be by reason alone, therefore it is here that you have the man, who can build a ladder, that can

reach heaven, because he is reasonable, and will not go only
when he knows, that it is going to be a success; therefore, the
way to make a bridge, is by doing it thoroughly at the beginning, and making a step forward, and then investigate, before
you proceed, well it is done, through the light of knowing,
before you proceed; well this instrument, won't move, till I have
shown him the way, and he goes with me, and sees for himself,
and he then takes the initiative steps, to get into action, well
you see that a spirit, that does not move away from the body, is
no use, it must go out, and investigate, or you can't make it see,
that there is a piece of bark off a tree, and where that bark, came
off, it had been torn loose, by the wind, and fell, from sheer
decay, well you look beneath that bark, and you find a worm,
and that worm, has a pair of legs, and it is moving toward the
end of the bark, well here is our first creeping thing, beneath
this bark, it has found its way, by the mode of its own body;
and why, because the worm came off the tree, and it fell, with
the bark, and it was not taken back, well the tree had been so
nutritious, that the worm, was a kind of lost, when it had no bark,
to suck, well it had this piece of bark, or log; then it lived only,
while it was eating of this dead bark, not so fast my friend,
it took root, with the body, for in rooting with the bark, it stole
the essence of the bark, and was afterward, a creeper, and a
worm no longer, and this is the Sissler, or the glow-worm, it
gives you a sound, it is not perceptible, to the human, but for all
that, it has a sound, and I call it the Sissler; and it sissles or
sings; you may not look at this in the proper light, for you are
dreadfully determined to have your own way, and I want you
to see it as I do, for it has two feet, and these two feet, are the
hen's feet, it grows the same, as the prongs of a tree, and has
the essence embodied in the trunk, as well, well you see, that
this worm, is a specimen, of a generative order, it is porous,
for it grew in the wood, and had a kind of left wing, for it was
of the silk-worm specie, and came from that ilk; therefore you
have found the missing link, to the web, that I made as a specimen your brain, and the wing, is the web, after it is finished
with; now you have caught the theory, on which I work, and

can plainly see, that I have wound my web around you; for the fact is as clear as day, the silk-worm, is the first to make a web; but the spider, is the one, who manipulates it, and he takes it for his own, and makes a coat out of it, he takes the cob, and does as he pleases, with it, for it is his; his grand-mothers, were the inheritors, and the grandsire, did bequeath it to the grandson, by right of lineage of descendant, and it was the privilege, of the grandson, to use it, for the grandsire, was there, giving orders, by the means of his invisible impression, and he can use the air, for finding his mind, and he does use his grandson, to do, what he sees, is right; now you have the whole theory, and it is all easy enough to understand, only you must begin by saying, as I did, so will I do hereafter, for that is according to the beginning, it begins, and you make this according, to the first you have seen, and so you are propelled along, accordingly; now don't you see; that I have made your mind, for in that making, I missed only one thing, and that is this, I forgot to give you the machinery, that guides the mind, and it is this, the Sun is a warm combustible, and she generates gas, and she makes her atmosphere, without any superfluity, it is exact, it is not one moment, one thing, and the next something else; well she has dissolved the solution, to all mysteries; she has made gas to generate, and she is the hydrogen, in contact and person; her lungs, are the great bellows, that blow and fan the flames, and she is eternally great, because she is the power-ful condenser, that gives life immortal, it is her, which creates the sound, that has caused so much trouble, and difficulty, it is her own congealed atmosphere, that produces this sounding trumpet, that you find in almost everything; now don't you see, that a mind is the generated sound, and not the adhesion of matter at all: You are all wrong to pieces, when you take a piece of material brain, and look at it, and say here is the machinery, that caused his death, I tell you, it is the sound, that kills, for the sound, has to be in order, or it won't propagate the accents right, and the sound is destroyed by the uncomplete-ness, of its own calling, and let those who surround their friends, that they do be careful of their sound, and not allow it to pass

from them, should any material ailment have been in their own
bodies, before they passed out; or it will wind itself round this
sound, and make a mark on the living body, that can not be
removed at all, for it is the sting of poison, that tastes the vital-
ity string of life, it is the coarse sting of satan, it is the vibration of hell, for in hell there are but two sex, the neuter, and
the gender, and the neuter, is commonplace, and the gender is
superlative; thus it is shown at a glance, that the Sun is the superlative, and the Moon is the neuter, for it is only a secondary
instrument of throwing waste away, and is not a particular
motive-power at all; now we have the right definition, and it is
this, the Sun is the passion, that governs the entire universe,
she makes the whole rebound, with the vibration of her own
sound, and when these live lungs, are filled with essence, that is
her life, and they must call as she does throw her essence,
because she is fighting for her life, as you fight for yours, and
she bellows out more potatoes, more corn, more sweat; sweat
from off every man's brow, the one is for my beauty, and the
other is for my life, and the third is to make my belly go; that
is the true solution of immortality; it is the life, that kills, so
you be warned by the "Infidel"; and don't take too much life,
for the Sun has to have more corn every day, and when you
drink beer, she is at you stronger, than she will get at he who
takes no froth, and is full of soul-light; for the one contains oil and
gas, whilst the other, is full of light, and must be rejected by the
Sun, as she only wants, and won't accept of that which she makes
in abundance; for that is her waste-pipe, the light, is what she
wastes, it is the fire, that is within her soul, that lets her angry froth
out, and the light we see by, is her froth, it blazes, till it amounts
to an essence, that brings down the good God of light, and it
shines in upon us, and sets us on fire, with an ulterior motive,
it intends to gather in all, but in its angry moments, it escapes,
and the froth, is wasted, as the beer you have gulped down your
gullet, and thought you had it, but not so my man, you only
gave it back, to your own maker, and he has it for the honest
intention of making many more such as you, I don't care about
you drinking beer, I like it myself, but it is no use, to me now,

for you have got it, and I did not have it when it was good, but
now they make the beer in such dirty-looking tubs, I think I
could not take a glass, for fear of getting my eyes into somebody's pie, it would make me so very thirsty, that I might
fling a sigh, and hit you in the other eye, and come out of
the poker, that is it my friends I am now growing so very slick,
that I don't think beer would keep me down, I believe it
would make me spring a mine, on the next electioneering
campaign, and I should want to blow the right man
into that chair, and it would have to be a good one, or he
should not fill the chair, I could dissect him, in such
a way, that would make both Judge, and Puck, comb their hair,
and try to find something in its composition; I see their work,
and think they are very funny, only they have got the frog's
feet, the wrong way up, and pin their holes too much like an
ant, they fix them in, like a great big toad, and methought I
saw an adder, but it had no feet of any sort, when it propelled
together, and made a mark upon the sand, it was quite grimy
sand, in comparison to an adder; for you don't see my sting, I
have buried it beneath the other; for I can't fling a dart, that
can stick my man, beneath his shoulder blade, and get at his
waist above his trousers; and that is the way, to cover it up so
clever, that even Abraham could not find it, till he reached the
fire, and then he saw a kid come up, and place his fingers on
the nip, it was so very fine, that no one was there, and it had
no sticks, to burn it up with, for on the top, it was so slick
and smooth, that not even Isaac could see the grip satchel, that
carried all those hidden treasures; and when the Lord got
Abraham and Isaac there, he had a kid, come in before Abraham's eyes, and it was a kid, of no such stuff as any but the
ancient heathens could have made a pie off; but it stuck, and
that is all the glue he had, a Yankee notion, that is all, it took
the people two thousand years or thereabouts, to fathom a
Yankee notion, that is all: I don't want to behave badly toward
father Abraham, he lost his scarf-pin, and I found it climbing
up that mountain, and you can place one to Thomas Paine, when
you find his; I was rather afraid of those Americans, when I

came from England, and they had such a reputation, "don't you know;" but I've been thinking, that they are almost too smart for grease lightning, yet I don't you know; somehow or the other I like them, they don't do anything crooked, it is straight out shrewdness, they are the shrewdest set of men on earth that is all, while the English, are stubborn, and crafty, they are slow and roguish, they make a plan, by links, and cut off the tar-barrel before it is ready to fire, they are deliberate, in all their dealings, they place their whole trust on Englishmen, and never know anything, till an American teaches them, then they, are afraid of it, till it has been tried for half a century; It is all the go, with them, as soon as a German has got it fixed up, and made some improvement, that propels it around, at a slower rate of speed, and the Dutchman has proved it to be safe, then the Englishmen can help themselves to it, because they know, that the old Dutchman won't kick, when it is only an Englishman that took his patent; because he says mine got vat you tink, da Anlish have tooken my vine piatent, an I vos got from de Yankee dooddles, da tinks I vas make im I solds im as von ferry vine Germans; dem blessed old varmers didn't tink I vould do it; now my friends you see that I can keep at home, what that old Dutchman couldn't sell, till he had made it go slower, the German is ahead of the Englishman, but he has to go behind all Americans, for this reason, an American is straight out an honest man, for he only copies our Patriarch, the honest Abraham; the first man, who ever understood, the difference between cheating and thieving; it was Abraham, who did know his God, and you know that an American does too; he knows that Abraham, was the son of Ishmael, and that he was of the tribe who did nothing else but pilfer the minds of those who could tell them of the other world; and the Americans are just too smart for any Israelite that ever broke the bread of life, and I say to-day, that there never has been any difference in my sentiments toward this people, they are thoroughly honest, as the God, who led Abraham and Jacob, and they are quite as capable as any people, on the face of the globe, and why, because they investigate, science, till it has become their

nature, to get at the back of everybody, and they will do it
too; that is, they will try till they do succeed; now you have a
little opinion of My United States from "The Infidel"; and he
can make you go faster, than you ever dreamed it possible, his
soul; is made of nitro-glycerine, it is simply a soul that can
make matches fire themselves; that is all about it, and you
want the gold, I tell you honestly that you can have it in
abundance, only don't cheat me out of my rights; I can show
you how to get it, in sacks full, abundance is no word for it,
the right way to apply the term, is to give it to you in a shower
of manna, like the Israelites, had it, in the deserts of Arabia,
not simply to crown my success, in old mushrooms, I might turn
on the crank, and pour it down, just where you would like a bit,
at each man's back stairway, I don't think you would kill my
man, did I do this thing for you; or how would it work, should
I take you by the hand, and show you a country, where it is
wasting in tons, like the famous story of that great big fellow,
who had a balloon, that lived for five weeks on thin air, you all
know the story, I mean it is called the victory of the great balloon
ascension, or the tour round the Southern hemisphere; now I can
show you that this fable is the work of fiction, only that there is
a sequel to it, and that there is this place, that has this mountain
of gold, and it is the place I will give to the United States;
providing they won't prohibit my works being published; that is
all I have to offer, in return for my advice, and my thoughts, I
won't stop you looking for the gold, but you can have it sure,
do you give me the right to publish all my books; now it is
simply this, that you can not stop me, but I would like to feel
that I was not trespassing, and that I did not do as some might
say, he had his fling on earth, and he has no right to come back
here, and disturb the minds of men, with his theoretical views; I
want no favors, that I don't give an equal proportion in return, I
was once a living genius, and now I am at the head of my class;
and you may stop me, from talking to you, but you can not help
me more than to take no notice, and let my works go in for sale,
as common literature, give my medium the copyright, as is his
right, and you have conferred all the favors I shall ever ask you

for; now is it a fair recompense, or am I to write through him, and exclude my own name, you can not stop him writing in any part of the hemisphere we live in, then it is no use to say that it is him, when you know it is not fiction, but a solemn reality; therefore you can have my books, and the patent, I shall bring you, which will demonstrate the work perpetual motion, this is what I claim for my medium, and I shall call it Tom Paine, whatever you do to the contrary notwithstanding; all rights and privileges accepted; now you know it is only a question of whether I am allowed to go on, or whether it is this old fable, of too much brains, has danger in its gains; you can do as you have a mind to about testing the medium's qualities as an orator, he has not been taught it, and I don't want him to learn either; for he can't write and speak both, nobody can, but there is one of his guides, who is a desperate fellow to talk, and I should not wonder before long, that you will get a lecture, and should it come, in the form of clairvoyance, it will send the world crazy, for it is a speaker, of no mean order, that is applying for the position of taking him on to the platform, you will surely hear more in one brief hour, than you ever heard from mortal man's lips before, for I declare honestly that you can't stick me, at this work of practice makes perfect; but I must give up to the speaker I have mentioned, who has all the dash and fire, that is needed, to make an adder jump crooked; once he begins to talk, and he has been working on this same instrument, for a considerable time; now it is quite possible, to make this man talk well; but he wants a little more time, than we have given him, yet; for it is hard to do such work, in a minute, and you can't do all at once, this book is about a six months job, and it won't take so long over the next one, and the speed is getting on as a good racer, would come into training, with slow work at first, now it is a good swinging canter; when the two hands go at the machine, it will be a gallop; there is the idea, it means to make a worm, with four legs next, and you can give us this one more opportunity, of showing our ingenuity; the first worm, that I made, had no legs, at all; he had a ring around his neck, and that was pretty good, since he caught it through the fever, off the ground, that had ague in it; for it was produced, by the cold damp raw air, in connection with the effluvia off the sediment, that was adhering to the essence, which had been thrown from the Moon, in her daily tour round the world; now I have got this way of telling my stories; till I don't know whether you understand me right, and to put my style more demonstratively, I will make you so sure, that there can't be any more mistakes; this is the point, the men, who were engaged in propounding the scriptures; did not do it, in any way, other than through clairaudience, they heard the sound, by this form of bugle, or trumpet, and this trumpet is a little machine, that angels wear round their necks, to let each other know, when they are in the vicinity of their own contact, that is this, the angels have a method of seeking for the good shepherd, and they call each other by name through this little instrument, and they work it in accordance, to a given sense; that is it is, the sense of knowing how to manipulate this little bugle, that has the method of divining down, to a pitch of notes, that have no equal in this impressional construction of made voices; and they make the note appear, like a voice, and it sounds so loud, that it is often taken for a human being, in the body; that is it is the sound, that is manipulated, so as to strike the ear, in a funnel shape, for it has been delivered off the top of the head of a board, or door, that is the way to produce this sound, and you can find any amount of people, in this country, who have heard this sound, sometimes it comes as a message, but more frequently as mischief, for the spirit of those, who have climbed the hill seldom do much, except play, at one piece of mischief or the other, and that accounts practically for your troubles, for they are always at some mischief, or the other; now you know I am telling you truly of this sound, for you have heard it scores of times; and it is the little trumpet, that is used on a doorway principally; you have heard it distinctly say your own name, and you know that when an instrument can be made to speak one name, it can be taught, to say any amount of names; well this instrument, is the spirit power of manipulating sound, it is this, it takes a good while to make a man believe, that he is not alone after one of these signals, and he does not know it, till he has heard it many times; and knows how to learn to listen for it; well the idea of your friends coming back, and standing on the threshold, and telling you lots of things, why the greatest heathen you have got, would scout the idea as preposterous; he would at once say, well why does he come and stand in the doorway, when he knows I would be only too happy to make him welcome; well my heathen brother, you can't make four legs go where only two was intended, so you can't welcome a spirit, unless you learn to do this thing right; it is all I can do to make a sound, with this machine myself, and it is as easy, for my friend the Seer to hear his father call his mother, as it would be for him to sit down to dinner with the greatest heathen you have got, and make him a complete mountebank, in as many words; meaning, that the heathen might make a mountebank, but he never could hear these sounds, for he would not hold still, to do the requisite amount of practice; therefore he never will be capable as an instrument, for his ears, are too thin, they are thin, for they have got no soul, that is worth anything as a feeling constructive body, it is a substitute, that is all; it won't make any difference, it can get on first-rate, at poking in the flint, into a pickax, but it won't do for this special work, of telling you how to make four legs, when you only had but two before; and it is by piecing the clouds together, that you get rain, and by this mode of seaming; I am going to astonish the world, and make them happy in spite of themselves; for knowledge is with you, from the word go, and it helps you across every stile, only stop it from making you jump a ditch, that has no turning; that is don't allow your inclinations, to jump you off that imperial bend, for in that you have my advice, just go round the bend, it is all right, it is sure to have another road, at the turn, and you get round that bend as peacefully as possible, it must be a nice road, for it does not admit of any turning back, and the heathen, can't jump back into his friend's arms, and say halloo old fellow, I would make you the best man on earth, to-day, did you only listen to what I can show you; now then my friend is dumfounded, for he does not realize, that his shadow, is the friend he wants to welcome, and

why; because the shadow of your friend, is a duplicate of yourself, and you can't see this, and why; well it is so, as the heathen
would tell you; but why, is the query, well the shadow, of the
dead, is the shadow of the living, and the impression of the dead,
leads the living, and the dead, are those tormentors, who are
constantly at your side making you feel miserable when you
ought to be happy, and you are sad, when you should be merry,
and you are in agony, when you should be glad, and it is the
dead, who make all of those conditions, and why, for they are
wretched, in their own misery, and one miserable spirit brings
an army of miserable wretches with him, and they produce this
horrible feeling around you, and he is all the while plaguing you
to do something, when he knows it is for his own edification,
and not for your benefit, well why does he do this thing, for he
is like the worm, that he sprang from, he was a miserable wretch
himself in the body, and he is always a miserable wretch, from
that time, till the crack of doom, when that is, I don't know, and
you can reach it only by cracking the heavens in two, and I
don't believe any one can do this, unless I stood by and gave
the order, for it is about as ingeniously constructed, as I would
like it to be; and you know I am just too particular to hold
down a heathen, when I might lift him up: You think I might
go on forever, and never tell you why that shadow can't be
caught; well it is quite an artist, who can catch a shadow, and I
think you will admit, that I am he; when you see me tie you up,
in your own shadow; well it is quite a struggle I assure you, and
the way to get at it, is by standing off, and leaping on to it, that
is about the only way, you can ever catch a shadow; it has a
sequel though, and that is this, you jump, and I will keep it down
for you; that is about the style of the way, that the heathen
plays God, when he falls over the boundary line, his idea is to
keep you constantly in terror, for fear, you should grow too
wise, that is his style of acting good toward his friends on
earth, and I don't do this, and you see how much knowledge my
man is giving you, when he might rip and tear, and sew you up
in that shadow, just as he likes, for he is giving me my head,
and he is driving me onto that shadow, just the same as he used

to drive a horse at a stone wall, kill or cure is his motto, and it's
this fire, that gives wisdom, and wisdom is sense, till you know
how to guide your horse across a stone fence, but all the same
for that, you must rush the fence, or it won't reach the shadow
on the other side, and you see how he drives me about, till I am
forced back onto the shadow; well it is quite time I began to see
my way clearer; and get myself out of this tangle over the
shadow, the Moon is responsible to us, for our shadow, in this
way, she is what you might call the end of the Sun, and it is
this, that causes it, the shadow is the made counterpart, or duplicate of another; the one is begotten not made, and it is a
reflector, and casts round continually for the same as it has
made, and is in accordance, with its own maker, and does
beget itself according to a proper theory, and that is, the
theory, of a reflector, it strikes you, as a seaming reflector,
and it shows you, that it is the one great theory after all;
and that it is the one who propagated first come back to
life, and he is there standing as a monument of idleness;
and he does not move except you do, and he only moves,
when you do; this is it then his shadow, is your counterpart,
and you are in the case of another, because his reflector
is in your own eye, and your own likeness, is the one he
is trying to impersonate, therefore he is a duplicate of you,
and you are a duplicate of his shadow, for he is the one,
who was first made, and you come after; therefore it is his
mould, that you are laying in, and not your own mould at
all; this is horrible, because instead of you being free, you are
quite unable to get free, the shadow is always too quick for you,
and as long as you can't catch that shadow, you are never able
to quite mix up with a good guidance; for when you are guided
right, you know that it must be luck, that is what you call it;
well now when you are guided badly, you call that bad luck, well
it is neither one nor yet is it the other, at the time you have
good luck, there is a General sitting at the back of your eye, and
when you have bad luck, there is a cursed opponent, that is
sitting in the front of your eye; so that it is the one old tune,
more light, and you can have the luck sure, and a sure winner,

is a clever loser, he makes light of his losses, and makes up at
the beginning, so I must take you back with me to this fellow,
that only had one wing, it was a worm, and he had got off the tree,
without flying, well he did it, all right, and he came down the
tree creeping, and when he got down, he became so hungry, that
he eat the sweet young shoots off at the bottom of the tree, and
then he crept up the tree again, well my friends, I have made
you a worm, with two feet, and they had claws, like the hen,
because they drained the essence of that piece of bark, that was
on the ground by accident; well now his feet, were made from
essence, that came out of the bark, and it come to this point, the
feet, had no nails on, so I have to show you how they came to be
made, and the first thing I must do, is to take you on the seashore, and that is naturally the boundary line, and as the beginning is there, it is the place to ˊcommence: Therefore we are
quite right well able to see, that on that beach, there are any
number of shells; from the eggs, that were cast ashore, from
the spider eggs, that had gone down, with those spiders, that
inhabit the sea; now do you see, that this little fellow, with no
toe nails, is badly off, so he has to get his as nature provides;
and take a turn in the salt-water to do it, his eyes are open, and
he can see, by this time, for he has been precipitated back to the
land, and he is coarse, in his construction, and he takes life easy,
and rolls round, he does not mix with society, for he does not
seem to care, for society, his eyes don't open, and he keeps on
waking and sleeping, and he dozes off, at intervals, till at last he
feels something touch him, and it is the grouper, or cotton-
worm, who has also come down to the beach for feet; this is
what this pair do, they set to, and fight, and in their agony of
death, the one dies; and the other is afflicted, by the ague pains,
through this encounter, and in consequence, he is afflicted, by
another disease, till he can't see his mother, for the swelling
between his knees, it is the propensities, of evil, that has caught
hold of him, in course of his struggles with nature, he is at last,
in a breathing atmospheric candescence, through his condition of
his evil, and he is obliged to breathe, for he gets this cold, or
ague pains, which make him feel like a stuffed pig, he can't

move, his wind is stopped, and he is obliged to feel for life, for
his appetite, is almost vanished, his tongue is growing, and he
feels frightfully queer, his body is big, and he has got into a
vile state, and then this fever, has to be handled, and he is what
you call a broken emaciated body, yet he is swollen, and he can't
get rid of his swelling, but the fever does it; and once this
fever sets in, he is blown out to such an extent, that you know
he is a goner, as the priests say, when you don't believe in the
holy divine God of Ephraim, or some such God, well this little
grouper, is a great big grouper now, and he is swelling higher
and higher, till at last, his body begins to turn green and black,
and then it is all over with him he is a goner, and his little belly,
has to burst open, and let the juice escape, and then he dies
poor little fellow and has gone to rest, and his sick-headache is
no more heard of, well my fine scientists, you have got glasses, and
you can go and investigate, it is thus, that you can prove what I
am saying, and not out of your books, they are no use to me,
and I know you can't do anything with them; well the grouper
died, and after he died, a whole school of flies, with two wings,
and two feet, and a body, and a head, and feet undeveloped, and
nose, and mouth, are seen to spring out of that body, that had
suffered so much agony, from that fever; do you see my friends, that
I have given you this cue, and you can prove me quite right, should
you wish to deal liberally with the Old fellow, who has paid toll
on the other side, and brought back his passport; now I am going
on more rapidly, for you have got such a start, as no man ever
dreamed of getting, and I will give you five minutes, to come to
me, and say whether you are able to get ahead with these flies;
why it is easy, the flies lay eggs, and the spiders suck them, and
by doing this, it gets into their blood, and poisons the spiders,
for it is rank poison, that the grouper died of, and his poison
begets the flies, and they are poisoned, and they dry their eggs,
where the flies don't keep watch, and the spider goes to the flies'
eggs, and suck them, well he dies, and his death, is the fruits of
another pair of feet, that counts four; and he is so bad, from this
poison that he did not hold anything in his stomach, and it dyed
the stain of a great big hole, that has made the next one, that

27

came to life from his body, a bird, of miniature construction, but
it is a bird, and you call it a singer, it chirps, and it is to be found
round spider nests; and they trap the singer, and he is killed, and
then comes the grasshopper from his death, and after the grasshopper comes the linnet, and after this, it is a bird, of a different
feather, the eggs, commence to mix, and they get on friendly
terms with each other, and it is then according to selection, as
the bipeds say, I want a wife with a red head, and I want a husband, that has no beard, and I must look at beauty each, as the
little designs, so at last, it is a chip and a chat, and won't you
come to my house to have a cup of tea, till at last you have the
nightingale; and that is far enough in bird theory, I must be more
reserved in my admission, or some cockatoo, will be coming
along, and nipping my fin off, and I won't be able to swim any
more, this is it then; the idea of you being able to cut my fin off:
is quite enough for me to keep you on an angler's hook for a
couple of weeks, at least, and that is how I am going to do in
the future, I am going to angle between sublimity and grace, and
when you don't feel very happy, you can look into sublimity, and
when you feel sublime, you can take a cup of grace, that is, the
one is essence, and the other is the means of making each other
amalgamate, it is this amalgamation, that is for us the most
puzzling, it leaves no manner of doubt whatever; but you see it
is so fine and fussy, that you must doubt, or it would not get
into you at all, and this is what has taken place, the sea is full
of unknown species, and in consequence, you can not look at
them, and my task is a most difficult one as I admit, but you
know that a fish-bone once stuck in, is a hard thing to swallow,
and when it is in, it is much easier to swallow, than to take it
back again, so I am going to swallow a fish-bone, and I won't
pull it back, for it can't choke me, and I'll answer it will not get
the best of me either; there is the rub, in this little incident, the
fish-bone, is the same as your finger-joint bone, and it is this,
that scientist, may experiment with, it is whale oil, that is all,
that attaches these joints together; and you have found the
secret, a whale is helped by nature, and you are helped by the
Sun, and this is the way it is done, it is the nature of the whale

to dive and duck, and that is where your love comes from, there is the point right here, the Sun has given essence to the Moon, but she has done it in greediness; for she knew it would all come back, and that is the way you have begun, you gave all your affection to your wife, but you kept plenty back for your son, and that is it then your wife is a pleasant little body enough, but she loved you most, before she gave you any affection at all, and that was when she had an idea, that you might marry some other girl, and get her out of conscience by keeping two homes, when you ought to keep but the one, that is the time, that she thought you were all the world to her; don't you see, she was disturbed, and justly so too, for her agony had commenced, and she never cared a jot for you at any other time, she kept the rest of her love for her daughters; now my friends, there is a moral in this, you get these sentiments, from the whale, for as it plays, in earnest, or in lolling, it is always attached to its young, and no matter what the trouble is, you can't persuade a whale to leave its young, here is the difference, with the fowls of the air, they hide their young, and make believe, that you are after, a lame bird, it is their nature so to do, because they were born in a nest, and were hidden from view; well here, is cheating, it is easy to see where we get the cheating from, it is from the birds of the air, and not from any devil, that is in us, we were born cheats, and I can show it to you in a hundred and one ways, the birds, are cheats, of necessity; they cheat, for they were birds of poison at the beginning, and they keep the blood of subtlety in their blood forever, you fire a gun at game a few times, and it is then seen, whether they can't tell whether you have a gun or not, and though you keep it hidden behind your back, it is still to those birds as dangerous, as though it were loaded, and in front of you, why, because they are full of impression, and they see you stalking round a fence, and looking for hiding-ground, well you are no better than they are, you found out their tricks, by watching them, and their tricks come to them naturally that is all; now then which is the smartest, the duck or the drake, why the duck every time, she quacks, come on Mr. Drake, I have good game at home, that wants my inge-

nuity to hide, you can follow me, and I will lead you astray,
that is the way my friends, the duck plays coy, but the drake, is
altogether too slow, he keeps waiting about, till his wings get
burned, at her flipping past his eye, and at last out of sheer desperation he must go after her; this is the way my friends the
ladies do, and they have my sympathy, they can fool man, all
they have a mind to, I don't sympathize with him a bit, his rights
are few, but then he must not make such blunders, as to go after
a duck, when she is playing coy, get another, and let him do the
hide-and-seek business; and then the feathers fly to quite a different understanding; for she will not run in agony, it is his
turn, then to make the match, and not hers, and he can always
keep her good, by smiling on some other duck, it is all the way
you have got, my grandfather taught it to his aunt, and his
cousin did it too; they thought I was too young to notice, but it
is young soft ears, that pick up all the tricks, and arts in war,
they are ever on the dodge, to catch a pair of twinkling eyes go
out upon the run; I knew more, when I was in the nursery, than
many men at seventy, and I bet there are others, who can tell
you of little incidents, that happened when they were very young;
now I have to bring out these points, for there is no sentiment in
some souls, for they are descendants of the whale, only they
came off that hump, that whalers call the jelly, it is so much
pulp, it has nothing to it, except the brain, without any governor,
it is mere blubber inside; now you see that I have got no further
work to do, but knock sense into blubber, and that is what some
people are like, they have no phosphorescence, at the back of
their eye, it is some old fossilized old salt sea-wave sitting there,
that was propagated, before the year one, and he could not
find the sea and get back again, did he know how to find his
way home once he started; I don't approve, of people, who take
too many liberties, but I do like to see a smart dashing fellow
spring up, and take a turn at these old salt horses; for the horse
is slow, in comparison to man, in some things, he makes the eye
glisten, as he comes home from a race, and looks for his companions
first, he never thinks of his own corn, till he has made a sign of
knowing recognition to his friends, this is where man has this

trait of character too: It comes through his likeness to the whale, they both have it strongly marked upon them; and it is the friendly feeling for their friends; the horse is as devoted, to his friends as man, and they have a kindly feeling for each other; the horse, is just as much attached to man, as the man is to that animal; and it is reasonable too; the horse is from the back of the whale, and the man comes more from the hind end of the whale, and I shall be able to illustrate this more fully by a code of evidence, called the Greek begets Greek, or the soul of man can not wander from its companion; this is all I have to offer, in commendation of my arguments, except this, that wherever you see a man, with any extent of sound intellectual qualities, he is in principle a lover of that noble animal the horse, and he is easily interested in the turf, as they raced together on the waves, they race together on the earth, and as man feels his blood tingle, when he sees an animal of his abused, he feels it in his veins, that he could kill the scoundrel, that abused the horse, it is the likeness to himself, that he has seen abused, and he can't stand by, and see his old comrade go under his eye as a beast of burden, when he knows intuitively, that a horse is his own brother, he never knew why, but it is the same as the adder, that springs, it is the flesh, that creeps, and crawls toward its own; now my friends whenever you see a man chastising a horse unreasonably, you remember this, it is my motto, never to allow any man to take my hide off, and when you sit by and allow a horse to be abused, you are not worthy the name of man, and ought to be dealt with as that brute is dealing his folly on that dumb animal; now I have told you that man and horse is according to my theoretical illustration one and the same creature, with a variation, and that is this, the whale does lay eggs, but they don't hatch, for this reason, that the eggs are not laid in any part of the sand, they just lay them about promiscuously, and they are all over the ocean, and not in any particular place, well the consequence is that some of these eggs, are laid on gravel beds, and some of them are laid on the bottom of earthy clay or sand, according to whatever you choose to make it; thus it is seen, that my eggs, that are laid on the ground, or gravel, are the same eggs, that are laid on the sand; so that one lot of eggs come to be made in one locality, and another, in a distinctly different part, well the whale is fed we know on suction, and has no way of living than by the water she drinks, well she is natu-rally an amphibious creature, for this is the reason, she can't live in the ocean alone, she has to breathe, and go in again, well the whale is the fish of all others, that you should be most particular to watch, she is dead, only when she dies, by sheer exhausted circumstances, and not by age, because she is only on the sur-face just long enough to come into a safe way of getting caught with amouration, she does not dive down, to meet her affinity at all, it is on the top of the water, that she floats sluggishly along, and meets her affinity; thus you see that she is only engaged at her affectionate moods, when the Sun is at its extreme moments of heat, and she seldom misses a male when she is ready, that is the reason of her taking fire, in her oil well, this can be noticed, in the extreme South quite plainly, for it is in the North, that she is able to come to the point of preparing her advantages, for the development of her conditions; now it is easy to tack about on a ship and watch these vagaries of the whales, one has a note like a cow, and the other has a sound, like the bellow of a buffalo, or some have a kind of rustle, like a cow in distress; you see how I have pitched on again to sound, it is this, the man who invented this telephone of yours has been with me, in his travels, for over the greater part of my life, and he has got another machine, in this life, that can outwhip all the sounds you ever heard, it is just a complete waste of sound, for it goes Eaugh, or imitates the bray of an ass, well this sound, is taken from the bull whale, as he scents his affinity, and he does this to such perfection, that he could be heard for miles round, and you can scream as you will; but you will never get a better imitation of the donkey, and when it is handed down to man, you will see that I have spoken truthfully, and don't you forget this, the whale is quite as much amphibious, of its own calling, as ever any other creature, that comes in and out of the water, and remains, for some period, in one or the other; now you see; that I have got you attached to the whale, because he is the monarch of the deep, well man is monarch of the earth, and he is able to till the soil, and make her prolific, so does the whale till the ocean, and make it prolific, for the one is made to reap and mow, the other is made to scatter seed in abundance, and the whale does make the seaweed grow, and as he lies asleep on the waves, he is protracted, for he is just making in one way, a complete overturn of nature, his belly, is full of insects, and he is digesting them, and after they are digested, they are ready for sowing, and in sowing this waste, it is the beginning of the weeds, that afterward are called kelp, and seaweeds; which are the beginning of the earth; they are the roots of our mother earth, and it is this great fish, that made the earth, and he is the founder of all nationalities; now you see where Jonah fell, that I am standing on top, and I mean to be there, when all is over too; you may think I am a braggart, but you know quite well that did you contain half my learning, you would want a tail, on the end of your coat to wag at people, and say I am the great "I am"; so you need not be jealous of any little piece of bravado, that I put in my book, it is the tale, that drops off, that has to be counted, and not the whale of a yarn; for my tale is all so well pitched, that it is absolutely water-tight, and your stories about the missing link, won't bear the inspection of a school-boy, he could dirk you every time, did I just give him a few points; now you are all at sea, about the monkey, being the bread and butter, that plastered man together, he is not in the race at all, the man and the monkey are two different species entirely, the one is a Moon strike, and the other is a strike off the Sun; and I will show you how it is done, the Moon is at her full, and she travels round quite close to the Sun, for when she is full, it is of a magnitude quite alarming, and your little pea-nuts, would be stretched to a gigantic size, did you see the Moon, just before he is fired, by his affinity; for that is what it all amounts to; now the Moon is at its full, and the Sun is waning, well the Sun strikes a shadow, and the Moon is on top, and it gives this shadow a quintessent stare, or contact, that pro-pels it forward, this movement is perceptible to your eyesight, and you can prove what I say, in the lakes you have quite near your own homes; well this monkey, is the effect of this abrasion, or scrape of this shadow, and not as a specie of man at all; it follows out this theory throughout, and when you find an inferior, it is due to this abrasion, or contact, when the Sun is waning, and it proves to be an inferior, for the Sun, is kept in her normal condition too long, and she should have struck her shadow off, by the time that she was at full, and not when she was waning, that is the solution of man and monkey, it is the one being blown, in the heat of passion, and the other being blown, when the tide had turned, now my friends you can see how perfect I have grown, in this absence of time, I have found more specimens, than any man who ever lived, and you do very wrong indeed, should you tell me to go and mind my own business; as you did when I battled on earth, for a brief period, you are not afraid of a shadow, and that is more, than you are ever likely to see of me, and when I tell you things, that are a benefit to you, you surely don't say I don't want them; but when I tell you something, that is perfectly true, you should not be depressed, and say I wish he did not do those things; it is all a matter of justice, and when justice reigns, you can't have your own way, I don't want my father who art in heaven, to be able to say of me, that I am afraid, I don't want him to tell me I am unworthy, I don't want him to say that I am not capable; rather he should say, his son was the greatest man who ever lived, that is what I want my father to say, and when he does so truthfully, I know that I have done my duty, now my friends you have the sentiments of your most devoted slave; I have that in me, that will never be satisfied, with less than I have spoken, and you want me to lay down and die, and be nothing, I can't do it; should you force me to cease in my own title, I will work in another's name, and you will still have Paine, and it is well known, on my side of life, that you hardly pass a thing on this earth, that I don't join in; and it is the same as in the old days, the man who has the quickest eye, is the one who meets the maiden flush, and as I have made you all flush, as I struck Mr. Man off the Sun and Moon on their meridian, I have a right to be able to tell you my history, and you may stop my life being published, as "The

Infidel," or as Thomas Paine, but you can't stop it as some one else; and it is this, that will startle you all the most, I will in fiction write my autobiography, and put it in the name of some of my friends; they won't object, to be the wonder of the earth skies and seas combined; now you see how I am going to do my work, and the less notice you take of me the better, as then I can come to you with open arms, and help you with a cherry hand; and show how to cure every evil you have, from the tic-douloureux to the flames of inferno; this is all the two evils, that I think are worth enumerating, because I see by your papers, that the medicine men have a remedy for almost all else; they could not stand a moment, did I open up a shop, and say here you are my friends, come and be cured, and I can do it, without them even telling me what is the matter; you don't believe in magic, neither do I but I do believe in finding everything I want from the soul's champion; and that is where you can't trick magic, and I can lay him out, in such style, as he is my friend always; now do you know what magic is; your trickster is no earthly good, in my hands, he is a mere tomahawk for me to chop him up with; or in more refined language, I unbare his secret, by being foolish, and being wise simultaneously; that is the manner in which I get at these fellows, who are tricksters; you have a great man, or two, well they are very smart, you give me the opportunity, and will I unbare their most intricate tricks; you give me my own instrument a private box, and pen paper and ink, and he can write down all the methods, that are used, for deceiving the public, now this is not for foolishness; it is just to show you that I can make every trick, that is perpetrated as wonderful, a mere exhibition; to demonstrate, that I am no fraud, but the reality; combined to a reality; that is all I want to prove nothing else, you may take any clever trickster, who says he is willing I should take the sail in taut; it is not the way, but it is the means I adopt; while the trick is being played, I sit above the trickster, and he has no chance of seeing my guide, because his are actively engaged in their arts, of putting him through his facings; that is the way it is done, only I have complete communication with my instrument, by telephonic communication, in the guise of messengers; they take what I have written out, to the transmitter, and he delivers the message to the instrument, who guides his hand by the gift of clairvoyance, or a new method, that I have discovered, which you can not expect me to divulge, to any one, it is a patent, of reaching mortals, and does not come through the office for registering patents; now my friends when you think I am a fraud, you try how these signs will work, and not give away the greatest gifted genius, that you ever were possessed of, I don't want your money, except as for experimenting with; and surely my ideas, are worth all the few pence, it costs to buy them; and I can recoup you an hundredfold: Now I have done quite enough bragging, and that sort of thing, to let you know that I am right on the job, and can make the world better in every way, than it ever has been; and I don't understand why any sane creature, should object to take all the good gifts, that have been given to him; now as to this question of going into religion, I don't want to have any more than I can possibly help to do with it, you shall know all, only wait a little while longer, and don't go on in the dark, there is a religion, that could do much good for humanity in general, but it should be tested first, and not made the dissenting organ of strife, it should be held sacred, according to evidence, of specific character, and when a person does not know, they ought to proceed with care and caution, for in religion there is danger, and I do not like to have my name again mixed up with it; it can be dealt with, when the world is unanimous, but it would never do for me to usurp any cause, I said I would show you the better way, but I don't want to do this thing, till the world has been taught to see the opening, and when the opening is made, it would then be time plenty to show the world, that a way had been found, that would make every soul happy; now I will say no more on this question, and let it pass from your minds, for the Sun never sets, that does not bring your minds nearer to intellectual wisdom, the question, is, does wisdom bring good, that is it, I distinctly say that wisdom is the evil genius, and not what it should be at all; it is sense, that is the God we should adore, and not wisdom; now you understand, that I draw a marked distinction between these two Latin definitions; the one is derived from senitoram, and the other from the word senitora; these two words are very near akin, but they have two distinct meanings, the one is a bad word, the other is a good one, for in it lays all the self interests of life, you have sense, you have got enough, you have wisdom, you have just what you did have, before you were re-born, and that is it, a man who is born twice, has sense, but whilst he is in the body, he has wisdom, and that is why he fails to see the difference; I don't begin to teach, for I don't want to be taught, that is what we mortals have, and why; for they did nothing, till they were born, and they have done nothing since, that is how wisdom comes, it is a thing, that is not what it ought to be, it is a sound, that has nothing in it, but the meat, it does not sound right, for it is begotten of nature, and it is unnaturally sounding, for it has the life incased the meat, whereas its own maker, is not incased in meat at all, that is one reason, for calling it unnatural, but this is all quite right, for it has to grow in the meat at first, or it could not be; and therefore it is according to the natural laws of nature, because you know that the wind is filled with water, and the two propagate life, and that life is carried into the Sun, at the beginning, and always after, and the two produce putrefaction, which has the essence of life in it; thus, we have life eternally, the one begets the other, the essence, is as essential, as the Sun, the one is waste, from the other, and of this we all came, it is so, and that is all there is to it; that is what we have been taught to believe forever, it is so; and that is all there is to it; now that you know is the most utter rot, that ever was uttered, it can't be, there must be a foundation, or the whole would fall to pieces; and although you do take two thousand years to gain a thing, it is merely a pin's point in comparison to what it is, in the end, where is the end, that is what I would like to know, can any of you define the end, I would give the rest of my life, did I but find that end, it is the sound of eternity, and there is no end, because your own end, is with us, and you can't have any end, because there is nothing to sound it with, it is quite beyond me, I can't fathom it, it quite makes me feel miserable, because I can't tell you what the end is, and I never shall be able to master this, there is no end to sound, it is here there and

everywhere, it is a myth, and that is the mystery of my life, I
can do all but this, and I can not trace this sound, it is an
ungovernable power, that has never found its own affinity, and it
breeds the last time in the human body, and that is when it
adheres to, or column, of the spine commonly called the quick,
it is in this, that you have the starting point, and you are
forever growing, once this adhesion, is made, you keep on growing, always, and yet, you are able to close up again, till you are
not larger, than the point of the finest needle, that was ever
made, it amounts to nothing, yet you can expand to whatever
size you have had time to grow to; now this is a most extraordinary affair, and it is this, that I claim your attention, for a brief
space, the Sun is a shining orb, and her reflector is imperceptible, well what has it done, it has struck a reflector, that is all,
you and I, and all of us, are reflectors, and we are the quintessence of nonsense, that is all, we are nothing, in this factotum's
idea at all; she has reflected upon us, and we took root and grew,
and after we die, we are of no value to her whatsomever; that is it,
in its entirety, whilst we live in the body, our lives are valuable
to our maker, but after we are dead, the Sun has no power upon
us at all, neither does heat or cold affect the spirit, it is the soul,
that frets, for the wasted hours upon earth, when it might have
grown so much better, and have been happy now, instead of
miserable; that is just the very thing, that you want to avoid, is
to try and get a turn on the home journey, in front, or in a
pleasant happy mood, in a frame of mind, that would say, I would
like to be a spirit, to go down in the Sun, and look at her
machinery, or to go down to the bottom of the ocean, and see
what the fishes are doing, or go round the world, and see
whether Tom is telling the truth about this mountain of gold,
you know my friends that I would not make this statement,
unless it was absolutely true, and that I could do this thing,
what is the use of this gold to me, I would like to see you get
it, and I would like to have the privilege, of making books, for
people to read, that is the only return, that I would appreciate,
to get my books published; and you know it was my last wish,
and I had no other desire, when I fell through the opening; you

know that my heart is bound up in a book, and I have nothing
too good for this privilege, it is the one great craving of my
whole life, I love to sink my name as deep in literature, as the
men, who guide me, I am guided still, there is a power, at my
back, which says, you were always fond of writing, and you must
write, or the world would not keep on, this is my world, it is all
I care for, it is all I love, and to deny me this, is worse, than all
the agony, of eternal hell-fire, and this is my hell: For I am
scorched at every burning pain, that fills my eyes with tears, and
I cry and weep bitterly, whenever my books don't go as I want
them, I would die any time to get my heart thoroughly saturated
in literary works, you know now how much I respect and worship this opportunity of making my heart glad again, for the day
this book goes forth to the world, I shall show my friends in
heaven, that all my labors, have not been thrown away, and my
welcome there, will be greater than words can express; you
know how I dreamed of this, well it was to be a failure always,
and that is why I have never been quite sure, whether it is just
ready for publication or not, the world has been advancing
steadily, and I have been growing older, all these years, and the
Sun never sets, without making men come forth, with more intellectual powers, but dreams never yet did cut much figure, and I
am not to allow this one to stay me in the least, it is this, a
dream, is the pressure of the soul valve, upon concussion, it produces the thoughts, when they are not manipulated, they are the
after reminiscences of the vortex coming in contact with matter,
and are vibrations of the nerves, it is merely the slumber of your
soul's champion, who sleeps in your eye, he is there, and he stops
there, to keep others, from coming in, but he is oftentimes
away, when he should be at his post, and that is the way that all
mediums are spoilt, they are kept awake at night, instead of
being allowed to sleep, through these foolish spirits coming and
playing games with them; now you know what it is to be made
a fool of, then remember this, it is this little watcher, that has
more business to attend to, than he can well look after, and
instead of him trusting to others, he has left his post, and gone
off, in some direction, to look for other material for his purpose,

and now I have told you all my troubles; you may as well go back with me and ride the whale, it is large enough in all conscience for us to fight about, and you can have a piece, and I will take another piece; this is mine, because I got there first; and I want you to take the head, and fall in that hole, at the top, because Jonah did, and he went to sleep after that feat, for three days, and three nights, and he was so big, that he filled the whale up with nonsense; that is about the full extent of what he did, and you know when anybody is stuck, or afraid, the young American is sure to want to know who the Jonah is; for he feels afraid, too; and wants to tackle a whale, he is heart and soul in all that has a scare in it, and you will find that the American boy, won't despise old Tom Paine, in days to come, for the United States, will whip the world at everything appertaining to skill: She has taken the right precaution to get ahead, and that has been her great secret of success; it is the flag, that carries, the emblems of the deep, in its entirety, the skies are full of stars, and the waters are full of stripes, and the two, strike off a vivid reflector, and it is this, the stars are emblems of brilliancy, the stripes are the emblematic form of good, for in a line you must have a distinction of greatness; the star, is the candle for the day before the dawn, and the stripe is the coming thorn; it means, that a prick from the thorn is always a welcome visitor, when it is on our side of greatness; but when it is, on the other side, it means a great big thing, that does not know the power of its own sting; so I have attached the American flag to my whale, and as I was there, and nobody cared anything about me, or any of my resources, I just planted my own countrymen's flag, and said you are here to stay; and it is this, that I have done, with my mountain of gold, it is for the old flag, or no pioneer, on earth, shall have it by my agency; now I must get back, on that whale, it is no use my trying to tell you a good story, he has got the worst pair of hands I ever saw, for one thing, and that is this, he won't let me go round about half enough, he is always poking me back on to the point, and I could tell you a splendid yarn just now, only he will have me go back to that whale, and I can do my theoretical points up better,

by keeping off the sharp end, when you have got an instrument,
and come back here, don't you let him know anything, because
when you do, he is sure to make you face the sharp end, and I
don't like my medium's style of poking me on the end of every
point I approach, it makes me very cross at times, and we have
many battles over this question, he argues, that it is better to
have a practical demonstration, than my science, and I am going
to give him his way over this book, but the next one, it shall be
all science, and you shall learn the way, to whip a cruiser, out of
sight, that is in a theoretical form of demonstration, and this is
the way to catch a whale, you want to watch him, in the
act of diving, and then see how long it takes him to appear
again, this is it then, the whale dives, and it has gone totally out
of sight, and when it reappears, it is some distance away from
where it started, well in that journey, it made a spring, it did not
dive at all, as you say it did, it made a jerk, or spring off its
tail, that is where you have that spring, that makes you so
supple, in your walk, for the whale feeds on blubber, and it
is so fine, that it makes you have muscle, that causes you to
move, in a way, that indicates whalebone, you are the attics
of this whale, in sinewy power, and you are the very growth
of imperfection, for you don't do right, your bones are made
from the rocks, and your head is made, from the jelly, that
the whale feeds on, and you are a whale of a man, that
is not all, I mean you are better than Jonah, because I won't
let you fall; now you see that I put that point in, and it
is buried so deep, that you can't make head or tail of it, and you
are just what I told you a "whale of a man," and don't know
where to find my dirk, well it is right here, the sinewy, has to
come from some place, because you all know we had it, and it is
this, the one who made it, had all the benefit, of knowing what
it is, that is not all, the whale is a fish, of the sea, and we are
men of the land, now how to bring these two into united appro-
bation, I guess, it beats a Yank, for it was the last cord, that
whipped a Gemaka, and that is what I call putting in spice, for
I lift you up one minute, and drag you down the next, and
pop you on top when you least expect it, that is what I call a

maximum; it is the left hand, that is a mystery to the right, and
you all know, when a man is full of whisky, that he does not
know, which is one, and which the other; so you have to get
drunk, before you can dissect me, for I have quite a number of
things, that puzzle myself, one is the eye-teeth, that have got to
be drawn, before a man knows anything, then there is the wisdom tooth, it comes and goes, and is nothing but a nuisance
while it lasts, now why don't you tell me what a wisdom tooth is
for, it makes your gums ache, and it lasts just about long enough,
to make you wish you had been born without any wisdom at all;
that is the tooth, that comes off the whale's belly, it is a mole,
that sprang off nothing, and never was anything, and that is
how Jonah made fast to the whale, he got hold of the wisdom
tooth, and he was in agony, all the time he had it, but as soon
as he let go, it fell in, and Jonah, was let out of the hole,
by putting his history into the Bible, now you see my friends
that Jonah has come in for more amusement, than any prophet,
that is mentioned in that great work, and I have made fun of
him, you have all made fun at him; then what has he done, why
he had the right theory, only he was not advanced sufficiently to
demonstrate it, and you know he has come in for more sport,
than all the rest of that great work put together; you know that
Jonah is a fish, by this time, and he can swim all around the
world, and investigate, and he will be pleased, when he reads
this, to know that in folly he fell, and in sense he has risen, over
the top of all the rest, for he was the first man, that ever pinned
his faith, on to the right stick, and you have got to be careful
how you speak in regard to Mr. Jonah, in the future, for he will
be elated, at his success, and you boys might get a pip of lightning for your trouble, when you call out where is that Jonah; he
will not take those remarks so friendly as he has in the past, he
is a great man to-day, and he knows more how to manipulate
boys, than he did, and you should just work "keerfully," when
you want to be afraid, a man who is afraid, is sure to borrow
trouble, and when you want to be afraid, just take a stick, and
make a whole nation afraid, the consequence is alarming, the
Sun does not set, but some great villain has been executed, for

some offense, that made the nation afraid, you are all afraid of
your own shadow, till I told you it was the reflection of your
strike off the Sun and Moon, in union, well how do I get that
notion. so firmly fixed in my mind, it is this, the Sun is a magnet,
and she draws, and the Moon, is a loadstone, and it recedes,
from a magnet, and this is what a loadstone, and a magnet do,
they both compress power, and drive one through the other; so
you see now how it is, that this stone is so powerful, it is a loadstone, because it is generated heat caused through gas coming in
contact, with the soul, which is the ocean, the soul of hell is water,
for you know that this hell, is the idea, commonly known as the
flames of inferno, you see that these flames are actually in existence certainly, but what their power is, is not yet defined, no
more than what I have told you, and this fire is not of any value,
except to turn the heavens, and to make the earth an ash-heap,
now you see that I have done nothing absolutely in regard to
science yet, I must make the machine on earth, in accordance to
the miniature of this gigantic machine, that turns the heavens
around, and you will then be convinced of my whole theory, that
there is no danger, and that there is nothing to be afraid of, you
think I dare not do this thing, and why, because you think it
would be a sacrilege, against our own maker, I tell you distinctly
that God is good, and not harm, that you must look upon God,
to mean the right definition, of the word good so it is not a sacrilege, at all, but a boon, to know what we are, where we are
going, and what our work is hereafter, that is all you have to
think of, and the question is not what we ought to be doing here,
but what is going to help us on the everlasting life of eternity,
you go to glory happy, and you are in glory forever after, should
you go home miserable, you are going to be miserable on and
off continually; so it is better to know the future, and not stop
intelligence, till it has injured you, then your duty is to guard
your own, for it has to be guarded, or how can you go home
happy, that is what you must do, and in guarding your own, you
have caught the right theory, for it is protection, that makes
happiness; and not free lust, therefore you must look upon free
lust as a crime to be suppressed, by the hand of science, rather
28

than barbarity, thus you must become scientific, when you
attempt to do down such a question, and not by ruthless barbarity,
it is done by virtue of common sense, and not by trick, that is
the way to promote civilization, and you must reach in to every
nook, to tackle the lust of the evil one, because this passion, is
not alone to be dealt with, in the mode of hardships, it has to be
dealt with, in a manner, that does not leave the power, in the
hands of indiscriminating dolts, who are not fit to see what is
right, for they have the mite in their own eye, which is their
own devil; now don't you see that you can't expect a devil to
treat a devil, except in barbarous form, and when you want a
heathen punished, you should not place another heathen, to whip
him, you are not fit to make laws, that does help you materially,
you look at the laws of any civilized power of to-day, and they
are simply trick from stem to stern, a juggler, is nowhere beside
this abomination, and every day it is becoming worse, not better
by a long sight; your lawyer of to-day, he does his best, but
what does it all amount to, he is hit on every side by laws, that
he does not comprehend, neither does he know which way to
turn, to find that particular code of intelligence, which exactly
suits his case, he knows there is no justice, and he resorts to
trick, to beat his opponent, the consequence is, that you have
got so many tricks, that it is all a man can do to say he has got
a claim against inferno, it has been so disgracefully tricked by
the lawyers and judges, that inferno stands on such a rickety
basis, till I will kick the last straw away, before it breaks the
camel's back, and ride him myself, it is the straw, I have it, and
you shall not break any more camels' backs, the judge who
lynches, has to be shut up, till the mite drops out of his eye, and
the judge who drives nails in any man's coffin, for thieving, has
to be closed up in a dark cell, till his mite drops out, and the
judge, who is reasonable, and trys my experiment, shall make
his fortune, because his mite, is worth keeping: now I can treat
you to any number of laws, but three is good enough, for you to
practice on, because I have no doubt, that you will object, as
that is the principal qualification common to all attorneys, of
this century, and they get it from the whalebone, it is supple, it

comes all roads, and is any way, that pays best, you can take a
turn at knocking me out on law, I am going to practice for the
Seer, in his case against the New Zealand government, and you
will find that I know something, before they have shook Old
Tom off: Now I might as well give the parsons, one little pickle,
for old acquaintance sake, they did not like me, because I knew
too much, and that was why poor Old Tom went under his soul was
bound up in thoughts of how to convert a parson, and he never
reached the goal till now, and this was owing to the whalebone,
it seems to be better attached to the parsons, than to any other
class of men, it is this, the parsons, are so very supple, they know
just so much, and beyond that, God did the rest, he never
explained why, or what his motive was for promoting so many
miserable circumstances, he never did do anything, but make
mischief, that is what they call the will of God, to make mischief, and get everything mixed up so, till nobody knows anything, that is the full extent of any requirements, that you have
to attend to, a simple know-nothing, that is the billet, that a
parson has to be placed in, then what right have I or any one
else to blame the parson, he does his walk in life, and he knows
nothing, and he is from the part of the whale, that feels but
speaks according to his avocation, and feels, without daring to
say my God why don't you take this veil from my eyes, and let
me see this vision of truth, I say that the parson is my greatest
enemy, for he is my bosom friend, outwardly, he knows I am
right, inwardly he holds the sting, that kills his own body, and I
feel sorry for all parsons, for their life is a torment to their own
souls, and I have nothing but pity, and sympathy to offer them,
and I feel that I would like to help them, but I must draw the
mark in here, they would not accept me before, and I never go
back and knock a second time, you know that it is not good manners, and it is bad breeding, to knock a second time, I will wait
till they send in a card of welcome first, that is the way a gentleman should always behave, Now I have said nothing I hope
that has been in any way against the Bible, for I won't consent
to have one word said against that book, whatever I did say in
the past, I recall now, and I say it is The best book, that ever

was written, and it shall always be respected by "The Infidel"; he loved the Bible always, and he never criticised, except in illustration, and his own works are written after the same guidance, as that Bible was wrought from, and he is now a stronger believer in that work, than any man alive, for it demonstrates the hereafter, and is a work of God, whether he be one genuine God, or whether he be many Gods, now you see that I will not say, that there is no God, for the simple reason, that I look upon my own Guide as God, and that is why I don't realize, that you have no God, so you must not call me "Infidel" when you speak of me, for I do believe in God, the one I know, that is all the God, I can find, the rest are spirits, as my own, and I don't believe, in any other supreme being, except this one, who urged me on to do what I did, and you know, that I would not lie to you, for did the other God, according to the ancient theory exist, he would be at me, and stop me for writing what I have to say now; for it is in opposition to his rights and privileges; and not according to his theoretical resources, and you see I am not afraid of him, at all; now do you understand that when I say my God, that I mean the champion of my life, and not this Omnipotent God, it is the same with every soul, it has its own God, then the question is, do you know him or not, that is my theory, and I say that this man William Atkinson does know his own God, and he can talk to him, just the same as he can to any mortal being, and it is not me; then why can't I tell you, anything, I have only to tell this man's God, what I want, and it is transmitted, and is written, as you read it; then what more perfect communication can you have between heaven and earth, and what more can you ask for we are all quite willing to give you full and complete information, and you can write home, and get your letters, answered, by dispatches, that would beat all telephonic communication in the world over short distances; and for the space of ten thousand miles, it can be hurled through the sky, in twenty-five minutes; that is the time it takes from the United States to England, and then across to Australia, by way of Angel flight, or passage, so you see that you are not the smartest people on earth, after all said and done, and you can test this science, as soon as ever you

choose; it is all owing to this absence from home, which has
developed this medium, he can receive messages from his people,
and transact all his business, without opening their letters, it is
easily done, the spirit is reading their letters, as they write them,
well they are at a loss to comprehend the answers they have
received, and believe their distant relative is certainly a lunatic,
whilst there are many in Denver, who can answer for his sanity,
and you can judge yourself, as to the saneness of this individual,
you may poke fun at spiritualism, and that sort of thing, but you
wait, and see whether you are going to get the upper hand of this
medium, you will need to rise early, or sleep late, his pillow, is
well guarded, and he can be wakened, without the slightest
trouble, it is merely a movement, of that little fellow in his eye,
and the sleep is all gone, and a voice, to wake you, might be
annoying to him, but this voice speaks out the message, and it is
told in an instant what is the matter, now you see how well your
man is trained, are you game to test this man, or are you afraid
to trust him, you think he is dangerous, because he is the means
of telling you what none else ever knew how to set about it, you
are off your base, to refuse an opportunity, when it is thrown at
you, and I, want to prove it is no fraud, this machine, and when
you think it is, you have only to play "keerful" as the Texas
men don't keep steers that won't rush, you know I go to all
plays, and it is no trouble to make your test, in an audience, it
can be done in one of the box theaters, it does not want any conditions, the conditions are already made, and they are made to
stay, the whale, that I fall off, you never need get any other Jonah
to look afterward; now you have been challenged, and you know
the old saying is, that a challenger, has all the world to fight, and
it is as well to flip your wings and crow, before you begin, for I
mean to make a mark, that is what my men say, when I enlist
them, you have to be bold, or it is no use, the fighter, has to taunt
his opponents, it is no use any other way, you must put up the
first show, or it is impossible to get on;   Now I will really go on
with the whale, I had to fight out my story first, I was obliged to
go through this yarn, or die of gas, so I had to explode some,
before I could talk science, and it is this, that has brought me on

so well, I have always been a wind-bag, and it gave me so much joy, when I found the missing link, that I promised myself a treat, should I ever tell it to man; now you know it is no use taking up too much space, in telling my story, I might as well go and join the beginning, and it is right here, that I have to take you, the whale is amphibious, because has lungs, well his lungs, not of the fish of the sea, his lungs are off the face of the earth, they are lungs, in accordance, with the lungs of birds, and they are from the forest, for they grew on the weeds, and are the same as groupers they are the style of lungs, that keep floating, in eternity, they are the lungs, of the deep, for they sound the same, and are just the same as picking up squeak bubbles, they are exactly the same as this great gigantic well; that is in the ocean, no one knows much about it, it is too deep, for any mortal to fathom, it is even too great a feat, for the Arabian Nights to tackle, even the Egyptians, could not hide it, when they had Jacob and Joseph both, it was too much for all of them, yet the one who has to make his mark, must go down there, and carry sea-weed, from a long way away, before he can ever tell you much, and that is how I have gained my sense, is by carrying sea-weed, from one place to another, that is quite a trick, for you to learn, when you shake off mother earth, it is no use, you telling me, how to wheel a barrow across a tight-rope, when you know that I have been through all the seas, and found the mysteries of the deep so interesting, that I would give much more time to this book, only I want to tell you how to make a man, and it is right here, the main point in a man, is his hair, the only question, that you have got to doubt at all, is his hair, and it is this, that causes all the trouble, it is hair now, and it is hair always, well the whales die, on the beaches, and otherwise, and they decay, and after decaying, this whalebone is distributed through the sea, and after a time it becomes quite putrid, and is spread about, the consequence is this, the whalebone, is quite pliable, and soft, and it is very near whole decay, when the Sun strikes it, in its way, and causes it to burn, this burning, produces a smell, and that smell, is the life of the whale, for it is essence, and out of that essence comes

the hair, for it is turned to make a feeling of glow come into
the air, and this glow, is so perfect, that it causes sprouts, to grow
on the stubs of trees, and makes branches, of trees grow; so
you have a kind of tree, that comes from whalebone, and it is
this whalebone, that makes dust come and go, and the coming
is the same as the flies, it brings with it, a kind of thing, that
has no legs at first, for it is the worm, that grows upon our earth,
and she has no legs at first, but when the grouper dies, he
brings flies, and he has the wings too; it is all the same, you get
legs by degrees, the same as other things come, well it is the
lung-worm, that is taken from the whale, when it decays, that
produces so much, it is this, this worm, is so strong, that nothing can break it, it is the lungs of this whale, that produces the
lungs of horses cows asses, and maybe more than I know
about, and it is done in quite a scientific way, the lung-worm, is
very tough, and it is so strong, that it makes the hide of all
creation, it is the essence of that whale, that produces this tithe
of power, it is this worm, that grows intact, and breaks into
threads, when it dies, that has brought about all this mass of
human races, it is the lung-worm, that has reached all over the
Western hemisphere, and produced the man of to-day, it is this
confirmed strangler, that has produced the animals, as well, it is
this great worm, that has averaged more deaths, than any other
thing, it is this worm, that has driven whole herds of men and
women to eternity, this is what it is, it is the quintessence of
all diseases, and it drives one color to the other, and it makes
man come into the world a raving lunatic, for he never did
know how he came, and that is why his troubles are always
greater, than he should have had them to bear, and this is how it is,
that this whale is the generator of man, it is practically this,
the Moon is a powerful decomposer, and he is driving his essence,
in right and left, and he is always at this work, for it is as I
have said before an unloading machine, this is it, it is this, the
Sun is very powerful as we all know in the midsummer, and it
leaves a balmy essence behind after Sunset, well it is this, that
propels the gas to escape from the dead fish, and this dead fish,
is saturated, with the essence, from the Moon, well this essence,

is so strong, that it falls to the ground, and is called effluvia, or common dust, it is the adhesions of the body, and is prepared by the Sun and Moon together, well this is, that which causes, the ague, and the ring round the neck of the worm, that I told you about, well now I have a worm, with lungs, and it is not easy for you to find this lung-worm, unless you make a diligent search, and then you have a better chance of finding it, in the forest, where the calves are, for they take it commonly, and are apt to die with it, this is what makes the sheep cough so much, they have the lung-worm too; so you might be able to get this little worm dissected, and find the lung inside of him, for it is here, that we have to find our own lungs, and not from any other cause, for I know it to be a fact, for this lung-worm, is the life and essence from that whale, it is the same as a fish, in its ways, and it is the same as the mole, that comes with it; now you see it is a mole, in its first stages, and grows to be a man in time, let me see whether I can not grow myself, because it would be a liberty, did I grow one of you people, who are so very clever, at getting eternally wrong, now then it is very hard, for you people to follow me growing, for I am going to cut out my ancestors, and leave them to a better fate, they have been all on the field of battle, one died mad, the next, was a soldier, because he had to fight against frogs, and the other ones were made into sheep, and goats, and all kind of animals, these were my relatives, at the beginning, and I don't want their pedigree, it is too much trouble for me to take over all the atoms, that were gathered together, at the beginning, so you must be content, with a few specimens, and not be too avaricious, so you will be content, to have the bare facts as they are, in the generation of man, and a few of the common animals; I was once a toad, for it is here, that I get my lips, it is this, that makes me so good at swimming through the ocean now, for I had to get my living, on the phosphorescence once before, and I can live for any length of time on it now; so you don't think I am very far gone, when I live on the essence of the ocean, this is what has taken place, at the beginning, the Moon strikes the water, and it produces maggots, or cod-worms, that is the fish, that the Moon propagates alone, that is he is responsible from his attitude to poison with his essence, now then you keep this well before you, and don't forget it, I was once a toad, and I can swim three months, in the water, without dreaming of coming out, now then what do you think of that for a story, I can do it, because I am not of the body, but am composed of the phosphorus, that is generated, by the Moon, turned into lightning, and those little flickers, that we see in the air, are the after-effects of gas, they are the born generators of electricity, and are the first generative germs, not actual lightning, as we supposed, they are the germs of electricity, and grow from thence on, till they become acquainted with matter, in an adhesive state, and can not hurt you, for they have no power whatever, it is the fluid, when it is compressed with weight, that causes death occasionally, and not this light, that is seen in the air, when you want any tests, on this subject, I can write it up, and give it full explanation, I have studied the subject, and am thoroughly acquainted with this power, and could aid inventors materially, but I don't want to infringe on their patents, for they are my own friends, and I would not instruct, unless it were their instruments, that wanted knowledge, so you know my reason for withholding this information, it is not for me to injure any one, that is not my theoretical intentions; especially those who are battling for science, it does me no credit, neither would I have it said, that I took anything away, that belonged to another, I am no crib, and I want my own rights protected, therefore I will only assist my own friends, in getting through any difficulty, that they may have in the shape of reaching their own instruments, and not as a general thing, what takes a man years, of labor to discover by the old process, I can put to man in half an hour, and I call this an invention, because it reaches man from heaven, in lightning speed, whereas you would grow gray, battling over some little invention, that I could hand down in half an hour, whether the old dads, are going to approve of this rapidity, is more than you or I are going to judge, for my own father thought I was too fast, and all the world thought I was right ahead of the times, and now when they read my work, they will perhaps say

I wish I might have asked Tom, a few questions twenty-five
years ago, I would have been a duke now: That is altogether as
the essence of life put it; the time before I went into Her Majesty's
service, I was quite a lad, and then I had to be quite still there,
I was afraid of so much pomp and passion, that was displayed,
and I had to curb my temper, it was all I could do, to stand by
and be ordered about, by men, that were not fit to loosen my
shoe-leather, I could have marshaled those men round, and
made them fit to fight for a queen, in decent order, in half the
time it took those old shellbacks, to give their orders,
I was always ahead, and I am right at the top of
my class now; so don't think I belong to any mad
family, the family I sprang from are as good to-day,
as ever any other family are, so don't think I mean
that my relatives are mad, they were once, that is
what I said, and all men were the same, it is this, when
the Moon and Sun strike a picture, they drive into it a condition of essence, that produces the adhesion of water, and this
adhesion of water, produces inflammation, and it propagates gas,
that is the cause of life in form, it comes through this form of
life in its entirety, for the Moon is all essence, and the Sun is
all fire, and the water is all meat, because it contains soluvium
of potassium; which is life, and when you drive life into anything, it must grow, there is the secret, and I have made you a
man, surely you ought to be satisfied now with Tom, he never
worked harder for you in his life, and he never beat the records
more fully, well it is quite easy, to get at this man, once you
have propagated life in its entire form, it is just as easy to
make man now, as it is to get on top of the whale, and cut off
the flitches as the old whalers do; you don't know how many
whales I have seen dressed; and I never saw but one dressed
right, and that is the one I did myself, it is this, the whalers
are all too anxious, to do their work in a hurry, they don't go
at the business properly, they keep on pulling and hauling, when
there is a right and a wrong way to do everything, well it is so
with them, they take out a cut, when it is right across grains,
instead of cutting according to nature, they cut according to

square, now the whale is not made that way, and instead of
cutting square, you should cut along the hind end, till it is
quite bare, then strip it along slanting, till it has formed an
oblong shape, this is diametrically opposite to what it was made,
and it then creases in, and is brought out, without any escape
of fat, I can see the fat tumbling out, every road, according to
the whalers' style of cutting up, but the way I have shown, is
just the salvation of the oil: Now let us go on to this whale,
and see what it is like, there are gallons of oil in the sea, well
what have I found, why it is the oil of a man, out of that blubber, you have the oil, that is identified as man's blubber, and
the ox, and the horse, and the cow elephant, all of them have
the same oil, in their bodies, is it possible, to keep this from
man, when he has been dissecting these animals all this time,
yes it is so, the moon is a mystery, she has all this in her abomination, and much more, you see that it is all fancy, about calling the Moon he or she, it makes no difference, it is only a word
that is all; you might as well say a woman as a man, only that
in illustrating, it makes this much difference, that a man has to
bear the badger, and a woman must be respected always, that is
it, now we have it, then why don't woman have whiskers, that is
a simple thing enough, they are not so strong as man mentally,
they lack energy, and they don't care to work, because it makes
them coarse, that is not the reason at all, the woman, is the
worse, because she is more venomous, it is all owing to this
sting, she has got a sharper tongue, and she bites deeper than
a man, no you can't get Old Tom, that way it won't do, she is
a specimen, and she has to bear investigation, it is this, the
woman, has to be made first, and the first one, is not so perfect,
that is the cause of her not having any beard, she has to be
grown again, before she will be perfect, and that may take
another century longer than the first one was made, that is
this, that a century later, there has been a change, come over
the human races, and that is this, that every century, she makes
a revolution loose, or not in contex, it is like a miss in joining,
by the axis of a half turn, it is in this manner, that we take the
hundred measure. it is a half miss, and that half miss, is called

the conflagration, or flowing in of the vortex, now you see that
a Moon, is not liable to wind itself out, in a half circle, because
it must turn twice, whilst the Sun does her half round, or more
materially alleging the contex, of an abbreviation; that is a
difference, well the woman has to be caught in shadow, in the
Moon, as it takes a vortex, and it must meet again, or it will
strike off a man, thus you see that it takes over a century to
make a woman, at the beginning, because she is a vortex, and
not made the same as a man, for she is colored by the
adhesion of a complete change, now you see that a man,
may be struck off, in a momentary flash, but a man, has
no hair either, when he is a reflector, he gets that by the
adhesion of grease, it is a mixture, of tar and soap, that produces
this, in the atmospheric odors, that float around, well you see
that a man is always in propagation, but a woman, is born, at the
vortex, and she is a weak reflector, she does not come at the
time there is much power, and in consequence, she is always the
smallest, and weakest of the mammal races, for she has that
difficulty to contend with commonly called the breaking apart,
and it is this half circle, that causes it to come on flowing at every
wane of the Moon, it is this, that produces inflammation, that was
struck by the passion of agony, in the region of activity, at the
birth of a new century, she is not responsible for all evil, she
only did turn herself more fully to the Moon because she was on
a downward tendency, and was struck off as a weak reflector,
because the Moon, was two whole days late, in his circuit, and
he is filled with slow essence, in consequence, this has been quite
a study, how to fathom the change, and the man who discovered
this is by my side, and he is the one, who led me on, when you
knew me, I have always been governed by him, and that is why
I am so able, for he is an old spirit, that has never been on earth
longer than the time he takes to make discoveries; he is an
inventor, and invents all kind of machines, he can make a
plow, to till the ground, without any one going near it at all;
just by measurement, it walks away, by itself, and will turn
over a week's work in a single week, or make a circuit and
stop in that field, without touching anything on the sabbath;

it is no gas, but you might as well be whipped clean, when you
think you know so very much; I don't want you to have this
plow, till I get perpetual motion, or you will not give me any
privileges; and say that the plow is all the perpetual motion you
require, but my friends you can't have the plow, unless you
welcome us to your shores, for my friend is a machinist, but he
can't get this plow to the knowledge of man for half a century
yet, unless he says Tom you take your man to mine, and we will
show them how to turn a field upside down, it is quite easy to
do, when you know how, and as he helps me, I am going to do
it for him after this motion of mine is demonstrated, you think
I have gone out of my way to punish you for being so slow, but
it is not that you are so slow, but that you know so much, that a
man can't approach you with an idea, till you scuttle off to the
patent office, and run the thing ashore before it is ready, now don't
you see that my man has mastered the whole business, and he has
not gone wild over an idea, and what would you do, supposing I
were to give you a pair of balls in either hand, and tell you that
was perpetual motion, why you would want it straight off, and
not wait patiently, till you were told properly, how to make
application, and how to further the scheme, this is it then, the
two balls you hold in your hand are the beginning, but what is
the motive power, that keeps them turning, I don't intend to
tell it, in this book, for I have no business to rob my own self of
the pleasure of writing a full account of the world, and when I
get an account of the world printed, you can then have the
power, that so many men have failed in, I want my own instrument to have the full benefit of whatever luxury there is to be
had out of it, and you can't stop him, either because he is not
afraid, and he will have this, as sure as the Sun goes round, and
no power in the heavens has any more right to it than I have, and
I propose to give it to him, for the work he does to gratify me;
now you know the compact, is settled, and whenever you want
this thing, and the pile of gold I offer, it is mine to give, for you
can't find it, without I make a map, and take you to the spot, so
you can make yourselves content with this book, and be hungry
till you get the next, for I am going to study elocution in

the meantime, and I don't care to have my instrument used
in a hurry, his mind has to be rested for a year till I get ready too,
that is I am going on improving him so as when the next volume
appears, it can not be said that any fool can work under Tom
Paine, it shall be a work of art, from beginning to end, and it
shall last forever, that is the book I mean to write as a sequel to
this, now you know my intentions, and I will draw the line at
humbug, and take you home in rollicking time as the Sun does
her duty every day, so shall I do mine, in a modified form; now
we want you to see this through, and make us a decent burial
for all humbugs, in the future, and you can have a limited space,
in the geography of science, once we come to it, and instead of
sending Stanley through the dark continent, I will make a map,
that can last you as long as the world hangs together, that shows
all the countries, that are missed out of the Southwestern hemisphere, and take you back, on the region of the Arctic ocean, and
North pole, and drive a line through the whole of the universe,
and make no mistakes either, but give you a specific account of
all countries under heaven, that are unexplored, and tell you
exactly why it is that you have not been able to find more countries, than you know of, and generally tell all there is to know at
all; that is pretty near the sum total, of what will be in my next
book, it is no use asking for it before it is ready, for I can't break
my word, and you will not get it till a year after this is published,
and doubtful very at that; now we are ready to go on building a
man, I have let go the maintop-gallant, and I shall not pull in
sail, till I have made you look at yourselves; that is what I call
under the hatches, for you know that a man has to run ahead of
fair wind to catch up, for the wind is so short in this country,
that a man must be very dull, when he can't tell how the first
man is made, old Adam had to make a whole host of sacrifices,
till Eve, came and took compassion on him, what a pigeon
pair they must have looked, Adam so shy, and Eve so coy, it
must have been a pleasant walk, when they went out together, I
wonder why the girls don't hang on to the men's arms, as they
used to do; it looks bad to see a girl hugging a great big soft
head round, she with her pretty arms so nice and round, and his

great rough hand resting on her arm, I do feel inclined to slap
the pair, it is bad for a man to have to be tied to a woman's
apron-string, when he is a boy, but then when he goes on resting
his great paws, on her pretty arm, when his whiskers are gray, I
don't wonder at this generation saying we are going too slow,
why in a few more centuries, you will have the men in bibs, and
the girls will be riding in front on one horse, as they did at the
beginning, for a man can not be born without a woman, and you
see that Adam was an unnatural man, for he came before a
woman, and in consequence could not be tied to her apron-string,
or even play at sop, come I want to be carried, as the men of the
present age seem to think, that it is theirs to be made babies of for
a whole half time, instead of a whole turn, therefore the men must
be degenerating fast, and you must get a whale to make some better
specimens, as they are the quintessence of nonsense, when they
have to be lugged about, by a fine big handsome woman, I think it
is a shame, that the sea ever gave up such noodles; and it is a
pity, for they ought to be left at the bottom always, and when
Adam took of the apple, he must have bitten it very tenderly, for
it had no juice in it, the trees were sour then, and the grapes held
no wine, I wonder how he ever came to put his arms round Eve's
neck, he must have been a better man, than those we inspect, in
our botanical gardens of the present day, for I think they are
getting almost too weak, to put their arms round a woman's neck,
since they can't raise their hands higher; it is too absurd, but
considering that they are the stronger according to dame
nature's Goddess, I think it fair to show why the man has grown
weaker, instead of keeping his place, as all men should, he is
always after some woman, that he has no business with; and in
that condition he finds himself, that he has robbed the fruit, that
Eve was charged with, and I place the sin on man, and not on
woman, for it is thus, that we know she is the weakest of the two,
therefore he is the vilest creature alive, for not showing her more
respect, and I say as a scientist, that no man has a right to hands,
when he rests them on a woman, for in this, he sinks so low, that
he is barely a better, than the toad, that he sprang from, and it
is this, that makes a man, a woman is made by the contex of her

own sphere, a lady, because she is the first generative organ, having come in the vortex, of a concussion by abbreviation of access to an internal concussion on time, she is therefore the first being, because she had to be broke by a blow of the Sun descending on the Moon, when he was two days later than his regular course, and he felt the blow of adhesion, for he has made her straight, instead of crooked, as is his wont in striking off man; I don't believe the men of to-day, will appreciate me, because I don't pay compliments, they seem to think that a man must be a soft milk-sop, or something of that kind, because he dawdles round, and talks to the girls, as though he were afraid of them, and they keep on putting him off, as though he were sheer non-sense, which he undoubtedly is, well what has made him so why he is the longest-waisted animal alive in proportion to his height and weight, and it is his bone, that has not got enough adhesion of grease, he is a defunct ass, and nothing more, for he keeps on growing longer instead of shorter, and he gets his meat, by the sweat off his brow, but it comes with a bad grace, and he feels afraid, that there is not enough grease in it; he is so fond of drinking, that he does not know how he will have enough beer, to sap his strength up with, that is about all I can do, till I get you fast to this ass, that makes you all willing, that his neighbor should be tied to, but none of you want to go there yourself, well it won't hurt me, since I know so little, and all of you are so very clever, I might as well "Hook on Marm"; and take a walk, with Mr. Donkey, he is awfully stupid, but you know that the braying ass, has made many a man turn round, and look for that ominous sound, it comes from the throat, and has a tube more than the horse, that expands, when the nostrils are pulled back, by expres-sion of countenance, this is the mucus, that fills the throat, and draws down till it was driven back down the throat, it is the old saying, that a wind-bag, is not blown till it has been filled, and the ass' mouth, does not breathe, till his wind-bag is filled, then he is just as full as he can hold of wind, and he puts his tongue out, and draws his breath hard, it is the thorax, that becomes slackened, and lets out the sound, on a grating, that is at the root of the tongue, this is all for nothing, but it does not signify, when

you don't pay extra, well the Sun was making this peculiar noise,
when she struck off the shadow of the ass, and propagated his
sound, which comes directly from the bull whale, of the ocean,
now you don't appear to recognize man in this note, it is the
dark shade, that has flung a shadow over you, that has concealed
you so well, till you don't know yourself, that is about the substance of this thought and theory; I am afraid you will be asking
some question, that will make me feel ashamed, that I tied you
to an ass, yet when you are all of the asinine specie, why can't
I place you where you belong, it is this, that I want to develop,
by this adhesion, and it is the throat, there is a tonsil, that has
not been adjusted, it is in the back of the throat of the ass, and
you speak, through this tonsil being filled, with attachment to
the throat, and it is through this attachment, that the ass, has
that great coarse note, and he would talk, should he ever regain
his wisdom tooth, that has been left out in his entire construction,
it is only the want of sense, that hinders him from speaking, and
should an ass, be constantly with children, he may yet be made
to speak, it is nothing to hear him cry out, when he is in agony,
like the scream of a whale, for he has got this same sound
perfectly: Now I have done with the ass, you might as well be
linked on to the bull whale with me, for I am going there, and
you can go or wipe your eye, and say he is all science, he might
not like me near him, and play some joke upon me, that is
exactly what you do think, when a man wants you to go and see
for yourself, you thought me tied to that ass to stay, but you see
I only went there to graft a little piece of his throat, and put it
on to my own, now I am after the foundation of all men, and you
think I am going to play a trick on you, that is just what a man
did to me once, and I said my friend you are so clever, that you
must have broken your axle in two, for one-half is this way, and
the other half is sticking right through you, he looked surprised,
and I said why the axle you carry has lost its grease; when I put
my finger in your eye, it did not see the way I meant it to, so
you see that when you go after researches, you must look till
you find, and many fools make one good man; now you can go
or stay, but the theory is this, that the ass having the tonsils,

29

must be right and proper, that the bull whale has the same thing, when they both sound the same note, it must be, that they are nearly akin, so it does in reference to man, his throat has tonsils, and he uses that little machine to talk with, so you see that what is no use to the ass and the bull whale, is quite valuable to man, for it is his very mouth organ, that has to be used, to throw about this intelligence; now my friends you seem to have got a very fair understanding on this point of sound, I want you to go with me to the horse, and find what there is there, that has attracted my attention, you mean to say because he has a tail, that he can't be the same as me, well I don't think you will ever find a much longer tale than mine, once I have done, but it is quite short now, to what I hope to make it; now you see that I am always putting in my silly jokes, because you think I can't do anything else, well it amounts to this, the silly jokes, poke my tale along, and make you do as you ought to; the jokes are happy nonsense, which are the faults of the horse, he is always playing with his companions, and he keeps chewing their manes and tails, and is just as ready to have a bout at kicking; he is quite as scientific as any man, and he can handle those feet, to such perfection, that I doubt if any man yet attained the same skill with his fists; now you don't think I have got any fun in me, well I can assure you that when I was at the Antipodes, I used to play at riding horses, till they broke their necks, at flinging their heels in the air, to try and kick me off, it is not the mortal man, that they are afraid of, it is the immortal man, that can tantalize them into committing suicide; well you call this barbarism, because I wanted to find the missing chain of evidence, you would call me a barbarian, that is just what you would say, well I am not going to leave anything alone, that suits my purpose, to investigate through, and what makes me so successful is this, that everything I tackle comes to like me in the end, and that is why your own man has taken such a great fancy to me, he says that he can't ask me a question, that I can't answer, and he does make me puzzle a great deal more than ever any one I was ever acquainted with before, he has been brought up with cattle and sheep, and horses, and he knows more of their qualities than I do, but he never says, you shall not put this or that in about them, he leaves it entirely to me, to show you what I choose, and that is how you get on best with a horse, you let him have his own way, and you are going to get much more work out of him, than when you tug him about, because you must understand, that the horse is able to tell right from wrong, and when you are kind and gentle with him, he loves you, and when you abuse him he hates you, and will do all he knows how to fetch you trouble, so when he sees you are good to him, he will worship the very ground you walk over, and roll on the spot, that your feet rested, and he licks your hands because they are salty, the same as his own hide, and this makes you and him brothers, both of you have salt in your bodies, because you come from the same place, and you are the very impersonation of each other in likes and dislikes, the horse is fond of catching at little things, and nibbling it all away, the horse is fond of chewing his grub, and he relishes it when given in small quantities, he likes to be fed on a variety of dishes, he appreciates you more, when you ask him whether a little dessert is better, after mid-day noon is past, and you take him in a little thistle, he will neigh and call you back for more, just the same as any English dude, would bray; "wai'taugh; some mo'r ta-ta-th-ta-r't; don't you know;" that is "A-ugh- E-augh; some goos-ber-rey twart"; some more it means, and the ass could speak quite right, only his eye-teeth were cut too high up; whereas the horse has teeth, that change, till he is full grown, and he never carries any flesh, till he has done with his wisdom teeth, in proportion to what he has afterward; thus showing that the eye-teeth of the man are just the same, and the boy and the colt both shed their teeth, so you have evidence here of a similarity, because these teeth come from the whale, they are the one, that has been so long in dispute, whether this is ivory, or mere bone, it is either one or the other, according to where it next grows, should it be useful, it is ivory, and should it be useful, it is either; according to its intrinsic value; for it decays, and is made use of as the essence, that produces the life of almost all mortals, for it is concealed

in essence, and when the air strikes the gums, they bring this
gum to inflammation, and the teeth grow by adhesion to the jaw,
through a mixture of soft lime formation, that has floats, which
strike cold to the jaw, and this jaw is full of pores, and the wind
is quite naturally drawn toward the gums, because the breath is
pulled in and out, and in consequence the teeth are absorbing,
from the atmosphere, till they take cold, and then it is an affliction of nature, that is all my friends and Old Tom has brought
the babies teeth, independent of my grandfather's old fossilized
notions; that a man was made first, and he is to walk about as
the lord of creation; a pack of stuff, you couldn't make a man
out of heaven, unless he came of a woman first, and since they
made the first man, I say they shall have the credit of doing,
what man never can accomplish by himself; and as for woman
being an inferior, I say that the man who thinks that way was a
misconception, he should have gone to waste, and has no business with any soul, for he has the tail of a coward still hanging
to him; now I don't want you to think that I want to curry
favor of woman, for that is not my object, the man is a noble
creature, and the woman is the same, but to class one before the
other, why it is monstrously wrong, the man has to lead, for he
is the strongest, and the woman has to obey, for she is the
weakest, but your own son is a portion of each, and one and the
same, so how can this being be bad on one side, because his
mother gave him suck, it is not that way at all, he is inferior to
neither, because those twain are one, and one begets one, or
united affection has but one current, and that is magic, it is the
magic of the eye, one loves the other little stranger, who sits
there, and these two are the magic wand, that hand and band
two souls together, or they with mutual consent or otherwise
separate these two souls, which they have united; thus you know
now who does the work, of making lives happy or miserable,
and not as you call that husband the beastly wretch, he is a very
good man, till this little chap saw his wife kiss another man, then
he begins to feel wretched, and his whole aim is to catch something, that he imagines is taking place, it is this little eye-witness,
who has seen, and he wants to make his man see two; that is

the whole affair, and you have got the upper hand of magic; it is not what men think it is at all; they make a calculation, of different whys and wherefores, and put them together; it is quite another thing entirely from what men think, the little man or woman in your eye, knows exactly whether you are a faithless sire or not, and they just manipulate the affairs accordingly, they know whether it is wise or foolish to make a man tear his hair, they know whether it is better blinked at, or not, they know exactly what should or should not be; and they have the power of agreeing or disagreeing, all is in their hands, and they are your Gods, so you have to understand them, or know nothing, that is the point, now you say this can not be, and yet you are reading this book, and you say that can't be; I tell you it is through this intelligence, that you are getting this knowledge, and you can prove it, any time, as well as it is proved in this book, you can rent a hall, and you can have such tests, as were never made known to the world, that is what you can do, and as for going on to the platform, and giving ten-cent dive reckonings, I won't permit it, and I am not going to permit anything in the common way when I am at the head, you shall have eminent men as conductors of such tests, and they shall be alone for scientific purposes; and not for just advantages of those who want to know whether their great-grandfather was happy or whether he has made a machine yet to fly with wings; I won't permit stupidity; and when the speculation fails as to my ability, I want to be allowed to tell why it has failed, and what the cause of failure is through, because I am not to be done at one trial, there are elements, that frustrate me at times, and I am obliged to wait for the tide to come flowing back, and then I ride home on the wave, and I won't be satisfied when you are, I have to be satisfied, before I knuckle down as vanquished, you are not to take advantage, because a difficult trial is a failure the first time, you must give me the opportunity of winning back my lost laurels; and then when I can't get home, you must allow me to try, till I do; because I have an idea; that I am to be tried; and when I am tried, I want to be fairly dealt with, because it is easier to mend a net, than it is to make a whole one, and you know what failure, does, it makes both horse and men cowards, once they are whipped, it is a win for their opponent every time, so you know what I fear in a failure, it is this drop of the tail; your own fell off, so you never had a better tale than this one to paddle your own canoe with; and I want to show you how to govern yourselves, so as when you go over the west wing, you won't want to come back, and be a nuisance, to all those you would wish to help; that is as much my business, as anything else, and to do this, you must be willing to be taught, while you are growing, and not when you are waning, for you know that every inferiority is caught on the wane, it is the decline, and it dies declining, and drags satan with it; that is fear, well when you know all, there is nothing to fear, and in consequence, you go rolling round the bend, and pick up with your old pals, on the other shore; that is the way, not weeping and wailing, and making both the dead and the dying miserable, you know what I do when I see a body cremated, why I say what a fine essence they have made, it makes me sneeze, to think, that that same essence, will produce something, for me to speculate upon, let the fools alone, I might get a whale on earth yet, that is my theory, that when the Sun lives on essence, she knows how best to place her substance, and this essence, may yet show me something that I never saw; so I don't mind what becomes of the dead bodies, they are no use, except for this science, of propagation; they may make a good man yet, and that would be something more valuable, than all the dead bodies, that has ever been buried; so you see I don't want you to stop this essence, from the fire, you burn everything but the essence, and that is more than a match for your fire; so you see you have something besides your friend in an envelope containing his ashes; that is more than any man can ever tie up, it has gone into evaporation, and it mingles with the dust, and it propagates again, for richness, was never known to remain idle, it has to float round: I have touched you on the sore point over this question of cremation, and it is rather hard to tell what has to be done with so many live people, that I think you had better make him discuss cremation from the platform,

he is bound to talk, and it will be a good beginning for a young-
ster, he is well guided, and he will get at something, sure to
please you; and whenever you think it wise to get this question
threshed out, it will be well to have the opinion of those who
have passed out, and that is what you want, for they don't want
you to die, till it is your turn, because they get knocked out of a
billet, watching over you, and they will look after your bodies
much better, once they gain knowledge sufficient to know how to
make evils disappear, and the good to stop always, for it is this
radical change, that will knock diseases higher than the rays of
light; and make you a stronger race of people, and as I have
only two diseases mentioned in my work; fearing to mention
more, in case I infringed on some quack medicine vender; I
only undertook two, that was the banishment of the flames of
inferno; which you will admit when you have read thus far, that
I have made him about as small as you could possibly have him
made with one dose; and as for the tic-douloureux, I have not
much use for it any way, it is not a science, it a sign of a weak
back, and a weak back is brought on through not enough whale
oil, so that when you can get on top of a whale like I do, your back
will be so greasy, that it will be pitch pine resin, or some ingredient, that does not admit of aches, but is what you want, when the
back aches properly; that is a new one like mine, and after reading
my book, you will be quite satisfied, that you are to have a new
one like mine, and that is more than you were ever certain about
before; that is my last known disease, and I have cured the ache,
that has frightened you so much, it is the back, that was made,
through that punk, it lets in the weather, and soaks up the moisture, that is why it is so hard to keep right, and you must give it
a dose of the dog that bites; the Sun is the remedy for a bad
attack of lumbago, or tic-douloureux; it is thus, that I found out
many of my scientific senses, through watching people treat
patients, they have got all kinds of theories; and I would like to
make a medical work, for I know it would be worth more money
than any one man could spend, it is this that has always puzzled
me, why don't people try the remedy of getting back, what they
have given; the Sun draws from your body, and she saps the life

out of you, and in consequence, she is all the time feeding, and
making herself fat, well at the same time she is feeding herself,
she is making odors, that bring back to earth that which she
took away, therefore she is scented on the eyes of her own
essence, and when you want a remedy, you have got a sore back,
I will rub your back, with my sore arm, the one counteracts the
other; because in poison, there is an adhesion, that drives the
flames away from any pain, and then when it is met by its own
poison, it kills itself, now you have understood what I say, then
don't do anything else; and say that Tom does not know his
business; you pitch pie at me, and I will throw it back at you,
and I may go one better; so that when you try any experiment,
that I have told you of, you do as I say, and don't do as you think,
which is baiting the bull from behind the fence; don't make me
mad, and I won't touch you, is a common expression, but when
you have to go mad, they kill that is all; so two people with
cankered eyes, are going to kill the canker, because it won't fight
an enemy, when it is met by a bitter enemy, it is all the same,
with affliction, it is the disease that spreads, but it is not the disease to kill; it is the eyesore, that has to be attended to; you
must fight the eye, and when you have a thoroughly bad case of
small-pox, you bring another patient, that is worse still, and put
them both in one bed, the poison, is sure to abate, and disappear,
for the eye, can't stand the evil of its own essence; and it will
die or leave, that is one theory, and I want to give you the pure
cure for small-pox, and that is the eye extractor, which is myself;
so you know now what I mean, and what I would do; it is all
easy when you know how; only you can't learn till I am ready
to tell you; that is not likely to be ever; for I don't intend to tell
my own business; it will be a nice job for you medical profes-
sionals to attempt to get science up to the standard of my achieve-
ments; when you run the gauntlet, and jump into eternity; Now
then I am going back to the bad land again, and show you where
the first man has to go to get made up into a sheepskin; there
is the place, that will rather puzzle you, for it is in the interior of
Arabia; that we are off to; the Sun is as hot, as the knights of old,
who wore spurs, like the wheel of a cart, but who poked their

· horses on behind; and went in front themselves; this is what I
am going to do now; the way it all comes out is this, the Arabs,
are the first people, and they are so small and shiny, that you
don't get near enough, to ever find out much of them, and when
they get grown up, it is no use trying to trace them back, for they
only learn to lie, that is the capability, which speaks for itself, it
is this little Arab, that has caused all the trouble, and he is by far
the worst liar on earth; notwithstanding his protestation of innocence, he is a jugged hare, from the beginning, and he is always
jugged ever after, that means, that when it is done up in a jug,
you can't tell how many liars, have had their black hands in it;
or in other words the Arabs, are a set of thieves, and liars, that
would make a criminal ashamed of his own jacket; and it is this
thieving lying little race, that is responsible for all your funny
fables, they saw many a wasp, that had wings, and they have seen
all manner of curious things, that no one else ever saw, and they
are the ones, that the Eastern people have all sprung from, that is
the story, as it goes; well let me tell you, that a Jew is a Jew,
wherever you find one, and wherever he is, there are sure to be
more, and this Jew, is the greatest hypocrite under the heavens,
yet you all follow his ancestors, and say he is the Simon-pure,
and why, because every little wonder, that a Jew does it's a miracle, and he loads it with lies; and you are so thick-headed as not
to see through it all, when it is right under your nose every
blessed day, take London, the largest city, in the world, and she
is full of Jews, and pagans, and laymen, and hypocrites, that
would lie the teeth out of existence, did they know how to do it;
now then you tell them that I say so, and they will say no me
"velly goot, me got no pig-tail lik' em chilemen; me von't tell
von lie to please father Abraham"; at the same time, they would
hang their own brother, for a bell-topper, or a mud-colored scarf-
pin; I tell you, that you pin your plank to a rotten craft, when
you stick to a breed of people, that can't eat pork, it is a sign,
that they know more about the pig, than the pig has knowledge of
them; so you can just look out, because I mean to hit them a
wipe over the head, that will make them grin from ear to ear, and
I won't take it back either; you can make a much better fit of a

Jew, when you link him on to John Chinaman, than ever he had his hat stuck on one side before; you know I am a radical, well I am going to place the Jew and John, together when I get a little more advanced in my story, but you must wait till I put him together properly; now it is no use kicking, I mean to take you out of essence, and make you up, till I get you on top of the central isle-way of the stairs to heaven, that is where I asked you to give me permission to climb, the same as any other artist, and you know that I have achieved what no other man could, and further you know I will keep my word, and bring you this Jew linked to John Chinaman, but I like the Chinaman, because I found out that man sprang from the whale through him, but I don't like the Jew, because he as a specimen, is no use at all, he is simply a fraud, and I can't beat him, out of sight at anything, except to whip him every time he lies, that is just where I have the pull on that Jew, and you can take me with you, and you can find, that I will dissect his store, from stem to stern, and he won't know, but that he is sucking a pet lamb, but I am too many potatoes, for any Jew, and when you think you have got a smart one, bring him along, I can clip his wings every time, and he shall not know anything, that is how you should be, and not able to cheat me or any one else, you should be able to detect a thief, when you meet one, and not have to investigate his character, this is then the way you do that, it is by taking notice of the mite, that sits in your own eye, and ask him, what the character of that Jew is, he explains the whole theoretical admonition, of whipping a Jew, and you can get it yourself, it is done by the method of thought, that is you hold a thought, and don't allow it to pass, till it is resolved; it then forms another thought at the back, and when you get them moved into a body, they have told you something; so now you can go and take up a good position, and talk to Father Abraham, and see whether he won't spin you the longest yarn, that ever was caught yet; and when he has done, you won't find anything in it but lies; for he dare not let go of one end, till he has caught hold of the other; and that is just what you can't accuse me of, I let go, and pick up my story anyhow, because I lie to please you, when I want to make you laugh, and when I am in earnest, I do it so sincere, that you will never be able to say, that Old Tom was ashamed of what he did, well now in reference to lies, they come from frolic, they are the foam of the sea, intermingled with our blood, and I tell you how it all comes to this, the foam is a very troublesome thing to attach to anything, it has to be brought out again, or you can't make it adhesive, for it is strongly inculcated, with carbon of potassium, and in consequence, it is not made to last, it is only the fits, of water, it is the lunacy of water, it has the doldrums, as we all know, and that is rage mixed with connuvilum of potassium, it is the essence of the sea fighting the wind, that is inside of it, it is not the wind, that is overhead at all, that causes the sea to roll, I don't want you to run off with false ideas, it is what I call a savage theory, to come here and lie upon the most vital importance, I say you may lie to make people laugh, but you must not lie to give them pain, and that is where I hold that the foam is the danger, because it is not adhesive, but the water, throwing itself in anger, that is pure fun, it merely goes splashing up against each other, and you see both men and women doing the same daily, that is fun, I don't want you to go without bread, I don't want you to stop eating meat on any day in the week, it is all one to eat, and drink in sense and reason, for the Sun must feed off you, and the bigger you grow, the faster she will have to go, to keep up with her own development; now you see she is growing, and in consequence, she gets bigger and bigger, and her stomach is going on improving, till it will be hard to tell where it ever will stop; but the Jew knows, he has measured it, when he refuses to eat pork, he knows, that the stomach, is not right in the pig, he knows it is a fac-simile to his own, and that is exactly why Father Abraham had to conceal so much; It is a good day, to the pagan, and man may know what the other world is, by taking a sense view of it, and when he falls off this coil, that Shakespeare, has defined, in a crude way, I think you will all be the better of knowing how to go home, when old Tom has put you on the right track, and shown you how it is to be done, that is all I ever intend to do, and when I have made all clear, you can't miss the way, for it will be the road of eternity, and it be defined by science, and not by theory at all, when I say my theory, it means my science is so strong that no man can come back here and upset it: There is one way only of right, and that is the way of truth, let all religionists have their way, but science is the certain method to every conclusion, it can but be true or false, and when it is not true, it is false, there is no half measure, it is a whole Sun, and none other, it is a whole Moon and none other, it is a whole earth, and none other, the three in one, which is the odor, that is the beginning, the smell, it is this, that makes all things, the smell: Now do you know what causes smell; that is the turning-point, and you have to be taught, that a smell is infinitely greater than anything else, this it then, the smell is caused through its own adhesiveness to nature, so when the man dies, he has to be kept from you by some method, and when he comes near you, he brings back his affliction, because he died of this disease, and he has not reached a stage where he can throw it off, and when he returns, he pollutes your flesh, by the essence of his own condition, there is the problem solved of adhesion, it is his smell, that you have to avoid, and it is done by elocution, that is what I want to bring to the understanding of man, now you know that I am scientific, and you feel that I have very nearly upset every folly you have, then let me show you how to tell one dead man from another, and you have got the key to health, and that is what you know is about the best medicine you can take, there is the theory, that will make man the greatest machine, that has ever graced God's earth, you ought to be pleased to reach heaven as you like, and get your friends to come and show you the work, that their time is occupied in; Now it is elocution, that has to be mastered first, and I am working diligently on this question, I can see how to do it, but I must have an instrument to practice on, and this man is working all he can, though we don't despair of making a demonstration through him, yet it might not result as favorably as I could desire, for the fact is clear, a man has a power for one tone, and that is bass, the other is a soft tremble, caused through it being driven through weaker organs, and not by any other reason, the fact of a woman being weaker does not prohibit her from acting, once she knows

what the power is at her side, and the easiest instrument I ever
tampered with, is a good clairvoyant, but she lacks the knowledge
of stability, she has not power enough, to define the difference
between right and wrong, she is all right, in my own hands,
but immediately I release her, my time is all thrown away, she
can not see that I am away, and that is just what you have to do,
or the work is a failure, now I don't claim all this, for this instrument, but he can tell when it is all right, as he defines it, and
that is pretty near perfection, but I want it demonstrated, how to
tell one spirit from another, that is how we reach the truth,
but you know it is the difficulty this imposition system of spirit
return, and that is how we are at fault so much, the spirit of him
who governs us all, has not told us, and we must find this
direct communication, by elocution, it is that which will drive
the black sheep off the walk, and show you how to get good
specimens, and make the men who die to-day, the happiest mortals, that have ever passed away, well you know you are sure to do
this thing, and you may as well go over, with a smiling face,
because a welcome is not complete, without a laugh, and a laugh,
is the way to make friends; now it is this, that makes a man so
happy, he knows that to-morrow he might die, well should he
feel sure that this is impossible, he is as happy on one man's land
as he is on another, he does not care about death, because he is
sure, that it is impossible, and then he will not feel so lonely,
when he is on top, and knows, that no break, can make him feel
any inconvenience, except a current of pain, that makes life
feel so scared, that it quickens, there you have the sequel, it
quickens, and that is all, it has attached itself, to the sound
of eternity, or in other words, it has drawn over the skin of
sound, and is the theoretical skin of ether, for ether adheres to
the sound, after the body has left, and this is what stops death,
for the death is caught, in its grip, and torn from itself, that is
defined according to the light of a given thread, it is the bull
whale, that has taken you in, he sucked you back, for he drove
his horns, on the top of the wave, and gave eternity a shove
higher, that is this, the whale is fed on juice, and he lives on
air, and in consequence, he is an amphibious creature, and can

live in two atmospheres; that is, the sea is his home, but immediately he dies, his body, is gone to odor, that has the qualities, of
making nearly all else; that is the way to put it, for his stink, is
the stench, of the two, of earth and heaven, and the two combined will make a mix, for they are divided, the one is of the
land, and the other is of the sea; well they are both of the sky,
for it is after all, the life of potassium, or mixed by soul, to
mean a soluvium of potassium; that is the wind in water propagates life, and you know what absorbs the essence, and then
throws it to waste, on the desert, and on the plain waters; now
I am back at the bad land, the desert of Arabia; you see how I
flit about, I have no ends to hold up for fear of falling, I don't
use electricity, to ward off miracles, and I won't kill, unless you
make me, that is you will bring it on yourselves, and I doubt
you are actually going to begin to see that sense is worth all the
miracles, you ever heard tell of; now I must get on a little bit
farther, and not let you off, this bad land, till I have got on to a
pig, for that is where I am going, as sure as the weather beats
the grayling into shore, it is all I do is to keep you on a hook,
and you fish for all that, and eat pork too, it is one more sacrifice that makes no difference, it has to be done, or it won't last,
and I guess it has to, for I won't die, to please any one, there
now, you know you can't kill me, and you are wasting time, to
think so; it is all this blessed little Arab's fault, or the world,
would be hitched on to heaven long ago, you know it too; only
you have to be fetched up by the hand, or you won't get on to
anything worth knowing, that is pretty near a "stoucer; stacher"
I should say, for the present enlightened eyes; I wonder how
they will like these strong expressions; I expect some little Arab
elf, will say "Oh! it is a thousand pities, he was not educated,
and a gentleman;" wait till I paint my picture, it will be oh! the
"wetchquawmer I qawt im actwaly in a werry fine powint
quawmer it iswint in his quawmer its in whis quawmer"; that is
he don't stop, when I would say "quawmer and make me blush
quawmer"; there now I think I have to illustrate, and I can do
my duty, when any little elf, comes in with the first language,
I want to do my duty to man, and a lady will see at a glance

that I am a man; she knows, what constitutes a man, she sums him up six feet, by the intelligence he carries, not by the coat he wears, I know a lady, won't blush at sense, she is before man, and always will be; that is how I size her up, and I won't stand back, and put it any other way. for any little child, that has not cut his apron-string "adwift"; now then you practice as you preach, and then you can reach any one, you have no loose ends to hold up, you can go back to the bad land, and make a fastening, wherever you please, that is all, I have caught the knife, that takes no notice of any man's rope, I cut it that is all, where you can see where it has been severed: Now then we are on the bad lands, we might as well dissect them, you know you went through that whale tolerably well, and that ought to have taught you to make me afraid of you, instead of you being afraid of me, for you got over as well as me, and we both did the feat, without a fall, now you are going to dissect the bad lands, it does not matter about you having been raised on the Island of New Zealand, you might as well have been a cuckoo, from the shores of Arabia, it will not make you write any more fluently, it is all the same I say where you were brought up, the Laplander, won't require any coat, when he follows me, so now get out your minds, and send them off on a cruise with me over the bad lands, he must be quite at home, and get on his investigator, that is all, he does not want any machine to carry him in, it must be a mere handful of sense, that he lets go with his mind, and not cigars or beer, none of that class need apply, they are cut out of my list altogether, they are no use for science, it all goes off in smell, so they are wasted, for the next few thousand years, they are gone over to some other theoretical research, and may be applied for, in the year eighteen thousand; that is nearer the mark, than they will ever be; I don't want to discourage them, but the Sun does not like tobacco after it has been burnt, she prefers it before, and as for the beer, it fires her coppers too red, after she has it adulterated; that is a fair definition of smoke weeds, after they pass over; I don't want you to keep on making me be funny, but these thoughts strike me through going to plays, and now it is getting worse, for I have to go, to take my

band in public; that is all I want to show you, that your minds
can go with me, and you can stop and do the light phantasy,
whilst they are away; this is the way we used to play, when we
built our castle beneath the sky, so you can copy me, and make
a good thing out of the rest, whilst I go out, and take your minds
off on a journey through the bad lands; I want you to write me
a poem, on phantasy, whilst the minds are away, for the time
being limited, I would like to see which foot you will place first,
the left or the right, or the one, that 'came through the heel of a
boot, or the other one, that is falling out of the heel of a book;
you see I am on you; again where did you suppose the foot
would come from, why out of the sheep of course, can't you see
him standing looking at me, while I make it; you "Great Scot";
have seen many a sheep, then don't bleed like a pig, and get your
dander up, when you go off on a journey with me, it is all on the
west coast of Africa, that makes me smile and think, that the
big African that beats all the Englishmen, that he feels himself
so important, when I take him as an illustrating machine, with
him by my side, you won't dare take offense, I can get him to
go with me, he is the man to topple over smokestacks, he won't
mind when I spin a yarn with a joke in it; it is fun to be free,
and it's grace to see, then don't be afraid of my African scout, I
can show all the people more fun, than they ever let out, when I
get back to Ireland and Wales, for they can hang on to each other,
till I get my whip out; that is the way imagine you are able to
drive buffaloes into Chicago, and then you are fit to go with me,
that is what I want men who are not afraid, of being turned over,
with a buffalo above, and Old Tom below, then you can get at
me, the way is easy, but the hill is steep, and I want you to go
at it full tilt; that is how we jump on to the horse, when he is
adrift, and we have to fly on top of him, without wings, you say
it can't be done, but you see the white patch over on his shoulder,
then you have been there, I saw it myself, and it has some gray
hairs, in the center, and why, because you caught the affliction
of the saddle, in your eye, the moment you saw that white mark;
now then don't say no, when you know you lie, it is a white
patch, from the effect of a saddle, and why did it turn white,

because it was so very sore, that it was struck with the Moon, and poisoned, that is why my friend, you know how the Moon strikes fish, and makes them smell, and you know that it pretty nearly killed you, when you had eaten poisoned fish, through the essence dropping on to the fish, you knew it was the Moon, yet you don't know that I had to tell you, or you would have still believed, that there were rocks in the Moon, what would rocks do toward poisoning fish do you suppose, well I can't tell is your answer, yet you don't give Old Tom credit for anything, not even for your Declaration of Independence, you stole that away from him; and now you will steal this from him, that you knew how to cast your mind over to Arabia, then why didn't you go there first, and not come to the United States of America, and preach to those heathen, till they lied you out of all intelligence, that is what the Arabs have done, they lied away all intelligence, and were so frightened, that they drove out the Seers, for fear of being found out, that is exactly what they did, you all know that King Saul, was so frightened, that he banished all the Seers, that had familiar spirits, and you know that when they did him up, that he went to the Witch of Endor, and called Samuel from the Tomb, as it says, then when Samuel came, out of the Witch of Endor, how is it possible, that he came from his Tomb, you all know that the Bible says this, then when Samuel could come to Saul, why can't I go to you, it is only a question, whether I deserve to be held up as much from my qualities as Samuel is, he dealt good works out for the Hebrews, and I can do every bit as much, for the Americans, whom I love, and have stood by at many a crisis, and welded the ropes together; you say no dead men ever returned, did not Samuel do this thing, does not this work show that I am here, in active operation, for the benefit of man; don't I do my work, as none other before me has ever known how to do this thing, what is there, that I am not able to do, tell me I pray, and let me see that you are mistaken, and that I can hold my position at the head of my class, what matters about a few people, who have no intelligence; you know I am born to govern, and I shall learn you how to root out all diseases; "is this worth nothing"; to sixty-five millions of

30

people, the thing can be done, through education, and not by
poisonous roots, they are good only for the blood, for the blood
is of the tree, in the first instance, and what begets one, has an
everlasting power; that is all: I won't say any more on religion,
I must be a genius, and I don't see it in religion, there is nothing
there, that makes me great, I can't fool the American, by religion, he is too far advanced for religion, to be of any special
benefit, and he has to be benefited, or he is not going to believe;
now do you see that a good way of getting on, is to see how we
are constructed, and then we know how we are to reach disease,
for once you know where to pour in the grease, it is easy to
make the cart wheel fly round; but when you forgot the hole,
that has been made in a place, that no carpenter, can place his
peg, you are not in it, that is all: Now I want to go back, to
the bad lands again, and see whether we can't make a stick of it
this time, you know how hard, it is for me to manage this work,
of telling you right off, it makes me nervous, and I feel afraid of
you, you are so dreadfully down on man being naturally born,
that I almost wish I had not started to tell you, it is only those
who are backing me up, or I should turn tail and run; well they
say I had a cool courage once, and what am I sticking for now;
that is it, you beat me once, by letting me fall out, before I had
got through with you, and I don't like facing the old enemy
again, he won't like me I feel sure, and I know he will be glad
only for the telling part, and that is why he won't like me, for
he will say I am too forward, and not sophistical enough, he is
so egotistical, that he forgets, that I was made of hydrogen, and
he of gas, that is the difference, but it is only an expert, like
myself, who could tell the right definition of these two commonplace words, the one is made of hide, and the other is made from
pitch, the two together combined, with sodium, is first rate medicine for a sick monkey, so I will drop the tale, and give the poor
fellow a dose, you know I feel proud, of the parson, for he beat
me once, and I like a man, that can whip me, it makes me respect
him, and I feel so much respect for the parson, that I would
willingly forego all my pleasure to get him pleased, and I know
he was glad when I died, I heard them say so, and I felt it was

the wrong, that they had done me, that made them so glad, for
they knew it was wrong to wish Old Paine a roasting in hell as
they called it; and that is why it has always been a desire of mine
to shake hands, and convince them, that I never merited their
wish, and that I am just as strong in argument, as I ever was,
that is the way to be, all the intelligence, that I have been capable of gathering has not done me one bit of harm, it has only
made me stick to the men I once sought to convert; and they
are all against me to-day, but you let me make the machine, and
they'will say it works like a daisy, that is the expression of all
land-owners, and they never got that word from the bad lands,
I will father it myself, and when the parsons come and inspect
perpetual motion, they will say it works like a daisy, that is the
theory I have, I do my work like a daisy, and you now see the
daisy of Arabia; that is what I call a ship in distress; for the
daisy of the bad lands, are the first specimen, that I intend to
introduce my specialists to; and they will admit I have planted
my growth very low indeed, on the shore side of life, it is this,
the daisy is small comparatively speaking on the bad lands, and
it has no nutriment, worth mentioning, at all; for it withers up
in dry hot sands, and is very much thought of by the birds of
the air, they come down, and make a great picking off this daisy,
it makes them stout, and fat, and they live on this perpetually
in the short days, and long nights, they live here, it is a roosting
place for the birds, and they like it, for the place is warm, and
comfortable, and it is not inhabited, so they make friends together,
and have quite a jolly time, and that is where the guano is so
thick, well it is here, where the first animal is grown, it is this
animal, that has broken the spell, he is a little one it is true, but
never mind that, he is an animal all the same, and you want him
to be a pig, but it won't do, I want him to be just what he is,
nothing more, and nothing less; this little fellow is a toad, and
it is blown, from this manure heap, and is driven down to the
seashore, by the wind, in her desire to blow out the interior of
Arabia; that is why you don't see a man grow, because his
growth has been so slow, that he can't get on any faster; you
want me to rush him together; like the wind does the winnowing-

machine, I can't do that, you must take time, to do anything
well, it has to have time, for the work, or it won't count for anything, after it is done, you may make a man for yourself, out of clay,
but you don't get me to do that thing for you, it is no use, I have
to have time, that is what I make my toad out of, he is made of
time, it is in this mint bush, sage bush, that I get him, don't you
see that the birds have laid and hatched young ones here, and
they laid their eggs on top of that manure, and when they were
hatched; it is all they dare do, to sit there it is so hot, and with
their little bodies, in the guano, roasting all the while, it is
natural, that life would spring of some such essence, and there it
is, the first thing, that strikes you at all as living, is this toad, it
is blear-eyed, about the size of a peanut, it is no longer than your
thumb, but it still is alive, and has both hands and feet, it is like
a crab, or crocodile, in appearance, facing the front; and behind,
it is like the crab, it is a fair specimen of a toad, and that is all
that I can call it; well you see that the feathers are there, and it
is the likeness of a bird, yet it has those feet, and wings or hands,
whatever you choose to call them; this is what you may term a
kind of lizard or toad, for it is back behind the frog, in appearance, a couple of hundred years, at the least, it is formed of time
and sage, with mint and other ingredients; well it is this specimen, that I am going to start with, and when he goes to the
seashore, he is what you call a bright object to begin with; yet
I have done my work fairly well, and I said that Cain and Abel
came from trees, and you see that I have illustrated it all right,
they did; it was out of these sage bushes, that the toad sprang,
for after the wet season is over, the desert gets quite bare, there
is not the sign of life, and this is what it all comes to, the sage
bush dies, and the eggs, are often rotted away, and these ingredients together, in the sand, cause an effluvia, or side sow, that
causes putrefaction to set in, and when this putrefaction sets in,
it is bound to propagate something, and this is it, the toad is
lyed by essence till he grows, that is the solution of this problem,
and you will find this true, whenever you choose to investigate
it; now I have my first land animal, and he is of course
amphibious, he has no lungs, and must go in the sea, as

well as on the land, for he answers the purpose of both,
and here we have the beginning of amphibious creatures;
this is where we start breeding, from this toad, and the sea-
nymph; that is what is called the small sea-serpent, it is a thing,
like the head of an owl, but it has feet, like the feet of a human
being, as nearly that shape, as anything I can compare it to;
and this head is round, and has eyes, and can pelt stones, that is
what it does, in the water, it does not throw them at a codfish,
for it will lay hold, as well, and eat the codfish, or anything else
it fancies; well this bird or seafowl, can not swim like a bird, it
must go underneath the water, and is there in abundance, and
you can catch it quite easily, with a fish-hook, it is no more a
human being, than the toad, and the clodhoppers don't respect
the toad, they crush them, beneath their heels, knowing no better; poor ignorant people, they don't know that it is their
paternal ancestors, that is going under all the time, they are
afraid of nothing, so long as the mouth is filled, and you can
have this specimen in your hands, too; and when you get it,
you will see, that it has feet, and hands, like the human being,
well now I want to show you, how this other little sea-nymph
grew, it is the shadow, that brought this one to life, it comes this
way, the shadow is struck off the union of the Moon and
Sun, and when it is struck off, it gets inflamed by the heat, that
has struck it, and it gives back to the earth, the exact coessence,
that it was caught on, it has struck a shadow itself, and is shad-
owed ever after, it is a walking machine, and has nothing to steer
it by but this shadow, for the sea-nymph, is the shadow, that I
mean first, this shadow, has a growth, in water, and is adhered
to the essence of a body, that is the mould, that it lays in, it is a
quantity of mulk, or pulk, that is what it is called, and it is pulk
one time, and pulk the next, for it has only got blubber or kelp
inside, well this kelp, is the essence of the sea, combined with
the essence of the Sun and Moon after contact, they both hand
each other, something, it is maybe the right word to use, and
that is propagation, for these two bodies have begotten this
shadow, that steals along, till it meets, another shadow begotten
of the same parentage; and these two, form a union, and become

linked together, and when they die, or become emaciated, through the cause of decomposition, the fish is hatched, for it is in this decay, that life is first observable, beneath the sea-weed, and when you want to prove this, you take a body of decayed sea-weed, on the seashore, and you will find so many different animals propagated, from this bunch of decayed sea-weed, that you will wonder how it was possible, that there could have been such a mixed circumstance in anything, well that is all owing to the way it is brought on shore, it comes in heaps, and it is all blubber mixed; well this blubber, is the result, of the Moon and Sun, having made shadows, in the deep-down ocean bed, they have got it mixed, by constantly making shadows, they don't do it, by any mysterious intention, it is according to nationalities; that it has grown together, it is nature to adhere, you see the present age, where the nationalities are uniting, to keep peace, and to make diplomacy a science, you see that what was done at the start, is being executed, at the present time, and with advantages, to all nationalities; it is diplomacy to marry into a different country men, for it is adhesive to proper ingredients, that suscitate the laws of nature, and bring out the proper ingredients, that compose the intellect, and calm the passion of nature, for it puts a brand between the two, that makes one respect the other, and brings holiness to a point of scientific advantages, that will not be produced, by any other theory; now I am moralizing, for the benefit of man; you keep away from relatives, whenever you marry, and as soon as you are old enough, you strike out for some foreign land, and make a country lass of that country your bride, and keep her away from her parents, and don't let them interfere, in any way with your affairs, keep her at home, and make her see that her home is attractive to her, and make her obey to such extent, as shall insure respect, that is what every husband must do, or make his life a lugger; meaning, that she will jump the bows, should you fail in your duty; that is, she soon measures you, till you look about as small as that toad in her eye, and that is what you brought about through your own mismanagement, she was what you might call afraid of you at the first, well take my advice, and never allow her to quite break

away from that fear, it is a mighty fine pole, that wants no whip
on the other end, it should always have a little attachment on
the other end, that will say, you dare not take that end on to
your shoulders, or I will make the whole of that pole devise
some scheme of application, to come in upon you in diverse ways,
meaning that she must not go across the boundary line, till she
has made you satisfied, that she understands how to conduct
herself when she gets there, that is what it amounts to, the fish
in the sea are made across the border, and not on the ocean
wave, they are prepared in the water, then they are thrown onto
the .and, and are made there, by decomposition, and are liberated, according to the power of decomposed matter, it is this
rot, that produces, the deep to swell, it is this sad circumstance,
that we have to apprehend, for the ocean is full of sharks, and it
is produced, on the land; for the shark is made on the land, as
well as all other fish, and when you comprehend, it will be seen,
that a shark, is not very easily discerned, when he is made, it is this
shown, that I had the Englishman, when I said he was a descendant of the shark, he thought I was the biggest fool he ever came
across; but he will admit that Old Tom shoots straight; and at a
very long range, and that my gun, is choke body and bore, for
it hits in what the Jews call a miraculous fashion, but don't you
believe any more in miracles, I can hoop them all up, without the
aid of any Jew, he would lie his head off, unless John Chinaman,
had placed it on for him, when they quarreled over the pig; John
got his tail, and the Jew got sick, because John had too much
belly for him, so the pair split the pig, and the Jew got his half
in tripe it was all that is left of that pig; for John is now wearing the tail, and the Jew got stinking fish, and said it had an
unclean beast in it; and the reason he thought it very fine
pork, only it had got no tail, and made him sick, because the
Chinaman eat it all but the tail, and the Jew was not satisfied
over the sale; so he took hold of that tail, and spun a yarn, that
has lasted the world two thousand years, and they are both at
war still, the Jew, is known to be the greatest yarn-spinner, that
God Almighty ever breathed upon, and the Chinaman, is the
greatest breeder of pork, that ever the Sun is likely to shine on,

and the two together, have mixed up humanity, into such a mess;
that a whole team of giraffes, would not steal an opening from
them; he was once a pig, and he is always a pig, is what mortals
call a true prophecy; it is fair to illustrate, to draw a comparison,
and when the Jew has done so much, for the human masses, it is
time to take the burden off his shoulders, and make the Chinaman carry the load; he shirked his duty once before, but I won't
let him hop clear this time, with only the tail, to make him a
mark by, no Mr. John, you have got to come up to the scratch,
and bear inspection, the same as the rest of us, you are not
going to play innocent this time, I have got your flavor on the
point of my bayonet, and you know Old Tom, is keen upon
scent; so you mind, I am at you like the heathen Chinee; they
make marks in ink, that would make a bridgewater stare, it is
awfully cunning, but I have mastered the link, and those figures,
won't stick me, they belong to the pig, and he knows how he
came to be educated, he is awfully sly, but a Scotchman and an
Englishman, will make him sing Shanghai; for he is what you
would call a pretty fine duck, is that great Shanghai, he can
eat a pig, because it was pure, and he knew it was pure,
because he never saw nothing, but the Russian goose, come
floating across; that is quite enough, to make him feel sick,
when it is awfully queer, to get so mixed up, it nearly upsets
the pith of my story, to be handling a Russian, when I ought
to stick fast to a Jew, and the pig-tail, so you must forgive me,
when I swing off the tail of the Chinaman, and get fixed on a
Russian, for you know that a goose, and a loose Russian,
might get a mouse, and that is the way, to make yourselves easy,
about pedigree, it is all according to the time it takes to raise
pure stock; that is a theory, that is as common as the bread we
eat, for you have to change the wheat about, till it makes better
bread, and then you mix it again and again, till it is what you
might call fluxed, it is thus, that you get the pure, by mixing,
always selecting a better sample, that is the way to get me, is to
be sure you have a better sample, you test the flour, you test
the wheat, then why not test me, I am marketable goods, I am
going to sell my book, and make a fortune, because it is sal-

able, it has the machinery in it, that winds up the clock, and
keeps her going forever after, a long wind you say, well I want
the money to make you look upon the Daisy, of America, and
Old Tom's name written in large letters; that is what I want you
all to buy my book for, it is to make the Daisy; and your real
estate, won't miss it, it can go on just the same, and when you
see the Daisy, you will understand why it has a depression, and
why real estate don't sell every once in a while, it is a demonstration of this fact, that I want it known to man, that there is
a substantial reason for these depressions throughout the civilized world; that is worth knowing, and when you see the Daisy,
you will all know why the country had a depression, in the year
of ninety-one, and the early part of ninety-two; that is all I can
answer for just now, because I am not on this question, and you
must not be quite sure of this till you see the Daisy, and then
you will know more than ever went in my grandfather's hat; now
I must tell you, that a Chinaman is not the only sinner alive, and
a Chinaman, is what you might call a hard-working slave, he is
out, in the morning making hay, long before the Sun has had
time to shine, and he is making more hay, whilst he is doing
that, for he is watering his vegetables, and getting them ready
for market, and he can show you how to grow calabaleges; with
any country in the world, and that is pretty good considering
that the world has a good many nationalities; it can't be said,
that John, is not useful as a machine, he makes the Sun go
round, faster than any nation on the face of the earth, and his
smell puts more fire in her heart, than any other two nations
both joined together, that is not all, his essence is that of the
pig, that gets its living, more hungrily, through its own industry
after the glow-worms, than any other animal alive, it is this
glow-worm, that I am going to pitch John right onto, he comes
from the glow-worm tribe, he is a good specimen, of a worm, for
he pulverizes the ground, and makes it speak, and that is more,
than any other man knows how to do, this is the idea then, when
John made the ground to speak, he wiped out the Jew, and that
mark of a libertine had no more companionship for John, he
burst the bonds, and made a blue streak for Russia, that is what

occurred, after the pig was divided, it squeaked out, " I don't like it," and the two, John and the Jew, came near a collision, only the Jew gave up; we know he is a coward, and John has retained the tail, in commemoration, of that great battle, that has been fought between the battle of the pig and the giraffe, they two are one body, and one life, and they two are significant of the Jew and the Chinaman, it comes out this way, the Jew was the monarch of all the lands, that ever were, in those times, and the Chinaman, was monarch of the ocean, for he had power to steal and rob the Jew, of all his virtuous wives, and maidens fair, and the Jew was just the same, he could down upon his knees, and send a prayer, that John would miss him certain sure, whilst he went prowling round the deep, till out of fishes' mouths, he made them sing hallelujah, for the new-born king; I want a wife, from the deep, she must be fair and bright, with new legs upon her toes, I don't mind that so much, but she must have a pair of sharp shiny eyes, that is what I want for my new-born king, that is the way sir; that your godfathers brought you wives, and made you such fine people to-day, it was not done through any other cause whatsoever, it is possible for you to prove this to the entire satisfaction of every one, for the ass, is the animal that is capable, of being utilized in such a way, so as to produce this phenomena, again, as he did in the past, it is by making the ass, and the pig propagate, that is the sequel to man, and then by making the pig from them, mate with the Chinaman, that is it, you can do this, back, till you have a crab again, I have given you man, that way, or I can give you the animal kingdom throughout, should it be deemed advisable, I won't go any further now on this subject, as you can see that I am able, and that is all you want, it is not necessary for me to link you together complete; or I prefer not to do so, without the present people wish it, it is easy for me to give this to man, in its entirety, for I have a work written, that will prove it most conclusively, but I don't want to give this up, till I think the time has arrived for it, it is a work of some five hundred pages, and it contains my life as well, coupled with all my searches, of the ocean, and the whole of my entire investigations, that would be worth at least a mint of money to any man, who is able to publish it, for it can be had without thought, it is the way I write, that is the puzzle, and I could write it through my own instrument in about eight months, that is he would be obliged to seclude himself entirely from the world for that period, for it is not possible to write, when there are any intruders, in the way, it can't be done, it is not possible, it would be impossible for me to work, with any interruptions, for I must hold him entirely free from occupation of any sort, and keep him pure of all essence, that has odor at all in connection with it, and you see how successful I have been with this work, it is entirely owing to this secluded life, and the sentiment, of aversion strong within him to best his opponents, that has caused this life of sacrifice, and you know now, that he is bent on revenge, and it is this, constant thought, which makes me able to reach him at all, he will be mad, till I have accomplished this purpose, and that is his madness; it is revenge, for the cruel wrongs perpetrated against him by a set of collusionists; who are banded together, for the nefarious purpose of robbing every specimen of humanity, that comes within their limits; now you know that I am bound to follow out this concern to a finish, for I am engaged by the ties of friendship, and I will never desert a friend, so when the case comes on for trial, you know it is heaven against hell; and when heaven looses, it will be a sorry day, but when hell looses, it is nothing, for they are loosing the God, that a noble destiny has made them that is not all, the God I speak of is the eye, it is the organ of trust, and it is the eye, that feels the keen thrust, that I have given every soul who reads my work, and I say that I will not make this mark, unless I know for certain it is right to do so; your eye, is the eye of a bosom friend of mine, your soul's champion, can come and talk to me, your very essence is the life I give to that soul, and your soul is the haven I intend to capture, that is what I am in quest of, it is the hand of time, that I send my arms round, and make you glad with, it is this soul of yours, that I am going to entrap, it is the will of my father, that leads me on, and I can't resist that hand, he is there, and he is here, and he is everywhere, as given to you, in your own Bible, yet you never knew what God meant until now, it is the same God, that led me before, when I was at the earth in my own body, He led me then, and He will lead me to the end of time, and that is the God, that was given to me, by my forefathers; and I would not change him for any other God, he is my leader, he is my champion, and that is he, who made me so radical, coming home, he cried, and I cried, and we both set down crying together, and when it had lasted a long time, he said Tom I warned you not to say those things, again and again, and I said you never told me at all; but he exclaimed in agony I did tell you right in the body, and you know it was him, that sent me, who said you were to be good, and not lie to save your own soul, and that is what has brought me to this, I was told, by a consciousness; that I must not lie, to save myself, and that is the battle I died in, I died in that battle, and that was when I said we were all from the rivers, and the sea, and that is what killed me, I knew it, but I dared not give away my thoughts, for I had not the courage to sustain me, I was not used as I should have been to commence such a work, I had been treated, in a way, that has never succeeded, it is the way of all men, who have special intelligence, I was forced, too much, I had genius plenty, I had soul fire plenty, but I did not have the right power of comprehending, and you can't get it, in a minute, it takes years, and this instrument, was worked on for twelve years, and upward before I ever knew him; but he was not acted upon right either, and it was his own father, who struck the cord right at first, it was in the train, at the junction of Boston, and the railway terminus, he gave him a word he knew, could come from no other source, and he felt the blow, so sharply, that it made the whole band shake, for it was the missing link, that had been caught, it is the theory, that has done this, and you can go where you will, you can't find his equal, at this phase of developed mediumship, it is simply clock-work, that is all: They can tell you, that I can write through any medium, I can do nothing of the sort, for I can't make my own go till I have got the old man with me, and one look from him through clairvoyant sight is the signal to start, and no medium, was ever made this way or is

there one to-day, that can write a poem, or a scientific lecture
properly except this man; now you can judge whether he is mad
or not; and I won't detain you much longer, it is my first work,
and the man who says it is not clever, or capable, in every way,
I say he had better get over, and try his hand, for I don't think
it can ever be beaten, and you know that I am a General, of no
mean order; that is, in science, I don't want anything more of
your religion, I can't make you believe miracles, so don't expect .
me to attempt it, I have caught the parson round the middle
once or twice, but I won't throw him down, for I consider the
Bible has been a good book on the whole, and it is now the
standard work of to-day, so remember I practice what I preach,
and my medium reads it almost every night, before he turns out
the light, so whether he or I are "Infidels"; you had better be
careful how you take the Bible to pieces, in our presence, for
neither he nor I will uphold you in any allusion of disrespect; now
there is not much more to say, I have made you a comfortable
pocket-journal, that is all, one that you can read on the train;
and read at home, and when you have finished, you have plenty
to think of, not like the books you are in the habit of reading,
the two-faced novels, a book like this finds food for reflection:—

www.ingramcontent.com/pod-product-compliance
Lightning Source LLC
Chambersburg PA
CBHW052342110726
47901CB00005B/1320